D0548626

WITHDRAWN FROM STOCK

A SONG FOR
NERO

By the same author

THE WALLED ORCHARD
ALEXANDER AT THE WORLD'S END
OLYMPIAD

EXPECTING SOMEONE TALLER
WHO'S AFRAID OF BEOWULF?
FLYING DUTCH
YE GODS!
OVERTIME
HERE COMES THE SUN
GRAILBLAZERS
FAUST AMONG EQUALS
ODDS AND GODS
DJINN RUMMY
MY HERO
PAINT YOUR DRAGON
OPEN SESAME
WISH YOU WERE HERE
ONLY HUMAN
SNOW WHITE AND THE SEVEN SAMURAI
VALHALLA
NOTHING BUT BLUE SKIES
FALLING SIDEWAYS
LITTLE PEOPLE
THE PORTABLE DOOR

I, MARGARET

LUCIA TRIUMPHANT
LUCIA IN WARTIME

A SONG FOR
NERO

A NOVEL

THOMAS HOLT

LITTLE, BROWN

A *Little, Brown* Book

First published in Great Britain in 2003 by Little, Brown

Copyright © Tom Holt 2003

The moral right of the author has been asserted.

A CIP catalogue record for this book
ia available from the British Library.

ISBN 0 316 86113 8

Typeset in Bembo by M Rules
Printed and bound in Great Britain by
Mackays of Chatham plc, Chatham, Kent

Little, Brown
An imprint of
Time Warner Books UK
Brettenham House
Lancaster Place
London WC2E 7EN

For my mother and father
But for whom.

ONE

So there we were in the condemned cell in Damascus – which is in Syria, and believe me, you don't want to go there, it's scalpingly hot and the people are not friendly – waiting for the soldiers to come back and take us off to be crucified.

I tapped him on the shoulder (he was huddled in the corner, sulking) and I said to him, 'Lucius Domitius, can I ask you a question?'

'Piss off,' he grunted, so I tapped him on the shoulder again. 'Look,' I said. 'We've been going around together now for, what is it, seven years or is it eight, I lose track, and all this time I've been wanting to ask you—'

'Ask me what?'

I shrugged. 'Well, it's a bit personal and you know how uptight you get talking about the old days. But any minute now they're going to take us out and kill us, so I thought, it can't do any harm. So?'

'What?'

'Do you mind if I ask you a question?'

He didn't turn round, but his shoulders sort of wobbled. 'Yeah, why not? What did you want to know?'

'Is it true you murdered your mother?'

'For God's sake, Galen.' This time he did turn round. 'Of all the things to come out with at a time like this.'

'Yes, all right,' I said. 'Keep your hair on. I'd just like to know, that's all.'

He sighed. 'You'd just like to know.'

'That's right. Come on, just to please me. Like I said, we've been friends a long time now.'

He was wearing that words-fail-me expression. 'No,' he said. 'No, I didn't.'

'Ah, right,' I said. 'Only, everyone says you did.'

'Then everyone's wrong,' he replied. 'Not for the first time,' he added. 'You don't want to believe everything you overhear at the bathhouse.'

'Fine,' I said, holding up my hands. 'I believe you. If you say you didn't do it, you didn't do it. Only you must admit − killing your own mother, it's not the sort of thing people make up out of their heads. Usually, when people say things like that, you generally find there's a grain of truth in it somewhere.'

He scowled at me. 'Ah,' he said. 'You mean, probably I murdered her just a little bit?'

I sighed. 'There you go again,' I said, 'being hostile. Every time I ask you about the old days, you get hostile. You know, a lot of people would be offended by that. Lucky for you I'm hard to offend.'

'I know,' he said, in a funny sort of a way.

'Well, there you are. And if you're telling me you didn't kill your old mum, I believe you, not a moment's hesitation. So, what about your wife?'

He stared at me as if I wasn't making sense. 'What about my wife?'

'Did you kill her?'

'No I bloody well didn't,' he snapped. 'Either of them,' he added.

I peered in the water jug, just in case someone had crept in while our backs were turned and filled it up since I last looked, two minutes before. Let me tell you, Syrian prisons are the worst place on earth, hot as hell and they give you one piddly little jug of water to last you all day. 'Thank you,' I said, 'that's all I wanted to know. Only, you do hear all those stories, and you can't help wondering. Well, you know.'

'No,' he said, 'I don't. What's the matter, does the thought of being locked up with a psychotic killer bother you?'

I laughed. 'Never has in the past. And you think I'm kidding, I was in a cell with a murderer once. Real nasty piece of work he was, stole a slave boy from a barracks on one of those big country places, cut him up into little bits, fried him in oil and ate him. Said he was hungry, apparently, and he didn't have the price of a plate of whitebait. Anyway, I was in this cell with him – Beneventum, I think it was, or maybe it was Ancona, anyway, it doesn't make any odds – and a nicer man I never spent time with. We scratched a chequers board on the floor and made the pieces out of little pellets of bread from our rations.'

He frowned, like he was thinking about something. 'So what happened to him in the end?'

'Oh, they executed him,' I replied. 'Well, you can see their point. Can't have a vicious bastard like that roaming the countryside. But he was really pleasant to me.'

He turned round again and faced the wall. 'I'd like it if you'd shut up now. We're going to be dead soon, and it'd be nice to take a little time to compose my thoughts.'

'Fair enough,' I said. 'And I hope you don't mind me asking, it's just curiosity. Are you sure about the wives, by the way?'

He made a funny noise; I couldn't quite make it out. 'Pretty sure,' he said.

'Only,' I went on, 'your first wife – gods, what was she called?' Memory like a colander. Olympia? Orfitia?'

'Octavia.'

'That's right, Octavia. Wasn't she executed or something?'

'Yes.'

'Oh, so you did—'

'No, I did not.' He was rubbing at his eyes with his thumbs. He tended to do that when he was upset about something. 'She was found guilty of adultery and the court sentenced her to death. I had absolutely nothing to do with it. In fact, I was horrified when they told me. All right? Or do you want me to swear an oath or something?'

'No, no, I believe you,' I told him. 'After all, why would you lie to me? Especially now, when we'll both be dead in two shakes. I mean, what'd be the point?'

Anyhow, that's what he told me, and like I said, why would he lie? It's not like I'm anybody, and God knows, he had enough dirt on me to have me hung, drawn and quartered a dozen times over, even if we weren't both of us about to die as soon as the sergeant got back from lunch, so he couldn't have been afraid I'd blackmail him or anything; and if I'd wanted to blackmail him – well, you get the idea, I'm sure. So yes, I believe him. Liars can't fool liars, my old mother used to say, and in all the time we were going around together, I can't remember him lying to me once. Not that I ever found out about, at any rate.

Well, you can believe me or not as you like, and there's magistrates and city prefects and watch captains from London to Babylon who'll tell you they wouldn't believe me if I told them fire was hot, and fair enough, since they only ever knew me in what I'd call my professional capacity. Even so, it comes down to what I said to him – why would I lie? I've got nothing to gain, except maybe looking after the good name of my friend, except he hasn't got one. Doesn't matter. As far as I'm concerned, Lucius Domitius Ahenobarbus Nero Claudius Germanicus Caesar Augustus didn't murder his old mum, or his first wife, or his second wife; and I don't think he did half of that stuff they say he did, like burning down the city on purpose or things like that. Not the man I knew, anyhow. And when you've been through good times and bad with a person, sleeping in ditches and under carts and in and out of dungeons and prisons and condemned cells and gods only know what else, I reckon you get to know a man fairly well. So there you have it, and whether you want to take my word for it or not is up to you.

And anyway, even if he did do some of those things – and you never hear the full story, only what they want you to hear; for a start, his mother was a vicious old bitch by all accounts and I don't suppose his wives were much better, all the nobility are savage as fighting cocks and three parts off their heads because of the inbreeding and stuff like that – even if he did do what they say he did, I can't judge him on that. After all, I'm no vestal virgin myself, I'd be the first to admit it. All I can go by is how he treated me, and my poor brother, rest his soul. And on that score, I'm going to stick my neck out and say no, he wasn't a villain or a monster or any of those other things they call him. He was all right.

In case you were wondering, we got out of that condemned cell, no bother at all. It was a stroke of luck, I won't argue about that – another quarter of an hour and we'd have been dead men. But just before the sergeant was about to collect us – he told me afterwards, he had the keys in his hand, if he hadn't stopped for a quick shit he'd have been right there and we'd have been crowbait – up turns a herald from the governor's mansion saying His Excellency's wife had just had twins after twelve hours' labour, and he'd promised Our Lady Diana (that's Artemis to you) that if she came out of it all right he'd set free all the prisoners who were due to die that day. So there we were, and that was all right. You know, when you stop to think of it, it's amazing how often things like that have happened to me over the years. The gods must like me, or something.

Well, if you want an example of that, there's the first time I ever set eyes on Lucius Domitius, and that was a close thing, I'm telling you. There we were, Callistus and me, they'd tied us to the crosses and hoisted us up, and I was saying to myself, Galen, this time you're really in the shit. And the crowd was yelling at us and throwing things – why have they got to do that? it's none of their business – and the watch sergeant was grinning nastily at us and he'd got that big wooden mallet they use for breaking your legs so you can't push yourself up to breathe, when suddenly there's this movement in the crowd, like everybody's getting out of the way in a hurry, and this covered chair appears, with four enormous Germans carrying it, and a dozen guardsmen trotting alongside, and the chair stops suddenly and a face shoves through the little window and asks what's going on.

'Just an execution, Caesar,' one of the guardsmen told him. Bloody silly thing to say. I mean, he could see that for himself. But he beckoned the man over and whispered to him, and the man went and whispered to the watch sergeant, and he goes over and talks to the man in the litter.

'What have they done?' the man in the litter asks.

'Very serious crime, Caesar,' replies the sergeant.

'Really? Murder?'

'Worse than that, Caesar.'

'Good heavens. Worse than murder? That's pretty bad. So what was it exactly?'

'Impersonating you, Caesar.'

For a moment nobody says anything, then there's this extraordinary noise from the litter, which of course is Lucius Domitius laughing. 'Is that so?' he says.

'Quite so, Caesar.'

'Oh, I think I'd better take a look at this,' he says. So the Germans lower the chair and the door opens, and out he gets. And you know, even though I was hanging off two bits of rope by my wrists and couldn't hardly breathe, I forgot all that for the moment, because the man in the litter – and I'm not stupid, I knew very well who he was by then – well, it's not every day you get to see the emperor of the Romans. And besides, he was the spitting image of my brother Callistus.

I say spitting image: actually, seeing them together you could tell them apart all right. For one thing, Callistus' hair was dark and he wasn't so jowly or thick round the neck. But there was one hell of a likeness, and when he saw it, Lucius Domitius was obviously tickled pink. 'Get him down this instant,' he said. 'It'd be a crime to execute such a good-looking fellow.'

Of course, everybody laughed like the pantomime had come to town, and to this day I'm not sure whether Lucius Domitius really meant for the watch sergeant to let us go, or whether he was just being funny. But the sergeant wasn't taking any chances, not when the emperor of the Romans had just given him a direct order. He was up that cross like a polecat up a drain, and they were helping Callistus down like he was made of Chinese pottery.

Which was all very well, but it wasn't doing me any good. 'Hey,' I shouted out. 'What about me?' And I guess I must've sounded pretty comical because everybody burst out laughing, and Lucius Domitius looked up at me and said, 'Who's he? The little rat-faced chap, there on the left. He seems very upset about something.'

'That's the impersonator's brother, Caesar,' someone said, and Lucius Domitius shrugged and said something like it'd be a poor show to save one brother and leave the other one up there for the crows, and the next thing I knew, I was standing on the ground on my own two feet, which I'd never expected to do again, that's for sure. Bloody terrible pins and needles I'd got, of course, after dangling up there by my wrists, but I decided I'd keep my face shut and not mention that. Luck is a wonderful thing, but it doesn't want to be pushed if you can help it.

★

We Greeks talk a lot. We're famous for it. If you've been to Greece, you'll know why. If you haven't – well, it's quite simple, really. Greece is a few patches of flat dust wedged in between far too many mountains. The soil is thin and it never rains. If you spend all day every day bashing baked clods with the back of your mattock head, you can just about scrape a living. So when it comes to things – nice things, like gold and silver and furniture and clothes and bread that isn't hard enough to sharpen chisels on – we've never had very much. Now, when you've got nothing worth having, life can be pretty miserable, unless you take your mind off it by being sociable. Outside of an anthill, you can't get more sociable than a bunch of Greeks. One of my earliest memories is walking from our village to the next village down a straight, dusty road with dozens of little tiny fields on either side. In each field there's a shrivelled little man, leaning on his mattock or his hoe while he chats over the boundary wall to the shrivelled little man on the other side. I promise you, the sound of Greek farmers nattering is like the hum of bees: you hear it long before you see them, and it's all round you wherever you go.

Ask anybody who knows about these things, they'll tell you that the Greekest Greeks in the world are my lot, the Athenians. You name a typically Greek thing, you can bet we do it or we've got it in Athens, twice as much as anywhere else. We've got more mountains per square mile, and our mountains are drier and rockier. We're the best at trading and doing deals. We're the cleverest, and the too-cleverest-by-half. We'll go to greater lengths than anyone else to get out of having to scratch dirt for a living. We talk the most. And we have the most glorious and fascinating past of any Greek city in the world. No future worth spit, on account of trying to be way too clever for our own good for far too long, but a great past, which we're extremely proud of.

Take our family, for instance. Nowadays we aren't anybody, but we can trace our ancestors back hundreds and hundreds of years, right back to the incredibly famous and astoundingly wealthy comic poet Eupolis of Pallene. It's been downhill all the way since his time, of course, and the astounding wealth got mislaid over the years, along with the social position and the respect and all that. But it's one of the laws of nature that fathers are better men than their sons, and that year by year in every way everything gradually gets shittier and shittier, so we've never been ones to go round sulking and whining about our lost heritage and stuff.

When I was a kid we lived with my grandfather in the ward of Phyle, which is about as far as you can get from the city and still be Athenian. He had a grotty little farm, twelve acres or so scattered right across the ward, and he also kept an inn. Besides him there was my mother, my brother Callistus and me, and our cousins Therion and Plutus, the sons of our uncle Adrestus who joined the legion and never came back. All the time I was growing up I always knew there was something not quite right about Callistus and me, because we stayed at the inn and peeled the onions and saw to the horses, while Therion and Plutus went out to the fields with Grandad. We accepted it, of course, the way kids do when they don't know any better – besides, it was far less work peeling onions than growing them, so we didn't care. But it was always understood that when Grandad died, we'd be out on our ears and have to go and make our own way in the world, while Therion and Plutus sorted out between them who got the farm and who got the inn. Luckily for us, Grandad managed somehow to keep going till he was an old man of sixty-five, by which point Callistus was seventeen and I had turned sixteen. When Grandad finally turned up his toes – I always liked him, though he had a filthy temper – Therion got the land and Plutus got the inn, and we each got a pair of sandals, a cloak, a loaf of bread and directions to the city. Mother cried a lot when we left home, but that didn't really mean much coming from her, and off we went to seek fame and fortune in Athens.

Fortune was out when we got there, but we quickly made ourselves very famous, mostly with the watch sergeants and the market stewards. I'd always had the rather naive idea that I had a talent for thieving. I don't know where this notion came from – some vicious bastard of a god with a warped sense of humour, probably – but it wasn't long before I had to face up to the fact that I'd been sadly mistaken. Truth is, I'm not a naturally gifted thief. If anything, I'm two or three notches below average. It's a great shame, and I wish it wasn't so, but you've got to face facts in this life.

It's not even as if I started off too ambitious and got cut down to size. The first thing I tried to steal was an apple. I can picture it to this day in my mind's eye. It was small, wrinkled, a bit waxy from being stored over the winter, and it was sitting on the edge of some vendor's stall in the main marketplace in Athens on the day Callistus and me first hit town. We'd finished off the last of our food the night before and we didn't have any money or any practical ideas about how to get any, and suddenly there was this apple, just lying there. Nobody seemed very interested in it. The stallholder was having a row with some woman about a duff pomegranate and the people standing around were earwigging on the argument, the way Greeks do. The way I saw it, all I had to do was lean nonchalantly up against the table with my hands behind my back, grope around with my fingers till I connected with the apple, then walk slowly and casually away. Piece of cake. Child of three could've done it.

Yes, but I wasn't a child of three. Kids can get away with murder in the thieving line, because they look all sweet and innocent and nobody suspects them. But my face is against me, for one thing. I look like a thief – loads of people have told me this over the years, and I expect it's where I got the idea from in the first place – and I was nervous as hell, this being my first attempt outside the family circle, as it were. Upshot was, no sooner had I got my little clammy digits round that apple when a great big hand, frying-pan size, clamps down on my shoulder and some clown starts hollering for the market police. Turned out that the man having the slanging match with the pomegranate woman owned the next stall down, and the real stallholder, the one whose apple I was pinching, had had his eye on me right from the start.

So there I am, first day in the big city, lying on the floor of the market district lock-up and wishing I'd stayed in Phyle and starved to death, because if you're going to die horribly you might as well do it among friends. By this stage I'm feeling rather sorry for myself, not to mention distinctly pissed about being left in the lurch by my dear brother, who'd somehow managed to make himself invisible as soon as the trouble started. I was keeping myself occupied thinking of all the rude names I was going to call him when we finally met up again on the other side of the Styx, when the guard sergeant – long, thin Corsican type, as I recall – looms over me and tells me I've got a visitor.

Of course, the visitor is Callistus, only you'd never have

recognised him. He was wearing this absolutely stunning green and orange tunic, embroidered seams, the lot. He had fifty-drachma sandals on his feet and his head was dripping with that really expensive oil that smells like violets and stale armpits. Anyhow, he thanked the sergeant in a loud, grand voice and gave him a drachma.

'This him?' the sergeant said.

Callistus sighed. 'I'm afraid so,' he replied, and it was enough to bring tears to your eyes, the sadness and disappointment in his voice. 'Really,' he went on, 'I can only apologise. It's the third time since we got off the boat at Corinth. I keep telling him what'll happen to him if he keeps this up, but he won't listen. It's like some kind of illness, really.'

The sergeant pulled a face. 'You want to sell him on,' he said, 'before he gets you in real bother.'

'I know.' Callistus clicked his tongue, just like the rich people do. 'But I can't, and that's all there is to it. You see, he was my poor dear father's favourite, and I promised him, during his last illness, that I'd look after the wretch, try and keep him under control.' He shook his head, spraying little drops of oil on the deck. 'The least I can do is give that poor stallholder something for his trouble. Do you think ten drachmas would be enough?'

The sergeant grinned. 'You bet. That Mnester'd sell his own father for ten drachmas, if only he knew who he was.'

'Splendid,' Callistus said. 'Look, would it be all right if I gave you the money, to give to this Mnester person? Only, I'd be rather embarrassed having to face him myself.'

From the way the sergeant smiled, I knew for sure that if Mnester got to see any of that ten drachmas ever, it'd only be because the sergeant was at his stall buying fruit. 'Sure,' he said, 'no bother at all. Right, you,' he called out to me, 'on your feet. It must be your lucky day.'

There you go, you see. Callistus didn't look like a thief. Callistus looked like a gentleman – well, he looked just like the emperor, though of course we didn't know that then – so nobody ever dreamed of suspecting him. Which meant he could just stroll into the bathhouse, take off his clothes, go for a nice swim and a splash about, have his hair done, get a massage, the whole bit. Then he wanders back into the changing room, starts putting on the smartest-looking kit he lays his eyes on, and if the attendant comes up and says anything, all he needs to do is look down his nose and the poor bugger slinks off to avoid getting whipped for annoying the gentry. Mind you, it was a stroke of luck there being a nice fat purse along with the clothes, because it made getting me out of there a damn sight easier.

'Shut up,' he hisses to me as we're walking out the door, 'and for God's sake try and look like a slave.'

Well, that wasn't difficult. We kept it up as far as the next block, just in case someone was watching, then we drop down in the shade and both started shaking like leaves.

'That does it,' Callistus said. 'From now on, we're going to be honest. My nerves can't hack this.'

'Bullshit,' I said. 'You were fucking brilliant. But where the hell did you get all the clobber from?'

So he told me what he'd done, and immediately I knew, like some god had appeared out of the sky and told me in a vision: no more thieving for us, we were going to be swindlers. Far grander, and a much better living, too.

'You must be out of your tiny mind,' Callistus said when I explained it to him. 'Just that one time was bad enough. It's taken years off my life. I was so scared I nearly shat myself.'

Well, that was my brother all over. I looked him in the eye and said, 'Don't be so pathetic. You strolled through it, you're a natural. You even had me convinced, and I've known you all your life. Sure you were nervous,' I went on, 'that's perfectly all right. You're a performer, an artiste. All artistes get nervous before they go on, it's a well-known fact. Hell, I'd be worried if you *weren't* nervous. But you'll get used to that, I promise you – and when have I ever let you down?'

He narrowed his eyes. 'How much time have you got?' he said.

That wasn't a very nice thing to say, but I'm bigger than that. 'The trouble with you artistes,' I told him, 'you don't have any confidence in yourselves. It's the same with all the world-class flute-players, they never believe they're any good.'

'Really,' he replied. 'And how many world-class flute-players do you know?'

'One,' I told him. 'Chrysippus, who used to come to our place when we were kids. I remember him saying once, he always threw up every time just before he went on to play. Nerves, you see.'

He frowned. 'Chrysippus used to throw up all the time,' he said, 'mostly because of drinking neat wine on an empty stomach. And he was hardly world class.'

'He played in Naples once,' I pointed out, 'and Antium, and once in Capri, in front of the emperor Tiberius himself. If that isn't world class, you tell me what is.'

Callistus shook his head, like a dog trying to get water out of its ears. 'Fuck Chrysippus,' he said. 'You're trying to change the subject, like you always do. The point is, I'm not doing it. And that's final."

'You don't mean that.'

'Yes I do.'

'No you don't.'

'Shut *up*, Galen, for crying out loud.' He rubbed his eyes. He always did that when he couldn't make his mind up about something. 'Anybody else would have learned his lesson,' he went on. 'The first and only time you try breaking the law, you get caught. Not only that, you get caught straight away, faster than a dog with a rat. Doesn't that tell you anything?'

'Of course it does,' I said. 'It tells me that thieving stuff off market stalls is a mug's game, while conning people is as easy as treading in cowshit, especially,' I pointed out, 'for a naturally gifted artiste such as yourself. Surely you can see that. It's as obvious as a hornet up your tunic.'

'For the last time,' he said, and by now he was almost whimpering, 'I'm not going to do it, and that's that. Getting you out of stir was one thing, but doing it for a living is something else, and I don't want any part of it.'

'All right,' I said. 'Fine. So what else can we do?'

I'd got him there, of course, and he knew it. He didn't say anything, just sat there looking miserable, but he knew I was right. Two young lads from the country, no money, didn't know anybody – well, there was our cousin Antyllus who always reckoned he'd give us a job, but would you fancy spending your life scraping down the insides of tanning vats? The way I saw it, we had two choices: a life of crime, or join the army. And when you put it like that, it's not really a choice, is it?

Oddly enough, I got a chance – years later, of course – to talk about this with the wisest man in the world, and I asked him what would he have done if he'd been in our shoes, and he told me, probably exactly what you did. Well, that cheered me up no end, as you can imagine, because I'd thought a lot about it over the years and there were times (mostly when I was sitting in condemned cells or waiting my turn in the queue for the gallows somewhere) when I wondered if I'd made the right decision, that hot afternoon in Athens. But apparently I did, and that's always meant a lot to me. It's one thing deciding something off your own bat and hanging on grimly hoping it'll turn out that you were right, but getting it confirmed by the wisest man in the world is another matter entirely.

In case you were born in Britain or your dad kept you locked up in the stables till you were thirty, the wisest man in the world was Lucius Annaeus Seneca, the philosopher, and I met him back when Callistus and I were hanging round the imperial court after that day when we first met Lucius Domitius. In those days, as I'm sure you remember, Seneca was pretty much running the empire, on account of having been Lucius Domitius' tutor when he was a kid. Needless to say, Lucius Domitius was supposed to be in charge, he was the emperor and all that kind of thing, but he was still only a young lad who didn't know what time of day it was, except he had the common sense to leave all the important stuff to people who knew what they were about, and who he could trust. Mostly this was Seneca – after all, he was the wisest man in the world – and he did all the paperwork and the money and negotiating with foreign kings and what-have-you, while the military side of things was left to the guards commander, a miserable old bruiser by the name of Burrus. Anyway, that's beside the point, and I'm only telling you about it because you need to know how come a low-life like me found himself talking to a fine gentleman and a scholar like Seneca.

It was one of those lazy afternoons around the palace when everybody was either sleeping off lunch or doing something they didn't want anybody else to know about. On days like that you could walk up and down and round and round through all the corridors and courtyards and cloisters for hours at a time and never meet a living soul. I was at a loose end – nothing unusual there, of course – and there was nobody about apart from a few clerks scuttling back and forth with their arms full of scrolls and tablets, and I was just wandering round looking for someone to talk to. Eventually I ended up in a courtyard by a rather pretty little fountain and I'd been there a while, just sat there with my mouth open thinking of nothing much, when this old, sad-looking type flops down next to me on the seat and starts cleaning out his ear with his fingernail.

I knew straight away who it was, so I stayed perfectly still and kept my face shut, looking down into the little pool under the fountain. He didn't say anything either. Soon as he'd finished cleaning out one ear, he started on the other one, and I guess he was concentrating on the job in hand, which is what you'd expect from the wisest man in the world. Then quite suddenly out of the blue he turns to me and he says, 'So, which are you?'

I thought I understood what he was going on about. 'I'm Galen,' I replied. 'I'm Callistus' brother.'

He frowned, then laughed. 'No, that's not what I meant,' he replied. 'I meant, which are you, a Stoic or an Epicurean?'

I hadn't got a clue what he was talking about. 'Neither,' I said, 'I'm from Phyle, in Attica.'

You could see it cost him a lot of effort not to laugh. 'I'm sorry,' he said. 'I was miles away, thinking about something else.'

I may not be the sharpest razor in the box, but I'm not stupid. If you find yourself sitting next to the man who runs the world and he looks like he's in the mood to chat to somebody, you chat. Also, like I said, I'm a Greek, we don't need a reason. 'That stuff,' I asked him, 'what you said just now – what does it mean?'

He smiled. 'Stoic and Epicurean?'

I nodded. 'That's the ones.'

He leaned back, clasped his hands round his knee. 'They're the names of the two main schools of orthodox moral philosophy,' he replied, then he must've realised that everything he'd said had gone whistling over my head like the geese flying south. 'Ways of looking at life,' he explained, 'of figuring out right from wrong, good from bad. The Stoics think that everything that happens to us in life is already decided, even before we're born. They hold that each of us has his destiny and we don't really have any say in what happens to us. The only thing that matters is our intentions, whether they're good or bad. We can't change what we do, because it's already been worked out down to the smallest detail, but what we can control is our own attitudes.' He stroked his beard for a moment. 'Look at it like this. Suppose you're an actor in a theatre. You haven't got any choice about what you're going to say, because all the words come direct from the playwright, and you aren't allowed to change so much as a syllable. Your job is to say those words as well as you possibly can. That way, it can be a truly rotten play, but you can still shine and excel because you said the truly rotten lines but in a clever and interesting way. Well, that's what the Stoics believe.'

'I think I see,' I lied. 'So what about the other lot? Ep-something, wasn't it?'

'Epicureans,' Seneca replied. 'They believe something quite different. They reckon that everything in life is random, nothing's got any meaning apart from what you bring to it. That being so,' he went on, 'the rights and wrongs of everything we do rest fair and square with us, and the only valid or sensible reason for doing anything at all is because you enjoy it, or because it's to your advantage.'

Well, right up to the point where he said that last bit, I was pretty sure I was a Stoic, because of nothing I did being my fault. But as soon as he got on to the part about enjoying yourself, I realised I was definitely with the other lot, the Epicureans. Odd how easy it is to make a mistake over something so very basic and straightforward. 'Right,' I said, 'got you. Thanks for explaining.'

'That's all right,' he replied, smiling, and I thought, this is a case of the old nut and sledgehammer. Here you've got the smartest thinker in the world, and he's wasting his time telling me something that any street-corner lawyer could've told me. Like sending for the Prefect of Aqueducts to bring you a drink of water. 'I get the impression,' he went on, 'that you aren't a student of moral philosophy.' He paused, and looked at me. 'Did I say something funny?' he asked, and I realised I was grinning like a thirsty dog.

'Sorry,' I said, 'private joke. You see, for a long time, before I lucked into this courtier lark, I was a full-time thief. Well, no, that's not true, we tried thieving and we were bloody awful at it. No, *I* was bloody awful at it, let's be accurate. So instead we did scams.'

He looked puzzled, so I explained (my turn to be the teacher). 'You know, the bathhouse dodge and the three nutshells caper and the Spanish silver mine sting and the old stolen necklace fiddle—'

'How absolutely fascinating,' Seneca interrupted. 'You know, I've met a lot of interesting people in my time, but never someone in your line of work.'

'Oh, we don't do that stuff any more,' I said quickly. 'Honest as the day's long, we are now,' I added, not bothering to mention that the day in question was the first of January in Caledonia. 'But the point is, if it's moral philosophy you're after – well, you've come to the right stall, because that's exactly what my brother and me have been studying ever since we got slung off the farm.'

He raised a snow-white eyebrow. 'Really? How's that?'

'Obvious, isn't it?' I said. 'Morality's all about good and evil, isn't it? Right and wrong. Truth and lies. That's right, isn't it?'

He nodded. 'Broadly speaking, yes.'

'There you are, then. We're professional liars – *were* professional liars, I mean. These days we're as pure as a mountain stream. But you can't spend your working life telling twisters and not get to know a thing or two about the truth.'

'I see what you mean,' Seneca said, rubbing his chin. 'I'll confess, I wouldn't have seen it in those terms myself, but your position is essentially valid. Do go on.'

I shrugged. 'Not a lot more to it than that. Thing is, where does the truth end and the lie begin? Here's an example. If I tell you an out-and-out whizzer, like I'm the King of Armenia, you aren't going to believe me for a moment. So I don't do that. I try and trim my lie as close to the truth as I can get it. All right.' I went on, 'suppose I wanted to make you believe I'm really the King of Armenia, right? This is how I'd go about it. I'd make out like I'm the king, only I'm going round in disguise for some reason, and I'm frantically trying not to get recognised. So I drop a few hints – inadvertently, if you get my drift, say some stuff that makes it sound like the king talking, but sell you on the idea that it just sort of slipped out because I was careless, or smashed, or whatever. Then I pretend like I've just realised what I've done, so I rabbit on about how I'm *not* the king. I'll say that now and again people have been known to mistake me for the king, since we look a bit alike. Then

I'll stop myself, and make a big fuss about how I don't think I look anything like him, it's just that some people – quite a lot of people, actually – somehow get the impression that I look like him, or our voices are a bit alike. You see what I'm getting at? Most of the time I'm telling you the solid gold truth – I'm not the king, I don't look like him one little bit – and the clever bit is that by telling you the truth, I can make you believe my lie much better than if I came straight out with it. That's what we call drawing the lie out of the mark, rather than trying to stuff it in. I guess the idea behind it is that everybody's full of lies – the honest folk, I mean – and that what you've got to do if you want to con someone is to charm one of their own lies up to the surface, like tickling a fish. Which means,' I went on, 'that nobody's really honest, when you come down to it. See what I mean?'

Seneca sat there for a moment looking like he'd just had his head stuffed full of new wool, then he burst out laughing. 'Exactly,' he said. 'You're absolutely right. You're saying that it's no good you telling me a lie, because I won't believe it. You've got to make me tell myself a lie, by telling me the unblemished truth.'

'You've got it,' I said.

'Wonderful.' he replied. 'And, taking that argument to the next level, we can say that it takes two men to make a lie: one to suggest it and one to believe it, and both of them are equally at fault.'

I wasn't sure I followed that. In fact, that sounded to me like he'd got the whole thing arse about face. But you don't go saying that to a man who can get you top billing in the circus just by clicking his fingers. 'You betcha,' I said. 'That's all there is to it, really.'

Anyhow we had a long talk after that, and gradually I ended up telling him all about our adventures, Callistus and me, from when we left home, when I was sixteen, through our nine years together on the road right up to the point five years ago where we were about to die and Lucius Domitius showed up. Well, that seemed to tickle the old bugger no end. He laughed, and said, 'So what you're telling me is, precisely because everything you did was wrong, everything turned out right in the end. In other words, you're a stone-cold Stoic.'

That shut me up for a moment or so. 'I am?' I said.

'Absolutely. Think about it rationally for a moment. Nature, or the gods, never wastes effort; everything happens for a reason. If we accept that – which is what the Stoics teach – then your destinies were set cold in the mould the instant you were born. Why else would Nature go to all the trouble of creating a spitting image of his majesty, and then weave a web of circumstances that brought that facsimile – against all the odds, mark you – to the one place and time where the copy and the original could be brought together to interact for their greatest mutual advantage? To claim that it wasn't predetermined would be like acknowledging the existence of the elephant and the intricately carved ivory scent bottle, but denying the existence of the ivory carver; and insisting, furthermore, that the scent bottle is a natural rather than an artificial thing, owing its shape to the random erosion of wind and weather.' He reached out his hand and clamped me on the shoulder. Where I come from we bust people's noses for that, but he was a Roman senator, so I guess he couldn't be expected to know better. 'Thank you, my dear friend. That must be the most compelling piece of evidence in support of the Stoic argument that I've heard in thirty-five years. I'm most deeply obliged to you, and your admirable brother.'

Goes without saying – as soon as he got started on all those long words and big beetlecrusher sentences, I stopped trying to understand and let it all wash over me. Oh, I remembered it all right, because coming from him it was obviously the good stuff, the real onion gravy, but it struck me that the sensible thing to do would be to tuck it away in my mind, like sneaking a couple of cutlets into your hanky at a posh dinner party, and see if I could crack it open later, as and when I had the time. So I did.

Anyhow, after that we nattered back and forth for a bit, till suddenly he realised what the time was and had to scurry off to some departmental briefing or whatever. And after he's gone I'm sitting there thinking, yeah, right. Clearly he's been funning with me, pulling my tail, spouting a whole lot of camel feathers and making me believe it actually made sense – just the sort of thing that'd tickle a smartarse Roman, conning a conner. But then I got to thinking, so what? Doesn't matter if he's having me on and he's so far up himself he's practically poking out through his own ears if what he said does turn out to make a bit of sense. And the more I've thought about it over the years (and for some reason I've never managed to flush it out of my head), the more I reckon he smacked the peg square on the head, and what he told me wasn't far off being the truth—

—And you can't go planting stuff like that in the head of a Greek without expecting something to come up out of it. Because, think how it'd be if there was this poor fool who went through his life telling the truth and everybody thought he was lying? And wouldn't it be even worse if there was another poor fool – maybe even the same one – who went around trying his very best to tell lies, and it always turned out that everything he said was actually true?

TWO

So there we were in Syracuse, hiding under a table.

Sorry. You can tell I'm new to this storytelling business – an amazing confession for a Greek, but like I told you just now, these days I make a point of only telling the truth – it's just dawned on me that I've been talking for half an hour and I haven't even started the story properly.

We were in Syracuse, Lucius Domitius and me. Syracuse is in Sicily, in case you didn't know. Sicily is a terrible place: it's all big estates worked by chain gangs, and everybody knows everybody else, which makes it really hard for people in our line of work. Anyway, we were in Syracuse, and we'd just tried the old one where one of you pretends to have discovered a load of buried treasure but you've had a bang on the head and lost your memory – you know about that one, I'm sure, it had whiskers on it when King Priam was getting chased out of orchards for stealing apples – and it hadn't gone very well, which was why we were hiding under this table, which was the front of a cheese merchant's stall in the market. I think it was the soldiers who were after us, them or the rich senator's bodyguard – anyway, we were being chased, and it was only a matter of time before we got caught and dragged off for a chat with the magistrate.

Lucius Domitius was wetting himself, as usual. He never got the hang of handling stress. What bothered him was the thought that the magistrate or the rich senator or one of those people would recognise him for who he really was. Now I wasn't too fussed about that. It's been my experience that people only ever see what they're expecting to see, and nobody would be expecting to see the former emperor Nero Claudius Caesar because everybody knew he'd been dead for ten years. It might just possibly occur to someone that one of the prisoners looked a bit like the late unlamented emperor, but the thought that it might actually be him wouldn't cross his mind, and even if it did he wouldn't dare mention it for fear of people thinking he was nuts. No, what was making me feel uncomfortable was the prospect of being found guilty of obtaining money by deception and being sentenced to twenty-five years in the slate quarries. Now it's a fact that nobody's ever actually done a twenty-five-year stretch in the quarries, and you might think that's reassuring, until you find out that the reason for this is that most people tend to die after five years down there, and the really tough old leatherbacks only make it to fifteen.

'So this is it, then,' he was saying, as we watched the sandals of our pursuers tramping backwards and forwards in front of our noses. 'This is where it finally grinds to a halt. What a bloody stupid way to go.'

'Don't be so miserable,' I told him. 'We'll get out of this, don't you worry. And when we do, we'll go to Africa.'

'Africa?'

'Should've gone there years ago,' I told him. 'Wonderful place, by all accounts. Glorious weather, beautiful cities, loads of money about, and the people are all overfed and dumb. Inside of a couple of years, we'll be so rich we can retire.'

'What the hell makes you think that?' he asked.

'Oh, I keep my ears open. Remember that wine shop in Massilia, where you had those bad olives? Well, there were a couple of Spaniards in there, just off a ship from Cyrenaica, and they were going on about how great it is out that way and how it's toe to heel with gullible rich silphium growers. Did you realise that nine-tenths of the silphium grown in the empire comes from Cyrenaica?'

He shook his head. 'I'm not sure I even know where Cyrenaica is.'

'You should do,' I replied. 'You used to own it.'

'Maybe. But you know perfectly well I never went anywhere in those days. Anyway, that's beside the point. What the hell makes you think we'd do any better in Africa than here? You told me the Sicilians were gullible, but it didn't take them long to figure us out.'

I sighed. 'All right. If you don't fancy Africa, there's other places. Lusitania, for instance. They have huge great silver mines in Lusitania.'

'No doubt,' he replied gloomily. 'And if I'm stupid enough to listen to you, we'll end up down one of 'em, with a pick and a crowbar and half a mouldy loaf a day between us.'

'Don't talk like that. You know what your trouble is?'

'Yes. I allow myself to get talked into things by bad people.'

'Your trouble is,' I went on, 'you're an Epicurean. You can't see that everything is part of a vast prearranged plan, and every little detail was figured out and set in stone centuries before you were even born. Now, if you were a Stoic, like me, you'd realise there's nothing at all else we could've done, we'd still have wound up here in the end. It's not what happens that matters, it's how well you cope with it. Which means,' I explained, 'staying calm and together, and not pissing down your leg every time you hit a rough patch.'

I expect he'd have said something downbeat and depressing only he didn't get the chance, because that was when the soldiers found us and winkled us out from under the table by prodding our legs with their spears.

I could have told him there was no fear of us being recognised by the magistrate. He scarcely even looked at us. He just listened to what the prosecutor had to say, and passed sentence – which may be your idea of the due process of justice, but it definitely isn't mine.

'Fifteen years hard labour in the slate quarries,' he said. 'Next case.'

Well, I told Lucius Domitius, it could have been far worse. I was sure we'd get at least twenty years, maybe even twenty-five, and we'd got off with fifteen. He must have liked our faces, or something.

Be that as it may. There we were, huddled in back of a rickety old mule cart, bumping along a narrow road winding its way round the side of a horribly steep mountain. The cart was so packed with poor bastards on their one-way trip to the quarries that we could hardly breathe, though since most of our fellow passengers didn't smell very nice that was something of a blessing. Nobody said much. We were all too miserable and the soldiers got nasty if we tried to chat. There were five Gaulish cavalry troopers in front of the cart and another five following on behind, and we were all chained together just in case we took it into our heads to jump off the side and make a run for it, though they needn't have worried about that, since there was nothing over the side except a bloody great drop. The best you could say for it was that it was better than walking.

It's hard keeping track of time when you're in that kind of situation. You're cramped and uncomfortable and every time the wheels go over a rut or a pothole you feel like your spine's just been broken, but after a while you find yourself drifting off into a sort of trance, just to take your mind off your troubles. So I don't know how long we'd been on that road, and I certainly haven't got a clue where we ended up. The best I can manage is somewhere between Syracuse city and the quarries, which isn't very precise, I know. But wherever it was, that's where it happened.

First I knew that something was up was when the cart suddenly jinked drastically over to the right, and all of us sitting on the left side found ourselves tumbled into the laps of the poor fools opposite. It was a wonder nobody got shot out and over the edge, and because we were all chained up together, it's a fair bet that if one of us had gone, the rest would've been dragged out too, and that would've been a bloody mess. I heard the cavalrymen yelling at the carter, and he shouted back something about the right front wheel going over the edge. Anyhow, the cart stopped and one of the cavalry troopers from behind shouted at us not to move or we'd all be dead. We'd figured that one out for ourselves, but it was nice of him to care.

What had happened was the edge of the road had got a bit crumbly and come away, damn near taking the cart with it. As it was, we were perched there, half on the road and half dangling over the drop. One of the troopers had the wit to draw the linchpin and get the mules clear: if they'd spooked and started backing up we'd have been over in a flash. But thanks to those damned chains there was no way to get us off the cart – we were all too close together and couldn't move – and they didn't dare try dragging the cart back off the edge, it was too finely poised. All in all, we couldn't have been more delicately balanced if we'd hired a top-flight Alexandrian engineer to draw it all out on paper and do the calculations.

No disrespect to you, but if you'd been in our shoes you'd have been pissing yourself; but it was different for us, we were all dead already as far as we were concerned, and when you've got sod all to lose you can afford to see the funny side. I was finding the way the soldiers were scatting about distinctly amusing, and Lucius Domitius was grinning like an idiot.

'I was just thinking about what we were discussing under that table,' he said, when I asked him what we found so hilarious. 'About Stoics and Epicureans, and predestination and all that. I was thinking,' he went on 'if everything is predetermined down to the smallest detail, like you were saying, that must mean this mess was, too. And I thought, Destiny must be pretty damned smart to be able to balance a cartload of condemned men so absolutely precisely on the edge of a precipice. Getting it inch-perfect like that, and first time, too. With a talent like that, she's wasting her time being a goddess. She should be raising triumphal arches or building pyramids.'

'You can mock,' I said. 'But this is exactly what I was talking about. I knew when we were under that table that it wasn't over quite yet, and the same when we were in the dock. Whatever happens next, it won't be what was supposed to happen, that's for sure.'

'Shut up a minute,' he interrupted. 'I want to hear what they're saying.'

The troopers had come up with a plan. They were thinking about putting a rope through the spokes of the back wheels and making fast to a stumpy old thorn tree, and then passing a second rope through the nearside front wheel and hauling the cart up off the edge that way. It wasn't a bad idea at all, and it might've worked if only they'd had two ropes, or even one. As it was, all they had was a long steel chain, and that wasn't a whole lot of good to them because of all the people attached to it. The best they could do was send one of the troopers back down the road as fast as he could go for some rope, and take a chance on him getting back before somebody sneezed and we all got smeared across the valley floor like birdshit.

Our part in this jolly adventure was to stay absolutely still, and to do us credit, we took to it like we'd been apprenticed seven years in the trade. Mind you, I don't suppose there was a single one of us in that cart who wasn't trying to figure out how to turn the situation into a chance to escape. Luckily for all of us, we were smart enough to realise that it wasn't on, not for us or Archimedes or Pythagoras or the clever men who make those moving bronze statues powered by steam. Nevertheless, it was something cheerful to think about, and kept us from getting restless.

Some time later (again, don't ask me to be precise), we heard voices up ahead. Nobody tried to take a look and see who it was, since that would've meant moving, and we were wise to that. But luckily the voices carried well in the air – still day, no breeze – and we could hear what was going on.

'Hey,' someone said in Greek, 'what the hell do you jokers think you're playing at? Get that bloody cart out of the way.' Typical landlord's voice: loud, confident, didn't give a damn about all the emperor's legions if they happened to be blocking a road he wanted to ride along. Did me good to hear it just then, that tiny faint suggestion that there are other powers in the world besides the senate and people of Rome, and very occasionally, on their own turf, they win.

Long pause, which I put down to the cavalrymen being savages and not understanding Greek. Same thing must've occurred to the mystery voice, because he repeated what he'd said, only in Latin.

'We can't,' called back one of the troopers. 'Cart stuck on edge of cliff. We trying to move, fall off bump, everybody die.'

'Bloody hell.' The voice sounded amused. 'What've you got in there, anyway? Slaves for the quarry, is it?'

'Ya, ya.' The trooper again. 'Criminals, bad people, going to quarry. Only getting stuck in the cart, and not to be moved.'

'Poor bastards,' replied the voice, and neither of them said anything for a while. Then the Greek said, 'You know, if you passed a rope through the back wheel—'

'This we thinking of,' interrupted the trooper irritably, 'but not have rope.'

The Greek laughed. 'Shows you aren't from round here, then. Nobody takes a cart out on these roads without rope.'

Pause, while the trooper thinks about it. 'You got rope?'

'I got rope, sure. I got brain, so I got rope. You not got rope, go figure.'

'You give rope.'

'I not give rope. Me give anything to the government if I don't absolutely have to? Not bloody likely.'

The trooper made an angry sort of noise. 'We soldiers. You give rope.'

'You Roman soldiers. I not give rope. You fuck yourselves.'

'Oh, for crying out loud,' muttered Lucius Domitius. 'A patriot. The gods must hate us.'

'Seems that way,' I agreed. 'Mind you, your uncle Claudius is a god now, so maybe we shouldn't be surprised.'

'That settles it. then. If Uncle's in Heaven, give me the other place any time.'

The trooper was gabbling away to his mates in Foreign, and they sounded pretty upset about something. Then a different trooper called out. 'You give rope. It is the law. We requisition.'

The mystery voice answered back in Greek. What he said is pretty well untranslatable, and probably just as well, but the troopers seemed to have got the message anyhow. 'If you not giving rope, we take.'

'No fear of that,' the Greek replied. 'You take one step in this direction, the rope goes over the edge, and you can go and fetch it from the bottom of the valley. If you get a move on, you could be there by this time tomorrow.'

Wonderful, I thought. Talk about your equipoise of opposing forces hovering in space. There was the cart, teetering on the edge of the gorge, and there were the troopers and the Greek, equally delicately poised. One tiny shove anywhere and the whole lot would go down. It was turning into an interesting day.

After a long quiet spell – I could hear the buzzing of the bees and the steady sound of horses chomping their bits – the first trooper piped up again. 'We buy rope,' he said.

'Now we're getting somewhere.' The Greek sounded positively cheerful. 'Giving to the government is one thing. Selling to the bastards is something else. Twenty drachmas.'

Pause. You could almost hear the graunching sound as the troopers calculated drachmas into sesterces in their heads. 'Too much. We give five sesterces.'

'You know what you can do with your five sesterces. If you don't, ask a good doctor.'

'Five sesterces,' the trooper repeated, only louder. 'Fair price for rope. Same as market.'

The mystery voice laughed. 'That's right,' he said. 'And if anyone ever catches me selling to the government for a fair price, may the crows pick the sinews off my bleached bones. Twelve drachmas, take it or leave it.'

Actually, I'm surprised that the patience of those troopers held out as long as it did. Soldiers aren't exactly known for their long-suffering forbearance, especially your northern auxiliaries. I don't know what the troop sergeant said, because he said it in Gaulish, but you didn't have to be a linguist to figure it out. A moment or so later we heard the mystery voice shouting, 'Right, I warned you,' at which point, I guess, he must've chucked the rope over the cliff.

I'm sorry I missed the next bit, because if there's one thing I enjoy, it's a good fight – provided I'm watching, of course, not taking part. Judging from the outcome, that must've been the fight of a lifetime, because the next thing we heard was the mystery voice saying, 'All right, that'll do. Leave them alone, and let's see to this cart,' and it wasn't long before we could feel the cart moving. In the right direction, I hasten to add, or I wouldn't be here telling you this.

I had my eyes firmly shut all the time, of course. It's a sort of superstitious thing with me in moments of great danger, all my life I've had this unnatural fear of seeing my own death happening. Anyhow, when I opened them again, the first thing I saw was this amazingly shiny bald brown head gleaming in the sunlight over the side of the cart.

'Now then, you lot,' he said – his was the mystery voice – 'let's be having you. It's your lucky day.'

So we stood up – took some of us several goes, because cramp and blind desperate terror combined really screw up your knees – and we finally got a look at what had been going on.

My guess is that it was the dozen or so men standing behind the bald-headed character who'd done the actual fighting, because several of them were bleeding and all of them were dusty from rolling about on the ground, whereas the bald-headed man was still as clean and freshly laundered as a page boy. The soldiers were lying on the ground, and they had that flattened out, slightly comical look that tells you they won't be getting up again (there were two of the Greek's men lying the same way, so it hadn't been entirely one-sided). How the troopers got that way was explained by what the Greek's men were holding in their hands: mattocks and picks and chunky oak mallets, heavy-duty farm tools that just happen to make first-class weapons (after all, if you can use them to gouge a living out of a goddess like Mother Earth, it stands to reason they're more than up to the task of sorting out a few mortal soldiers).

'What happened here,' the Greek was saying, 'is like this. Your cart lost a wheel.' The sound of a big mallet scrunching spokes showed the Greek's admirable attention to detail. 'You villainous lot of desperadoes took advantage of this to escape, pausing only to massacre these brave, loyal soldiers. My boys and I tried to stop you, public-spirited types that we are, but you just swept us aside, stealing a valuable sledgehammer and cold chisel as you went. Well, that's how I'm going to tell it when I make my report and put in my claim for damages – two premium-grade field hands killed, damage to clothing and property, not forgetting the hammer and chisel, which you'll find in the box of tools at the back of the wagon. If any of you worthless bastards get caught, it'd be nice if you did me the courtesy of telling it my way, though no bugger's going to take your word over mine if you don't. In the meanwhile, enjoy the rest of your lives.'

I'll say this for Lucius Domitius: he was as strong as a carter's ox. Give him a sledgehammer and point him at a length of chain, and he'd get the job done. He'd just freed the last of our travelling companions and was leaning on his hammer having a well-deserved blow when the Greek called to him, or rather us (I'd been holding the chisel). 'Here,' he said, 'you two.'

About half a dozen of us looked round, with that gormless who-me? expression on our faces.

'Yes, you two. The little rat-faced type, and the bruiser. Don't I know you two from somewhere?'

Now he said it in Greek, but if he'd been talking Latin, if he'd had any sense he'd have used the grammatical form unique to that language, the Question Expecting The Answer No.

'What, us?' I said. 'Don't think so, sir.'

He scowled. He was one of those solid, chunky-faced types

who manage to look jolly even when they're scowling, but I didn't let that fool me. 'Balls,' he said. 'I'm sure I've seen you before. Faces as ugly as yours, I don't tend to forget.' His frown got deeper, then he burst out laughing. 'Sure I know who you are. You're the pair of toerags who tried to con my cousin Thrasyllus in the fish market. I helped catch you bastards.'

Lucius Domitius gave him a look. 'Oh,' he said. 'Really.'

'That's right,' the Greek said, grinning all over his face (and he had a lot of face to grin all over, as I think I mentioned). 'Damn straight that's who you are. Bloody hell.' He shook his head. I don't suppose he'd had so much fun in his whole life, outside of public executions. 'Comical do that was, when those idiot soldiers ran straight past where you were hiding behind that barrel. If I hadn't told 'em where to look, they'd never have seen you.'

'Fancy,' said Lucius Domitius.

The Greek started roaring again, like a bull with the bellyache. 'Oh, this is too good for words. Here,' he went on, pulling a purse the size of Hercules' scrotum out of his belt and throwing it at us, 'take it, you've earned it, and thanks for the laugh. You've made my day.'

Lucius Domitius looked like he wanted to pull the Greek's head off and play handball with it, but there's a time and a place for everything. 'Thank you,' I said quickly, and I darted out and scooped up the purse before he could change his mind. 'Time we were going,' I hissed to Lucius Domitius, grabbing him by a handful of his hair, and – just as well for all concerned – he took the hint and followed me.

Once we were out of sight we started running, down the road and up a miserable stony little goat track that wound up into the rocks. We kept going until Lucius Domitius tripped over a rock and went splat on his face.

'All right,' I said, looking round, 'this'll do for a moment. Well, now,' I added, dropping onto the ground like a sack of onions, 'didn't I tell you it was going to be all right?'

Lucius Domitius called me a rude name, which was quite uncalled for. I wasn't bothered, though, because I'd pulled open the Greek's purse. It'd been a long time since I'd seen that much money all in one country, let alone snuggling in the palm of my hand.

'You see,' I went on, 'isn't that exactly what I've been telling you, about philosophy and all that shit? You look after the attitude, and Destiny'll take care of the rest.'

Lucius Domitius shook his head. 'I don't see that at all,' he said. 'Your attitude was pitiful. You just stood there in that dock looking like a badly stuffed olive.'

'I was being calm and dignified,' I told him. 'What did you think I was going to do, stand up and make a speech? Anyway, you can't talk. You were whimpering.'

'I was not.'

'You bloody were. I was so ashamed, I didn't know where to look. Really, if you're the stuff those fine old Roman families are made of, it beats me why we aren't all speaking Carthaginian.'

He made an impossible suggestion involving my head and other bits of me, and I left him to get on with his sulk. When you've been around with someone as long as I'd been with him, you get so you don't even notice stuff like that. Water off a duck's back, as the saying goes.

The crazy thing was – and I'm telling you the truth, straight up – I'd known all along that we weren't for it that time. I knew for a fact that we'd get out of it somehow or other, just so long as we played it cool and waited for God to yank our nuts out of the fire. Now it could be your Stoic philosophy, or maybe I'm prophetic like the crazy old women who work in oracles, or maybe some god appeared to me in a dream and told me the whole story of my life, and for some reason it'd slipped my mind. Maybe it's none of those things. Maybe it's just instinct. But I knew, sure as the runs after eating too many plums. I always know. Like I knew that time in Italy, when Callistus died —

Well, yes. Maybe I ought to tell you about that. I mean, now's as good a time as any, if there can be a good time for something like that. Truth is, I've been putting it off, because even thinking about it depresses me, let alone putting it into words. But I suppose you've got to know, sooner or later.

Bet you anything you've been wondering how in hell a scruff like me and the former emperor of the Romans came to be traipsing round together cheating honest men of their hard-earned money.

For one thing, you're asking, what could two such different men possibly have in common?

Well, that's easy. We both loved the same person, namely my poor brother Callistus, rest his soul.

As far as Lucius Domitius was concerned, the whole thing started more or less as a game. Back then, I have to say, he was a very different man in all sorts of ways. Creature of his environment, as the philosophers would say, because up till then his whole life was sort of creased down the middle: everything on the left-hand side being work, everything on the right being fun, and never the twain shall meet. Work entailed ruling the world, or at least trying to look like he ruled the world while Seneca and that ox-necked thug Burrus actually did the job, when, that is, they could spare the time from playing high politics and pass the hemlock soufflé with Lucius Domitius' ghastly mother. So work was a real pain in the bum: audiences and meetings and state receptions and trying to stay awake through all those mind-numbing religious services and smiling sweetly at ambassadors from the King of the Snake People and freezing your nuts off at trooping the colours in the cold light of a February dawn on the Field of Mars. Well, yes, it beats digging ditches or scraping out poultry sheds, but unless you happen to be a real old Roman with dried laurel leaves where your brains should be, it's hardly a barrel of laughs. Meanwhile, on the other side of the ledger, there's fun, and not just fun as in playing knucklebones or getting completely honked at the chariot races. When you're the last of the Julio-Claudian dynasty, heir to the likes of Tiberius and Caius Caligula, you're pretty well obliged to measure up to a fairly high standard of debauchery. It's expected of you, like wearing the toga and being able to recite your Homer. When they bring on the Libyan eunuchs on all fours dressed in goatskins, you can't turn round and say, No, thanks, I'd rather read a book.

Not that Lucius Domitius would rather have read a book – written one, possibly, but that's another tale. I'm certainly not trying to imply that he was in any sense backwards when it came to dunking his sausage in the gravy. But, as the old saying goes, if you get served up nightingales' livers in truffle sauce every meal for twenty years, you can be forgiven for daydreaming about a boiled egg and a stick of celery. Lucius Domitius told me once that after months and years of evenings spent at home with two dozen hand-picked Cappadocian virgins and characters with nicknames like Mylon the Human Flagpole, and always getting told when he asked whose idea it was, Well, that's how it was done in your uncle Caligula's time, and he was following on from your great-great-uncle Tiberius, it's *tradition* – well, he said, he reached the point where the dividing line between pleasure and duty was getting more than a little blurred. When you get to the stage where you can only tell one kind of ritual from another by whether or not the people taking part have got their clothes on, it's time to find yourself another hobby.

Now you don't need me to tell you what Lucius Domitius' hobby was, and of course he chose it precisely because it was the most shocking thing he could think of. Duty, you see: the Claudian family's always prided itself on being as outrageously offensive as possible, right back into the mists of prehistory, and the one thing a Roman aristocrat can never do is let the side down. So Lucius Domitius took up playing music and singing and writing poetry, like a slave or a Greek, and when people had sort of got used to that, he started doing it in public. Only, that was where he went that one step too far that makes all the difference. He was young, of course, still just a snot-nosed kid, so he can't really be blamed for it. Nevertheless, once he'd started down that track, there was no way he could ever go back.

In case you're wondering what was such a big deal – sure, noble Romans are expected to behave like wild animals in their free time, just like they're supposed to be absolutely prim and proper when they're on duty. But the whole point is, they're supposed to keep the private stuff private. Everybody knows what they get up to, there'd be no bloody point in doing it if they didn't. But what's not allowed, under any circumstances, is to do it in the road where the many-headed and the smelly-footed can see you. And as for standing up in the theatre or the circus and making a public exhibition of yourself – let's put it this way. Nobody really gave a second-hand breakfast about what Caligula got up to with his sisters behind closed doors. But when Lucius Domitius announced his first public concert, you'd have thought the world had come to an end.

Well, yes. That's Romans for you, and if every last one of them suddenly got eaten by giant killer ants, I'm not saying the world wouldn't be a much nicer place to live in. But they've been around a fair old while and there doesn't seem much chance of getting shot of them in the immediate future, so the sensible thing is to get to know how their bizarre little minds work. Besides, we Greeks aren't all that much better in some respects, though don't tell anybody I said so.

Anyway. When Lucius Domitius first set eyes on my brother Callistus and noticed the striking resemblance, it struck him as a splendidly Julio-Claudian sort of notion to have a boyfriend who was the spitting image of himself. All sorts of possibilities, as you don't need me to tell you. I expect he could almost picture the ghosts of his uncles and his great-great-uncles sagely nodding their approval and saying he was a chip off the old block. Trouble was – once again, typically Lucius Domitius took the thing one step too far, and screwed up everything. He fell in love.

Mind you, if you're going to go around falling in love with people, Callistus was a logical choice. I'm biased, of course. But ever since I can remember, I'd always somehow known that our kid was something special, like he was a different species or something: the improved model, the perfected strain, what people would be like if we lived in Plato's Republic instead of the septic tank of the nations we call the Roman Empire. It wasn't just that he was tall and well-built and muscular and all that shit, he was also all those things you'd expect would make someone a serious pain in the arse, like good and kind and brave and wise and generous and unselfish, except that you couldn't help liking him. When we were kids together, of course, I hated his guts. But I always loved him, better than anybody ever. He was like that.

So there you are, that's what the Emperor Nero and I had in common, and for some reason I can't begin to fathom (I loved Callistus, but I never ever understood him), he loved both of us, completely and straight from the heart, no mucking about. I couldn't even feel jealous, though I did my level best. Also, if we're going to be honest, when you go from starving in the gutter all night and running away from the guard all day to living in the palace and eating white bread off silver dishes, you're inclined to think nice thoughts about whoever is responsible for your change in lifestyle. So, as far as I was concerned, Lucius Domitius was all right, and if he was in love with my brother Callistus, it only went to show what good taste he'd got.

So there we were, Callistus, Lucius Domitius and me, all living in the palace along with several hundred other people, and generally speaking, things could've been a whole lot worse. Don't ask me how long I was living in the palace, because that kind of life does funny things to your sense of time. It was years, certainly: five or maybe even six. Funny thing. Either the time was whizzing by because I was living in the lap of luxury and everything was fine, or else it was dragging by like a lame snail because I had nothing to do all day and I was bored out of my skull. Whatever, it was a long time, and I'd got pretty well settled in when things suddenly started to go wrong.

Living in a palace, you haven't got a clue what's going on in the real world. Actually, in the *real* real world, where you and I and all the rest of the little people have to live, things weren't too bad at all. True, there were Romans all over the place, governing everything that couldn't get out of the way quick enough, but since Lucius Domitius had been sitting in the big chair, taxes had gone down, or at least they hadn't gone up; he didn't start any wars, so the countryside wasn't swarming with recruiting sergeants poised to swoop on the unwary; and for once there were half-competent people in charge of the grain supply, so people weren't starving in the streets. Pretty cushy all round, unless you happened to be a noble Roman. Unfortunately, noble Romans are the only ones who matter worth a damn, and they weren't having a nice time. Lower taxes meant they couldn't cruise round the provinces ripping off the locals and taking their slice off the top. No wars was a total disaster, of course, since if you don't have wars it's very hard for ambitious second lieutenants to earn medals. Worst of all, though, as far as they were concerned, was an emperor who stood up in front of twenty thousand dock workers, cheesemongers and professional layabouts in the theatre and sang songs about the fall of Troy, with harp accompaniment. Given a choice between that and an invasion by a million plague-infected Germans, they'd have taken the Germans so fast it'd have made your head spin.

Oddly enough, the conspiracy that had us all scared shitless was about the only one that didn't come to anything. That was the plot to give the throne to Julius Vindex, the governor of the province of Gaul. I have no idea why anybody thought Vindex would make a good emperor; in fact, I don't know anything at all about the man, other than his name and the job he did. But we were so busy worrying about him that we hardly noticed the Spanish governor, Sulpicius Galba, until his soldiers were inside a long spit of the city. Silly mistake to make – on a level with being so fussed over a missing roof tile that you fail to notice that the house is on fire.

Now, unless you were born in a cave and raised by wolves, you know perfectly well what happened next. Galba's army closed in on Rome and Nero killed himself before the cavalry could get to him; Galba became emperor and was killed by Marcus Salvius Otho; Otho became emperor, reigned for ninety-five days and killed himself before Aulus Vitellius' men could get at him; Vitellius wasn't so lucky when the governor of Africa, Titus Vespasianus, rolled into town: he was chopped up into little bits and slung in the river, and I'm in no hurry to tell you that it didn't serve him right.

And that's stone-cold history, which you heard about from a very reliable source in the barber's shop while it was going on, or learned about from your elders and betters, who you're duty-bound to believe. The truth is slightly different as regards some of the peripheral details, but nobody's going to stop a galloping horse, as my uncle used to say.

I can tell you a funny story about the Year of Five Emperors, as it's come to be called. One time, several years later, Lucius Domitius and I were in this wine shop in Apamea, which is a horrible dump of a city in northern Syria. So there we were, nursing a small jug of rotgut and minding our own business, and we got talking to this clerk, who was something trivial and boring in the Roman prefecture there. Anyway, he was fairly thoroughly tanked up, and after a bit he suddenly started cussing and ranting and carrying on about how he was the unluckiest man who ever lived, and how all his troubles were the fault of that miserable no-good bastard Nero.

At this point, Lucius Domitius topped up his cup from our jug and said there was a coincidence, because Nero had completely fucked up his life, too, and the clerk said, well, there you go. Then Lucius Domitius said, 'Excuse me asking, but what exactly did Nero do to you?'

Well, the clerk – can't remember his name, and it isn't important – he pulled a very sad face and explained that he hadn't always been a poxy little clerk, once upon a time he was the secretary in charge of production at the Mint in Rome, where they make all the coins. It was, he told us, a very responsible and important job, and he did it very well. His bosses told him how many of each type of coin would be needed each year, and it was his job to commission a sculptor to engrave the dies (for stamping the coins out of sheet metal), get dozens of identical copies made, and make sure the coins were made on schedule and all ready when they were needed for paying the soldiers, and so on.

As you can imagine, he said, it was a major part of his job to keep up with what was going on in the world, particularly anything that might mean a change of emperor. Like the rest of us, when things started going brown and smelly at the end of Nero's reign, he naturally assumed that Vindex was going to be the next emperor, but he was ready for that. He sent one of his house artists right up to Vindex's headquarters in Gaul to take a good look at him, make a few sketches, generally get an idea of what the man looked like so the Mint sculptors would be able to get some dies made up in plenty of time for the start of the new reign. No flies on him, he told us, as a big fat tear wobbled its way down his nose. He knew perfectly well that as soon as Vindex got in, the first thing he'd need would be barrels and barrels of freshly struck coins to pay off his soldiers with. So he put his top man on engraving Vindex's portrait, and a bloody wonderful job he made of it too. In fact, this sculptor reckoned it was the best work he'd ever done, totally lifelike and outrageously flattering at the same time. Only problem was, of course, that Vindex never got to be emperor; so there's our new friend, trashing those beautiful new dies – something told him that if Galba ever saw them, he'd be explaining to the palace guard exactly what he wanted them for – and chivvying his sculptors for portraits of Galba. Luckily for him, his chief engraver was a quick worker, and pretty soon lovely new denarii and sesterces were tumbling off the die-stampers' benches, ready for despatch to the army barracks.

Then, of course, Galba got scragged and Otho was in charge; and Otho was a pretty-faced type half Galba's age, so there was no chance of just firkling the dies about. In the scrap they went, and all those lovely new coins ended up in the melt, while the chief engraver sat up all night chipping out a suitably impressive portrait of Otho.

Being caught on the hop like that nearly gave the poor bugger a stroke, since what he liked best of all was to get his work done calmly and sensibly without having to rush. But he could get a wiggle on when he had to, and in just three months he'd got new dies installed and was all set to go, just in time for Otho to top himself and leave the way open for Aulus Vitellius.

At this point, the chief engraver walked out on him, and went to work for his brother-in-law mending bagpipes. So his assistant got an unexpected promotion, and slaved away night and day in order to come up with a really top-class likeness of Vitellius. It really was a triumph. So good, in fact, that one of the first things Vespasian did when he took over shortly afterwards was send the sculptor and our friend into exile, on the grounds that nobody could turn out such an admirable portrait of someone they didn't really admire.

So, said the clerk, there he was, doomed to spend his last few years scribbling inventories in the flyblown heat of Syria, and none of it would have happened if only that criminal lunatic Nero hadn't screwed things up to the point of being slung out of the palace. People in important, responsible jobs should have more consideration for others, he told us. It was their sacred duty to think of the consequences of their actions on innocent, hard-working people who only ever did their best in really appalling circumstances. In fact, he said, it was a bloody disgrace that Nero had been allowed to kill himself in quiet and peace, because he'd have enjoyed ripping the selfish bastard's lungs out with a blunt trowel.

Well, even though we weren't exactly flush right then, we reckoned it was the least we could do to buy this wretched sod a quart jug of the house blended red; and we ended up drinking Vespasian's health well into the wee small hours. Coincidentally, next morning we got the news that Vespasian had conked out and his boy Titus was now in charge; and strangers in the marketplace were so upset at the way the three of us took the news that they pulled horrible faces at us and asked us what in hell we thought was so funny.

★

Oh yes, there's a funny side to everything, if you're in the right place at the right time to appreciate the joke. There were probably quite a few people grinning like camels on the last night I spent in the palace, but I wasn't one of them.

First I knew of it was when someone woke me up out of a deep sleep (I've always had the knack of getting to sleep, even when things are at their hairiest). You know what it's like when you're dead to the world and suddenly you're bounced into being awake, it's like a real bitch of a hangover, distilled into a few seconds of intense pain and bewilderment. So there I was, and there was this shape looming over me with a guttering oil-lamp in its hand, but I couldn't see well enough to tell if it was my brother Callistus, or the emperor himself, or some god appearing to me in a dream looking like one or both of them.

'For fuck's sake, Galen,' the shape hissed at me, 'get up, it's an emergency,' and since it was talking Greek with a thick up-country Athenian accent rather than a poncified Roman one, I guessed it had to be my brother.

'Piss off, Callistus,' I yawned at him. 'It's the middle of the night.'

'Correct,' he snapped at me. 'It's just after midnight, and the whole place is deserted. There's nobody in the whole fucking palace except you, him and me.'

That woke me up, better than having the chamber pot emptied over my head. The palace was about the size of a large town, hundreds of people lived there, maybe even thousands. As well as the servants and the office workers and the cooks and hairdressers and laundry staff and gardeners and God-only-knows what else besides, there ought to have been a hundred or so palace guardsmen on duty all hours of the day and night, not to mention all the guests and hangers-on. 'Are you sure?' I asked him. 'We can't be the only ones here, it's not possible.'

'Come and see for yourself if you like,' he replied. 'And I'll give you a thousand sesterces for every man you can point to.'

'Shit,' I said. 'So what's going on?'

'Guess,' Callistus replied, throwing my tunic at me. 'And when you've done that, meet me by the kitchen door. Get us a sword each, and any money you can find. I'm going to fill a sack with bread and cheese. There's no knowing where it'll be safe to buy food.'

Now once he started gabbling on about swords, I knew we were really in trouble, since Callistus had always been one of those people who has involuntary bowel movements at the sight of anything sharp and pointy. His idea of martial arts was flopping down on his knees screaming 'Please don't hurt me!', and I'm pretty much the same. And a very satisfactory method it's proved to be, over the years.

Anyway, he buggered off before I had a chance to get any further news out of him, so I had no option but to do as he said. I pulled on my tunic in the dark — he'd taken the lamp with him — and I eventually managed to find my boots, groping about on the floor with my hands. To be fair to myself, I did try and find the stuff he told me to get, but everybody else in the place must've had the same idea: no money and no swords to be found anywhere. After I'd wasted loads of time looking, it struck me that if I didn't get down to the kitchens straight away the bastards might leave without me, so I packed in the search and hurried off as fast as I could go. He was absolutely right, of course. The whole building was as empty as a tinker's purse, and the echoing noise my boot heels made on the marble floors was the scariest sound I'd ever heard in a lifetime jam-packed with scary sounds.

'Where the hell have you been?' Callistus barked at me, when I caught up with the two of them at last. 'We thought something bad must've happened to you.'

Oddly enough, I was under the impression that something bad was happening to all three of us, right then and there, but I wasn't in the mood to argue the point.

A bloody comical sight we must've looked, so it was just as well there was nobody to see us. At least Callistus and I had our tunics and boots on. Lucius Domitius was still in his nightgown and slippers — crazily exotic slippers they were too, silk and seed-pearls, embroidered with the Rape of the Sabine Women in gold thread — with a ratty old cloak on top and a battered old leather hat that I'd last seen on the head of one of the gardeners. Considering how finicky he'd always been about how he looked, that was another very bad sign.

'Now then,' Callistus was saying, 'let's pull ourselves together, there's no reason why we can't get out of this if we only keep our heads. I say we head over to Phaon's place.' (Phaon was an ex-slave, freed by Lucius Domitius as a reward for twenty years' faithful service to the family; since then he'd made an obscene amount of money out of highway contracts and aqueduct concessions. He lived about four miles out of town, in a villa that looked like the sort of thing Zeus might have built for his retirement, if only he could have afforded it.) 'Anyone got any better ideas?'

Truth was, neither of us had any ideas of any description, so we set off for Phaon's house. Now, Lucius Domitius wasn't used to walking. Running, yes. He liked taking part in athletics and all that shit, and he wasn't half bad for an amateur. But walking wasn't something he'd ever had to do, especially not in the dark, down cobbled alleys and rutted lanes, in thin-soled pornographic sandals. As a result, our progress was a bit more leisurely than any of us would have liked. It got worse. For one thing, the shortest route to Phaon's place took us right past the gates of the Guards' barracks, and it was a year's wages to a second-hand mackerel that if the soldiers recognised Lucius Domitius we'd all be for the chop. We put our heads down and hurried past, which was a bloody silly thing to do, since it made us look furtive and suspicious – what we should have done was lurch along singing objectionable songs, as if we were plastered, but we didn't think of that. Anyhow, we got stopped by the soldiers and asked to explain ourselves.

Looking back, the expression on the soldiers' faces when they shoved their lantern under our noses and saw not one but two apparent Lucius Domitiuses was one of the most comical things I've ever seen. Wasn't quite so droll at the time, though. Fortunately, Callistus' brain was still just about turning over. He grinned like an idiot, and told them we were entertainers.

The guardsman wasn't expecting that. 'You what?' he said.

'Entertainers. Actually,' Callistus went on sheepishly, 'we're professional Nero impersonators, and this is our manager.' He nudged me savagely in the ribs and I nodded three times. 'What we do is we show up at parties and weddings and stuff, and we do Nero impressions; you know, singing and playing the harp and doing little dances. It's not a bad gig, so long as you're careful not to overstep the mark.'

The soldiers were staring at us as if we had three heads each. 'You can make a living doing that?' one of them said.

'Sure. Twenty sesterces a night, plus nosh and a drink or two. Better than digging ditches. But we sort of got the impression that the bottom's about to fall out of the Nero business, so we're clearing out of town for a while.'

The soldiers just stood there gawping at us for a scarily long time, then one of them shrugged, as if to say that nobody could possibly make up a bloody stupid story like that so it must be true. 'Good idea,' he said. 'In fact, if I was you I'd put a good long stretch of road behind you as quick as you can.'

'Thanks,' Callistus said, 'we'll do that. Have a nice day.'

That wasn't all. No sooner had we got out of earshot of the barracks but the ground started jumping up and down, and there was a terrific crash of thunder, followed by lightning. Too much for Lucius Domitius, who'd always been pathetically superstitious; and I can't pretend I didn't feel a sharp twitch in the bladder, even though I'm savvy enough to tell the difference between a mild earth tremor with thunderstorm accompaniment and the wrath of the gods. It took us several minutes of comforting, cajoling and arse-kicking to get Lucius Domitius back on his feet, and even then he was gibbering away in Latin under his breath all the way out of town and into the country lanes.

Did I mention I hate the countryside? May sound odd coming from a farm boy like me, but the great outdoors gives me a pain in the tush. It's horrible all the time, but at night, when you can't see spit and you don't know where you're going, it's at its unspeakable worst. We walked into brambles and went in up to our knees in reed beds. We wandered into an abandoned gravel pit and couldn't find our way out. In the end we had to scale a small cliff: Callistus on top, me bringing up the rear, and the two of us pulling and pushing Lucius Domitius like a pair of dung-beetles. Eventually, just when we'd convinced ourselves that we were hopelessly lost, we walked straight into the outer wall of Phaon's place (literally). That was all right, but we couldn't find the gate. We trudged up and down, following the wall, but if it was there we contrived to walk straight past it. This was getting ridiculous, so we dropped down on our heels and tried to figure out what to do. Climbing the wall was out of the question, with Lucius Domitius doing a wonderfully life-like impression of a three-hundredweight sack of onions. Then Callistus laughed and said, 'Not to worry. If we can't go over the bugger or through it, we'll go under.'

That bothered me a lot. Things were bad enough already without Callistus cracking up and starting to babble. But he was quite serious. We'd get down on our hands and knees and scrabble away with our fingers and burrow under the wall.

And that's what we did; and it worked. Turned out we were sat right next to the spot where a drain ran under the wall. We cleared away a bit of mud and shit, and there was a nice big hole for us to crawl through – even big enough for Lucius Domitius, and he was quite a size back then, especially round the bum.

So, we were through. Lucius Domitius was all for striding up to the front door, assuming we could find it, and banging on it like gentlemen. But Callistus didn't like that idea. He'd been turning things over in his mind ever since we left town, and he'd come around to thinking that maybe Phaon wouldn't turn out to be quite as friendly as we'd thought. Well, we weren't too happy about that, and I might have suggested that it'd have been better all round if he'd thought of that earlier. Anyway, while we were discussing the point, Lucius Domitius happened to find some gardeners' tools – actually, he stood on a rake and got smacked on the nose by the handle – and that set Callistus off again. If we could dig under the outer wall, he reckoned, we could bust into the house the same way, and nobody would know we were there; and if you don't know someone's there, you can't turn him in to the soldiers, however treacherous a bastard you may happen to be.

You can tell how tired and screwed up we all were from the fact that that line of reasoning seemed to make sense. So we prodded and groped around until we found tools to dig with: a pick, a double-tooth mattock and a shovel, to be precise. This isn't the tool kit of choice of your career housebreaker, but it was better than using our hands and risking Lucius Domitius breaking a fingernail. We chose a spot at random just under the back wall of the house and began to dig, and we'd hardly got started when the ground just seemed to give way under us, and there we were, sitting on our rear ends on the cold flagstones of Phaon's cellar.

Long silence, then Lucius Domitius pipes up. 'Well, here we are, then,' he says. 'Now what?'

Things are different in real life to how you imagine they'll be. Needless to say, all that racket didn't pass unnoticed. Phaon turns up at the cellar door holding a lamp. He peers at us through the darkness and says, 'Oh, it's you,' like he'd met a poor relation at the racetrack. 'What do you want?' he says, and we get the impression he's not thrilled to bits to see us – though it's understandable, I guess, because how would you feel about a party of uninvited guests who've just caved in a hole in your cellar roof?

Well, we'd achieved our objective against all the odds: we'd got to Phaon's villa, and you'd have thought we'd be pleased with ourselves. Not so, because it dawned on us that even though we'd completed our mission, we were still just as much up to our knees in cowplop as we'd ever been. At best, all we'd done was buy ourselves a little time.

Phaon told us the news from town; it wasn't good. Apparently there'd been a special emergency meeting of the Senate, at which Lucius Domitius had been declared an enemy of the people and a warrant had been issued for his arrest. As soon as he was found, they said, he'd be punished in the old-fashioned way—

'What does that mean, exactly?' Lucius Domitius interrupted.

'It's the ancient traditional punishment for treason,' Phaon told him. 'They strip you naked, wedge your neck in a wooden fork and beat you to death with sticks. Apparently it's been so long since it was last done they had to look it up in the old records.'

Another thing Lucius Domitius hadn't had much experience of was pain. Toothache a couple of times (though he had remarkably good teeth; anyway, far better than he deserved after spending his early years stuffing his face with honeycakes. Where I grew up, we couldn't afford the stuff that rots your teeth but I've been a martyr to toothache all my life). Nothing worse than that, though, so the idea of being tortured to death scared him rigid. That's your Roman nobility for you. Soft as a pancake.

'It's all right,' Callistus interrupted, 'it's not going to come to that. Oh, for pity's sake,' he went on, as Lucius Domitius produced a pair of very small, extremely fancy daggers from his sleeve. 'Put those things away before you cut yourself.'

'I'm not going to let them take me alive,' Lucius Domitius said. Then he got a fit of the shakes and dropped the daggers on the ground with a clang. The jewelled knob on the end of one of them came off and rolled across the floor. 'But maybe you're right,' he added quickly. 'Maybe we can get out of this after all. What do you think, Phaon? Can you hide us here until everything settles down?'

'No,' Phaon replied. Well, at least he was honest about it. 'You must be out of your tiny mind bringing him here,' he went on, addressing Callistus (presumably because he recognised that my brother was the only member of the party with enough common sense to smear on a biscuit). 'This'll be one of the first places they look, and if they catch you here, I'll be feeding the crows along with the rest of you.'

I must say, disaster is a wonderful way of getting to know people. The couple of times I'd met Phaon before, I'd put him down as just another Imperial brown-noser: polite, charming, anything-you-say-is-fine-with-me-Caesar. A pain in the bum, in other words. I never knew he could be so refreshingly straightforward.

At this point, Lucius Domitius burst into tears. 'It's all my fault,' he said. 'I brought it all on myself, and now all of you – the only true friends I've ever had – you're going to be killed along with me. It's all because I'm such a pathetic coward. If I had a scrap of decency about me, I'd kill myself right now.'

Callistus sighed. 'Shut up, will you, for God's sake, I'm trying to think.' He scowled for a moment, then grabbed Phaon by the sleeve. 'You,' he said, 'get upstairs, watch the road, the moment you see anything, you let us know. Right?'

Phaon nodded and fled.

'I wouldn't trust that arsehole if I were you,' I muttered. 'If the soldiers show up, I bet you he'll be running down the road yelling, "This way! Over here!" as fast as his feet'll carry him.'

Callistus looked at me. 'That's what I'm counting on,' he said. 'Now shut up and listen, both of you. I think I've got it figured out, so for crying out loud pay attention. I don't know how long we've got.'

He sounded so confident that for a moment I really believed he might have thought of something. After all, hadn't he winkled me out of the shit a dozen or so times over the years, starting with that stunt in the bathhouse? All right, Callistus was no Aristotle, but he could think on his feet. 'What's the plan?' I asked hopefully.

'All right.' Callistus stooped down and picked up the funny little daggers. 'I think Phaon's probably right. Sooner or later they'll look for us here. I should have seen that back in the palace, but I didn't, so I'm the one to blame. I want that understood before we go any further. I'm the one who's got us in this mess, so I'm the one who'll have to get us out. That's the plain truth, and I don't want any arguments from you two. Clear?'

Of course, Lucius Domitius had never seen him in this mood before. He was a bit stunned, I think, at being spoken to like a foot-man or a stable-boy. Probably just as well, because it made him keep quiet. Anyway, we both nodded to show we agreed, and Callistus continued: 'We could try and get away, but I don't like the odds. The three of us, on foot – if we stick to the roads we'd never cover enough ground before the soldiers find us. It's a simple matter of walkers against riders. If we go across country, we won't have a clue where we are, we'll be strangers, sticking out like a maggot in an apricot. You know what it's like in farm country, Galen. If there's a stranger in the district, everybody knows about it before the poor bugger's gone a mile. Long story short: I think running for it is out.'

'So's hiding,' I pointed out. 'You heard the fat man. We can't stay here.'

But Callistus shook his head. 'That's not what I'm proposing,' he said. 'Think for a moment. What'll it take to get the soldiers to fuck off and leave you in peace?'

'That's easy,' Lucius Domitius groaned. 'My head in a basket.'

'Fine,' Callistus said, with a slight nod. 'Then that's what we'll give them.'

I have to say, forget about the context for a moment, the look on Lucius Domitius' face was something quite comical. 'You *bastard,'* he said, backing away until his arse bumped into the wall. 'You're going to give me to them after all. You *bastard.'*

(See what I mean about disaster? This from the same fat slob who was all set to slash his wrists two minutes earlier so Callistus and I could escape. And the rest.)

But Callistus shook his head again. 'That's not what I've got in mind,' he replied calmly. Then he turned to me. 'Galen,' he said, 'you remember that polecat we had when we were kids? And the bloody thing got loose and scragged Anaxarchus' prize rooster, and he came storming over our place swearing at Mother, and unless we gave him the polecat so he could pull its neck, he'd have the archon and the soldiers and the governor-general on us, and see us all in the galleys?' He grinned. 'And you remember what we did?'

I didn't like the way this was going. 'Sure,' I said. 'You made a little wicker trap and went up the hill to where you knew there was a polecat nest, and you trapped a stringy old gill and gave that to Anaxarchus, and he never knew the difference. But—'

'Exactly.' My brother's grin melted into a smirk. 'He got a polecat to kill, we got to keep ours, and everybody was happy.'

'Except the other polecat,' I pointed out.

'Screw the other polecat. Besides, this is better. This time, we don't have to go snaring a decoy, we've got a volunteer.'

I was afraid that was what he'd meant. Really afraid – you know, that cold griping feeling in your bladder that makes you want to pee all down your leg. From anybody else, I simply wouldn't have believed it. But coming from Callistus – well, he was that sort of person. He didn't mess about, and he was straight down the line, always.

'Just hold on, will you?' Lucius Domitius had that dumb, bewildered look on his face. Really, for two coatpins I could have banged his head against the wall. 'I don't understand. Will someone please explain what you two are talking about?'

Callistus swung round on him. 'Oh God,' he said, 'have I got to spell it out for you? Listen. You and I look pretty much the same, right? Not shoulder to shoulder, maybe, but anyone seeing me on my own, without you there, would take me for you. Certainly it's a good enough likeness to fool a guards captain who's only seen you maybe half a dozen times on parade or in the theatre.'

'Yes,' Lucius Domitius said. 'How's that going to help us?'

Bloody fool, he still hadn't seen it. Callistus had to explain. 'Simple,' he said. 'You kill me. When they get here, they find my body and think they've got you. You're hiding up in the hayloft, but of course they won't bother searching, they'll think they've got the genuine article—'

Lucius Domitius screamed. I kid you not: a full-blooded scream, like a pig being slaughtered with a blunt knife. 'No,' he whimpered, 'no, no, you can't. No, I won't let you. Don't even say such a thing, it's horrible—'

Callistus slapped him round the face, put a lot of wrist into it. It worked. Lucius Domitius stopped squealing and stared at him in horror.

'That's settled, then,' Callistus said. 'Right.' He held out one of the little daggers. 'Come on, then, we don't know how long we've got. It'd be best if you can scuff my face up a bit, not so much that they won't recognise me, just enough to blur the edges a bit. Well, come on, for pity's sake.'

But Lucius Domitius was sliding down the wall like a slug and sobbing helplessly. He wasn't going to be any use. 'Callistus,' I said, 'what the hell are you thinking about? You can't chuck your life away for – for *that*.'

'Fuck you,' he replied savagely. 'It's my life. When I think how many times you nearly got us killed with your bloody stupid scams, and I had to risk my neck to save you.' He must have seen from the look on my face that I was suddenly going all to pieces. It was as if someone had peeled me open, taken out all my bones, and sewn me up again. 'It's all right, really,' he said gently. 'This is what I want to do, for his sake, and mine. And it's not as if we've got any options. It's either me or all of us, so it's as broad as it's long.'

'Bullshit,' I said. I was starting to shake all over. Odd thing. Ever so many times I've been sure I was about to die, and with good reason; I was always scared shitless, yes, but there was never that feeling of absolute total despair – because, I guess, I knew that if I got snuffed it wouldn't really matter (because what bloody good am I to anybody? None at all, not even to myself). But the thought that Callistus would die – that he'd die and I'd be left on my own – I'd never had to face that before, and I'm telling you, I couldn't take it. It was only being frozen stiff with horror that stopped me blubbering helplessly like Lucius Domitius was doing.

And then he said: 'Galen, I want you to do this thing for me. I've never asked you for a favour before, ever, but I'm asking you now, because it's important. Will you do it for me? Will you?'

And I heard myself answer, 'All right,' because, fuck it, I couldn't really say anything else. That was Callistus for you: sometimes, just occasionally, he made you want to be like him.

'Will you?' he repeated, and I nodded my stupid head, and let him stick one of those ridiculous little knives in my hand. He had to fold my fingers round the handle just to stop me dropping the thing.

Then he took a step towards me, and of course I shrank back, like he was the one who was about to knife me, and not the other way about. 'Pull yourself together, Galen,' he said sharply, 'let's get this over and done with.' Behind him, Lucius Domitius started wailing and boo-hooing like a fractious two-year-old; it'd have made a cat laugh to hear him, but not me. Callistus came closer; I tried to stay put, but I couldn't, and then my back was to the wall and there wasn't anywhere else to go. 'Come *on*,' Callistus shouted – he was *annoyed*, of all the things to be – and I opened my eyes very wide and stabbed him.

Of course, it was a bloody shambles; I screwed it up, like I screw up everything. I got him all right – there was blood everywhere, all over my hands, on the floor, you name it – but he was still alive. He was hurting, you didn't have to be a doctor to see that, but he was trying very hard to keep his temper. 'It's all right,' he said, 'you've got to try again.' He reached out and took my hand, pushed it away so as to pull the knife out of his gut. 'Go on,' he said, 'up here, look.' I suppose he meant his heart or his neck, but I was completely lost, I couldn't even breathe. So he lifted my hand until the point of the knife was pressed up against that little hollow where the collarbones meet the neck, and then he put his arms around me and hugged me.

I tried to grab hold of him as he fell but he was too slippery with blood, he slithered down my front and landed at my feet in a heap, and all I could do was look down at him. I wanted to scream, but I didn't have a voice. It was the worst thing ever.

God knows how long I stood there, but at some point that little shit Phaon came bursting in, yelling something about the cavalry, and then he saw the dead body, and me, and he said, Oh God. Then I guess some part of me I don't know much about seemed to take over, and I heard myself say, 'It's all right, I killed him.'

Fortunately, Phaon was too busy staring at the bloody mess on the floor to look round and see Lucius Domitius. So when he said, 'Who? Who've you killed?' I said, 'Caesar, of course, who the hell do you think? He didn't want to be captured, so I killed him.'

Phaon tore his eyes off the thing on the ground and looked up at me. 'Now what?' he said.

'Now you go out and meet the cavalry,' I said. 'And you fetch them down here and you show them the body, and you tell them a slave did it.' I don't know who was saying all this stuff. It sounded like the sort of thing Callistus would say, only it was my voice I could hear, but when was I ever that bright or that resourceful? 'You tell them,' I went on, 'that the slave who did this was Epaphroditus – you know, that evil little wanker who used to write his letters for him. This is very important: Galen and Callistus were never here, you never saw them tonight, it was Epaphroditus the secretary who killed him, and he ran off before you got here. Do you understand?'

Phaon was too fuddled to argue. 'Epaphroditus,' he repeated, like he was learning his lines for a play. 'All right.'

'Good,' I said. 'Because if you tell them different, if you say it was Galen and Callistus, and we get caught, we're going to tell the magistrates that it was you who helped him escape from the palace, and you brought him here, and you were going to hide him – you get the idea.'

Phaon was too scared to talk, so he just nodded.

'Right,' I said. 'Now piss off.'

So he ran out, and I grabbed Lucius Domitius by the collar, and I pretty much had to drag him out of there, up through the hole we'd made in the cellar roof, and I had to push him to make him start running, and I had to keep shoving him in the bum to keep him from stopping and flolloping down in a big messy heap, and we ran out through the orchard and under the wall, and once we were on the road we kept running, and running.

And, basically, that's what we've been doing ever since.

THREE

Where were we? Oh yes.

So there we were in Sicily, on the run, having just escaped from fifteen years in the slate quarries (which was good), all because some crazy Greek had massacred our guards (which was bad, since we were going to get the blame, and pretty soon every soldier in the island was going to be looking for us). We had a big purse of the crazy Greek's money (also good), and the clothes we stood up in (also bad, because the fashion statement they made was unmistakably Escaped Convict). We hadn't got a clue where we were, or what we were going to do next. By our standards, in other words, just another day at the office.

'The first thing we need to do,' I told Lucius Domitius, as we picked our way down a rocky hillside, 'is get out of these clothes and get a wash and a brush up. Next, we go to Mauretania.'

He stopped dead in his tracks and stared at me. 'Mauretania,' he repeated.

'Mauretania. It's the answer to all our problems. All we have to do is go there, and we'll be free and clear, all our troubles will be over.'

'Oh, good,' said Lucius Domitius. 'Would you mind awfully telling me why?'

I scowled at him. 'It's obvious. First, it's easy to get to from here, there's ships going backward and forwards every day. Second, nobody knows us in Mauretania, we'd be off to a fresh start, and we wouldn't be looking over our shoulders every two minutes. Third, the Mauretanians are a nation of born marks.'

'What?'

'Marks.' Was he being deliberately obtuse or something? 'Suckers. Not very bright people. Rich, fat, friendly and gullible. We'll do well there.'

He looked at me as if I was dribbling at the mouth. 'Where the hell did you get that idea from?'

'It's common knowledge,' I told him. 'Everybody knows that. It's, what's the word, proverbial. Rich and thick, like buttermilk. You go to any of those places, they're all the same. Tingis, Icosium, Cyrene—'

'Cyrene's in Libya.'

'Is it?' Trust Lucius Domitius to split hairs, just when I was getting a flow going. 'Well, it's all the same thing, isn't it?'

'No, it isn't,' he replied snottily. 'They're a thousand miles apart.'

'Let's not quibble over details,' I told him. 'The point is, it's a long way from here. Also,' I went on, because this was the good bit I'd been working round to, only he'd interrupted me, 'it's border country. Basically, you've got your long, narrow coastal area which is your Roman province, and behind that, there's the vast expanse of free Mauretania, which is an independent state. And you know what that means.'

He nodded. 'They don't speak Latin,' he said.

'Which means,' I told him patiently, 'it's outside the jurisdiction. If things get hot for us and we need to clear out in a hurry, all we've got to do is nip over the line and we're safe. No extradition.'

He shook his head. 'You're wrong there,' he said. 'There's a treaty between the empire and the free state.'

'No, there isn't.'

'Yes, there bloody well is. I should know, I signed it.'

I shrugged. 'Well, anyway,' I said. 'It's got to be better than here, with soldiers looking for us under every bush. What do you say?'

He looked doubtful. 'I don't know,' he said.

'Don't be such a pain in the bum. It's wide-open territory out there. And a fantastic climate.'

He raised an eyebrow at me. 'It's all deserts, isn't it?'

'Only when you get inland a way.'

'Didn't you say that's where we're headed? Besides, they've got lions in Mauretania, and scorpions the size of cats. And savage

nomadic tribesmen who'll kill you for what's under your fingernails. We don't want to go there.'

'Yes, we do.'

'No, we don't.'

' "No, we don't",' I repeated. 'I'll say this for you, Lucius
Domitius, all those years you spent honing your debating skills
with the finest minds of your generation, they really paid off, didn't
they?'

'Oh, shut up.'

All this time we'd been carrying on down into the valley, until we
reached the flat plain where the farmland started. We still didn't
know where we were, of course, and my instincts were telling me
we should stay up in the rocky bits, away from where people lived
and we'd stick out like pimples. Actually, my instincts were bickering like an old married couple, because they were also telling me
that up in the rocky bits was where the soldiers would expect us to
be. What we needed to do was get out of those clothes, stop being
runaway quarry slaves and become something else. That's one of
the good things about not being anything at all: you've got flexi-
bility.

Pretty soon we found ourselves on a dusty little road between
small, stone-walled olive groves, with a little river chortling along
somewhere close on our right. This wasn't good, since anybody
seeing us would know we weren't local. I was wondering what we
could do about this when we heard voices coming from a little
patch of beech trees dead ahead. Bugger, I thought; I grabbed
Lucius Domitius by the sleeve and pulled him down behind a wall.

'Now what?' he said.

'Voices up ahead,' I told him. 'Shut up, I want to listen.'

So I listened, and then I started to grin. There were two of
them, a young man and a girl, and it was pretty obvious what they
were doing; no threat to us, anyhow. Lucius Domitius started to get
up, but I pulled him down again.

'Oh for pity's sake,' he muttered. 'You might get off on eaves-
dropping on young lovers making out in the fields, but now isn't
the time. We're running for our lives, in case you'd forgotten.'

I sighed. No attention to detail, you see. You've got to pay attention in this life, or you'll walk past all your golden opportunities and never know they're there. 'Listen,' I said.

I don't have many talents, but I can place people by their voices, it's a knack I have. The girl was easy enough, some local farm kid; probably she'd been doing the family laundry down by the river when she met the boy. He was rather more interesting. Admittedly he wasn't saying much, she was the one making all the noise, but when he did say anything, he said it in Latin. It's my experience that in these moments of high passion, people don't tend to muck about with foreign languages. What we'd got here was a genuine, twenty-carat Roman.

The rest of it was easy enough to figure out. Personally, I blame the schools. If you send your kid to one of those fashionable places where they set them reading Theocritus and all that stuff, all about handsome young noblemen out hunting who run into lovely, willing peasant girls in idyllic pastoral settings, what the hell do you expect? It's always worse the closer you get to a big city, of course. Where I come from, near Athens, it's getting so you can't duck in behind a bush for a quick shit without tripping over a Strephon-and-Amaryllis act in among the daisies and buttercups.

So, there we were, and what I needed most of all, of course, was a bathhouse creeper's hook.

Sorry, I'm getting technical. You know what a bathhouse creeper is, right? Just in case you don't, think of one of those low-life characters who make their living stealing things from the changing rooms of the public baths. It's an ancient profession with a rich heritage of tradition, though I've never done much good with it myself. The principal tool of the trade is your small bronze hook mounted on a long, thin, flexible shaft, which you stick through the bathhouse window and use to fish out purses, cloaks, hats, whatever. I'm told they make the best ones in Alexandria, with three prongs and a shaft that folds up so you can stash it under your cloak, but any old hook will do, and if you haven't got a hook, you can always use a suitably shaped branch off a tree.

That's assuming you can find one. The nearest trees were the beeches where the Sweet Young Things were still hammering away at it (which reminded me, I had to get a move on; they couldn't keep going for ever), so I crept up as quietly as I could and had a snoop round for a fallen branch. No joy, but they didn't seem to have heard me, so I took a chance and broke a long, whippy shoot off a sapling. Just the job, right down to the handy little fork near the tip, which would do just as well as any fancy three-tined Egyptian bronze hook.

Another thing I've observed about your young Roman buck: when he goes al fresco bonking, he always takes his clothes off – so they don't get dusty and covered in grass stains, I guess. Wouldn't do for everybody to be able to tell at a glance where he's been or what he's been up to. Amazing streak of prudery in the high Roman character, which is a real blessing for a bloke in need of a change of clothes.

Like I said, I've never really done much with creeper's hooks. The real artists – ticklers, they call them in the trade – can winkle out a ring or a brooch through a narrow window with their eyes shut, standing on their mates' shoulders. I'm not in that league, but I'm good enough to snag a tunic and a belt on the flat. For some reason, the bastard had kept his sandals on, but there wasn't anything I could do about that.

'Right,' I whispered to Lucius Domitius, once I'd got safely back behind our wall. 'Time we weren't here.'

So we hopped it, back up the road in the opposite direction for a hundred yards, then across the river on stepping stones, up the other side and into a handy stand of fir trees. Only then did we have a chance to examine our haul.

'Nice,' Lucius Domitius said, fingering the cloth. 'Good weave. Mainland Greek wool.'

I nodded. 'And get a load of the buckle on the belt,' I said. 'That's ivory, not bone. Let's see what's in the purse.'

Less than I'd expected: fifteen in silver and some copper, but every bit you get makes a little more, as my old mother used to say. 'Right,' said Lucius Domitius, 'I'd better try them on.'

That wasn't what I'd had in mind. 'You?' I said. 'Don't give me that. You want a change of threads, go steal your own.'

'Don't be stupid,' Lucius Domitius replied. 'Think about it for a moment, will you? We've got one high-class tunic between the two of us, right? So one of us is going to be the master, and the other one's his faithful slave. Do you really think anybody's going to believe in you as a smart young city type?'

He had a point, unfortunately. You don't get Greeks swanning round with Italian slaves, not even in Sicily. 'All right,' I muttered. 'But just till we get to a town with a tailor's stall. Understood?'

He grinned. 'We'll see,' he said, pulling his tunic off over his head. 'Now then,' he went on, putting on the nicked tunic, but he got half of the way in, then stopped. It was way too small for him.

'You were saying,' I said.

He tried again, twice, and only gave up when we heard the ominous sound of stitching giving way under the strain. 'All right,' he conceded, 'you try. Though it's probably too small for you, too.'

Fitted me like a glove. Well, like a small glove, but at least I could get my neck through the head hole without ripping it to shreds. 'There,' I said, 'how do I look?'

'Like a Greek tickler who's just stolen a Roman's shirt,' he replied. 'I suppose you'll pass as an ex-slave who's come into money, though the ear's a bit of a giveaway.' Valid point, and it just went to show he could pay attention to detail when it suited him. It's a good tip for telling your genuine ex-slave, by the way: look for the mark on the ear lobe where the piercing's healed over. A bit of free advice for you, to help you when dealing with rogues and unscrupulous characters.

'It'll do,' I said. 'All right, I'm a wealthy freedman on a business trip, and you're my personal attendant. What line are we in?'

He thought for a moment. 'Dried fish?'

'This far inland? Not likely. What else have they got in Sicily?'

'Wheat,' Lucius Domitius said, trying to remember his geography lessons, 'wool, figs. Cheese. Sicilian sheeps' milk cheese, those big cartwheel jobs with the thick plaster rinds.'

'That'll do,' I said. 'All right, I'm a Mauretanian cheese merchant—'

'Oh for pity's sake.'

'Well, everybody's got to be from somewhere. I'm a Mauretanian cheese importer, my name's Pittacus – our neighbour next door but two down the valley at home,' I explained, before he could ask me where I'd got the name from. 'You're a slave, obviously. Galatian, you'll pass for a Celt with that hair – know any Celtic names?'

'No,' he said. 'Let's just stick to Lucius, or we'll get confused. That's the trouble with you, always making it too elaborate, so we forget or muddle ourselves up, and then—'

'Yes, all right.' I took a moment to get myself into character. 'Fine,' I said. 'Now, let's get some more space between us and the owner of this shirt, just in case. An extra mile never hurts, as my brother used to say.'

I can't say as I like Sicily much, but one thing it's got going for it, you never have to walk terribly far before you get to somewhere. It may not be anywhere exciting, or the place you want to be, but so long as you keep going you'll find yourself in a village or a town. Other places I've been, you can walk all day and never see anything but rocky mountains, or desert, or moorland; and one place I was in, I remember walking for three days and seeing nothing but row upon row of beans.

The place we fetched up in was either a fat village or a thin town. Anyhow, there were a couple of dozen houses, a smithy, a wheelwright's shop and a tower, all perched on a hilltop like a pimple on a Roman's nose. It was a bit like the poxy little towns in Attica where I grew up, except that you got the impression that people only went there if they had a reason, or couldn't avoid it. Oh yes, and there was a little thatched shrine to some minor local hero or other (but then again, there always is, isn't there?).

Obviously, we headed for the smithy, as being the place where the local deadheads and time-wasters would be likely to hang out. Village smithies in predominantly Greek communities are remarkable things. You can spend your life going from one to another and I'll bet you ten drachmas you'll never ever see any work getting done. But they must make a living somehow, and if you want your hoe straightened or your ploughshare fixed, the man'll give you a long, cool stare and tell you he might be able to get round to it at some point in the second half of the month after next, with a following wind and barring a plague of locusts. What you will see, on the other hand, is half a dozen old-timers with five good teeth between them, a bloke with a wooden leg who talks to himself all the time, three or four farmers who look at you as if you're something they've tracked into the house on the sole of their boot, one blacksmith sitting on a stump drinking, and one skinny twelve-year-old boy leaning on a fifteen-pound sledgehammer. The moment you show up, of course, they'll all immediately stop talking, except the guy with the wooden leg, and they'll stare at you for a very long time, and then the smith'll say, 'Right, then,' or something like that.

Now, this is where you need to be careful. If you come right out with it and say what you want, like, 'The wheel's come off my cart, can you possibly fix it for me?' or, 'Is there anywhere I can get a bed for the night?' or, 'Where the hell is this?' or whatever, they're all going to look at you like you've got six heads, and a four-year-old girl you hadn't noticed before's going to burst into tears and run into the house yelling for Mummy. No; what you want to do when the smith says, 'Right, then,' is stand there leaning on your walking stick and nod your head just the tiniest bit, with a little upwards flick. If you've done it right, there'll be a silence that lasts about as long as it takes a cat to throw up a furball, and then they'll carry on with their conversation where they left off, and you're in. It's all right, they've accepted you, and sooner or later someone's going to pipe up and ask you what you want. Just follow these simple rules, and there's no reason why you can't get yourself an overpriced dinner of sausage and leek broth and a night's sleep in a hayloft in any village in the Eastern Mediterranean.

Anyway now that you know the drill, I don't need to take you through it step by step, so let's skip to the bit after the smith says, 'Right, then,' and on to where one of the old farmers says, 'And what'll you boys be after?'

The good thing about this ritual is that it gives you time to get yourself together, which is handy if you're being someone else for the first time. 'Just a bite to eat and somewhere to doss down for the night.' I said, 'And could you tell me if we're on the right road for Leontini?'

The old farmers looked at each other. The kid with the hammer sniggered. 'Leontini,' said the smith, as if we'd asked him if he'd seen any pink-winged hippogriffs lately. 'Nope. Can't say as you are.'

'Oh,' I said. Not that I cared a damn, you understand, I just wanted to find out where we were. 'So where are we, then?'

'Heracleia,' said one of the farmers. That was a fat lot of good. It's a fact that nine out of ten villages in the Greek-speaking world are called Heracleia, and the ones that aren't are called Aegae.

'Right,' I said. 'So where does this road go, then?'

Short pause. 'Syracuse,' said one of the old men.

'Yes, we just came from there. What about in the other direction?'

'In the *other* direction.' The shortest and stockiest of the farmers frowned, like he was doing long division in his head. 'Well, if you keep going long enough, reckon you'll wind up in Camarina.' And serve you right, he didn't add, but it was all there in his tone of voice.

'Ah, right,' I said, like I knew where the hell Camarina was. 'We must've taken a wrong turn back at the ford.' It's always safe to say that. Well nine times out of ten, anyway.

'That'd be right,' grunted the smith. 'You want to get to Leontini, your best bet'd be to go back the way you just come, then head west where you went east and carry on up over.'

I shrugged. 'Camarina's just as good to us,' I said. 'See, I'm just going round looking for places where I can buy good quality Sicilian cheese. That's my business. Actually,' I went on, 'maybe you gentlemen could help me out here. Does anybody make cheese in these parts?'

Stunned silence, then they all shuffled half a step closer. 'Best cheeses in Sicily,' croaked the oldest of the farmers. 'Known for it, in fact. You won't get a better bit of cheese this side of Acragas.'

It all went like a dream after that, of course. Somehow, about half an hour later, the whole village knew that there was some lunatic stranger in town willing to pay actual silver money for anything round with a plaster rind on it. Never been so popular in all my life. Of course, I had the wit to play it cool. Gnarled old men came bustling up shoving cheeses under my nose, but I kept on frowning and sucking my teeth, and saying, 'Well, I did hear they do a pretty good strong cheese out Lilybaeum way,' whereupon they'd out with their knives and hack off huge great wedges and practically shove them down my throat. Pretty good cheese it was too, though personally I prefer the stuff they make back where I was raised. It's got that light, delicate flavour, and what you don't eat you can use to sharpen chisels on.

So it was all working out pretty well. Quite apart from all the buckshee cheese, there wasn't any nonsense about having to pay for a place to sleep or kipping down among the cows and goats. Some fat bloke with a lot of cheese to get rid of insisted that we go on home with him, and I got an actual bed, with a pillow and sheets, while the family slept on the floor with the dogs. Lucius Domitius didn't do quite so well – he had to muck in with the livestock – but, as I explained to him afterwards, it would've been totally out of character for me as a major cheese baron to give a toss about where my slave got billeted for the night.

Next morning, after a leisurely breakfast and a refreshing dip in the river, we set off on the road to Camarina. I explained that since I'd come so far I might as well press on a bit further, but it was almost a stone-cold certainty that I wasn't going to find anything even half as good as their cheese, and I'd be back in a day or so with a cart, ready to load up everything they could possibly spare, payment in cash on the spot. They seemed genuinely sorry to see me leave, which was a rare treat for me.

'Which just goes to prove what I was telling you,' I explained to Lucius Domitius, as we lost sight of the village behind some mountains. 'The vicissitudes of fortune, and all that. In the space of one day, we went from being condemned men on our way to the quarries to honoured guests of the village, nothing too good for us, help yourself to another plate of biscuits. That's what life's all about,' I went on, 'bad fortune, good fortune, down one moment, up the next; and the mark of your wise man, your true philosopher, is treating the rough and the smooth like they're really all the same thing. Which of course they are,' I pointed out, 'essentially speaking.'

'Oh, shut up, Galen,' he replied. 'You're making my head hurt.'

Of course he was just snotty about having to sleep with the dogs while I had the bed, but I didn't say anything. It was a nice day, for Sicily, and I wasn't in the mood for bickering. We were walking down a good, level road with cornfields on either side, the sun was shining and we had a quart of drinkable wine the farmer had given us for the road. There was even a woman singing somewhere in the distance, probably some old bat doing her washing or fetching water. Pleasant little tune, too.

Lucius Domitius stopped dead like he'd just stepped in a cow turd. 'Do you hear that?' he said.

'Hear what?'

'That woman, singing,' he said. 'There, listen.'

I shrugged. 'Yes, I can hear it,' I said. 'So what?'

He had this look on his face. 'That's my song,' he said. 'I wrote that.'

Oh God, I thought, here we go. 'Nah,' I said, 'I don't think so. Probably just sounds a bit similar, that's all.'

He scowled at me. 'That's my bloody song,' he said. 'Niobe, among the wavy reeds. You think I don't know my own music?'

'Oh well,' I said. 'If you say so. Can we get on now, please? Or have we got to stand here like a couple of prunes till she's finished?'

Now's probably a good time to tell you about Lucius Domitius and his music. Well, I'll do my best, anyhow, because I'm damned if I understand it, the way he used to carry on. Me, I can't ever see why people make such an almighty big deal about music and poetry and stuff. It's just something that people make, the way I see it, like furniture or pottery or hardware. Sure, it comes in lots of different grades of plain and fancy, just like everything else. Same goes for cutlery or shoes, only you don't get people drooping about in raptures of ecstasy about a beautifully crafted pair of boots. But really, what difference is there between a boot and a hendecasyllabic ode, except that a good pair of boots keeps your feet dry? It's just stuff that people make, and if they're really lucky, they get paid money, though as far as I can see most poets and musicians and the like end up giving the stuff away to their friends, assuming their friends hold still for long enough.

Be that as it may. Now, I've got an ear for music like a cabbage has teeth, but I dare say that Lucius Domitius' stuff was as good as anything else, maybe even a bit better. Big deal. As far as I was concerned, this didn't actually help us much. Now, if he'd been prepared to use his divine gift to make us a copper or two along the way, like by singing in people's houses or playing the bagpipes outside country inns, I could have seen the point in that, and I'd have been right behind him, every step of the way. But he wouldn't ever do that. His reason was, he was terrified that someone who'd heard him in the old days, when he used to give these recitals in front of thousands of people packed into theatres and racetracks, would know in a flash it was the Emperor Nero, who wasn't dead after all but still alive and taking a hat round outside a carters' brothel in upper Paeonia. Well, quite. I don't think that was the real reason, either. I think it was all in his head, because music and poetry made him think of the old times, who he used to be and what he'd lost, and he just couldn't bear to be reminded of that. It's as if he felt he had to pay a price for getting out of the palace alive that night – and for Callistus, of course – and the price he thought was fair was the thing he loved most in all the world, or maybe second most. And fair play to him, who's to say that wasn't the right thing to do? After all, we're all supposed to make sacrifices to the gods when they do something for us, and sacrifices are supposed to mean something, like you're giving up something valuable, to show how grateful you are. Most people, of course, they send the cook down to the market to buy the cheapest, scrawniest couple of chickens he can find, because any old rubbish'll do for the gods, and what they don't want will make a casserole for the servants. That's not my idea of giving thanks, though I won't pretend I'm religious or anything like that. Lucius Domitius, though, when he gave thanks for the life of my poor brother, he did it properly, gave up something he really valued, and I have to say, that was all right by me. Also, of course, it meant I didn't have to listen to him practising, which was also a blessing.

So there we were, on this otherwise perfectly agreeable morning, stood there in the middle of the road like a lopsided triumphal arch, while Lucius Domitius listened to this old boiler singing his song. It seemed to go on for a very long time but eventually she ran out of verses and it ground to a halt.

'Right,' I said. 'Now, do you think we could possibly get on with running for our lives? If it's absolutely convenient, I mean.'

Of course, I was exaggerating a bit, because we hadn't seen hide nor hair of any soldiers, but there was nothing to say they wouldn't show up at any minute, and besides, strolling for our lives wouldn't have sounded nearly so good. But it didn't matter. I was wasting my breath anyhow, because he wasn't paying any heed to me. He was too busy wallowing in self-pity, the bastard. Eyes all red and puffy, and a big fat wet tear rolling down his cheek. That was a bit much, from where I was standing. I mean, it was a nice enough little tune and the old woman had an all-right sort of a voice, but it wasn't anything to get you sobbing your eyes out.

'Hey,' I said, 'Lucius Domitius, pull yourself together. This isn't the time or the place.'

He turned his head and looked at me. A proper sight, he was. 'I guess you're right,' he said. 'I'm sorry. Very unprofessional of me, like laughing at your own jokes.'

Well, I could've said something pretty amusing at his expense right then, but I let it go. No point picking a fight. It'd only have delayed us further, and by this point I'd had enough of standing still in the open. 'Don't worry about it,' I said, grabbing him by the sleeve and hustling him along.

But he was still brooding about it at midday, when we sat down for a rest under a chestnut tree and ate some of the food our hosts had kindly given us (cheese, needless to say). 'Bloody strange,' he said, 'hearing that song, right out here in the wilds of Sicily. I'm amazed it got this far.' He grinned. 'Someone must've liked it, I guess.'

'Quite probably,' I said. 'Catchy tune. Nice words. And it only takes one satisfied customer to go prancing round humming it and suddenly the whole village knows it. There was a song like that back home when I was a kid, something about a wandering knife-grinder and a farmer's daughter—'

He gave me a poisonous look, for some reason. 'Well, anyway,' he said. 'That's quite enough about that. Let's just put it out of our minds for now, shall we?'

Well, he shouldn't have said that, because all the rest of the afternoon I was humming that stinking tune under my breath. I just couldn't get it out of my mind. I was still humming it when we kicked our boots off under the table at a scruffy old two-room inn that evening.

'Will you shut up that row?' Lucius Domitius hissed at me. 'People are staring.'

I was about to point out that that was bloody fine, coming from him, when to my amazement I heard the same tune coming from the back of the room. There was nothing for it, of course. We had to go and see who was singing it.

Turned out to be this smelly old carter, who was sort of stacked up in a corner, drinking his way through a small bath of the gorgon's blood the management had the nerve to pass off as red wine. No point talking to him if you wanted a rational answer, but sitting next to him on the bench was another man, presumably his mate – a little bit younger and less mothbitten round the face, and to all appearances moderately sober.

'That tune your pal's singing . . .' I began.

He looked up at me and frowned. 'Yes, I know, I'm sorry about that.' He leaned across the table, tugged his chum by the wrist and shouted, 'MENIPPUS, SHUT UP, YOU STUPID OLD FART,' so loud that heads turned right across the room.

'It's all right,' I said politely, 'he wasn't bothering us. It's just that song he was singing, it's familiar from somewhere but I can't think where I heard it.'

He looked at me sideways and laughed. 'Obviously you two aren't from round here,' he said, 'or you'd know that song. It's famous in these parts, that song.'

Lucius Domitius didn't say a word, but he was glowing so much the back of my neck got burnt.

'Really?' I said. 'Traditional, is it?'

He grinned. 'You could say that. Good story, too.' That was a hint, so I sat down next to him and waved to the innkeepeer for more booze. When it came, the man went on, 'That song is by the emperor Nero himself. The fat, ugly, murdering bastard,' he added, with feeling. 'So I expect you're surprised to hear it being sung by respectable folk. But it got famous around here because of the stone quarries.'

'Stone quarries,' I repeated. 'There are stone quarries nearby, are there?'

He nodded. 'You bet. Bloody terrible place, by all accounts, though I've never been there. Anyway, it's one of the places where that evil shit Nero used to send people to die. Hundreds of 'em he put in there, thousands even, and not more than one in twenty made it past the first year, or so they reckon. All the rich and powerful Roman lords who pissed him off, or else he was after their money and trumped up some phoney charge against them. He was always doing that.'

'I remember,' I said with a sigh. 'Nobody was safe.'

'Too bloody right. Anyhow,' he went on, spilling some of the wine as he poured it, 'one of the things that creep Nero did was, he'd hold these parties for all the high-up Romans, and when he'd got them trapped in that huge palace of his in Rome, he'd make 'em all sit there for hours and hours while he played his harp at them and sang. Sheer murder it was, by all accounts, because he couldn't play the harp worth pigshit and his voice was something like a cat in an olive press. So he's doing one of these parties, and there sitting in the front row is this fat old Roman senator. I can't remember his name, not that it matters worth a fart. So this old senator's been there for three hours or more, on top of a big dinner with a lot to drink, and the music's going on and on, and finally he can't keep his eyes open a moment longer, and he nods off to sleep and starts snoring. Well, that turd Nero catches sight of him and does his nut, what a terrible insult to his singing and all that crap, and he calls for his guards and sends the poor old fat bloke off for five years in the quarries.'

'How terrible,' I said. 'Carry on.'

'Well,' said the carter, 'a couple of years go by, and one day Nero's sitting on his golden throne chatting to some people, and he asks, whatever became of old So-and-so, haven't seen him round here in a camel's age. Well, of course, everybody gets very twitchy, until someone says, don't you remember, Caesar, you had him chucked down the pit for falling asleep during your wonderful concert. Now old Nero, he's had a drop to drink already that day, he's feeling a bit soft, so he says, We can't have that, send a messenger and have him released at once. So off the messenger goes, and back he comes with the senator, who's still just about alive but not nearly as porky round the tum as he used to be; and he's still wearing the rags of his senator's purple gown, and everybody's real sorry for him, and there's this big sloppy scene where Nero forgives him, and everybody's sobbing their eyes out, and it's all fine. But then Nero says, I've got an idea, let's have a nice party to celebrate old what's-is-name's getting out of the can, and everybody thinks, Oh shit, because they know what's coming, but they all say, What a clever idea, Caesar, let's do that. So they bring on the booze, and as soon as everybody's sat down, up gets Nero and he starts doing a concert. Well, he's done one song and he's halfway through the next when the old senator gets to his feet and slowly starts walking out of the room. Nero's absolutely furious. He swings round and he says to the senator, Where the bloody hell d'you think you're going? And the senator lets go a great big sad sigh, and he says, Back to the stone quarries, Caesar, where do you think?'

I didn't look round and I didn't say a word. Had to bite a dirty great chunk out of my tongue, but I managed it. Anyway, the carter went on, 'So that's exactly what he did; and every day for the next three years, until Nero finally got what was coming to him and some bugger finally slit his useless throat, which meant all the poor prisoners in the quarries got let out and sent home again, that old senator used to sing that same song, the one Nero'd been playing when he walked out, over and over again, till everybody in the quarries and the villages around knew it by heart. Well,' he finished with a shrug, 'I guess folks round here must be the only people in the world who still know any of that fat arsehole's music. Reckon you could call that immortal fame, if you were so minded.'

Immortal fame. That old thing.

Now the other day I was in the market square, leaning up against a bookseller's stall reading the *Odyssey*. Now before you get the wrong impression of me, I wasn't doing it for fun; I was checking some facts for this story I'm telling you, though that's by the by. Anyhow, there's this really weird bit in the *Odyssey*, where Ulysses is on his way home from Troy, and it's taken him ten years to get nowhere and he's had all kinds of really horrible adventures with monsters eating his friends and now he's been shipwrecked and everybody's dead except him, and he gets washed up on this island that nobody even knew was there. And the locals, who must've been a damn sight more soft-hearted than most islanders I've come across, take him to the king's palace, where he gets a cracking good feed and a change of clothes and a nice warm fire to dry out his bones – all without anybody asking who he is, because of course hospitality is its own reward, and a good man's always ready to help out anybody who's in a bad way on the road, regardless of whether the unfortunate guest is a prince or a beggar. Yeah, right. Anyhow, so there he is, incognito, stuffing his face with good wheat bread and cheese, and the palace minstrel gets up and starts singing a song about – guess what – the remarkable adventures of the great hero Ulysses, who sailed for home after the fall of Troy, had marvellous adventures, and then was never heard of again.

Immortal fame, see. Ulysses gets to be famous, even while he's still alive – but you can bet your front teeth that the adventures the minstrel was telling the tale about weren't anything to do with the real Ulysses. Either it was stuff that had happened to somebody else who wasn't famous, so the minstrel told the story but made it about Ulysses instead, or else he just made it all up out of his head and pretended it was about Ulysses just to make it more interesting.

Same with Lucius Domitius, as I'm sure you've figured out for yourselves. Just as the Ulysses listening to the song wasn't the same man as the Ulysses the song was about, so Lucius Domitius was never the Nero Caesar the carter's mate told his tale about. Same in my line of work, too. The Galen who tells everybody in the village he's a wealthy cheese importer is just a cheap crook; but for all I know, to this very day there may be people in the arse end of Sicily who're still waiting for Galen the cheesemonger to come back, buy up all the cheeses in town, and make them all suddenly rich, so they're free and clear, and all their troubles are over. It's like I left a little bit of me behind, and it's grown and changed, like a shoot grafted onto a tree, into something with a life of its own. Which is more than I've ever had, at that.

'Of course,' Lucius Domitius said next morning, after we'd left the inn, 'it's a very old story.'

'Really,' I said.

'Oh yes.' He nodded firmly. 'In fact, it's at least four hundred years old. In the earliest version of it I've come across, it's set in the court of Dionysius, who was the dictator of Syracuse back in Plato's time.'

'Oh,' I said. 'It's not true, then. I mean, you didn't . . .'

He looked uncomfortable. 'I never said that,' he replied. 'I'm just saying, it's an old joke, that's all.'

'But you did – I mean . . .'

'I'd rather not talk about it.'

Well, it was none of my business. Still, it struck me as a bit farfetched that anybody, even a Roman senator (and they're all as crazy as a barrelful of polecats), would set himself up for a second term in the slate quarries just for the sake of an apt quotation. Then again, I'm just a farm boy from the back end of Attica, so what would I know about Roman noblemen?

'Anyway,' I said, 'at least we know where we're headed.' I'd done some discreet asking around in the inn, and found out that we were no more than three days' walk from Camarina, and once we got there we stood a fair chance of finding a ship bound for the African coast without having to hang around for too long. Truth is, I was getting a bit sick of the sight of Sicily. As things had turned out, the place had seen us right, but luck's a bit like a heap of rocks piled up on the edge of a cliff directly above your house. It doesn't do to push it.

'Three days' walk,' Lucius Domitius was saying. 'I don't think these boots are going to make it that far. I say when we reach the next village we buy a couple of mules.'

I shook my head. 'We don't want to do that.'

'Why the hell not? We've got money. And anyway, we can ride them to Camarina, sell them when we get there, get our money back and save ourselves a walk.'

'Bad idea,' I said.

That annoyed him. 'What the hell's wrong with it? And another thing,' he went on. 'You keep saying, the sooner we're off this road the better, before the soldiers come up here looking for us. We'll cover the ground a hell of a lot quicker if we ride.'

'Absolutely not,' I said. 'We'll get to Camarina on our own two feet, thank you very much. No mules.'

'What's wrong with mules?'

He was starting to get on my nerves. 'I don't like 'em, all right?'

'I see. Going to tell me why?'

'No.'

'Please yourself.'

Actually, there's no secret about it, and Lucius Domitius knew perfectly well, or he should have done if he'd ever listened to me over the years. Plain fact is, I can't be doing with mules. I think it's got something to do with the time Callistus and me were in Bithynia, and we'd done something or other to make ourselves unpopular in this town we were passing through, so much so that some git had called the guard, and we had reasons of our own for not wanting to explain ourselves to a parcel of soldiers right then. But it was all right, because tied up outside the town's knocking shop were these two mules, and we thought, hop on them, we'd be out of town and gone long before the soldiers got there. So we help ourselves to these mules, and off we go, and we're almost out of the danger area when suddenly my mule decides to stop running and stand there still as a rock, like he'd just seen the gorgon's head or something, and nothing I could do would get the miserable creature to move. So there I was, shouting and kicking at this completely stationary mule when the soldiers show up, and next thing we know we're in the cooler, with stealing mules added to the charge sheet (and stealing livestock on its own'll get you strung up in Bithynia, which is a horrible place at the best of times, you just take my word for it). Anyway, that's me and mules. Now if Lucius Domitius had said donkeys or an ox-cart or even horses, I might well have said, yes, fine, because I'd far rather ride than walk any day of the month. But mules – no way on earth, never again.

So we went on walking, and at the end of that day we fetched up in this town. Proper-sized place it was, with two inns, bathhouse, bakehouse, even its own diddy little theatre and racetrack. Another time I'd have said, let's hang around here a day or so, see if we can't work a decent fiddle. But we had money in our purses and what I was interested in after a hard day's walking wasn't sizing up marks, it was getting my boots off and resting my feet on a footstool for a few hours. So we put in at the less evil-looking of the two inns, paid cash in advance for a jug of the local poison and a couple of plates of pot luck, and settled down for an evening of lounging around like a couple of gentlemen.

It's important when you're doing what we were doing always to make sure you keep in character. Like, if you're being a cheese merchant and you blow into a new town, you've got to spend some time asking about the local cheeses, doing deals, whatever. Otherwise, two gets you one that someone'll tell someone else, We had two cheese buyers in our place the other day but they didn't seem to be very interested, and you can be sure that the bloke they say this to is a captain of guards or a market commissioner who's been after us for days, and he'll ask his mate: These two strangers, they wouldn't happen to be a rat-faced little Greek and an Italian with a neck like an ox, and next thing you know, we're getting our collars felt.

So the very least I could do was start asking round the inn about cheese, and who had any for sale, and once I'd got the point across I was suddenly knee-deep in farmers again, not to mention the steward from a big estate, all trying to get me to go up their place next morning and try a slice or two. So I was saying yes, we'd really like to do that, only we're pressed for time a little bit, anxious to get to the coast as soon as possible to be sure of catching our boat home before it leaves without us, but we'd be back in a month or so, and maybe then'd be a good time to go round looking at stuff. They all seemed happy enough at that, kept promising me that it'd be worth my while, because each and every one of 'em just happened to produce the finest cheeses in Sicily for flavour and texture and God only knows what else. All in all, I did more work that evening than your genuine cheese merchant does in a week, and not a green copper to show for it at the end, of course. Strikes me, if I'd put half the time and effort into being an honest businessman that I've put into lying and swindling over the years, I'd be a rich man by now, with my own villa by the sea, drinking wine from my own vineyards. But there you go.

Needless to say, Lucius Domitius wasn't pulling his weight in all this – fair play to him, it wasn't his job, since he was being the humble and self-effacing slave, sitting quiet in the corner with his jug of etching fluid and his half-loaf of barley bread. Credit where it's due, over the years he'd got it about perfect – not that there's a lot to it, sitting still and keeping your face shut – but he had talent, no doubt about it. Sometimes, when he was really putting his heart and soul into his performance, I'd look round for him and not even see him till he stood up, he was that good. No, his job (aside from just being, like slaves do) was keeping his ears open, picking up the little stray snatches of conversation that can make all the difference in our line of work. It could be anything: some clown shooting his mouth off, suggesting he'd be a good mark; something we could use in a scam, like there's these merchants expected in town with letters of credit, but they're strangers, so nobody knows what they look like; advance warning, like the prefect's cracking down on tall-story men, or someone we'd had dealings with before is arriving on the next boat.

So, when I'd done my rounds and it was time to go to bed, we went out into the yard, like we had horses to see to or something, and I asked him if there was anything doing.

'Too right,' he said, with a worried look on his face. 'There's a Roman senator on his way, visiting his estates or something. We'd better clear out first thing.'

I could see his point, of course. A Roman senator would know the former emperor of the Romans by sight. Now I wasn't as bothered about that as he was. I know for a fact that most people only ever see what they expect to see, and none of your purple-stripe boys would ever expect to see a dead Caesar togged out like a garlic-nibbler in a country inn in the back end of Sicily. Rich men don't see slaves, unless they want them for something, and even if this senator happened to notice Lucius Domitius and see the resemblance, he'd just think, Oh look, there's a slave who looks a bit like Nero. He might mention it to his chums or write a poem about it, but you'd never get him to believe. No way.

But yes, it wasn't worth the risk. After all, there wasn't anything we wanted to do there, it'd just mean hauling ourselves out of bed at first light instead of having a lie-in. No big deal. 'All right,' I said. 'Any idea where this character's coming in from? Syracuse, presumably.'

He jerked his head up, Greek style (nice touch). 'They didn't say,' he replied.

'Oh well.' I shrugged. Like I said, I wasn't really worried. 'We'll keep going for Camarina. We'll just make sure we're on the road bright and early. Don't suppose his lordship's going to shift his aristocratic bum while the dew's still on the grass.'

So, come cock-crow, we were up and washed and ready to go. Paid the landlord, slipped out before the stable-boys started work, no fuss. Just to be on the safe side, I'd given in to Lucius Domitius whining and splashed out on a couple of mules. We'd cover half as much ground again riding as walking, and a man I'd got talking to the night before had offered me a pretty good deal on them. It was a pleasant enough morning, the road was good and flat for a change, and I was explaining to Lucius Domitius why Mauretania was such a good idea. A couple of hours down the road and I'd forgotten all about the Roman senator.

Well, you couldn't fault my logic, could you? I'd done my best: figured it all out, weighed up the odds, chosen what seemed like the sensible way of handling the situation. Short of having Pallas Athene come to me in a dream and tell me my fortune, I don't see how I could've been expected to see what was going to happen. That's what's so unfair about life. You follow the proper drill, do it all right, you ought to be able to expect that things'll go your way and you won't end up knee deep in the shit.

No warning, of course. One minute we were walking our mules up a gentle little hill; the next, over the brow comes this bloody great procession, coming straight at us. Nowhere to hide, we were right out in the open, nothing else on the road for a mile behind us.

Your Roman senators, being the richest men the world has ever seen, they've got to find stuff to spend all that money on. You and me, we reckon we're ahead of the game if we've got enough to eat for today and tomorrow, and a change of clothes if we're really lucky. For your Roman senator, life's never that simple. If he stays at home, he's got to have a villa the size of Troy, with enough footmen and houseboys to man a full-strength legion. If he goes anywhere, it's either a coach with six milk-white horses, or a sedan chair carried by eight identical Germans, with the labours of Hercules in full relief on the doors, picked out in gold leaf. Nor is there any risk of his lordship getting lonely as he travels from A to B. Aside from his four coachmen or his eight bearers, there's his valets and his secretaries and the two Syrians who wipe the snot off his chin when he sneezes, and a half battalion of bodyguards with great big clubs just in case the King of Persia decided to sneak up behind him with his entire army and try to steal his ivory pedicure set.

So there we were, the two of us, and bearing down on us like Hannibal and all his elephants was this column: footsloggers at the front, then two blokes with the bundles of rods and axes (showing that this one was some kind of high-up government official as well as a rich bastard), then a dozen cavalry outriders, then the coach, and another wagon behind that, presumably to carry his worship's clean underwear.

Now what you do in a situation like that is you get off the road as quick as you can, doffing your hat and looking down hard at your feet, to show you know your place. This is no bother to me, I don't mind it in the least, and I'd have been happy as a pig in shit to do the usual thing and carry on my way a few moments later. Unfortunately, it was taken out of my hands, so to speak, by my goddamned contrary mule.

I knew, as soon as I tugged on the useless creature's bridle and my arm nearly came out of its socket, I knew I should never have let myself get talked into breaking my number-one rule of survival in the cold, cruel world: no fucking mules. Needless to say, as soon as mine dropped anchor, Lucius Domitius' did the same. So there we were, obstructing the highway, and the Roman getting closer to us every moment.

The front man was yelling at us, 'Get those bloody animals off the road.' Well, that was helpful. I was hauling away with every last bit of strength I had (but that wasn't worth much, a skinny little runt like me) and so was Lucius Domitius; and if he couldn't shift his mule, what chance did I have?

Well, the procession came to a dead stop about a foot from my big toe, and it was pretty obvious that they weren't pleased. The footsloggers grabbed us and shoved us out of the way. I landed on my bum; Lucius Domitius banged his head on the paved road. Then they tried to shift the mules, but they didn't have any luck either. One of the cavalrymen rode up, but my mule must've said something nasty in Horse, because his fine white mare suddenly got all skittish and tried to buck him off over her head. Then the carriage door opened and this perfectly round head appeared, shouting, 'What's the hold-up? What's going on?' Wonderful, we'd met the senator.

The lead thug shouted back, trying to explain. 'It's these mules, sir, they won't budge.'

The senator frowned and thought for a moment. 'Kill them,' he said. 'I haven't got all day.'

So the cavalryman hops off his horse, gives the reins to a thug to hold, strides up drawing his sword, and slices it across my mule's neck, just like that. Before the poor thing hit the deck he'd done the same to the other one, and a moment later the footmen had got both carcasses dragged onto the side of the road out of the way.

Problem solved.

Well, I'd have been quite happy to leave it at that. But your Roman senator's a devil for fair play when you don't want him to be. He had his people bring us over, and there we were, looking up at him, hemmed in on all sides by his flunkeys so we couldn't make a run for it.

'Sorry about that,' said the senator, staring over the tops of our heads as if looking straight at us would've made his eyes dirty. 'But I'm in a hurry, official business. Give these men a fair price for their animals.'

Some Greek in a flashy green tunic hops down out of the coach and sticks money in our hands. I didn't even bother to look. I was keeping my eyes on the toes of my sandals, and praying Lucius Domitius had the good sense to do the same. I was waiting to hear the click of the carriage door shutting, maybe someone shoving us out of the way, but nothing happened. Finally, I looked up.

The senator was looking me over like he was out fishing and he'd found me in his net. 'Don't I know you from somewhere?' he said.

Shit, I thought. 'I don't think so, sir,' I said. 'I'm sure I haven't had the honour.'

He wasn't buying it. 'I'm sure I know you,' he said. 'Have you been to Rome?'

I shook my head. 'Never, sir.'

'You're sure about that?'

Bloody silly question, like it's something that'd slip your mind. 'Positive, sir. My name . . .'Screw me, I couldn't remember what my name was supposed to be. 'Pittacus,' I remembered, just in time before it looked funny. 'I'm a cheesemonger, sir, from Mauretania.'

The senator clapped his hands together. 'That must be it, then,' he said. 'I served there on my last posting. Whereabouts in Mauretania do you come from?'

I didn't look round, but I could feel great waves of hate crashing into me from Lucius Domitius' direction. 'Icosium, sir,' I answered, mostly because it was the only place in Mauretania I could think of.

'Really.' The senator was beaming. 'I know it well. And you're a cheesemonger, you say. So what are you doing in Sicily?'

Given the choice, I'd rather have been eaten alive by beetles than carry on this conversation. Sadly, nobody gave me the option.

'Buying, sir,' I said. 'Stock.'

'Oh.' The senator frowned. 'How odd. Is there a market for Sicilian cheese in Iconium?'

I nodded. 'Oh yes, sir, they can't get enough of it. Goes like shit off a shovel, sir, pardon the expression.'

'Really.' He shook his head. 'How peculiar, when the local variety is such a delicacy. I don't remember ever seeing Sicilian cheese for sale when I was there.'

Bastard, I thought. 'It's a new thing, sir,' I said, 'very new. Fashion, you know.'

'Oh well.' He thought for a moment, then rubbed his nose on the back of his hand. 'Well, anyway, that explains that. I knew I'd seen you before, you know. Never forget a face.'

Then, mercifully, the carriage door slammed and the procession moved on. I was still clutching the coin I'd been given. Don't suppose two strong men with crowbars could've prised my fingers apart, I was that tense. I stayed there without moving till the last man had disappeared over the brow of the hill.

'Do you know who that was?'

I'd clean forgotten about Lucius Domitius. 'Stinking fucking bastard Roman,' I replied, 'that's who that was.' I opened my fist and saw what I'd been give: a whacking great gold piece, enough to buy a whole string of mules. 'Bastard,' I repeated.

Then Lucius Domitius was grabbing me by my shirt, twisting the collar so I could hardly breathe. 'Do you know who that *was*?' he hissed.

'Let go of me, you lunatic,' I said. 'What the hell are you throttling me for?'

He let go, but he was bright red in the face. 'That,' he said, 'was him. The senator.'

'Yes, I'd gathered that.'

'No, you clown. *The* senator. Him. The one I sent to the slate quarries.'

FOUR

Once, a long time ago now, I was in Egypt or one of those places, broke as a tinker's fiddle, to the point where I was hanging round the market looking for actual work, and this fat bloke wearing what looked like a carpet came up to me and asked me did I fancy being a beater in a lion hunt? And the answer was, obviously, no, but if the job paid money, count me in; and next thing I knew, I was standing in this long line of people, all deadbeats and losers like me, and we were walking across this slice of desert rattling sticks and bashing old copper pans and making a hell of a racket. When we'd been doing this for a very long time, out of a little clump of scraggy bushes jumps this lion. Well, he takes one look at us and bolts off the other way, which is exactly what I'd have done in his place, and he's running flat out, thinking, well, that was easy, when suddenly the ground gave way under his feet and there he was at the bottom of this deep pit, which the hunt people had dug the previous day and covered over with dry grass and bits of twig.

I'm only telling you this because I knew exactly how that poor bugger felt. One moment he's doing fine, showing the bad guys a clean pair of heels; the next, everything's turned to horseshit and he's comprehensively stuffed. Just like that time with Lucius Domitius and me in Sicily.

'You're kidding,' I said.

Lucius Domitius looked at me. 'Yes,' he said, 'I'm pulling your leg. That's my idea of a funny joke. Pull yourself together, will you? That was him. Gnaeus Sulpicius Asper, the poor sod I sent to the slate quarries.' He waved his hands like he was trying to shake them off his arms. 'We've had it,' he said. 'This time, we've finally run out of fools' luck. We're dead.'

I could see where he was coming from, but even so. 'Don't talk soft,' I told him. 'Sure, it got a bit warm back there, but we got away with it. Take a couple of deep breaths, and everything'll be fine.'

He just looked at me.

'Oh for God's sake,' I said. 'Look, he thinks I'm an African cheese dealer, this time tomorrow he'll have forgotten the whole thing. All we've got to do is keep out of his way, and that's the end of it.'

He didn't say anything, which was a really bad sign. Well, I wasn't putting up with that. 'It's all your fault, anyhow,' I told him. 'You were the one who insisted on bloody mules. Haven't I always told you, no mules, not ever? And did you listen?'

He didn't look like he was in the mood to talk about mules. He stood there for a moment or so, making an effort to stop quivering. Then he said, 'All right, which way?'

'What?'

'Which way do we go now? Straight on, or back the way we came?'

'Talk sense,' I told him. 'Obviously, we keep heading for Camarina. Seaport, boat out of here, simple as that. Why, what did you have in mind?'

He shook his head. 'Sorry,' he said, 'my brain's stopped working. Yes, let's do that. You never know, we might still get away with it.'

We didn't talk much the rest of the day, which was probably just as well. He was just plain miserable. I was trying to think ahead, figure out the sort of unforeseen shitmines we might stroll into, but for the life of me I couldn't think of any, apart from a company of cavalry thundering down the road after us because his lordship had just remembered where he'd seen Lucius Domitius before. Nothing we could do about that if it happened. The trouble with Sicily is it's all open country. You can't just duck off the highway and hide out in the bush when you catch sight of a nasty-looking dust-cloud coming up the road behind you. It's all just fields full of dirt-scratchers just waiting to say, 'They went that way,' to any passing cavalryman. But that was all right, because it wasn't going to happen, for the reasons I just explained. His lordship wasn't going to turn round suddenly and say, Bugger me, that slave we just passed in the road was Nero in disguise. Things don't happen like that. Looked at calmly, there was nothing to worry about.

So we kept on down the road, walking as fast as we could go, and come evening we crawled into yet another poxy little Sicilian town and parked ourselves in yet another poxy little Sicilian inn. This time, I didn't do the cheesemonger bit; in fact, we kept our faces resolutely shut on the whole subject of cheese, and you don't need to be told why. We found a quiet corner, tried to make ourselves look as unfriendly as possible, and rested our feet.

There were a couple of carters behind us, talking to someone I couldn't see. Naturally I started earwigging, because it's second nature.

'Just arrived,' one of the carters was saying. 'Don't know what to make of the bastard yet, but chances are he'll be no better and no worse than the other bastard. They're all pretty much alike, anyhow.'

His mate laughed. 'Not so sure about that,' he said. 'Reckon this one might have a bit of an attitude, at least to start off with. You heard about his son?'

The other carter and the bloke we couldn't see hadn't heard, so he told them. 'What I heard was, his son arrived a few days ahead of his old man, wanted to do a bit of hunting or whatever before knuckling down to his job on Daddy's staff. Anyway, a couple of days ago he was out wandering about in the villages, and he only goes and gets himself robbed, the dozy young sod.'

'Get away,' said one of the others.

'Damn straight. What I heard was, they snuck up behind him when he wasn't looking, smacked him over the head, took the lot. Even the clothes he was wearing.' He sighed. 'Well, you can guess what that'll mean. The new governor hasn't even taken office yet, and his son's the victim of a brutal robbery. It's going to mean soldiers everywhere, random stop-and-searches, and if you can't prove you're on legitimate business, in the guardhouse you go till they can find someone who'll vouch for you.' The man we couldn't see grunted, like he was saying, That's right, that's what'll happen. 'I mean, it'll wear off after a few months, I dare say, 'specially if they get the toerags who did it, but don't be surprised if things are a bit tense for a while.'

The other two seemed to find it all pretty amusing. 'What, they even nicked his boots, did they?'

'So I heard. The kid reckons he didn't see them, but some blokes in the fields saw a couple of dodgy-looking strangers acting a bit funny – big, broad, thick-necked Italian type, and a little Greek bloke with a face like a ferret. Word is, they're a couple of those convicts who did in the guards on the way to the quarries; there were two blokes answering those descriptions in that batch.'

'Ah,' said the one who hadn't said anything yet, presumably the bloke I couldn't see. 'That explains that then. Only, our sergeant was saying something about going and checking out some village where they'd seen a couple of strangers, and none of us knew what it was in aid of. That'll be it then.'

So there we were, Lucius Domitius and me, not daring to move in case this bloke who'd turned out to be a soldier looked up and saw us. Luckily, they all pushed off not long afterwards. We gave them a count of twenty, and got out of the inn quick.

The hayloft seemed a safe bet, for the time being, so we went there. 'This is terrible,' Lucius Domitius said. 'I can't believe it. It's like someone's doing it deliberately.'

It was my turn to sit quiet. I like to be upbeat about things, but this was beyond me.

'Really,' he went on, 'if it wasn't so fucking awful, it'd be hilarious. We've got one lot of bogies after us for murdering Roman soldiers and escaping from the quarries; we've got the governor about to put two and two together and send his personal guards out after us; and now it turns out that you stole the shirt you're wearing from the governor's son. Between that lot, every single soldier in the entire Roman army's going to be looking for us by this time tomorrow.' He made a funny sort of gurgling noise. 'It's amazing,' he said. 'Just like that, we've turned into the most desperate criminals in Sicilian history, and we haven't even done anything.'

Normally I'd have pointed out the bright side, but there wasn't one. 'You got any ideas?' I asked, which shows how depressed I was feeling.

'Sure,' he said. 'Let's kill ourselves and save them the trouble. About the only good thing I can see in all this is that we'll have been crucified as common criminals long before Sulpicius Asper figures out who I am, which means I'll be spared all that really nasty stuff they promised to do to me if they ever caught me. Thank heaven for small mercies, really.'

'Hold your bloody water,' I snapped at him. 'They haven't got us yet. There'll be a way out of this, you wait and see. There's always a way out, so long as you don't lose your nerve, and have faith.'

'Really.' He looked at me as if I was something he'd found in an apple. 'Next you're going to tell me you've been in worse fixes than this.'

'Well, yes,' I told him. 'And so have you. It's not so long since we were in a cart on our way to the quarries, and look at us now. Free and clear. No reason why we shouldn't stay that way, so long as we stay cool and don't panic.'

I thought he was going to shout at me, but he didn't. 'All right, then,' he said, 'so what's the big idea this time?'

'I'm not sure. Probably the best bet would be the original plan. We can't be all that far from Camarina by now. If we could just get on a boat, all our troubles'd be over. But,' I went on, 'I've got a gut feeling that that'd be a bad idea. Like, if they already know out here about us stealing the kid's clothes, it's more than likely they've sent riders all along the coast telling the bogies to watch out for us, so Camarina could be putting our heads in a noose.'

Lucius Domitius nodded slowly. 'Makes sense,' he said. 'So, what's the alternative"'

'Head inland,' I said, 'maybe. It's what they're not expecting us to do, so that's in its favour. On the other hand, it won't be long before everybody on this island's going to be looking out for us, especially if they put up a reward. We'll be strangers wherever we go, so we'll stick out like a boil on a camel's bum. If this was back home I'd say head for the mountains. I know loads of caves and places like that around Phyle where a bloke could stay out of sight for months. But wandering about in these hills would be asking for trouble – assuming we could get across the plains without some bugger seeing us, which isn't likely.'

'Bloody hell,' said Lucius Domitius thoughtfully. 'And you're the cheerful one. I'm right, aren't I? We're dead.'

'No we're not,' I said. 'It just needs thinking about, that's all.'

'That's all,' he repeated. 'Well, fine. You get thinking. Personally, I'm going to try prayer.'

So there I was, in this hayloft in Sicily, trying to think of some simple but ingenious way of staying alive, and I guess I must've thought so hard I sprained my brain and knocked myself out, because next thing I knew, I was waking up, with sunlight pouring in through the loft door.

Now it could be that I'd been thinking in my sleep, or maybe Lucius Domitius' prayers had got through for once and the gods sent me the answer in a dream. Dunno. And I don't suppose it makes a blind bit of difference. The point is, as soon as I woke up, I *knew*. Simple as that.

'Hey,' I called out. 'You there?'

I heard him grunt and turn over. 'Wassmatter?'

'I've got it,' I said. 'Our way out of here.'

He groaned. 'Whenever you get that confident, self-assured expression in your voice, I know I'm in for a bad time. Go on, then, what's your brilliant idea?'

Just as well I'm the thick-skinned type, or I might have taken offence. 'Shut your face and listen,' I said. 'Where's the last place they'd think of looking for us?'

He thought for a moment. 'Ecbatana,' he replied. 'But that's no good, it's three thousand miles away.'

I pretended I hadn't heard that. 'Who's looking for us?' I asked. 'Soldiers, that's who. So, what we need to do is we need to be soldiers. I mean,' I went on, 'when you look at a soldier, what do you see? You see the armour, the shiny helmet, the red cloak, the big shield, all that. Never look at his face, do you? I mean, you can't see much more than the tip of his nose past those big cheekpieces, and besides, you don't bother to look. It's like I keep telling you when you worry about being recognised – people see what they expect to see. They look at a man sat on the curule chair, they see the emperor. They look at a bloke dressed as a slave, they see a slave. And a bloke in armour, with a red cloak . . .'

He stared at me like I was dribbling. 'Are you out of your tiny mind?' he said.

'Also,' I said, 'there you are sitting outside an inn, or herding your cows, or spitting up your field, and these two blokes come up to you, in uniform, asking if you've seen two blokes. It's never going to occur to you that the blokes asking the question are the blokes they're looking for.'

He scratched his head. 'Say that again,' he said. 'Slowly.'

'We dress up as soldiers,' I said. 'We pretend we're looking for us. Think about it.'

He thought about it. 'Just one problem,' he said. 'Where are we going to get two sets of army kit from? Or were you thinking of strolling up to the barracks and asking the quartermaster sergeant if he's got anything in our size?'

I shook my head. 'Don't worry about that,' I said, 'I've got that all sussed. Least of our problems. So, what do you think?'

He had this look on his face like he had really bad wind. 'I don't know,' he said. 'It's so bloody stupid, we might just get away with it. But—'

'That's settled, then. All right, let's get going. No point sitting here waiting to get caught.'

Now if you're racking your brains trying to figure out my brilliant plan for getting hold of two sets of infantry uniform, you're in good company, because so was I. Oh, I know I'd told Lucius Domitius I'd got it all worked out, but that was a little white lie, because otherwise he'd have kicked up a fuss and we'd never have got anywhere. As we climbed down out of that loft, I've got to say, I didn't have much idea of how to go about it. Well, I was pretty much resigned to the fact that we were probably going to have to bend the law a bit, but apart from that, I was trying to keep an open mind, as it were.

My first thought was that Lucius Domitius' crack about the quartermaster sergeant wasn't as dumb as he'd tried to make it sound. It's a well-known fact that the Roman army is there for two reasons: to keep the peace, and to get ripped off by anything that moves. If you've got a dying horse, or three tons of mildewed beans, what do you do? Sell 'em to the military. Or suppose you're a building contractor, or you've got a factory making hobnails. Who's your favourite customer, the one you know you can screw over any day of the week? The boys in red. And if there's anything you want, and the army's got it, all you need to do is buy the quartermaster or the stores clerk a drink, and you can call round the barracks with a wheelbarrow and the soldiers'll help you load it up. I love the army. Really, it's enough to make me wish I paid taxes.

Only trouble with that as a game plan was that I didn't know where the nearest barracks was, and for some reason I wasn't keen on the idea of wandering round town asking people the way. A pity, but you've got to be realistic. So I remembered what my old mother used to tell us when we were kids: what you can't buy, steal.

Well, that's all right to say, but I didn't like the idea of following a half platoon of squaddies down a dark alley and mugging them for their kit. A direct frontal assault was out, I reckoned. That just left stealth. And that was when I started to wish that when I was young and starting out in life, I'd had the chance to knuckle down and learn a trade. You see, it's one thing hooking a cloak and a belt off some young git while he's shagging the local fauna. Tickling off the military, on the other hand, is skilled work. You need to have had a decent education if you want to play that sort of game.

Still, it was all I could come up with, so I applied my mind and thought it through: when do soldiers take their kit off? Answer: they don't much, and if you don't believe me, stroll up to the next sentry you see and take a good sniff. And then I thought, Galen, you're thinking small again, it'll be the death of you, your lack of vision. True, your bacon-chewing, flat-footed Mule of Marius only sheds his togs twice, his wedding night and his funeral. Your officers, on the other hand, are a cut above that. They're gentlemen. They wash.

'Now then,' I told Lucius Domitius, 'keep your eyes peeled for the bathhouse.'

He looked at me and started whining, but I was expecting that. 'Oh for God's sake,' he said, 'you're not planning on tickling for the stuff, are you? Don't you ever learn? That's what got us into this mess in the first place.'

'Sure,' I said. 'It's like the old country saying: fuck-ups are like a door, they get you in and then they get you out again. Now, we're going to need a long pole, and something we can use for a hook.'

'No.'

'And some string,' I added, because I'm dead keen on attention to detail. 'Start looking.'

The long pole was easy. You know those things shopkeepers use for snuffing the lamps outside their shops? We found one of them, just leaning up against a wall. The hook was a bit harder. I figured a pot hook would do, but all the ones we saw had pots hanging off them, and it'd have taken too long to snaffle them. Just when I was getting nervous strolling through the market holding a long stolen pole, we saw this ironmongers' stall, and there on his table was a row of brand new meathooks, still black from the fire. 'There,' I said. Just the job.'

Lucius Domitius looked worried. 'How the hell are we going to steal one of them,' he said, 'with the bloke standing there watching? And if you say start a diversion—'

'Don't be stupid,' I told him. 'We've got money, remember. We buy one.'

So we did, and then we snuck round the back of a butcher's shop and unpicked a yard of thread from the hem of Lucius Domitius' tunic, and used that to tie the hook on the pole. Of course, that made another problem. It's not smart to wander round the place with a hook tied on a long stick, asking people the way to the public baths. In the end, all I could think of was tearing the sleeve off Lucius Domitius' tunic and wrapping it round the hook. A bit obvious, you'd have thought, but we got away with it.

Luckily, the baths in that town weren't hard to find: posh new building, probably only been up a year or so. It was still fairly early in the morning, early enough for there to be a fair chance of catching an officer preening himself before setting out for a day's shouting at the men. (Now if you're smart, you'll have noticed that suddenly I'm talking about one officer, singular. That was the clever bit. Your officer, of course, wouldn't dream of leaving the camp and going into town without his faithful batman trotting along at his side. The only drawback was that I was going to have to be the slave this time; but I'd seen that one coming. After all, say what you like about Lucius Domitius, he was a Roman aristocrat, something I could never pass myself off as in a thousand years.)

When will they ever learn, these bathhouse keepers? Anywhere you go, from Hibernia to Sarmatia, every bathhouse you see, you'll find a little window round the back just the right position and height like it's been put there specially for the local ticklers. Actually, that's not far off the truth. The architects will tell you it's there to let the hot air out, or some such garbage. Truth is, the bathhouse keepers get a slice of the action from the ticklers, and everybody's happy.

Quick scout round first. Nobody about, so I hopped up on Lucius Domitius' shoulders, stuck my head through the window and looked to see what I could see. It was promising. I had a direct line into the changing room and, sure enough, among all the gowns and tunics I caught sight of a nice shiny Greek-style breastplate, all gilded and cute, the way the rich boys like them. Better still, there was nobody about, apart from a doddery old wreck of a changing-room attendant, and he was having a quiet kip in the corner. It was all too good to be true. Well, no point hanging around. I stuck my tickling pole through the window, and it reached just fine. Then it was simply a matter of poking about until I got the hook round one of the breastplate straps and reeling the bugger in, and all our troubles would be over.

Well, almost. Probably you're way ahead of me. A breastplate, you're thinking, that's a bloody heavy thing to winkle out of a building on a long, thin pole. Too right, only I hadn't thought of that. I did manage to get the rotten thing halfway across the room before the leverage ripped it out of my hands and it went clattering on the marble floor, making a row like the battle of Marathon.

Even the changing-room guard couldn't sleep through that. Up he jumped, looked round, saw the breastplate on the deck, rocking backwards and forwards, while the hook end of my pole was disappearing through the window.

Naturally, he makes a grab for the pole, and of course he misses, but the stinking hook gets snagged in his sleeve. So there's me, hauling like a fisherman on a good day, dragging this old fart across the floor by his sleeve. He starts yelling bloody murder, and straight away the changing room starts filling up with angry-looking blokes, not a stitch on, of course, but all of them baying for my blood.

Well, I had the wit to let go of the pole, but that put me off balance. I rocked to and fro for a second, then I slowly toppled off Lucius Domitius' shoulders and landed hard on my kneecap on the pointy cobbles. Lucius Domitius fell over too, and there we were, sprawled on the floor howling with pain, while inside the building some evil shit starts hollering for the guard.

This would have been an ideal time to hop it, quick, only I'd buggered up my knee by falling on it and I couldn't move. Lucius Domitius didn't seem much better off, but nonetheless he hops up, grabs me like I'm a sack of charcoal, swings me over his shoulder and sets off as fast as his legs can carry us.

Fair play to him. Probably he thought he was being brave and noble, like that bloke in the poem who carries his old dad on his shoulders to safety out of the burning ruins of Troy. Unfortunately, it didn't quite work out that way. After about a dozen steps, Lucius Domitius' legs caved in under him and we both go crashing to the floor. Goes without saying, I pitch on my buggered knee. All I can think about is how much it hurts; Lucius Domitius is scrabbling around trying to get me off him so he can get up. Hardly surprising, we're still there thrashing about when out pop the guards.

Of course, the first thing they do when they see us is burst out laughing. The second thing is they scoop us up by the scruff and drag us inside, me still howling about my knee, Lucius Domitius calling me a bunch of stuff he never learned from Seneca. All in all, we were in a bit of a state.

(Now you'd have thought that, what with me being a bit of a philosopher, I'd have handled this unfortunate reversal with calm dignity. Sorry to disappoint you, but I didn't. First, I'm not that much of a philosopher. Second, it's hard to be dignified and calm when you've got three soldiers dragging you along by your ankles while you're frantically trying to cling on to the doorposts. Try it, and you'll see what I mean.)

Anyway, there we were, in a cell in the lockup in this poxy little town in Sicily, and this time, believe it or not, I really did think we'd had it. Your Roman soldier may not be a genius; in fact, it takes all his concentration to eat a dish of beans without half of them going up his nose, but it seemed a pretty safe bet that sooner or later they were going to look at us and think: big, thick-necked Italian, small scrawny Greek with a face like a polecat, and realise they'd just earned themselves a promotion. Then it'd be up in front of the magistrate, and it wouldn't matter a toss whether Lucius Domitius got recognised or not, we were facing enough capital charges to kill a legion. Speaking as one who already knew how it feels to get roped up on a cross with the sergeant swinging the big wooden mallet I told you about earlier, I've got to admit I wasn't happy.

'It's all your fault,' I told Lucius Domitius. 'You should have told me trying to tickle a breastplate was a bloody stupid idea.'

He looked at me, then shook his head and lay down on the floor.

'Really,' I said, 'I rely on you to do that. Yes, I know sometimes I get an idea and I'm all carried away with it, but that's where you come in, it's your job to say, don't be so bloody daft, Galen, that's a terrible idea. And you didn't. And that's how come we're in this mess.'

'Go to hell,' he said.

'Yes, right,' I replied. 'Because of you, that's exactly what I'm about to do, thank you ever so much.' I'd been pacing up and down but there didn't seem any point, and besides, the cell was too small for serious pacing. 'Lucius Domitius,' I said, 'you ever think about that?'

'About what?'

'You know,' I said. 'What happens to us when we die. Well, what do you reckon?'

He yawned. 'Can't say I've given it much thought.'

That struck me as a bit poor. 'Oh really,' I said. 'That's funny, because I seem to remember that in the old days you were the supreme high priest and in charge of all the religion right across the empire. Seems to me you can't have been doing your job properly, in that case.'

'True.'

I wasn't having that. I really wanted to have an argument about something. 'Bloody hell,' I said, 'that's a fine thing to say. If anybody ought to know about religion and stuff, it's you. Your uncle's a god, for pity's sake. Come to that, half your rotten family are gods.' I thought about that for a moment. 'Here,' I said, 'do you think that when we fetch up on the other side they'll put in a good word for us?'

'I doubt it,' he said. 'All my relatives always hated me. Even the ones I didn't have executed.' He sighed. 'My uncle's going to be convinced I murdered him; and even if he isn't, I don't think he'll be too happy about what I did to his wife. Who was also,' he added, 'his niece. So I don't think we can count on him being very sympathetic. Now, who does that leave? Well, there's my great-great-great-grandfather Augustus, he was very fond of my grandfather, so there may be a bit of hope there. On the other hand, he was always bloody strict, so I've heard. If he knows about me playing the lyre in public, he'll have me in Tartarus before you can say knife. That just leaves his uncle Julius, and he was a vicious bastard at the best of times.' He yawned again. 'If I were you, as soon as we get there, I'd pretend you aren't with me. It'll probably make things a lot easier for you.'

'Thanks a lot,' I said; then I paused. 'So you really believe in all that, then?'

He laughed. 'No, of course not,' he said. 'My great-uncle Claudius can't be a god; he needed two footmen and a surgeon every time he had a shit. Besides which, I don't think I've ever really believed in the gods. It's all just politics, as far as I can see.'

'Shut up, for crying out loud,' I shouted, and I spat into the fold of my tunic for luck. 'That's a bloody stupid thing to say at the best of times, and the way we're fixed right now . . .' Well, I couldn't believe it. Of all the things to say. What if Jupiter had heard, or one of the others?

'Calm down.' He sighed. 'One thing's for sure, I'm going to find out the answer pretty soon, one way or another. So where's the point in speculating about it now?'

He was starting to get on my nerves. 'Could make all the difference in the world,' I said. 'Like, I heard about one lot who reckon that so long as you tell the gods you're sorry for all the bad stuff you did just before you die, you get to go straight to the Elysian Fields, just the same as if you'd been good all your life. If there's any truth in that, it could be important.'

He shook his head. 'I don't think so. That wouldn't make any sense. You could be an absolute shit for seventy years, like – well, like my great-great-great-uncle Tiberius, for example, and so long as you had a moment or so to apologise before you snuffed it, you'd be free and clear. It'd be chaos.'

Something had been striking me as odd, and I finally realised what it was. 'You're being very calm about all this. Usually when we're about to die you go all to pieces.'

'Yes,' he admitted. 'But this time it's – well, so final, if you see what I mean. All the pieces slotting into place, if you like. It's got to mean that this time we really have come to the end of the road. Somehow, that doesn't bother me nearly as much as when I still believe, somewhere deep down, that we might be getting out alive after all. There's a lot to be said for not panicking. I wish I'd known about it before.'

I shrugged. 'I'll say this for you, back in the old days you'd never have been this calm.'

'True,' he said. 'But in the old days I had something to live for.'

'What's that supposed to mean?'

'Oh for pity's sake, Galen, look at me. Look at what I've turned into, ever since we ended up in Phaon's cellar. I'm a joke. I'm dressed in rags, I've got hands like the soles of a boot, I'm sunburnt up to the shoulder, I spend my life running away from soldiers and sleeping in ditches, and all I've got in the way of human companionship is you. Call that a life? Why the hell should I be bothered about losing something like that? If it was a punishment, I wouldn't do it to my worst enemy.'

I breathed out slowly. 'I'm going to pretend you didn't say any of that,' I said. 'I'm going to pretend that even if you did say it, you didn't mean it, you're just ranting away because deep inside, you're scared out of your mind and it's making you say the first thing that comes into your head. All right?'

'Suit yourself. I still reckon it's a pretty poor go when I've got to spend my last hours in this life locked up in a cell with you. When I think how it used to be . . .' He stopped and sighed. 'Actually,' he said, 'I'll tell you a secret. I hated having to be emperor.'

'Bullshit,' I said.

'No, absolutely straight. It was a foul life, and I loathed it.'

'Sure,' I said. 'All that partying and boozing and screwing around. You only did it because you had to.'

He laughed. 'That's not far off the mark, believe it or not. It seemed to be the thing to do. I'd spend all day in the law courts hearing appeals, or in some meeting with advisers – advisers, that's a joke, they were telling me what to do. That's when they bothered to let me know what they were up to. Oh, they were very polite, it was always, May I suggest, Caesar, and Perhaps you might consider doing this, Caesar, but if I came up with something I wanted to do, or I suggested a way of dealing with whatever it was, it was as though they hadn't heard me. And then there was the endless bitching and fighting, wherever my mother was concerned. I reckon she fed on melodrama, like a bee on honey. And then, at the end of the day, in would come all my so-called friends – though I wouldn't trust them not to steal snot, they were an evil bunch – and then I'd be obliged to go out with them, getting drunk and beating people up in the street. I think I only went along with it because it was the exact opposite of what I'd been doing all day, only it wasn't. It was the other side of the same coin, another thing that was expected of me. And so finally I thought, what is it I *really* want to do, and I knew, I wanted to write poetry and music and perform in front of people. Can you believe it? All I wanted to do was stuff any tart's son can do but I wasn't allowed to. Well, I made up my mind, I wasn't having that – it was Callistus who helped me do that. He said, if there's something you want to do, then you go right ahead and do it, and to the crows with what anybody thinks. And I was just starting to get the hang of it when Galba shows up and suddenly I'm hiding in cellars.'

'My heart bleeds.'

He wasn't listening. 'I'll tell you another thing that damned near broke my heart,' he went on. 'Every time I played something or sang something, it'd always be the same, even if I'd played like an elephant and sung like a crow, everybody in the room would start clapping and cheering and carrying on like I was Apollo himself, and the only reason they clapped was because they were afraid for their lives, didn't want to end up in the slate quarries, like Sulpicius Asper. And you know what?' he went on. 'That just wasn't fair, because – well, I'm not Homer or Pindar or Anacreon, I'm not even Virgil or that smug little creep Ovid, and my voice is all right but nothing special, even when I was young and everybody was telling me how wonderful I was, I knew *that*. But some of my stuff was good, I know that too. Once or twice, just occasionally, I got it right and I produced something with some quality to it, but nobody plays my stuff now, of course, and everybody thinks it must all have been rubbish, and that's simply not fair. Like I said, if I'd had the camp whore for a mother and I'd grown up in the Subura, chances are that I could go into a wine shop in the city and mention my name, and someone'd turn round and say, Hey, aren't you the chap who wrote that thing, the one that goes ta-tumpty-tumpty-tum, and he'd buy me a drink. You know, that's all I ever wanted, and it's the one thing I could never ever have.'

'How sad. How utterly fucking tragic. Oddly enough, all I ever wanted was to sleep in a proper bed and go into a wine shop and have enough money for a jug of wine and a plate of tripe, and not have to keep looking over my shoulder in case the guard drops by. And that's what I could never have. But then, I never learned to play the flute, so what would I know?'

He looked at me and shook his head. 'You don't understand,' he said.

'Too right I don't,' I replied. 'Of course, there were things I did have. I had my very own hoe, back on the farm, and any time I wanted I could walk up the mountain and spend all day smashing bloody great clods of dirt with it. Blisters, now, I could have all the blisters I liked, and there was never anybody saying, It's not fair, why does Galen get to do all the hard work and not me? Dammit,' I said, 'I even had a brother once. Not for as long as I'd have liked, mind you, but it was better than nothing.'

Then he looked at me again and I was sorry I'd said that. But, like I mentioned, I was in the mood for a good fight. I wanted him to get angry. But he wouldn't play, just slumped back on the floor and stared up at the roof

I sighed. 'It's all right. I'm sorry, I didn't mean that. And yes, in a way I can see what you're getting at, because you had so much and you lost it all, and I never had anything worth spit, so big deal. It must've been hard for you.'

He shook his head. 'That wouldn't have mattered. Oh, you don't believe me, but it's true. There's been times, this last ten years, when I wake up in the morning and I can't remember what it was like, living in the Golden House and never wearing the same shoes twice. It seems so bloody ridiculous – all that effort and money, and I never actually noticed. It amazes me how little I've missed all of it.

So yes, I know that if only I could've been me, instead of always having to be someone else, some character in a scam, or nobody at all when we're on the run and keeping our heads down – if I could've been me, and gone around the place singing and playing, passing round a hat or standing up on a cart outside inns, I could've been so happy. I'd never have wanted anything more. But instead . . .' He shrugged. 'Too late now,' he said, and then he grinned. 'You know what they say I said? My famous last words, before I stabbed myself? "What an artist dies with me." You know, that's quite good, it puts it pretty well; shame I never had the talent to come up with something like that. And now here I am, about to die, and it's not even my own words, it's somebody else's, it's a *quotation*. That's the bloody awful truth. I'm not even as good as the lies they tell about me.'

'Not as bad, either,' I said gently. 'For what it's worth, I know that. You're a bit of an idiot, Lucius Domitius, and you do some pretty dumb things and you fuss like an old woman sometimes, but basically you're all right. I just thought you'd like to know that,' I added awkwardly.

He laughed. 'Wonderful,' he said. '*Couldn't find his arse with both hands but basically all right.* What a wonderful thing to have carved on your headstone. You've got no idea how good that makes me feel.'

He'd clearly made up his mind to be miserable, so I left him to it, and went back to walking up and down. But that wasn't any more help than it had been before. Also, I was feeling very hungry, since we hadn't had anything to eat since the inn. 'This is no good,' I said. 'So we're going to die. They still ought to feed us.'

'Oh, they'll feed us, all right. The only question is, what to?'

Then the door opened, and a short, square sergeant with no neck told us it was our time to go up in front of the magistrate. Never mind, I thought. And then I had an idea. Not one of my best, I didn't need to be told that, but better than nothing. 'Lead on, then,' I said to the sergeant. He grinned. He could see I was up to something. I could see him figuring away behind his little round black eyes.

'No you don't,' he said. 'After you.'

So I let Lucius Domitius go first, then me, then, as the sergeant came up close behind us, I kicked the cell door backwards with my heel, hard as I possibly could. For a moment there I didn't think I'd got enough oomph into it, or else he wasn't where I needed him to be, but then, as I was turning round, I heard a lovely chunky noise, like a huge apple falling off a tree. Sure enough, I'd got the bastard right on the nose, and the bump had been him falling over.

'Well, don't just stand there,' I hissed to Lucius Domitius as I dragged the door shut and shot the bolt. 'Run.'

'All right,' he said. 'Where to.?'

'How the fuck would I know?'

'Oh for—' He scowled at me, like I'd just done something really embarrassing at a diplomatic function, then he spun round and started running – up the corridor, when I'd reckoned on going down. But it was broad as it was long, since I didn't have a clue where the passage went to, up or down. The sergeant was back on his feet already, because I could hear him thumping the door with his fist while he yelled for help. Wouldn't be long before the corridor was packed with soldiers, all of them extremely pissed off at us for bashing up their mate. Whether they'd come up the corridor, or down, or both at once, remained to be seen.

'You might have told me,' Lucius Domitius yelled back at me over his shoulder as we ran, but I was too winded to explain that I'd only just thought of it on the spur of the moment, so I panted, 'Drop dead,' and left it at that.

Just as I feared, we ran into a soldier. Luckily, though, we *ran* into a soldier, or rather Lucius Domitius did, and he was a big bloke, and the soldier was only little, though pretty tough and wiry, at that. But in a head-on collision it's sheer mass that gets the job done. Down the soldier went, with Lucius Domitius on top of him. I just managed to pull up short and jump over the pair of them, and I stopped myself by slapping both arms against the wall. Something rolled by my feet, and I saw it was the soldier's helmet – lazy sod hadn't bothered to do up his chinstrap. But that was all right, because it meant that when I kicked the soldier in the head, I didn't bust a toe.

Anyhow, I kicked him good. 'What the hell are you doing that for?' Lucius Domitius shouted.

'Get his cloak,' I said, scrabbling for the helmet. It wasn't a great fit, but it was all right. 'And what's he got under it, a breastplate?'

'Mailshirt,' Lucius Domitius answered. 'How do you get those things off? I can't see any straps.'

'Pull it over his head, I guess,' I replied. 'I don't know, do I? I wasn't the commander in chief of the Roman army for fifteen years.'

It turned out to be a bit like skinning a hare. 'We haven't got time for this,' Lucius Domitius muttered as he lugged the soldier about. 'What do you want the bloody thing for, anyway? It won't do you any good when they string you up on a cross.'

The mailshirt was a better fit than the helmet, though I can tell you, it's damned hard to breathe in those things, they squeeze all the puff out of you. 'We're back to the original plan,' I said. 'Here, pass me the sword belt. Come on, it'll only take a moment if you don't stand there nattering.'

He stood up and looked down at the soldier. 'You just said it was a bloody stupid idea.'

'No, tickling the stuff from the bathhouse was a bad idea. The rest of it's fine. Help me with these chinstraps, I can't reach.'

We'd been longer about it than I'd have liked, but we weren't doing so bad for country folk, as my grandad used to say. Also, I'd have liked to have got the soldier out of sight, but there wasn't anywhere to put him. 'Come on,' I said. 'Let's keep going. This must lead somewhere.'

Well, of course, he'd been quite right, it was a bloody stupid idea. On the other hand it worked sort of, because we came round a corner, past a whole lot more cell doors, and saw daylight. That had to be good. But before we could get out there, a load of soldiers came up behind us.

Not so good, I thought. They've got to have seen the bashed-up guard and know what we'd done. Running for it was about all I could think of, and I didn't reckon much to it.

Then something wonderful happened. The soldier in front stopped dead, stuck his chest out, tucked his chin in, and saluted.

Well, like I said, I'm not the former supreme commander of twenty legions, I can't tell a lance-corporal from a regular squaddie just by looking at his belt buckles, or whatever it is you tell rank by.

'You got one of them, then,' the soldier said.

'No thanks to you,' I snapped back. 'Don't just stand there, for crying out loud. The other one's bound to be somewhere close.'

The soldier did the saluting thing again. 'Do you need any help with that one, chief?' he asked.

'I can manage,' I replied. 'Now get on and do as you're told.'

'The other one, chief, he's armed and dangerous. Left one of our mob out cold just down the passageway.'

'What, that little Greek squirt?' I said. 'Stone me, he didn't look like he could bust his way out of a cobweb.'

And then, mercifully, they buggered off. I waited till they were out of sight, then I nodded to Lucius Domitius and we sort of strolled across the courtyard like we were taking the air after a nice meal. Only goes to show – if you look like you're doing something you're not supposed to be doing, every man and his dog'll jump on you. Make it seem like you're going about your business, all normal and boring, and they don't even see you.

I'd like to pretend that finding the stores was all part of my original plan, and that I figured out where it was likely to be from first principles and made a beeline for it like a dog after a weasel. After all, you weren't there, so you'd never know I was lying. But then, I'm not like the people who write history; I tell it like it was, not like it ought to have been. Truth is, I heard a lot of soldiers coming up behind us, so I pushed open the first door I came to, and got lucky.

Weird place, the stores in a barracks. I don't suppose there's anywhere in the world where you'll see so many things that look exactly the same. There were stacks of identical blankets, rows of identical shovels, piles of identical boots, and a whole wall covered in shelves loaded with identical helmets, swords, breastplates, belts (all rolled up, like an army of giant snails), tent pegs, pot hooks, shield covers, bow cases, every bloody thing you can think of and a bunch of stuff you'd never recognise—

('What the hell are those?' I asked, pointing at a rack of polished iron bits.

'Spare ratchet mechanisms for catapults,' Lucius Domitius replied. How he knew that, I have no idea.)

—everything exactly the same as the one next to it, from palisade stakes to spoons, all neatly arranged, everything straight and tidy and ready so the quartermaster's clerk could lay his hand on it without having to look. Forget your aqueducts and your triumphal arches and your gilded chariots drawn by four milk-white horses. Whenever I think about what the empire actually means, that's the picture I see in my head: every single thing you could ever think of, and hundreds and hundreds of each of them.

'Don't just stand there gawping,' Lucius Domitius said. 'Let's get what we need and get out of here.'

I'd thought we had the place to ourselves, but no such luck; a huge bloke came out of the back room and scowled at us. 'Well?' he said.

That wasn't good, but I gave it my best shot. 'This man needs a full set of kit,' I said. 'Everything, the works.'

The big bloke looked at me as if I was mad. 'So?' he said.

Wasn't expecting that. 'Well, then,' I said. 'This is the stores, right?'

'Yes, this is the stores. Where's your requisition?'

Decision time. He was a big bloke, but Lucius Domitius and I could probably have handled him. He wasn't expecting trouble and that's half the battle. So yes, we could have thumped him, grabbed the stuff and made a run for it, but somehow I didn't want to push my luck that far. That just left talking to the bastard. 'No time for any of that bull,' I said sharply. 'You can take it up with the captain later.'

'Crap,' he said. 'You know the rules. No requisition, no stuff.' He looked at me. 'Can't say I've seen you before,' he added. 'What's your unit?'

I could feel Lucius Domitius getting tense, but we'd gone past the point where bashing the bloke was a viable business proposition. He was looking at us a bit sideways, and we wouldn't have the element of surprise. I didn't know enough army stuff to kid my way out, and of course they'd relieved us of our ill-gotten gains, so offering him money wasn't on the board. Turning and running out of the building was tempting, but luckily I had more sense. Beyond those options, I couldn't think of anything.

Luckily, I didn't have to, because suddenly Lucius Domitius barked out, 'Name and rank,' in his best Roman voice.

The bloke told us his name: Marcus something, buggered if I can remember, rank: quartermaster sergeant. I noticed he'd stood to attention without even thinking about it. Anyway, Lucius Domitius was scowling. He took a step closer to the bloke. 'Do you know who I am?' he said quietly.

The bloke looked at him. Poor bastard, he was obviously scared rigid. 'No, sir,' he said.

'Better that way,' Lucius Domitius said. 'Who do you report to?'

He muttered some name.

'Right,' Lucius Domitius said. 'I'll see to it that he gets the necessary dockets. Now listen to me, soldier,' he went on. 'I haven't got time to explain and you don't want to hear what I've got to say, so we'll skip all that. One set of kit, and do try and get it as close to my size as possible. I've got enough to contend with without hobbling round Sicily in boots two sizes too small for me. Understood?'

The sergeant's eyes looked like they were going to pop out of his head any moment, and his hands were twitching, but he shook his head. 'Sorry, sir,' he mumbled, 'but I got to see a docket. Otherwise—'

Lucius Domitius punched him on the nose, and he fell straight backwards, like a chopped-down tree. Then we helped ourselves to what we were after: armour and helmet and stuff for him, a new pair of boots each, that sort of thing.

'Marvellous,' Lucius Domitius sighed, as he did up his boots. 'Now we've added robbery with violence to the collection. And this time we're actually guilty, though I guess that by now it doesn't matter a damn.'

I was in no mood to listen to that. 'You're crazy,' I said. 'Stark staring nuts. I can't believe what you just did.'

He looked surprised. 'What, belting the sergeant? Seems to me we didn't have much choice.'

'No, not that,' I replied angrily. 'What you said back there. "Do you know who I am," for crying out loud. And you're the one who's always petrified of being recognised.'

He shrugged. 'Maybe. But I don't think he got wise. He was too busy wondering what had gotten into you. Actually, I'd be interested to know what you thought you were playing at.'

We left the stores and walked across the yard. Of course it was anyone's guess which way the main doors were, leading out into the town. Pretty soon the soldiers would catch on, or the magistrate'd get tired of waiting and send some men to hurry us up, or the quartermaster would wake up and start yelling the place down. The way I saw it, we'd used up an entire lifetime's worth of luck, along with all the unused good fortune I must've inherited from my ancestors, and pretty soon it was all going to fall apart round our ears. On the other hand, they hadn't got us yet.

Bugger me if the main doors weren't straight across the courtyard. Of course, they were shut, and there was a brace of sentries in front of them, looking dead miserable, the way sentries generally do, but what the hell, I thought, I'm game if they are.

We doubled back and walked round three sides of the yard so they wouldn't see us. Then we broke into a run as we came up to them, yelling, 'Quick! Open up.'

'Hold on, mate, where's the fire?' one of them said.

'Get those fucking gates open!' Lucius Domitius shouted. 'Couple of prisoners've escaped. Got into the tower and shinned down the wall on a rope. If they get away, we're all going to be in the shit.'

He may have been useless at pretty much everything else, but when it came to telling the tale, Lucius Domitius had the knack. The guards looked at each other, then they started shooting the bolts back.

'Get a move on, will you? They're getting away,' Lucius Domitius bawled, and they did as they were told. They believed him. Hell, I believed him. Mind you, he was telling the truth, because a few moments later, the prisoners had got away, and if anybody in the whole province of Sicily was more surprised about that than they were, I'll buy him a drink, with pleasure.

'The depressing thing,' Lucius Domitius said, as we jogged round the corner and darted down an alleyway, 'is that that was probably the easy bit.'

He was being miserable again, but I could see his point. 'One step at a time,' I told him. 'Let's get out of this horrible bloody town, and then we can see about getting off this horrible bloody island.'

One good thing about living under the iron heel of a cruel and ruthless oppressor is that people don't think twice about seeing soldiers on the street. Better still, they do their best not to look at them; instead, as soon as they're aware of them, they tend to shuffle past as quick as they can, looking the other way. Naturally, that suited us just fine; and we found that the more we stomped along, making ourselves as conspicuous as we possibly could, the more invisible we became. By the time we reached the outskirts of town, people were darting out of our way like we were a couple of runaway carts and we practically had the roads to ourselves.

'These people must have guilty consciences,' Lucius Domitius muttered, 'or else why are they so scared of us?'

I didn't answer that. It was one of those things where, if you need to be told, you're never going to understand.

Once we were back in open country it didn't take us long to click back into the old routine. After all, we still had to eat, and that meant practising the only trade we had, namely kidding. Dressing up as a soldier is an old scam and pretty reliable, though the take is always poor. You can bluster free food, booze and lodgings out of innkeepers, and that's about it. It's a living, but I wouldn't call it a career. One good thing about it, as far as we were concerned: it meant we had no trouble finding out what was going on. We'd prance into an inn or a farmhouse and do our have-you-seen-two-men routine, and we'd get the latest news, or the latest rumours, at any rate, about how the hunt for us was going. It didn't take long for the word to get out that we'd busted out of the guardhouse. It was bloody alarming to hear that we'd been credited with killing at least two soldiers, and in some cases as many as five. But we were pleased to find that, apparently nobody had twigged that we might be togged out as soldiers. On the other hand, they had put two and two together and figured out that the two hooligans who tried to tickle the bathhouse had to be the same ones who robbed the governor's son, which also meant that they had to be two of the cons who escaped from the quarry gang. To Lucius Domitius' delight, we didn't hear the name Nero anywhere, and he started to get a bit more cheerful as we put more and more distance between ourselves and that town.

On the negative side, we hadn't got a clue where we were or in which direction we were headed. I figured we were heading west, towards Camarina. Lucius Domitius was certain sure we were going south, in which case we'd be walking into the sea at any moment (which we didn't). All he had to do was look up at the sun and he'd have known I was right, but Lucius Domitius was never one to let a few poxy facts choke him off a nice juicy opinion.

It was only after we'd been on the road for four days, bludging off innkeepers and farmers and sleeping in barns, that I started to wonder where Camarina had got to. It was bloody annoying, like being stood up for a date with your best girl. We'd walk and walk, and still the wretched city wasn't there. Eventually it dawned on me what had happened. We'd gone right past it, above it to the north.

'Right,' I said. 'You're the one who went to school. What's in this direction?'

Lucius Domitius looked at me. 'How should I know?' he said.

'Don't give me that,' I told him. 'I'll bet that somewhere in the palace there was this huge great bronze map of the empire with all the places marked on it, and you must've seen it hundreds of times. You must know the principal towns in Sicily.'

He shrugged. 'Not me,' he said. 'And it's the first I've ever heard about any map. Whereabouts in the palace would that have been, then?'

'I don't know, do I? I was just a house guest, I didn't own the place. You sure there wasn't any map?'

'There could have been, I suppose,' he said. 'It was a big palace. There were loads of rooms I never went into. But nobody ever mentioned anything like that.'

'Oh.' I was shocked, for some reason. I mean, you'd have thought it was the sensible thing to do. Think about it: some messenger blows in, says there's trouble brewing in Cyanopolis. Nobody's ever heard of Cyanopolis, it's just some border fort, so it stands to reason, there'd be a big map, and everybody, all the advisers and general staff and what not, they'd troop off and take a look at it, and then they'd know. Otherwise, you'd have a major crisis on your hands, decisive action needing to be taken straight away, and nobody'd know whether it was in Cilicia or Upper Moesia. What the hell kind of a way to run an empire would that be?

'I think,' he went on, 'that if we've overshot Camarina, we should be headed straight for Gela. Only, if that was the case, we should be following the course of the river Anapus, and if we are, I haven't seen any sign of it.'

I looked round. No river.

'If we're north of the Anapus,' he went on, 'any moment now we're going to run into some horrible great mountains. But if that's where we're headed, we should be right up close to them by now, unless we're following one of the lower river valleys that feed down off the central block. But I don't think we are, because there'd still be damn great big mountains on either side of us, and there aren't.'

'Right,' I said. 'What you're saying is, you haven't got a clue where we are.'

'I never said I did. Look, it's been years and years since I learned all this stuff in school, and I wasn't paying attention then. I was too busy looking out of the window or making up tunes in my head. Of course,' he went on, 'it's possible that that big road we were following for a while back there was the military road across the mountains – only I'd have thought it'd have been bigger and wider – in which case, we should have spent last night in Hybla, though it's just possible that we left the road a mile or so short of there. In which case, this ought to be the flat plain that runs down off the mountains to the sea, halfway between Camarina and Gela. But I wouldn't bank on that, because everything's in the wrong place for that.'

'Thank you,' I said. 'I wish I hadn't asked now.'

But he was right, amazingly enough, because early the next day we found ourselves back on his military road, and sure enough it wound up at the sea. We got off it before that, of course, since we didn't want to be on the main road where there were likely to be people about. Anyhow, the long and the short of it was, we fetched up at the seaside, our toes practically in the water, looking out towards (if I'm not mistaken) Tripolis, on the African coast.

'It's at times like this,' I said, 'I really wish I was a seagull. Then we'd be in Sirtis by nightfall.'

'I don't think that'd be such a good idea. They eat seagulls in Tripolis.'

'You know what I mean,' I said. 'All right, now what? We've got a choice. Left or right. What do you reckon?'

He shrugged. 'I'd toss a coin for it, if we had any money.'

'No,' I said, 'I want a sensible, reasoned decision. If it was blind guessing, I'd do it myself. Which do you think, Camarina or Gela?'

'Broad as it's long, as far as I know,' Lucius Domitius replied. 'Seeing as how both of us know fuck all about either of them. Well,' he added, 'that's not strictly true. I seem to remember that in Gela, every summer solstice, they have a big crab-eating competition down on the sea front. They pile up all these crabs, and each contestant's got a pair of tweezers and a little brass hammer, and the first one—'

'What's that got to do with us?'

'Search me. I'm just telling you because it's the only thing I know about Gela. Unless,' he added, 'I'm thinking of the other Gela, the one in southern Macedonia.'

I changed my mind about the map. If he'd had a chance to study a map, instead of just piecing it together from what he remembered, he could've bored me right off my feet and straight into the grave. 'Gela, then,' I said.

'All right. Why not?'

'Right.'

So that was that. We'd made up our minds to head for Gela. It only goes to show, really, how pointless it can be, making big decisions, because we hadn't been on the road more than an hour when we saw a ship.

It was close in to the shore, quietly bobbing along, one of the big grain freighters that make the run from Sicily to Italy, final destination Rome. I'd seen enough of them at anchor at Ostia. Seen from a distance, they look like a floating city, scores of them all tied up in a row along the specially built dock, and as soon as one gets emptied it pulls out and another one slots neatly into its place. It's a hell of a business, feeding a place the size of Rome, and to do them credit, they've got it figured out pretty well. Mind you, it's one of the few things they really care about, because a grain shortage can turn Rome from the hub of the civilised world into a wall-to-wall hunger riot in about three days.

Anyhow, there was this ship. Lucius Domitius, who knew a thing or two about the grain trade for obvious reasons, reckoned it had loaded up at Camarina and was working its way round the east coast on its way home. (The big freighters don't like crossing any more open sea than they have to, but they don't like having to shove their way through the straits of Rhegium, either. They'd rather take another day and a half over the trip, even though time is money, than risk pranging the ship on a rock. Most of the freighters on the grain run are on the elderly side, and you only have to sneeze in the wrong place and they start shipping water in seven places.) He pointed out how low she was riding in the water, which backed up his theory that she was full and making for home. That seemed like a reasonable conclusion to draw, from my limited knowledge of such things (and what I know about ships and international trade you could carve on a toenail).

'Well,' I said, 'what do you reckon?'

'What do I reckon about what?'

'The ship, dummy. Us getting on it and getting the hell out of Sicily. What do you reckon?'

He frowned. 'Well,' he said, 'it'd be nice if we could manage it. But I don't see how.'

'Bloody hell,' I said. 'And you're supposed to be the educated one.'

'All right,' he said. 'You tell me, how do we go about hitching a ride on a grain ship?'

'Easy,' I said.

And yes, I was pretty confident that it would be, or at least, it'd be a damn sight easier than staying alive and free in Sicily with the whole island after us. True, when I said that to him, I hadn't actually got a plan or anything like that, but figuring out each last painful detail before I make a decision isn't my style.

'Easy?'

'You bet,' I said. 'What we need is a small boat.'

He looked at me. 'What do we want a small boat for?' he asked.

I clicked my tongue. He could be a bit dense sometimes. 'You fancy swimming out that far, be my guest. Me, I'd rather row.'

So, the next thing was, find a small boat. Luckily for us, that's not too hard when you're right next to the sea, in an area that's so dirt-poor they eat fish all the time. The first one we came to had a little prune-faced old man in it, fooling about with a fishing net.

I walked up to him. 'Sorry, mate,' I said, 'we're requisitioning your boat.'

He looked at us, took in the armour and uniforms, didn't seem all that impressed. 'No you bloody well aren't,' he said.

'Sorry,' I repeated. 'But it's a military emergency, we need that boat. You'll get it back when we've finished with it, don't worry about that.'

'I'm not worried,' he replied, turning his back on us. 'You're not having my boat. Now fuck off.'

It wasn't going the way I'd expected. Where I come from, you see, if a soldier comes bouncing up and tells you he's taking your cart or your mule, answering back will get you a thick lip, and that's if you're lucky, so people don't tend to do it. Obviously the Roman garrison in Sicily wasn't quite so straightforward when it came to military procurement.

'Hey, you.' Lucius Domitius reached out and clapped the little guy on the shoulder. 'We're talking to you. Now, get your arse off this boat, or I'll do it for you.'

He winced and turned round. 'What d'you want my boat for, anyhow?'

Thanks to the delay, I'd had time to think of an answer to that. 'See that big grain ship out there? We have reason to believe there's two wanted criminals on board. Our orders are to search the boat and arrest the scumbags. All clear?'

The old boy scowled at us. 'Why've you got to have my boat, then? Haven't you wankers got a navy for that sort of thing?'

'Yes,' I said, 'but not here. Last I heard, it was saving civilisation from the Parthian menace. Which doesn't make any odds,' I went on, 'because we don't need a couple of squadrons of battleships. All we need is your boat. All right?'

He'd probably have carried on arguing the toss, but Lucius Domitius slowly started drawing his sword, and in the right time and place the sight of a couple of inches of Spanish steel is worth a few thousand words.

'It's all right,' I called back to him, as Lucius Domitius pushed us off and then scrambled in behind the oars, 'we'll have it back to you by nightfall.'

I think the old boy may have shouted back a reply, but I didn't hear it. I could guess what it was.

'Here,' said Lucius Domitius, after we'd gone a couple of dozen yards from the shore, 'have you got any idea how you set about driving these things?'

'What, boats?' I said. 'Dead easy, piece of cake. You just sort of dip the oarblades in the sea and pull on the handles. Nothing to it, really.'

'Ah,' he replied, shooting a bucketful of water up my nose, 'that's all right then. You can row, since you seem to know so much about it, and I'll sit in the back here and steer.'

'Me? I don't know spit about rowing.'

He frowned at me, the git. 'Don't be silly,' he said, 'you're an Athenian, proud descendant of the victors of Salamis, rowing's in the blood. You know perfectly well—'

'I do not,' I replied, straight off. 'Rowing in the fleet was what the poor people did. My lot were upper crust, cavalry class. We were riding into battle on thoroughbreds when your lot were still hoeing turnips in Latium.'

'Really?' He grinned at me. 'How are the mighty fallen. Now get rowing, or I'll push you in the sea. You can swim, can't you?'

'Of course I can swim,' I lied. 'All right, you get hold of the steering thing, and I'll see what I can do.'

Like I'd said, nothing to it, rowing a boat. It's like skimming the shit off a vat of newly fermented wine, only the spoon's six feet long. I don't know why Lucius Domitius made such a fuss about it.

'Right,' I said, as we skimmed across the water like a great big beetle. 'Get that armour off, and dump it over the side.'

He looked at me as if I was crazy. 'You what?'

'Get rid of it,' I said. 'Quick, before we get there.'

'After all the trouble we went to getting hold of it in the first place? No way.'

I sighed. 'For pity's sake, why is it you've got to moan and whinge about every damn suggestion I make?'

'I don't know,' he said. 'Maybe it's something to do with the way you keep landing us in the shit. Or perhaps I'm just an old fusspot.'

'The armour,' I said. 'And the cloak, and all that stuff. Get rid of it.'

He gave in, and started ditching metalwork into the sea. I did the same – bloody awkward, since I was trying to keep the boat going at the same time. Here's a tip for you, by the way. If you try and row a boat with one hand while unbuckling a helmet strap with the other, the boat goes round in circles.

Lucky for us the grain freighter was just wallowing along. Even so, I had to stretch my back to get us up next to it. By that time, we'd dumped all the army stuff except the swords and belts. 'Hey,' I shouted, loud as I could manage, 'you there in the ship.'

Just when I was sure they hadn't heard, or they were pretending they hadn't seen us, someone stuck his head over the rail. 'What do you want?' he called back.

'Where are you headed?'

The bloke on the ship shrugged his shoulders. 'Ostia,' he replied. 'What's it to you?'

'Can you give us a lift?'

'No.'

That caught me a bit by surprise. 'Oh,' I said. 'You sure about that? We'll pay.'

'That's different,' the bloke shouted back. 'Thirty drachmas each. Forty with food,' he added.

I smiled, though I don't suppose he could see me very clearly at that distance. 'Actually,' I said, 'I thought we could trade.'

'Trade?'

'We have valuable stuff,' I told him. 'Worth a lot more than forty drachmas.'

'Have we?' Lucius Domitius muttered. 'News to me.'

'Shut up,' I told him. 'Well?' I said to the ship bloke. 'What do you reckon?'

'Depends. What've you got?'

Good question. 'Well,' I said, 'for a start, we've got two really nice swords, with scabbards and belts, top of the range stuff.' The bloke didn't say anything, so I went on, 'Best Spanish steel, lovingly crafted by dedicated artisans, absolutely guaranteed—'

'No,' said the bloke.

'What?'

'No. Not interested.'

'Oh.' I looked around quickly. 'Well, how about a nice, tight little rowing boat? One owner from new, lovely handling, throw in a pair of oars absolutely free.'

'No, thanks.'

This was starting to get desperate. 'All right,' I said, 'and this is my final offer. How about a best quality, home-bred, fully certified male field hand? Excellent condition, prime of life, turns his hand to anything.'

'What? Where?'

'Him,' I replied, pointing to Lucius Domitius. 'Here, look at the shoulders on him, just the thing for lugging great heavy jars of corn about. You interested or not?'

'You *bastard*—' Lucius Domitius started to say. I kicked him on the shin, and he shut up.

'I dunno,' said the ship bloke. 'Shirt and boots go with him?'

'Yeah, go on,' I said, 'why not? But I'll want wine with the food.'

He was still thinking about it. 'Teeth?' he said.

'What do you mean, teeth?' I asked.

'What're his teeth like?' the bloke said. 'Has he got them all, or what?'

'Sure,' I said. 'Loads of teeth. Look, you want to deal, or do I wait for the next freighter?'

The bloke hesitated for a moment or so, then nodded. 'Deal,' he said. 'But you sleep on deck with the crew, right?'

'Suits me,' I said. 'I like the fresh air.'

The bloke disappeared, and somebody threw a rope over the side of the ship. 'Looks like we've done it,' I said cheerfully. 'Next stop, Italy.'

But Lucius Domitius didn't seem pleased at all. In fact, he was pulling the most horrible faces at me. 'You shit,' he hissed, 'You total arsehole. You just *sold* me to that man.'

I shrugged. 'So what?' I said. 'Look, don't worry about it—'

'Not worry about it? Are you out of your tiny mind?'

'Calm down, will you?' I said. 'It's quite simple. It just means we leave the ship a bit early, that's all.'

'No way,' he whined. 'Have you any idea what they do to runaway slaves?'

'Sure,' I said. 'More or less the same as the soldiers'll do to us if we don't get the hell out of Sicily. Now shut your face and try to act like a slave. You've done it loads of times, it shouldn't be a problem.'

'Yes,' he whimpered, 'but then I was just pretending.'

'Well, now it's for real, so that ought to make it easier. Come on,' I said – I was reaching for the rope – 'it'll be all right. Like, when have I ever let you down?'

He may have said something, but I was scrambling up the rope and didn't hear.

FIVE

I have to say, it's not bad, travelling on a grain freighter. They're not like most ships, where everything's cramped and if you sneeze everybody on the boat gets wet. You've got room to stretch your legs, and freighters don't sway about as much as your little merchant ships. They're still pretty basic, mind – if you want to take a shit you've got to squat down in this chair arrangement at the back end, with your bum hanging out over the ocean – but there are worse ways to get about, believe me.

Lucius Domitius wasn't so keen, of course. Once they'd stripped his clothes off and had a good poke about to see if he was all there and so on, they made him ship's cook, on account of the real cook had jumped ship in Camarina and they hadn't had time to find another one. I tried to tell them he hadn't done much cooking before, but they didn't seem too bothered about that, and I got the impression they didn't care who did the job so long as they didn't have to. As we went along, I figured out why that was: it's no fun looking after great big cauldrons of hot oil and boiling water when a ship starts rolling about. Still, he got the hang of it quite quickly, with nothing more than a few minor scalds and such like. What really pissed him off was having to be chained up at night, but the captain insisted on that, since we were so close to the shore and all, and he didn't want him jumping overboard in the middle of the night and swimming for it. I told him there was no danger of that – which was true, so long as we were in Sicilian waters – but he said he'd rather be safe than sorry, and I didn't want to make a big thing about it.

At first sight, the crew struck me as a bunch of pirates, but it turned out that they were all right, more or less. About half of them were Greeks, and they never stopped gabbing; the other half were a mixed bunch, Spanish and Egyptians, a couple of Italians, and they never said a word. Most of the time they were busy pulling on ropes and scrambling about up in the rigging, like sailors do, but of an evening they'd all squat down on the deck next to the galley and gobble down their bacon and beans and have a natter – or at least, the Greeks nattered and the rest listened, or not, as the case may be. The first couple of nights out, when I went over to join them they all shut up and stared at me, even the Greeks; but then I guess the strain of keeping their faces shut got too much for them, and one of the Greeks asked where I was from. I said Phyle, in Attica, and of course that was enough. Two of the Greeks were Athenian, and next thing they were asking, did I know so-and-so, and it didn't take them long to decide I was an off-relation, twelfth cousin nine times removed, like everybody is in Attica. Of course, I hadn't been telling the truth when they asked me all these questions, because the last thing I wanted was for anybody to tumble to who I really was, but of course I knew enough people in Phyle to lie so they'd never know the difference. Once they'd made up their minds that I was all right, they even started talking to Lucius Domitius, which made life a bit easier all round. He'd had the sense to figure out who he was going to be in advance, so he had all his answers pat. He was always smart that way.

'I'm from Galicia,' he said, when they asked. It was a good answer, because he could pass for a Celt with his reddish hair and enormous neck, though he was a tad on the tall side. 'Back home I was called Brennus, but nowadays I answer to pretty well everything.'

They laughed at that, but one of them frowned a bit and said, 'You speak pretty good Greek for a Celt. Actually, I'd have put you down for an Italian, myself.'

Lucius Domitius pulled a very sad face. 'Ah, well,' he said, 'that's a long story.'

'So?'

'Well,' he said, as he scraped out the bean pot, 'if you must know, I come from one of the best families in Galicia. In fact, by rights, I should be a prince in my own country. But when I was just a kid, the Romans came round taking up hostages for good behaviour, and I was chosen, so they packed me off to Rome, and I got raised there, along with all the other hostage kids. Went to Roman school and everything.'

They were impressed. 'Is that right?' one of them said. 'So how come you ended up here?'

Lucius Domitius shrugged. 'My folks back home must've screwed up somehow, because when I was fifteen, one day when we were in philosophy class, these soldiers came in looking all grim and solemn, and all us Galician kids were stood up and marched off. Half of them, I never did find out what happened to them, but I guess they got the chop – they were all the really important ones, the king's sons and nephews and so on. The rest of us wound up in the slave market and well, no offence to you folks, but it's been sort of downhill ever since.'

Obviously they reckoned that was really sad, because they looked at him and nodded gravely, and one of them poured him a drink. 'That must be a shitty thing,' one of the Athenians said, 'being born a genuine prince and ending up a slave. Makes you think, really.'

Lucius Domitius shrugged. 'It was a long time ago,' he said. 'And I've been a slave much longer than I was a prince, so I've had time to adjust. It's just the way things go, that's all.'

I think they were impressed with his courage and modesty. I know I was, and I knew full well he was just bullshitting. 'Maybe you were well out of it, at that,' piped up another of the Greeks, an Illyrian with a nose busted two ways. 'I mean, at least you're still alive. Them other kids weren't so lucky.'

Lucius Domitius sighed. 'You said it,' he replied. 'Whenever I catch myself thinking about the old days, I tell myself, it's better to be alive and be someone's slave, even if your master's just a small-time chiseller, than to be the Lord High Emperor down among the dead men.'

That really got to them, and a couple of them started nodding like billy goats and saying, that's right, that's very well put. I reckoned so, too, at the time. Since then, I found out it was straight out of Homer's *Odyssey*, with a few of the old-fashioned words taken out. Should've guessed, I suppose.

So we carried on, nice and quiet and peaceful, pottering along the Sicilian coast; and then one day, a small boat comes alongside and it's an old man and a couple of women selling stuff, and while they're trying to kid the sailors into buying their junk, they're telling them this really exciting news. I could tell it was something pretty hot by the way they all acted when they heard it. Now the old man and his outfit were giving me a pretty wide berth, since they'd somehow figured out just by looking at me that I didn't have any money, so I had to creep up on someone else and eavesdrop.

'Straight up,' the old man was saying. 'Heard it the night before last in town from a mate of mine, he'd heard it off a carter who'd had it off a bloke in the market, who'd heard it off a barber who'd given a shave to a bloke off a ship from Rome; and this bloke, the sailor, he'd left the city the same day as the news broke, so it's fresh as apples.'

The sailors were shaking their heads, like something bad had happened. 'And he was no great age,' he said. 'I mean, he was getting on, but he wasn't that old.'

'Sixty-nine,' said the old guy. 'That's six years younger'n me, and I'm still going strong. Still, it's the life they lead, all that boozing and whoring. Does them in while they're still in their prime.'

There was a bit more stuff like that, and then the captain showed up and told the old bloke to piss off out of it, so I didn't get to hear any more till that evening when they were all discussing it, even the Spaniards and the Egyptians. Like I'd thought, someone important had died. In fact, it was about as important a someone as you could get: the Emperor Vespasian.

Soon as I heard that, of course, I looked across at Lucius Domitius, to see how he was taking it, but he just stood there stirring the beans, like he didn't understand what they were all talking about.

'He was all right,' one of the two Italians was saying. 'Sure, he wasn't perfect, he had his faults like the rest of us. Basically, though, he was all right.'

'You can say that again,' one of the Greeks put in. 'At least, when you think of who we could've wound up with.'

'Too right,' said one of the Spaniards. 'I mean, think what it'd be like if that arsehole Galba'd stuck around.'

'Or Otho,' said one of the Greeks. 'He was a really nasty piece of work, Otho was.'

'Or Vitellius, come to that,' someone else said. 'He was the worst of the lot, by all accounts. Old Vespasian did everybody a favour when he knocked that creep on the head.'

Behind them, Lucius Domitius cleared his throat. 'Forget about Vitellius,' he said. 'And the rest of that lot. If you're looking for a really evil bastard, what about Nero?'

That set them all off nodding and muttering, that's right, he was the worst of the lot. Of course, I was sat there speechless, thinking he must've gone off his head, but he didn't look like he was throwing a crazy fit. Quite the opposite. Just goes to show, you can't judge by appearances.

'I mean,' Lucius Domitius went on, 'that other lot, they weren't around for more than a day or so, there's no way of telling what they'd really have been like. They might even have settled down, turned out all right in the end. Unlikely, I'll grant you,' he added, as some of the crew started shaking their heads and pulling faces. 'But anything's possible, they could've reformed, turned over a new leaf once they'd got their backsides on the curule chair. But Nero – well, we had fifteen years of that bastard, so we know for sure exactly what he was like.' Lucius Domitius sighed, like he had toothache or something. 'I'd like to see someone get up and try and make excuses for all the stuff he did, as if anybody'd try.'

One of the Greeks nodded so furiously I thought his head'd come off. 'He was an evil shit, that Nero. He had the right idea, killing himself like that.'

'I don't agree,' Lucius Domitius said (and I thought, hello). 'No, a quick, easy death like that – too good for him. They should've caught him and strung him up by the balls outside his own palace gate, and let the crows peck his eyes out.'

Nobody disagreed with that. 'Would've served him right,' said one of the Spaniards, 'the things he done.'

'Only murdered his mother, didn't he?' said one of the Italians. 'Only had his own mother put to death, like she was a criminal or something. A man who could do something like that—'

Lucius Domitius shuddered. 'Doesn't bear thinking about,' he said. 'Though, mind you, she was an evil bitch as well, or so I've heard. Still, that doesn't excuse what he did, does it?'

'Oh, pure poison, that Agrippina was,' said one of the Athenians. 'No doubt about it, she'd have done him in if he hadn't got to her first.'

'She'd have done the world a favour, then,' Lucius Domitius said sharply. 'And anyway, it doesn't matter that she was a vicious, scheming bitch. Doesn't even matter that she'd have killed him if she'd thought of it first. She was still his mother, and there's absolutely no excuse.'

'Oh, I don't know,' piped up one of the Greeks. 'What about Oedipus?'

Confused silence. 'How do you mean?' I asked.

'Oedipus,' the Greek repeated. 'His mum did in his dad, so he killed her. It's in plays and everything.'

'You mean Orestes,' one of the other Greeks said. 'Oedipus was the one who killed his dad and screwed his mum. Though they do say Nero did that, as well.'

Lucius Domitius sighed again. 'I wouldn't be surprised at anything that bastard did. Though I don't know why he'd have wanted to. She was no vase painting, so I've heard.'

That stopped their conversation dead for a while, and I was just about to try changing the subject when someone said, 'Well, I never heard where he murdered his father, but they do say he did in old Claudius, and wasn't he his uncle or something?'

'Great-uncle,' Lucius Domitius said, 'though technically he was Nero's father, since he married Agrippina. She was his niece, you see.'

'What, Nero's niece? I thought she was his mother.'

'No,' Lucius Domitius said patiently, 'she was Claudius' niece.'

'And he married her? Dirty old bastard.'

Lucius Domitius shrugged. 'Well, they see things differently, the Roman nobility. But yes, I don't see how Nero couldn't have been in on Claudius' murder. Mind you, he was only, what, sixteen, seventeen at the time, but that doesn't mean much in those circles. And Claudius was a good emperor. At least, he wasn't so bad.'

Everybody laughed at that. 'Give us a break,' someone said. 'Claudius was a real vicious old sod, executed people right, left and centre. Whoever done him in, he had it coming.'

'That's right,' someone else said. 'He let those advisers of his, ex-slaves the lot of 'em, go around killing people for their money. And didn't he ever get through wives at a hell of a rate? Best you can say for Claudius is, he was better than the bloke before him.'

'Yeah,' said one of the Egyptians, then he added, 'Who was that? I can't remember.'

A Greek laughed. 'Caligula, you clown. You know, the nutso who thought he was a god. I reckon he must've been the worst of the lot.'

'Apart from Nero,' Lucius Domitius said firmly. 'Nero was the worst.'

Everybody nodded again. 'He was the pits, Nero was,' said a Spaniard.

'Glad you agree,' said Lucius Domitius. 'For instance, you take taxes.'

A Greek frowned. 'Actually,' he said, 'you're wrong there. Taxes weren't so bad in Nero's day, in fact they were lower, at least out our way. I remember, because my dad was on the local board in our village, and he said Nero actually lowered taxes from what they'd been before. Still,' he added, 'that's neither here nor there.'

'Exactly,' Lucius Domitius said. 'After all, what good are lower taxes when the price of everything keeps going up all the time? Like when Nero was in power.'

'Did they?' One of the older men lifted his head. 'I don't remember that. In fact, they went down when Nero came in. I know that because there was a drought in our district about that time, and the government stepped in and fixed the price of grain. Still,' he added, 'I don't suppose that was any of Nero's doing. One of his advisers, more like.'

'Bound to have been,' someone else agreed. 'Don't suppose Nero knew what was going on in the empire from one day to the next. All he cared about was writing poetry and playing the harp. What sort of emperor is that, I ask you?'

'I was just going to say that,' Lucius Domitius said. 'Mucking about enjoying himself, dressing up in silks and prancing about on a stage when he should have been doing something worthwhile. Do you know, there wasn't a single war while he was in charge? Pathetic. And he was proud of it too, the gutless coward. Boasted about it, while the soldiers had nothing to do all day but loll around the barrack yard playing dice.'

'Shocking,' said an Italian. 'Still, that all changed when Vespasian got in. He really sorted out those Jews, didn't he?'

'And the British,' a Greek pointed out. 'Killed thousands of 'em, the savages. There was always plenty to keep the army busy while he was around.'

'No wonder the taxes had to go up, then,' I said. 'Got to be paid for, wars.'

'Yes,' Lucius Domitius admitted, 'but at least he didn't go spending it all on building fancy palaces and temples and all that shit, like Nero did. He was obsessed with all that stuff, art and architecture and rubbish like that. No wonder he couldn't afford to fight any wars.'

'Yeah, it was all right if you were a painter or a plasterer,' an Italian pointed out. 'Like my uncle, he did plastering and fresco painting, that line of work. Very comfortable, he was, in Nero's time. But he didn't like doing it, he said, not working for that arsehole. It made him feel guilty, he told me, all the time he was doing it.'

'No wonder,' Lucius Domitius said. 'And don't forget, it was Nero who started the Great Fire, just so he could get rid of the old slum buildings and put up poncy new ones.'

'That's right,' said a Greek. 'That was him, that fire. Him and the Christians.'

An Egyptian nodded. 'They were in it together,' he said, 'or so I heard. Nero gave 'em all torches and sent 'em out setting light to people's roofs while they were asleep. They like doing that sort of thing, Christians. It's because they're Jews.'

'And slaves,' added a Greek. 'Slaves or ex-slaves, the lot of 'em. It's time something was done, if you ask me.'

Lucius Domitius picked up a knife and started slicing leeks. 'What really put the tin lid on it for me,' he said, 'was the hypocrisy of the bastard. Just as soon as the fire'd died down a bit, he was out there on the streets, directing the fire crews, heaving buckets of water, as if he cared what happened to people. And all the time, he'd started the bloody fire himself. I don't know how somebody could behave like that.'

'Well, he was wrong in the head, wasn't he?' a Greek said. 'Must've been. Otherwise, he wouldn't have done all that dressing up and singing in public. Rotten voice he had, too, though my dad always said he played the lyre well. He heard him once, actually, that time he came to Greece. But he couldn't sing any better than our old cat.'

'Your dad?'

'Nero.'

'Oh, right. Actually,' whoever it was went on, 'I heard he used to make all the senators go to the theatre and listen to him caterwauling, and as soon as they were inside, they'd lock the doors so they couldn't leave, not till he'd finished.'

'I heard that,' someone said. 'By all accounts, there were people asleep and having fits and heart attacks, right there in the stands, and nobody was allowed out for any reason. What a bloody farce.'

'Too right,' Lucius Domitius chimed in. 'I mean to say, what a disgusting way to treat Roman senators. Absolutely no respect.'

Several of the men sniggered. 'Fuck the Roman senators,' one of them said. 'Respect? Come on, this is rich bastards we're talking about here, the men who own all those huge estates right across the world, with slaves working them so free men can't compete and get forced off the land. I should know, or why do you think I'm here and not back home, pruning my vines? They get no sympathy from me if they had to sit through a boring concert or two. Them and Nero, they deserved each other, is what I say.'

That made them laugh. 'Pity he didn't scrag more of them, really,' said a Spaniard, 'or we'd all be better off. Should've done the lot of 'em in, and nobody'd have missed them. Not that I'm saying murder's right, of course, but you've got to admit it, there's some people are better off dead.'

'Couldn't agree more,' Lucius Domitius said. 'Nero, for one.'

'What the hell was all that about?' I asked him the next day, as soon as I got the chance for a quiet word. 'Have you gone off your head, or something?'

But he just smiled and went on slicing onions. 'Quite the reverse,' he said. 'I don't think I've been this sane for years.'

'Funny idea you've got of sane,' I muttered. 'Saying all that stuff about yourself like that.'

'I enjoyed it,' he replied. 'It set my mind at rest. All these years, you see, I've had this nagging feeling at the back of my mind that I must've done something wrong, something really bad. Now it seems like I didn't, and the worst that could be said of me is I made a lot of Roman senators listen to music. Quite good music, some of it, though I say so myself.' He flicked the sliced onions into the pot and wiped his knife on his sleeve. 'So finally,' he said, 'I was able to make up my mind, about what I want to do.'

'Oh, really,' I said. 'And what's that, then?'

'Simple,' he said. 'I want to go home.'

For a moment or so, I couldn't think what he meant. 'Home?'

He nodded. 'That's right,' he said. 'Home. Where I come from, where I was raised. I've been thinking about it a lot, and I'd really like to see Rome again before I die.'

You could've knocked me down with a grape skin. 'Tell you what,' I said, 'if you go anywhere near Rome, you might just get your wish. Especially the dying part.'

He shrugged. 'So what?' he said. 'Big deal. Oh, think about it, will you, Galen? Ever since we've been going round together, since that night in Phaon's cellar, we've been half a step ahead of the hangman every inch of the way. We've been in half the condemned cells in the empire, and every time we manage to scrape out by the skin of our teeth, straight away we're being hunted down for something else.' He shook his head, like he couldn't believe it. 'And you know what?' he went on. 'The crazy part of it is it's all for little stuff, trivial little offences, thieving and swindling, or even stuff we didn't actually do, chickenshit stuff, and all so bloody unnecessary. Damm it, Galen, if I'm going to spend the rest of my life dodging a horrible death, I might as well do it back home where I belong as in some filthy alley in Pannonia or Cyrenaica, or some other place I've scarcely even heard of. And if I'm going to be strung up on a cross or torn limb from limb, why can't it be for something worthwhile? Like being who I am, for example.'

I was stunned, no other word for it; it was like someone had just bashed me over the head with a big lump of lead pipe. 'You're crazy,' I said. 'You can't go back there. You're a wanted man, for God's sake.'

'Sure,' he said, 'in Italy. And Pergamum and Raetia and Lusitania and Illyricum and Liburnia and Pamphylia and Bithynia, and now Sicily as well.' He laughed, though I couldn't see what was so damned funny. 'You know,' he went on, 'it's got so that Rome's probably the safest place in the world for me right now. After all, I'm already dead there. That's got to be an advantage.'

Well, what was I supposed to say to that? Still, there was nothing to be gained from losing my rag with the idiot, so I just said, 'Well, you've changed your tune, haven't you? You're the one who's always shit-scared of being recognised wherever we go.'

'I know.' He nodded. 'But it was this last time, when we were in that cell in Sicily, I finally realised. And it's all thanks to you, of course, you and your brilliant schemes and your sideways career moves. Thanks to you, it's even more dangerous not being me than it is being me. And then, when I thumped that soldier – you remember, that big, ugly bastard in the stores – I didn't plan on doing it, it just suddenly seemed the obvious thing to do, and I did it, and it worked; and you know what? I wasn't afraid. Ten years ago, I'd never have dared, I'd have been frozen with fear, trying to take on a trained soldier half a head taller than me.' He could see I'd lost the plot some time back, because he went on, 'It's simple, really. I'm not afraid any more, because suddenly I think I know who I am. And I don't mean who I was, I mean who I am now. Isn't that something, Galen? I knocked out that huge great bruiser with just one punch, and he never knew what hit him.'

I guess he was making some kind of point, but buggered if I knew what it was. After all, I was the one who'd put down the other guard, when we were leaving the cell, and I'd been absolutely terrified every single moment. And I knew exactly who I was, and it didn't make me feel any better at all. Quite the opposite.

'Look,' I said. 'This is all very well, and if you've managed to achieve inner peace, bloody good luck to you. Right now, though, what I'm mostly concerned with is how the hell we're going to get you off this ship before it docks at Ostia. Unless, of course, you want to spend the rest of your days slicing onions.'

He grinned. 'Is that so?' he said. 'I was sure you must've solved that problem before you sold me to the ship's captain, because otherwise you wouldn't have done it, would you? I mean, nobody'd be so recklessly stupid as to do something like that without figuring out a completely watertight plan first.'

'All right,' I said, 'spare me the brilliant sarcasm. There are times when you've just got to think on your feet, that's all. Or would you rather be back in Sicily, dodging soldiers?'

'You know,' he went on, ignoring me and laying into the last onion, 'if it wasn't for wanting to see Rome again, I'd be perfectly happy staying put on this ship. I mean, I've got enough to eat, somewhere to sleep, and I expect they'd give me a new tunic when this one falls to pieces. Oh yes, and they seem to like me, and we've been on this boat three days and nobody's tried to kill me. What more could you possibly ask out of life? Except a chance to go home,' he added. 'That's the one little bit that itches. It's like a nail working up through the sole of your boot; the further you go, the worse it gets.'

'I'm not listening,' I said.

'Big deal,' he replied, 'you never listen. You talk instead.' He slashed at what was left of the onion like he was a Thracian cavalryman cutting off someone's head. 'God almighty, am I ever tired of your incessant bloody talking. It'd be different if you ever, just once in a while, said something worth hearing. Even if it was only twice a year, Kalends of March and Ides of September, something like that. But you don't, you just drivel.' There were tears running down his face, but it must've been the onions. 'You know,' he went on, 'I've travelled the world with you, I've seen men whose skins are black with the heat and blue with woad, I've seen deserts and forests and oceans, and everything, every bloody thing, was drowned out in a sea of your never-ending chatter.' He spun round, and his knife was level with my throat, though that was just coincidence. 'I could've heard music or listened to philosophers or storytellers in the markets. Instead, I got you. And you know what? Because of you, I've kept silent. I haven't sung, I haven't played. When I was sixteen years old I used to walk along composing poetry under my breath, I chewed my food to an iambic rhythm, I even dreamed in metre, and when I woke up there'd be little shards and snippets of pure, clean hexameters left in my mouth that I'd have lost by the time I opened my eyes. And then,' he said, scowling at me, 'you came along. Through some horrible error, some ghastly case of mistaken identity, your brother – the only person I ever loved in my whole life – your brother died and I got you instead. Wonderful.' He threw the knife across the galley; it clattered on the decking. 'I got you, and your constant hum of dogshit driving everything out of my mind, every verse and every tune, until – bloody hell, until I stopped listening to me and started listening to you instead. I tell you what, Galen. If the Senate and People of Rome wanted to make me suffer like nobody's ever suffered before, all they had to do was shackle me to you for ten years; only I did it for them. And all this time, I've been keeping you alive, saving your useless neck over and over again because *he* would have wanted me to. I'm rotting in hell, Galen, and hell is you. Do you understand that? Are you actually listening to me, or are you allowing your attention to wander?'

You could've pulled out my spine and shoved it up my bum, and I wouldn't have noticed. It was like I'd bumped into some nutter in the street, the sort who follow you around screaming at you and won't go away. And the sheer bloody ingratitude of it – I tell you, if we'd been alone somewhere, out in the open where nobody could see, I'd have smashed his teeth down his neck, even though I'd have had to stand on something to reach.

'You finished?' I said.

'More or less.'

'Fine,' I told him. 'You know what, Lucius Domitius? You're an arsehole. You're a selfish, ungrateful, stupid arsehole, and if it wasn't for the fact that Callistus died for you, I'd turn you in to the captain, and me with you for being such a bloody fool as to look after you all these years.' Oh, I was angry all right. 'You saved my neck, did you? Fuck you. You wouldn't have lasted a day on your own. They'd have caught you and pulled you apart, bit by bit, you'd never have had a chance to starve in a ditch because you aren't capable of fending for yourself. Well,' I said, 'that's all right. If you want us to go our separate ways, let's do it. I'll take care of me, and you can look out for yourself. Starting with getting your useless bum off this ship. You think you can do that, all by yourself?'

'Sure,' he replied. 'And I can do it without making everything ten times worse, which is more than you can say.'

I laughed. 'Really?' I said. 'Is that right? Let me tell you something, Roman. All over the world there's thousands and millions of slaves, and you know why they stay slaves, instead of just slinging their hook and going home? It's because they haven't got any choice. It's because it's bloody difficult and dangerous, a slave running away, and they only hang around because they know that if they try and make a dash for it, they're going to get caught and strung up on a cross, and they're going to die painfully. Now, if you're so much smarter than all those thousands and thousands of poor bastards who never even had a chance, you go ahead and you do it. But you're so thick, you can't pick your nose without sticking a finger up your ear. You try it, you're a dead man. As if I cared.'

'You reckon?'

'I don't reckon,' I told him, 'I know. Oh, you think you've had it hard because you can't ponce around in silk dresses playing the harp any more. Big fucking deal. I've had it hard because I never had anything, not even enough to eat. I didn't wind up stealing and cheating for a living because I pissed off a whole empire so they couldn't stand the sight of me any more. I wound up this way because I was born. And you talk to me about having it hard.'

He pulled a face. 'You said it,' he said. 'You were born to this life, because it's all you're fit for.'

I don't know how I kept myself from decking him. The only thing I can think of was knowing he was right. But that's got nothing to do with it, has it?

'Listen to you,' he went on. 'You tell me how incredibly hard it is for a slave to escape, and then you stand there telling me that if I stick with you, you're clever enough to figure out how to do it. You honestly want me to believe that *you're* smarter than all those millions of people. For crying out loud, Galen, don't you ever listen to what you say?'

I'd stopped being hot angry, I was cold angry now. 'All right,' I said, 'that's up to you. From now on, you're none of my business. If you can manage to get away from this ship and stay loose long enough to go back to Rome, then bloody good luck to you. I mean it,' I added, 'I wish you all the luck in the world, I really hope you'll make it. I owe you that,' I went on, 'because finally, after all these years, I'm free of you, free and clear. It's wonderful. Ten years, I've had this grindstone the size of a cartwheel hanging round my neck, because Callistus wanted me to keep you alive. And now you turn round and tell me I don't have to do that any more. You know what? It's better than all the jailbreaks and the last-minute reprieves, because I haven't just saved my life, I've actually got it back. *My* life, Lucius Domitius. Thank you.'

He looked me in the eye. 'My pleasure,' he said. 'We should've had this talk years ago.'

'I wish we had.' Suddenly I felt cold all over, because this wasn't just a row, like we used to have all the time. This meant something. It was like having a tooth pulled – hurts if you do, hurts if you don't, but you know deep inside that you're better off without. 'Goes to show, doesn't it, how dumb you can be. That's ten years of my life I'll never have again. But it's worth it, to put things right.'

He nearly said something, but he stopped himself, and his face was all stiff, like he'd been dead for three days. 'Good luck, Galen,' he said. 'I hope we never see each other again, but good luck anyhow.'

'And to you, Lucius Domitius,' I said. 'Hope the music and stuff come together somehow.'

'Thank you.' Suddenly he looked at me. 'Galen.'

'What?'

'Just tell me one thing, will you?'

'All right.'

He took a deep breath, like he was nervous. 'Tell me,' he said, 'is my voice really that bad? Or is that just another piece of shit they say about me?'

I paused before I replied. 'It's really that bad, Lucius Domitius. Sorry, but you did ask.'

He lifted his head. 'That's fine,' he said. 'I don't mind. Just so long as I know. And you're the only person who wouldn't lie to me about that.'

'Well,' I said, 'I'm glad you realise that. I may have done some shitty things to you over the years, but I'd never lie to you.'

I turned and walked out of the galley, and it must have been those awful bloody onions, because my eyes were hurting. Or maybe I really did feel bad about something, I don't know. It was almost enough to make me wish I'd told him the truth about his singing.

★

Time went by, and the brown splodge on the right-hand side of the ship stopped being Sicily and turned into Italy, and I found myself having to face up to the fact that this journey wasn't going to last for ever. In spite of my falling out with Lucius Domitius and everything else, it had been one of the most relaxing times in my life (which gives you some idea of the complete mess I've made of it) and the thought of having to go back to work — starting at the bottom again, with a completely empty purse and nothing but the clothes I stood up in, etcetera — took the shine off the last few days of the cruise. For two pins and a clove of garlic, as my old mother used to say, I'd have asked the captain if he had a job going, only he'd have wondered why a supposedly prosperous merchant like me suddenly wanted to join the crew of a grain freighter.

I don't think I said more than a dozen words to Lucius Domitius from the time we had that fight until the day when the lookout told us that we were coming up to Circei, next stop Ostia and Rome. I went to the galley to get my meals, held out my plate, and walked away without saying anything. Silly, really, but my anger had turned septic, and even looking him in the face made it ache. In the back of my mind, I was worried sick about how he was going to get off the ship (assuming he still wanted to, and hadn't made up his mind to stay on board and cook bacon and beans for the rest of his life; and somehow the fact that he had that option and I didn't made me resent him more) but I tried not to think about it. Not my problem any more.

One day out from Ostia, the sea got crowded. Nobody else thought anything of it, but to me it was a sight to see: dozens of grain freighters, as big as ours or bigger, sitting in the water like giant ducks as they waited their turn to put in and unload. When you see something like that, it makes you realise how enormous Rome is, the sheer number of people who must live there.

About midday we dropped anchor and settled down to wait. There wasn't any of that buzz you sometimes get on a ship when it's about to put in after a long journey, as the crew start talking about what they're going to do when they hit town. Grain freighters aren't like that. As soon as they're unloaded they're off again, time is money, a quick turnaround makes all the difference between profit and loss when you're shaving your margins to the bone. As far

as our crew was concerned, party time was at the other end, at
Camarina, where the ship would have to lay over two nights waiting for the next load to be put on board. I wished that I could be
with them, but I knew I couldn't risk showing my face in Sicily
ever again. No, by the time they were getting slung out of taverns
in Camarina, I'd already have been back in my own personal slate
quarries for a fortnight: back to the daily grind of pulling scams,
snatching stuff off market stalls, running like hell from the guard.
What a wonderful life, I thought.

And then it struck me, as we sat there on the water with nothing to do but look at the scenery: actually, I don't have to do that
any more, I can do something else. It hit me like a bolt of lightning
out of a clear sky. What I could do, I had no idea, but what the hell,
it wasn't possible that I could be the only man in my position in the
greater Roman area, home to millions of the world's poorest
people. There had to be thousands like me, and they managed
somehow. I'd never heard anybody talking about carts going round
the streets of Rome picking up the emaciated bodies of down-and-
outs who'd starved to death during the night. No way. It was
simple: all I had to do was go into town and get a job.

Of course, I'd never done anything like that before. Twenty-four
years since I left home, and all that time I'd watched people working in countries all over the world, but I'd never walked up to
someone and asked him for a job of work, or hung around at a
hiring fair, or anything like that. I knew how it was done, in theory,
but I'd never done it myself. But, I reasoned, it can't be difficult, or
how would all the deadbeats and brickheads manage to do it? If
they could do it, a resourceful bloke like me ought to have no
problem, surely. The more I thought about the idea, the more I
liked it. In my mind's eye, I started picturing myself, ten years, fifteen years on. There I was, in a nice wool tunic, standing in front
of a busy workshop with a dozen or so blokes beavering away in the
background, and I could hear me saying, *When I first came to this
town, I had nothing but a ragged old shirt and the boots on my feet.* Of
course, I had my back to the workers, so I couldn't see what it was
they were doing, which was a pity, since I'd have liked to know, it
might have given me some ideas. Still, at the time it didn't seem
important. Didn't matter what work I set my hand to so long as I

worked. It was all so blindingly simple: put the effort in, and at the end of the process out pops a comfortable, stress-free old age. A bit like making sausages, really.

And (I couldn't help pointing out to myself) none of this would have been possible – already I was thinking of it as safely in the jar – none of it would've been possible if I hadn't finally got rid of Lucius Domitius. Sad to say, but the fact needed to be faced. It was him who'd been holding me back those last ten years, the worry and aggravation of looking after him, keeping him out of harm's way. Without him on my back like a sack full of stones, I could finally crack on and live my life, I could finally find out what it was I was supposed to be doing in the world, I could finally be me. Maybe I'd miss him, a bit, to start off with, but there comes a time when you've just got to turn your back on the past and start looking at the future. So there.

Well, you get like that when you're stuck on a ship going nowhere for hours on end. It's like when you wake up in the middle of the night and can't get back to sleep, you start thinking too hard about things, and before long it feels like your brain's itching and you can't scratch it. Then all the crazy stuff starts seeping out from wherever it is you keep it stashed away the rest of the time, and the next thing you know, you've made up your mind to do something really crazy and stupid. When this happens in the wee small hours it generally doesn't matter, because eventually you fall asleep and when you wake up it's all gone. But on a ship in the Ostia roads, absolutely still on the water and no way off if you can't swim, there's a very real danger of taking some of this dogshit seriously.

Well, that was the frame of mind I'd managed to work myself up into. At some point, not quite sure when, I realised that one of the things I'd have to do before I could draw a line under my useless, wasted past and press onwards to my bright new life was make my peace with Lucius Domitius – not that I wasn't still mad as hell about some of the things he'd said, but I didn't want to wake up one night and lie there fretting because we'd parted enemies and I'd never said goodbye. Besides, there was nothing else to do, and I'd been sitting on a big coil of rope for several hours, and my arse was going numb. So I got up and went looking for him.

Grain freighters are big, but there's not much room on them. All the space is filled up with jars of corn. Usually, you can find anybody you're looking for in less time than it takes to eat a bowl of soup. But he wasn't in the galley, he wasn't on deck or down in the hold, and he wasn't sat out back in the shitting chair; it was a pretty safe bet that he wasn't in the captain's cabin. So where the hell was he?

I asked around, but nobody had seen him for ages. Eventually, one of the guys I asked must've got to thinking, and asked the captain, because suddenly he was charging round in a blazing temper, searching under empty sacks and up in the crow's nest and prodding about in the huge man-sized grain jars with a spit – and no sign of Lucius Domitius anywhere.

'Bastard can't have gone overboard,' he was muttering, 'because he was still cooking breakfast when we dropped anchor. Anybody remember hearing a splash?'

Then it dawned on me. At some point that morning, while we were lazing around with our brains turned down, he'd taken his chance and buggered off.

'Must've sneaked off over the side, nice and quiet,' the captain said. 'Probably swam underwater as far as the anchor rope of the next ship down, then made his way ship to ship as far as the shore. Well, I hope he got a stitch and drowned.' He kicked a pile of old sacks. 'Serves me right for being too bloody soft-hearted, I guess.'

For some reason, the captain seemed to blame me – not that he came out with it and accused me of helping him escape, or anything like that. I think he was just extremely angry at losing a slave, and I was the one who'd put him in the position of having a slave to lose, so it was all my fault. As usual, the crew took their mood from the skipper, and by the time we finally tied up at the dock, I was only too glad to get off the ship and away from all those scowling faces. I was so upset and pissed off at being hated for something I hadn't done that I'd walked the length of the pier and started up into the town when suddenly it hit me.

Damn, I thought. He'd gone, and I'd missed him.

I didn't know what to do, so I sat down with my back to a wall, and for some reason I suddenly burst into tears. I was squatting there, bawling my heart out, when I noticed there was someone standing over me. Short, round bloke with a bald head and a scrubby white beard. Face like a full moon, with a little piggy snout for a nose.

'What're you making that filthy row for?' he asked me, in Latin.

I looked up at him. He was all blurry round the edges, because of the tears.

'I just lost the only real friend I ever had,' I said. 'He up and buggered off, and never even said goodbye.'

The round bloke frowned. 'Oh,' he said, 'right. Well, there you go. Have a drink, it'll make you feel better.' He fished about in his purse and flicked a coin at me. I caught it one-handed without even looking. It turned out to be a good silver denarius, which'll buy you a really bad hangover any day of the week in Rome, with enough for a good meal left over, so that was all right. Of course, it had to be an old coin, with the Goddess of Fortune carrying a Horn of Plenty on one side, and the head of the emperor Nero on the other.

SIX

So there I was, down and out in Ostia, without a copper to my name — actually, that's not true, because when I woke up the next day, after my denarius' worth of debauchery, as well as a real classic of a sick headache I had precisely one copper farthing (and I damn near swallowed that; never been able to get out of the Greek habit of carrying my small change in my mouth, see). Somehow, that one completely useless coin — there's nothing you can buy with a single farthing — made it even worse.

Anyhow there I was, with a bad head and a stiff neck after a night's sleep in a temple portico. Wonderful way to start off the rest of my life. Still, it was my own silly fault, and I had no sympathy. I sat down on the temple steps and tried to figure out what I was going to do.

Well, I could stay in Ostia. Always plenty of work around a grain terminal, if you don't mind ending up a cripple after a year or two. Or I could stroll up the military road to Rome; or I could pick a direction, head out into the countryside, and see if I could get a job doing farm work.

Maybe it was the hangover and the stiff neck, but the more I thought about it, the more I liked the third option. After all, I told myself, deep down where it matters I'm a farm boy, and if it wasn't for the cruel vicissitudes of fate (Seneca's line, not mine) at that very moment I'd be home in Attica, sitting down under my own fig tree with my breakfast in a basket before putting in an honest day's work hoeing between my vines. A city wasn't the place for me, I told myself; in a city I'd get into trouble, have the guard chasing me down narrow alleys in no time flat, and I was done with that kind of thing, thanks all the same. Good healthy farm work, though – of course, I knew farm work from nothing, ploughing and sowing and pruning and all that stuff, nothing anybody could teach me about growing things in the bosom of our mother Earth. Screw cities, I told myself. Give me the feel of newly turned soil under my feet, the sweet smell of apple blossom in the evening, the quiet, friendly chatter on the way home from the fields, and a fat hunk of cheese and a wodge of fresh home-baked barley bread in front of the hearth before turning in for a refreshing night's sleep. That's the way people were meant to live, after all, not cooped up in brick boxes like pigs in winter.

Once you get away from the docks, Ostia's not a big place. Just keep walking for an hour or so and you're out into farmland. As the fresh air cut my hangover and the exercise loosened up my aches and pains I realised that, for once in my life, I'd made the right choice. On either side of the road I could see people working at that slow, unstressed, enduring pace you get once you leave the town behind. Just occasionally, a big cart rolled by, piled high with greens or fruit or winejars, off to feed the insatiable maw of Rome. Hah, I thought, how pathetic; all those millions of people who can't even feed themselves, have to pay someone else to do it for them. The hell with all that, I thought. That's the joy of farming. You just put stuff in the ground and go away, and when you come back there's a tasty meal, sitting there just waiting for you to pick it and take it home.

Well, all this time I was keeping my eyes open for a village or a big farmhouse, somewhere I could go and ask if they had any work going. Of course, I knew that Italy wasn't quite the same as my part of the world. I'd heard all about that, many times; how the small farmers had all been conscripted into the army or put out of business by the rich senators and their big, slave-run estates. Yeah, I thought, sure; I'd heard all that from ex-soldiers and other low life, blokes who'd never done a real day's work in their lives. If they'd lost the family farm it was because they were basically no good. There'd always be plenty of real farmers, men who ate what they grew and grew what they ate. You can't just sweep them all off the face of the land, and sooner or later I'd find one, and he'd give me a job. Or even if I didn't, well, all these rich absentee landlords, they'd need men to do their work for them, and the blokes in the fields I could see from the road didn't look like slaves. I couldn't see any chain gangs or overseers with stockwhips, just blokes in homespun tunics and broad leather hats, quietly getting on with the job in hand.

But on I went, and no village or farmhouse, just more and more fields, not even a cowshed or a linhay. Obviously I was missing something. So I decided to ask someone.

The first man I saw was leaning on a two-tine hoe, having a blow. He could've been my next-door neighbour from Phyle, the type was that familiar – long, stringy bloke with big nubbly hands and a faraway look in his eyes. 'Morning,' I called out.

He turned his head and looked at me. 'Mphm,' he said, or something like that.

'Nice day,' I said. It doesn't do to rush things when you're talking to country people.

'Mm.' He looked at me without blinking, like I was a nasty case of leaf rot.

'Good rap you've done there,' I said, waving my hand at five neatly spitted rows of turned earth.

'Mm.' He frowned slightly, but I wasn't worried. It's like with horses or cats, you've got to earn their trust first.

'Well,' I said. 'This your place, then?'

He didn't move for a while. Then he shook his head.

'I see,' I said. 'Tenant, then?'

He shook his head again. That's Italians for you, they aren't as forthcoming as us Greeks. Still, salt of the earth.

'I'm only asking,' I went on, 'because I'm in the way of looking for a bit of work. Any going up your place, do you know.?'

He thought about it for a long, long time. 'Mphm,' he said, and then, just as I was about to ask him if that was mphm-yes or mphm-no, he added, 'Reckon so. What's your game, then?'

I shrugged. 'Oh, I'll turn my hand to anything, me. So, where should I go?'

'Hm?'

Salt of the earth, Italians, but as thick as shit. 'Who should I go and see?' I explained. 'The steward, or the foreman, or whatever.'

He jerked his head sideways at nothing in particular. 'Try the house,' he said.

'Right, I'll do that, thanks.' I hesitated, just in case he was about to say something helpful. No chance. 'So, where's the house, then?'

'Up over,' he replied, with another sideways jerk.

'Pardon.?'

He frowned. 'Up over,' he repeated. 'Then down along. Big house, can't miss it.'

I had no trouble at all finding the big house, mostly because it was the only house I'd seen since I left Ostia. House is maybe not the right word. It was bigger than a lot of villages I've seen, and what it reminded me of most was an army camp. Bloody great big barracks, for one thing, right next to the barns and sheds; also its own watermill and a damn great big smithy. The house itself was one of the smaller buildings on the site. It had an odd look about it, old-fashioned and brand spanking new at the same time.

One good thing was, there were loads of people about. I stopped a bloke who was pottering along prodding a mule in the ribs with a bit of stick, and asked him where the foreman might be. He shrugged.

'Dunno,' he said. 'But your best bet'd be to go up the long barn and ask there.'

A bloke in the long barn said, try the presshouse. A bloke in the presshouse thought he might be in the stables. A little skinny bloke in the stables reckoned he'd just seen him leaving the mill-house, probably headed for the tool store. The two blokes in the tool store just looked at me. On my way back across the yard, someone yelled at me from behind and I turned round to see who it was.

'You,' he said. 'I don't know you. What're you prowling round for?'

He was a short bloke, wide as he was tall, no neck, shoulders like two pigs side by side. Ex-sergeant; you can always spot them 'Sorry,' I said. 'I was looking for the foreman.'

'I'm the foreman. What d'you want?'

Well, I'd got off to a good start, hadn't I? 'I was looking for a job.'

'You?' He made it sound like I'd made a bad joke. 'You're not from round here, are you?'

'No,' I admitted.

'Thought not. So, where are you from? You look Greek to me.'

'That's right,' I said. 'I'm from Naples originally, spent some time in Asia—'

He scowled at me, and I got the impression he didn't want to hear my life story, which saved me the trouble of making one up. 'What're you doing in these parts, then?'

That was an easy one. 'Looking for work,' I said.

'Ex-slave?'

'Freeborn,' I replied smartly. 'Raised on a farm,' I added, 'not much I can't do around the place.'

'Really.' His scowl got deeper, till it nearly met in the middle. 'Well, normally we don't hire in from off the road.'

Normally was good; suggested that this might be an exception. I kept my face shut and let him talk.

'But,' he said, 'just so happens we could use a few more hands, what with—' He stopped and lifted his head, Greek style. 'All right, go on. Get yourself down the barracks, ask for Syrus, he's the lead hand. He'll tell you what to do.'

So that was all right, I was in. Now, I could tell that something was up, because of that *what with* he hadn't finished, and a general twitchiness about his manner. Also, I wasn't too keen on a barracks for the hands, and a lead hand called Syrus was either an ex-slave or a slave – Syrus is just a name Romans give to someone from Syria, because they can't pronounce his regular name. Can't say I blame them for that. Syrian names sound like someone blowing his nose in a handful of wet grass.

So I went and asked for Syrus, and a bloke with one eye missing said he wasn't there, what did I want him for, and I explained, and he said, more fool you, but get a blanket from the pile in the corner, soup's in the big pot. Soup sounded good, because I hadn't had anything to eat since I got off the ship, unless you counted the meal I had out of the kind man's denarius; and I seemed to remember parting company with most of that somewhere between the last tavern and the temple steps. But the soup turned out not to be so good after all. In fact, it was very bad, mostly water with a thick skin of grease floating on top. Still, it was better than nothing, so I slurped down as much as I could bear, got a blanket (old and frayed round the edges) and sat down in a corner to see what'd happen.

I'd been there a while – long enough to lose track of time, can't be more specific than that when I saw an old bloke coming towards me. He can't have been as ancient as he looked, or he'd have croaked from old age shortly before the Trojan war; he was crooked and bent, the way very tall people get when their spines wilt, and he had a completely bald head, little bleary eyes and maybe one and a half teeth. His skin was all mottled and blotchy, but there was enough colour in it to show he wasn't Italian; some kind of Easterner, I guessed.

'You there,' he said.

'What, me?'

'You. New man. I am Syrus.'

Wonderful, I thought, this is the lead hand. 'Hello,' I said, because it never hurts to be polite.

'Overseer is telling me, new man arriving.' He blinked at a patch of wall behind me, to my left. 'You with me, please.'

So I got up, and he carried on looking at the patch of wall. 'Be following, please,' he said, then he turned round and started tottering off the way he'd just come.

'This very good place,' he said, without looking round. 'This very good place to be working. I am working here sixty-seven years, since I am being fetched here from my family's home in Apamea. I am lead hand here thirty-one years. Boots you will be finding in bin next to window.'

From the look of the boots, they'd been there longer than he had. I found two that looked like they might be distant cousins; they were scruffy, but they had to be better than what I had on my feet. Besides, they were free.

'I am serving master,' Syrus droned on, 'and master's father, and his father before him. Very good family, very glorious and honourable, very fair and kind to hard worker. When first I am arriving, crying, crying all the time, but soon finding out this is very good place. Tunics in box in corner, all sizes, very good.'

'Thanks,' I said, pulling out a few specimens and putting them back. 'So,' I said. 'What's the food like, and what's the pay?'

'Working in fields very hard,' Syrus went on, 'soil very good, not like Syria, where is no water, very dry. Growing good vine, good fig, good olive, doing everything best way, like it says in book. This is new master's way, very good way, all is in book, very wise. You be following, please.'

'Sure,' I said. 'About the wages, do we get paid by the day or the month, or what? Only, if it's possible, I was wondering, a little sub up front would be really helpful—'

'Master is very good man,' said Syrus, like I wasn't even there. 'Much learning, much understanding in books. Always reading, reading, very good.'

We crossed the yard – for someone who could only take little teeny steps, he covered the ground damn quick – and he led the way into the tool shed. 'Here is tools,' he said, 'very fine, all made here on farm. You be taking from stack in corner double-tine hoe.'

I groaned. I hate those bloody things. 'Look,' I said, 'I don't suppose the foreman mentioned it, but actually I'm better suited to working with animals – you know, leading the team, or maybe a job in the stables. Anything to do with horses, I'm your man.'

'From stack in corner,' he said. 'Stack in corner.'

I got the impression that unless I picked up a hoe, he'd have to stand there all day repeating *stack in corner* for fear of losing his place and having to start all over again from the beginning. I picked up a hoe just to shut him up, and then he was off again like a polecat down a drainpipe. No kidding, I had to walk a damn sight faster than I'd have liked just to keep up with him.

He may have been blind as a bat, but he obviously knew his way around the place. After we'd been walking for maybe half an hour, he stopped dead in the middle of a huge ploughed field, and announced. 'Is here.'

I was afraid he'd say something like that. Stretched out across the field in a long line were maybe three dozen blokes, all with double-tine hoes, all doggedly bashing away at the clods of dirt turned over by the plough. My least favourite job in the whole world: clod-busting (and guess what I spent most of my childhood doing).

I looked round to tell him I'd got this terrible shooting pain in my right shoulder, but he'd gone; I caught sight of him scuttling back towards the house, still nattering away about something or other. Then some bloke who looked like Management caught my eye and gave me a look like fresh mustard; so I sighed, got a firm grip on my hoe, and started swinging.

Never let it be said I'm shy of pulling my weight; an honest day's work for a fair day's pay, that's all I've ever asked out of life. But there's all sorts of honest work that don't involve stooping down all the damn time, and I particularly despise stooping down. I have a delicate back, the slightest thing can set it off sometimes, and once it goes sort of 'click', that's it for the rest of the day, I'm in agony. Anyhow, I've always found that when you're in excruciating pain you quickly lose track of time, so I don't know how long we were out there bashing clods. It felt like twenty years, but it was probably just a few hours. Then everybody suddenly stopped and looked up, so I did the same. Straightening up was no fun at all, but I wanted to see what was going on.

There was this bloke sitting on a big horse, watching us. He was a sight to see all right. Try and picture a little kid who's died and been pickled in brine, like the Egyptians do, so he's all wrinkly and blanched. Top the mess off with a mop of fluffy grey hair, and there you go.

The overseer yelled out, 'Who said you could stop working?' and everybody snapped back down, like those water cranes they have out East. But I was curious to know who the bloke on the horse was, so I kept glancing up at him whenever I could, and of course I kept my ears open, because he was muttering something under his breath. I couldn't make out the actual words, but it sounded a lot like poetry.

Then he stopped muttering, because the overseer bloke was talking to him. 'I was thinking, boss,' he was saying, 'time's getting on, how'd it be if, instead of going over all this lot by hand, we got the harrow out and just—'

But the bloke on the horse interrupted him. His voice was very high and shrill, and he sounded extremely pissed off. 'No, no, no,' he said. 'How many times do I have to tell you people?

> *But when thy fluttering hand hath sown the seed,*
> *Breaking the soil becomes thy greatest need;*
> *By delving deep strive to appease the gods,*
> *And with the ponderous hoe assault the clods.*

Ponderous hoe,' he continued. 'The book specifically states, the ponderous hoe. Or do you presume to know better than the poet?'

Short silence. 'Well,' said the overseer slowly, 'that's as may be, but where I come from—'

There are some sounds you can identify straight off without

needing to look, and the noise a riding whip makes when it hits a man's face is one of them. Of course, I sneaked a look. The overseer was staggering back, with his hands up round his mouth. The bloke on the horse had a whip in his hand, and was carefully rolling it up again. 'Remember,' he was saying, 'the ponderous hoe. Not the harrow. Really, is it too much to ask for you people to do as you're told?'

Well, I got my head down bloody quick, because one thing I've learned in life is not to draw attention to yourself when things start getting stroppy. Next time I dared look up, the bloke on the horse had gone and the overseer was standing there mopping blood off a nasty long cut across his cheek from his lip to his eyebrow. Marvellous, I thought, I've really landed on my feet here.

Finally, after a couple of lifetimes with time added for bad behaviour, we reached the headland and the overseer called time for the day. On the way back to the barracks, I asked one of the blokes what all that had been about.

He looked at me. 'You're new here, aren't you?' he said.

'Yes, it's my first day. Who was the nutso on the horse, and why did he belt the overseer?'

The bloke laughed. 'Him on the horse,' he said, 'that's Marcus Ventidius Gnatho, and it's him as owns this lot. And a whole lot besides, but this is where he lives, most of the time.'

'Ah,' I said. 'Well, that's handy to know. But what made him go beating up on the overseer? And what was that poetry he was spouting?'

The bloke grinned. 'Ah, well,' he said, 'our Marcus Ventidius, he's a bit of a scholar, see. Always got his head in a book, or else he's making up his own books, poetry and stuff. Well, about five years back, his old man dies and Marcus inherits, and he gets the notion of running the farm like it says in this big long poem, by one of them writer chaps from the city. Seems like they've got nothing better to do with their time up there than sit around making up these poems all about how you're supposed to do things, like farming or sailing or doctoring the sick, any damn thing that comes into their heads. Course, they don't know bugger all about it, they just copy it all out of some other book and pretty it up so it scans and all, but our Marcus, he gets hold of this damned old poem, that he calls *On Farming*, by Publius Virgilius Maro, and the long and the short of it is, we got to do everything like it says in his book, whether it's the right way or not. Now this overseer, Cleitus his name is, Spanish chap, he's not been here very long – they don't hardly seem to stay here any time, overseers – so he don't know any better than to go telling master how his book's all wrong; and Marcus, he don't like that at all, like you just saw. Course, we could've warned him, but then, where's the fun in that?'

I thought for a moment. Now, you probably wouldn't put me down as a literary type, and you'd be right enough at that, but you couldn't hang round the palace any time back in the old days without overhearing people banging on about this poet and that poet – bored me half to death, of course, and mostly it went in one ear and straight out the other side, but bits of it couldn't help sticking – and I particularly remembered Virgilius Maro because Lucius Domitius couldn't stand his stuff, not even for ready money, and he was always reciting bits in silly voices and generally taking the piss. So when the bloke said the name, I nodded and muttered, 'Oh, him,' or words to that effect. Not that I'd recognise the works of Virgilius Maro if you painted them blue and stuck them up my bum with a forked stick, but there you go.

'So,' I said, 'that's not the first time he's done something like that, then?'

The bloke grinned. 'Overseer before last, he tried to tell old Marcus you can't go pruning in September, you'll kill the vines dead – well, stands to reason, everybody knows that. But master, he flies into a right old temper, smacks overseer round the face with the back edge of a billhook, busts his jaw for him, tells him it says in his book, start pruning when Arcturus is rising, and if he won't do what he's told, he'd better clear off out of it. Well, overseer's gone the next day, and we do the pruning like he says, and all the vines on the north slope, dead as boot nails inside of a week. The heat, see. Laugh? We nearly shat ourselves.'

I nodded. Actually, I could see what'd happened there, because they do start their pruning when Arcturus rises in Ionia, which is where a lot of the old Greek poets came from, and it must've been one of their books Virgilius Maro was copying out of. I thought about trying to explain this to the bloke, but I decided not to bother.

'Well,' I said, 'no skin off your nose, I guess.'

The bloke shook his head. 'Master blamed us for the vines dying,' he said. 'Picked out three blokes, had 'em flogged till they damn near died. Still, you can't go telling these fine gentlemen what to do, they always reckon they know best. Lords of all creation, that's what they think they are, and if something goes wrong it's always got to be some other bugger's fault. But you can't complain, can you? I mean, that's the way things are.'

The food turned out to be rubbish, and nobody said anything about wages, or if they did, I didn't hear them. But I was too knackered after a long day with the ponderous hoe to be bothered about that. I found a corner of the barracks that nobody wanted for anything, curled up in my blanket and went to sleep.

Next day we were booted awake at daybreak and marched out for another spell of ponderous hoeing. By midday I'd just about had enough, but the overseer was in a filthy mood and skiving didn't strike me as a sensible idea, so I gritted my teeth and got on with it. Come knocking-off time, all I wanted to do was crawl under a stone and die. The next day was pretty much the same, and the day after that. I'd hoped that after a day or so I'd have got back into the swing of field work and the aches and pains would start to ease off, but I was kidding myself. If anything it was getting worse and worse, and still nobody had mentioned money or anything vulgar like that. On the other hand, I kept telling myself, at least I was eating regularly, and I hadn't had to hide from a half platoon of soldiers ever since I'd arrived in Italy. There wasn't much in it, but on balance I reckoned I was better off, just about.

On the tenth day, we were still clodbashing. By this point, I was pretty certain that I'd done something nasty and permanent to my back, and my arms and shoulders weren't all that wonderful either. Also, the boredom was starting to get to me in a big way. At first I hadn't minded it so much, since you can have too much excitement in life, but when you've been used to keeping your wits about you, living on your nerves and your instincts – well, it's like a bloke I once got talking to in a bar somewhere. He said he'd been born and raised in a big city in Asia Minor somewhere, and then he'd moved for some reason and wound up in the depths of the country, on his own all day, and he told me the peace and quiet was slowly driving him round the bend. All his life he'd been used to noise – people in the streets in the day, carts rumbling and creaking through the streets all night, having to dodge and weave in and out of the crowds and the traffic just to get from one side of the market square to the other. Standing in the middle of a wide open field all day, no sounds except the tweeting of the larks and cows farting in the distance, it was sheer torture to him, he said. Well, I guess it was the same with me and excitement, or, if you prefer it, danger. My brain was going numb from not being used, and I was getting so bored during the day that I couldn't sleep at night, even though I was completely shattered. Crazy, of course. I mean, whoever heard of anybody pining away because they weren't in mortal peril all the damn time? But then, I never pretended I was right in the head.

So there's me, on the tenth day of my new career in agriculture, and we're in our usual line belting great big lumps of caked dirt with the ponderous fucking hoe, when who should turn up but that doddering old pest Syrus? Hadn't seen hide nor hair of him since the first day, not that I'd missed him, but there he was, still twittering on into space, and behind him there was this other bloke. Big man, broad shoulders, enormous neck like an ox, reddish-brown hair starting to go thin on top. Lucius Domitius.

Well, I didn't know what to make of that. First thought was, he must've come looking for me; and though I was still very angry indeed about the stuff he'd said, really bloody angry, I found myself thinking, Well, that's all right, then, as if everything had just been put straight. But he didn't seem to be looking for me, or anybody much. He was just stood there, looking at the double-tine hoe in his hands like he was trying to figure out how you made it work, with a look on his face like he'd just woken up after being bashed over the head down a dark alley. Then I tumbled to what had really happened. He hadn't come looking for me after all. He'd just happened to show up here looking for work, and it was all sheer coincidence.

Needless to say, breaking line or wandering over to chat to someone was definitely not on, not while the overseer was about, so I had to wait till knocking-off time before I could hurry across and say hello. By that point, he looked like he'd been tortured for military secrets by the Parthians: his mouth was hanging open, and he was shaking slightly all over. At least I'd done farm work before. Don't suppose he ever had.

I came up behind his left shoulder and said, 'Hello, Lucius Domitius,' in a quiet, everyday sort of way. He stopped dead, then swung round so fast he nearly lost his balance.

'Galen,' he said. 'What the bloody hell are you doing here?'

I grinned at him. 'Earning a living,' I said. 'Good, honest work, you can't beat it. How about you?'

'What?' He looked like he hadn't understood the question. 'Oh, me too. I mean, I've been wandering about since I got off the ship, trying to make my way to the city, but this is, well, as far as I've got, and I hadn't eaten for two days, and someone said there was work going here, so . . .' He shook his head. 'Galen,' he said, and his eyes were going all red like he'd got dust in them, 'you've no idea how glad I am to see you. I – oh God, this is stupid.' And he flung his arms round me and gave me a hug that came close to busting all my ribs.

'Leave off, for fuck's sake,' I gasped, 'you're killing me. And the other blokes are staring.'

'Huh? Oh, right.' He let go, and suddenly we were both grinning like complete fools. 'I thought I'd never see you again,' he said.

'Me neither,' I replied. 'So, when you jumped ship, what happened?'

We started walking. 'Oh, nothing much,' he replied. 'I climbed down the anchor rope when nobody was watching, then I swam underwater as far as the next ship down, came up, caught my breath, and so on right into the harbour.'

'That's what we thought you must've done,' I said.

'Oh.' He frowned. 'Oh, right. And I was thinking how clever I'd been. Well, no matter. So, how long have you been here?'

'Ten days,' I said. 'And in case you hadn't noticed, this is a fucking awful way to live. I wouldn't wish it on a dung beetle.'

He lifted his head. 'I'd sort of got that impression myself,' he replied. 'I mean, is it always like that?'

'Today was one of the better days,' I told him. 'The master wasn't about, the overseer's been in a relatively good mood.'

'Oh.' He frowned. 'So, who does this place belong to? I asked the old, mad bloke, but he didn't seem to be listening to me.'

'Marcus Ventidius Gnatho,' I replied, and told him all about the poetry and Virgilius Maro and the overseer getting smacked in the face. He looked very thoughtful.

'Ventidius Gnatho,' he repeated. 'Oh God, I remember him, he was a right creep. Very boring, but with a vicious streak.' He frowned. 'Came to all my readings and recitals,' he added. 'Didn't even need to be invited, he came of his own accord.'

'Well, that proves it, then,' I said. 'Obviously he's completely mental.'

'Quite. Always looked like he was enjoying it, too; or at least, I don't ever remember him falling asleep or sticking pins into his hands to make himself stay awake. I remember one incredibly long evening where he started telling me why he liked my use of the double caesura in trochaic hexameters, and it was dawn before I managed to get him to shut up. I think he hated me as much as the rest of them, but he was a genuine virtuoso when it came to crawling: never let his personal feelings get in the way of his work.'

I pulled a face. 'You're thinking he might recognise you, then?'

He shrugged. 'I wouldn't have thought so. It'd never cross his mind that someone working in his fields could be a dead emperor. But it's not a risk I'd want to take, all the same. Does he hang round the workers very often, or is it just once in a blue moon?'

'I've seen him three times in ten days,' I replied. 'From what I gather, he likes to spend a couple of hours each afternoon riding round making a pain of himself, but it's a big place and there's loads of other field gangs beside this one. So long as you keep your head down and your mouth shut . . .'

But he was frowning. 'I don't like it,' he said. 'I mean, just my rotten bloody luck, I wind up on the only estate in Italy that hasn't got an absentee landlord.' He stopped, and looked at me. 'If I move on,' he said, 'will you stay here, or what?'

I hadn't given it any thought. I mean, as soon as I saw him again, I must've automatically assumed we'd stick together. After all, it seemed meant. We'd been apart eleven days, and then the gods scoop us up and shovel us back together again. Not that I go a lot on the destiny stuff, but it's hard to ignore the subtle machinations of fate when a giant hand descends from the clouds and rubs your nose in them.

'Maybe,' I said. 'I mean, this is a really shitty place, but I've sort of got used to not having soldiers chasing me all the time.'

He started walking again. 'Well,' he said, 'maybe it'd be safer if we did split up – for you, I mean. After all, nobody's after you in Italy, you've got a clean slate. But if someone recognises me and you're with me, it'd only take one person from the old days . . . I mean, you two weren't very popular around the court.'

This was news to me. I mean, I didn't think anybody even knew who I was back then. 'Really?' I said.

He nodded. 'All my friends – my hangers-on, they called them, and that was the polite term – the senators and the army people hated the lot of you, because you were with me. I suppose they blamed you for me going to the bad, or you made a convenient scapegoat for people who'd supported me or Agrippina in the early days. I don't know; the point is, so long as you're with me, you're running a risk you don't need to run.'

Even at the time I was pretty sure, deep down, that it was genuine concern, that he really was worried for me. But I didn't want to take it that way. I wanted it to be an excuse for ditching me. 'Well, fine,' I said. 'If that's the case, maybe we would be better off if I stayed and you slung your hook. Like we said, Gnatho's probably not bright enough to recognise you, but if you think it's dangerous for you here, then you'd better clear out while you can.'

He looked at me. 'You think so?'

'It's your decision,' I said. 'I don't like it much here either, but it's not like I've got a lot of choices of places I can go.'

'Nor me.' He sighed. 'Another thing,' he went on. 'If I do leave here, I'm definitely heading for the city. It's important to me, I've set my heart on it. And Rome's hardly a safe place for me, so . . .'

Suddenly I didn't want to talk about it any more. 'Whatever,' I said. 'You decide. After all, every single decision I ever took for the two of us landed us in the shit.'

'That's not true,' he said. He was lying, but I liked that he said it. Ten years is a long time. I defy anybody to go around ten years with a person and not get used to them being there. 'We were just unlucky a lot of the time, that's all,' he said, rather lamely.

People didn't tend to make friends in the barracks. It wasn't the kind of place where people talked to each other a lot, and we were making ourselves conspicuous chatting away like that. So we kept our distance that evening. We sat apart during the evening meal, and he took his blanket to the other side of the barracks when it was time to go to sleep. To be honest with you, when I woke up the next morning I was half expecting to find he'd buggered off during the night, but he was still there when we lined up for the work detail. When we stopped work at midday, I went over and sat next to him.

'You're still here, then,' I said.

'Yes, well, I haven't made my mind up yet.'

'You sounded pretty definite about it yesterday.'

'There's no desperate rush,' he replied. 'Rome'll still be there this time next week, probably.'

Sounded to me like he was changing his tune again, but then, being decisive and resolute weren't exactly his strong suit at the best of times. Which made me think: if he stuck around for a while, maybe he'd forget all about the going to Rome nonsense, and we'd both be better off.

Just my luck, we were three days into a heatwave, and no sign of it ending any time soon. Apparently Virgilius Maro never considered putting in a bit about how important it is to give the field hands plenty to drink when it's hot, or else he couldn't get it to scan or something. Anyway, we got a cup of water at midday, and that was our lot till we returned to barracks at night. This was a fucking awful arrangement. Every day we'd have a couple of blokes keel over in the heat, and two or three more pretending to keel over so they could skive off for an hour and go sit in the shade while the rest of us got on with it. Lucius Domitius and I couldn't do that, of course, on account of not making ourselves conspicuous. Bummer.

The next day, it was even hotter, and the day after that was hotter still. On the good side, though, we hadn't seen anything of Marcus Ventidius Gnatho, and if it was the heat that was keeping him indoors, I reckoned it was a small price to pay. Not that I was really worried, of course, but it'd have freaked Lucius Domitius out, and then he'd start banging on about leaving again, and what with one thing and another – well, you can put up with having a dry throat and being all sweaty.

A curious thing I've noticed about life. The longer you stay in one place, no matter how shitty it is, the harder it gets making your mind up to leave. In my experience, about the only places this rule doesn't apply to are prisons, but as luck would have it, I've never been in a prison long enough for the effect to set in, so maybe it's the same with them too. Not that I'm in any tearing hurry to find out, mind.

So we'd been there a month, maybe a month and a half – hard to say exactly, because each day was pretty much like the others, though some were better and some were worse – and oddly enough, it was starting to get easier all round. For one thing, we'd been taken off busting clods, which was good, and put on levelling the ground between the rows by sitting down hard on the newly turned earth and wriggling about (see *On Farming* by Virgilius Maro, book two, line three hundred and fifty-seven for details. I have an idea that whoever Virgilius Maro paid to copy out his poem for the bookseller made a spelling mistake there, and what the poet really wrote was 'and straining bullocks roll the earth full flat'. Easy mistake to make, and all that). On balance, I reckon I preferred the ponderous hoe, but at least we weren't on our feet all day long. After that we skipped down to lines three-fifty-nine to sixty, which was building trellises, and that was no bother at all.

It was late afternoon on a day that wasn't much different from any other day, and we were all in a pretty good mood, because the overseer had told us that come knocking-off time, we were finally going to get paid. He hadn't gone into details, like how much we were going to get, but we didn't mind that. Not knowing just stretched the treat out longer.

And then the bloke showed up.

I remember looking up from the vine prop I'd just tied in, and there he was, just like that, sudden as a thunderbolt out of a clear blue sky, or a chamber pot emptied out of a tenth-storey window just as you're passing underneath.

He was sat on a huge black horse, and he was talking to the over-seer, very quiet and discreet, like he didn't want anybody to hear what he was saying. Behind him were about a dozen men; by the looks of them they were either ex-soldiers or gladiators, big ugly bastards, all muscles and scars. They weren't the same ones he'd had with him the first time I saw him, so my guess is he'd hired local talent when he arrived in Italy. Not that that mattered worth a damn.

By sheer fluke, Lucius Domitius was standing next to me in line. I leaned over and prodded him hard in the back. He turned round, asked what the matter was.

'Over there,' I whispered. 'No, don't turn round. Just move your head slowly, like you're stretching or something.'

'Oh for crying out loud, Galen,' he grumbled, 'don't be so bloody melodramatic, it can't—' He stopped, froze for a moment or so, then looked back at me. 'Shit,' he said.

I nodded. 'It is him, isn't it?' I said. 'That lunatic from Sicily. The one who blocked the road when we were being taken to the quarries, and killed all those soldiers—'

'Keep your voice *down*,' he barked, so loud that a couple of the other men on the line turned to see what was going on. 'Yes,' he said, 'that's him, all right. Bloody hell, Galen, what's he doing here?'

'Search me,' I replied. 'But something tells me he isn't here to give us large sums of money or introduce us to his daughters. Get your head down,' I hissed, as the bloke on the horse looked up and started casting his eye over the line. Could be he was stretching his neck, or wondering idly why in hell's name we were building our trellises two months later than every other farm in Italy, but then again, could be he was looking for someone.

I haven't got a clue how long he stayed there nattering with the overseer. I kept glancing sideways out of the corner of my eye to see if he was still there, and eventually he wasn't. I straightened up, and saw him and his blokes riding off down the track in the general direction of the house (though it was also the way back to the main road). 'It's all right,' I said, 'he's gone.'

Lucius Domitius stood up, and made a groaning noise as he straightened his back. 'May be your idea of all right,' he said, 'but it sure as hell isn't mine. What do you think all that was about?'

I lifted my head. 'No idea,' I said. 'I mean, it could all be perfectly harmless. Maybe he's on his way to the city on business and got lost, and all he was doing was asking for directions.'

'Don't think so,' Lucius Domitius muttered. 'How long does it take to say, back the way you came, left and left again, then follow your nose? They were stood talking there for at least half an hour.'

I frowned, trying to get my brain to work (but after however long it was, it was slow getting started). 'Well,' I said, 'if he was looking for us, he didn't look very hard. Just sat there jawing with the overseer. If he was looking for us, all he had to do was ride down the line.'

Lucius Domitius bit his lip. 'Yes, all right,' he said. 'I don't know. Unless he simply wasn't expecting to see us in a line of field hands. But if he goes up to the house and asks, have you seen two men, a big sandy-haired type and a little bloke with a face like a rat—'

'You know what?' I said. 'I'm really not interested. All I'm concerned about is being some place he isn't. Don't know about you, but as soon as work's over, I'm for slipping away quietly and making a run for it.'

But Lucius Domitius lifted his head. 'Not sensible,' he said. 'Think about it, Galen. Can you think of a better way of drawing attention to ourselves than skipping out half an hour before we finally get paid? Half an hour after, maybe, that's perfectly reasonable, but before – well, there could only be one reason for that, couldn't there?'

He had a point, the awkward bugger. 'Sure,' I said, 'all right. But I really don't fancy marching back to the barracks and finding him waiting there for us, with the blacksmith standing by to rivet down the fetters on our ankles. If we push off right away, we'll have a half hour's start on him and his muscle. And I've got a lifetime's experience in being chased by armed men telling me that half an hour's start is a perfectly good business proposition.'

Lucius Domitius made a show of adjusting the lie of a vine prop. 'Maybe,' he said. 'I don't know, maybe he's a lawyer and he's looking for you because your long-lost uncle just died and left you a half share in a silver mine. Although,' he added, 'I can think of other explanations.' He scratched his chin, for all the world like he was trying to decide which evening cloak to wear, the dark green or the blue and white stripe. 'So what do you think we ought to do?' he said.

I scowled, thinking hard. 'I don't know,' I said. 'You're right, running for it may well be as good as nailing a tablet to the barn door with "We're the ones you're after" on it in big bronze letters. Or we could go back to the barracks and find we've strolled right into a trap. It's a tricky one, this.'

Just then the overseer called out, 'Time,' and everybody in the line started picking up their tools, ready for going home. That was, of course, just what I hadn't wanted to hear, since it meant we'd run out of time for making a decision.

'Well?' said Lucius Domitius.

Sometimes you've just got to trust your instincts. I hate times like that, because my instincts are about as reliable as the men who come up to you in the marketplace and ask if you're interested in buying cheap silver tableware. Still.

'We hop it,' I said. 'We walk back with the rest of 'em as far as the little copse of olive trees, then we hang back like we're diving in the bushes for a quick shit, double back, strike out for the main road and run like buggery.'

He frowned. 'The main road, are you sure? Isn't that exactly where they'll head for?'

'No,' I replied, 'because they know we aren't dumb enough to do a stupid thing like that. Besides, if we get a move on, we'll be on the military road before they realise they've missed us.'

That line of reasoning seemed to convince him, which was odd, since I thought it stank. 'Then what?' he said. 'Which way, Rome or Ostia?'

Good question. Ostia – stow away on a boat that's just about to leave, non-stop across the open sea to Greece or Spain, and we'd be laughing. Or we'd get there and find the weather had closed in and nothing was getting out for a week. Rome, on the other hand – very big place, crowded, nobody knows anybody else. What chance would anybody have trying to find two people out of a million?

'Let's go to Rome,' I said. 'Looks like you're getting your wish after all.'

SEVEN

It's a fair old hike from Ostia to Rome, especially if you happen to be wearing someone else's boots. If the boots are older than you are, and were made for someone who had talons for feet, it's a very long walk indeed.

'It's your own silly fault,' Lucius Domitius told me, more than once. 'When we left Sicily, you had a perfectly good pair of boots, but no, you had to go and trade them in for those miserable objects, just because you thought you were getting something for nothing. That's the trouble with you. You keep grasping at opportunities that turn out to be complete disasters.'

He was always at his most annoying when he was right. 'Well, what about you?' I said. 'You did exactly the same thing.'

'Yes. And have you seen me limping? No. That's because I traded my clapped-out old boots for a decent pair of new ones, which fit.'

'Exactly,' I said. 'You were born lucky, and I wasn't. Unfair, or what?'

He frowned. 'You make your own luck in this life,' he said, 'good and bad. I've made more than my fair share of both kinds, so I know what I'm talking about.'

Well, I was going to say more or less the same thing, only probably not as neatly as that (but then, I never had a classical education). That's another annoying thing he used to do. How can you insult somebody when he's forever beating you to it?

'Well, anyway,' I said. 'The point is . . .' I shut up. I couldn't remember what the point was going to be. 'We must be nearly there by now,' I went on. 'What I was thinking was, our best plan would be to hang about till dark and slip in along with all the carts. That way, if there's anybody watching the roads for us—'

'Oh, smart idea,' Lucius Domitius interrupted. 'The first thing we do in Rome is break the curfew. On the other hand, we could just stroll in, packed in the middle of a crowd at the gate, and nobody would be able to pick us out, even if there is anybody watching. I figure the best time would be an hour before the gates close. There's always the most terrific squash at the gates at that time. Even if they saw us and identified us, they'd never be able to get to us through all the people.'

Well, yes, he had a point there. 'Fine,' I said, 'we'll do it your way. Just don't blame me if we walk straight into a trap.'

'Don't worry about it,' he replied, 'it'll be fine. Back in the old days I was always wandering about the city incognito. I learned a thing or two about not being seen.'

God, I thought, that old stuff again. Over the years we'd been going round together, he'd boasted about how he used to roam the taverns after dark and nobody recognised him, time and again. He was so proud of this master-of-disguise thing that I'd never had the heart to tell him that he never fooled anybody, mostly because of the platoon of plain-clothes guardsmen that Colonel Burrus had trailing him wherever he went. Your average Roman street person can smell the guard a hundred yards away with their eyes closed, which may account for the fact that Lucius Domitius and his cronies never got their teeth smashed in when they were out making nuisances of themselves. I met a bloke once who used to do guided tour parties: two denarii a head, and you could follow round with the guards watching the emperor making an arse of himself in public. Quite a profitable line, while it lasted.

'Well,' I said, 'you're the expert. Though I still reckon we ought to take a detour and go in at the Appian gate. If they're expecting us, the Ostian gate's where they'll have put their watchers.'

He shrugged. 'If you like,' he said. 'Or we could be really clever and hike round to the Asinaria. Save a lot of walking uphill, too.'

Made no odds to me. As far as I was concerned, the longer we put off strolling into the city, the happier I'd be. 'Anyhow,' I said, anxious to change the subject. 'Since we're basically on a sightseeing trip, what do you want to go and look at first?'

He smiled. 'I was just thinking about that,' he said. 'Well, first stop, the palace, naturally. No, really,' he said, when I pulled a face. 'It's been, what, ten years. They might have got round to finishing it by now.'

Fair enough, I thought. After all, he'd always been ridiculously proud of the palace architecture, a lot of which he'd designed himself – well, not the actual drawing lines on a piece of paper, he had Greeks who did that. His input consisted more of waving his arms in the air when they showed him the drawings and saying, 'Can't you make it a bit more sensuous?' and crap like that. 'All right,' I said. 'What next, after the palace?'

He furrowed his brows, like this was some really important decision. 'I'd like to go and see my bridge,' he said. 'And then we can cross the river and take a look at my racetrack. And we can stop off and see my baths on the way.'

'Sure,' I said. 'Good itinerary. Is there anything else you want to see, apart from the ones you built?'

He grinned. 'Not really,' he said. 'Oh, don't pull faces at me. I'm here trying to make some kind of sense of my life. At least I can stand next to a really cute building, something that'll still be standing and looking good a thousand years from now, and say, I built that.'

'Fine,' I said, 'so long as you say it quietly.'

He nodded. 'Yes, well. Oh, and if we take a dog-leg up Scaurus' promenade, we can see my arches, too.'

'Of course we can,' I muttered. 'And when we're through gawping at your immortal legacy, have you thought where we're going to doss down for the night, with no money?'

He shrugged. 'There's always a doorway in the Subura,' he replied. 'Isn't that the regular place for down-and-outs?'

'Not if you want to be still wearing your boots when you wake up,' I said. 'It's a pretty rough neighbourhood, in case you didn't know. Full of thieves and muggers and other undesirables.'

'We should fit in pretty well, then.'

I sighed. Ten years and still he hadn't got a clue. 'Talking of money,' I went on, 'how do you propose we get hold of some? Only it's bound to come in handy, for buying food and things.'

He smiled patronisingly. 'Oh, that's easy,' he said. 'We sit down outside a temple and look pathetic, and people will give us money.

It's called begging. Actually, it'd be a smart plan to wrap a bit of old cloth round your leg, pretend you lost it on active service. You wouldn't believe how soft-hearted Romans are where veterans are concerned.'

'For pity's sake,' I said, 'you really haven't got a clue, have you? Do you really think that anybody can sit down with a hat on any street corner that happens to be free?'

He looked puzzled. 'Well,' he said, 'the guards are supposed to move them on, but—'

'But they don't,' I told him, 'because they're organised, almost like a trade guild or something, and the members of the guild pay their dues, and the guild pays off the guard. Which is why bad things tend to happen to offcomers who try to set up on an empty pitch without joining the guild or handing over a fifth of their take. We wouldn't last a day; they'd be fishing our bodies out of the river by nightfall.'

'I had no idea,' Lucius Domitius said. 'But hang on, can't we just join up, like everyone else? I happen to think trade guilds are a pretty good idea. I mean, someone's got to look after the working man . . .'

I laughed. 'There are lots of good ideas in the world,' I said. 'Ever so many of them; and you look at any really shitty situation, anything that's gone so badly wrong it can never be put right, and somewhere in the background you'll see the mangled remains of the good idea that caused the whole mess in the first place. Like wars,' I went on. 'Eight hundred years your people have been fighting wars, and every single one of 'em started because the Romans were afraid of somebody, some bunch of woolly-backed savages who were bound to come raping and pillaging throughout the empire unless they were smacked down first. Eight centuries of pre-emptive strikes, millions of people dead and mutilated, because you Romans reckon peace is a good idea. Or take your governments,' I went on – I've got no idea why I suddenly felt like I had to preach a sermon, but it was as if something had been building up inside me for a long time, and it was suddenly bursting out, like a volcano. 'Everything that's wrong with the world is because of some idiot's good idea. Like, five hundred years ago, you Romans thought it was a good idea to get rid of your kings and be a republic, and what did you get? The most corrupt regime the world's ever seen, run as a private business by a load of aristocratic thieves and swindlers. So what happens? A hundred years ago, your great-great-great-uncle or whatever he was, Julius Caesar, thought it'd be a good idea to get rid of all that shit and have good government, in the hands of one good man. And what did we get? We got Tiberius, and Caligula, and that murderous buffoon Claudius—'

'And Nero,' he muttered. 'Don't forget him.'

'Well, quite,' I said, 'my point exactly. A whole lot of people said, let's get rid of Nero, that'd be a good idea. And the result? Four civil wars in the space of a year. Don't give me your good ideas, they suck. For crying out loud, you should know that better than anybody. You thought, let's stop wasting all our money on killing savages, let's spend it on cute buildings and teaching people to appreciate art and music and shit. And here you are.'

He laughed. 'Yes,' he said, 'but that was a bad idea. And besides, I may be reduced to wandering the streets with the likes of you, but the buildings are still there. And it may be a bad idea to try and run a farm according to a book of poetry, but the poetry still survives, and always will. And you know how that came about? Because my ancestor Augustus was a patron of the arts, and as long as people read Virgilius Maro, they'll remember Augustus. So maybe it wasn't such a bad idea after all. Mind you,' he added, 'personally I think Virgilius Maro is completely overrated, but that's just my opinion, and who am I to argue with history?' He lifted his head. 'Besides,' he went on, 'who's to say that if my ancestors hadn't conquered the Gauls and the Carthaginians and the Teutones, that they wouldn't have smashed through our defences and burned down the city? But as it is, the city and the empire will last for ever.'

'You say that like it's a good thing,' I grumbled.

'Well, of course it is. Maybe not for you and me, personally, but for the benefit of the whole human race. Just imagine what the world would be like if the Empire were to fall and the Germans or the Persians were to get control. We'd sink from being humans to being animals in the space of a few generations. You know what?' he went on. 'It's one of the few things that keeps me going, the thought of what the empire means. Like the story of the Spartan candidate.'

I frowned. 'Is that the one with the farmer's daughter and the goat?'

'There was once a Spartan,' said Lucius Domitius. 'He belonged to one of the great ruling families, and all his life it'd been his ambition to be picked as one of the three hundred royal body-guards, the best and bravest men in the land. So, every day of his life he trained at sports and combat practice till he was as fit and good at fighting as it's possible to get, and the day came when he went to the palace for his interview, to see if he'd be accepted. That evening, his wife and children were waiting for him at the front door, and they saw him coming down the street with a huge happy grin on his face. So they asked, Did you pass? And he beamed at them and said, No. Well, they couldn't understand why he was so happy, and they asked him, So what are you grinning for, you failed? And he said, Yes, but isn't it wonderful to know there are three hundred better men than me in Sparta?'

I thought about that for a moment. 'On balance,' I said, 'I prefer the one with the farmer's daughter and the goat. And besides, I don't see the point.'

'Don't you? How odd. The point is,' said Lucius Domitius, with a soupy expression on his face, 'I don't mind that they stopped me being emperor, not really. Because, well, the empire's still here, bigger and stronger than ever. I'm glad that there was someone better at the job than me, and that he eventually got to do it.'

I shook my head. 'You know,' I said, 'it must be really nice to be an idiot, like you. It must be really great to look at the world and honestly believe it makes sense. I wish I could, but I'm not an idiot, so I can't. Great pity, but there it is.'

He smiled. 'Nobody's perfect,' he said.

I wasn't going to let it go on a cheap one-liner. 'Seriously, though,' I said, 'you don't honestly believe all that crap, do you? About the empire and Rome and it's all worthwhile because of the future of the human race?'

'Well, yes,' he said.

'Really? After everything you've seen these past ten years, going around with me?'

He shrugged. 'True, going around with you for ten years does make me apprehensive about whether the human race has a future.'

At this point I pulled a face, ha-ha-very-funny. 'If you mean, has it made me cynical, well, yes. I've seen that most public officials are corrupt or incompetent. I've seen that law-enforcement officers all across the empire are so pathetic they couldn't even catch *us*, which would stop me sleeping at night if I was an honest citizen. But it hasn't changed my mind about what Rome means, not a bit, quite the opposite. You see, with you I've had a peek under the flat stone, I've seen what human beings are like, the sort of things they can do if they aren't stopped. I tell you what; if I got my throne back tomorrow, after what I've seen, I'd be the best bloody emperor they've ever had.'

I changed the subject after that, because it was starting to get a little bit scary; it was the first time in ten years he'd talked about being emperor again, even in a joke. I'd always reckoned that he never even thought about that stuff, the same way as a man who's saved from the cross at the last minute – like me, for instance – doesn't go around saying, Next time they get me up on one of those things, I'll put on a better show for the crowd.

Like I said, Lucius Domitius wasn't just an idiot, he was a colossal idiot, he was an idiot the way an elephant is an animal. My old mother used to say, everybody is the best at something. I guess Lucius Domitius was the best idiot in the whole wide world.

Rome sucks.

Not for everyone, maybe. For your fat-cat, purple-striped senator breezing into town in his gilded ivory litter carried on the shoulders of two brace of thoroughbred Germans, I can see where Rome is the best place on Earth, what the Elysian Fields could have been if only the gods had had a bit more taste and vision. For your sharp-nosed Tyrian entrepreneur, bouncing into town on the box of a cart laden down with the finest in exclusive fabrics for the discerning society hostess, Rome is the only place to be. For the down-and-out Italian-trash peasant (assuming he hasn't got a price on his head, of course), Rome's the place where you can earn a living just standing in a line outside a rich man's house, waiting for your little goody-basket of bread, wine and figs. If you're a Spanish nouveau riche after a spot of instant dinner-party credibility, or a Calabrian artichoke magnate who wants top dollar for his wagonload of wilted greens, or a sailor off a stone barge looking for neat wine, broad-minded women and the latest cutting-edge developments in social diseases (in which case, check out the Grand Circus district, or so my sources tell me), or a Greek hairdresser or a Syrian doctor or a Thracian masseur or a Batavian flute player or a newly fledged lawyer in a hurry to make his first million before he's thirty, the Seven Hills are where it's at. No question. Just walk right in and help yourself.

Far as I'm concerned, though, you can stuff it. I don't like the noise, or the fact that you have to wade ankle-deep in the contents of other people's chamber pots (no kidding; especially when it rains and the cart ruts fill up). I don't like the crowds – everybody's tense and wary all the time, like deer in open country, and if you happen to stumble and fall they'll trample you into the mud so deep nobody'll ever know you're down there – or the darkness at noon in the narrow alleys between the tenement blocks, which are so high that a newly minted turd slung out of a top-storey window will smash your skull with the force of a fifteen-pound sledgehammer if you're unlucky enough to be walking underneath. I don't like the way the ground shakes at night as the timber-wagons and brick-wagons lumber through the streets, so close that the lead ox has his nose squashed right up against the tailgate of the cart in front. I don't like having to flatten myself against the wall every time a half-platoon of rat-arsed city guards swaggers past after a day of bludging free drinks in bars, hoping they won't trip over my toe and then beat me to a bloody pulp for obstructing police officers in the execution of their duty. I don't like the pace of life, the attitude, the priorities or the mindset. And I really, *really* don't like the smell.

'You have no idea,' said Lucius Domitius, sidestepping just in time to avoid treading in an ox-pat, 'how great it feels being back here. All the time I've been away, trying not to think about it, I was kidding myself – it's not so hot really, all big cities are pretty much the same, that sort of bullshit – and now I'm here again, it's like getting my eyesight back after being blind for ten years. It's amazing, really it is. I feel like I'm me again.'

A few yards behind us, a tile slid off a rooftop and glooped into the muck, spraying our backs with stuff I really didn't want to know about. If I had to live in Rome long-term, first thing I'd do if I had the money would be go out and buy myself a nice, well-padded army-issue helmet, to guard what little brains I've got against all the bits that fall off buildings.

'Wonderful,' I snarled. 'So long as you're happy, that's all that matters, really.'

I was wasting my breath, of course. One thing I've learned over the years, it's no bloody good trying to talk sense into a bloke when he's in love; and Lucius Domitius was head over heels in love with the Niffy City, you could tell from the way he was drooping along with his mouth open. Absolutely crazy, of course, but that's love for you. Personally I've always reckoned it's a really bad idea, but I know most people don't agree with me there.

'When you've quite finished drooling,' I went on, 'maybe you could give some thought to what we're going to do about getting something to eat, silly little things like that. I know I'm just an old fusspot, but the fact that we haven't got any money whatsoever, and—'

I didn't finish the sentence. Lucius Domitius didn't notice, of course, because he hadn't been listening to a word I'd said, not since we walked in through the city gate, so there wasn't any point in trying to get him interested in what I reckoned I'd just seen.

Besides, I wasn't at all sure I'd seen it. Just a glimpse through a dense tangle of arms and heads and shoulders; I could easily have been wrong. I decided to keep my face shut and make sure before I started shooting my mouth off.

If there's one thing worse than being wrong, it's being right; because a while later, just when I'd more or less convinced myself that I'd been seeing things and there was nobody there, I caught sight of him again, and this time there wasn't any doubt at all about it. I'm good at faces, and this was definitely the same man.

'Here,' I said, grabbing Lucius Domitius by the shoulder and shaking him. He stopped, like he'd been woken up while sleep-walking, and stared down at me. 'What?' he said.

'Bad news,' I said. 'There's a bloke following us.'

He scowled at me. 'Bullshit,' he said. 'It's a crowd. You've probably just seen someone who's headed in the same direction as us, that's all.'

'Not that simple,' I said. 'You see, I know him from somewhere.'

'Well, that's possible. I mean, you did live here for a few years. Probably he's just some shopkeeper you used to buy things from.'

'Oh no,' I said. 'I know exactly where I've seen him before.' And I told Lucius Domitius about when I arrived in Ostia off the grain barge, and the kind gentleman who'd given me the denarius.

'Him?' Lucius Domitius frowned. 'You think that's him you just saw?'

'I don't think it's him, I know. I don't ever forget faces, you know that. Basic survival instinct in our line of work.'

Lucius Domitius looked unconvinced. 'All right,' he said, 'let's say for argument's sake it is the same guy. Now, which explanation is more reasonable: that he's followed your trail all the way out to the Gnatho ranch and then back here again, or that it's just a coincidence you seeing him again, and he's no bother to us at all? If you were making a book on it, what odds would you be giving?'

'I don't believe in coincidences,' I told him. 'It's a religious thing. Tell you what, why don't we duck down an alley and see if we can shake the bastard off? I mean, if you're right and he is just some bloke who happens to be going the same way as us, it won't have done us any harm. And if he really is following us—'

'Bloody hell!' Lucius Domitius stopped dead in his tracks, like he'd just seen a ghost, or his wife and his best friend making out in a doorway. 'Galen, what in hell's name is *that*?'

He was pointing at something, but I was buggered if I could see what it was. I did look, but all I saw was a load of old buildings.

'What's up?' I asked.

'There.' He was pointing with his arm stretched taut, and shouting so loud that people were looking round. 'It's gone, and there's that *thing* there instead.'

I sighed. 'All right,' I said, 'explain. What's such a big deal? And for pity's sake keep your voice down and stop waving your arms about.'

'The palace,' he said, and he was genuinely upset, nearly in tears. 'The palace. My palace, my Golden House. It's gone.'

'Balls,' I said. 'Something that size, it'd take twenty years just to cart the stone away.'

'Are you blind? Look for yourself.'

Truth is, I hadn't even noticed we were in that part of town. But I looked round, got my bearings – the Grand Circus away to the southwest, Claudius' temple over on our left, the Esquiline Hill in the distance on our right, the Caelian Hill behind us, which meant that the Golden House should indeed be straight ahead, right under our noses. But it wasn't. Instead, there was a huge round thing, like a stack of cheeses.

'You're right,' I said, 'it's gone. And that hat-box thing's since our time, as well.'

Then someone coughed behind us, and we both spun round like we'd been jabbed in the bum with a branding iron. And there he was. Short, round bloke with a bald head and a scrubby white beard. Face like a full moon, with a little piggy snout for a nose. My benefactor from Ostia.

'Excuse me, gentlemen,' he said, 'but I couldn't help overhearing. Am I right in thinking you're new in town?'

I was staring at him like he was the gorgon or something. Of course, Lucius Domitius hadn't seen him before, didn't know there was anything wrong. He nodded and said, 'Yes. Well, not new exactly, but we've been away.'

'I see. A long time, by the sound of it.'

'Twelve years,' Lucius Domitius said quickly. 'What happened to the Golden House?'

The round bloke smiled. 'Pulled down,' he said. 'One of the first things Vespasian did, because it was so unpopular. It reminded people of Nero, you see.'

'Oh.' Lucius Domitius looked like his best friend had just died. 'Good job, too,' he said. 'Terrible waste of money, typical of that bastard Nero.' He shook his head, but I don't think he was fooling anybody. 'So, um, what's that round building?'

'That?' The round bloke was grinning. 'You are out of touch, aren't you? That's Vespasian's great gift to the people of Rome,' he went on. 'I'm amazed you haven't heard of it. It's the greatest sports arena in the world. The Colosseum, surely you've heard of it.'

'Oh, that,' I said, pulling myself together with a snap they must've heard in Naples. 'Of course, how stupid of me, I remember now. We heard all about it at the time. Nobody talked about anything else, not even in Bactria.'

'Bactria?' The round man raised an eyebrow. 'Good heavens,' he said, 'what on earth were you doing out there?'

'Oh, trading, that sort of thing,' I said. 'Wonderful place, but very hot. So, that's the Coliseum, is it? I've often wondered what it looks like.'

'Colosseum,' the round bloke corrected me, with a grin I didn't like. 'Yes, it's a sight to see, isn't it? And just beyond it's where Titus is going to build the new bathhouse, which also promises to be a sight to see, or so they reckon. It's remarkable how they've managed to transform this whole quarter in so short a time.'

'Fantastic,' I muttered. 'Sort of like healing the wounds, really. Symbolic.'

'Quite,' the round bloke said. 'Well now, since you're strangers in Rome, perhaps you'd like to see round the new developments? It so happens I'm at a loose end for an hour or so, it'd give me great pleasure to—'

'No,' I yelped. 'Thanks,' I added, 'but actually we're in a bit of a hurry. Business meeting,' I went on, 'in the forum, and we're late already. Very kind of you to offer, but we'd better be getting along.'

'Of course.' The round bloke nodded gravely, but he was look-ing at our boots, and you didn't need to be a mind-reader to tell what he was thinking. 'Well, if you're headed for the forum I'll walk with you, I'm headed in that general direction. And I can point out some of the other changes since your day as we go.'

I was stuffed. The only way I could think of getting rid of him was to kill him, and it was a bit public for doing that, even in Rome. Just as well Lucius Domitius was a bit clearer-headed than me – well, of course, he could afford to be, he hadn't seen this bloke before. 'We'd really like that,' he said, 'but first we've got to stop off at our bankers', and that'll take a while. We've only just got back, you see, and there's heaps to do. New clothes and boots, for one thing. We must look like a dreadful pair of scruffs in our old trav-elling things.'

The round bloke laughed. 'Of course,' he said. 'I won't hold you up any longer, then. It was a pleasure meeting you.'

'Likewise,' Lucius Domitius barked over his shoulder, as I hustled him off into an alley. As soon as we were out of sight in the shad-ows, I dragged him into a run and we didn't stop until we'd put four or five turnings behind us.

'What the hell's got into you?' Lucius Domitius said, as soon as he'd caught his breath. 'What did you want to go haring off like that for?'

I was leaning forward, hands on knees. 'That man,' I said.

'What about him?'

'Ostia.' It's hard to talk when it feels like someone's got your lungs in a screw-clamp. 'You remember, I told you. I was sitting against a wall feeling sorry for myself, and some perfect stranger wanders up and gives me a denarius.'

Lucius Domitius nodded. 'So?'

'That was him.'

'What?' He stared at me. 'Are you sure?'

'Absolutely bloody positive.'

'But . . .' He stood there for a few moments opening and closing his mouth, as if he was trying to talk but all the words had been repossessed by the bailiff's men. 'You're kidding,' he said.

'Yeah, sure. I made the whole thing up. Fuck you, Lucius Domitius. I swear to you, that's the same man. Scraggy beard, little round pot belly and a face like a rabbit.'

'Must be a coincidence,' he said, and it was so obvious from the way he said it that he didn't believe that either, so I didn't bother correcting him. 'So,' he went on, 'who do you think he is?'

'No idea. But I have this lurking suspicion he's probably not our friend.'

'But it's crazy.' He rubbed his chin so hard I'm surprised he didn't draw blood. 'Didn't seem to me like he'd recognised you. I mean, if it was the same man and he'd been tracking us down, surely he'd have known, since he's crossed your path already, that if he walked up to us like he just did you'd be bound to recognise him.'

'Obviously he didn't care,' I said. 'I reckon he's doing it on purpose, so we'll know he's on to us. Just to torture us, scare us out of our wits before he closes in for the kill.'

Lucius Domitius frowned. 'You say that,' he said. 'But when all's said and done, he was only a little fat guy, we could take him out with our hands tied behind our backs.'

'Oh sure,' I said, 'unless of course next time he shows up he's got two platoons of city guards trotting along at his heels.'

'He's got to find us again first.'

'Well, he didn't make too bad a job of it this time.'

Lucius Domitius sat down against the wall. 'I reckon it's got to have been a coincidence,' he said. 'Either that or, if he really is trailing us, he's got the most amazing luck. I mean, how on earth could he have found us? We haven't been staying at any inns, or anything like that.'

I shook my head. 'What about the Sicilian who showed up at Gnatho's estate? Or was that a coincidence too?'

'Yes, but . . .' He frowned. 'All right,' he said, 'even if someone did manage to track us as far as there, how'd he get the message to his buddy here in the city to look for us exactly here? It doesn't add up.'

'It does,' I replied. 'Think about it. First he sees me in Ostia—'

'Sees you,' he pointed out. 'Sorry if this sounds rude, but who the hell would bother tracking *you* all the way from Sicily to Rome?'

'First,' I repeated, 'he finds me in Ostia. My guess is, he's working for the Sicilian, the nutcase who killed all the soldiers – he's chasing us, he figures out that we must've been on board that particular grain freighter, so he sends his mate there ahead on a faster ship to catch us when we reach Italy, right? But you've jumped ship, remember? So Rabbit-face is waiting for the grain boat at Ostia, he doesn't see you but he sees me—'

'And gives you a denarius. We could do with more mortal enemies like that.'

I ignored him. 'He sees me,' I said, 'but not you – I'm assuming you're the one they're after, him and the Sicilian – so he goes off to find out what's happened to you, probably goes and asks the grain freighter captain, who tells him you've jumped ship. By this time, the Sicilian's arrived in Italy—'

'All right,' he interrupted. 'So why did he send Rabbit-face by the first ship, and then wait for a later ship himself?'

'Be quiet, will you, I can't think if you're nattering away. The Sicilian arrives, finds out from Rabbit-face that you skipped before the ship got in; they split up and go round the countryside checking up on places where we could've found work, and that's when we saw the Sicilian at Gnatho's. Then we give the game away by bolting without even collecting our pay – I told you that was a bad idea, but you wouldn't listen – so the Sicilian figures we must be heading for Rome. He sends a rider ahead to tell Rabbit-face to look out for us—'

'And Rabbit-face just happens to bump into us in the street. In a city of a million people. Sure, right.'

'No, you're missing the point,' I said. 'It's you they're looking for, right? They know who you are. So, of course, they'll know that the first thing you'll want to do is go and take a look at your old house, the palace, like bloody Ulysses in the fairy stories. All Rabbit-face has got to do is hang around near the site of the Golden House, and he's got us. It all makes sense.'

He thought about that for a while. 'If you're right – I'm not saying I agree with you, but if you're right, we're in the shit again. But the Sicilian, that's what I don't understand. If the Sicilian's after me, why did he turn me loose on the way to the quarries? Why not just go to the magistrate and say, You know who you've got there, mate? Only the most evil man in history. But all that crazy business about killing the guards, and then letting us go, for crying out loud. He even gave us money.'

I shrugged. 'Maybe he didn't realise who you were till afterwards, I don't know. Maybe he didn't want anybody else to know he'd found you; maybe he wants to kill you himself, in some horribly imaginative way, and an ordinary public crucifixion simply wouldn't cut it. Or maybe he doesn't want to kill you, maybe he thinks you've got some secret information he can get out of you—'

'Bloody hell.' Lucius Domitius had that startled-weasel look on his face that I'd come to recognise as Inspiration. 'Dido's treasure.'

I looked at him. Fine time for him to start gibbering, I thought. 'You what?'

'Dido's treasure.' He'd gone as white as ewe's milk cheese. 'Oh come on, you must've heard us talking about it, in the old days.'

'No, I think I'd have remembered something with the word treasure in it. What are you talking about?'

He shook his head. 'Amazing,' he said. 'What the hell did you do all day, back in the palace?'

'Dido's treasure,' I said. 'Explain.'

He grinned. 'The legendary fortune of Dido of Carthage,' he said. 'You do know who Dido was, don't you?'

'Of course I do,' I lied. 'But what's he got to do with anything?'

'She,' Lucius Domitius said, with a really irritating smirk. 'She was the *queen* of Carthage, who fell in love with Aeneas. The founder of Rome, in case you haven't—'

'Get on with it.'

'Queen Dido,' he said, 'had a huge fortune in gold and silver and precious stones, and the old stories say it was hidden somewhere and forgotten about, and never recovered. Well,' he went on, 'I found it.'

I did a double-take. 'You found it?'

'Well, as good as. There was a chap called Viniculeius – equestrian order, nouveau riche, made his money speculating in grain futures – and he'd seen it, in a deep cave on a headland on the African coast, near Utica. But it was so amazingly huge he hadn't been able to take away more than he could carry, so he had to leave it there, and the very next day, as luck would have it, he got arrested on a poisoning charge; he'd killed his three brothers and their sons so as to get sole control of the family firm, really nasty business. Anyhow, at his trial he sent word that he needed to see me desperately urgently, so I had him fetched in, and he told me the whole story. Said that if I let him off the murders, he'd show me where the treasure was.'

'And you believed him? Come on, you're not that dumb.'

'Sure I believed him,' Lucius Domitius replied, 'because in his baggage when they caught him was this amazing collection of ancient Phoenician gold plate – cups and wine jugs and dishes and God only knows what else. I had some people who know about these things take a look at them, and they all said, definitely Phoenician, and very old indeed.'

I frowned. 'I thought you said this Dido was queen of Carthage, not Phoenicia.'

'The Carthaginians were Phoenicians, idiot. Which meant,' he went on, 'that the stuff he had with him was exactly the sort of thing you'd expect to find in Dido's treasure. Well, I was pretty excited, as you can imagine. For one thing, I was still finishing off the palace, and money was getting short. And beside that, nobody can resist buried treasure, it's human nature.'

'So, you let this bloke off?'

'Certainly not,' Lucius Domitius replied. 'He murdered seven people, out of sheer greed. No, I handed him back to the judges and let them get on with the trial, and he got what was coming to him. But I didn't tell him that, of course.'

'You didn't.'

'Course not. I said we'd have to let the trial run its course, but then I'd see to it that he was smuggled out of jail and given a new identity somewhere a long way away, so he could start a new life.'

I raised an eyebrow or two. 'And he fell for that?'

'No problem. It's one of the advantages of everybody thinking you're a bit simple, they don't expect you to double-cross them. Anyway, he gave me very detailed directions how to get there, drew me a map, all the rest of it.'

'But you never collected? Why the hell not?'

He sighed. 'Well, to begin with, I wanted to go myself, you know? Silly, really, but I wanted to be the one to find it. Also it'd have been good publicity – me finding this huge fortune, historical links to the founder himself, and then nobly handing it all over to the exchequer and not keeping any of it for myself. The way things were at the time, I needed something good like that to stop people hating me so much. And then, of course, things started to come apart all over, and what with practically all my generals and provincial governors setting their sights on being the next emperor, obviously I couldn't trust anybody to go and fetch it for me. All I'd have done was hand some wannabe emperor the money to pay his troops for seizing my throne. And then, of course, I had to leave in a hurry, and that was that.'

It was quite some time before I could manage to get a word out, and when finally I did, it was 'Bastard!'

He looked surprised. 'What?'

'Bastard,' I repeated. 'You stupid, selfish, shit-for-brains bastard. You're telling me that all these years we've been rattling around, starving hungry and the guard chasing us, and all along you've known where there's this vast hoard of treasure, just waiting to be scooped up.'

He grinned feebly. 'To be honest with you,' he said, 'this is the first time I've thought about it in years. I mean, the stuff from the old days, it's got so it's all like something out of fairy stories. But yes,

I guess it probably is still there, unless someone's beaten me to it. What're you pulling that strange face for?'

'Never mind,' I groaned. 'You were saying.'

'Oh, right. All I was going to say was, you were talking about someone possibly being after me because of some secret or other, and that made me think, Dido's treasure.' He shrugged. 'That is, it's possible. I can't think of anything else that'd mean someone would want to catch me alive without letting anybody else know.'

I didn't really want to talk to him any more, not for some time, for fear I'd lose my rag completely. 'Well,' I said, 'there you go. It's a possibility, yes. Did a lot of other people know about this treasure thing?'

He nodded. 'Only people around the palace,' he said, 'people I was sure I could trust with my life. But you know as well as I do, I was very wrong indeed about most of them. And come to think of it, of all the people who were in on it, I made sure I was the only one who knew all the details, the directions and so on. I learned them off by heart, then I burned the map. So, yes, I guess I'm the only person in the world who knows, unless Viniculeius told anybody. And I doubt that, he wasn't a very trusting man.'

I shook my head. It was all too much for me. 'I told you we ought to go to Africa,' I said, 'I bloody *told* you, but—'

'You said Mauretania,' he interrupted, 'and that's the other side of the province, nearly a thousand miles from Carthage.'

'Just shut up, will you?'

We spent the rest of the day getting deliberately lost.

Logical thing to do, when you think about it. After all, if you haven't got the faintest idea where you are, how can anybody else be expected to? Luckily, getting lost in Rome isn't exactly difficult. We just headed north-east till we hit the Subura, and dived into the maze of funny little streets and courtyards and whatever. No problem.

By the time we'd done that, it was getting late, we were both exhausted, not to mention starving hungry. In the end, we ducked in under the portico of some horrible scruffy little shrine, lay down and went to sleep, along with about a dozen other tramps and low-lifes. I can't remember what I dreamed about, but I do remember waking up, because when I opened my eyes there was this bloke with a knife standing over me.

I hate it when that happens.

Fortunately I had the presence of mind to kick him in the nuts, which made him fall over. Then, as I was jumping up, something heavy fell off my chest onto the deck and went *chink*. There's only one thing in the world that goes *chink* when you drop it.

The bloke started to get up, so I kicked him in the ear, and that sorted him out. By the looks of him he was just one of the tramps, anyway, he was out of it now, and I wasn't minded to hang around there till he came to again.

Talking of which, Lucius Domitius chose that moment to wake up, in mid-snore. He sat up sharpish, and I heard another *chink* just like the first one.

Now there's weird, and there's just plain bizarre. I picked up the thing that had gone *chink* and loosed off the little bit of string tied round the neck, and peered inside. There had to be at least forty denarii in there.

Which meant that during the night, while we were sleeping, surrounded by all those street people, someone had crept up nice and quiet and, without disturbing us or them, had tucked a fat purse of money inside my shirt.

EIGHT

A lot of stuff you can learn to cope with, such as being hounded by the authorities, or thrown out of taverns because they don't like the look of your boots, or pelted with stones because you talk funny. Move around enough in this world and you'll come up against something of the sort, unless you're incredibly lucky or a Roman senator. You come to expect it. You get the knack of starting to dodge even before the punch gets thrown.

But this one took me completely by surprise. I mean, what kind of sick bastard tracks you halfway across the known world, sneaks up on you while you're asleep and gives you money? You could drive a man crazy doing stuff like that. It's inhuman.

Lucius Domitius looked at me. He was holding something in his hand. 'You too?' he said.

I nodded. 'I say we get out of here,' I told him. 'Quick.'

'Good idea,' he replied.

Eighty denarii we had between us. That's good money. We weren't used to lugging that sort of weight of coined silver around with us. The really bizarre thing was that it was eighty denarii we hadn't nicked or swindled, or even (God help us) earned. As we hurried through the streets in the general direction of the Ostia gate, I turned over in my mind the various possibilities. Like, maybe it was forged money – death penalty in Rome for passing off duff coinage, it'd be a crafty way of getting us crucified – only I can sense a bad coin five hundred yards away, in a thick fog, and the stuff in our purses was the genuine article. So, I thought, maybe the coins are marked in some way that shows they're the loot from some robbery, maybe where a guard or a servant got killed. But I looked at the coins and I couldn't see a damn thing, they were just money – some old ones, with Tiberius' head on them, right down to shiny new jobs with Vespasian's ugly mug squinting sideways at you through the Latin. All right, I thought, maybe the wise guy's a Greek, and he assumes that everybody carries their money in their mouth; maybe the coins have been smeared with poison . . . At that point, I decided I'd better stop thinking, before I sprained my brain.

'You realise,' Lucius Domitius said to me as we passed the Bona Dea, 'they're probably watching the gates for us.'

I shook my head. 'Listen,' I said, 'this has gone way beyond that kind of shit. If they wanted to nab us or cut our throats, they could've done that last night. Talk about your perfect opportunities. If they wanted us dead, two more murdered tramps in the Subura, nobody would even have noticed. No, there's something else going on here, and I don't know what the hell it can be, but it's making my guts pucker.'

He thought about that. 'So you reckon it'll be all right, then,' he said, 'going through the gate?'

'Search me,' I said. 'Probably not. But unless we're planning on staying inside the city for the rest of our lives, we've got to go through a gate sooner or later. The way I see it, our best bet is to get on a ship going somewhere a long, long way from here, and Ostia's got to be the best place for that. There's ships leaving Ostia every day for every country in the world, and unless they see us get on board, how can they know which one we've got on and where we're going?'

'I like that,' Lucius Domitius said. 'That's a smart idea.'

'Don't sound so bloody surprised. I do get good ideas occasionally.'

So we kept going; and the further we went, the more I realised how perishing hungry I was. Now in all honesty I don't think you can blame me for that, since the last meal I'd had was the usual greasy soup and wilted greens back in Gnatho's barracks, and that seemed so long ago that it might as well have been cooked by Hercules, with Achilles washing the dishes. We'd gone hungry all the while simply because we'd been broke, but now we weren't, and I couldn't see the point in saving our skins by running away if we starved to death in the process.

Needless to say, when I mentioned this to Lucius Domitius he was about as sympathetic as a stone adder. But I made it clear that unless he gave in and we stopped for a quick bite of something, I was going to keep on moaning at him till his eyes started popping out.

'All right,' he sighed eventually. 'We'll pick up some bread or something off the next stall we come to. Will that do you?'

'No,' I said, 'it bloody well won't. At the very least I want bean soup and chickpeas with a hunk of bacon and a pint of wine. God only knows where our next meal's coming from after that, so we'd better stock up while we can. It's basic common sense. A fat lot of escaping we'll be doing if we're too weak to move.'

He wasn't impressed by that argument, I could tell, but he also had the wit to realise that it'd be quicker to give in than argue. Luckily we came across an open tavern before he had a chance to change his mind.

The house special of the day was a sort of grey slop with hard bits in it. Unfortunately, it was also all they'd got, apart from bread with the texture of army boot soles and some dry, crumbly cheese. You wouldn't feed it to a dog. We had seconds.

'The next question we've got to consider,' I said, with my mouth full of bread, 'is where we go from here. I was thinking, Africa.'

He whimpered. 'Not again,' he said. 'Oh, I get it, you've set your heart on Dido's treasure. Well, don't you think it'd be a good idea to get shot of whoever this loon is who's tailing us first?'

I didn't like his tone, but I couldn't be bothered to make an issue of it. 'We'll do both,' I said, 'at one stroke. I mean, we've got to go somewhere, and Africa's a long way from here.'

'Yes.' He nodded, spilling grey slop down his chin, 'and to get there, you've got to go via Sicily, or had you forgotten that? There's one place I never want to go back to.'

'The ship's got to go to Sicily,' I said, 'but we don't have to get off it. In fact, it'd be a sight better if we stayed on the ship till we get there. Less chance of being seen, and all.'

He lifted his head. 'Forget about Africa,' he said. 'There's a whole world out there, places we've never heard of, places that've never been discovered, or where nobody's been for so long, everyone's forgotten how to find them, like the land of the lotus-eaters in the *Odyssey*.' He frowned. 'I was thinking of Gaul or maybe even Germany. I mean, who in his right mind would ever choose to go there? It's the obvious place, really.'

'Germany?' I repeated. 'Are you out of your tiny mind? I'd rather stay here and get crucified.'

'Anyway,' he said, 'I don't suppose it'll be up to us. What we need to do is get on the first ship to leave, and screw where it's going. I just want to get out of Rome as fast as possible.'

'Isn't that exactly what they'll be expecting us to do?' I said craftily. 'Whereas if we bide our time a little, hang around the docks keeping our heads down—'

'They'll find us, and we'll be screwed. No, first ship out of here, it's the only thing to do.'

I thought about it for a moment or so. What the hell, I told myself, that treasure's been there hundreds of years, it can hang on a bit longer – assuming there really was any treasure, which I didn't believe for a moment. If all the buried treasure I've heard rumours about over the years was to fall out of the sky, it'd cover Rome like a snowdrift. And he was right, of course. Given the spooky way they'd been able to find us, even after we'd gone to all the trouble of getting lost in the backstreets of the Subura, getting out of town as quickly as we could was the only way. 'Fine,' I said, 'we'll do that then.' But we didn't, because immediately after I'd said it, a house fell on me.

Sorry if that sounds a bit melodramatic. People tell me it's one of the hazards of living in Rome, where half the buildings are so old they're only standing up through force of habit, and the other half have been slung together in the last few years by slum landlords who don't give a damn. If that wasn't bad enough, it doesn't help to have endless processions of huge great carts rumbling past all night, every night, literally shaking the buildings to bits. Shocking, really, and if I was the emperor of Rome I'd do something about it, you can bet your life. Light a bloody great fire, probably, and start again from scratch

I'd like to make a big thing about this, because it must've been pretty thrilling stuff, and I love telling the tale, as you've probably gathered by now. Unfortunately, I missed the whole show, on account of being bashed on the head by a chunk of falling masonry.

Typical of my luck, that: something really spectacular happens, and I sleep through the whole thing.

So you'll have to make do without my keenly observed eyewitness account, and do the best you can with what Lucius Domitius told me later. He said that the front wall of this building – one of those horrible tenement blocks that are gradually filling the place up – suddenly started to bulge, like a frog's chin. He reckons he stood there watching only for a heartbeat or so, trying to figure out what on earth was going on, and then, when he finally tumbled to it, there wasn't time to yell and tell me to get out of the way. I suppose I've got to believe him, though I can't help thinking that anyone with the gumption of a small piece of stale bread could've reached out, grabbed me by the arm and yanked me out of the way. Wouldn't have taken much. After all, he was stood right next to me, and he didn't get so much as a bruised toe.

Anyhow, the wall sort of bellied out and went pop, like a mud-bubble in a swamp, whereupon whacking great big slabs of brick and stuff fell off the upper stories – which by some miracle didn't come down, it was just a patch of wall the size of the sail on a merchant ship that fell in – and it was one of these slabs, rather than the wall itself, that nailed me. Caught me a glancing blow on the side of the head, apparently, just above the left ear, and if it'd been a finger-length over to the right it'd have smashed my skull like an eggshell. Well, some of us were just born lucky, I guess.

I know what happened next without Lucius Domitius having to tell me. I can picture him, standing there like a huge stuffed olive, in the middle of all the dust and stuff, while I'm pinned down by a damn great chunk of wood (which fell on me after I'd been knocked out, apparently). So much for comrades through thick and thin, it was a couple of strangers who went in and pulled me out. Rather a brave thing to do, since obviously they had no way of knowing the rest of the building wasn't going to come down on their heads while they were at it. But I get the impression that your long-term resident Roman learns how to handle this sort of situation, what with falling-down buildings being such a common thing. Whatever. These two men who just happen to be strolling past dive in, grab my wrists and drag me out, well clear of the building just in case it decides to finish the job, and there I am. We heard later that a couple of other people weren't quite so fortunate: one killed outright, the other had his back broken, paralysed from the neck down. Horrible, really, when you think of it. Like I said, Rome sucks.

Anyhow.

Back to what I remember, and the first thing I saw when I opened my eyes was this gorgeous-looking bird leaning over me with a worried look on her face. That frightened me, a lot, because I'm a realist, I've got no illusions about myself, so the chances are that if I wake up out of an unexpected sleep and see a cute female looking down at me, the only probable explanation is that I have died and gone to the Elysian Fields. And – well, I'm sure it's really great in paradise, you're free and clear, all your troubles are over and there's nothing to do all day but stroll about on the grass eating fruit. Me, though, I'd rather be alive, thanks all the same.

But this theory of mine turned out to have a flaw in it, thank God, because it specifically says in the book of words that the blessed souls in the Elysian Fields feel no pain, and I had a headache so monumental that they were probably going to have to draw it in on all the maps. This took some of the shine off the being-stood-over-by-luscious-women thing, but it made me feel a whole lot better. If you see what I mean.

Besides, when I looked at her again, I realised she was more in the nice-looking category, rather than the classic all-time greats. Nice eyes, very big and round and dark, but she had a nose on her like one of Hannibal's elephants. Well, that's a slight exaggeration, but it was a hooter and a half, no two ways about it. Smaller than an Egyptian obelisk or the ram on a warship, but that was the most you could say for it. That aside, she was about nineteen, very pale skin, like fresh milk in the pail, wearing a plain old dress that'd probably belonged to her big sisters and her mum before that.

'He's awake,' she said, and damned if I could place her accent, though usually I'm sharp as a razor when it comes to voices. She spoke Greek, but with a sort of snorty croak, like she had a bad cold.

So there I was, lying on my back, admiring the view (or what I could see of it past the nose) and wishing my head didn't hurt so much, and of course Lucius Domitius has to come barging in and spoil it all. Next moment, instead of the cute girl I'm looking at his crow-scarer of a face, peering down at me like I was somebody's bad handwriting. At least he looked worried, which was something.

'Are you all right?' he said.

Bloody stupid question. 'No,' I said, 'my head hurts. Where are we? What happened?'

'You're in a room in an inn,' he replied. 'A wall fell on you.'

'A what?'

'A wall. A building collapsed, and you got hit on the head. Luckily, it doesn't seem to have done you any harm. At least, I don't think it has—'

'Excuse me,' someone I couldn't see interrupted, and I noticed he had the same accent as the nose girl. 'I have a small amount of expertise in these matters, perhaps if I could examine him.'

Made it sound like I was a dodgy horse at an auction, the daft prick. Anyhow, Lucius Domitius got out of the way and there was this stranger looming over me. First thing I noticed – couldn't help noticing it, really – was that he had a nose just like the girl's, if anything, even bigger. He was dark, suntanned, about twenty-five; almost certainly the girl's brother.

'Who's this?' I mumbled.

'This is the very brave man who saved your life,' Lucius Domitius said, making it sound like I was an ungrateful sod for not knowing that. 'He and his brother went in and pulled you out of the ruins, just before a whole lot more of the building fell down. If they hadn't got you out, you'd have been crushed to death.'

'Oh' I said, 'right. Um, thanks,' I added, since it always pays to be polite.

The nose bloke smiled, very wide, masses and masses of glowing white teeth. 'Think nothing of it,' he said, 'I'm sure you would've done the same for me.' He bent low over me and before I knew what he was up to he'd pushed back my right eyelid with his forefinger. 'Any dizziness?' he asked. 'Nausea?'

'I've got you breathing up my nose. Does that count?'

He laughed, as if I'd said something really funny. 'He'll survive,' he said. 'That head's going to be a bit sore for a day or so, but there's no real harm done.'

Well, that was good to hear, assuming the bloke knew what he was talking about. 'Are you a doctor?' I asked.

'For my sins,' the bloke replied. 'Perhaps I'd better introduce myself. My name's Amyntas, this is my sister Myrrhine, and my brother, who's just gone to find the innkeeper, is Scamandrius. My brother and I are both doctors, with our own practice back home in Memphis, in upper Egypt.'

Myrrhine, I thought, nice name. Actually it's not, it's a boring, droopy sort of name, and what I was really thinking was, it's the same as it is with clothes. A pretty girl can look good in anything, even a cabbage-sack with three holes cut in it, and any name can suit her, even rotten old Myrrhine. Also I was dying to ask, has your brother got an enormous nose too? But on balance I thought I'd better wait till he got back, and see for myself

'Memphis,' said Lucius Domitius. 'You're a long way from home.'

Amyntas smiled. 'Don't we know it,' he said. 'Everything here's so strange, so different. So *big*,' he added, with just the faintest hint of a shudder. 'But my brother and I, we've always wanted to see Rome, ever since we were little boys. And then my aunt died – she was the widow of a well-to-do freedman here in the city, we're the only family, so we had to come over and see to her estate. And here we are.'

Good God, I thought, cute and an heiress too, but that couldn't possibly be of any significance to me. Not even worth thinking about. Bash on the head or no bash on the head, I didn't have any problems with my memory, and I could remember that I was a small, skinny, middle-aged Greek, wanted on capital charges in a dozen provinces (but not Egypt), not a bent copper to my name apart from what'd been given me by some lunatic assassin after my blood, and with a face like a rat into the bargain.

And then I had an idea.

What can I say? It seemed like a good one, at the time.

'Fine,' I said. Then I pointed at Lucius Domitius. 'And who's he?'

Both of them stared at me like I was crazy. 'Excuse me?' Amyntas said.

'Him over there,' I said. 'The guy with the thick neck. Friend of yours? Personal slave?'

'But—' Amyntas' eyes narrowed. They had a lot of scope for it. 'You don't recognise him.'

'Never seen him before in my life,' I said.

'Oh.' Amyntas nodded slowly. 'Excuse me asking, but can you remember your name?'

'Me?' I acted puzzled. 'Well, of course I – Well, no,' I went on, pretending I'd suddenly been struck all thoughtful. 'No, I can't.'

'Ah!' Amyntas nodded twice, very quickly. 'I know what's happened. It was the bump on the head. I'm sorry to tell you, you've lost your memory.'

'What?' I acted all panicky. 'But that's—'

'It's all right.' Probably he was a good doctor, he had a nice, soothing manner. 'In nine cases out of ten it's a purely temporary thing, only lasts a day or so, a month at the very most. Nearly all patients who lose their memories after cranial trauma make a full recovery.'

I looked at him. 'Nearly all?'

'Ninety per cent, at least.'

'You mean there's a one-in-ten chance I'm stuck like this?' I made a show of trying to sit up. Amyntas pushed me slowly back. 'That's terrible,' I said. 'Give me some medicine, quick.'

He smiled. 'I can give you a soothing draught,' he said. 'It'll calm you down, relax you. That's the best thing in your condition.'

'Bugger being relaxed,' I said. 'I don't want to be relaxed, I want my memory back. You're a doctor, give me some medicine for that.'

His smile was like taking a bath in warm oil. 'Honestly,' he said, 'the soothing draught is the best medicine. The loss of memory is mostly due to shock and anxiety. Calming you down and making you feel relaxed should deal with that, and you'll have your memory back in no time.'

'You're sure about that?' Lucius Domitius interrupted. He sounded as frantic as I was pretending to be. That made me feel a bit guilty. I know, mostly he was panicking because, well, we were in enough shit as it was without me going all crazy, and besides, it was a safe bet that he'd told this Amyntas the tale, how we were itinerant sardine merchants from lower Pisidia or some bullshit like that. If I suddenly got my memory back and started gabbling about how I was a fugitive con artist and he was the emperor Nero, things could get a bit tense all round. Of course, I wasn't going to do anything of the kind, but he wasn't to know that.

(And while I was at it, I thought: Why *am* I doing this, just out of interest? And the answer was, no getting past it, because I thought the only way I'd stand a chance with the girl was to hang around her for a while, her presumably being the nurse, she'd be by my bedside mopping my brow with a damp cloth and looking concerned, and then I could be really grateful and say how wonderfully good and compassionate she was, and that's exactly the sort of thing girls like, gets their juices flowing like nothing else. Completely crazy, the whole idea; doomed to failure, right from the start. Obviously I was acting just a little bit nuts. Probably because of the bang on my head.)

Still, I'd started the caper now, so I couldn't back down. Also, it was going to be very ticklish telling Lucius Domitius, even if I managed to get him alone for long enough to explain, so on balance it'd probably be better if I didn't. Rough on him, of course, but that's what friends are for.

'Here,' Lucius Domitius said, 'I'll tell him who he is, that might jog his memory. Might that work?' he asked.

'Try it, by all means,' Amyntas replied.

'Fine. Well,' said Lucius Domitius, not actually looking at me, 'your name is Euthydemus, you're my business partner, we deal in quality dried fish, and we live in Corinth. That's in Greece,' he added, and I thought, you prat. I'm supposed to have lost my memory, not gone stupid. Besides, I couldn't help thinking, if I'd really lost my memory, feeding me all this bullshit just to back up the tale you've been telling could do me permanent damage. There I'd be, really believing I'm a prosperous dried fish merchant, and when my real memory started creeping back, telling me I was a failed bathhouse tickler and petty swindler, I'd start thinking I must be going off my rocker. And he didn't even have the excuse of wanting to get off with some big-nosed chick. Dear God, I said to myself, how bloody thoughtless can you get?

But clearly I couldn't say anything there and then, so I just looked helpless and pathetic, and said, 'Oh, right,' or something of the sort. Amyntas peered at me down his nose and asked if that rang any bells, and I said no, not really, and he said, Well, early days yet, and now he thought I really ought to get some rest, and he took Lucius Domitius gently but firmly by the elbow and steered him out of the room.

So there I was, me and the beaky but adorable Myrrhine. She sat on the edge of the bed looking at me for a while, like I was the saddest sight she'd ever seen, and then she said, 'How are you feeling now? Any better?'

I thought, yes, right. 'A bit,' I said. 'But my head's still hurting.'

'Of course,' she said, getting up. 'Really, I ought to leave you in peace, so you can get some sleep.'

'No,' I said quickly. 'I mean, um, it's all right, it's not that bad.'

'Would it help if I bathed your forehead with a damp cloth, do you think?'

You betcha, I thought, but I didn't put it quite like that. 'Yes, that'd be really nice,' I said, trying to sound nonchalantly brave, or some such shit. 'Unless you've got other things you should be doing. I mean, I don't want to be a nuisance.'

She smiled. Nice smile. 'Oh, it's no trouble,' she said. 'I'm used to this sort of thing, helping my brothers with the patients.' She picked up a bowl and a bit of rag off the table and started splodging my face. A bit like being kissed by a mackerel, but it's the thought that counts, as Plato said to Aristotle.

'It must be interesting work, doctoring,' I said.

'Oh, it is,' she replied, looking at me dead soulful. 'It's wonderful to see all those poor sick people getting better. Most of them, anyway. My brothers are very good doctors, you couldn't be in better hands.'

'I'm sure,' I replied, as a bit of water dribbled down off my eyebrow into my eye. 'I can see that. He's got a very good manner, your brother.'

'Oh, he's famous for it, back home. People come from miles around.'

'So,' I went on, 'how do you like Rome? I expect it's quite different from what you're used to.'

'Oh, it is. Everything's so big and bright and wonderful, it's like something out of a story. Though there's a lot of sad things too, all those poor people in the streets. I felt very sorry for them, sitting there with their little bowls begging for coppers.'

'It's tragic,' I agreed. 'But that's life for you.'

'Oh yes. Life can be very sad sometimes.'

Well, great, I thought, we're getting along like a house on fire here. What with the being hunted like a wild animal by the law all the time and the never having any money or being able to stay in one place for more than five minutes, one way and another, I'd never had much time for chatting with girls, and the kind of girls I'd mostly found myself chatting to hadn't been like this at all – barmaids, principally, and the sort of girls who hang round outside bathhouses. Not that I'm knocking them, they're absolutely fine as far as they go (all the way very quickly, in my experience), but not the type you can sit and talk to meaningfully about important issues, like Myrrhine and I were doing. Besides, a bit of fun is a bit of fun, but there's more to life than that. I'd always wanted to kiss a girl without having to worry about whether her tongue in my mouth meant she was fishing about for my small change.

'Still,' I went on, 'there's lots of nice things to see in Rome too. Have you been to the Circus yet?'

She frowned. 'Yes,' she said, 'but I didn't like it much. All those poor gladiatiors and people getting eaten by lions. Actually, I think that sort of thing's rather horrid.'

'Absolutely,' I said, 'I can't stand all that myself. Give me a good play any time.'

'You like plays?' She clapped her little hands together, spraying me with water from the bit of rag. 'Oh, I love plays. We get them sometimes in Memphis, very occasionally, when a touring company comes round. My favourites are the comedies. Which do you like best, Menander or Diphilus?'

Never heard of either of them was the truth, but of course I wasn't going to say that. 'It depends what mood I'm in, really,' I replied (and you've got to admit, it's a damn good answer, especially for a man with a bad head). 'Sometimes I feel like a spot of Menander, sometimes only Diphilus will do, if you see what I mean. What about you?'

'Oh, I'm the same,' she said, 'absolutely. And the Latin writers too – I can read Latin, you know, my mother taught me. I just adore Plautus, though don't you think Terence is a better observer of human nature?'

'Damn straight,' I said. 'Not much about human nature he didn't know.' Just then it occurred to me that I was supposed to have lost my memory. 'You know, I feel sure I must have gone to the theatre quite a lot, because all this stuff sounds very familiar. Maybe my memory's coming back.'

Her eyes were shining. 'Oh, good,' she said, 'isn't that wonderful? Do you think it's because of us talking about plays? It'd be so splendid if that helped you remember, wouldn't it?'

'Fantastic,' I said, 'let's keep going. So, what other plays do you like?'

'Apart from comedies, you mean?' She frowned. 'To be honest, I don't really like tragedies much, they're all so sad and gloomy. Do you like tragedies?'

'Not really,' I replied. 'I always think there's enough unhappiness in the world without making up any more.'

'Oh, that's so true,' she said. 'I think that's why I like comedies, they're so bright and cheerful, and everything turns out all right in the end. Not like real life,' she added, with a sigh. 'How about poetry? Do you like it? I do.'

'Very much,' I said, and for what it's worth, I was telling the truth. Some poetry, anyway. There was this one my uncle used to do about Leda and the swan that always had us in fits. He had a filthy mind, my uncle. 'What sort of poems do you like?'

'Oh, Theocritus and Anacreon and Alcaeus, Sappho of course, and Theognis, though some of his poems are a bit difficult for me, I'm not terribly bright, I know—'

'I wouldn't say that,' I said. 'I think anybody who likes Menander and Theocritus must be pretty clever, don't you?'

She blushed, right down to the tip of her nose. 'Oh, I don't know,' she said. 'I'm sure I don't understand all the complicated bits. You should hear my brothers talking about poetry. They can see all sorts of clever things that just go right over my head, I'm afraid. I just like the nice, cheerful bits, myself.'

'Same here,' I said. 'After all, it's there to be enjoyed, poetry. It's not like you're taking a test or something. You don't get a crown of bay leaves or a medal if you figure out all the hard bits.'

She laughed. 'Oh, you do say some funny things,' she said. 'It's almost as good as watching a comedy. You must be very clever to be able to think of things like that.'

'It's just a knack I've got,' I replied modestly. 'I guess,' I added quickly, since I wasn't supposed to be able to remember. 'I just say the first thing that comes into my head, really.'

You can see for yourself that things were going pretty bloody well, so it was a pity Lucius Domitius had to pick that moment to come barging in; also the brother, Amyntas, and another bloke I didn't recall having seen before. Not that it was hard to figure out who he was. One glimpse of the enormous thing jutting out of his face like the great mole in Ostia harbour was enough to tell me that this was the other brother, Scamandrius. Just in case I was blind or stupid, though, Amyntas introduced him. I remembered my manners and thanked him politely for saving my life. He just grinned shyly. Not the talkative kind, I guessed.

'I'd just like Scamandrius to examine you,' Amyntas said. 'He's had rather more experience of these cases than I have.'

So Scamandrius examined me, and asked me exactly the same questions his brother had (only he had one of those little tiny quiet voices that drive you spare after a while), and when he'd finished he nodded a couple of times and whispered something to Amyntas, who nodded back and said, 'Just as I thought.' Then he faced me and said, 'So, have we remembered anything yet?'

Before I could say anything, the girl piped up 'Oh yes, we've been having such an interesting talk, all about theatre and poetry and things.'

Now I don't know how they do things where you come from, but if your sister suddenly told you she'd been nattering away about poetry to some bloke you'd just dragged in off the street, I have an idea you'd maybe frown a bit and possibly get a little up tight. Certainly that's what'd happen where I was brought up. But apparently not in Egypt, or anyway Memphis, because both of them beamed and said, 'Splendid, splendid' (at least, I assume that's what Scamandrius said, because he was muttering again and I couldn't hear), and I began to think I'd probably like Egypt if I ever got to go there. 'But,' Amyntas went on, 'it is rather important for the patient to get plenty of rest, so I do think we ought to leave him alone for an hour or so. Come along, Myrrhine.' And they all shoved off.

Well, I was sorry to see her go, when we'd been doing so well, but my head was still hurting like buggery, so I closed my eyes, and I was just starting to drift off (because I was having this dream where Myrrhine and I – well, never mind) when the door opened and Lucius Domitius came in. He waited for a moment, like he was listening out for something, then he shut the door quietly.

'Listen,' he whispered.

'Mmm?'

He looked at me. 'I haven't got much time,' he said. 'They're harder to get rid of than a stone in your boot. Have you really lost your memory, or is this some scam you're working?'

When I was a kid growing up in Attica, there was this old bloke who lived on the edge of our village, and I remember talking to him one time, during the olive harvest I think it was, and he told me, 'Son, nothing bad can ever happen to you in this life if you always do the right thing and tell the truth.' He died not long after that – I can't remember if he died of some horrible disease or got murdered by thieves, it was one or the other – and I've never forgotten that bit of advice. The crucial word, of course, is always. Doesn't work without the always. If you go through life cheating people and telling lies and then suddenly try and stop, you end up in the cowplop.

So, yes, I really wanted to tell Lucius Domitius the truth, because it was the right thing to do, but it was too late for that; I'd missed out on that always part by thirty-odd years. Besides, if I'd told him that I was pretending I'd lost my memory so I could hang around some girl, when we were being chased by some nutcase who tracked us across the length and breadth of the empire to give us money in our sleep, he'd have done his block. And quite right too; if it'd been the other way round and he'd been lying to me and I'd found out, I'd have ripped his lungs out with a soupspoon.

So I gave him my extra-special blank stare. 'What the hell are you talking about?' I said.

'Oh God.' He rolled his eyes, not a pretty sight. 'Well,' he said, 'this is going to sound a bit weird. Are you ready?'

'Depends,' I said.

'Fine.' He took a deep breath 'It's like this,' he said. 'You know I told you that your name's Euthydemus, and you live in Corinth, and you and I are in the dry fish trade?'

I nodded. 'That's right,' I said. 'Actually, I think bits of it are coming back to me.'

'I doubt it,' he said, 'because it's all lies. It's not true, any of it.'

I raised my eyebrows. 'Really?'

'Really. And my name isn't Pisistratus, and I'm not your second cousin by marriage.'

Well, nobody had told me he was, so that was all right. 'So why did you say—?'

'I was lying.'

'Oh.'

I wasn't making it easy for him, no. Don't know why, but he was stood there with this desperately serious expression on his face, and I was still buzzing after chatting up Myrrhine. No excuses. I was being a bastard. Comes of not knowing who my father was, I guess.

'The truth is,' Lucius Domitius went on, 'you and I are a pair of confidence tricksters. We swindle people, that's how we earn our living. Only, we aren't trying to swindle Amyntas and his brother, and they really did save you from a collapsing building.'

'I see,' I said. 'So why are we lying to them?'

'Ah. Well, this is the bad bit. There are some men after us.'

'What, chasing us, you mean? People we swindled?'

'Could be,' Lucius Domitius said. 'The scary part of it is, we don't know who they are. But they followed us here from Sicily – that's where we were last – and they searched us out while we were asleep, and gave us some money.'

'I see,' I said. 'They gave us money, and you're saying we're running away from them. Why?' He pulled a face. 'It's complicated,' he said. 'But let's just get a few things straight. Your name,' he went on, 'is Galen.'

'Galen, right.'

'And my name – well, you call me Lucius Domitius . . .'

'But that's not your real name?'

'Well, yes,' he said, 'it is. At least, it's a bit of it. My real name is Lucius Domitius Ahenobarbus—'

'That's Roman, isn't it?'

'Yes. I'm a Roman. I was saying, my real name is Lucius Domitius Ahenobarbus Nero Claudius Germanicus Caesar Augustus.'

I giggled. 'That's a very long name,' I said.

'Isn't it? The point is, you're the only person in the world apart from me who knows that.'

'Do I? Well, I guess I must do, if you say so. Only I can't remember, see.'

He closed his eyes for a moment. 'Look,' he said. 'Do you know about the emperor Nero?'

I nodded. 'That bastard,' I said.

'Quite. Well, the truth is, I'm him. That's me.'

'Don't be silly,' I said. 'Nero's dead. Good riddance, too, by all accounts.'

'No, he's not. I mean, I'm not. I'm very much alive. I faked my death, with your brother's help, and you and I have been going around together ever since. Ten years, in fact.'

'Making a living by cheating people out of money?'

'Yes.'

'And you're really the emperor of the Romans, in disguise.'

'That's right.'

'Sorry,' I said, 'I don't believe a word of it.'

Broke my heart to do it, mind. The expression on his face was so tragic it'd have made a bailiff weep. But it was much, much too late by that stage to own up, so I was more or less stuck, and if I had to play the part, I had to do it convincingly. It's not easy, lying to someone you've known ten years (unless, of course, she's your wife).

'I'm sorry,' he said, 'but I can't prove it. I mean, I can't show you a sworn statement countersealed by the praetor's office, or anything like that.' He laughed, rather grimly. 'Dammit, I've spent so long not being Nero as hard as I possibly can, I guess I've lost the knack of being me. All I can say is, if I'm not Nero, why in hell's name would I pretend to be him? Can you think of a single good reason why someone should want to pass himself off as the most hated man in history?'

He had a point there, of course. 'It's all very well you saying that,'

I said, 'but it could be an elaborate counter-bluff. Like,' I went on, 'maybe you really are a con merchant and maybe I'm a rich mark you're trying to swindle. Pretty far fetched, maybe, but a damn sight more likely than you being a dead emperor.'

Well, it was good enough to shut him up for a moment or so. Actually, it was pretty neat, because it was just the sort of thing that'd make a reasonable scam: you get chatting in a tavern with some bloke, make it look like you've had a skinful, blurt out that really you're some desperate wanted criminal and you've got a huge stash buried somewhere, only it's no use to you because you daren't go back and get it, so you offer to sell the mark your map of where it's hidden for a few lousy gold coins. I filed that one away for future use. Waste not, want not, as we used to say back home.

He was getting really uptight, poor bastard. 'Look, you stupid Greek gallows-bait,' he said, 'if you think you're a wealthy man, just take a look at the palms of your hands, tell me if they belong on a rich man. You've just spent a couple of months bashing dirt with a mattock, because it was either that or starve.'

I looked down at my hands, just to show willing. 'Doesn't prove anything,' I said. 'For all I know, I could be a hard-working yeoman farmer, with a nice little nest egg salted away for my daughter's dowry.'

He made a rude noise. 'I promise you,' he said, 'as soon as you get your memory back, I'm going to kick your arse from here to Praeneste for that. You a hard-working farmer.'

Now that was unfair, because, if it hadn't been for the unfairness of Fate, that's precisely what I could have been. 'No more unlikely than you being the emperor of the Romans,' I said. 'All it needs is one look at you. No, I'd say you're either a retired gladiator or fresh off the galleys.'

I thought he was going to lose his temper, but he managed not to. 'Listen,' he said, 'with any luck and the god's blessing, you'll get your head unscrambled in a day or so and then you'll remember, so I'm not going to waste time and breath trying to convince you. I'm just telling you this so when you do remember, it won't come as too much of a shock. Also, if you could possibly avoid saying anything that'll get us both crucified, I'd be much obliged. All right?'

I looked him in the eye. I'm a professional, but even so it wasn't easy. 'You're weird,' I said. 'If you ask me, you're the one who needs a doctor. Still, if anybody asks, I'll tell them you aren't the emperor Nero. After all, it's the plain truth.'

He was about to say something, then he didn't, and I thought I saw a little gleam in his eye. It was only some time later that I figured out what it could be – namely, I was the only person in the world, except maybe Phaon, if the worthless little shit was still alive, who knew for sure that he was the emperor Nero. If I'd forgotten that, it couldn't exactly hurt, could it? If I genuinely didn't remember, they could put me on the rack and stick thorns under my fingernails, and I wouldn't say a thing.

'Fine,' he said. 'Just bear that in mind, and everything'll be all right.'

He left the room, and I turned over and tried to get some sleep. Fat chance. I lay there, feeling horribly guilty. Not on, I said to myself. Lucius Domitius and me, we'd been through a lot together, and hadn't I promised Callistus I'd look after the stupid idiot? All it takes is a pretty face – a pretty face with a gigantic nose, yet – and all that was going out of the window. Marvellous. And leaving that on one side for a moment, what about this mysterious threat hanging over us? When that wall fell on me, we'd been on the point of skipping Rome, jumping on board the first ship we came to, and getting as far away from the city as we could get. What was I planning on doing when the bad guys turned up – telling them they couldn't touch me because I'd just fallen in love? Yeah, right.

But it was like arguing with a little kid. You point out all the facts, make a really good case, and the little bastard just looks at you and carries on eating the worms or drinking out of the puddle. I knew I was acting crazy and dumb, but I couldn't stop myself. That's when it hit me, like a tile off a roof. I was in love. Shit.

Well, quite. It's all very well for your young sprigs of the nobility to go swanning round the place sighing and soppily grinning because some girl's just smiled at them. They've got nothing better to do with their time. They've got money dangling off their belts, and sure as hell they haven't got merciless killers or the praetor's guards trailing round after them. Love is strictly for the idle and the honest; for the likes of me, it's just not an option. Pity it doesn't know that, really, it could save a lot of unpleasantness.

I'll say this for being dead stupid, though, it means you can put deep thoughts right out of your mind pretty much at will. Useful survival trait, actually, given the number of condemned cells I've been in.

So I stopped thinking about that, and tried to figure out what I could say to Myrrhine next time I saw her, and while I was doing that, I must've fallen asleep, because the next thing I saw, apart from the insides of my eyelids, was Myrrhine herself, poised over me like a crow on roadkill with a bit of wet rag in her hand.

'Oh, I'm so sorry,' she said. 'Did I wake you up?'

'That's fine, really,' I replied. 'What time is it?'

'Oh, just after dinnertime. My brothers and your friend are finishing off the wine, so I thought I'd come and see how you're getting on. Are you feeling any better?'

Well, my headache had gone, for a start. On the other hand, since it seemed likely that me being ill was the main reason for her being nice to me, I wasn't in a hurry to admit it. 'A bit,' I said. 'My head's still very sore, of course.'

'Oh dear. Does this help?' she said, splodging me with the rag again. Actually, it was bloody annoying.

'Wonderfully,' I replied. 'If you don't mind, that is.'

'Oh no, it's no trouble.' And she stuck a corner of the rag in my eye. 'I've got some good news for you,' she said.

'Really? What?'

She smiled at me. 'Some friends of yours have turned up,' she said.

I sat bolt upright, which meant I got her little finger up my nose. 'Friends of mine?' I asked.

'There, I thought you'd be pleased,' she said. 'Who knows, as soon as you see them, maybe your memory will come back, it's often the way in these cases, according to my brother Amyntas. He was telling me, one patient he had—'

'What sort of friends?' I interrupted. 'I mean, what were they like? What did they say?'

'Well.' She put down the damp rag, not a moment too soon. 'I went down to the front room to get some more water—'

'When was this?'

'Oh, about an hour ago, while you were still asleep. Anyway, I went down to the front room, and there were these two men, a Greek with a lovely red cloak, frightfully expensive I'd say, and a little man, probably an Italian, with a bald head and a little scrubby beard. And they were asking the innkeeper, had he seen two men: a big Italian with a thick neck – that's what they said – and a Greek with a pointed face and small eyes.' She paused, looking sheepish. 'Well, what they actually said was, a Greek with a face like a polecat. I don't think you look a bit like a polecat, but—'

'That's what they said, was it? Their exact words?'

She nodded. 'So of course I said yes, they're here in the inn, only the Greek gentleman's had a terrible accident, a wall fell on him, he's upstairs in bed. And I was about to tell them about how Amyntas saved your life and wasn't it lucky, him being a doctor, when the men said thanks and they'd be back later. They didn't say how long—'

I jumped out of bed and started looking for my boots. Myrrhine gave a little squeal and spun round, probably because I wasn't wearing any clothes. 'Have you seen my boots?' I said.

'Under the bed,' she replied, without looking round. 'Really, you shouldn't be getting up, Amyntas said—'

I buggered Amyntas under my breath. 'It's all right,' I said, 'I'm feeling much better now. Have you told Lu— Have you told my friend?'

I saw the back of her head lift. 'No, he's in having dinner with my brothers, I thought I'd tell him when they've finished.'

'Wonderful,' I muttered. 'Hang on, you said this all happened an hour ago? Why didn't you tell me before?'

'You were asleep,' she said, 'I didn't want to disturb you.'

Stupid bitch, I thought, and then I thought, No, she was being considerate, she wasn't to know. 'Would you do something for me?' I asked, dragging my tunic on over my head. 'Could you nip down and tell my friend? I'm sure he'll be interested.'

'All right,' she said. 'They'll have finished their wine soon, I'll tell him then.'

'Now!' I shouted. 'I mean, I think it'd be better if you told him now, if it's all the same to you. I'm sure he'll want to be told as soon as possible.'

'Oh,' she said, 'very well. Only Amyntas gets quite annoyed if he's interrupted before he's finished his wine.'

'He won't mind,' I said, 'just this once. Please?' I added, just managing not to yell at her.

She left the room, and I looked round, trying to figure out the best way to get out of there. The window was easily big enough to get through, but there was an awful lot of empty air between the window ledge and the street below, so I didn't fancy that. The only alternative was the stairs, leading down (presumably) into the front room. Well, I thought, if I get out now, maybe it'll be all right, or I could wait for Lucius Domitius, because he'd be sure to wait for me if he was in my shoes.

The point is, some of us are naturally good people, and some of us are no good. I know I'm one of the second lot; people have been telling me this for many years, and they needn't have bothered, because something like that, you can feel it in your water. It's sad as hell and I'd far rather be good and brave and noble, but after all this time I'm resigned to it. I'm not good or brave or noble, and I never will be, and that's that. Just got to face facts and make the best I can of a bad job, namely me.

But it's not all guilt and wretchedness A good bloke – Lucius Domitius, say, and deep down he was all right, as I may have told you before – a good bloke would worry about ditching his best mate at a time like that; he'd have real trouble doing something so mean and nasty. But when you're no good, like me, you don't have to beat yourself up over stuff like that. It's my nature, you say, and you just get on with it. I remember talking about it with a philosopher back in the old days – not Seneca, one of the other philosophers, but Seneca'd have said exactly the same thing, I'm sure – and he said I was bang on the nail, because the glorious Aristotle had said pretty much the same thing, like everything's got its own nature and it can't help doing what its nature tells it to. Well, my nature was telling me to get the hell out of there, and if Aristotle says it's all right, it's all right. Right?

So there I am, scuttling down the narrow stairs like a very fast-moving crab, and I come out into what was obviously the front room. They're all the same, city inns, you can walk round them blindfold and not bump into a pillar. Unfortunately, I'd got the timing a bit wrong (probably a judgement on me for not waiting for Lucius Domitius), because standing in the middle of the room was the Sicilian bloke, the one who'd had all those soldiers killed. He had a lot of men with him, a dozen at least, and they made your champion gladiators look like flower girls.

I stopped dead, like I'd just walked into an invisible tree. The Sicilian looked at me and grinned.

'Hello, Galen,' he said.

NINE

There's a lot of people in this world who aren't particularly bothered about having their names known by strangers. Emperors, for instance, and kings, and provincial governors. Poets and singers. Artists. Gladiators. People who do running and jumping in the Olympic Games. You see one of them in the street and you call out, 'Hello there, Mylon,' or whatever his name happens to be, he doesn't swing round and say, 'How the hell do you know my name?' because he expects it, it's part of being who he is.

But when you're someone like me, hearing your name spoken by someone you don't know is generally bad news. Granted, the Sicilian wasn't exactly a stranger. I'd seen him twice before, but I hadn't precisely introduced myself either time, so if he knew my name, it was because he'd taken the trouble to find it out, and it couldn't have been easy, at that. People don't tend to waste that much effort on yours truly unless they want to do something horrible to me.

Well, I could've spun round and bolted for the stairs, I suppose, but there didn't seem to be much point. At best, we'd have met up again on the flat roof, and that'd have been wonderfully convenient for chucking me off. Also, I couldn't see me outrunning the Sicilian's men, they all looked horribly fit and agile. The idea of putting up any sort of a fight was just plain silly. Face it, I told myself, this time you're in the shit, right up to the ankles. Actually, that's not a very clever expression. I know people use it all the time, but it's not that smart. I mean, I've been up to my ankles in shit many a time, back home on the farm or walking down the street in a big city on a rainy day, and all right, it's not exactly my idea of fun, but there's worse things in life, such as having a large number of unfriendly people getting ready to grab you. Compared to that, wading about in cowplop is no big deal, trust me.

'Right,' the Sicilian said, and his blokes started to come towards me. Well, I know the drill, you stand still and don't try and fight or run, don't give them any reason to get unpleasant. The thing was, did they know the drill or were they just a bunch of amateurs? Before I could find out, though, someone right behind me at the foot of the stairs said, 'What's going on?'

Didn't have to look round to know it was Amyntas' voice. Oh dear, I thought, silly sod's going to try and intervene, which means they'll probably kick the shit out of him, and that made me feel bad. I mean, it wasn't exactly a priority in the pecking order of my emotions just then, but I spared a thought for him, even so. All he'd done was save my life, introduce me to his sister, and give me a whole lot of free medical treatment, and what was he about to get in return? Pretty unfair, I thought, though it just went to show what I'd always thought: go through life being good and kind and unselfish and helping others, and you'll end up getting your arse kicked, along with us deadbeats.

But the Sicilian raised his hand, and the heavies stayed where they were. I couldn't read his face very well, but something was bothering him. 'Hello,' he said, and he must've been talking to Amyntas, because he'd already said hello to me.

'I asked you,' Amyntas' voice said behind me, 'what you think you're doing.'

And the Sicilian didn't say a word. He just stood there, like a war memorial or something.

'Well?' Amyntas said, 'I'm waiting for an explanation.'

Me too. What I wanted to know was, why was Amyntas still alive and in one piece? Remember, I'd seen this Sicilian order his slaves to murder Roman soldiers, for no readily apparent reason. Someone who had the forged steel balls for something like that wasn't going to be scared of one solitary Egyptian doctor. Hell, even I wasn't scared of Amyntas, and every bloody thing terrifies me.

'I need to talk to this man,' the Sicilian said eventually (and his voice was all quiet and mumbly), 'It won't take a moment, if you'll excuse us.'

Amyntas pushed past me, stood between me and the Sicilian. 'I'm afraid I can't allow that,' he said. 'I'm this gentleman's doctor, and he needs his rest, he's not to be tired out with questions. If you want to talk to him, you'll have to come back later.'

The Sicilian looked at me, then at Amyntas. 'How much later?' he asked politely.

'Oh, several days,' Amyntas replied. 'He's had a very nasty bump on the head. Overtiring himself at this stage could be very serious indeed.'

I was still reeling at the shock of hearing myself referred to as *this gentleman* – thoughtless bloody thing to do, people have been known to die from laughing too much – so I wasn't even trying to figure out what was going on. Something obviously was. Mob-handed psychopaths don't tend to shrivel up with terror at the sight of small Egyptian doctors unless there's a hidden subplot. But I'm not one of those people who can't be confused and happy at the same time. Far from it. Give me food or money, or stop hitting me, and you can bewilder me as much as you like.

The Sicilian sighed. 'Fine,' he said. 'We'll come back in a few days' time, then. After all, if he's as sick as you say, he won't be going anywhere in a hurry, will he?'

Amyntas lifted his head. 'Not unless his condition deteriorates,' he replied. 'In that case, obviously, I may need to take him to one of my colleagues, someone with more expertise in this field than me.'

'I see,' the Sicilian said quietly. 'Is that likely, do you think?'

'Oh, you never know,' Amyntas said. 'They can be the very devil, head injuries.'

For some reason, the Sicilian didn't like that, or else he didn't like the way Amyntas had said it. Anyhow, he pulled a grim face. 'Let's hope he makes a speedy recovery,' he said. 'After all, he's my very dear friend. Aren't you Galen?'

I swallowed something that appeared to be taking up valuable space in my throat. 'I'm sorry,' I said, 'but I honestly don't know who you are.'

'Really? That's sad. Oh well, never mind. I'm sure with the doctor here taking care of you, it's only a matter of time.'

One of his heavies chuckled at that. Private joke, presumably. I hate those. 'Well,' the Sicilian said, 'we'd better be getting along, then.' He made a small gesture with his hand, and the heavies backed out of the doorway. He treated Amyntas to an extra special stare, then followed after them, leaving me alone with Amyntas. He frowned at me, like I'd just farted in the middle of his dinner party.

'As for you,' he said, 'I think you ought to get back to bed.'

'Really,' I said.

'Really. I don't want to worry you, but perhaps you don't realise just how serious your condition is.'

And that's no lie, I said to myself. 'Oh,' I replied. 'Well, in that case, I'll get back upstairs again.'

'Good idea. I'll come with you.'

'No, really. I can manage.'

'Are you sure?'

'Very sure, thanks.'

Soon as I was back in my room, I went to shoot the bolt, only there wasn't one. There were six nail holes in the woodwork, and a discoloured patch just where a bolt ought to have been, but no bolt. If I'd been paranoid, I'd have said somebody had taken the bolt off the door, and quite recently, too. But who'd do a thing like that?

There was, however, a tripod. Call it a tripod, more like a watchman's brazier, but in Rome it'd be a tripod, and two coppers a night extra on the price of the room because of it. Wonderful people, the Romans. You can't buy a secondhand hat in Rome, only heirloom-quality collectable headgear.

Anyhow, it had three legs and it was sturdy enough to do some good wedged diagonally against the door so I jammed it in place, lay down on the bed and did something I don't do often and am not very good at. I thought.

Mostly I thought, shit, and, Oh bugger, what've I got myself into? and a load of stuff along those lines. In the gaps between that sort of thought, I tried to fit in something a bit more constructive. For example, down the stairs probably wasn't going to get me anywhere, but up the stairs would bring me onto the roof. Rome being the crowded place it is, the gap between rooftops is often small enough that you can jump it, if you happen to be an Olympic athlete. But I didn't feel up to that sort of thing. I knew me, I'd be bound to trip over my feet as I jumped and end up in the street below, looking all flat and boneless, the way people do when they fall off very tall buildings. Or, I thought, I could go down a couple more floors, into one of the other rooms, and jump out of the window from a safe height. That had a certain specious charm to it, but I decided not to. I'm not a born gambler, but I was prepared to bet money the Sicilian's boys were watching the building from a discreet distance just in case anything interesting dropped out of the windows. That, unfortunately, was about as constructive as I could get, under the prevailing conditions.

I was lying there, toying with a bloody stupid idea about starting a fire as a diversion, when something went thump outside my door, followed by a curse and some unrefined language, in Greek.

'Go away,' I said. 'I've got a sword.'

'Fuck you, Galen,' Lucius Domitius replied through the timber-work. 'And open this bloody door, will you?'

I jumped off the bed like a cat hit by an apple core and wrenched the tripod out of the way. One of the legs came off, which tells you all you need to know about the furniture in Roman inns.

'What the hell are you doing, barricading yourself in like that?' Lucius Domitius grumbled as I opened the door. 'I walked straight into it, expecting it to open, and I've given my nose a hell of a crack.'

'Serves you right, for barging in. Listen—'

'No,' he interrupted impatiently, 'you listen for a change. You know who I've just seen, out of my window? That maniac of a Sicilian, that's who.'

'I know,' I said, and I told him what had just happened. 'So, you see—'

'Hold on.' He lifted one hand. 'Got your memory back, then, I see.'

'What? Oh, yes, it was a miracle. Aesculapius came to me in a dream and cured me.'

'Handy, that.'

'Real stroke of luck,' I agreed. 'Listen, what're we going to do? We can't stay here. It's obvious now – we weren't rescued, we were captured. We just didn't know it.'

'Quite.' Lucius Domitius nodded. 'Actually, I'd pretty much fig-ured that out for myself before I even saw the Sicilian. For one thing, whoever heard of a doctor who'd so much as look at you without money up front? I don't know Egypt, but if they've got doctors there who pay your inn bills for you, it's a weirder place than I ever imagined. And then there's the bird, the one who's been fawning over you like a lovesick dove. Obviously that can't be genuine.'

I didn't say anything. No point in getting uptight in the middle of a crisis. 'Whatever,' I said. 'The point is, how are we going to get out of this building?'

He frowned. 'We could try walking out through the door,' he said. 'I've tried it before, several times, and it works.'

'Sure,' I said. 'And even if Amyntas lets us go—'

'You think that overgrown vol-au-vent's going to stop us? Unlikely.'

'Even if Amyntas lets us go,' I repeated, 'we'll be strolling right into the welcoming arms of the Sicilian and his charm-school graduates. Let's not do that.'

'Good point.' He sat down on my bed. 'How about the window?'

'Do me a favour, we're ten stories up.'

'Oh. Roof?'

'Fuck the roof.'

He nodded. 'Yes, it's a stupid idea. We could always disguise ourselves as washerwomen and get past them that way.'

I sighed. 'For crying out loud,' I said.

'All right, all right, I'm brainstorming. Just let me think aloud, can't you?'

'Go on, then.'

'Can't think of anything else. I know,' he added suddenly, 'how'd it be if we started a fire, as a diversion? Just a small one, enough to make lots of smoke, but no actual—'

'No thanks. Burning to death is a horrible way to go.'

'True. Well, that more or less cleans me out of bright ideas. How about you?'

I sighed. 'Same here. I guess we'll just have to wait and see what happens.'

Wish I hadn't said that. I'm not a religious man, God knows, but even I know that saying something like that is asking for trouble. It's like walking up to the biggest, meanest bloke in the village, spitting in his drink and betting him five drachmas he can't bust your nose with one punch.

At least, with the gods, you don't generally have to wait too long before they kick you in the nuts. I'd hardly said those very stupid words, when Lucius Domitius raised his hand to shut me up, and sniffed.

Excellent nose he had. Well, excellent for smelling with, it wasn't exactly a thing of beauty or anything like that. But he could smell army-issue harness oil on a soldier's sandal ten heartbeats before the soldier came at us out of a dark corner yelling, 'Hey, you!' (A talent that'd saved our skins on at least three occasions over the years.) So when it came to precision sniffing, I was prepared to trust his judgement. 'What?' I asked.

'Something's burning,' he replied. 'The building's on fire.'

'Are you sure?'

He looked at me. 'You think I don't know what burning buildings smell like? Me, of all people? Shut up, I'm trying to—'

And then someone down the passageway started yelling, 'Fire! Fire!' He gave me one of those smug told-you-so looks, then jumped up and yelped, 'Bloody hell, the inn's on fire.'

Well, that's the gods for you. Really sick sense of humour, if you ask me, but don't tell them I said so. 'Fuck,' I said. 'Now what do we do?'

'Leave,' said Lucius Domitius, hurrying to the door and tripping over the remains of the tripod.

So we left.

Outside in the passageway it was thick smoke. Hits you like someone punching you in the guts, smoke. Suddenly you can't breathe, and everything stops while you try and find a mouthful of air from somewhere. So there I was, gasping like a landed fish, and some lunatic running down the passageway crashes into me and knocks me backwards, right onto Lucius Domitius. He falls down, the way you do, and I land on top of him. Well, it jolted the smoke out of us all right, and down on the floor there seemed to be rather more air, so that wasn't so bad. We took on supplies, as they say in the navy, and started crawling on hands and knees towards the stairs. A couple of other blokes dashed past us, luckily not tripping over us. Down below, I thought I heard Amyntas' voice yelling something, but he was the least of my worries just then. What was bothering me most of all was the thought of the Fire Brigade. Famous Roman institution: soon as there's a fire, they send out these lunatics armed with hammers and big hooks on poles, and they start pulling down the burning building so the fire won't spread to the surrounding houses. Good idea, unless you happen to be inside while they're at it.

'For God's sake,' Lucius Domitius spluttered behind me, 'can't you crawl any faster? I don't want the last thing I see in this life to be your wiggling arse.'

I was going to reply, because there's never any call to be gratuitously offensive, when some blokes came running up behind us, dragged us to our feet by the scruff, and boosted us down the passageway at a brisk trot. Not the way I'd have gone about it. I misplaced my lungful of clean air while I was being hauled up off the deck and caught a whole bunch of smoke instead. But next thing we knew we were being shoved down the stairs, into the front room (which was full of fire) and out into the street and the fresh air. Now that was good, let me tell you and I was just about to turn round and say thank you very much when someone bashed me on the head.

I hate getting knocked out. The getting bashed isn't so bad. It only lasts a split second and then you're fast asleep. The bummer's when you wake up. It feels like a really, really bad hangover, but without the fun of the truly epic piss-up the night before. And I don't suppose for one moment that Amyntas would've approved of me getting clobbered, not while I was still recovering from the last lot.

But what the hell. I opened my eyes anyway, just to see if they still worked, and I saw that I was in what looked like the dining room of a big, grand house, only it was rather the worse for wear. On the walls were the remains of some cute frescos: a bunch of blokes with no clothes on chasing some girls across a flower-carpeted meadow. Sadly, the panel where they caught up with them had suffered quite a bit from the damp, and all you could see was the tops of their heads and their feet. There were enough cobwebs up in the corners of the ceiling to patch up an army after a big battle, and the dust was thick on everything.

So much for the scenery, I thought, what about me? I tried to move, but found I couldn't. Well, I didn't like that at all. You can get seriously damaged, being bashed over the head. There was a bloke in our village who was stood under a tree when some clown was up in the branches doing some heavy pruning. A log fell on his head, and he was paralysed from the neck down for the rest of his life. I was just about to panic when I realised what the problem was: I was trussed up with rope, which was why I couldn't move my arms and legs. So that was all right.

Someone next to me groaned. I managed to turn my head enough to see who it was: Lucius Domitius, needless to say, all wound round with rope like a capstan on a ship. Bloody comical he looked too, though I suppose I was just the same.

'What's happening?' I asked.

He groaned again, and said, 'How the hell should I know? Where is this, anyway?' And then he caught sight of the blokes-and-birds fresco and said, 'Hang on.'

'What?'

'I know where we are. This is Cassius Longinus' house. I came to dinner here once.'

'Wonderful,' I said. 'Who's Cassius Longinus, and what're we doing in his house?'

'No idea. Only, it's not his house any more. He's dead.'

'You're sure of that, are you?'

'Positive. I ordered his execution.'

That wasn't what I wanted to hear. 'Well, it was his own fault,' Lucius Domitius gabbled on. 'He was plotting against me, absolutely no question about it, I saw the evidence and it was clear as daylight. It was me or him, and—'

'Listen,' I said, 'I don't give a stuff about some dead Roman. I don't give a stuff why you had him killed. Just a pity you didn't kill the lot of 'em while you were at it, if you ask me. What I want to know is, did he have a large family? Lots of friends? Anybody who might bear a grudge?'

He thought about it for a moment. 'Probably,' he said. 'Very popular man, I suppose that's why they thought he'd be a good choice for someone to overthrow me. Oh, I see,' he added, 'you're thinking that whoever brought us here—'

For crying out loud, I thought, I've seen statues who were quicker on the uptake. 'That's right,' I said. 'Which is why I asked the bloody question.'

Long, awkward silence as both of us realised that, even if we had figured out who it was who'd nabbed us, there was very little we could do about it, trussed up like carpets. 'Well,' Lucius Domitius said eventually, 'at least we weren't burned to death in the fire.'

I'd forgotten about the fire. Straight up. Only a short time before, we'd been moments away from a horrible death trapped in a burning building, the kind of situation honest folk have night-mares about, and what with one thing and another it'd slipped my mind, like a second cousin's birthday. It's what happens when you're having nasty adventures all the time. You get absent-minded.

'Sure,' I said. 'It's like surrendering to the enemy and winding up getting fed to the lions. I mean,' I went on, 'if this Cassius person wants to see us dead, why didn't he just leave us in there to fry? Too much time on his hands, obviously.'

'Cassius Longinus hasn't got any time at all. He's dead, remember.'

I growled. 'Well,' I said, 'when you see him on the other side of the River, any moment now, you can smash his teeth in for him. That's if they've got teeth in the afterlife.'

'I don't think so,' Lucius Domitius said. 'At least, nobody's ever mentioned it.'

'Good,' I said, 'I think I've got an abcess coming. It'll be nice to avoid that.'

Then the door at the far end of the room opened, and two of the biggest men I've ever seen in my life walked in. Not just big, as in you'd have to stand on a table to punch them on the nose. *Big* big.

'Thought we heard you talking,' said one of them cheerfully, in an unexpectedly high voice. 'How're you feeling, both of you?'

The bloke who said that was the shorter of the two, maybe by as much as a whole finger's breadth. He had high cheekbones, arms like six fat snakes having a race up a tree, and a completely bald head, not even any eyebrows. The other bloke had a face like a vulture, with long black hair tied up in a ponytail. That aside, he could have been the bald guy's big brother.

Neither of us said anything. This seemed to worry the bald man. He asked, 'Are you all right?' and sounded like he really cared. Strange, I thought.

'Of course they're not all right,' said the other one, in an accent you could've blunted a knife on. 'They're all tied up with rope. Probably got pins and needles.'

He came over and started untying my ropes, while his friend saw to Lucius Domitius. When they'd finished, and I was flexing my ankles to see if they still worked, Lucius Domitius (who'd been staring at the bald man like he'd seen a ghost or something) cleared his throat awkwardly and said, 'I know you. You're Alexander, the gladiator.'

The long-haired bloke laughed. 'Good memory you've got, chum.' Meanwhile the bald man was looking at his feet, like he was embarrassed or something.

'It is you, isn't it?' Lucius Domitius went on. 'I saw you fighting loads of times. You were really good.'

Something else I didn't want to hear. Now if he'd said, 'You were so pathetic, even I could've done you over with one arm in a sling,' that might have cheered me up.

The bald man was blushing, would you believe. 'Yeah well,' he said. 'That was a long time ago.'

'I'll say,' put in his friend. 'We been retired, what, ten years? That's right, nine going on ten. Our last fight was just before Otho got done in.' He laughed. 'That dates us,' he said. 'Half the kids you meet nowadays probably don't even know who Otho was.'

'Is it as long as that?' said Lucius Domitius. 'Good God, doesn't time fly? Seems like only yesterday I saw you take down the two German brothers – what were their names?'

Something else had just occurred to me, though it probably didn't matter. Still, he should've known better than to let on he knew who the bald bloke was. Knowing the name of the man who's just kidnapped you isn't what you'd call a survival skill.

'Segibert and Runthing,' said the pony-tail bloke, grinning. 'Don't ask him, he comes over all shy when you talk about the old days. Not me, I like remembering.'

'Just a moment.' Lucius Domitius turned and looked at him. 'Of course, I recognise you as well. You're Julianus Bolius, the two-sword man.'

Shit, I said to myself, but if Pony-tail was bothered about being recognised, it didn't show. Bad, bad sign; made it look even more definite they were going to kill us.

'That's right,' he said. 'Fancy you knowing me without my helmet on.'

'You were very good,' Lucius Domitius said. 'Wasn't it you who had that amazing bout with the Spanish net-and-fork man, Nicias or Nicomedes or something like that? You remember, where he had you flat on your back with the fork-tines at your throat, and then you did this really neat little sideways roll, knocked him off his feet, skewered him with his own fork?'

'That wasn't me.' Pony-tail shook his head. 'That was my brother Julianus Saphax, rest his soul.'

'God, yes.' Lucius Domitius was nodding frantically. 'I remember him all right. He had this move with the left arm that nobody ever seemed to be able to figure out.'

'Almost nobody,' Pony-tail interrupted, nodding his head towards his mate. 'Alexander here, he was the only one who ever managed to read it.'

'Of course, yes,' Lucius Domitius exclaimed, 'I remember, I saw that one. Your brother had Alexander up against the boards, and then quite suddenl—' He broke off, his eyes as round as soup bowls. 'My God,' he said.

The bald man had tears running down his cheeks. 'It's all right,' Pony-tail said, 'we sorted that out years ago. He knows I don't blame him, don't you, Alexander?' The bald man nodded, too upset to say anything. 'That's how it goes in the arena, you don't take it personal. I mean,' he went on, 'look at us, best mates, been together now, what, seventeen years?'

'Eighteen next February,' Alexander snuffled.

'Well, there you are,' Pony-tail said. 'See, when you're really good mates, like we are, even stuff like him killing my brother, it doesn't matter a damn. You just put it behind you and carry on.'

Alexander sat down on the floor and burst into tears. 'Still,' Pony-tail went on, in a loud whisper, 'it's probably best if you stay off that subject. He gets upset, see, and I'm the one that's got to put up with him.'

Lucius Domitius nodded, as if to say, I know what you mean. Bloody nerve. Not to mention the fact that his two heroes of the sanded arena there were the men who'd snatched us out of the inn and bashed us over the head. Somehow, I wasn't convinced that they were on our side.

Maybe Pony-tail sensed my misgivings, because he looked me in the eye and said, 'Well, I guess I owe you two an apology. About bumping you on the head, I mean. Only, what with the crowd and the fuss and all, there wasn't time to explain. Easier to fetch you here first and explain afterwards.'

Lucius Domitius looked like he was about to say, Oh that's all right, don't worry about it, so I nipped in first. 'Explain what?' I said.

Pony-tail shrugged. I guess that's what landslides on the slopes of Etna must look like. 'Not a lot I can tell you,' he said. 'Bloke we do jobs for occasionally, he comes round to see us and he says, two friends of mine are in a spot of trouble, they're being held prisoner in an inn down by Ostia Gate, I want you two to nip round there and get them out. Only be careful, he says, remember, they're my friends, and you boys don't know your own strength sometimes. So,' he went on, 'it'd be really nice if you didn't say anything about the bumps on the head, right? He'd get really snotty if he knew, stop our money and all. And let's face it, times are hard. We wouldn't be doing this sort of shit if they weren't.'

The expression on Lucius Domitius' face said he thought it was a crying shame that two famous heroes of the Grand Circus were reduced to bashing people in inns just to make ends meet. Once a pillock, always a pillock, as my old mother used to say.

'This bloke,' I said, 'the one who hired you. He wouldn't happen to be a Sicilian, by any chance?'

Pony-tail frowned. 'Don't think so,' he said. 'At least, I don't know where he's from originally. Never known him leave the city, though.'

That didn't sound right, but I carried on anyway. 'Tall bloke,' I said, 'straight nose, square jaw, dark curly hair.'

'No, that's not our bloke,' Alexander put in. 'Short, tubby little chap, bald, about four chins. Goes by the name of Licinius Pollio.'

A short, tubby chap. Shit, I thought, *him*. 'Oh,' I said, 'him. Well, you're right about one thing. He'll be pissed off if he hears you clobbered us.'

Pony-tail pulled a face. 'That's no lie,' he said. 'Nasty temper he's got, for a bloke who looks like a fattened lamb. You won't tell him, will you?'

'Of course not,' Lucius Domitius put in, before I could say anything. 'Don't worry about it. But did he say what he wanted with us?'

Pony-tail shook his head. 'Nah. Just fetch 'em to the old house and wait for me to show up, that's all. Mind you,' he went on, 'I'm surprised he hasn't shown up by now. We were supposed to meet him here at midnight and it's well past that now. I heard the cabbage carts go by outside, and that was some time ago.'

'He's a funny bloke, Licinius Pollio,' said Alexander. 'Don't suppose I should be telling you this, but he's had us following you about for the last few days. Bugger of a job finding you, we had. I mean, a big, good-looking ginger-haired Italian and a small, rat-faced Greek – not my words,' he added quickly, 'that's the description he gave us, and no names, of course, that'd have been too much like your actual help. You got any idea how many people there are answering to that description in Rome?'

Not to mention misleading, I thought. Lucius Domitius, good-looking? 'You managed it, though, obviously,' I said.

'Oh, we know our way about,' Pony-tail said. 'In our line of work, we know everybody.'

'Not the bashing people on the head business,' Alexander amended. 'That's not what we really do, except when times are hard. Really, you see, we're cooks.'

I managed to get in ahead of Lucius Domitius, though only just. 'So you've been trailing us,' I said. 'Did he say why?'

Alexander lifted his head, Greek-style. 'No. Just follow them around, was what Licinius Pollio told us; keep an eye on 'em, make sure they don't get into any bother.'

Pony-tail was grinning, which seemed to annoy Alexander. 'Sorry,' Pony-tail said, 'but we've got to tell 'em. I mean, it's the funniest thing. You won't tell Licinius Pollio we told you, will you?'

'Told us what?'

Alexander shrugged, and Pony-tail went on 'I don't know,' he said. 'I've known Licinius Pollio come out with some pretty weird stuff but that's got to be the weirdest. He said, follow them around – that's you – look out for them, and when they're asleep, he says, I want you to sneak up on them and leave this money where they can find it.'

I looked up sharply. 'Money?'

'That's right,' Alexander said. 'And then, when you dossed down for the night surrounded by all those low-lifes, I said to Julianus, we can't leave 'em there with all that money on 'em, chances are they'll never wake up again. So we had to hang around all night, just in case someone tried to rob you. Which they did,' he added, 'or they tried to. Couple of blokes, nasty-looking types they were. But we bashed 'em, and they slung their hook.'

Well, now at least I had a name for the vicious monster who'd been playing such cruel games with my head, and I don't just mean hitting it: Licinius Pollio. Never heard of him. 'Did he say anything else about us?' I asked. 'Where he knows us from, anything like that?'

Pony-tail shook his head. 'But that don't mean anything, I mean, we don't exactly chat heart to heart much, what do you expect? He doesn't invite us to dinner and introduce us to his teenage daughters, either. And before you ask, that's a what's-his-name, hypothetical. I don't know if he's got daughters, or if he's even married. I couldn't care less, either.'

'Anyway,' Alexander chipped in, 'I thought you said you knew him.'

For some bizarre reason, God only knows why, I got it into my head that I could trust these two. Anything more unlikely this side of flying elephants it'd be hard to imagine, but there it is, sometimes you get these crazy notions. I think it was because, if you ignored their extreme size and savage appearance, they reminded me a lot of my aunt Callirhoe. 'Never heard the name Licinius Pollio before in my life,' I said. 'I know a short, tubby bald Italian guy, like the one you described. I've seen him at least twice. But why in hell he should be interested in us, let alone hiring people to give us money in our sleep or rescue us from burning inns—'

Pony-tail coughed, and he had an embarrassed look on his face, along with all the fencing scars. 'In case you're getting the wrong idea,' he said, 'we didn't rescue you from the inn because it was on fire. More the other way round.'

'Excuse me?'

He pulled a weak grin. 'The inn was on fire because we were rescuing you. What I mean to say is, we started the fire. Diversionary tactics, I think they call it in officers' training. Well,' he went on as I gave him a scowl that'd have etched bronze, 'we could see there was this hired muscle staking the place out, and we didn't want to make a scene fighting our way in and out. And you might have got hurt—'

'More hurt than a heavy blow to the head,' I muttered. 'Well, couldn't have that, could we?'

Alexander made a wounded noise, like a kicked dog. 'I told you, didn't I, we shouldn't have bashed them. I said they wouldn't trust us if we did, and now look. You, you're always after the quick fix, that's your problem.'

'Don't listen to my friend,' said Lucius Domitius soothingly. 'It's just because he's short, he gets nervous around tall people. Probably I'd have done exactly the same thing in your shoes.'

That seemed to cheer Pony-tail up a lot. 'Well,' he said, 'so long as you understand. Truth is, we aren't all that clued up on this line of work. Like I said, we're only doing this because times are hard. Anyhow,' he went on, 'that's about all there is to it, really. We've been following you around, and when that building fell on your friend—'

'Oh, so that wasn't you as well, then?' I asked. I was still upset about that being-short thing. 'Only I did wonder. Seemed to me it fitted in quite nicely with your way of going about things.'

'Ignore him,' Lucius Domitius said. 'I generally do.'

Alexander grinned, while Pony-tail went on 'When that building fell on your friend, we were a bit stumped. You see, Licinius Pollio made a point of saying, keep out of the way, don't let 'em know they're being followed. Well, it's a bit bloody obvious, isn't it, saving someone from a falling building? On the other hand, he did say make sure no harm comes to them. But then those two blokes darted in and pulled you out, so we thought, well, that's all right.

But then they whisked you away like that, so we followed, and, well, you can imagine what we thought when we saw who it was'd rescued you. Didn't know what to do, did we?'

'Hold on,' Lucius Domitius interrupted. 'You recognised them?'

'Course,' Pony-tail said. 'Everybody in Rome knows those two.'

I frowned. 'You mean Amyntas and what's-his-name, his brother? The Egyptian doctors? They said they'd only been in town a short while.' I turned the frown into a scowl. 'Why are you two grinning?' I said.

'You tell him,' said Alexander, after a pause.

'Those two,' said Pony-tail. 'What did you call them?'

'Amyntas,' I said. 'And the other one, I can't remember offhand. Anyway, they're doctors, from Memphis in Egypt. And they've got a sister called Myrrhine.'

Alexander lifted his head. 'They may be from Memphis originally,' he said. 'I mean, everybody's from somewhere. Like, I'm from a small village in Thessaly, and Julianus is from Ecbatana, in the Persian empire. But they've been in Rome certainly as long as me, and I've been here twenty-two years.'

'He's right about them being doctors, though,' Pony-tail put in. 'That's what they used to do, apparently.'

'Fine,' I said impatiently. 'So what do they do now?'

Pony-tail pulled a face. 'Oh, they run one of the biggest street gangs in the city,' he said. 'The Pincian franchise, they call it. Seriously unpleasant people.'

'Hooligans,' Alexander grunted. 'Into thieving and mugging and the political stuff. And receiving, too, and kidnapping. They do a lot of that. Quite a few of the blokes we used to fight with've ended up working for them over the years. Not us, though. We don't hold with that sort of thing.'

'They're gangsters?' I said.

'Yeah, that's what I just said,' Alexander replied. 'So, as soon as we realised they'd got you, we zoomed back to Licinius Pollio and told him.'

'Didn't he ever give us what for,' Pony-tail interrupted. 'What the hell were you two thinking about, he said, letting those animals get their hands on them?'

'And then he told us to get over there right away and have you two out of there,' Alexander went on. 'But like we told you, when we got there we saw all these bad guys hanging round the place. Some of 'em were Scyphax's people—'

'Scyphax?' Lucius Domitius said.

'That's his real name,' Alexander explained, 'the one you called Amyntas, for sure. And his brother's called Biacrates.'

'What about the sister?' I asked. 'Myrrhine. Is that her real—?'

Alexander lifted his head. 'Never heard anything about any sister,' he said. 'I mean, they might have a sister, for all I know, but I never heard anybody mention one. Anyhow, some of them were Scyphax's mob, we recognised a few familiar faces. But some of 'em were Strymon's blokes, and of course Scyphax and Strymon aren't exactly what you'd call friends.'

I sighed. 'Strymon?'

'He's another big man in the gangs,' Pony-tail said. 'Heads up the Esquiline faction. They're not as big as the Pincians, but they make up for it by being extra antisocial. There was a big turf war, year before last, between their lot and Scyphax, so I can't see where the two outfits'd be working together on anything.'

Alexander nodded. 'And on top of that,' he went on, 'there was a whole bunch of 'em we don't know from anywhere. Either they're new in town, or they were brought in specially. God only knows whose side they're on.'

My head was starting to swim before he said that. 'Bloody hell,' I muttered. 'And all this because of us? Really, they needn't have bothered.'

'Anyhow,' said Pony-tail, 'with all that lot out there, we had a Samnite's chance in a brothel of just strolling in the front door and collecting you. So we snuck round the back and started the fire. Seemed like a good idea.'

'Well, it worked,' said Lucius Domitius. I noticed he'd gone all pale and thoughtful, and no wonder. One thing I felt absolutely sure of, it wasn't me that all these high-powered gangsters were after. 'And you've got no idea why they were after us,' Lucius Domitius went on, 'these gang people, I mean, Scyphus and whatever the other one's called.'

'Scyphax,' Alexander corrected him. 'And Strymon. Sorry, no idea. I mean, we could get hold of one of their people and see if we could squeeze it out of him, but I don't think it'd get us anywhere. One of the gangs' strong points is the grunts don't ever know what the bosses are up to. Security, you see.'

'Anyhow,' Pony-tail said, 'you don't have to worry about them any more, or at least not for now. Licinius Pollio isn't a gang boss, if that's what you were thinking.'

'Fine,' I said. 'So what does he do, then?'

'Slaves, mostly,' Alexander said. 'All honest and above board, mind. Mostly he leases building workers to the government. He's got half a dozen brothels as well, and he deals in the better grades as a sideline, houseboys and clerks and pages, that sort of thing. Wealthy man, by all accounts.'

Somehow, that didn't make me feel any better about Licinius Pollio. But Lucius Domitius said, 'You know, now you say that, I think the name's vaguely familiar. Didn't he start out in a small way about twenty years ago, buying and selling gladiators?'

'That's him,' Pony-tail said. 'And that's how we got to know him, of course. It was him sold us to the tribune when we started off in the fight game.'

'Practically family,' I muttered, but nobody took any notice of me.

'Talking of Licinius Pollio,' Alexander yawned, 'where the hell's he got to? Not like him to be so late, usually he's really punctual.'

Pony-tail shrugged. 'Got held up somewhere,' he said. 'Busy man like that. Or I suppose Scyphax or Strymon could've caught up to him, but I doubt that, he's too sly. Got to get up with the shepherds to pull one over on Licinius Pollio.'

He didn't seem particularly worried at the thought, so I decided I wouldn't worry about it either. After all, if I wanted to worry (which I didn't) I was pretty much spoiled for choice. If I felt like it, I could worry about why not one but two Roman street gangs were fighting over our worthless carcasses, or why in hell Licinius Pollio had appointed himself our personal defender and welfare bureau, or whether Lucius Domitius was too hopelessly smitten with hero-worship to take a chance to escape if one presented itself, or where our next meal was coming from. Stuff like that: ordinary, humdrum concerns. I expect you lie awake at night fretting about much the same thing. But I was buggered if I was going to worry about the well-being of some rich Roman nutcase I'd seen twice, even if he had bought me a skinful of disgustingly bad wine that night in Ostia. Life's too short.

'Anyhow,' Pony-tail yawned, 'doesn't look like he's going to show up tonight, so we might as well turn in. Afraid we didn't think to fetch along any blankets, didn't think we'd be spending the night here.' He glanced at Lucius Domitius. 'You can have my cloak if you like,' he said. 'I don't feel the cold much.'

Lucius Domitius said he wouldn't dream of it, he'd be perfectly comfortable as he was; and, since nobody seemed inclined to offer me anything, that was that. The two uglies sort of propped themselves up against the wall, like trestle tables when dinner's over, and started snoring in counterpoint. The door, I noticed, didn't seem to be locked.

Well, I thought. Mercury helps them as helps themselves, as they say in the thieves' guild. Both of them looked like heavy sleepers, we'd be well away by the time they woke up. Go for it, I thought. So, like a fool, I crept over to the corner, where Lucius Domitius was trying to make a pillow out of his boots, and nudged him in the ribs.

'Time to go,' I whispered.

He lifted his head and looked at me as if I was a mosquito who'd just bitten the tip of his nose. 'What?'

'The door's open. Your two pals are asleep. Let's get the hell out of here, while we can.'

He yawned. 'Why would we want to do that?' he said.

There were times when I could've strangled him, if only my hands weren't too small to fit round his big fat neck. 'Don't be bloody stupid,' I said. 'We're prisoners. Escaping is what prisoners do.'

'No we aren't,' he replied, a bit too loud for comfort. 'We're guests. Something like that, anyway. Besides, it's late and I'm knackered.'

'You moron,' I hissed, 'what's happened to your brain since we got here? Or did your gladiatior chums knock it out your ear when they kidnapped us?'

He clicked his tongue. He could click his tongue more annoyingly than anybody I've ever met. 'You aren't still going on about that, are you? Weren't you listening when Julianus Bolius explained? It was the only way to get us out of there without attracting attention.'

I could've screamed, only I had more sense. 'This is crazy,' I said. 'Just because these two bruisers were your pin-up boys back in the old days—'

'Rubbish.' He scowled at me, and even though the light from the lamps was getting dim I could see he'd gone a sort of Tyrian purple colour. 'Just perfectly ordinary straightforward admiration for two great sportsmen. It's one of the finer things in life, so naturally you wouldn't understand.'

Well, they say owners get like their pets over the years, but for the life of me I couldn't remember Lucius Domitius ever keeping a tame idiot. 'Let's not argue about that now,' I said. 'The point is, we're free to go. So let's go.'

'No'

What I should have done is left him there. God knows, that's what I ought to have done. Wouldn't you? I mean, suppose you and your brother are being chased by a pack of wolves, and suddenly your brother stops dead and turns round and walks towards the wolves saying, 'Hooza *good* doggie, den?' Surely that's where brotherly love and family duty stop, and you can walk away without any risk of the Furies coming and nagging at you in the wee small hours. I never got around to discussing the point with Seneca – pity, really – but I'm sure he'd have been right behind me on this one. We all have an obligation to look after our family and our friends, but not when they're acting like stupid arseholes.

But I didn't. Instead, I said, 'Why the hell not?'

'Because,' Lucius Domitius replied, as if he was explaining something simple to a backward child, 'these people are on our side. I can feel it, in my bones. After all, if they'd wanted to kill us—'

'Balls,' I said. 'They could just as easily be taking us to be horribly tortured by some noble git who hates you from the old days. There's enough of 'em, God knows, the sort who'd reckon that you burning to death or getting stabbed by mobsters'd be the next best thing to giving you a free pardon.'

He wrinkled his nose at me, the bastard. 'Bit far-fetched, isn't it?' he said. 'I think it's much more likely that this Licinius Pollio's someone I did a good turn for in the old days, and he's repaying the favour. Everything I've heard so far makes me feel sure he's a friend.'

'You haven't got any friends,' I said. 'Nearest thing you've got to a friend is me, and I hate you. Now stop pissing about and shift your useless bum, before you wake up the gladiators.'

He sniffed. 'Nothing stopping you going,' he said, 'if that's what you want to do. You bugger off out of it, and try not to get caught next time you try stealing purses, because I won't be there to rescue you.'

I ask you. Why would a man, an ordinary bloke like me with no great pretensions at being good or brave or any of that shit, why would a normal bloke like me stick with such an ungrateful, mean, stupid arsehole? Because Callistus told me to, maybe. But if Callistus himself had talked to me like that (he never would have, so it's a bad example), I'd have turned on my worn-down little heel and left him standing there. Honest, I would. I'd never have forgiven him. So why – *why*, for crying out loud – didn't I take my chance and go, right then, without another word?

Beats me. I guess I must be really, really, really, really, really stupid.

'Fine,' I said. 'We'll stay here. And when they're hanging us upside down over a roaring fire and beating us to death with thin sticks, maybe you'll say you're sorry, you should've listened to me. It'll be something for me to look forward to.'

He sighed. 'Really, Galen,' he said. 'You do go on sometimes. Look,' he added, in a thoroughly offensive attempt to make up the quarrel, 'it's all very well being cautious, we've had to be very care-ful who we trust, I know that. But give me some credit for being able to judge human nature. These two are all right, take my word for it.'

'You,' I said. 'A judge of human nature. Now I've heard every-thing.'

'Well,' he replied, 'I didn't want to bring this up, but I'm not the one who was mooning around like a lovesick calf over some gang-ster's moll.'

Gangster's moll – where did he pick up an expression like that? 'Sure,' I said. 'And whose word have we got that that's what she is?

Your two bosom buddies over there, and that's all. Personally, I wouldn't believe them if they told me cowshit stinks.'

He yawned, and stretched. 'If you're going,' he said, 'go. If not, push off and let me get some sleep. It's been a long day.'

It was either clear off and leave him, or crawl away into a corner and keep my face shut. And I thought, all right then, Zeus, you made me the way I am, you sent me into this world with a face like a rat and enough brains to fill half a walnut shell. Presumably you had your reasons, and I'm not going to try and guess what they were. Now it's up to you, Zeus. I've done my best. I've been doing my best with this shit you gave me for forty bloody years. It's time for you to mind the store, Zeus, and I'll just cruise along for a while and see how well you get on, and maybe after a bit you'll realise what rotten bloody hard work it is being me, and what I've got to put up with. And maybe then you'll stop emptying your chamber pot of horrible adventures over my head every time it gets full.

I don't suppose Zeus was even listening. I've been talking to him on and off ever since I was a kid, and I've never seen or heard anything to suggest he's listened to me even once.

So I snuck away into the opposite corner, wedged my back into the angle of the wall, drew my knees up in front of me and sort of half-closed my eyes, so I could go to sleep without taking my eyes off the door. Sounds difficult, but I must've managed it somehow, because the next thing I remember was sunlight streaming in through a hole in the roof, and a strange smell I hadn't come across in years. A really good cooked breakfast.

TEN

Straight up. Would I lie to you about a thing like that?

We didn't go in much for cooked breakfasts back when I was a kid. For one thing, for a cooked breakfast you need to have something to cook, and usually we didn't. For another, we were always up at the crack of dawn, out in the fresh air weeding the vines or leading the goats up the mountain, with a little wicker basket with the stale end of a loaf and a small onion in it, if we were lucky. But they had cooked breakfasts in the Golden House, back when Callistus and I were living there as honoured guests of the emperor Nero, and I can't say as I remember them smelling anything near as good as what was wafting in through the door.

Well, I thought, if I'm going to cross the River today, might as well do it on a full stomach. So I got up and wandered over to the door, limping because of the cramp and the pins and needles. You try sleeping hunched up in the corner of a derelict dining room some time, and you'll see what I mean.

'There you are.' Lucius Domitius was standing in front of a big brass tripod, stirring something in a fat round copper pot. 'Just in time for the food, as usual. You must have a little voice in your head, like Socrates, to tell you about meal times.'

'Fuck you,' I replied affably. 'Where have your friends got to?'

'Alexander's fetching water from the pump,' he replied, 'and Julianus Bolius has nipped out to the market for some fenugreek. Won't be long.'

'And what do you think you're doing?'

'Stirring the fish sauce,' Lucius Domitius replied, as if it was crazy to imagine he could possibly be doing anything else.

Bizarre. No other word for it. Because the crazy fool still hadn't tumbled to the fact that we'd been kidnapped by those two – snatched, abducted, taken prisoner, whatever. He seemed to be under the impression that this was some kind of house party, and that any moment now this Licinius Pollio would come tripping in through the door and ask us if we fancied joining him and the others for a quick game of handball in the courtyard. So there he was, helping the two thugs to fix breakfast. And to think, a complete shit-for-brains like that was once in charge of the entire Roman empire. There's got to be a better way of running things than that.

'Right,' I said. 'Fish sauce. Great. And I suppose there's sweet and sour pork and honeycakes to follow.'

'With fish sauce? For breakfast? You're weird.'

On the other hand, I thought, the fish sauce did smell rather good, and my stomach felt like I hadn't eaten since Theseus grew out of bedwetting. I guess Seneca would've called it pragmatism: if you're stuck with a madman cooking up a fish breakfast waiting to be horribly killed, you might as well eat the fish breakfast as not. Well, it's a philosophy. Everybody needs a philosophy, after all.

Then Alexander came in with the water jug. He didn't seem to notice me, which suited me just fine, but he peered over Lucius Domitius' shoulder to see how the fish sauce was getting along, and nipped a pinch of some yellow powder out of a little wooden chest lying on the floor. To see him sprinkling it over the pot, scientific as a Cretan doctor opening a bloke's head, you'd have thought that getting the fish sauce just right was the only thing that mattered in the whole wide world.

Pony-tail came breezing in with a basket of greens and stuff, and Lucius Domitius was relieved of duty while the two bruisers fussed over their creation. Actually, it wasn't hard to believe that they really were cooks first and hired killers second. I've been in enough market squares in my time to know that if you're after a cook, look around until you find the biggest, toughest, most evil-looking blokes present, and they'll be the cooks. There's something about the profession that attracts large men with violent dispositions, apparently. It's the big knives, if you ask me.

It seemed to take them for ever to get it just right; but in all fairness I've got to say, those two were good at their job, and if I'd been a senator's steward organising a big dinner party, I'd have had no hesitation about hiring them. Tuna steaks on wheat bread with a rich cream sauce, garnished with stuffed songbirds and crisp garden vegetables, as good as what we'd been used to up at the Golden House, if not better.

Well, we'd eaten the meal and were finishing up the sauce with the last of the bread, when the door opened and a girl walked in—

Come on, Galen, you can do better than that. Just because something you say is more or less true, doesn't mean to say it's *really* true, because simply reciting the facts is sometimes not enough. For instance, I could say, there was this bloke who got lost on his way home, but he got there in the end, but it wouldn't be the *Odyssey*. It'd be true, because that's what happened, but I'd have left so much out and done so little justice to the story that it'd be misleading.

Let's try that again.

The door opened. Right, that's fine, it didn't fly open or slowly drift open with a sinister creak. And yes, a girl came in. Short, dark complexion, hair piled up on top of her head, about nineteen years old. And yes, this girl wasn't spectacularly beautiful or anything like that, she was nice-looking in a cutesy sort of a way, no more than that. And she didn't come in dancing or balancing a blazing torch on the tip of her nose, she just sort of walked through the door, the way people walk, until she was about three feet from where I was sitting cross-legged on the floor, and then she stopped. That's a pretty accurate description of what happened, but it's still not *really* true, because you could read that and think to yourself, Well, a girl's just walked in, so what, big deal. If you've been eating fried food and smudged the page with your greasy fingers, you could miss the whole thing; or maybe the rats have got into your cupboard and nibbled holes in your book. You could pass the whole incident by without really taking any notice, and then, when the important stuff starts happening later on, you wouldn't have a clue how or when or where it started. Well. I'm no artist, I'm not good with words, so I can't think of a way of doing this subtly. All I can do is tell you that a girl walked in, and it's a really big deal, so pay attention.

'There you are,' she said.

Alexander looked up. 'Hello, Blandinia,' he said. 'Where's Pollio got to?'

She looked at him and clicked her tongue. 'He's been waiting for you all night,' she said, 'over at the old house, where you're supposed to be. He's not happy.'

'But this is the old house,' Pony-tail interrupted.

She sighed. 'No,' she said. 'This is the old ruined house. The old house is two doors down from the temple of Luna, five minutes north of here. You've screwed up again,' she said.

Alexander and Pony-tail looked at each other.

'Fuck,' said Pony-tail.

'I thought so,' the girl went on. 'We've all been hanging around the old house like a flock of geese waiting for the spring. There's flute-players and harpists and actors and cooks and waiters and a couple of exotic dancers, on time and a half, the lot of 'em, and all this time you've been here. Next time you're given your instructions for a job, you might try listening.'

'I'm sure he said the old ruined house,' Alexander said lamely, though his heart obviously wasn't in it. 'I guess I must've got the wrong end of the stick.'

The girl grinned spitefully. 'You'll be lucky if that's all you get when Pollio gets hold of you,' she said. 'And usually he's such a nice, easy-going man. Don't know when I've seen him so upset. Now then,' she went on, turning to look at Lucius Domitius in a way that suggested that the two gladiators had suddenly ceased to exist, 'you must be Nero Caesar. My name's Blandinia, I'm Licinius Pollio's freedwoman. If you're ready to leave, we really ought to be getting along.'

Something hurt my toe. It was only some time later that I figured out it must've been the heavy red earthenware dish I'd been holding in both hands. And if I was poleaxed, you can guess how Lucius Domitius reacted. He sort of shimmered from head to foot, like a reflection in water when someone throws a stone in the pool. 'Excuse me?' he said.

The girl Blandinia frowned ever so slightly. 'I'm sorry,' she said. 'You are Nero Caesar, aren't you?'

There were a lot of things Lucius Domitius could've said at that moment, but instead he chose 'Yes.'

'I thought so,' Blandinia replied. 'You're just how Licinius Pollio described you.' Then she turned her head and looked at me. 'And you must be Galen,' she said. 'Are you ready?'

There was something about her. You know in the fairy stories, the way that looking into the gorgon's eyes was supposed to turn you to stone. Well, looking Blandinia in the eyes was a bit like that, only instead of changing you into a block of marble, it made you tell the truth. Main difference being, they had the sense to kill the gorgon, first chance they got, while this Blandinia was not only alive, but apparently allowed out in public without an armed escort.

'Yes,' I said.

'Come along, then,' she said briskly, like I was the family dog, and that seemed to be the finish of her interest in me. She turned back to Lucius Domitius and said, 'Well, at least you've had something to eat. I hope these two have been looking after you properly.'

'Oh, yes,' Lucius Domitius replied (which makes me wonder if the truth thing only applied to me). 'They've been really kind and helpful.'

'That's all right, then,' she said. 'Maybe we won't have them killed, after all.'

To be fair, it probably was a joke. It just didn't sound anything like one, that was all.

Anyway. Next thing I knew, I was hoppiting along behind, trying to keep up with this girl and Lucius Domitius as she led the way out of the house, round the back and out onto the street. 'It's a great shame you missed the reception,' she was saying, 'Licinius Pollio'd gone to a lot of trouble to make sure everything would be nice. Never mind, though,' she said, 'can't be helped now.'

Alexander and Pony-tail were following on behind me, so if the thought of making a run for it crossed my mind, it didn't hang about there long enough to take its boots off or wash its hands. We marched down an alley, through a courtyard, up another alley – by that time my sense of direction was completely fuddled, so I stopped trying to keep track of where we'd been and tried to get talking with the girl hoping I'd be able to get some kind of clue from her about what was going on. But she was as smart as a lawyer, and I got nothing out of her.

We hadn't been walking all that long when, quite suddenly,

Blandinia stopped dead in her tracks and pushed open a little narrow door in a plain brick wall. It looked like the entrance to some warehouse, but on the other side was a magnificent entrance hall, with mosaics on the floor and amazing painted plasterwork – a lion hunt in Persia, a storm at sea with ships rolling about, the wooden horse of Troy being dragged in through the city walls, and a load of other stuff, very tasteful and not long painted, judging by the damp smell of the plaster. It all seemed a bit odd, such an extravagant display of wealth tucked away behind a miserable little door in a grotty alleyway, but then I remembered something I'd overheard in an inn a few years back, about how the rich Romans were getting cagey about being conspicuous – something to do with the unusually high proportion of rich men who found themselves in court on treason charges (where the guilty party's property gets confiscated by the emperor if he's convicted). Fair enough, I thought. If flashing your money around is going to land you in the dock, there's a lot to be said for making yourself hard to notice. Of course, these trumped-up treason charges were supposed to have been one of the great evils of Nero's reign, which the noble Vespasian had put a stop to, but maybe nobody had told Licinius Pollio that, or maybe he was just one of those paranoid types who never trust the government. Some people are like that, apparently.

A porter met us at the threshold (which was decorated with one of those beware-of-the-dog mosaics with a picture of a huge lifelike Spartan hound; a lot of people like them, though I reckon they're too cutesy for words, almost as bad as the dinky little silver skeletons people have as centrepieces for dinner parties) and led us into the dining room. Nice place Licinius Pollio had, I'll give him that. There was an enormous double lamp hanging from the ceiling on a gilded chain so you could see right around the room. The furniture wasn't very old but it was all good stuff, lots of gilding and ivory panels, and loads of cushions everywhere – real Levantine purple, not the cheap imitation. One nice touch I noticed in particular: the ceiling was painted blue, with flying birds and a big yellow sun and everything. Made the place seem light and airy, like you were having your dinner outside.

And there, standing in the middle of the room fussing over something with the chief steward, was that same tubby little man I'd first met in Ostia, the one who'd given me a whole denarius to get zonked on. He raised his head as we walked in, looked straight past me as though I wasn't there, and started gazing at Lucius Domitius like he'd seen a god or something. 'Welcome, welcome,' he called out, scurrying across the room to meet us, 'do please come in, make yourself at home. And your friend,' he added, as an obvious afterthought.

Tactically, we were badly placed. Alexander and Pony-tail had parked themselves in the doorway, like Horatius and his buddies getting ready to hold the bridge against the Etruscans. Aside from getting past them, which would've been tricky without cavalry support at the least, and probably elephants, it didn't look like there was any other way out of the room. If we'd been fetched here to be horribly put to death, I couldn't see there was much we could do about it.

If he was planning on killing us, either he was going to feed us first, like farmers do with pigs before sending them to market, or else he hated us so much he was planning on eating us afterwards. The place was rigged out for a high-class dinner, little tables dotted around the floor with silver dishes of interesting little concoctions involving dead birds and sausages, two rather fancy bronze donkeys with panniers full of fresh olives, that sort of thing. Expensive and tacky, unless they were presents from people he didn't want to offend. Not that I gave a damn. Personally I like tacky. What else would you expect from someone like me? No, the only reason I even bothered looking was because you can tell so much about a person by the things he puts on display when company's expected, and at that precise moment, I wanted any hints I could get about who we were up against. All in all, the decor and effects seemed to suggest either someone who'd been poor and come into money, or a man who knew what he liked and didn't give a toss – the boss of a street gang, for instance, someone like that.

I had plenty of time to look around, because the tubby little guy, Licinius Pollio, was stood there in front of Lucius Domitius like he'd taken root, staring. Just when I was starting to get fidgetty, like you do when you've been standing in one place for a while, the tubby little guy cleared his throat and said, 'This is indeed an honour,' or something like that. Lucius Domitius smiled feebly and said, 'Oh, right,' and the tubby guy beamed. Honestly, you could've snuffed out that fancy lamp of his, and we'd still have been able to see.

'In fact,' he went on, 'this is a lifetime's ambition for me.' He paused, like he was trying to swallow a whole apple. 'I'm sorry,' he said, 'that must sound very crass, but the truth is, I'm rather at a loss for words. I'm not usually like this, I promise you.'

'That's all right,' Lucius Domitius said awkwardly, 'don't worry about it.' He gave Pollio his best stuffed-frog look, and then asked, 'Sorry if this sounds rude, but what are we doing here?'

For a moment, Pollio looked like he didn't understand. Then he blinked like a lizard and said, 'Well, really, I just wanted to meet you, really. I know, it sounds silly, but it's true. You see,' he went on, speeding up suddenly like a cart rolling down a hill, 'the fact is, I happen to think that your music and your poetry – well, they're wonderful. I've got copies of all your poems I could find, I've been collecting them for years, and whenever I meet someone who'd been at one of your recitals, I pester them to hum me the tunes, and I've got a slave, a Sardinian, wonderfully clever fellow, who writes them all down in little marks and squiggles on a wax tablet, and works them up so my musicians can play them. I've got twelve full-time musicians, you know, and all they do is play your music, and I sent to Antioch specially for a very famous singer I'd heard about, he wasn't cheap but I felt that only the best would be worthy of your songs – Diomedes of Antioch, maybe you've heard of him? No? Well, never mind. Anyway, he sings and the musicians play for me three times a day, after breakfast, lunch and dinner, and I've got a couple of quite decent flute-players who do medleys of your work at other times during the day, when I'm alone or exercising or having a bath. And also, something I'm really excited about, I managed to get hold of the harp you played when you gave your first public recital at Naples; it took me ages to track it down, a captain in the guards had it and it cost me an arm and a leg, but now of course it's one of my most treasured possessions. And—' He stopped and caught his breath, as if he'd just run the foot race at the Olympic games. 'Well,' he said, 'like I told you, I just wanted to meet you and, well, say thanks, for all the wonderful hours of pleasure you've given me.'

Well. I've got to give Lucius Domitius his due; he took it very well, considering. Me, in his place, either I'd have strangled Licinius Pollio right there on the spot for scaring us half to death and having his tame thugs bash our heads in, or else I'd have burst out laughing so hard I'd have split a gut. Not Lucius Domitius. He just stood there, mouth slightly open, didn't say a word. I've seen livelier corpses in plague pits.

'Anyway,' Licinius Pollio went on, 'that's all I wanted to say. And now, if you'd care to join me for a bite to eat, I'd be honoured. Epaphroditus, water and towels for our guest.'

A little skinny kid with curly hair bounded forward with a silver bowl and started washing Lucius Domitius' hands, and I don't think he noticed until the kid started trimming his fingernails with a little silver knife, he was so stunned by the whole business. Then another bloke, who for some reason was got up as Cupid or Ganymede or someone like that, steered him over to a couch and shoved him onto it in a duly obsequious manner, whereupon a whole bunch of slaves swooped down and shoved dishes of food under his nose, until he was surrounded by them and I couldn't see him any more. At this point, a rather less elegant bloke tapped me on the shoulder and pointed to a smaller, plainer couch stuck behind a pillar. Well, only a mug stays standing up when he can lie down, so I went where I'd been told and waited for the food to come round, which it did eventually. I was still pretty well stuffed with Alexander's fish sauce, but one thing you learn when you're on the road is to eat first while it's going and worry about digesting it later. Very tasty, those snacky things, though maybe a bit salty for me, and you had to eat a whole plateful of the little savoury things in pastry to fill yourself up.

Our host, meanwhile, was perched on the couch next to Lucius Domitius. He wasn't eating anything, he was too busy chattering away, about how *The Fall of Troy* was probably his favourite of Lucius Domitius' works, either that or *Orestes The Matricide*, depending on what mood he was in, though he really loved that long, slow bit in *The Transformation of Arachne*, and why was it he'd never done anything like that again, it was a pity, not that he didn't like the later stuff, don't get him wrong, but there was something special about the early works, he must've heard *Telemachus at Pylos* forty times if he'd heard it once, it was pure genius – I stopped listening after a while, because even a country boy like me knows it's really bad manners to throw up at a posh dinner party.

'Have some tripe,' said a voice beside me. It was Blandinia, the girl who'd fetched us. She was grinning.

'Don't mind if I do,' I said. 'Can I ask you something?'

'Sure. What's on your mind?'

I jerked my head at Pollio. 'Is he for real?' I said. 'I mean, this isn't some horrible ruse, is it, to soften us up or lull us into a false sense of security?'

She lifted her head, Greek style. 'Hardly,' she said. 'If you need proof, I'll hum you the whole of *The Bed of Procrustes*. I've heard it so often, I know the rotten thing by heart.'

'More than I do,' I said. 'In fact, I don't remember that one at all. Truth is, I wouldn't know it from a vaudeville number. I'm not really musical.'

'Me neither.' The grin softened into a smile. 'In this house, though, you don't get much choice. So,' she went on, 'you're Galen.'

'That's right,' I said. 'How come you've heard of me, then?'

'Oh, I remember you from the old days.' She laughed, though it wasn't the friendliest noise I've ever heard, if you see what I mean. 'You haven't got any idea who I am, have you? Well, no reason why you should, I was just a kid back then, obviously.' As she said that, she looked past me at Lucius Domitius, who was still listening to Pollio telling him how clever he was, rather like a harbour wall listens to the sea. 'Hardly likely really, that you'd notice a slave's kid running round the kitchens. My dad was a cook, you see, and my mother worked in the laundry. Slaves aren't usually noticed at the best of times. As for their kids, unless they smash a vase or make a noise when there's company in the house, they're pretty well invisible.'

'Oh,' I said. If I'd thought it'd have helped, I'd have said how good the food always was and how clean the sheets were, but I got the impression that she wouldn't have been impressed. 'So that's how you know me, then,' I said.

She nodded. 'You and your brother,' she said. 'Actually, I liked him. One day, he caught me stealing grain out of a jar in the store-room, and I thought he'd tell on me for sure, but he just smiled and gave me an apple. I'd never had an apple before, would you believe?'

That sounded like Callistus all right, doing good deeds all over the shop, harvesting hearts and minds wherever he went. Nothing like that ever happened to me. I mean, I never caught kids thieving from jars or any of that stuff, so I never got the chance to be generous and lovable. What I always say is, if you don't get the breaks in this life, what can you achieve? Bugger all.

'Ah, right,' I said, or something equally memorable.

'I was sorry when I heard he'd died,' she went on. 'I remembered him very well. You can imagine: you see, I was convinced the nice man who'd given me the apple was Nero Caesar – after all, they looked so much alike, didn't they? – and then when I told my dad he just laughed and said no, that must've been the emperor's Greek friend, Callistus. And then when I met Nero Caesar the second time – well, I realised Dad must've been right. Anyway, that's why I remember him, and you too, for that matter. I think your brother was the first person I'd ever met who was nice to me for no reason – not being family, I mean, or a friend of my parents.'

'Excuse me,' I interrupted, as something she'd said sank in, 'you heard that Callistus was dead? Who from?'

She looked at me for a moment, completely blank-faced. 'It was about five years ago,' she said. 'I wasn't with Licinius Pollio then, I was still a slave. Actually, I was working in a brothel, but we won't go into that. Things weren't very nice for Nero Caesar's household after he was thrown out, people seemed to blame us for what'd happened. I suppose it was because he'd gone and we were still there. Anyway, one of my clients—' She looked away as she said the word. 'He was a soldier, and he'd been one of the men who went to Phaon's villa to arrest Nero Caesar – only they got there too late, of course, didn't they, and he was already dead. The soldiers all got into terrible trouble for that, needless to say. The officer was cashiered, if that's the right word, and the men were posted to all sorts of horrible places, very cold or very hot, and nearly all of them were killed or fell sick and died. But this man – he'd been sent to the German frontier, which is the worst posting you can get, apparently – he'd survived and finished his tour and come back, which is when I met him. Often the clients get talking when they're done, they're often the sort of people who don't have anybody much to talk to, and when I told him in passing I'd been raised in the Golden House, he started telling me the story, about going to Phaon's villa and seeing the dead body, and everybody taking it for granted that it was Nero Caesar, because it looked pretty much like the face on the coins and the statues. But when they took the body back to the city and had various people examine it, just to make sure, there was this Greek doctor who was absolutely certain the body wasn't Caesar, because he'd treated Callistus for a burn on his arm a few weeks earlier, a lamp that got knocked over or something, and he saw the scar.'

I looked at her. I remembered; it'd been me that knocked the lamp over. 'Go on,' I said.

'Well,' she continued, 'the Greek doctor told the sergeant who'd brought the body in, and the sergeant scowled at him and said, Are you sure? And the doctor said, Positive, the scar's exactly where the burn had been, and he'd also examined Caesar for a strained elbow tendon, caused by too much harp practice or whatever, and there hadn't been any scar there that he might have mistaken for the one on Callistus' arm. The sergeant didn't like that at all, because everybody else he'd asked had sworn blind the body was Caesar, but he reckoned he couldn't keep quiet about a thing like that. So he went to his officer and told him; and the next thing they all knew, they'd got their new postings and never saw each other again. But there was another funny thing, the soldier told me: that doctor, the one who noticed the scar, he got sent to Africa as the governor's personal physician, and he hadn't been there a week when he was stabbed to death in the marketplace by some robbers. Strange, really, don't you think?'

'Odd coincidence,' I agreed. 'Assuming it was all true, that is. I mean, you're right, it was Callistus who got killed, not Lucius Domitius, but for all you knew your soldier could've been making things up, him or the man he got it from.'

She nodded. 'I wondered about that, too,' she said. 'So a while later I asked around, people I'd known in the old days – some of us managed to keep in touch, friends of my parents mostly – and it so happens that a boy I grew up with had become a clerk at the palace; and I was talking to him about this, and he suddenly went quiet, so I asked him what the matter was, and he told me there's a whole file of letters and reports in his department, which he'd been told to make copies of three or four times, all about a pair of petty criminals who keep turning up all over the empire, and they look uncannily like Nero Caesar and one of his hangers-on from the Golden House. Well, I told this clerk, there's a simple explanation for that, and didn't he remember Callistus, who looked just like Caesar, and that brother of his (meaning you); and you'd disappeared the same time as Nero Caesar died, so wasn't it likely that these two petty criminals were Callistus and Galen? But my clerk friend said they'd thought of that, soon as the first reports came in, and there was a letter on file sending an officer to investigate, and a few pages on, the officer's report, where he said he'd been out and found the two men and talked to them—'

'Excuse me?' I said. 'That's not right.'

She nodded. 'I know,' she said. 'Remember, I said this was a while after I'd met the soldier. Well, in the meantime I'd been bought from the cathouse by Licinius Pollio, who'd apparently been to some trouble to track me down, because I'd known both Callistus and Nero Caesar. Anyhow, the name of the officer who made out the report was Licinius Macer, who just happens to be our Pollio's nephew. In fact, Pollio had bought him his commission not long before.'

'I see,' I lied. 'So it was Pollio who found out—'

She lifted her head. 'He had a pretty good idea by then,' she said, 'but it wasn't till I told him about the soldier I'd met that he was absolutely sure. Then he told me to go back and chat up my friend the clerk, and see if I couldn't get a copy of the whole file out of him. Well, he didn't like the idea, but he'd always been soft on me, from way back, and I asked him very nicely, and so Pollio got his copy. Meanwhile, my clerk kept me up to date on further sightings of you two for about two years, and then one day he told me he couldn't help me any more, because the file had been taken away and rewritten in code. And then, not long after that, he fell ill and died.'

'Oh,' I said.

'Quite. Though,' she went on, 'two of the other clerks in his office had the same bug, and they were very sick for a while and then got better. But Palamedes – that was my friend's name – he was the only one who died of it. Bad luck, don't you think?'

I nodded. 'So then what happened?' I said. 'Pollio followed up the trail where it'd left off, did he?'

'Sort of. Actually, he found another clerk, in the cipher department, the one who had the job of coding the latest entries in that file, and he gave him a lot of money. That's how he found out you were in Sicily.'

That shook me. 'He knew that?'

'Oh yes.'

Not good, I thought; because if Pollio's spy in the palace knew where we were, it was because he'd read it in the official reports, so whoever those reports were written for had to know too. Probably several people, not just one. 'Right,' I said. 'So then what did he do?'

She frowned. 'I'm not quite sure,' she said. 'I was helping him with the search, me and a dozen or so others in the house, but he didn't tell us everything, only the bits we needed to know to do the jobs we'd been given. I gathered that he'd sent a letter by express courier to some friend or business partner of his in Sicily, asking him to rescue you from whatever mess you got into next and bring you home, but apparently it all went wrong, some soldiers got killed or something, and you sort of slipped through the net.' She sighed. 'No, it was pure chance that we found you when you turned up at Ostia. Pollio just happened to be down at the docks that day – this is what I've been told, though I didn't have it from Pollio himself – and who should he bump into but you? He thought he knew you from somewhere, so he gave you some money just in case you were an old friend fallen on hard times; it wasn't till he got home, wondering out loud who it was he'd met, and I heard him describe you to someone—'

'I know,' I put in. 'Scrawny little Greek bloke, I expect he said, with a face like a ferret.'

'Like a weasel, actually,' Blandinia replied, 'but close enough. Anyhow, to cut a long story short, soon as we'd figured out who you were, we all went scurrying down to Ostia after you, picked up the trail at Gnatho's estate, followed it on to Rome, and hired half the layabouts and street people in the city to look for you.'

I nodded thoughtfully. 'So you found us,' I said. 'So why didn't Pollio scoop us up and bring us in right away? What was all this shit about Alexander and whatsisname following us around to keep us safe, and giving us money in our sleep?'

All this time, I'd been feeding my face with the grub the slaves brought round, but I wasn't paying attention to it, just stuffing it into my mouth and chewing. Typical of the way things go with me. I can truthfully say I've had goose stuffed with partridge and honey-roast thrush wrapped in escalope of hare with fennel sauce, and I haven't got a clue what it tastes like. Might as well have been bacon and beans.

'Well,' Blandinia replied, 'I wondered that, too. But Pollio — well, he's basically a good man, pretty decent and considerate, not at all like your average Roman knight. A bit strange in some ways, but fundamentally all right, if you know what I mean. But when it comes to Nero Caesar, it's like he's spoiled in the head or something — like he's been out in the rain without a hat once too often, and the damp's got into his brains and turned them mouldy. The way he saw it was, he couldn't go grabbing Nero Caesar off the street and having him dragged here like a runaway slave or something, it'd be the most appalling liberty. What he was planning on doing was biding his time till you two started cooking up scams again, and then he'd offer himself as the mark. That way, when you two were working him over, pretending to be sardine kings or parsnip barons with a lucrative trade deal up your sleeves, he'd have a pretext to invite you to dinner, maybe get you to stay for a few days, and he'd pretend to be taken in by your scam, which'd be his way of giving you a large sum of money without Nero Caesar feeling he was accepting charity. It was only when he found out you'd fallen into the hands of gangsters, and there were rival mobs about to fight a pitched battle over who got to keep you, that he decided he'd better get you out of there quick, and the hell with the proprieties. So he sent for Alexander and Julianus Bolius — and, well, here you are.'

'My God,' I said. 'What a devious man he is, to be sure. I tell you what, he'd have done well in our line of work.'

Blandinia nodded gravely. 'He has,' she said.

That shook me. 'What, scamming? But he's so rich. Nobody ever gets rich doing what we do. Crucified, yes, but not rich.'

She lifted her head. 'You're wrong there,' she said. 'Can I be absolutely honest with you? The truth is, it's quite easy to make a lot of money cheating people, provided you're good at it. Licinius Pollio's good at it. You aren't.'

'True,' I said. 'Well, about us, anyhow. But is that really what Pollio—'

She nodded. 'He was a legacy hunter,' she said. 'Back before he got tubby and lost his hair. His father was a respectable knight in the grain trade, but he got on the wrong side of Claudius Caesar and ended up broke. Licinius Pollio made his pile by sneaking round rich, elderly widows and getting them to leave him all their money in their wills. He was very good at it, I gather; he was good enough looking to get their attention, and cute and funny enough to get them fond of him, and that's basically what it takes. Oh, I'm not saying he didn't forge a will or two when an old bat didn't turn out as susceptible as she ought to, and there's some people who'll tell you that one or two of his old dears may have crossed the River a bit before their time, though I haven't got an opinion on that point. Mostly, though, it was sheer charm and personality. If you've got those, you see, swindling people's a piece of cake. If you haven't – well, I won't make a song and dance out of it, but he's here and you're where you are, and that more or less says it all, doesn't it?'

I nodded. Not a lot you could say to that, really. Still, the thought that this obviously rich and respectable Roman whose venison pasties with coriander and chives I'd been gobbling down all the while was really no better than us made me wonder why the world works how it does. I mean to say, cheap trash like me and Lucius Domitius, we pull a few scams, the guards get on to us, and the next thing we know is, we're hiding under a cart or inside a water butt, penniless and hated by the whole world, and somehow that's sort of comforting; it shows that the gods really are watching and keeping score of who's nice and who's nasty. But if a man can go around cheating old ladies, forging their wills, maybe even murdering them, and wind up as rich and comfortable as a genuine member of the noble equestrian order, then where the hell's the sense in that? I don't see how even Seneca could've explained that one away.

'Fair enough,' I said. 'But straight up, you're telling me that

Licinius Pollio's gone to all this trouble and expense just because he likes the way Lucius – I mean Nero Caesar sings?'

'That's about the strength of it, yes.'

I ask you. Dumb as cowshit, some people. All that money and time and effort just to find Lucius Domitius, when for a fraction of the cost and aggravation he could take a hike down to the slave market, or even get on a boat to Delos, and buy himself a top-flight band, flute-players and harpists and zither-botherers and the whole bunch of them, plus a crackerjack singer, and they'd play and sing Lucius Domitius' words and music just as well as he could, most likely a damn sight better. Just goes to show how weird people can be when it comes to art and music and bullshit like that.

Anyway. 'That's a relief,' I said. 'Hard to believe, but if that's all he wants us for, that's fine. Absolutely great. I mean, we're not proud. You tell Licinius Pollio, if he wants to hire Lucius Domitius to sing and play for him, chances are he'll be delighted to work for board, lodgings and pocket money, let alone the going rate. We aren't proud, Lucius Domitius and me.'

She gave me a funny look. 'I'd gathered that,' she said. 'You know, that's a funny thing: the former emperor of the Romans, working as a field hand. That's something I'd have liked to see.'

I frowned. 'It was better than a clown show, I'll grant you,' I said, 'watching him trying to swing a hoe. He's got the strength, you see, but bugger all coordination, plus he doesn't know the work. What I mean is, he's a piss-poor field hand, just as he was a piss-poor emperor of the Romans. Stick a harp in his paws, though, and he'd be worth all of a drachma a day. If you ask me, people are born to a particular line of work. I was born to scamming and thieving, and that's who I am. Nero Caesar's a born catgut-fondler – not the best, not the worst, but then again, when the soles of your boots are peeling off, you don't insist on having the very finest cobbler in the empire see to them, anybody who can do the job is just fine.' I shook my head. 'Sounds like your Pollio was born to be a knight, and I don't suppose it really matters how he got there. And by all accounts, the late lamented Vespasian was born to be the emperor. If only people had some way of knowing what it is they're supposed to do before they start doing it, the world would be a happier place, and no mistake.'

She looked at me. 'You're wrong on one score,' she said. 'I think you were born to be a philosopher. You haven't got the legs for standing about looking impressive in a short woollen gown, but otherwise I'd say you were ideally suited.'

She was making fun of me, but I'm used to that. 'And then there's you,' I said, turning my line like a wise general counter-attacking from a position of weakness. 'You were obviously born to be a rich knight's confidential freedwoman. It's obvious you're good at it.'

She turned bright pink, then said, 'I don't know what you're suggesting, but as a matter of fact, Licinius Pollio's tastes run in a different direction. You don't believe me, come and look round our place some day and count the rosy-cheeked fifteen-year-old page boys. I *work* for a living.' Actually, I hadn't been suggesting anything of the sort, but apparently I'd trodden on a corn. Still, it got her off my back for a moment. 'Anyhow,' I said, pressing home with my heavy infantry, as it were. 'What's the plan from here on?'

She frowned. 'I'm not sure. To be honest with you, I don't think Licinius Pollio's thought much beyond this. I mean, his life's been devoted to getting to the point where he could sit Nero Caesar down and tell him how wonderful his music is. At some stage, he'll probably screw up enough courage to ask for a song or two. After that, I don't know. I rather get the impression that Pollio was planning on dying after that, on the grounds that anything else would be a pathetic anticlimax.'

'Oh,' I said. 'Only I was hoping we could sort of spin this one out for a while – twenty years or so, for choice. It's not like either of us has got anything better to do.'

'I expect that could be arranged,' she said. 'Or if you don't want to spend the rest of your days hanging round our house, I could always have a word with him for you. He'd be far too shy to offer, for fear of giving mortal offence, but if I told him that what Nero Caesar would like best in the whole world would be four hundred thousand sesterces and a boat trip to Trapezus, I'm sure he'd be only too pleased to oblige.'

I nearly choked on my rabbit with fruit sauce. 'Four hundred thousand?

'All right, six,' she said. 'Say what you like about Pallio, he's no piker, he'd want to do the thing properly.' She smiled at me, though there was something about her expression that reminded me of a growling dog. 'I think it's probably safe to say that all your troubles will pretty soon be over. Now isn't that nice?'

Six hundred thousand sesterces, I thought, fuck a stoat six ways to Nicomedea. And all my troubles over, too; no more sleeping in ditches or eating cheese with green fur on it or hiding from soldiers in middens. Just because a creep who swindled old ladies liked the way Lucius Domitius played the harp. Crazy.

'Would you mind?' I said hoarsely. 'Having a word with Licinius Pollio, I mean? I think it's a tremendously good idea.'

'Thank you,' she said. 'I'll do that, then, as soon as he's through nattering with your friend. Meanwhile, eat up, there's still plenty of food left, and if we run out, we can always send Alexander and Julianus Bolius out to the kitchens.' She sighed. 'It's a pity they're so useful as hired muscle,' she said, 'because actually they're very good cooks. They're even better at beating people up, though, so by your theory that's what they ought to be doing, full time. Or is your theory flexible enough to allow for a person being really good at two things at the same time?'

As it happened, I had an answer to that point, but I never got to tell it, because that was when the door flew open and the room filled up with people.

I recognised the Sicilian, of course, and a couple of his button men who I'd met back at the inn. The rest of them were cut from the same cloth, as we say back in Attica, and besides, you didn't need to look further than the swords in their hands to see what they were there for.

I may not be much of a human being. I'm not brave, or clever, or good-looking, or gifted with any useful skills. But I've got a small collection of instincts that see me through when the shitrain starts to fall, and that's more than a lot of people can say. By the time the boarding party was through the door, I was invisible. I'd slid off the couch, landed on my knees, slithered sideways across the floor and wormed my way behind a handy floor-length curtain. Another thing I have a certain flair for is attention to detail, because I remember remembering to tuck my toes in (unlike Claudius Caesar, in very similar circumstances, who left them sticking out under the hem of the curtain and got caught straight away; and they dragged him off and made him emperor, so let that be a lesson to you). Anyhow, there I was and there I stayed, and because I had the sense not to poke my head out to see what was going on, I missed the details of what happened next. I heard a lot of shouting, which didn't last very long, some screams, and quite a bit of that sound that's not really like anything else, really sharp metal slicing into flesh and grating on bone. I suppose they could have been carving the saddle of roast mutton in a hurry, but I don't think that's what it was. In any event, it didn't last very long. About the time it takes to eat an apple, give or take a bit. Then someone spoke.

'The other one,' he said, and then I heard Blandinia reply, 'What, you mean the Greek?'

'With a face like a rat,' said the first voice, 'yes. Where's he got to?'

'Oh, you've missed him,' she said, sounding very unimpressed. 'He bolted off through the door like a polecat. You might just catch up with him if you're quick.'

'Fuck,' said the first voice, and then, 'All right, get after him. We'll come back for this lot.'

Sort of a stampeding noise, then nothing. After the nothing had been going on for a good long time, I took a deep breath and stuck my nose round the edge of the curtain.

Well, the good part was, the room was empty. Apart from dead people, of course. There were plenty of them.

ELEVEN

When I was a kid, I used to have this nightmare. I was in our house, and there was just me, and I'd go round the place for ages and ages (our house was a lot bigger, in the dream) and there'd be nobody, just me. Then suddenly I'd go round a corner or walk into a barn, and there'd be everybody I ever knew, lying in a great big heap, dead. Sometimes they'd be all chopped up in bits, other times they'd be covered in boils, like they'd died of plague, and once or twice they were all dried up and mouldering, like they'd been dead for a year or so. It was a really horrible dream, and it usually came on after I'd eaten green figs last thing.

Well, maybe it was just the figs, or maybe it was one of those prophetic dreams the gods send us, to let us know we're in for a really shitty time and there's nothing we can do about it. Anyhow, if it was a prophetic dream, that was what it must've been warning me about: the sight I saw when I came out from behind the curtain.

I've seen dead people; who hasn't? I've seen them lying on beds, or face down in ditches, or sat up against walls with their heads drooping down on their knees. I've seen them carved up and smashed in, or bent and twisted in the wreckage of carts, or bobbing just under the water like huge white carp waiting to be fed breadcrumbs. I've seen them hanging off wooden crosses beside the road, with their bones poking through their skin. I've seen glimpses of them under a blanket of feeding crows, I've seen them dry and crispy and brittle like duck crackling where they've been turfed out of ancient tombs and stacked outside like trash, I've seen them in bundles of bits, jumbled up and mismatched, where someone's ploughed up an old graveyard. I've seen them carried on doors with everybody crying their eyes out, or stepped over in the marketplace because it's nobody-in-particular's job to clear them away. I know dead people from nothing, and most of the time they don't bother me at all.

But there was something about this mess. I'm not soft-hearted or sentimental. So long as it's not me who's dead I generally don't give a damn. But that was pretty bad. It upset me. You know what it reminded me of most? Well imagine a little rich kid, a spoilt brat who goes in for temper tantrums and throwing things about the room – everything just chucked on the floor or against the wall, or left lying and trodden on, dolls bashed against the doorframe till they're busted, good clothes torn, nice things spoiled just for spite – and you look at it and you think how wicked it is, such a waste, how unpleasant. And it wasn't just the dead people, either; oddly enough, it was the wonderful food and the gorgeous silverware and everything of the very best, carefully chosen with love for a really special occasion, and some bunch of bastards had come in and smashed it all up, like big bad boys spoiling a little kid's birthday. It was all rather nasty.

Pollio wasn't hard to find; whoever'd taken him out had given him an almighty chop with a sword, starting at the collarbone and going right through to the middle of his chest, through all that bone and gristle. It takes a strong man in a temper to do that, even with a Spanish-pattern sword. I was looking for Lucius Domitius, of course, so I didn't pay him much heed (though I distinctly remember thinking as I stepped over him, Well, there go my six hundred thousand sesterces; fuck, fuck, *fuck*). But Lucius Domitius wasn't there, not even under a fallen table or in bits. That had to be a good thing, I told myself; he wasn't dead, or at any rate he wasn't dead yet (and, when you think about it, that's the most any of us can say about anybody).

All your troubles will be over, I thought. Yeah, right.

And then I thought, well, she didn't see me running out the door, because I haven't, yet. And then I thought, they sounded awfully pally, Blandinia and that voice, like they knew each other from somewhere. And then I thought, 'All your troubles will be over pretty soon'. The bitch, I thought.

So there I was.

It was time for a decision. I could get out of the room, or I could stay where I was. I could go looking for Lucius Domitius, maybe make some sort of effort to save his life, or I could piss off out of there and out of Rome and out of Italy, and keep going until I fell off the edge of the world or stubbed my toes on the pillars of Hercules, like Ulysses but in reverse. My decision. Nobody to say, Don't be a bloody fool, Galen, or, You can't do that, Galen. Nobody else to stick their oar in or talk me into doing something I'd rather not do. Just me, on my ownsome.

Just me.

Fuck it, I thought. Because, I know me. I know I'm not a hero, or a good man, or very much of a man at all. I'm a little Greek thief with a face like a rat. People know what to expect from me. I know what to expect from me, and what I'm capable of. Oh, I knew what Callistus would've done. He'd have gone off and found them, found Lucius Domitius, got himself killed trying to rescue him. I knew what Lucius Domitius would've done, if it'd been the other way round and I was the one who'd been dragged off. He'd have gone off and found me, got himself killed. But I knew me, and I knew exactly what I was going to do. I was going to run away.

So that's what I did.

It was a good plan, too, one of my better ideas. Shame it didn't work out.

I got as far as the main gate. I stopped, looked round, listened carefully – attention to detail, see – and then I took one step into the street, at which point someone grabbed me by the shoulder and pushed me up against the wall.

'Right,' he said. 'Name.'

That was an odd question. Either they already knew who I was or they had no reason to care, so long as they had me. 'Name,' the voice repeated impatiently, and it occurred to me that maybe I was in the shit but in some different shit, not the shit I'd been expecting.

'Hyacinthus,' I replied, picking a name at random.

'Fine,' said the voice. 'Now, what were you doing in that house?'

And then, of course, I knew who it was pushing me up against the wall. Only the bloody watch. I could have wet myself laughing, if I hadn't widdled it all down my leg out of sheer terror when I was hiding behind the curtain. Oh, didn't I mention that? Well, it didn't seem the sort of thing you'd want to know.

'What house?' I said, stupidly.

'The house you just came out of,' the voice said. 'Turn round, slowly, and let's have a look at you.'

Yes, it was a watch sergeant. Typical specimen of the breed: big, craggy-faced Italian with a hard, round paunch under his coat of rings. Behind him, five bored-looking troopers, with spears and swords. And where were you bastards when we needed you?

'Only,' the sergeant went on, 'I know for a fact that house is empty. Been empty for years, ever since Philippus Maro was put to death for treason. So what were you doing in there?'

And then it dawned on me, like a beautiful sunrise. 'All right,' I said, 'you got me. I was looking for something to steal, only the place is empty, like you said. Nothing in there but cobwebs and dead birds.'

The sergeant laughed. 'You aren't from round here,' he said, 'or you'd have known that. God, you're pathetic. There's thousands of houses in this city, and you get done trying to rob an empty one. The gods must hate you.'

'Yes,' I said. 'Still, they can't hate me that much, or they'd have had you catch me coming out of a house that wasn't empty, with half a dozen silver plates stuffed up my shirt. Then I'd really have been in the cowplop.'

The sergeant frowned. He hadn't seen it that way. Because, you see, I hadn't stolen anything, so he couldn't have me for thieving. I hadn't busted in, the door was obviously open and the lock wasn't damaged, so he couldn't do me for housebreaking. In fact, I was innocent as fresh green oil, straight from the press, and he knew it.

'Yeah,' he said. 'Maybe the gods like you after all.' He let go of my shoulder, but he hadn't said anything about being free to go. It's best to wait for them to spell it out, in my experience. It saves you from getting a spear in the back, for one thing.

'Actually,' I went on, 'it's a bloody good job I ran into you, because I was just on my way to find you.'

That took him by surprise. 'Get away,' he said.

'Straight up,' I said. 'You see, the house isn't all that empty. In fact, it's full of dead bodies.'

He blinked. 'Dead bodies?'

'Couple of dozen, I'd say,' I said, 'though I didn't count them. Murdered, by the look of it. That or they had a really good fight among themselves and there was no one left standing at the end. But that's for you to say, isn't it? After all, that's your department, dead people.'

He must've been an old hand, that sergeant, because he didn't turn a hair when he saw all the blood and bodies. One of his squaddies took one look at the scene and rushed out to throw up, but that sergeant didn't seem bothered at all. 'Well,' he said at last, poking at Licinius Pollio's corpse with his toe. 'At least I can be sure you didn't do this, you're far too skinny and weedy to go cutting people in half. Besides, whoever chopped this one, he'd have been sprayed up and down with blood when he went through the poor fucker's neck artery.' He looked round at me, with an expression on his face that told me he'd just thought of something. 'So,' he said, 'if you didn't kill them and you don't know who did – I'm assuming you don't know,' he added meaningfully.

'What, me? Haven't a clue, sorry.'

'That's all right then,' the sergeant said, frowning, 'because if you did know and you weren't telling me, that'd make you an accessory after the fact, and you wouldn't like that one bit.'

He was lying, actually. I know a bit about the law, the same way mice know a bit about cats. But I wasn't going to tell him that.

'Anyhow,' he went on, 'so you're innocent and you don't know who did it and it's nothing to do with you. So why tell me about it?'

Good question, in the circumstances. Hardly the way you'd expect an incompetent thief to carry on. 'Just being a good citizen, I guess,' I said feebly.

'Oh, you're a citizen, are you?' He looked at me. 'Funny, I'd have had you down for a Greek, myself.'

He was wrong there, too, because as it happens I actually am a fully fledged, genuine, no-messing Roman citizen, with rights and everything. I got made one by the emperor himself, what's more – well, by Lucius Domitius, back in the old days, he made Callistus a citizen, and made me one too so Callistus wouldn't moan about me being left out. But that, of course, was another thing I wasn't going to let on to a sergeant of the watch, who might not approve of bosom buddies of the late Nero Caesar. 'Just a figure of speech,' I said. 'What I meant was, I considered it my duty. Like I told you, I was just on my way to find you when you found me.'

'Right,' he said, as if I'd just told him he was really a girl. 'Well, you can feel very proud, I'm sure. Meanwhile, I'm arresting you as a material witness. Since you're such a dutiful bloke, you won't mind a bit.'

Fuck, I thought. Still, as far as he was concerned I was Hyacinthus the feckless housebreaker. There was a better than even chance that I might end up in the galleys or the mines, but a threat like that hanging over you is cuckoospit when you've been in as many condemned cells as I have. 'Only too pleased to help,' I said, forcing a grin. 'Meanwhile, you've got a mass murder to investigate.'

'Yes, haven't I ever,' he grunted. 'Well, it's out of my league, so we're going back to the watch house, fetch the prefect. Maybe even the city aedile, for something like this. Here,' he called over his shoulder to his men, 'any of you lot recognise any of these?' Dead silence. I guess his squaddies didn't mix with high society very much, for some reason.

So we went to the watchhouse, and on the way, since nobody seemed to want to talk to me, I turned over a few things in my mind: things I'd seen back there in the house, and a few things I hadn't. You'd have thought I'd done enough thinking for one day, but apparently not. With a brain like mine, I can keep it up all day if I have to.

The sergeant – his name was Marcus Trebonianus, for what little that's worth – had been right; the watch captain called the prefect, and the prefect called the aedile, and while we were waiting for him to tear himself away from whatever dinner party he was at, they parked me in a little cell out the back where they wouldn't have to see me and be offended by my unprepossessing features. So there I was, back in the cooler again, just me, four walls, a low ceiling with things growing out of it, and a heavy wooden door. I propped my back against a wall, stretched out my legs and tried to relax.

Fat chance. Oh, it wasn't the being in the coop that had me all nervous and edgy. One cell is pretty much like another, and there's bugger all you can do in them, so after a while you learn to sit still and conserve your energy, like a lizard on a warm rock. Generally when I'm locked up on my tod, I close my eyes and imagine sea battles. I can do that for hours and not get bored, not that I'm much of a military buff. No, what was making me antsy was not knowing what'd become of Lucius Domitius; was he dead yet, or were they slowly torturing him to death, or what? It made me itch all over to think he might still be alive, even if only just. Any of the moments dripping away from me could have been the moment when he closed his eyes and breathed out the long sigh that empties the chest of the last remaining air; and here I was stuck in a cell, unable to do a damn thing. It was stupid, of course, my being there; it wouldn't help solve anything, even if the idiot watch had a flea's chance in an oven of catching the killers, which they didn't, of course. Honestly, I wonder why the hell cities bother with watchmen and guards. They're no bloody good. Think about it – if they were even a tiny bit competent, I'd have been dangling off a cross years ago. They don't keep the streets safe, they don't catch thieves and murderers, all they do is make life miserable for people like me, who never did them any harm personally. And sometimes, like then, for instance, they make it impossible for honest, decent folk to rush off saving their friends' lives and stuff like that. If ever I get to be emperor, first thing I'll do is send them all home, without severance pay.

I was thinking about that, and a whole bunch of related issues that were keeping my mind so fully occupied that I hadn't had to imagine so much as a rowing boat, when the door swung open and the sergeant came in. He had the same rather confused look on his face, only more so.

'Visitors for you,' he said.

'Really?'

'Apparently. Your sister and your cousins.'

'What? I mean, great, thanks. Show them in.'

The sergeant gave me a look you could've started a fire with if you'd had a flint handy. 'Beats me how they knew you were here,' he went on. 'You got any ideas about that?'

'Intuition,' I replied. 'Always been very close, my sister and me.'

'Oh. Well, here you go, then.' He stepped back into the passage and beckoned to someone, and who should walk in but my brave rescuers from a day or so back: Amyntas, Scamandrius and the girl, Myrrhine.

'Here's your—' the sergeant started to say, then there was a blur and a scurrying sound, and something shot past him and landed on my chest. 'Oh, thank God,' it said, sounding very much like Myrrhine, 'thank God you're all right, we were so worried.'

'Thanks,' I said, as the other two squatted down on either side of me, looking grave and solemn. 'Um, how did you find me, out of interest?'

'Yeah, I'd like to know that,' the sergeant put in, but Myrrhine gave him a nasty look, and he shut the door behind him.

Amyntas waited to hear his footsteps before he said anything. 'Right,' he said, 'this is what you've got to do. Myrrhine, give him the knife.'

At once Myrrhine stood up and lifted her skirt in a most unladylike fashion. I won't tell you how she'd managed to smuggle a dagger into the cell, but if I hadn't seen it for myself I'd have said it wasn't possible; at any rate, not without doing yourself a nasty injury.

'Hang on,' I said, 'what is all this?'

'It's a jailbreak, you clown,' muttered the other one, Scamandrius. 'Now, you take the knife and as soon as we've gone, you get the guard in here on some pretext or other, and—'

I lifted my head sharply. 'No way,' I said. 'I won't do it.'

Amyntas sighed. 'Don't be such a chickenshit,' he said. 'So long as you pick the right moment, when he's looking the other way, it'll be a piece of piss. Just under the ear's a good place; or you can grab his head with one hand, give it a little twist, and—'

'No !' I said. 'Look, I don't know what's going on, but if you think I'm going to murder a Roman soldier, you're out of your minds. The trouble I'm in at the moment is sparrowshit compared to something like that.'

Amyntas smiled. 'That's what you think,' he said. 'Actually, your case is so absolutely fucking desperate, it's probably just as well you didn't know, or you'd be a nervous wreck by now. You see,' he went on, 'in an hour or so's time, a bloke is going to show up here and tell the prefect that the little Greek thief he's got in the cells is actually an intimate crony of Nero Caesar's, from the old days.

Furthermore,' he went on, before I could say a word, 'roughly the same message'll go out to a number of prominent citizens in this town, all of whom have urgent reasons of their own from back in the old days for wanting to get hold of you. I may be wrong, but I think that's about as much trouble as it's possible to be in, short of being halfway down the throat of a lion. Of course,' he went on, 'if by some chance you happen not to be here at that time, there won't be much point in sending all those messages. Have you got the picture?'

I looked at the dagger. It was short and thin-bladed and looked like it was everything a top quality functional dagger should be. You could kill somebody with a thing like that. 'Look,' I said, 'you still haven't said what you want me for. Maybe I can do whatever it is you want without leaving this cell, and no need to go around scragging watchmen.'

'Nice thought,' said Amyntas, 'but no dice. Now, soon as you're out of here, I want you to go down the street, like you're heading for the river, and you'll see a couple of guys carrying a small closed sedan chair. Get in the chair, and everything'll be fine. You got that, or shall I run through it for you one more time?'

I frowned. 'How did you know I was here?' I asked. 'And why are you here, anyway?'

'Never you mind about that. There'll be plenty of time to go into all that later.'

But I lifted my head. 'For pity's sake,' I said, 'you've got to tell me something; not the whole deal, maybe, but at least you can tell me if you know what's happened to—' I nearly said, 'Lucius Domitius,' but I didn't. 'My friend,' I said.

Amyntas laughed. 'Let's not kid around,' he said, 'we all know the score. You mean, your brother Callistus. Well, of course you're worried. But don't be, we've got all that in hand. Now, let's run though the drill one more time. Knife; out the door; head for the river; sedan chair. All clear?'

'Perfectly,' I said.

Yeah, well, I said that, but it was just to get rid of them. I'd have laughed like a drain, only I didn't want to make him suspicious. 'Fine,' Amyntas said. 'See you soon. Good luck, not that you're going to need it.'

He banged on the door, and the guard opened up and let them out. I waited for a good long time, then banged on the door myself. The guard opened it a crack and stuck his head through.

'Excuse me,' I said, and held out the knife, its point pinched between my thumb and forefinger, like a cook adding ground cumin to a stew. 'My visitors seem to have dropped this. I thought I'd better hand it in.'

The guard stared at me like I'd grown a tail where my legs should have been. 'Where'd you get that?' he rasped.

'Like I just said, one of my cousins dropped it. Careless bugger, I could've cut myself on it.'

'But I searched him myself—' He scowled. 'All right,' he said. 'Stay there, don't fucking well move. I'll be right back.'

He wasn't long, and when he reappeared he had two other guards with him. They hung back in the doorway, swords drawn, while he crept forward at me, like a dog stalking a partridge. 'Right,' he said, when he was just over an arm's length from the knife, 'drop it on the floor, then get back against the wall. And if you're up to something, God have mercy on you.'

I shrugged and relaxed my fingers, letting the knife drop. He sidled up to it like a nervous crab and kicked it across the floor to the doorway, where one of his buddies picked it up. 'All right,' he said, relaxing a little but not much. 'You two, search the cell, I'll see to this bastard.'

I hate being searched, it's undignified. One of the advantages of being small and ratlike, as opposed to tall, willowy and slim or big and muscular, is that soldiers and the like only tend to search me when they're actually looking for something, but even so, it happens to me rather more often than I like. Still, at least on this occasion I was clean as snow and pure as milk, as they say in Attica. Likewise the cell, as the other two proved after a short, pointless display of energy.

'Fine,' the guard said eventually, 'so that's all right. But I'm warning you,' he added, with a bewildered look on his face. 'Just don't try anything, that's all.'

The door slammed behind them, and I went back to lying against the wall, like I'd been doing before I'd been disturbed. Now, though, I had a lot more to think about.

Your brother, he'd said. Your brother Callistus.

It's a bugger, being human. Birds and deer and mice and foxes, they don't have to put up with the kind of shit people do, their lives are simple and straightforward. You watch where you're going, sniff three times before breaking cover, spend your days trying to eat without getting eaten. If a predator shows up, at least you know what he's after, and you can run or fly or do what you have to do. And if your sister or your uncle or whatever is a bit slow off the mark one day and ends up as a link in the food chain, well, that's the luck of the draw. At least you know where you crouch, so to speak. Being human is much more difficult, because your enemies don't wear bushy red tails or grey fur overcoats to let you know which side they're on. You've got to figure it out as you go along, try and keep track of who's who, you've got to think all the damn time. Oh, I suppose you could go up into the hills and live in a cave and throw rocks at anybody who comes within a hundred yards, but then you'd have nobody to talk to (and for a Greek, that'd be worse than being dead). I don't know, there's got to be a way of figuring all this stuff out, but I'm buggered if I know what it is.

Your brother Callistus, he'd said. Crazy. Did that mean that Licinius Pollio and all his people had been slashed to death over the venison crêpes just because someone thought Lucius Domitius was my dead brother? And why, for pity's sake; what for? It was hard to imagine anybody, let alone two Roman gang bosses, spending the last ten years muttering, 'So help me, I'm going to get that bastard Callistus,' into their pillows every night for ten years, because he'd never actually done anything to anybody, apart from steal a few tunics and help Lucius Domitius escape. Now a tunic's just a tunic, and it couldn't have been the helping Lucius Domitius that'd got them riled up, because if they knew about that, they had to know Callistus was dead. Assuming he was, of course. Maybe – well, maybe at the last moment, when I wasn't looking, Callistus and Nero Caesar had swapped back, just to make a monkey out of me, and it hadn't been my brother I'd killed after all.

Well, I wasn't in the mood to write off any possible explanation, but that one did seem just a trifle far-fetched. Other than that, though, I couldn't think of anything. Proving nothing, mind. After all, I hadn't dogged Callistus' footsteps all round the Golden House every hour of every day we were there. It's possible he'd done something to piss off somebody at some time when I wasn't around, and so I never got to hear about it. But *Callistus*, for God's sake. He wouldn't knowingly have done anybody down, except a mark in the course of business, and of course we'd been retired from all that all the time we were Caesar's guests. I could just conceive that at some stage, purely by accident, I'd done something horrible to somebody, enough so he'd bear a grudge. But Callistus? No, not possible.

Anyhow, there was no way I was going to murder any prison guards, not even if Amyntas was serious about telling everybody who I was – and I couldn't see that, not in a hundred years. For a start, who'd believe him? He couldn't very well offer any proof, not in his line of work, for fear of drawing attention to himself. Furthermore, if I'd made sense of any of what seemed to be going on, the last thing he'd want to do is put the idea into anyone's head that Galen was alive and in town, with the implication that if Galen was here, Callistus couldn't be far behind. No, I said to myself, right now, the only safe place for me is right here, behind a nice stout door in a tight stone cell with armed men outside to protect me. God bless the watch, I thought, Rome's finest.

As I arrived at that conclusion, the door swung open again, and the guard came in. He looked like a man with a bad headache.

'Guess what,' he said. 'You've got visitors again.'

I looked at him. 'Really?'

'No kidding,' he replied wearily. 'And fancy who's here to see you. Your sister,' he said, with a flogged-out ghost of a smile, 'and your two cousins from out of town.'

'What, the ones who were here just now?'

He shook his head. 'Different ones.'

'Oh,' I said.

'Large family, is it?'

'Huge,' I answered.

'Right.' He clicked his tongue. 'I'll show them in. That's after we've searched them,' he said nastily. 'Thoroughly,' he added, 'so it may be a while.'

'Take your time,' I told him. 'I'm not planning on going anywhere.'

He looked at me as if he'd just found me in his salad. 'You can bet the rent on that,' he said, and he stomped out, leaving me to wonder what I'd said to offend him. Well, some people are just sensitive, I guess.

When he'd said it could take a while, he wasn't kidding. In fact, I'd made up my mind that whoever it was had been put off by the searching and the attitude, and had buggered off. I'd just started a chariot race in my head, as a change from sea battles (Greens leading the Blues by a nose coming into the turn, with the Blue favourite coming up fast on the outside), when the door swung open, and there was my pal the guard once again.

'I've been thinking,' he said. 'If this bird out here's really your sister, what's her name?'

I frowned. 'I don't know,' I said. 'It depends which of my sisters you've got out there. Want me to go through the whole list? Could take some time.'

He sighed. 'Large family. Yeah, you said. All right, which sister would be about nineteen or twenty, short, sort of dark skin, hair piled up in one of them beehive jobs? Or are they all identical twins?'

That sounded familiar, and I thought, Shit. Except, she might be able to answer a question for me, and I was fairly safe in my cell, and, as I'd just proved, I didn't have to leave it if I didn't want to.

'Sounds like my kid sister Blandinia,' I replied. 'Fancy that, I didn't even know she was in town.'

'Blandinia,' he repeated. 'You're sure about that.'

'Sure I'm sure.'

'Fuck. All right.' He turned and called into the passageway. 'In here,' he said.

There was a blur and a whirring noise, and guess who was kneeling down beside me, making an awful fuss – was I all right, what had that horrid man been doing to me, it was all right, they'd sent for Uncle Thrasymedes, he'd have me out of there in two shakes. I looked under her armpit towards the door and nearly shouted for the guard, who was just on his way out. Standing on either side of the door were my two least favourite gladiators, Alexander and Pony-tail.

'Shout out if you want anything,' the guard grumbled. 'Wine, biscuits, little cheesy things on sticks. We're here to please.'

He slammed the door, just as I was about to call him back. It's true what they say, never one about when you need one.

'You,' I said.

'Oh be quiet,' Blandinia said, turning off the worried sister like a tap in a barrel. 'God, how feckless can you get? Can't even walk out of a house without getting arrested.'

'You betrayed us,' I snarled. 'I heard you, talking to that bastard; he knew you. It must've been you who told him where we were.'

'Sure,' she replied. 'Big deal.'

I crawled backwards an inch or so till I was flat up to the wall. 'And now you've come to clean up the loose ends, right?'

'Yes,' she replied. 'Oh, don't start slobbering, I didn't mean that, we aren't going to hurt you. If I'd wanted you killed, I'd have told Strymon you were behind the curtain, instead of covering up for you. Even a nitwit like you should be able to figure that one out.'

Well, she had a point there, I suppose. 'So what are they doing here?' I asked. 'Or did you fetch them along just to cook something?'

'Don't be silly. They're going to get you out of here.'

That seemed to be news to Alexander and Pony-tail. 'You what?' Alexander said.

'Don't you start,' she said over her shoulder, without looking round. 'Now listen to me, this is how we're going to play it. You start screaming, like you're in mortal pain. The guard comes in. The boys thump him—'

'Just a moment,' Pony-tail objected, but I don't think she was listening.

'—and we make a run for it. We've got a sedan chair waiting out in the street, so we haven't got far to go.'

'Another one?' I said. She ignored me, too.

'Right, got that?' she went on. 'Fine. So, on the count of three—'

'Hold it.' I raised my hands. 'If you want me to leave here, you'll have to drag me. I may not be very smart, but I know when I'm well off. I'm not going.'

She frowned at me. 'Fine,' she said. 'Alexander, come here a minute. Now, grab his ankle and when I say twist—'

When you're trying to sound like you're in mortal pain, it always helps to be in mortal pain. I was pretty convincing. In fact, it was probably the best agonised scream of my screaming career. Sure enough, in came the guard; a heartbeat later, down fell the guard on his nose, fast asleep. Alexander lifted me over his shoulder like he was a shepherd and I was a poor little orphan lamb, and we were out in the passage. I couldn't see much from where I was, but I heard a sound like an apple getting run over by a cartwheel, so I guess Pony-tail must've hit someone else. Then we were out in the street, and I remember shooting through the air and finding out what a sack of onions feels like when it gets loaded on a farm cart. Then it got dark, as you'd expect inside a closed chair. I couldn't move, probably because Blandinia was sitting on me.

Short, fast, bumpy ride, and then the weight eased off my neck and a huge hairy arm grabbed me and fished me out into the light again. I landed on my feet and the arm pulled me upright.

We were in a courtyard, in what must've been a big, grand house. Alexander was on one side of me, Pony-tail on the other, and Blandinia was marching across the yard towards the cloister. I didn't say anything as they frogmarched me along. I may be a Greek, but I can keep from talking if I make a real effort.

'Right,' Blandinia said, and they pushed me into a chair, their enormous hands on my shoulders. 'You two, clear off and fix something to eat. I'm starving.'

So there I was, in some rich bastard's house, sitting on the grass with a beautiful girl while two extremely skilful cooks whipped up dinner. Strange how things turn out; for most of my life, I'd have reckoned that was a good deal. Pity, isn't it, that when you eventually get what you wish for, it usually turns out to be a horseshit omelette.

'Now then,' Blandinia said. 'I expect you'd like to know what's going on.'

I had one question to ask her. I asked it. 'Where's Lucius Domitius?'

She raised an eyebrow, then: 'Oh, you mean Nero Caesar,' she said. 'I'm not totally sure. But he's safe. More's the pity,' she added.

'What's that supposed to mean?'

'Do be quiet,' she replied, 'or we'll never get anywhere. Do you want me to explain, or don't you?'

You can't argue with women. It's like trying to put a fire out with oil, the more you argue, the worse it gets. An old bloke I knew once said there's only three ways of dealing with them when they get argumentative: kiss them, bash them or walk away. Probably very good advice, if any of the three had been on the cards, which they weren't.

'Go ahead,' I sighed.

'Thank you so much. Right,' said Blandinia, 'this is the house of Lucius Regalianus. He's in Crete at the moment, buying and selling things, but his steward is an old friend of mine, from the Golden House. You may even recognise him, though I don't suppose you will. Guests don't notice footmen, and that's what he was back then. All clear so far?'

I nodded.

'Splendid,' she said. 'You see? I knew you'd got enough intelligence to follow a simple story. Now, you want to know exactly what all that was about with Licinius Pollio.'

'Yes,' I said.

'It's like this.' She yawned. 'Just as you guessed, I set it all up, with Strymon, the gangster. As soon as he heard I'd got a lead on Callistus—'

'Just a moment,' I said. 'You know perfectly well Callistus is dead.'

'Sure,' she replied, 'but they don't. They think he's alive, that Nero Caesar is in fact your dear departed brother. So does Scyphax and his mob, for that matter.'

'Why would they think that?'

'Because that's what I told them,' Blandinia replied. 'When they all found out that Pollio's people and I were taking an interest in two men who were thought to be the infamous companions of Nero Caesar – actually, they knew about the intelligence reports my friend the clerk saw, but they hadn't read the reports themselves, so they were pretty much in the dark. Anyhow. Strymon came to see me and asked if it was true I was on the trail of Callistus and Galen. I said yes, what of it? And he offered me – well, quite a lot of money, if I kept him up to date. Then Scyphax came and made me the same offer.' She sighed. 'What's a poor ex-slave girl to do? I said yes please, to both of them. Then, when we heard you'd been seen in Sicily, I told Strymon, and he zoomed off after you. But sad to say, he's not the brightest lamp in the temple, if you follow me, he found you all right, on your way to the slate quarries, and he killed the guards to get hold of you—'

'That was Strymon,' I interrupted. 'The Sicilian bandit.'

'That's right,' she said. 'Oddly enough, he was born in Sicily, though nowadays he's as Roman as any other Greek who happens to live in the city. Anyhow, he had you right there, but the idiot didn't recognise you, even though he had a good description I'd sent him, plus you'd have thought anybody would've been able to tell Nero Caesar from the face on the coins. But there you go. He thought a couple of other men were you and Callistus, and he turned you two loose. He found out his mistake soon enough thanks to your idiot friend Nero Caesar, managing to get himself recognised by the provincial governor, no less. Honestly. When you two screw something up, you don't do things by halves.'

'He recognised us,' I repeated.

She nodded. 'Not straight away, of course,' she said. 'He thought he'd seen a face he knew, and then he got to the governor's office, and there on his desk in with the official despatches was an all-points bulletin from Rome telling all provincial officials to be on the watch for two men, believed to be intimate friends of Nero Caesar and wanted for questioning, and one of them the spitting image of Nero himself'

'Ah,' I said. 'So the governor thought Lucius Domitius was Callistus, too.'

She nodded. 'Anyway,' she went on, 'as soon as he'd made the connection in his mind, he sent his soldiers looking for you, but by that time you'd managed to kid your way onto that ship. Luckily, Strymon's people were a step or two ahead of him. They asked around and figured out which ship you had to be on, then they got a fast yacht and zoomed back to Ostia to be ready for you when you arrived. Only,' she continued with a sigh, 'your clown of a chum messed all that up by jumping ship, of course.'

'How thoughtless,' I muttered.

'Quite. And then Strymon got it wrong again. He'd briefed his men to watch for Nero Caesar – or Callistus, as he thought – because he'd be the easy one to spot. So Strymon's men were looking for two strangers off the boat, one of whom would look like the face on the coins. When you strolled off the boat on your ownsome, they didn't look twice at you. Even Pollio – he'd got the same news, of course, from me – even Pollio was expecting the two of you, and when he bumped into you in the street he really wasn't sure if you were one of the men he was after or not. Still, he gave you some money, so you can't complain.'

'Can't I? Oh dear.'

'Anyhow,' Blandinia carried on, 'Strymon realised what'd happened, and he went tearing up and down the country looking for you. He nearly caught up on you at that farm, only he missed you yet again and didn't realise until you helpfully bunked off without waiting to claim your wages. Stupid thing to do.'

'Seemed like a good idea at the time,' I said.

'Really? What funny minds you two must have. So there you were, strolling up to Rome. Pollio – who had more brains than Strymon, bless him, though he was terribly naive, especially when you think how he made his money – Pollio figured out that you must be headed for the city, so he concentrated his efforts on picking you out when you came in through the gates. That's where Alexander and Julianus came in, and they did a good job.'

'I take it,' I said, 'they've been working for this Strymon all along.'

She shook her head. 'Don't be silly,' she said. 'They're working for me. Oh, they probably don't know it, but they are. If you're a girl trying to make something of yourself in a man's world, it's ever so helpful to have the two biggest, meanest fighters in the city to look after the primitive side of things. Anyway, where was I? Oh yes. Pollio was watching the gates for you; so, by this time, was Scyphax. He's clever, Scyphax, we underestimated him. That's how he managed to get hold of you both, thanks to that stroke of luck, with the wall falling on you. And that,' she said, 'is about it, really. As soon as I knew I'd got you at last, I sent word to Strymon to come and pick you up. He had to dispose of Licinius Pollio, of course, since Pollio knew about you. Also from my point of view,' she added blithely, 'since Pollio's the only one apart from you and me – and maybe a few people in the government, but we aren't sure about that – who knew that your friend is actually Nero Caesar and not Callistus the Greek, he had to go. Pity, I quite liked him, in spite of everything.'

She didn't explain that 'everything', but I didn't ask. Actually, I was a trifle shocked; she'd had that man, her master, murdered just like that, because he was inconvenient. Him and his entire household. Well, you expect that sort of thing from gods, and kings and emperors as well, I guess, but not from pretty little girls young enough to be your daughter. Nice world, isn't it?

'So Lucius Domitius is with this Strymon,' I said.

She nodded. 'Unless he's contrived to lose him again,' she said mournfully. 'And there's Scyphax to consider, too. Trouble is, Strymon has the delicacy of touch of a bull elephant. Like when he tried to barge into that inn and grab you. Scyphax could outsmart him easily, only Strymon's got me on his team, and I'm brighter than Scyphax.'

'That's right, is it? You're working for Strymon?'

She lifted her head. 'No,' she said, 'I'm working for me, silly. I'm just using Strymon to do the heavy lifting, if you follow me. With Scyphax in reserve, if I need him for anything. Not bad, really, for a girl from the kitchens. Of course,' she added, with a little shake of her head, 'it could all go horribly wrong and I could end up being fished out of the river on a long hook, with my face just starting to flake off the bone. But there you are. Can't ford a river without getting your feet wet, as they say.'

There was something about the way she said that, all flippant and devil-may-care, that made me think that maybe, deep down where it didn't show, she was almost as shit-scared as me. In which case, served her right. Of course I may have been kidding myself. We do a lot of that, us Greeks, particularly if there's nobody else around we can kid. We talk to ourselves as well, though I expect you've noticed that.

'All right,' I said. 'So, since we're being all frightfully civilised and chatting away like this, maybe you can tell me what's going to happen to Lucius Domitius. And,' I added, remembering something vitally important, 'me. Are we as good as dead, or is there some way we can possibly get out of this alive?'

She considered the question gravely, which frightened me so much I nearly pissed down my leg. 'I think your friend isn't long for this world,' she said eventually. 'You, on the other hand, I'm not sure about. You might make it, you might not. I don't want to build your hopes up, of course, but really, it's too early to say.'

'Oh,' I said. 'Any idea when you might know for sure?'

'It all depends,' she said, wrinkling her nose. 'There's a long way to go yet. If it was up to me, I'd probably let you go. I'm not sure why, maybe it's because you're so pathetic – and I don't mean that in a nasty way, but let's face it, you are what you are. Unfortunately, there's only so much I can do.'

I thought, Big of you, I'm sure. Now, what if I were to jump up suddenly, grab you round the throat and tickle you under the chin with that dinky little bone-handled knife you've got hanging off your belt? Would that make it easier for me to get out of this house, or would it guarantee I'd never reach the street alive? And this is where I've got a bone to pick with the gods. They ought to tell you stuff like that. You listen to the old poems, your *Wrath of Achilles* and your *Man of Many Wiles*, and the gods are always stopping by to whisper good advice in people's ears. But where were they when I really needed them? Well, exactly. If you ask me, the gods are just another lot of rich bastards who happen to live for ever and know how to do conjuring tricks. Screw the lot of 'em, I say.

'Well,' I said, 'thanks for that, I appreciate it. Now, another question for you. What the fuck do you and this Strymon and Scyphax want with Lucius Domitius and me? Particularly if they don't know who he is.'

'Ah.' She grinned. 'And I had you figured for a clever man. Never mind. Come to think of it, clever man is one of those figures of speech they teach you about in law school; like hot snow or cold fire. You really don't know, do you?'

'Me? Nah, I'm just a dumb peasant. You're going to have to tell me. Otherwise,' I added, 'how can I do what you want, if I don't know what it is?'

She looked at me as if I was a sea bass she was thinking of buying. 'I believe you when you say you don't know,' she said. 'And besides, it doesn't cost me anything. Does the name Dido, queen of Carthage, ring any bells?'

Bloody hell, I thought, so that's what all this is about. It's a damn fool bloody stupid treasure hunt. That huge fortune in gold and stuff that was supposed to be sitting there in a cave somewhere on the African coast – just as well Lucius Domitius had seen fit to mention it, or I'd have been screwed.

I thought quickly. 'No,' I said, trying to sound like I was lying through my teeth. 'Sorry, haven't got a clue what you're on about.'

'Really?' She smirked at me. 'What a pity, because that makes you far less valuable than you were a moment ago.'

'Fine,' I said. 'No reason to keep me, then.'

'Nice of you to see it that way. I'll call Alexander and have you killed.'

The way she said it, I got this picture in my mind of Alexander wringing my neck like a chicken and filleting me neatly with a sharp knife for escalopes of Greek, marinaded in garlic butter. 'You can if you like,' I replied, wanting to sound like I didn't believe she'd do any such thing, though of course I knew she would, if she believed I didn't really know (and of course I didn't, not the details anyway). 'But honestly and truthfully, I don't know anything about any Queen of Carthage.'

She frowned. 'Don't be silly, Galen,' she said. 'Both of us know Nero Caesar found out where Dido's treasure's buried from that knight he had tortured. Why else do you think you've been allowed to wander round the empire for the last ten years, miraculously not getting strung up on a cross every time you bungle a scam? It's because the whole world's been watching you, waiting for you to lead them to where the treasure is. To be honest, the one thing we haven't been able to figure out is why the hell you've waited all this time. All we could think of is you've realised that as soon as you make a move for it, we'll have you, while as long as you're drifting aimlessly around, it's in the interest of the government to let you stay alive and loose. Of course,' she went on, 'that doesn't explain why the government hasn't scooped you in and loosened your tongues with the rack and the hot irons, but I suppose they were afraid you'd die under torture or something idiotic like that. Anyway, they may have the patience of camels, but I don't. What scares me is the thought that some clown of a mule driver might stumble on it quite by accident, and then all our work'd be floating down the river, along with yesterday's wilted greens. Or else you're perfectly capable of dying of starvation or the plague, just to be insufferably difficult.' She leaned forward, like a cat crouching down before it jumps on some poor little furry bugger. 'Go on,' she said, 'why don't you tell me where it is? Just me, and then I'd be able to get it for myself, and there'd be nobody else involved. Then I could let you go. Why not? You haven't got anything to lose.'

Tread carefully, I told myself, you're crossing a plank bridge over a lake of ripe shit here. 'What about Lucius Domitius?' I said. 'Will he be all right, too?'

She scowled at me out of a pure sunny grin. 'No,' she said, 'he's not included in my good nature, I'm afraid. This is just you and me. So, how about it? Deal?'

I could tell she was getting excited – one up to me in the sparring match. 'Why don't you tell me why you're so down on Lucius Domitius?' I asked her. 'I get the feeling you really don't like him at all.'

She laughed, all dry and brittle. 'You're quite right,' she said, 'I don't like him. If it wasn't for Dido's treasure, I'd have seen him dead a long time ago, one way or another. But I don't want to talk about that.'

'Sorry,' I said, 'but I want to know. Else, how can I tell what you're serious about and what's just salad?'

'Very well,' she said, and you'd have sworn the gorgon had just turned her heart to stone. She'd gone as white as a statue that's been out in the sun and wind a long time, and all the paint's flaked off the marble. 'I'll tell you, though really you should be able to figure it out from what you've heard already. You know I was brought up in the Golden House, and my parents were slaves.'

I nodded. 'Is that it?' I said. 'Just a grudge?'

'Just a grudge.' She sighed. 'You clown, Galen. You were there in the Golden House, you obviously knew what went on there. You must know the sort of games Nero Caesar liked to play with little girls and little boys. For God's sake,' she said shrilly, 'I was seven years old. I still have the most horrible dreams, even now. And my parents knew, and there was nothing at all they could do about it because of what we were, slaves, just bits of property. Oh, I was lucky, I'm still alive. I suppose that's lucky,' she added, 'though there are times I'm not sure. Why are you looking at me like that? Are you seriously trying to tell me you didn't know?'

'Yes,' I said. 'I mean, I didn't know, this is all news to me. But I was just a hanger-on, Callistus' brother, nobody ever told me anything.'

'Really. So you never knew what sort of man you've been going round with these last ten years. You're really that stupid.'

I shrugged. 'I never said I wasn't,' I told her. 'I didn't know, really. I believe you, because why would you bother lying to me? But it's just sort of gone in my ear, I can't make any sense of it. I mean, I know Lucius Domitius has got his faults, God knows. But— Well,' I said. 'I believe you. I guess.'

She looked at me for a while. 'Who cares what you believe, anyway?' she said, cold as a dead body. 'I'd have had them kill you at the dinner party, only you're Callistus' brother. Oh, he'd have been able to tell you all right. That's why I loved Callistus more than anybody I've ever known. He rescued me, you see. He got me out of there.' She stood up suddenly. 'I'm going in now,' she said. 'You'd better stay there. If you try and leave, they won't kill you but they will break your arms and legs. If I were you, while you're waiting, you might care to think about what I've just told you.' Yeah, I thought. Right.

TWELVE

You may remember a while back I told you about the time I met the world's cleverest man, the great Seneca. We got chatting about Stoic philosophy and stuff, and I was able to fill him in on some things he didn't know about my line of work, thieving and swindling and so on.

Well, sorry to bang on about it, like I'm name-dropping or whatever, but the truth is, that conversation must've made a real impression on me because I can remember pretty much all of it, even now, including all the long words. I gave you the gist of some of it earlier, but I left out the interesting bit because it wasn't really anything to do with what I was telling you about, then. But you're going to hear the rest of it now; partly because, as I sat in Blandinia's garden with bugger all else to do but think about what she'd told me about Lucius Domitius, not to mention me being about to die, I went over it all in my mind and thought, Yes, well; partly because I've been lugging it round in my head all these years because it's too good to waste, and it's cracking stuff, really. Besides, you've put up with me chattering away all this time, you deserve a bit of quality as a reward.

Like I said just now, old Seneca and me, we'd been talking about good and evil and lies and truth and all that, and I think Seneca had pretty much forgotten I was there, or who I was – he was getting on a bit, after all. The other day I figured it out on my fingers. It was the same year he died when we had our chat, so he can't have been a day under sixty, and even the best of us gets a bit blurry round the edges at that age.

Anyhow – I don't know how exactly, but the conversation had

somehow worked its way round to the Great Fire, which had happened the previous year. I think Seneca brought it up as an example of some point he was making, and I must've said something like, Yeah, what about that? or, That was really something else, wasn't it? Doesn't matter what I said; point is, after a while Seneca went all thoughtful, or else he had an attack of heartburn from eating crunchy snacky things out of a finger bowl, because he went dead quiet and stared past me, and then he started talking about history.

Great, I thought, getting my money's worth here, and I hadn't even had to pay for my seat, so I pinned my ears back and opened my mind up like a rabbit-catcher's net, hoping that at least some of the good stuff'd stick in it. Unfortunately my left leg chose that time to go to sleep on me, and it's bloody difficult concentrating on the sublime and the profound when you've got pins and needles shooting through your toes and right up into your bollocks; so I missed a load of what was probably really good stuff, and by the time I caught up again he'd made at least one extremely telling point, probably two or three, because the first thing I remember him saying was: 'And for an example of this, of course, we need look no further than His Majesty, Caesar himself. I do believe his own circumstances illustrate my point exactly. Don't you agree?'

Well, naturally I said yes, of course, because a scruff like me can't go saying, Sorry, I missed that bit, would you mind going over it again? 'Absolutely,' I added, wiggling my toes about. 'Couldn't agree more.'

I remember him smiling – not at me, more sort of past me, like when the archers in a battle shoot high over the heads of their own side to drop the arrows down on the enemy. 'It's rather sad, actually,' he was saying. 'History will remember Nero Caesar as a bad man, quite probably as some kind of monster; or else they'll say he was mad, which saves the difficulty of trying to understand. And they'll remember me, ironically enough, as a good man, a wise and humane man born tragically out of his time, a flower blooming in desolation. The injustice of it all disgusts me so much, I'm delighted I won't live to see it.

'You bet,' I said awkwardly. 'Um, how do you mean?' I added.

'Oh, come now.' He frowned a little. 'Surely it's obvious.' He looked at me. 'Or not,' he added, with a slight click of the tongue, 'or you wouldn't be scowling at me like that. Very well. Let's set out the facts in the daylight, like honest lawyers – prosecution and defence. Only we'll let the defence open, shall we, just for a change? What do you think?'

Of course, I wasn't thinking anything, except what an idiot I'm making of myself and my foot hurts. So I said, 'Good idea, why not?', and he grinned, then went on.

'The case for the defence,' he said, sitting up straight like he had a javelin up his bum, 'is that Nero Caesar, on ascending the throne in his sixteenth year, immediately set about sweeping away the notorious corruptions and vicious practices that so marred the last years of his uncle's reign; the evil men who'd secretly controlled the empire during Claudius' dotage were winkled out of power, disgraced and punished; misappropriated public funds went back into the treasury where they belonged; corrupt colonial governors were brought to trial; even his mother – quite the worst of the parasites – couldn't escape what can only be described as justice. Meanwhile, the battered economy was nursed back to health, taxes cut, Rome's food supply secured, the vital interests of Italian agriculture safeguarded. In political life, all traces of Claudius' reign of terror were swept away, free speech was restored in the senate, the power of the army curbed, pointless wars of aggression abandoned, while at the same time genuine foreign threats to national security were promptly and efficiently dealt with – the Parthians, Armenians and the rebel British, to name but three. At home, of course, conditions are better than at any time in living memory, and even disasters, like last year's catastrophic fire, have been turned to good use – in place of appalling slums, clogged streets and derelict tenements, we now have a city whose beauty at last truly reflects the worth of her people. Accordingly, we live in a city where the rich and powerful no longer oppress the common man, where the foreigner can at last claim redress for his wrongs against the citizen, where the senate and people of Rome have taken back the reins of government from nameless, corrupt Greek bureaucrats and court favourites, where crumbling brick has been replaced with shining marble – and all of this in a mere eleven years since Nero Caesar came to power, and all this because Nero Caesar came to power, spurned the temptations of power, turned power against those who would abuse it, for the benefit of the entire commonwealth. Surely' – and Seneca pulled a funny face, like he'd just swallowed a wriggly snail – 'surely we live in the best of times, and the age of gold has come again.'

He stopped talking and looked at me, like he was expecting me to say something. Me, I was sat there with my face open, thinking, Stuff me, he's right, this is a wonderful time to be alive, and all thanks to Lucius Domitius; well, who'd have thought it?

'You see?' Seneca went on. 'All facts; all true; you can go and read the edicts, or sit in the library and look up the figures for corn supplies and public expenditure. All true – as true as the facts presented by the prosecution, which would go, I fancy, something like this . . .'

He paused, changed his expression, tightened his eyebrows, made his mouth thinner. Quite scary, he looked, and not nice and affable at all. 'We live,' he said, 'in a cursed city, in unspeakable times, ground under the heel of a monster whose name will ever after be a byword for savagery and wickedness. A murderer – the word is hopelessly inadequate, we must invent another to describe the sort of man who kills, first his uncle, then his uncle's trusted advisers, then the flower of our nation's noblest families – Lepida, Silanus, Rubellius Plautus, Cornelius Sulla – then his cousin, the innocent Britannicus, then on through a torrent of blood to his own wife, his own mother. A freak – what other word can describe a nobleman, a senator, an emperor who daubs his face with paint, curls his hair, dresses in the disgusting attire of a common actor and makes an exhibition of himself in front of the entire world, playing at poetry and music and theatre while the senate and people of Rome are forced to sit still and watch, yearning to look away from the degrading spectacle, but not daring to do so for fear of the stone quarries or the executioner's sword? A common fire-raiser – are you so pathetically naive that you can bring yourself to believe that the murderous inferno that consumed our beloved city was an accident, or the work of heathens or cannibal Christians, when the ashes were barely cool before the tyrant's Greek architects and Greek sculptors and Greek landscapers and design consultants were scuttling among the ruins, kicking aside the charred bones of murdered innocents as they pegged out the foundations of the tyrant's obscene palace, his blasphemous temple to his own evil megalomania? As to the other charges – the bestial perversions, the insatiable lusts, the reckless extravagance, the callous cruelty – words fail me, all words fail me, the golden voice of Apollo himself fails to convey in mere words what the eye witnesses infallibly for itself, in every alley, on every street corner poisoned by the monster's filth.'

Well, you could've knocked me down with a stick of celery. All those poor people he'd had killed, and starting the Great Fire, too because, when you think about it, there's coincidence and there's the screaming bloody obvious, right? – all that and the bestial perversions and insatiable lusts too. Bloody hell, I thought. The bastard.

'All true, actually,' Seneca went on, quietly, helping himself to a handful of spicy crunches from a finger bowl. 'And all lies, just like the statement for the defence – the facts are the same, but the interpretation differs slightly, and the golden age becomes the reign of terror, simple as choosing adjectives. And counsel for the defence will smile, admit the murders, point out that by any criteria the world's a better place without Lepida, Silanus, Rubellius Plautus, Cornelius Sulla, Narcissus, Pallas, Britannicus, Octavia, Agrippina. Even if a few of them were innocent, or as innocent as Roman nobility could ever be, if they'd been spared they'd have been used as figureheads of rebellion; thousands of lives would've been lost because Nero Caesar allowed himself the luxury, the self-indulgence of mercy. Quite true. And counsel for the prosecution will brush aside the corn supply and justice for the provinces and corruption stamped out and peace on the frontiers: "That wasn't Nero Caesar, that was all Seneca's doing, Seneca and Burrus, two honest men who had the misfortune to serve the tyrant, who eventually paid for their wisdom and courage with their lives"—' Then Seneca stopped suddenly and grinned at me, and said, 'Oh, didn't I tell you? I'm going to die soon. Suicide, it'll be, the decent way, without all the nastiness of a trial and execution. I got found out, you see, after all these years – stealing from the exchequer, manipulating policy to feather my own nest (I didn't get to be the fourth richest man in the world by writing philosophy, oddly enough) and, eventually, plotting with the indescribably awful Calpurnius Piso to murder the emperor. Actually,' he added with a wink, 'it's my sixth plot in five years, but that buffoon Tigellinus couldn't see an elephant if it was crawling up his nose; which is why I had him made chief of police, it goes without saying. You see?' he went on, with a rather graceful gesture. 'All true, and all lies; because I did do some rather fine things – no, Nero Caesar and I together did some very fine things for our fellow citizens, and Nero Caesar and I together and separately did some other things you'll have to make your own mind up about, if you can be bothered. Calpurnius Piso, for example – Piso will tell you we plotted to rid Rome of the monster, we're liberators like Brutus and Cassius. I might tell you I did it because of the power and the money; I'm absurdly pleased with my own profile, and I know it'd look simply wonderful on a ten-pence piece, looking down its aristocratic nose at all the fish-mongers and garlic-sellers in the Market Square.' He sighed, stood up, paused to rub his foot (cramp, probably). 'The one thing that neither prosecution nor defence will allow you to believe is that it's all true – all the good things, all the bad things together – and that men can be bad and good at the same time, and switch backwards and forwards between the two like a messenger running errands. And that, my young stealer of cloaks from bathhouses, is more philosophy than you could buy anywhere in this city for a gold sovereign, even a genuine one; and even so, it's mostly horseshit. The only truth—' and he stopped smiling and just looked at me, if you see what I mean. One of those looks. 'The only truth is what you stand up in on the beach after a shipwreck, and which of you's still standing after a fight on your own doorstep, and what your dog thinks of you when you come home. And now,' he added, 'I think I'll go and take a leak,' then, pinching a last handful of spicy crunches, he limped away towards the lavatories.

So there I was, sat in some garden in some house, all on my tod. Just me and my thoughts. You know by now I've been in some pretty dodgy places in my time – condemned cells and up on crosses and God knows what else – but that garden was one of my all-time least favourites.

For a long time I tried to tell myself, So what? So what, if Lucius Domitius got up to stuff back in the old days? I hardly knew him then, he was just the man who'd saved me from the cross because he'd taken a fancy to my brother. On balance I approved of him, back then. Yes, he was a rich bastard – *the* rich bastard of all rich bastards, emperor of the Romans, no less – and surely that says it all; you expect that mob to do every nasty rotten thing that it's possible to do, because that's who they are, rich bastards, and that's what rich bastards do. But, on the other hand, he'd got me down off that cross, which I richly deserved to be up on, because I was a thief and I'd got caught. He got me down off there, and it was my fault, not his, that I was up there in the first place. So, on balance, I reckoned he was all right, or at least, all right for a rich bastard.

And then all that stuff had happened. We'd escaped from the palace, Callistus (fuck me, I thought, it always ended up back with him, doesn't it?) – Callistus had given his life for Lucius Domitius, and Callistus couldn't possibly have been wrong about a person. If he reckoned Lucius Domitius was worth dying for, I wasn't going to argue, was I? Not me, the thick one in our family. And then we'd gone around together all those years, starving and running together; and all that time, he wasn't a rich bastard any more, he was just a poor bastard and a thief, like me, no better and no worse – so yes, I'd come to the conclusion he was all right, because Callistus reckoned so, and because I reckoned so, judging him as I found him. Now you could say: Of course Lucius Domitius didn't get up to anything nasty while you and he were on the road together because he never got the chance to carry on his old tricks, because the two of you were too busy dodging guards and trying to stay alive on a thimbleful of sprouting grain and there wasn't time or opportunities for that sort of shit. Well, I can't argue with that. Can't be bothered to, either. It's like if you were a magistrate and I got hauled up in front of you for hooking sandals at a bathhouse, and I was to say, Actually I'm not guilty, because really I'd have been an honest, hard working farmer and never screwed anybody, only I never got the opportunity. You'd laugh till you bruised a rib, and then you'd send me to the mines, of course you would. I'd do the same if I was up on the curule chair, not stood in front of it. So, right – where's your argument now?

And I tried to tell myself: Look, you're a pathetic little Greek swindler and everybody in the world is out to kill you, and the only person in the universe who might be on your side is Lucius Domitius, so who cares a screaming fuck what he may have done? If you were drowning, you'd take his hand. And besides, it's none of your business what other people do, so long as they don't do it to you. If the whole world's against you, screw the lot of them. And this Blandinia, this murdering thief bitch who might consider letting you live if she feels like it – whose side are you on, hers or your only friend in the whole world? Just a pity she got out alive, and lived to be the death of you.

And that was a bugger, too; because Callistus saved her, and Callistus couldn't have been wrong about a person, could he? If he figured she was worth saving, who the hell are you to call her a murdering bitch or whatever? Can't have it both ways.

So now do you see what I mean about the gods? Surely, if they're there for any other purpose besides being our rich bastard landlords, shouldn't they be there to tell us this is what's right, this is what's wrong, learn it off by heart because there'll be a test later? But I tell you, I sat in that garden, all alone, and I listened; and they didn't say a word. They didn't even fart. I think all the gods must be Romans. That'd explain a lot, if you ask me.

And – God forgive me – I started thinking to myself: if that's what gods are like, maybe Callistus was a god. You know how they get their jollies prowling about among us poor mortals, pretending to be one of us, like some low-life swindler, telling the tale; like me, even, and Lucius Domitius. Just suppose Callistus was a god in disguise; and I'd loved him, and Lucius Domitius had loved him, and the murdering bitch Blandinia had loved him, because that's how mortals react to gods, they can't help it, just like cats with catnip. And so this rich bastard of a god comes down and he sets us all this wonderful riddle, and once we're all tangled up in it like sheep in briars, he fucks off back to Olympus and settles down to see what kind of a mess we make of trying to get ourselves free. Maybe that's what love is, a nasty game that gods like to play on poor mortals, innocent and vulnerable as children. Maybe Callistus was a god, and then we'd all be in the clear. We could load all the bad things we'd done on him, and he could take the blame. In that sense, maybe he'd save us all. Again.

By this stage my brain was starting to hurt, so it was probably just as well that I was interrupted before it had a chance to boil over like porridge and come dripping out my ears.

Alexander and Pony-tail came out into the courtyard, carrying a couple of small tables with covered dishes on them. When I saw who it was, my first thought was, Oh shit, she's changed her mind and they're going to kill me, but then I thought, Yes, but the tables, and the nosh. Why bother to poison me, when a bash on the head is so much quicker and cheaper? And if they were going to kill me by feeding me to death with potted hare tartlets – well, there are worse ways to go, at that. The likelier explanation was she'd said, You'd better see to the prisoner, or something along those lines, and they'd taken that as licence to go and cook something.

'It's just a snack,' Alexander said, lifting the lid on shoulder of mutton Etruscan style, with creamed leeks and beans in gravy. 'Something to help you keep your strength up, that's all.'

Fine, except what would I be needing my strength for? Didn't say anything, of course, just, Thanks, that's really thoughtful of you, or words to that effect. Pony-tail said not to mention it, and I got the impression he was upset about something. Guilty, almost. A moment later, Alexander confirmed that by adding, Really, it was the least we could do. That was interesting.

'Oh?' I said. 'How do you mean?'

They looked at each other, like a couple of embarrassed mountains. 'Truth is,' Pony-tail said, 'we feel a bit bad about – well, you know.'

'It wasn't right,' Alexander said. 'I mean, he was so nice to us. Not a lot of people are, you know.'

So which one was he talking about, Pollio or Lucius Domitius? Could've been either, except if they were feeling bad about Pollio, why be nice to me? I took a chance. 'Yes,' I said, 'well. Does you credit, I'm sure, but where I come from we have a saying, fine words oil no greens. He trusted you.'

You know, even though they were so big and mean-looking, I almost wished I hadn't had to say that, because it obviously hurt. Alexander turned away; Pony-tail stood there staring at his toes. They didn't come across as angry or anything, just ashamed. This went on for some time (and all the while my shoulder of mutton Etruscan style was going cold, but I didn't want to spoil the mood; bitter reproaches don't come across so well when spoken through a mouthful of creamed leek). Then Alexander said, 'You know what makes it worse?' Pony-tail put a hand on his shoulder, but he shook it off. 'What makes it really, really bad?' he went on. 'He was my hero, you know? I worshipped him; all those wonderful songs and poems, and that voice – I went to all his public recitals, I even dressed up as a senator, purple stripe and everything, so I could sneak in to the closed concerts. People think that just because you're a gladiator and you were born in some village you haven't got any finer feelings, you can't appreciate music and poetry. Balls,' he spat angrily. 'Back then, I'd have cut off my right hand just for a chance to meet him and say how much I loved his music. Well, I say that. Someone said he'd introduce me once, back in the old days, but I couldn't, I was too shy. I mean, it'd have been like meeting Phoebus Apollo, what could I possibly have said? And then I actually do get to meet him

'Bashed him on the head,' I muttered. 'You must've felt so proud.'

'Don't.' Alexander shuddered. 'Look, you've got to believe me, we didn't know, either of us. Oh, we knew she was pretty much running the show, but we thought she was just doing what Pollio told her to. We didn't know she was involved with Strymon and his mob. Otherwise—'

'Really,' I interrupted. 'So where were you when they burst in and started killing people? You could've stopped them, you two. Or were you afraid?'

Pony-tail twitched when I said that, but Alexander just looked very sad. 'We were in the kitchens, weren't we?' he said. 'We were slicing onions, and suddenly these blokes came in, with swords and clubs and all. We had no idea. We thought it must be a robbery, only they said, stay right where you are and nobody'll get hurt. Look, we got through the arena without getting killed or carved up, we've done our share. The two of us, take on a dozen armed men without even knowing what it's about? No, we stood there, and they stood there, and then someone called them and they pissed off and left us, then we heard screams, so we ran to the dining room, but by then it was all over. Just dead people everywhere. We still didn't have a clue what was happening, but then Blandinia came in and told us—'

'We should have killed her,' Pony-tail muttered. 'Only it

wouldn't have solved anything, would it? And we don't want to get murdered by Strymon's men, thank you very much.'

'And then,' Alexander went on, 'she told us she was going to fetch you, and then we found out you'd been arrested, so we went with her to get you out. And that's all we've done, really.'

I sighed. Actually, I couldn't blame them, but I couldn't very well admit that. 'Too bloody right,' I said. 'That's all you did. Not very impressive, was it?' And while I was saying that, some god whispered an idea in my ear, and I went on. 'Now if I was a really famous gladiator, the best in the world like you were, and I had a loyal fan, someone who worshipped the ground I trod on—'

Alexander made a little whimpering noise, like a hungry dog, but I carried on. 'If he was in terrible danger and I was there, I think I'd have taken the trouble to save him, rather than just standing around like a prune. He believed in you two. He talked about you all the time, you know; how you were the best he'd ever seen, how he wished he'd had a chance to meet you, all that stuff. I bet he was thinking as they dragged him away, It's all right, Alexander and Julianus'll rescue me—'

That was too much for Alexander; he was crying, dripping huge fat tears into my bean casserole. 'I know,' he said. 'God, I'm so ashamed. It's true, we were scared. You're away from the arena so long, you forget what it's like, how scared you are at the sight of sharp metal. Back then, when I was fighting, every time I went out on the sand I'd be shivering so much I could hardly hold my sword. But you get used to it, something cuts in and takes over and you get through it somehow, till the next time. But it's been ten years, for God's sake, and thumping people from behind in dark alleys doesn't count; it's not the same thing at all as looking down a newly honed edge at some bastard who wants to kill you. When they came in our kitchen with swords, we were scared, and that's all there is to it.'

Shit, I thought, I'm in serious danger of liking these two nutcases. But I was still busy thinking. I was telling myself, Blandinia's made a mistake here with these two; she's got them down in her mind as just a pair of thugs. Only they're not, they're more like Lucius Domitius than anybody else I've come across. Under that muscle and scar tissue they're all delicate and sensitive, they're artistes. So who are they going to listen to, when the screws are on: her, or me?

'It's all right,' I said, and they looked at me like they were drowning and I'd chucked them a rope. 'I understand. It's not your fault.'

Gratitude's not something I've had a lot to do with, certainly not gratitude pointed at me. Funny feeling, makes you pleased with yourself and a bit guilty, like you're really just a big fraud, both at the same time. 'Thank you,' Alexander said. 'Thank you for saying that.'

I nodded. 'Don't worry about it,' I said. 'Everything's fine. Now, are you going to help me, or not?'

That made them go a bit thoughtful, but only for a second. 'How do you mean?' Pony-tail said.

'I'd have thought that was obvious,' I replied. 'We've got to get out of here and rescue Lucius Domitius.'

Pony-tail looked puzzled. 'Who's he?' he asked.

'Nero Caesar, you idiot,' Alexander snapped without looking round. 'But just a moment. We don't even know where he is.'

I looked at him all stern and hard. 'You could find out,' I said.

'Could we? How?'

'Well,' I said, 'you could try getting a hold of that bitch round the neck and squeezing till she tells you. That ought to do the trick.'

They didn't like the sound of that for some reason, so I went on: 'Or you could go round and ask Strymon, if you think that'll be any easier. Personally, though, I'd rather take my chances with Blandinia.'

They thought about it, but not for long. 'Yes, all right,' said Pony-tail. 'You wait here, we'll be right back.' They went off the way they'd come, and, since there was nothing else for me to do, I had a bit of the shoulder of mutton Etruscan style. It wasn't bad, at that, though it could've done with warming through.

Blandinia didn't look quite so cocky as she had the last time we'd talked; she was spitting-angry, no question about that, but she was also very scared. I think she realised they weren't kidding around. What gave her that impression, I'm not sure, though probably Pony-tail's enormous fingers on either side of her windpipe might have put her on the right track.

'You're crazy,' she said, in a rather strained voice, 'all of you. You're also three dead men, unless you pack this in immediately.'

Well, she had me worried, right enough, so it was just as well that Alexander and Pony-tail weren't chickenshits like me. But then, I never said I was brave. Quite the reverse.

'Tell us where he is,' Alexander said, 'or we'll pull your head off.'

You know, we all say stuff like that – I'll tear your head off, I'll smash your teeth down your neck, I'll kick your spine up out the back of your neck – and all we really mean is, I might possibly hurt you, or then again I might not. But when Alexander said that, it was rather obvious that he was just telling it straight, no melodrama. He'd nod his head, and Julianus would squeeze hard, snap her spine and give her neck a twist and a yank, and off her head would come, like a stopper out of a jar. It made me feel sick, but that's what I get for having a top-of-the-range imagination.

Anyhow, she got the message. 'No, listen,' she said, with rather less attitude, 'I'd tell you if I knew, but I don't. Really I don't. I mean, why would he bother telling me? I don't need to know; and it stands to reason, in this line of work, the fewer people know something, the better. Strymon may be dumb, but he's smart enough for that.'

It sounded like she was telling the truth, but it wasn't what I wanted to hear. 'She's lying,' I said. 'Of course she knows, she's the sort who wants to know everything, all the details, just in case there's something'll give her an edge. Squeeze her a bit more and she'll tell us, trust me.' Pony-tail looked doubtful, but he shrugged and tightened his grip; and for a moment I was afraid he'd overdone it, because her eyes started bulging out of her face and she made a revolting gurgling noise and twitched all over. 'All right,' she said, 'all right. Let *go*, for God's sake.'

I nodded – just think of it, me giving orders like a general – and Pony-tail eased off a bit, so she could breathe. 'Now, then,' I said.

'I'm just guessing,' Blandinia gasped, 'but Strymon's got a place on Long Lane, just past the tanner's yard. That's all I can think of.'

Pony-tail frowned. 'Which tanner's yard?' he asked. 'There's two.'

'What?' She struggled to drag air down her bruised throat. 'I don't know, I've never been there, just heard other people talking about it. A place on Long Lane, just past the tanner's yard, that's all I know. Really.'

I nearly burst out laughing. 'That's the best you can do, is it?' I asked.

'Please, let go. Make him let go, I can't *breathe*.'

She was going a funny colour, and I decided that she'd have to be cooler than the Alps in winter to keep up a good lie when she was that close to dying. 'Let her go,' I said, 'she's telling the truth. It's bloody useless, but that's all she knows.'

Alexander scowled, and nodded at Pony-tail (where did the chain of command suddenly appear from, I wondered in passing), and he relaxed his vast blood-sausage fingers by a certain carefully-regulated amount. 'Well,' I said, 'so what do we do with her?'

Pretty obvious I wasn't going to get any sensible suggestions out of those two. Born followers, the both of them. It was up to me to come up with a brilliant idea. I hate that.

'We'll have to take her with us,' I said.

Alexander looked dubious about that. 'What if she squeals and makes a racket?' he said. 'People'll stare; we don't want any trouble.'

And then Apollo shot me with a stroke of genius. 'Well, that's simple,' I said. 'You know what to do.' And I rubbed the back of my head, like it still hurt.

They weren't as slow on the uptake as all that. Alexander closed his fist and clubbed her on the base of the skull, and she went out like a snuffed lamp. Fast asleep in Pony-tail's arms, like a girl flaked out after a night's partying. Sweet, really.

'Brilliant,' Pony-tail moaned. 'Have I got to lug her all the way to Long Lane?'

'The sedan chair,' I said. 'The one I was fetched here in. It's still about the place, isn't it?'

Confession time. I love riding in sedan chairs. Bloody stupid, really. I guess it's because sedan chairs are the all-time essential rich-bastard thing. I mean, you see them swaying through the streets on the shoulders of a couple of enormous Germans or Libyans, up so high they're clipping the ears of the poor people as they jostle by – it's everything that being a rich bastard is about, if you follow me. Now I don't much care for rich people, but that's never stopped me getting a real thrill out of being one, just for a little while, peeking out through the curtains of a closed chair at the bald patches on the little folks' heads. And, well, if ever I get taken rich, which is about as likely as my old mother getting swept up to heaven and put among the stars as the constellation of the Drunk Old Bag, first thing I'll buy myself is a really swish sedan chair and six porters, all Thracians or Lusitanians, a matched set. And of course, when I ride through the streets in my chair, there'll be a beautiful young girl reclining at my side, because if a thing's worth doing, it's worth doing right, only, in this daydream of mine, the beautiful young girl won't be fast asleep, and we won't be on our way to rescue Lucius Domitius from the meanest street gang in the world, always assuming we can find their hideout. It's little things like that that fuck up a nice bit of wish-fulfilment.

Finding a tanner's yard in Long Lane wasn't hard at all. All that took was going to Long Lane and breathing in. Beats me why they allowed something that smelt that bad in a posh neighbourhood, but that's Rome for you: the grand houses stand up out of the slums and the trash like a man standing in a gutter. Anyhow, we found a tannery, and there were houses on either side that looked like they could be a gang's hideout, not that any of us had a clue what a gang's hideout looks like.

'So what do we do now?' I heard Alexander say, down below on street level. 'Start knocking on doors?'

I tweaked the curtain aside. 'All right,' I said. 'Now let's find the other one.'

Beats me why they'd decided to take orders from me, but they did. The other tannery was down the other end of the lane, and it had almost identical houses up and down the street. I was just about to give up, when I saw someone I recognised.

Very handy knack, a gift for faces. Of course, it's something you have to pick up if you're going to last more than a month in the scamming trade: you've got to be able to recognise a face immediately, out of the corner of your eye at fifty paces, and remember that that bloke was in the crowd when you pulled such and such a scam at such and such a place, which means it'd be a very bad idea to try the same scam again where he'd be likely to see it. Anyway, I saw this face, just for a split second, and I knew where I'd seen it before – namely, in the inn where Amyntas had taken me, and the bloke had been one of the Sicilian's boys.

'Stop,' I called down, 'we're here.'

I pinched back the curtain and watched where the bloke was headed. I saw him cross the street to the gate of a big old house, pause for a moment to look round, then knock on the door four times, rat-at-at-TAT. The door opened, he ducked inside, the door swung shut again; all over in the time you'd take to eat a grape. There's lucky, I said to myself.

'What about Blandinia?' Pony-tail said, once I'd got down from my floating eagle's nest and explained what I'd seen. 'We can't just park her in the chair. What if she wakes up?'

I sighed. 'Can't you bash her again?' I said.

'Not really,' Alexander replied, sounding like an expensive doctor. 'It's not, what's the word, cumulative, bashing people; I mean, you can't sort of top up a bash with a smart tap every two hours to keep it fresh.'

So I thought; and what I came up with was pretty thin, but let's see you do better on the fly, when most of your brainpower's taken up with being very scared.

Imagine you're the porter, right? You're sat in your little cubby hole, thinking about whatever porters think about, and there's this frantic banging on your door. You wake up, snap, and pull back the little slide; who's making that fucking awful row, you ask.

Through your little hole in the door, you can see this pointy-faced Greek bloke, and behind him there's two uglies, holding up a girl who doesn't look too chipper. In fact, she's slumping, and the two bruisers are holding her up.

'Open the goddamn door,' hisses the pointy-faced type. 'Come on, people are staring.'

You feel a bit panicky, because of the urgency in his voice, but there's such a thing as standing orders, including, *Don't let anybody in unless you know them, or they've got a pass.* 'Who're you, then?' you ask nervously.

Pointy-face spits a string of Greek names at you. They don't mean spit as far as you're concerned. You don't know what to do for the best. A porter can get the skin flayed off his back for letting strangers in, and the same for keeping important visitors standing out in the street. 'Who's she, then?' you ask.

One of the thugs in the background is asking what in hell the hold-up is; he doesn't sound happy. The Greek looks at you and says, None of your damn business, now open the bloody door. Of course, this is turning into a porter's worst nightmare – buggered if you do or buggered if you don't, and no way of knowing which. You start to say you're sorry, but—

'You bloody well will be sorry in a minute,' says Pointy-face, 'if you don't open the damn gate. You'll be off to the farm, with your hoe in your moist little hand, if our Strymon hears you made his little honey-apple stand out in the street, running a fever so bad she's fit to fall over.'

At that point, the girl groans pitifully (you aren't to know it's the first helpful thing she's done in her whole life, and she's only doing it because she's fast asleep on her feet and hasn't got the foggiest idea what's going on), and a helpful little voice says to you, Come on, they've got to be on the level; I mean, who'd be crazy enough to try and kid their way into our house, of all places? So you shoot back the bolts as fast as you can and haul the gate open, and soon as you do, one of the uglies shoves the droopy girl in your arms and says, Catch hold of this a moment, will you? And you grab her to stop her falling over, and then the back of your head hurts, and next thing you know – well, you don't want to imagine that, it'd give you nightmares. Anyway, you get the idea. Corny as Egypt and crazy as a tubful of polecats, but who gives a shit? More by luck than judgement, sure, but it worked.

So there we were: inside the walls all right, but feeling very conspicuous and terribly, terribly lonely. You've heard of the Seven against Thebes, I expect. Well, we were the Two against Strymon (I'm not counting me, for obvious reasons) and the odds on the Seven had to be better. Also, didn't all the Seven get killed? I don't know, I wasn't paying attention when our mother told us the story.

Just as well one of us had his wits about him. Say what you like about Alexander, he was like the hedgehog in the saying – you know, how the fox knows many tricks, but the hedgehog knows one good one. He only knew one scheme for situations like this, but he gave it a go. 'FIRE!' he started yelling – and he could yell, believe me; I was nearly blown over – and to make it a bit more convincing, he picked up the porter's brazier in one hand and pitched it across the yard. Pure fluke it happened to land on a stack of jars lined up against the wall. Even flukier that they happened to be full of lamp-oil. Fool's luck, you could call it, only if there is such a thing, how come I never get any?

If there hadn't been a fire before, there was a honey of one now, in fact, I remember thinking as I stood there watching the whole yard blossom into orange flames, looks like Alexander may have overdone the diversionary tactics this time. Not entirely his fault, mind you, because a sensible bloke wouldn't have stacked the month's supply of oil up against the stables, with all that hay and straw inside.

That's another thing I don't like about Rome. Bloody place is a fire trap.

I guess there was a sort of wonderfully stupid irony about the whole situation. A fire starts. Thanks to a stiff breeze which scoops up fistfuls of glowing embers and scatters them over the neighbouring rooftops like a man sowing barley, in the time it takes to eat an apple the entire block is up in flames, with people running around yelling and pushing and shoving and panicking, the way people do, some poor fools trying to be sensible and organise bucket chains, others running screaming in the wrong direction, or struggling to get back inside the burning buildings to get children or crippled relatives, not to mention the looters. When there's a fire, you get a wonderful display of pretty well everything that's right and wrong with human nature: courage and cowardice and greed and cool common sense under stress and a hundred subtly different strains of stupidity – the pity of it is, it all happens so fast right in front of your nose, with three or four absolutely fascinating exhibitions going on at the same time; doesn't matter how observant you are, you're bound to miss a gem or two, an inspiring display of selfless bravery or a collector's item in the way of sheer unparalleled selfishness. It's as good as the theatre for distilling what mortal humans are all about down into a ninety-nine-parts-pure essence. Pity about all the smoke and shit, but I guess you need that for ambience.

Well, there was this incredible show going on right under my nose – *Rome Burns*, a tragi-comic extravaganza in twelve simultaneous acts – and I wasn't paying attention, as bloody usual. No, I wasn't even thinking of myself as a member of the audience; nothing would do me but I had to clamber up on stage, so to speak, and gatecrash my way into the play. Thinking about it with the fabulous alchemy of hindsight, I can see now why the true-blood Roman gentry get so uptight about respectable people getting mixed up in theatricals and performing on a stage. Here's Rome burning, say, a tragedy of catastrophic proportions, ruining the lives of dozens, hundreds of miserable bastards, rich and poor; and here's me, an insignificant little Greek, who's so up himself he's got to use this terrible thing as the background to his own trivial drama, his own worthless private subplot. Worse still, in this case, because I'd gone one step further. I'd *caused* the damn fire, by bringing on as a plot device the moron Alexander, with his penchant for setting light to the scenery every time he runs into a minor difficulty in his work. You know how lots of people are firmly convinced that Lucius Domitius Nero Caesar started the Great Fire just so he could have a truly spectacular backdrop for his *Fall of Troy*, with harp accompaniment? Well, that happens not to be true; but it's a stone-cold fact that Galen the Athenian, an artiste in a wholly different genre of make-believe and performance arts, deliberately started the Long Lane Fire as a *mise en scène* (I think that's the right term) for his ballet for three idiots and a stunned girl, *The Rescue of Lucius Domitius*. No harp accompaniment, I'm afraid, but what do you expect if you engage a bunch of cheapskates?

I'm not quite sure what I'm trying to say here. I mean, there's a point to this, and your Senecas and Petronius Arbiters and Caius Juvenalises'd be on it like a snake, but instead you've got me. Maybe you can figure it out for yourselves – in which case, maybe you'd drop me a line and let me know what it is. Assuming I'm still alive when you read this, and you can find me.

Anyhow, there I was, standing in a courtyard with burning buildings all round me, people running hither and yon, bashing into me and treading on my feet, and there's Alexander and Pony-tail, not to mention the poisonous bitch Blandinia, who's sleeping through the whole show like your elderly aunt when you've been to great pains to fight your way to the front rows and get seats so she'll be able to see the swordfighting and hear the screams. And I was thinking, *Shit*.

Well, wouldn't you have done? Because we were there to save Lucius Domitius' life, and he was somewhere in that big house, moments away from burning to death. Not smart. Could do better.

'Don't just stand there,' I screamed at them. 'Do something.'

They looked at me like I was the captain of a ship becalmed in the middle of the sea, and I'd pointed straight up in the air and said, 'That way.' Well, they had a point, it wasn't the most helpful suggestion I'd ever made. But I couldn't think what to do, I was too bewildered by how fast it had all happened, not to mention the sheer unspeakable scale of the fuck-up I'd just perpetrated. I mean, it's not every day a provincial farm boy like me sets fire to the biggest city in the world. Call it stage fright, if you like.

Then a little bit of burning cinder lit on Blandinia's forehead, and she woke up with a shriek. She got up; stumbled forwards, staggered like a vaudeville drunk, found her feet, looked round and said something very unladylike.

'You *idiots*,' she said, proving she was plenty quick on the uptake. 'What've you *done*?'

Seemed to me she'd got it all plumb right at the first guess; woman's intuition, they call it. Anyhow, we weren't in the mood to explain, so we didn't say anything.

'Right,' she said, and you could almost hear her brain snapping into place, like one of those great big Molossian padlocks when you turn the key. 'Five gets you ten he's in the dining room, which ought to be there.' She pointed at a door vaguely opposite; it was outlined in fire, like on a wall painting, and rather graceful plumes of smoke were feathering up under it.

'You sure?' I asked.

'You can take it to the bank,' she said. 'Go on, move.' So we moved, for no reason I can see other than that she was telling us to, and she sounded like she was in charge. I guess it's like soldiers are trained to obey the words of command without thinking. Anyway, Alexander's side-of-beef shoulder crashed into that door, and the poor wooden bugger never stood a chance. It exploded into a mess of splinters and we were through, into a cloud of smoke so thick you could've spread it on bread with a knife.

I didn't get much further than that, because I tripped over something and went down on my nose, crack on the mosaic floor, ouch.

Turned out what I'd tripped on was a dead body, and I wish I knew who he was, because he saved my life, though I don't suppose he did it on purpose. Alexander and Pony-tail sprinted past me into the smoke, and a moment later there was a horrible crash as something fell in, a wall or a ceiling, something like that. Something heavy, any rate, and instantly fatal.

And that was the last I saw of them. One moment there they were, two enormous bouncy dangerous idiots but all right, fundamentally, because they were on my side, even if they did go around setting light to cities. The next moment, they were gone; and whether the falling masonry and roof-timbers got them clean, or they were pinned down and suffocated in the smoke, or whether they were still awake when the flames got to them, I'm sorry but I simply don't know. They charged out of my life as abruptly as they'd burst into it, and that was the end of them.

Bugger, I thought, as I scrambled up and shot out of there like a rabbit with its scut on fire. I couldn't see Blandinia either – it was entirely possible that she'd been under that roof or wall or whatever it was, but somehow I doubted that, because her sort don't die unless they're specifically killed. Didn't matter. We'd tried to save Lucius Domitius, but it was all doomed to failure from the very start, and I really, really wished I hadn't made the effort to begin with. A good idea at the time's the best you can say for it, and I don't know to this day how many lives it cost. All my fault. Sorry.

At any rate, that was palpably the end of that. Lucius Domitius, the two gladiator cooks, probably the bitch Blandinia, pretty well everybody I knew in the City of Rome was now dead, and there was me, on my own, at a loose end once more. I trudged across that courtyard, couldn't even be bothered to run. Where was the point? Wouldn't have bothered me unduly if a burning chunk of building had fallen smack on my stupid head and tidied me away out of the story.

'Galen?' said a voice behind me. 'What the fuck are you doing here?'

I spun round. Guess who. Not that anybody else but me would've recognised him, probably. He was covered in blood, for one thing; also he was wringing wet, his hair plastered down onto his head, and he was filthy with ash and plaster and God knows what else. In his right hand he had a sword, a German pattern with a long blade, bent almost to right angles.

'Galen?' he repeated. 'What're you staring at like that?'

Oh, nothing, I thought. Just you, that's all, the dead bloke who keeps on coming back to life. 'Are you all right?' I said. 'You look bloody awful.'

'So do you,' he replied. 'Look, is there any reason why you're standing there like the last leek in the patch? Waiting for someone, anything like that?'

I shook my head.

'Fine,' he said. 'Let's get out of here, shall we?'

Well, why not? He made it sound like dodging out of some boring family gathering or harvest festival; let's you and me slip round the corner to this great little wine shop I know. The others can sort out the fire and clear away the dead bodies, while we have a couple of quick ones. Absolutely, I thought, what a really good idea. Shame I didn't think of that.

The street was crowded with people, all of them getting under each other's feet in their hurry to get out of the way. We didn't rush (that's one of the good things about having a charmed life, you don't have to worry about getting accidentally killed – like having a wall fall on you, for instance, or being pinned down by a burning roof-beam. You just saunter past the scurrying little people, because everything's just fine, really). As we put the fire behind us, a large cart thundered past, with a gang of hefty-looking men crammed in the back, clutching long hooks and big hammers: the fire brigade, on its way to pull down enough houses to clear a firebreak. Lucius Domitius' idea originally, though it was Vespasian who put it through and took all the credit.

'Right,' I said. 'So what the hell happened to you?'

'What?' He'd been thinking of something else, by the look of it. 'Oh, not much to tell, really. One moment I was stuck there being talked at by that Pollio man – was he for real, do you know? Only I can't believe anybody could be that obsessed with anything I ever wrote, not even me. Anyway, I remember this crashing noise and I looked round, and then wham! and everything went black on me. When I woke up I was in this barn or stable, just a wooden shed sort of place with straw on the deck and a powerful smell of livestock. Some bastard had tied me to a beam, so I woke up with the most appalling cramp in my legs and my back; and before I could open my eyes properly and say, Hello, where is this? some big bugger started hitting me round the face and saying, Well, where is it, where's it hidden? God knows what he was on about. I assumed either he was crazy as a magpie or he'd mistaken me for someone else. But every time I tried to say anything, he'd just whack me again. Anyhow, he'd been at this for what felt like a very long time when guess who showed up? You'll never guess—'

'The Sicilian,' I said.

'What? Oh, you knew.'

'He's a gang boss,' I said. 'His name's Strymon.'

'Strymon,' he repeated. 'Come to think of it, that does ring a bell, I think he was in business back in my time. Fancy that. But anyhow, he turns up and gives the bloke who'd been knocking me around a fearful telling-off for starting before he was ready. Quite startled him; the bloke who'd been thumping me, I mean. I think he expected to be told well done for using his initiative. So he shrugs and pushes off, and this Strymon takes over, but all he does is ask me over and over again, Where is it, where's the secret hiding place, and every time I ask him what's he talking about, I don't understand, he bashes me. Better at it than the first bloke, too, though to do him credit he was taking care not to hit me where there was any danger of doing permanent damage. Like I was a valuable slave or something. Just when all this was starting to get on my nerves, there's this loud yell, Fire! and sure enough, we can all smell burning. The Sicilian, Strymon, if that's who he was, first thing he says is, Cut him down quick, get him out of here; then he pushes off to see what's going on. His two heavies cut me down, but while they're doing that, the fire's taken hold bloody quick in our stable, the roof's starting to burn through and there's bits of glowing cinder dropping down, setting light to the straw; also, the smoke's getting a bit much. One of the heavies says something like, Screw this, leave him, let's get out of here. The other one says, No, master wants this one safe, it's important, you come back here. But it's too late, his mate's slung his hook, so he's left to finish cutting me down. Serves them right for making such a thorough job of it, I guess. Anyway, as luck would have it, just when I'm about loose, a chunk of timber falls down and nuts the bloke, he falls over and just lies there. I get myself free, and so help me, I did my best to drag him out of there, but after all that getting knocked around I just wasn't up to it. And he's all-over blood from a nasty scalp wound, poor bugger, which makes him horribly slippery so I keep losing my grip, and the smoke's got so thick I'm choking my lungs up, so in the end I give it up and – well, I'm ashamed to say I just left him there and hopped it. And a few moments later, I saw you, and here we are.'

(And I thought to myself, Curious, isn't it, the number of people who die saving Lucius Domitius' life? All the way from Callistus, right down to Alexander and Pony-tail, and some nameless thug trying to cut him loose from a beam in a burning barn. Death must love him, I thought. The Black King's heart must leap up at the sight of him, like a shepherd's dog in the early morning, when he hears the door scrape.)

I nodded. 'You had it easy, then,' I said, and I told him what'd happened to me, including Dido's treasure and all about – well, most about – the unspeakable Blandinia, and how all the time we thought we were free and clear (except when we were in condemned cells, or the guards were after us) and nobody had a clue who we really were, in fact we were being carefully tracked by the government and at least two teams of private enterprise snoopers. He didn't like that one bit. Oddly enough, I left out what happened to Alexander and Pony-tail; and I didn't say anything about why Blandinia hated him so much, just made it sound like she was a greedy, vicious bitch – which she was, of course, so no harm done. I guess.

'Well,' he said, as we carried on sauntering through the streets of Rome like two gentlemen, 'the way things have turned out, it's not so bad, after all. I mean, who's to know I got out of there alive? Nobody, except you and me. They'll assume I died in the fire, and they won't be looking for me any more. But honestly, do you really believe they were only after me because of Dido's treasure? Well, not after me, even; after Callistus. That's weird.'

'Cuts both ways,' I reasoned. 'If Callistus looked just like you, stands to reason you look just like Callistus. Only you're the one still walking and talking, if there's any sense in that.'

He pulled a face. 'Not really,' he said. 'But it's crazy, all the same. Here's me, the most hated emperor of the Romans there's ever been, and all these people are trying to catch me because they think I'm a Greek tall-tale merchant who never did any real harm in his life. Just goes to show, it's not what you are or what you do that matters, it's what people believe about you.'

Well, I wasn't going to argue with that. It wasn't clever or profound enough to be worth arguing with, and besides, he was trampling on a great big bundle of raw nerve-ends in that area (though I don't suppose he realised that) and I just wanted to change the subject.

'So,' I said, 'here we are, genuinely free and clear for a change. What now?'

He shrugged. 'Well,' he said, 'if we weren't broke and destitute, we could do any damn thing we liked – go lion-hunting in Mesopotamia, or tour the Aegean looking at the cities, or retire to our country villa and spend the rest of our lives translating the *Odyssey* into Latin iambics. Trouble is, with no money and no way of getting any, we're still pretty well anchored in the shit. The only difference is, we're no worse off than the fifty thousand other broke, helpless buggers in this city. When you look at it like that, free and clear's not necessarily the be-all and end-all.'

It looked like it was his big day for stating the screamingly obvious. 'What now?' I repeated. 'Do we stick around here, or do we go somewhere else? If you want to know what I think, I've had enough of the big city for a while. Too many undesirable elements, in my opinion.'

He sighed. 'If we go anywhere else, we're going to have to walk,' he said. 'Which rules out most of the more attractive options, such as ranching in Bithynia or a pilgrimage to Athens to study moral philosophy.'

'I don't know,' I said. 'There's always ships.'

He lifted his head. 'I've had it with stowing away,' he replied. 'Asking for trouble.'

'Ah, but we don't have to stow away. We could work our passage, like normal people. Both of us know the ropes, after that grain freighter.'

'True,' he admitted. 'But why bother? If we're officially dead, there's nothing to keep us from stopping in Italy. We've done farm work as well as crewing a ship. If you recall, we only cleared off out of that because Strymon was after us.'

'Come off it,' I said. 'You couldn't stand field work. I was there, remember?'

'Only because of that clown of a landowner, him and his ponderous hoes. On a normal farm—'

I stopped him. 'On a normal farm,' I said, 'there'd be a normal bailiff. You wouldn't like him, I promise you. He'd work you to death and feed you pigs' scraps while he pocketed the hired help's food allowance. The trouble with farms large enough to hire casual labour,' I went on, 'is that they're owned by rich Roman bastards who think they're the lords of all creation. Probably,' I added fair-mindedly, 'because they are. Take it from me, you'd hate it.'

He raised an eyebrow. 'You're basing this on all the years you spent day-labouring in Italy,' he said, 'presumably while I was asleep or looking the other way. But I guess you're right,' he sighed. 'Pastoral idylls are strictly for the poets, like Virgilius Maro; and we both know how much harm that stuff does, if you take it seriously. Shame I'm a poet, really.'

'Agreed,' I said. 'Hang on, though, I've just thought of something.'

'Oh dear. Well?'

I thought for a moment. 'You're dead, right?'

'You could say that, I suppose.'

'As far as everybody else is concerned, I mean you're officially dead, you and Callistus. Nobody's going to be looking for us any more. Right?'

'Let's hope so, anyway.'

'Fine. So, what's there to stop you earning us a living by doing the one thing you're sort of half-way competent at?'

He frowned. 'Making trouble for people? Don't think that's a sound commercial proposition.'

'Singing,' I said irritably. 'Playing the harp, all that shit. You always said the only reason you wouldn't do that was because you were afraid someone'd recognise you. Well, that's not a problem now, is it? Like, just suppose somebody does think you sound strangely familiar – I don't reckon there's any risk at all, but just for argument's sake. Somebody hears you and starts thinking, God, that sounds just like Nero Caesar, I wonder if it could actually be him. So he trots off to the prefect's office and says, Guess what, Nero Caesar didn't die after all, he's alive and playing the harp in a roadside wine shop in Calabria. Now, let's suppose, also for argument's sake, that the prefect doesn't have this clown slung in the cells till he sobers up; suppose he takes it seriously. He sends off to headquarters, and they send back saying, Don't be ridiculous, it's here on file, Nero Caesar's dead, and so's the Greek lookalike we were keeping an eye on for ten years. Prefect's happy, tells busybody to fuck off. Like I said, free and clear. And we can go around earning an honest living for a change, instead of being chased down alleys by the market patrol.'

He lifted his head. 'I'm not doing it,' he said. 'Too dangerous. I mean, you heard that Pollio bloke; and the gladiators, Alexander and Julianus – I wish I'd had time to say goodbye and thank them, by the way. Seems like I owe them a hell of a debt.'

'Don't change the subject,' I said quickly.

'All right. Like I was saying, you heard them. Mad keen fans, they were. Suppose they'd heard me playing in some tavern courtyard or in someone's house, at a party. They'd have recognised me, you can bet; and they wouldn't have been put off by some blather from the prefect's office, they'd have *known*.'

'All right,' I said. 'But they wouldn't have done us any harm, either. Bought us a drink, probably. That sort of risk I could live with.'

'You're missing the point,' he growled. 'They'd go around telling people, guess who I saw at Pellegrinus' bar the other day—'

'And whoever they told would tell them to wear a hat next time they went out in hot sunlight. Even if these mythical fans of yours believed, nobody else would. Come on,' I said. 'Look at it sensibly, for God's sake. Which do you reckon is the bigger risk: the outside chance of tripping over some loon who really liked your music, or doing the hundred-yard dash against twenty soldiers next time we bugger up a scam and have to run for it? Oh, we've been lucky so far, but as far as luck' s concerned, we're about due to start seeing the bottom of the jar. And apart from scamming, and you singing and harp-playing, what the fuck else is there we can do? Nothing.'

He was quiet for a very long time. Then he looked past me, sort of over my shoulder. 'I suppose,' he said, 'if I stick to just harp-playing, and don't play any of my own compositions – now that I'm quite definitely dead, as you say – it might not be such a terrible risk, at that.'

I sighed with relief 'Well done,' I said. 'I was sure we'd get there in the end.'

'And it is what I'm good at,' he went on, starting to sound more than a little bit keen. 'And it's got to be better than swindling and cheating for a livelihood.'

I smiled. 'Safer, too.'

'Yes, all right, safer. And better than farm work, as you pointed out.'

'Most things are,' I said. 'After all, a job in the dry; board and lodging thrown in free, like as not. Beats all sorts of trades, if you ask me: house-building and making barrels and shoeing horses and fishing—'

'Not to mention giving pleasure to people,' he said enthusiastically. 'Bringing a little happiness into their dull and wretched lives.'

I wasn't so sure about that, but I wasn't going to spoil the mood. 'It's like we've said over and over again,' I told him, 'it's what you were born for, and now at last you've got the chance. You should be thrilled,' I said persuasively. 'You know what? It means you're freer now than you've ever been. Like, when you were emperor of the Romans, you still weren't really allowed to play music, so much so that it got you slung out on your ear, nearly killed. I'm telling you, this is going to turn out to be the first day of your life. Everything that's gone before's just been wasted time and having to pretend you were someone else.'

'Put like that, it sounds pretty reasonable,' he said. Then he pulled a terrible face, like he'd just remembered that yesterday was his wife's birthday. 'There's just one problem.'

'Oh? What's that?'

'I haven't got a harp.'

THIRTEEN

Hadn't thought of that, had I?

Bloody musicians, you see. Most people with a trade, it's not the sort of problem that causes much grief You're a stonemason? If you go for a job in a quarry and you don't happen to have your own hammer and chisels, that's fine, there'll be tools you can borrow. Shipwright? No problem, borrow what you need from your mates till you've got a few bob saved up, then you nip across to the smithy and have a set made for you, or hang around the auctions till what you're after comes up for sale. Tools aren't cheap, exactly; nothing's cheap, especially when you're broke. But in any trade you care to name, there's ways round the problem, and skilled tradesmen face it every day of the year, so how you go about dealing with it's tolerably well known.

Every trade you care to name, that is, besides harp-playing.

'All right,' I said, 'let's think about this calmly. You're a harp-player. Where do harps come from?'

'Easy. From the harp-maker.'

I scowled. 'Yes,' I said, 'but he doesn't just pluck them off the branches of the harp tree when the Pleiades are rising. He makes them. Can't you make one? I don't suppose it's all that difficult.'

'No,' he said. 'Actually, it's extremely difficult. You've got to get everything just right, or the thing sounds like a fight between two cats.'

I sighed. 'I see,' I said. 'So, how much do they cost, then?'

He shrugged. 'Search me,' he said. 'Never bought one in my life. I just said to someone, Fetch me a harp, and a few heartbeats later, a harp appeared, on a red silk cushion.'

He was being feeble at me. 'All right,' I said, 'but you must have some idea what they cost. More than a plough? Less than a warship?'

'No idea. Please bear in mind, before I went on the road with you, I didn't know the price of a loaf of bread, let alone a harp. A war in Bithynia or a harbour or boots for twenty thousand infantry, yes, I could tell you more or less what that'd cost. But not little things.'

This was getting silly. 'Fine,' I said. 'We can't make one, chances are we can't buy one. That leaves stealing.' I paused. 'We can do stealing,' I said.

'Fine. Who were you planning on stealing one from?'

Good point. You don't see many harps in the course of a day's walk. 'Yes, but we're in Rome,' I pointed out. 'Biggest city in the world. Stands to reason, there must be more harp-players to the square foot here than anywhere else. We just go where harp-players hang out, I guess. The market square, probably.'

'I don't know.' He was coming over all foggy again. 'I thought the whole idea of this was so that we wouldn't have to do stuff like that any more.'

'It'd just be one last time,' I said.

'No '

'Fine.' I shrugged. 'You'll just have to sing for a living, then, instead of harp-playing. Broad as it's long, really.'

So we set off to steal a harp. Now it sounds like something you ought to be able to do if you set your mind to it. After all, when you think of all the things human beings have managed to achieve over the centuries – building the pyramids, say, or melting glass out of sand – stealing harps should be a piece of cake for two grown men on a warm day. Well, it probably is, in Plato's Republic or some such place, where everything's as it should be and all is for the best. In the cesspit where the sons of Romulus hang out, on the other hand, it's almost impossibly difficult. I mean, you remember the old stories, where the hero wants to marry the wicked king's daughter, and the wicked king sets him three apparently impossible tasks, which he manages without breaking into a sweat. Just goes to show how dumb those wicked kings really were. Instead of all that buggering about with killing dragons and fetching three-headed dogs from the Underworld, all they had to do was say, Go steal a harp, and the hero would've have died an elderly bachelor, if he was that lucky.

Well, eventually we found some harp-players, after we'd tramped round the squares and the temple yards and all the other places where day-labourers hang out in the city: about a dozen of them, to be precise, along with twenty-odd flute-girls, eight or nine drummers and two rather alarming-looking Cilicians who did noisy things with bells. Presumably they were waiting for someone to hire them, though they didn't seem to be in any hurry; not like the poor sods at the hiring fairs we used to have out our way when I was a kid, where you'd find thirty or forty sad-looking blokes scrambling all over you if you hinted you might have a day's trench-digging to bestow on some worthy candidate. Maybe it's a musician thing, I don't know; anyhow, they were sprawled all over the paved court in front of Juno-on-the-Subura, passing round jugs of toothstripper wine and combing each other's hair, and when we strolled up and sat down on the temple steps, a few of them turned round and smiled, while the rest ignored us. I guess they could tell by our appearance that we weren't hiring, and they had us down as either fellow songbirds or general loungers.

The harp-players were easy enough to spot, because they had harps. Unfortunately, separating them from same looked like it was going to be beyond us. For one thing, carefree and bohemian they might have been, but every one of them kept his pride and joy right up close, either with his hand resting on it or tucked under the crook of his knee, so there wasn't any chance of just sidling off with one. Even if we'd had the brass balls to snatch a harp, we wouldn't have got two paces, since the musicians were bunched so up tight you'd have had trouble threading your way past them at the best of times. Lucius Domitius looked at me and sighed, and we were about to get up and walk away, when we noticed that there was a game of dice going on.

Clearly, we were in no position to start gambling, since we didn't have any money, or very much of anything else, except dust and fleas. On the other hand, what could they do to us if we lost and couldn't pay up? Well, they could smash our faces in, but what's mere physical pain when you're down and out anyway? Besides, Lucius Domitius was no slug when it came to rolling dice; he'd learned from one of the finest dice-players of his age, his uncle, the late Claudius Caesar – it was the one thing they had in common, and the only time old Claudius could stand to have Lucius Domitius in the same room with him was when they were throwing the bones. Now, for all that he had this wonderful gift, we tended to shy away from games of chance after a nasty experience we had after we'd been together on the road for about six months; I won't bore you with the details, but it involved a disputed throw of Venus, two very large Cypriot market porters, and a cesspit. We'd learned our lesson after that, and got into the habit of being somewhere else whenever a game started up. But here we were, with nothing to lose except our teeth, where a lucky fall of the dice might result in money, or a harp, or both. I nudged Lucius Domitius in the ribs, and for once he seemed to be on the same wavelength as me; he gestured to me to stay put, then got up and wandered over to where the game was.

'Excuse me,' he said, 'but that looks like fun.'

A harp-player looked up, and said, 'Fun?' like it was the last possible word he'd have thought of in that context.

'That game you're playing,' Lucius Domitius said. 'I seem to remember we used to play a game something like that when I was a boy, and we went down the mountain to visit my aunt and uncle.'

All the gamblers were looking at him now. 'Is that so?' said one of them, in a nice, clear, piss-off-we're-busy voice. 'Small world, isn't it?'

'Mind if I watch for a moment?' Lucius Domitius went on. 'I'd like to see if I can remember the rules.'

'Sure,' said one of them. 'Just keep your face shut, all right? We're trying to concentrate.'

So he sat down on his haunches and watched them for a while. Then, in a break between points, he said, 'Sorry to butt in again, but where does the money come into it?'

A drummer craned his neck and frowned at him. 'You what?' he said.

'I couldn't help noticing,' Lucius Domitius said, 'you keep handing round coins while you're playing. Is it like counters, so you know whose turn it is? Or is it something to do with keeping score?'

Me telling you what he said, it must sound pathetically corny, and you're thinking, what kind of nitwit would fall for an obvious spiel like that? Well, that's because you're not getting the delivery – which, all credit to him, was superb. Pure genius. It was so good, even I was ready to believe that here was some buffoon up from the country who'd never heard of playing dice for money. If they had their doubts, my guess is that greed overrode them, they wanted him to be what he seemed, the biggest natural mark in the history of the world, so much that they refused to listen to the nagging little voices in their heads. Amazing.

'Well,' said a harp-player, after a short silence. 'It's like this.'

Now obviously, there was a problem, and I'm sure you're way ahead of me and you've figured it out for yourselves. Just in case you haven't: before they'd let him play, mug or no mug, he was going to have to ante up the price of a call, and of course he didn't have any money, not one solitary copper farthing. I wasn't sure what I'd been expecting him to do. In his place, I expect I'd have tried to palm a few coins off the pot when I thought nobody was watching (and I'd have got caught, sure as winter, and there'd have been a nasty scene and quite probably violence). What Lucius Domitius did was far smarter. He listened patiently while the bloke explained the basic theory and practice of gambling, then he said, Thank you, that's very interesting, and stood up to leave.

'Where are you off to?' one of them said in dismay. 'Aren't you going to stay and try your luck for a point or two?'

Lucius Domitius looked terribly, terribly sad. 'I'd love to,' he said, 'but I can't. You see, I haven't got any money.'

General despair; all the worse because they'd all got their hopes up so. 'Oh,' one of them said. 'Pity, that.'

Lucius Domitius nodded. 'All I've got is five donkeys loaded with salt, down at the cooks' market – that's what we do, my brother and me, we pan for it down on the coast this time of year, when there's not much doing on the land. It's an interesting sideline and we make quite a good thing of it, especially when the price holds up, like this year. I think—'

The gamblers didn't actually want an insight into the workings of the salt trade right then. What they wanted was to fleece a sucker. 'Five donkeys,' one of them interrupted. 'So, how much salt can a donkey carry, then?'

Lucius Domitius shrugged. 'Depends,' he said. 'We don't like to overload them, they're getting on a bit, like we all are. So we keep it down to somewhere round one and a half hundredweight.'

You could see them all doing the figuring in their heads; five by a hundred and fifty, times five sesterces. The click when they all arrived at the same answer at more or less the same moment was so loud they probably heard it at Veii. 'Tell you what,' one of them said, trying not to quiver, 'why don't you bet us some of your salt against cash money? We don't mind, it'd be like the army.'

Lucius Domitius shook his head. 'Oh, I couldn't do that,' he said. 'What'd happen if I lost? My brother'd get upset if I go giving away our salt.'

'Ah yes,' said a harp-player, 'but think how pleased he'd be if you won.'

'Not much chance of that,' Lucius Domitius said. 'After all, it's the first time I've played in a long, long while. And this – gambling, did you call it? Funny word – this gambling's all new to me. I know,' he went on. 'How'd it be if we just played for stuff that isn't worth anything? Bits of gravel, or beans? That way, we could have all the fun, and I won't have to worry about my brother shouting at me.'

They weren't happy, but the thought of this once-in-a-lifetime opportunity slipping away was too much for them. 'Good idea,' one of them said mournfully. 'We'll play a point or two like that, until you've had a chance to see how easy it is. Then maybe you'll change your mind.'

Don't get the impression that I'm a great expert on dice-playing, because I'm not. But a child of three could've spotted they were cheating, doing every damn thing they could think of to make sure they lost. Goes to show how completely Lucius Domitius had 'em foxed, because they were concentrating so much on losing to him that they didn't notice the pretty raw strokes he was pulling to make sure he lost to them. No; all they saw was that in spite of the very best they could do, the mug was such a dead loss dice-roller that he couldn't help losing every third point. So, when finally Lucius Domitius (eyes shining like a bride on her wedding-day, cheeks rosy with excitement at this wonderful new game) said, All right, then, I think I've got the hang of this, let's play for stakes, they were hard put to it not to bust out grinning, like dogs who've slipped into a sausage shop when the owner's forgotten to put the catch on the door.

'Wait there,' Lucius Domitius said, getting up off his knees, 'I'll go and fetch some salt. I won't be more than an hour.'

That panicked them. An awful lot can happen in an hour, they were thinking. You could see them picturing the scene in their minds – Here, brother, where are you going with all that salt? Oh, I met some people over on the Subura, and we're going to do gambling. Not with our salt you aren't, you gullible clown . . . 'That's all right,' one of them called out in a rather hoarse voice, 'we'll trust you for it. Sit down and let's get on with the game, while you're on a lucky streak.'

Since Lucius Domitius had lost four out of the last seven points, 'lucky streak' was taking poetic licence a bit far, but he said, 'Oh, all right then,' in a cheerful voice and sat down again. They handed him the dice, and he proceeded to lose.

Boy, did he lose. By the time they'd been playing for an hour, he was down a nominal one thousand sesterces, or nearly a third of our mythical stash of salt. Then it was as if he'd just woken up out of a dream, to find he'd wet the bed.

'This is dreadful,' he said. 'What's my brother going to say? We were going to use that money to dedicate an altar to our step-mother, rest her soul. He'll kill me.'

Genuinely distressing to hear him, so much so that all the gamblers but one looked away and didn't say a word. But the one who'd been doing all the winning, and held most of Lucius Domitius' markers, grinned hungrily and said, 'Tell you what. I'll give you one chance to win it all back. The whole lot. What do you say?'

Lucius Domitius bit his lip. 'I don't know,' he said. 'I think I've done enough damage for one day.'

The gambler wasn't having that. 'Here's the deal,' he said.

'Double or quits. One point. You could get it all back. Go on, it's a wonderful chance.'

Lucius Domitius handled it well. At first he wouldn't hear of it. Then, as the gambler upped the stakes, he let himself get talked into it, one step at a time, until finally they reached a deal: the markers plus another five hundred sesterces' worth, against what was in the pot – two hundred sesterces, 'and I'll even throw in my harp. There, I can't say fairer than that, can I?'

Lucius Domitius went through all the torments of Sisyphus before he finally nodded and said, 'Go on, then.' The gambler beamed like sunrise over the Adriatic, and handed him the dice. There was dead silence. Lucius Domitius scrunched the dice together in his hand, and then he threw.

He lost.

'Oh well,' the gambler said, 'never mind. Better luck next time.'

Lucius Domitius was staring at the dice like he was Orestes facing the Furies. 'All right,' he said, 'one more throw. All the rest of the salt, against what you've won already. Just one more point,' he added pitifully. 'Please.'

But the gambler shook his head. 'Sorry,' he said, 'I can't do that. It'd be tempting Fate, and I'm very religious.'

There was a moment of dead silence; everybody staring. Then Lucius Domitius nodded, once. 'Fair enough,' he said. 'You wait there, I'll get the salt.'

The gambler scowled mustard at him. 'Oh no,' he said. 'Not likely. I'm coming with you.'

'Please yourself,' Lucius Domitius said with a shrug. 'Doesn't matter to me, one way or the other. Follow me.'

So off he went, with the gambler tight at his heels, like a well-trained hound. As they passed me, I waited a moment or so, then quietly got up and followed. As luck would have it, there was a dark, narrow alley quite close by. I tried not to hit the gambler harder than necessary; he was a greedy bastard, but it was us who set him up, not the other way round.

'Fine,' I said, straightening my back, 'now we've got a harp. Let's get out of here, before his mates come looking for him.'

We dragged him over to a handy midden and dumped him, then set off for the Praenestine Gate. 'We ought to remember that one for another time,' I said, jogging along to keep up with Lucius Domitius, who was putting in big, long strides. 'I mean, there's other things beside harps.'

But he lifted his head. 'We're giving up on all that,' he said, 'that's the whole point. Now I've got this,' and he hugged the harp like it was his baby son, 'we won't have to do this stuff any more. Free and clear; isn't that how you put it?'

If there was anybody watching out for us at the gate, they were subtle about it; we didn't get that hairs-curling-on-the-back-of-the-neck feeling as we left the city (though that's not a reliable warning sign, believe me; one of these days I'll tell you about that time in Noricum, when the bloke we'd spent an evening bragging to, thinking he was the head of the local thieves' guild, turned out to be the military prefect's batman).

The plan was to stroll the thirty-odd miles to Praeneste along the straight, level military road. Praeneste's the sort of place where a jobbing harp-player has his pick of engagements – plenty of knights and businessmen trying to act like knights have houses or villas there, handy for the city but countrified enough to play at being Cincinnatus in; failing which, there were inns and taverns where we could pass the hat round and be likely to find something in it afterwards, aside from apple cores and a few stray hairs. Comfortable, affluent Middle Italy. God's own country.

As we walked along, feeling those precision-cut military cobbles under our thin-soled feet at every step and dodging out of the way of speeding chariots and huge rumbling cabbage wagons, Lucius Domitius got in some serious harp practice. It'd been ten years, he said, and he hadn't so much as picked up a harp in all that time. Not that it was something you could forget, he was at pains to point out; but the fingertips get soft and the muscles get complacent. He was right, at that. To begin with, the only noises he could get out of the thing were tinny plunks, like the sound of a silversmith working over a cracked anvil. But he fiddled with the strings and the pegs for a bit, and eventually produced something that a deaf man might mistake for music, if he wasn't paying attention.

'Right,' he said (plunk, plink). 'So what do you think I ought to include in my repertoire? Nothing too grand or fancy, enough for an hour's set, with encores.'

I scratched my chin. 'How about "*The Spanish Centurion's Daughter*"?' I suggested. 'We always used to laugh at that when I was a kid.'

He frowned at me down his nose. 'I don't think I know that one,' he said. 'And anyway, I was thinking of something a bit more upmarket than taproom ballads. Some Heliodorus to start with, perhaps, and then maybe something a bit more meaty: Phrixus or Strepsiades. "*The Tears of Niobe*" always goes down well in the provinces.'

I yawned. 'Do me a favour,' I said. 'People don't want culture when they're sitting all cosy at home in the country, they want something they can sing along to, or hum. The old favourites, you know: "*Such A Man*" or "*I'll Hide My Sword*".'

'Oh, please.' He looked as if I'd just farted in his face. 'All right, if the only gig we can get is in an Egyptian brothel, where they want something to drown out the screams. But if I'm going to be playing for gentlemen . . .' He frowned. 'Well, rich people, anyway. I mean to say, if you're entertaining a few friends over a quiet dinner, you want something a bit refined, to set the tone.'

'Balls,' I argued. 'What they'll want is something with a bit of a beat to it, not all that long-haired stuff. Tell you what,' I added, when I saw him puffing himself up like a bullfrog. 'Practice a bit of both. Then when we get there, you can gauge the mood of the house and adapt accordingly.'

He pulled a face, but it made obvious sense, so that's what he did: For every precious little hendecasyllabic morçeau, a good old-fashioned vaudeville number with lots of choruses. By the time we stopped for the night at a nice-looking roadhouse, I felt a bit like Ulysses and the sirens, when his men tied him to the mast while the nasty women sang at him. Well, at least Lucius Domitius didn't sing. Just as well, or there'd have been blood on the cobbles before we reached the eighth milestone.

The roadhouse was doing good business: stables full, people in travelling clothes lounging about on the porch, potboys and kitchenmaids scurrying across the yard fetching wood and water and stuff. A quick glance at the tariff painted up on the outside wall gave me a reasonable idea of what sort of place it was:

Bread   *1a*

Relishes	*2a*
Hay: per mule	*2a*
per horse	*3a*
Wine: Falernian	*4a/6th*
House	*2a/6th*
Ordinary	*1a/6th*

Well, quite: fancy prices for the carriage trade. Good sign, I thought; someone who'll cough up twopence for a pint of drinking wine wouldn't think twice about flipping a farthing or two into a hat if he'd happened to like the tune. Actually, it always amazes me how people who wouldn't normally give you the dirt between their toes will happily throw away good copper money on a snatch of a song in a public place. Nearly everyone puts in something, apart from the very poor and the very rich. If I had my time over again, I'd be a harpist.

Obviously, it was good manners and common sense to ask the landlord before setting up a pitch. As we'd expected, he didn't mind; a nice cheerful tune would entertain his customers, he said, maybe pull one or two passers-by in off the road. Just so long as we didn't get under anybody's feet, that was fine. In fact, if we were good for business, he'd send the girl over with some of yesterday's bread when the rush was over, and we could doss down in the hayloft over the traphouse for free.

Lucius Domitius might have talked like an idiot half the time, but he had the common sense to lay off the Heliodorus and the Strepsiades and stick to ballads and showtunes. As a result, we did all right, which pleased us both, me because I like money, Lucius Domitius because (as he put it) there's no better accompaniment for instrumental harp, musically speaking, than the rhythmical clinking of copper in a felt or leather receptacle. A small crowd gathered after a while and asked if he did requests. Most of them were for 'Gone For A Soldier' or 'Agrippina's Dwarf' or the-one-that-goes-tum-tumpty-tum; but one old toothless git of an ex-soldier hobbled up and asked for 'Banks of Scamander'. If you don't know that one – and most people don't – it's a catchy little number by one Lucius Domitius Nero Claudius Caesar Germanicus, about the only thing he ever wrote that's got a tune you can whistle. Of course, the old soldier didn't put anything in the hat; in fact, after a moment or so he wandered off to the bar to cadge drinks. He made Lucius Domitius' day, even so, and I think if he'd tried to touch us for money, Lucius Domitius would've given him the whole hatful out of sheer gratitude.

Luckily, though, it didn't come to that; and, by the time we retired to our hayloft with our basket of stale bread (with some ancient watercress and a wedge of hard cheese thrown in out of sheer naked benevolence), we were only a farthing short of four sesterces. Not just good money, practically wealth.

'I told you,' I told him, 'we should've done this years ago. Sixteen pence, just for tickling a few strips of gut. It beats work, that's for sure.'

Lucius Domitius frowned. 'You can't have been paying attention,' he said. 'That was work. Bloody hard work. On my feet playing, four hours without a break—'

'That's not work,' I pointed out, 'that's what you used to do for fun. Dammit, you used to bribe people to come and listen to you. And even if it does count as work, three weeks' money for four hours' graft – next best thing to being a senator, I reckon.'

'Whatever.' He made a show of being tired, yawning, stretching, all that. 'Now would you mind shutting your face, please? I want to eat this garbage they've given us and go to sleep, if it's all the same to you.'

I wasn't offended, or at least not much. 'All right,' I said. 'We'll divvy up the takings, and then we can turn in—'

He scowled at me. 'What do you mean, divvy up?' he asked unpleasantly.

'Divvy up,' I repeated. 'You get your half, I get mine, same as we've always done.'

He laughed. 'You can forget that,' he said. 'I earned it, I'm keeping it. You be grateful you've got a feed and a roof over your head.'

I couldn't believe my ears. 'You what?' I said.

'You heard me. I work, I get paid. Or were you accompanying me on the flute, and I didn't notice?'

'You bastard,' I pointed out. 'Here, give me my share, before I lose my temper.'

You'd have thought he'd have apologised, said he was sorry for trying it on. Not a bit of it. He actually seemed upset at me. 'You thieving little Greek,' he snapped at me. 'What the hell do you mean, your share? You didn't do a damn thing, just sat there with your feet up. You didn't even take the hat round.'

I was telling myself, Stay calm, put up with it, losing your rag never helped anything. 'Arsehole,' I said, and I was starting to get all shrill and speechless. 'Whose idea was it in the first place, for fuck's sake? Who had to talk you into this gig, when you were saying, Oh no, we don't dare, someone'll recognise me? Who was it said we could steal a harp? Who was it bashed that bloke on the head? Come to that, who was it saved you from Strymon, when anybody else would've just left you there? You'd be dead right now if it wasn't for me.'

'I like that,' he sneered. 'All right, if we're playing that game, who rescued you from the prefect's men in Alexandria? Who went back and got you out of that prison in Damascus, when they weren't even looking for me?'

'Oh, right,' I said. 'And I suppose you got away from that tallow-chandler and his men in Istria all by yourself, I had nothing to do with it.'

'You got me into that mess to begin with, I'll give you that,' he said. 'But all I remember about that is how you nearly got us both killed, saying we could jump to the ground from the window.'

'Screw you,' I said. 'All right, what about the fishmonger in Halicarnassus? He was going to chop your hands off with his cleaver.'

'Balls. And since you started this, what about that time you were up on a cross, and I told them to let you go? Can't trump that, can you?'

'Yes, but that was only because of Callistus—' stopped short; we both knew that was far enough. Otherwise I'd have to say, What about the time my brother died to save you? and that wouldn't do either of us any good.

He stared down at the straw. 'Well,' he said, 'I guess you did help me choose the music. And getting the harp was your idea And—'

I lifted my head. 'Half's too much,' I said. 'I think we should change the split. How about three to one?'

'Straight down the middle, like we've always done,' he insisted.

'Otherwise it's too complicated. We'll only end up arguing over half a farthing.'

'Better still,' I said, 'you be treasurer, hang on to the money, and when we need stuff, we pay for it. I mean, where's the point splitting it up? It's not like we're going our separate ways or anything.'

'No, that's right,' he said, not looking at me. 'That's not likely to happen, not after all this time. If you'd rather carry the money—'

'What, get lumbered with all that extra weight? No fear. You're the big, strong one, you can do the heavy lifting.' I clicked my tongue. 'I'm sorry,' I said. 'I shouldn't have yelled at you like that. Wasn't called for.'

'Forget it. Eat your dinner before it rots.'

Always the same; it's not what you say that really buggers things up, it's what you don't say. Worse still is when you don't say it so loud that even a deaf man with his head down a hole can't help hearing it. It's not like we're going our separate ways, no, that's not likely to happen, not after all this time. What he didn't say was, well, this is what I've come to, even when I've had my second chance, my fresh start: busking outside taverns, stuck with you. I guess it was playing the harp again that started him off. So long as he hadn't done that, hadn't played music, sung, any of that shit, he'd been able to keep himself buried deep down inside. He'd concentrated on the running away and not getting caught – easy enough when you're starving and on the run, you have to pay attention, you can't let your mind wander off into the places you'd rather it didn't go. You've got an excuse. But when you're free and clear, and the novelty's starting to wear off, like the silver wash on a dud coin, you stop and think, Hang on; so I'm still alive and they haven't got me, but where in hell is this place, and how did I ever get here? And then you start thinking, and how exactly am I going to get home? A bit like Ulysses, really; you survive the Cyclops and the clashing rocks and the sirens and the kingdom of the dead and the witch who turns men into pigs and the shipwreck and God knows what else, and you come to an empty beach, where you stand up and find you've lost everything. All your ships sunk, your men dead, your treasure and weapons dumped or at the bottom of the sea, your clothes ripped off you in the reefs. You stand up on that beach naked in a strange country, and you say to the gods, Thank you very much, thanks for nothing; I did all that, I was a fucking *hero*, and look where it's got me. You stand there on the beach, and you've got nothing left but yourself, who you are. Only Lucius Domitius didn't even have that. On the one hand, he had a harp; on the other hand, he had me. Poor, unlucky bastard.

(And then I thought, yes, but when Ulysses told them who he was they gave him a ship full of treasure, more than he'd robbed off the Trojans, far more than he'd lost along the way; and they gave him a lift home and unloaded his going-away presents on the beach, and all his troubles were practically over. He was free and clear, and in the end he got back everything he'd lost, and lived happily ever after. Lucius Domitius – well, he'd got a harp again, he was playing music and people were listening, enjoying it, even; was that a ship-ful of treasure to him, far more than he'd lost along the way? Wouldn't be surprised if he saw it like that. Never did have much sense, my friend Lucius Domitius.

And then I thought, what about what Blandinia had told me, the things he'd done, the things he used to be. Suppose, when he stood up on the beach after the shipwreck, it turned out that that was what was left. Suppose that was the real Lucius Domitius, and the only reason he hadn't done any of that stuff in our ten years together was because he hadn't had the opportunity? You think you know someone. You think you can judge character, but you can't, and that's how frauds and swindlers and bastards like me make our living, pretending to be good when we're bad to the core. Now I've never been any good at that game – not because I'm a good man, but because I'm not even good at being bad; if either of us had any talent in that line, it was him. He could tell a tale, put on a charac-ter, make you believe he was something he wasn't. You think you know someone, but all you ever get to see is bits and pieces, and that's at the best of times. Except Callistus, of course. But he was different—

—And besides, I've always wondered about Ulysses. I mean, here's this bloke, so we're meant to believe, who gets dumped on by every god in the sky. For ten years, it's just one ghastly, horrible adventure after another. No sooner has he managed to slither out of one certain-death scenario but he slides into the next one, nastier and even more certain-death than the last one, chased by monsters and soldiers and probably market commissioners and pork butchers with big cleavers, though the poet doesn't mention them. All this time, he's scheming and scamming and lying to everybody he meets, tricking and cheating, ducking and dodging his way, right across the known world, from Troy to Sicily. Even when finally he gets home, against all the odds, it's not as if they're pleased to see him or anything. Oh no – it's still more lies and tricks and schemes, ending up with the most appalling bloodbath right there in his own dining room, him against the whole senate and people of Ithaca, and what for? All this heroism, all these amazing deeds that will live for ever in the memories of generations yet unborn; what does he get out of it at the end? Gold, silver, prizes, purple tapestries, a triumphal arch and a procession down main street, followed by the hand of the beautiful teenage princess in marriage? Like hell. All he gets out of it is the privilege of going to sleep in his own little room again, next to a faded old bag with a face like a prune who he hasn't seen in twenty years. I ask you – why bother? Stupid fool should've stayed in Phaeacia and got a job.

Still, I can't talk. Been there, done that; only I was never a king or a prince or an emperor of the Romans to begin with, and if I went home and started picking off my enemies there with a bow and arrow, I'd get nailed to the nearest tree, and quite right too. When I've stood up on that beach, naked and destitute, with nothing but me left, they've arrested me for vagrancy and slung me in the lock-up. I could roll up at the palace gate on Scheria wearing nothing but an embarrassed grin and say I was the long-lost king of Ithaca till I was blue in the face, but no one would ever believe me. I guess telling the tale only works if the tale is true, or if you can make them believe it is.)

We spent the day lounging about. We realised that we weren't in any hurry to get to Praeneste. In fact, we'd only told ourselves we were going there because people as a rule need to believe they're going somewhere, rather than just wandering aimlessly about. But it seemed silly to leave this safe, comfortable billet, where we had food to eat and a place to sleep, money to pick up by the hatful, and where the guy in charge didn't seem to mind us being there. You'd have to be as thick as army bacon to walk out on all that on the off chance of finding something almost as good twenty miles down a hard, dusty road.

'Sooner or later,' I told Lucius Domitius, 'they'll get sick of the sight of us and set the dogs on us, and then we can go to Praeneste. Meanwhile . . .'

He yawned. 'Sure,' he said, 'why not? Crazy, isn't it?' He laughed. 'It must be weird, stopping in one spot your whole life. People do it, though, so it must be possible. I mean, take this place. You can bet the innkeeper took over from his dad, who got it from his dad, and so on back to Aeneas and Lars Porsena. A bit like an empire, really, only it's smaller. And,' he added, chewing a straw, 'not nearly as much pain and effort. It'd be fun, running an inn.'

I laughed. 'Don't you believe it,' I said. 'I grew up in one, remember? It's bloody hard work, all hours of the day and night; and it's bad enough in regular jobs where you've got one or two bosses ordering you about. In the tavern business, every bugger who walks in through the door's your boss, and you spend your whole life being told what to do by strangers. Fuck that for a swim in a cesspit.'

He shrugged. 'That's just you, Galen,' he said. 'It's like every place we've ever been. Soon as we move on, suddenly it becomes a dump, the last place the gods made, the armpit of the universe; at least, until we go on somewhere else, and then that takes over as the most dismal spot on earth. In all the years we've been together, I can't remember you ever saying anything nice about a place.'

'Yes, but that's not me being miserable. It's just that all the places we've been were horrible.'

'Really?' He looked at me. 'You don't think there's a simpler explanation, maybe. Well, who knows? Perhaps you're right. What about here, then? Is this a horrible dump, or have we finally broken our ten-year bad patch and stumbled on somewhere that's slightly decent?'

'It's all right,' I said. 'I mean, there's nothing actually bad about it. Just a roadhouse, that's all; not bad, not good, not anything, really. If you were a regular citizen, like a trader or something, and you stopped here on your way somewhere, I don't suppose you'd even notice it.'

'True,' he replied. 'Extremely telling point you just made there, only it's not a point about this place, or even wayside inns in general. It's a point about people. Oh, I know; if I'd had to spend the night here in the old days, I'd have been furious at whoever was in charge of planning itineraries for stranding me for a whole night in a poxy little inn. Someone would've ended up in the stone quarries for that. But, like I said, that's a comment about me, about the way I was back then. Doesn't tell you anything important about this inn.'

The way he was then . . . Interesting, I thought. 'Sure,' I replied, 'but you were hardly a regular citizen. I'm talking about ordinary people. Not emperors of the Romans, and not poor unfortunate buggers like us with empty bellies and boot soles as thin as onion skins. You can't go by what the very rich think, or the very poor. They're always different.'

'Funny way you have of seeing things,' he said. 'Of course, by that way of reckoning, I never was ordinary people. An emperor and a tramp, the opposite ends, but never the in-between. You know, I probably have a very strange view of the world. Unique, even.'

I was getting bored with this discussion – just think of that, will you? A Greek, fed up with talking. If you'd told me such a thing could exist, I'd have laughed in your face. 'I expect so,' I said. 'Unique, and no bloody good to any body else. Sounds about right, for us.'

That evening, Lucius Domitius played and the hat went round. The take was rather less, three and a half sesterces as against a gnat's nibble under four, it was still more money than either of us had ever earned by honest work in our whole lives before. Good money, just for picking at a few bits of sheep's innards. If only, I kept saying to myself, if only we'd known about this racket earlier, like maybe nine years and nine months ago. For one thing, we'd both be rich by now; or at least, we'd have earned enough to buy a few acres, a little farm on a hillside with barley interplanted between the vine rows so as not to waste space. Only – back then, mind – if you'd said to us, work hard for ten years and, if you're lucky, eventually you might get to be small-time peasants – well, it's not the sort of offer that sets you quivering like a bird dog, is it?

The landlord was pleased, anyhow. According to him, bar takings were up, either because we cheered people up and so they spent more, or else because they came in the bar instead of sitting outside in the yard because of the godawful racket. Either way was good enough for him, and to mark his grateful thanks, he saw to it that we each got a raw onion with our stale bread and leftovers that night. Fantastic.

Wait, it gets better. The fourth night, we got pig's trotters, and the seventh night we were invited to move our stuff from the hayloft down into the coachhouse. I did some rough figuring and reckoned that at that rate, after a year we'd be running the place. Five years, and we'd be provincial governors.

'So what does he do?' the landlord asked my harp-player, as we munched our onion on the tenth night. 'I mean, you play the harp, pretty well if you ask me, and the customers like it. But I haven't seen him do anything, except sit around.'

'He's my manager,' Lucius Domitius answered, with his mouth full. 'Manager, personal trainer, harp coach. If it wasn't for him, I wouldn't be where I am today.'

'Is that right?' The innkeeper shrugged. 'Well, you wouldn't think it to look at him. Still, whatever works for you guys. Anyway, I was thinking. Instead of playing out in the yard, why not come in the bar? At least, we could try it out for a day or so, and if it doesn't work out, you can go back to how you were, no harm done.'

Lucius Domitius lifted his head. 'I like it in the yard,' he said. 'Good acoustics. A bit like the theatre at Tarentum. You ever been there?'

'Me?' The innkeeper looked mildly shocked. 'I don't go anywhere,' he said. 'Too much to do here. Never been further than the village in my life.'

'Really?' Lucius Domitius raised an eyebrow. 'You've never been to Rome?'

'Rome? God, no.'

'But it's only a day or so down the road. Less, if you ride.'

'When can I spare a day or so, busy man like me? This place doesn't run itself, you know.'

Lucius Domitius clicked his tongue. 'The greatest city in the world, on your doorstep, and you've never been. Aren't you even curious?'

'No.'

That seemed to settle that. 'Fine,' Lucius Domitius said. 'Why should you be, after all? It's just a lot of houses and shops, and a few temples and things. No big deal, at all.'

The innkeeper nodded. 'That's just how I see it,' he said. 'And anyway, if ever I want to see the world, I just look in my bar. Everybody comes here, see. I've had all sorts stay here. Merchants, business people, knights, foreigners even. Had a senator, once. I don't have to travel, they all come to me sooner or later.'

'Quite.' Lucius Domitius smiled gravely. 'You never know, one day you might have the emperor of the Romans, right here in your bar.'

'Wouldn't that be something,' the innkeeper said. 'Though I don't know as I'd fancy that. Good for trade, people coming to see where Caesar himself stopped the night; but he'd want everything the very best, and I don't suppose he ever pays for anything. When we had that senator, he made me send out for vintage Falernian and Hymettus honey, and we never saw any money off him. Bastard,' he added sadly. 'This whole place wouldn't keep his boyfriend in white lead for a week. Still, there you go. Doesn't do any good complaining.'

So there we were; and to tell you the truth, I've been in worse places. After a while it got a bit boring, with nothing to do all day but sit around. There were plenty of people to talk to, of course, and that helped. Found out a few things, too. The new emperor, Titus Caesar, was doing a grand job; likely to turn out better than his old man, they reckoned, him having been born a gentleman, while Vespasian Caesar had been nobody when he started out. There had been a lot of excitement in the city lately: open war between two street gangs, with a whole neighbourhood set on fire, loads of people killed – a fine gentleman hacked to death in his own house, even, though obviously he must've been involved with the rackets in some way. Of course, the guards had been down on the lot of them like a ton of bricks after that, and that'd put them in their place, because you can't have pitched battles in the street and fires and stuff, and Titus Caesar wasn't the sort of man who'd stand for that sort of thing. By all accounts, the biggest of the gangs, Strymon's lot, had been rooted out like bindweed, though they hadn't got the man himself (still, it was just a matter of time); and the other one, Scyphax, nobody'd seen him for a while, so chances were he'd done the sensible thing and got out of town. Anyhow, it was a good thing, cracking down hard on crime, and it just went to show how important it was, having a strong man for an emperor. Not like the bad old days, they all agreed.

I had mixed feelings about that. All in all, I reckoned, it was just as well Lucius Domitius and I were dead because otherwise, if I was Strymon or Amyntas, I might be feeling a bit hard done by, and in the mood to share my bad luck with someone. In fact, if I was still alive, I'd be thinking seriously about moving on, maybe heading for India or Hibernia or the Island of the Lotus-eaters, instead of loafing around the yard of an inn no more than a day's ride from the city. But when you've died and been burnt to ashes, probably had a building or two fall in on top of your charred embers, you don't have to fret about stuff like that. You could say it was probably the smartest move I ever made, dying.

Couple of times, I caught myself thinking about Dido's treasure. Well, quite; but I had loads of time on my hands and not much else to do. I thought, sure, it sounds like a load of centaurs' feathers, but men like Strymon and Amyntas don't go around believing in dumb old tales. If they set so much store by it, there had to be something to it, maybe something Lucius Domitius or his knight who told him about it didn't know. Maybe there was a huge pile of gold and silver parked in a cave somewhere, at that; and if so, it wasn't doing anybody any good just sitting there. Of all things, it set me to thinking about Ulysses again, how he'd been washed ashore on that old beach, and come away with more gold and silver and treasure than he'd had when he left Troy with all his plunder. I thought about what Lucius Domitius had said, how if he'd found this Dido's treasure, it'd have paid all the debts of the empire, put him right back in the black, and all his troubles would've been over. And I thought, What if Lucius Domitius and I happened to get washed up on that beach, with nothing but our skins and the dirt under our nails, and we happened to find that treasure? At one stroke he'd be every bit as rich as he'd been in the old days; more so, even. I thought, What if we were to happen to find Scheria and that lucky beach? (Only we'd have more sense than to go home after that. I may not be the sharpest razor in the case, but I'm not dumb, like Ulysses. We'd stay in Cloud Cuckoo City, between this world and the other one, like men who've died but not stopped living. Yes, I thought, I could get used to that. I mean, what's the point of travelling around, or even going home, when all the places I go to are horrible anyhow?)

The morning of the fourteenth day, I was sat on the mounting block in the yard, trying to figure out how two men would set about shifting a thousand tons of gold ingots out of a cave and up a cliff (I was thinking: block and tackle, mule-powered winches, how about those swinging crane jobs they use in Mesopotamia for pumping water?), when I heard a voice I recognised. I'm good at voices – had to be, over the years, for obvious reasons connected with my profession – and besides, this one wasn't hard. It was distinctive, you could say; and not so long ago I'd been putting myself out to get chances to listen to it.

I thought, as I slid backwards over the mounting block and cowered behind it, not daring to move, that maybe Lucius Domitius wasn't so dumb after all, with his endless fretting about people hearing him sing and recognising him. Voices are easier to tell apart than faces, if you ask me.

It was that bloody woman, Myrrhine; you remember, the sweet, caring, angel-of-mercy sister of Amyntas, aka Scyphax, the gangster. She was talking to one of the grooms, a nice enough bloke by the name of Marcus Mezentius. I'd played a few games of knucklebones with him over the past few days, he was pleasant company and a good loser. Anyhow, Myrrhine was asking him to take special care of her horse, because the poor thing hadn't been well lately; at least, there didn't seem to be anything wrong with him that she could put her finger on, but he hadn't been eating as well as he usually did, and sometimes when he looked at her, she got the feeling something was bothering him. Straight up, I'm not exaggerating, that's what she said. My pal Marcus was playing along, because it doesn't do to go telling guests they're off their rollers; he said he'd keep a special eye on Honeysuckle (that being the name she'd seen fit to lumber the poor creature with) and yes, he'd make sure he remembered to comb his mane from the left, the way he liked it.

Weird, how quickly your opinion of someone can change. Not so long ago, I'd have wanted to knock Marcus' eye out with a stone for daring to talk to her. Now, I just hoped he'd be able to put up with her idiotic babbling long enough to give me time to sneak across the yard and warn Lucius Domitius. I guess the way you see people depends on where you are, when you are, and what their brothers really do for a living.

My luck was in. Either Marcus liked listening to drivel, or he was so used to being polite to guests that he couldn't break the habit, or he reckoned a pretty girl is worth spending time with, even if she won't stop talking and you're unlucky enough not to have been born deaf. Whatever; I didn't know, didn't care. I was too busy pretending to be a tiny little mouse scuttling across the courtyard, and I did it pretty well, at that. Once I was inside the coachhouse, of course, I quit scuttling and went storming through the place like a drunken German, till I found Lucius Domitius, darning a hole in his shirt.

'Get up,' I snapped. 'They're here.'

He looked at me. 'Who's they?'

'Amyntas,' I said, and he did the sitting high-jump, stabbing himself with his needle and not noticing. 'At least, his filthy bitch sister's outside, nattering at Marcus the groom.'

'You sure it's her?'

I didn't bother answering that.

Lucius Domitius shuddered from head to foot, like a wet dog. 'It's just not fair,' he said. 'You know what? I'm getting sick of this. Everywhere we look, there's some creep after us, and we haven't even done anything wrong, for once, apart from stealing the harp. All right, what's the plan?'

'Plan? I haven't got any damn plan. You think of something for a change.'

'All right.' He stood up, looking round for something. 'We'll climb up in the loft, swing down on the bale hoist into that overgrown culvert down the other side, and cut across the paddock to the road. If we get a move on, we can be in Praeneste in a couple of hours.'

Sounded good to me. 'Let's go,' I said.

'Just a bloody minute, will you?' He was still looking for

whatever it was. 'Did she look like she knew we were here? I mean, was she asking that groom if he'd seen us, or anything?'

I shook my head. 'She was talking about her horse,' I said.

I could see him deciding not to bother thinking about that; then an idea plopped into his mind, like birdshit dropping in your drinking-water barrel. 'Horses,' he said.

'What about them?'

'We'll steal their horses,' he replied, pulling his shirt on over his head. The needle and thread were still dangling off his shoulder, where he'd forgotten all about them, but I couldn't be bothered to mention it. 'Two birds, one stone. We get to ride, they have to walk. Got it.' He picked up a little home-made satchel he'd been sewing out of unwanted sacking. 'Come on, follow me.'

He didn't give me a chance to say what I thought about that for a plan of action. As I followed him up the ladder into the hayloft, I could see all the things that'd be bound to go wrong, like I was watching the gladiators from the top row of the circus: they'd see us crossing the yard; while we were wasting time saddling and bridling, Amyntas and his men would catch us; the horses would bolt and get loose, and we'd be trapped in the stable while the whole household rounded them up; my horse would throw a shoe two miles down the road, and I'd be leading it along when Amyntas and his thugs rode up in a hired cart and caught us. I could see all these disasters happening right there before my very eyes. I wanted to warn myself not to be so bloody stupid, but I was too far back to make myself heard. Too bad.

We made the culvert without breaking any serious bones, and scampered across the yard like hares clearing out of the corn when the men start cutting it. Nobody about that we could see, so we headed for the stables. There were five horses standing in the stalls; no clue, goes without saying, as to which ones belonged to Amyntas and his party. Didn't think of that, did we?

'Bugger,' said Lucius Domitius. 'I know. We'll take the two best, and turn the others loose.'

You ever tried turning horses loose when they don't want to go? Can't blame them, really. Probably they'd all had a long day, clomping along the paved military road; all they wanted to do was stand still and eat. They were like elderly house-slaves, they didn't want to be set free; too much like hard work. We tried hitting them with brooms, but that just got them good and mad, neighing and kicking the partitions and carrying on generally. Too much noise.

'Screw this,' Lucius Domitius said. 'Let's just—'

He didn't get any further, probably because Amyntas walked up behind him and put a razor under his chin.

FOURTEEN

'Hello, lads,' said Amyntas. 'Not dead, then?'

Time to run away, I thought, but I didn't. Partly because I wasn't going to leave my friend in deadly danger, partly because some bastard was sticking a knife in my back. Couldn't be bothered to look round and find out who it was. Once you've seen one bastard, you've seen 'em all.

'Just as well my sister isn't here,' Amyntas went on. 'That's her horse you were clobbering with that broom handle. If there's one thing she can't be doing with, it's cruelty to animals.'

I remembered Seneca telling me once that, according to Plato, man is just a two-legged animal that can't fly. I suppose I could have mentioned this point, but I didn't. Slipped my mind, I guess.

'I don't know,' Amyntas went on. 'You people, you're something else. You start a fire, burn down six blocks, just to make us think you're dead; and then what do you do? You come out here and start passing your hat round, in public, on the main road, in an inn owned by me. Short of hiring men to walk up and down the streets shouting out your new address, I don't see how you could've made yourselves easier to find.'

Oh well, I thought. At least we've given the gods a good laugh, so maybe they'll go easy on us. Or maybe not. I reckon the gods are like the audience in the circus: they enjoy a bit of comic relief, but what they really get off on is the sight of blood. You know, a lot of the time, the gods remind me of Roman senators. Or the other way around. Whatever.

'You aren't going to kill us,' Lucius Domitius said, and if I hadn't known better I'd have reckoned he meant it. 'You know perfectly well my brother and I are the only ones who know where the treasure is.'

Amyntas laughed. 'Do me a favour, please,' he said. 'Do I look like the sort of moron who'd go for some kids' story about buried treasure? And as for that dogshit about you being rat-face's brother, don't insult my intelligence. I know perfectly well who you are,' he said. 'Your majesty,' he added.

He let that sink in for a moment. No point arguing, of course. As the old country proverb has it, when they've got your nuts in a vice, it's better not to struggle. 'All right,' Lucius Domitius said. 'So what are you going to do?'

'Actually,' said Amyntas, 'I'm not sure. It's difficult to know what to do for the best. Selling you to the senate and people of Rome ought to be the obvious course, but for that I've got to make them believe you really are Nero Caesar, and the truth is, I'm not sure how to go about that. On the other hand, I could get a small fortune for you from Strymon. He'd be really pleased to see you both, I know that for a fact. But,' he went on, 'I don't think I'll go down that road just now, even though it's tempting. The point is, why settle for a small fortune when you can get a big one? From, say, his excellency the governor of Sicily.'

Bugger me, I thought. There were so many people after our blood, I'd clean forgotten about him. In case you've forgotten too (though you haven't got the same excuse), he was the poor bastard Lucius Domitius had sent to the stone quarries back in the old days, for falling asleep during one of his recitals; the same man whose son's clothes we stole, that day we escaped from the quarry cart, and the same man we ran into on the road, the one who was sure he knew me from somewhere. Well, yes, I thought; he might well want to see us, too. So many people keen to get a piece of us; definitely a seller's market. Pity there weren't a few more of Lucius Domitius and me, really. We could have taken Amyntas into partnership and made – well, a killing.

So there we were, Lucius Domitius and me; trussed up like the goat at a society sacrifice, slung in the back of a cart under a load of smelly old blankets, on our way to make one man happy and another man rich. At least Lucius Domitius didn't moan at me as we bumped along the road back to Rome, but I think that was mostly because Amyntas' people had gagged him with a strip of old rag soaked in stale vinegar. Back in the shit again; it was almost like coming home, after being away for rather too long. What with all the earning an honest living and not having to hide from soldiers, we'd got soft, both of us. A few more days, and we'd have been spoiled rotten.

I think the idea was to take us to Ostia and charter a ship for Sicily. Well, we got as far as Ostia, because that was where we were turfed out of the cart and stacked up against a wall in some warehouse like so many bundles of vine props. But then the plan changed.

I must've been asleep when the debate started, because it was the sound of their voices that woke me up: Amyntas, that brother of his — Scamandrius, or something of the sort — and Myrrhine, sounding just the same as ever and starting off every sentence with 'Oh', but this time she was chattering away quite cheerfully about how to dispose of us for the best possible return.

'After all,' she was saying, 'if it doesn't work out and there's nothing there, we don't have to kill them. We can just get back on the boat and go to Sicily, like we'd planned. It's virtually on our way there.'

'It's not,' Scamandrius objected. 'Three or four days out of our way, at the least.'

'Well, there you are, then,' Myrrhine said. 'I mean, what's three or four days? It's not like they'll go off or anything. And just think, if there really is anything there—'

'It isn't just the time,' Amyntas said. 'They're slippery as eels, those two. I know they look like idiots, but they've been slithering out of trouble for ten years, somehow or other; and just look what they did to Strymon. Now you wouldn't call me the timid sort, but I won't feel easy in my mind till they're safely delivered and paid for and off our hands. Besides, they're a damned liability, with Strymon and the governor after them. I don't want to get my throat cut because His Excellency'd rather get 'em for free than pay money.'

'Hold on,' put in Scamandrius. 'He doesn't even know we've got them yet.'

'Don't you believe it.' Amyntas again. 'We can't keep secrets in a set-up like ours. I mean, just look what happened to that clown

Pollio. I expect he thought he was the only one who knew what he'd got hold of. And we know for a fact that Strymon's got his eyes and ears in our outfit, same as we've got ours in his – same as the Romans've got their spies on both our payrolls, come to that. I'll bet you a gold talent both of 'em know exactly what we're up to right now. Which is why we can't afford to muck about chasing buried treasure along the way.'

'Oh, but that's the point, surely,' Myrrhine cut in, in that simpering little-girl voice of hers. 'You said it yourself. The governor knows we're bringing Nero Caesar to him. Strymon knows we're taking Nero Caesar to Sicily. What's the riskiest thing we can possibly do right now? Go to Sicily, of course. No, what we ought to do is head somewhere they won't expect us to go. Like Africa.'

Short pause; danger, brains at work. 'Yes,' Scamandrius said eventually, 'but we know Strymon believes in this treasure bullshit. Won't he be expecting us to try for it?'

'Not if his spies have told him we're taking them to the governor,' Myrrhine said, sweetly patient. 'Think about it. If you're the governor, and you're planning to ambush us and take Nero Caesar without having to pay, where'd you do it? Here in Ostia, where you've got to explain what you're about if things go wrong? Or in your own province, where you can do anything you like?'

'Fair enough,' Amyntas sighed; I got the impression this wasn't the first time he'd had to put up with his sister's good advice. 'But the opposite goes for Strymon. He'd want to ambush us here, on his own turf.'

'So, the sooner we get out of here, the better,' Myrrhine said triumphantly. 'Whichever way we go, there's no earthly point hanging around here a moment longer than we have to. We push off; Strymon gets here and finds we've gone, so he hires the fastest boat he can find and chases off after us, in the direction he'd be expecting us to go. But meanwhile, we've gone in the opposite direction, to Africa.'

'You said it was practically on our way,' Scamandrius said, but I could tell his heart wasn't in it; he knew the debate had gone against him, and he was just going through the motions of a withdrawal in good order. Never had a sister myself; never had the plague, either, but I know what it can do to people.

'I said it's only two or three days out of our way,' she replied calmly, for the benefit of any members of the class who hadn't been paying attention earlier. 'Just long enough to throw both Strymon and the governor off the scent. Then – assuming we haven't found the treasure, of course – we dart across from Africa to Selinus or Lilybaeum, where they won't be watching for us, and take them by cart across the middle to Syracuse. Easy as anything.'

'I don't know,' Amyntas said wearily. 'God only knows what Dad'd say, if he knew we were trolling off on a jaunt hunting for fairy gold with the two most wanted men in the empire along for the ride. He'd kick our bums from here to Puteoli.'

'No, he wouldn't,' Myrrhine chimed in promptly. 'He'd say we were using a bit of savvy for a change, sending a bucket down the well instead of jumping down it ourselves. He wouldn't have turned his back on thousands of talents of clean money just for the sake of clipping a couple of days off a journey.'

'Yes, but— Oh, screw it,' Amyntas said. 'You win, we'll do it your way. I just wish the old fool'd had the sense to keep you out of the business. You always did have the knack of making us do things we don't want to do.'

'Exactly.' You could hear the smirk. 'And that's why he made you make me a partner. There's got to be someone in this firm with a bit of imagination.'

I could almost have felt sorry for them. In a couple of hours' time, they'd be asking themselves, how the hell did she ever manage to talk us into this? And by then, of course, we'd be on our way to Africa. Just goes to show how important it is to keep women out of business; same reason you keep the cat out of the fish pond.

Still. Their bad luck, our good luck. Not that I was getting my hopes up or anything, but three or four days more before we had to say hello nicely to the governor of Sicily had to be a good thing, surely. Every extra day was another twenty-four chances of wriggling out of it (and of course, wriggling out of certain death was something Lucius Domitius and I knew a thing or two about; but even a master craftsman needs tools and materials). There were all sorts of possibilities, if the gods were minded to give us a break, everything from sneaking quietly over the side in the middle of the night to dodging off in some nice dark cave. The more I thought about it, the happier I felt about Amyntas' old man making the boys play nicely with their kid sister. If I'd thought about it much longer, I might even have considered taking back some of the things I'd said about her under my breath.

Well, the debate broke up and we were left alone for a short while. Then a couple of hands showed up and started hauling us about like we were barrels of whitebait. The long and the short of it is, they dumped us in big sacks, like the ones you take piglets to market in, and that was all I saw of the proceedings. I had to work out what happened next by what I heard and felt and smelled, though it wouldn't have taken Archimedes to figure it out from first principles. Onto handcarts, up the ramp, and down into the hold. Not the way I'd choose to travel, I have to say. Better than walking, and that's about as positive as I can manage to be about it.

Well, I was the one who'd been dead keen to go to Africa. Good example of why you should be careful what you wish for, I guess. It raised a fine philosophical point in my mind, which I'd have been happy to discuss with Seneca himself, if he'd happened to be lying there beside me all bundled up in ropes and we'd somehow managed to spit the gags out of our mouths: is it worth it getting an extra three or four days of life, if you spend them in the dark, suffering agonies from hunger and cramp and seasickness, with rats nibbling the lobes of your ears? Is there anything about life that makes it worth hanging on to by your fingernails when you'd be far more comfortable dead, or is it just fear of the unknown, force of habit? Take it a bit further (I did, I had the time and piss-all else to do): suppose you were the luckiest, richest, most privileged man in the whole world, and the day came when either you could die, or you could go on living, but your life would be thoroughly miserable, trudging down dusty roads or hiding behind olive jars as the soldiers came looking for you. Or suppose you were the greatest hero ever, and you'd just plundered the wealthiest city in the world, and on your way home you're shipwrecked and washed up on a desert island, with nothing but the skin you were born with? As I lay there trying to scare off the rats by wiggling my ears (it didn't work), I made my imaginary friend Seneca reply, Yes, it's worth it, because you never know what's just around the corner. Your shipwrecked hero might find a great treasure buried on the island, and then get picked up by a passing ship. Your once-fortunate man might discover he's happier herding pigs or busking on street corners than he ever was in his fine house with his Chinese table-linen. And your poor sod tied up in the hold of a ship might wriggle free, or a rat might chew through the ropes thinking they were a particularly muscular ear, and he'd be able to jump off the ship and swim to shore. Yes, I told him, but I can't swim.

That's not the point, replied my imaginary friend. Listen. When Pandora opened the jar, and all the evils flew out to plague mortal men, the gods took pity on them and put blind, shivering Hope in the very bottom of the jar, to keep men from giving up and dying where they stood. Hope pulls us through, keeps us going when we're absolutely sure we're done for. The beating of the heart and the action of the lungs are a useful exercise in prevarication, keeping our options open.

I asked my imaginary friend what prevarication meant. When he'd explained, I said, Yes, that's all very well, but let's go back to that Pandora story for a moment. Leaving the gods out of it for now, I said to him, haven't you ever stopped to wonder, if Hope's such a wonderful bloody thing, what was it doing in the jar in the first place, along with all the other evils? Oh sure, it popped up its little fuzzy head and told Pandora it was her friend, the gods had sent it to help make everything all right, but that's what you'd expect Hope to say, and it proves jack shit about what it was really up to. I reckon (I said) that it was in the jar from the very start, and it stayed behind to kid us poor bloody mortals into hanging around and suffering all the other evils, instead of legging it across the River to where it's quiet and safe and all our troubles would be over. I think, I told him, that we're going to roll around in this shitheap of a boat till we get to Africa, and either we'll die there or in Sicily, but sooner rather than later. And no great loss, either.

Then my imaginary friend started getting snotty – typical, really, even people who aren't actually there lose their rag with me sooner or later. He said, Listen, Galen, while I tell you about death; because I've been dead a good few years now, and take it from me, you can stuff it. Oh, it's all right for you, you goddamned sightseer. You come here, to the very gates of the palace of death, and you look around, like you're some hick from the country hitting the big city for the first time, and you think you know, you think you understand. Like hell you do. This is what death is like. I used to be a Roman senator, adviser to the emperor, supreme power behind the throne, wisest and most respected man of my generation, loved and admired by everyone who read my books or heard me lecture. I'd rather be a fuller's slave, dragging round the streets from dawn to dusk collecting other people's shit and piss in a bucket, sleeping on a stone floor and eating stale bread with the blue mould all over it, than be the purple-gowned Caesar of all the glorious dead. Look round you, Galen; they've all come to see you, all the heroes and kings, the rich and the wise and the beautiful when they were alive. See how they're crowding round you – you, of all people, petty thief, son of a whore, bosom buddy of the most evil man who ever lived – and they're reaching out their hands, trying desperately to warm their chilled fingers over the little glow of your fading, guttering life. It's not much life, God knows, but down here among the dead it shines like the sun and blazes like Rome burning, and all these ghosts of your elders and betters would trade you all their glory and honour for one poxy little flicker of it. If you want to know about life, you're in the right place, here where there isn't any. Now go back, to your week or your three days or your three hours or your three heartbeats, go back to your shining palace and your roaring hearth and leave us poor people in peace.

Well, that was me told. Of course I wasn't convinced, but I had enough to put up with without getting yelled at by make-believe philosophers, so I quit thinking and tried to spook off the rats by banging my head on the deck. That didn't work either, but it did feel good when I stopped doing it.

At some point, some bugger came round and fed us. Well, he yanked down the gag, stuffed a ladle of something in my face (cream of grease soup, I think it was), then stuffed the gag back in before I could throw up and went away again. I guess it was enough to keep me alive, and at any rate it was better than mother's home cooking. Still.

So I guess we must've got to where we were supposed to be, because suddenly the hatch opened and this sharp painful stuff got in my eyes and made my head hurt (light, I seemed to remember it was called) and some bastard grabbed me and hauled me up out of my snug little nest into the salt air, where it didn't smell of piss-soaked sacking. And somewhere on the ship, someone called out to somebody else, 'Are you sure this is Africa?', and whoever it was called back, 'Don't ask me, I've never been this far before.' And I thought, Well, here we are, this is as far as I get to go. Call it a pattern emerging, if you like. Short, timeless interlude on a boat, and then straight off the gangplank into the deep shit. Last time, if you remember, the late Licinius Pollio gave me a denarius to get rat-arsed on. This time, no money and no booze, but otherwise not much difference, except that this time we were on our way *back* to Sicily.

I have to say, Africa's not one of my favourite places. For one thing, it's too hot. We have hot back where I was raised, in Attica; we have so much hot, we don't know what to do with it. But Attica hot's different; it makes you sweaty and itchy and bad-tempered, but it doesn't crackle up the skin on your face or make your eyeballs dry out. Also there's the sunlight. It's way too bright. It's so bright you can't see a damn thing, and what sort of service is that? There's other things I didn't like about Africa, but I'm just giving you those two as an example of what a complete dump the place was.

They dug Lucius Domitius out of the hold and slapped him awake, and then they started asking him for directions. Naturally, he didn't have a clue where he was (and if you don't know where you are, how can you be expected to show anybody where anything else is?). Amyntas got all up tight when the treasure wasn't there on the beach waiting for him, all neatly packed up in jars with the necks sealed with red wax; he was stomping around muttering and asking his brother if he was sure this was the right place, though how Scamandrius was supposed to know that (since all he had to go on was what Lucius Domitius had told him, namely nothing), I have no idea. Myrrhine was the only calm one, and she was floating around like some kind of big-nosed woodnymph, smelling flowers and acting like she was on a picnic at the seaside. I'd have wet myself laughing, except I was about to die.

'You said Africa,' Scamandrius was saying, 'this is Africa, what more do you want? And don't go snarling at me. If you want directions, go ask Nero Caesar. That's why we brought him, isn't it?'

So they asked Lucius Domitius; and he told them, without

needing to be hit hardly at all, that to the best of his knowledge, the treasure was in a cave under a ruined Carthaginian temple at a place called Oudepopote, on the coast five miles due east of Utica, wherever Utica was. And then he spat out a tooth and added, 'If you want to know how far we are from Utica, why don't you ask the captain of your ship? If anybody knows where we are, it's probably him.'

Well, Amyntas made a sort of Oh-for-God's-sake gesture and stormed off up the beach. He came back a few moments later, and the bloke he had with him was someone I knew, though I hadn't reckoned on seeing him again. It was the skipper of our grain freighter, the one that'd brought us from Sicily to Ostia. I was so surprised, I nearly fell over.

Could've gone any bloody way, at that point. For a start, Lucius Domitius was his slave, properly speaking; I'd sold him to him, if you remember, to pay for our passage, and Lucius Domitius had jumped ship and swum to the shore, leaving the captain feeling distinctly pissed off and hard done by. But at that moment, Lucius Domitius was on his knees in the sand with blood all over his face and Scamandrius standing behind him with a big wooden club. Me? I was standing very still, with my arms roped behind my back, looking as sorry for myself as I possibly could. Well, you never know. Most people are nicer than me, they go in for sympathy and compassion and stuff like that. I did manage to shake my head and mime shushing noises at him when he caught my eye, but I had no way of knowing if he got what I was trying to tell him, or whether he assumed I was just plain crazy.

'Well,' Amyntas was saying, 'where the hell is this place?'

The captain went all thoughtful, which seemed to annoy Amyntas even more. 'You said Africa,' the captain said, 'and then we'd be heading on to Sicily. That's all you said, so I thought, best thing'd be to put in between Hippo and Utica, so we wouldn't have to bugger about rounding Fair Point, and we could just nip back across to Lilybaeum and carry on round the coast from there.'

Amyntas had been acting very antsy while the captain said his bit. 'Fine,' he said 'Are we east or west of Utica?'

'East,' the captain said, 'about five miles. I made for here because I know this little bay. I got blown in here once when I was a lad, on my uncle's ship. There's an old fallen-down temple just round that headland, or was when I was here last. They may've bust it up and carted it away for stone, for all I know.'

Scamandrius looked up, and Myrrhine suddenly took an interest. 'This temple,' Amyntas said, 'you'd be able to find it again?'

The captain shrugged. 'Don't see why not,' he said. 'My uncle knew it, said it was put there to mark the shortest distance between Africa and Sicily, back in the old days, by the Carthaginians. You know, Hannibal's lot, the ones who beat the shit out of you Romans.'

I don't know what ticked Amyntas off more: the captain's chattering on when he was in a hurry, or being accused of being a Roman. 'Actually, I'm Egyptian,' he said quietly, 'and you'd better find this temple, or I'll cut your liver out. Understood?'

Now that was probably Amyntas' mistake, threatening the captain. Understandable, I guess. He was in a foul mood, because of being nagged into this jaunt by his sister, and then being told that they'd come all this way with nobody actually bothering to find out where they were meant to be headed (I suppose Amyntas assumed Scamandrius had sorted all that out, and Scamandrius had thought Amyntas was going to do it), then discovering that quite by chance they'd pitched up in more or less the right spot, but having to put up with the captain telling him his life story when he wanted to get cracking before nightfall. A bloke like Amyntas, a professional hard case with an image to keep up, I expect he was used to threatening people when he wanted something done, most likely did it out of habit, without thinking. But captains of ships are funny bastards, I've noticed. They think a lot of themselves, and they don't like having to deal with landlubbers who come all high and mighty with them just because they happen to own the boat or they're paying for the charter. You go around making threats, like you're talking to a slave or something, they can get very touchy indeed; and I guess this was what must've happened in this case. Also, there was Lucius Domitius, who as far as he was concerned was his property, not to mention a good ship's cook, kneeling there drooling blood and spit; and if anybody was entitled to knock Lucius Domitius around, he'd have said to himself, it's me, and not some snot-faced civilian. So he'd made up his mind, I reckon, that he didn't like Amyntas much; and if he'd been going to be helpful and cooperative, for example by letting on he'd seen us before, stuff like that, he was now firmly resolved that he was buggered if he'd tell Amyntas anything unless he was asked a straight question, and maybe not even then. Just goes to prove what I always say: it doesn't pay to beat up on the little people; one day you'll be sorry. Actually, of course, nine hundred and ninety-nine times out of a thousand you can kick shit out of the little people and nobody'll give a damn, but it's a saying I'm fond of, nevertheless.

Anyhow. The captain sort of looked sideways at Amyntas and said that if he wasn't mistaken, the temple was somewhere this way, and if they all cared to follow him, he'd see if he couldn't find it. So Scamandrius grabbed a handful of Lucius Domitius' hair and pulled him to his feet; I trotted up eagerly like a good dog, no need to kick me, look, I'm even carrying my lead in my mouth. Myrrhine brought up the rear, still bending down now and again to pick a flower or two, and off we went.

Turned out we weren't more than ten minutes' fast walk from that temple, or what was left of it. Hadn't been much to begin with, I dare say; not a proper temple, like the ones in Rome or back home in Athens. More like a biggish barn, only it was built out of rather boring-looking grey stone blocks, with a couple of straight pillars out front. At least half of it was just plain missing – you'd have found the stones in the walls of the local farmhouses, I guess, if you could've been bothered to look – and the rest of it was slumped sideways, like a man who's come home with a skinful and stands there in the doorway, leaning on the frame because he knows he'll fall over if he tries to move. Don't suppose any of our gods and goddesses would've been seen dead in a place like that, but I guess the old Carthaginian gods weren't so fussy.

'That's it, is it?' Amyntas said doubtfully.

The captain shrugged. 'That's it,' he replied, 'pretty much where it was when I saw it last.'

'Fine,' Amyntas said. 'Right, you go back to the ship and wait for us. Don't go wandering off or tell anybody where we've gone. Understood?'

The captain nodded, once; I could tell he was getting more and more uptight, but either Amyntas didn't notice or he didn't care.

Anyhow, the captain strolled off back the way we'd just come. Amyntas waited till he was out of sight, then led the way up a zigzaggy old sheep track to the temple.

'You're absolutely sure this is it?' he barked at Lucius Domitius. Of course he wasn't, but he had the wit to reply, 'Well, it certainly fits the description,' or some such thing. 'In a cave under the temple, that's what the knight told me.'

'Fine,' Amyntas said, as we walked in through where the doorway would have been if it hadn't fallen in years ago and been carted off to make pig sheds. 'How do we get into the cave from here?'

Bloody stupid question, of course. 'I suppose there must be some sort of trapdoor,' Lucius Domitius said, 'though it can't be too obvious. People must've been coming up here poking about for centuries. If it was plain to see, they'd have found the treasure.'

'Oh.' Amyntas obviously hadn't thought of that, which goes to show how stressed out he was. Normally I expect he'd have been way ahead, figuring out stuff like that well in advance, without needing to be told. 'Then I guess we'll just have to spread out and search for it.'

Here's something else he'd got wrong. He hadn't brought any of his button men with him, presumably because he wasn't prepared to trust them if there did turn out to be a whole bunch of buried treasure. Sensible, knowing the sort of people he had to work with, but dumb in another sense, since it left him short-handed for searching for the trapdoor. Of course, he could've told Scamandrius to leave us be and help him look, but that'd have been an even bigger cock-up, since we'd have been out of there like rats up a conduit. So he and Myrrhine had to do the spreading out and searching, while Lucius Domitius and I stood there and watched, with Scamandrius right behind us, digging us in the back with a knife. Did me good to see them scrabbling down there in the dirt and finding nothing but spiders and a few rats' bones. Trouble was, Amyntas soon got it into his head that either Lucius Domitius was holding out on him, or he'd deliberately brought him to the wrong place. 'I'll give you a count of fifty,' he yelled, grabbing Lucius Domitius by the ear like he was a naughty kid, and pushing him down on the ground. 'If you haven't found it by then, your mate here gets it.'

That meant me, of course, and quite suddenly my attitude changed somewhat. Now I started wondering if maybe Lucius Domitius knew more than he was letting on, and he was keeping it to himself so he wouldn't have to let Amyntas take the treasure, and to hell with whether I got my neck broken. Bastard, I thought, the treasure means more to him than I do; and then I thought, well, what do you expect? Rat-faced little Greeks you can get anywhere, but a fortune in gold is something else. That was just me panicking, of course, because I knew perfectly well that Lucius Domitius didn't have a clue where the trapdoor was, if there was one at all. Truth is, I don't suppose he ever really believed the knight's story about Dido's treasure; and if he did, he was planning on sending someone else to go fetch it, not looking for it himself. So if the knight did tell him how to find the cave (assuming the knight actually knew), I don't suppose Lucius Domitius paid any attention to the details.

Actually, it was me that found the cave, and I wasn't even trying. I was more interested in what Amyntas had just said, about me getting hurt, and I'd started to edge backwards, since Scamandrius happened to be prodding Lucius Domitius with his stupid knife at that moment. Anyhow, I took a step back and found I'd just put my weight on something that wasn't really there. Bloody stupid you feel, when you do that; and all your instincts tell you to wave your arms around, which is supposed to help you get your balance, though I don't see how. But I couldn't even do that, because my arms were tied up with ropes and all I could do was wiggle my fingers, which doesn't count, apparently. Whatever; a heartbeat or so later I wasn't standing on anything at all, and I sure as hell wasn't flying.

Turned out I'd stepped back onto a rotten old floorboard or something – maybe it was a trapdoor after all, I'm not actually interested – and it'd given way under my weight. If that makes me sound like I was a bit of a porkchop back in those days, forget it, I've always been the scraggy, wiry sort; it must've been a very rotten floorboard. Anyhow, I fell through it, landed badly, felt something go twang in my leg, and flumped down on my bum, only to find I was sat on something unpleasantly sharp. I howled, the way you do. Scamandrius was kneeling down beside the hole trying to slash me with his knife. I guess he thought I'd found some cunning way to escape. What with trying to get off the sharp thing and keep out of the way of Scamandrius' knife, and all this with a buggered ankle, I wasn't doing too well. Then Amyntas came over with the lamp; he peered down the hole at me, and then started swearing.

Myrrhine joined him a moment later, and looked over his shoulder. 'Told you so,' she said.

FIFTEEN

Course, I hadn't the faintest idea what they were on about; not till my good foot slipped on something hard and round, and I crashed over on my elbow. That hurt like buggery, so it was a moment or so before I could be bothered to look up, see what I'd fallen on.

Tableware. Gold tableware: cups and dishes and jugs and goblets and God knows what all, glowing amber in the light from Amyntas' poxy little lamp. I'm not talking about a few pesky little trinkets here, think of how a cornfield looks, just before they start cutting, and the orange-yellow blaze stretches so far in every direction it makes your eyes go funny. Or think of what it's like when you get a word in your head and catch yourself saying it over and over again, till it doesn't make sense or mean anything any more. That's how I felt, staring at all that stuff; it couldn't all be gold, because there wasn't that much gold in the whole world. Stood to reason; gold's only valuable because it's scarce, and there was so much of it down there, you could have roofed over every house in Attica with the stuff and still had enough left over to make a dozen large cisterns.

'See?' Myrrhine was saying. 'I said it'd be worth going out of our way for, but nobody ever listens to me. Well, Dad always used to say . . .'

She was right about one thing: nobody was listening to her, except me, of course, and I don't suppose I count. Scamandrius had stopped trying to scalp me with his baby cleaver and was squatting on the edge of the hole with his mouth wide open. Lucius Domitius was standing behind him, looking like the gorgon had just winked at him. Only goes to show he was a born idiot, because he could have snuck out of there and been a mile away before anybody noticed he was gone.

Anyway, long silence; everybody gawping like idiots, and me sitting on more wealth than the average senator spends in a week. Amazing. Then Amyntas sort of shook himself, and said, 'How the bloody hell are we going to get this lot out of here?'

Well, good question. Furthermore, it gave me an idea, but I hustled it away into the back of my mind, for fear it'd show on my face. Then Myrrhine said; 'Well, we can't shift it all ourselves, that's for sure. We'll have to get the captain and his men in here.'

Amyntas didn't like the thought of that. Funny thing: the more money there is at stake, the less people are inclined to share it. I mean, if there's a group of you and you find a drachma in the road, you don't have to think twice about it; off you all go to the nearest tavern, drinks all round in the name of Our Lady of Good Fortune. Find a hundred million sesterces, and the first thought that crosses your mind is, How do I get rid of the others so they won't want their share? You'd think that the more there was to go round, the less you'd be worried about keeping it all for yourself; apparently not.

But facts are facts. It'd have taken one man on his own a month of hard slog just to haul all that stuff out of the hole and stack it on the temple floor. 'We'll have to give them a cut,' he said. 'Can't expect them to lift this lot on day-labourers' wages.'

Myrrhine and Scamandrius looked very sad, but they nodded their heads. 'Unless' Myrrhine piped up, 'we leave it here, go back and fetch some of our people. I mean, it's been here this long without anybody finding it . . .'

You could tell from her tone of voice she didn't like the idea; and her brothers pulled faces like they'd just bitten into something rotten. 'Even if we did that,' Scamandrius said, 'we'd have to share with our lot, they're only human. I say if we've got to do a deal with somebody, it might just as well be these sailors as anyone else. If you ask me, we've got a wolf by the ears here.'

Well, quite. Instead of making them happy, all that treasure had really ruined their day. That's people for you.

'All right,' Amyntas said slowly. 'Here's what we'll do. You two, stay here and make a start shifting the stuff. I'll go back to the ship and negotiate. It's still going to take a long time, even with the sailors, so the sooner we start, the sooner we'll be done.'

Scamandrius' idea of making a start was grabbing hold of Lucius Domitius and putting his knife across his throat. 'You,' he said to me, 'get up and start shifting the gold, or your friend here gets cut. And don't even think about playing me up. You too,' he added, nodding at Myrrhine, 'get weaving, there's a lot to do.'

Myrrhine pulled a face. 'You give me the knife and I'll guard the fat boy,' she said. 'You can shift a lot more than me.'

He lifted his head. 'Do as you're told, for once,' he said, 'and don't argue.'

So Myrrhine had to get down in the hole with me and do some actual work, which didn't please her very much. There wasn't a lot of room, and standing on a pile of gold crockery wasn't easy; both of us kept slipping and sliding about, at least till we'd cleared a space to stand on. Myrrhine was sulking and didn't say anything, which was fine by me; I'd had enough of her to last me a long time.

I don't know what took Amyntas so long; it was hours before he came back with the sailors. But they brought lamps and torches and ropes and lumber and all sorts of useful stuff, and once they got started we were able to make some serious progress. Did they ever work, those sailors. You could tell by the look on their faces, they couldn't believe what they were seeing. Of course, they all recognised Lucius Domitius and me, but they couldn't figure out whether they were supposed to say anything, so they just looked at us all bewildered and kept their faces shut.

One thing we didn't have was anything in the way of a cart; not even a wheelbarrow. That was bad news, because it meant that we were going to have to carry every single bit of gold from the temple back to the ship. If getting it up out of the cave was a big job, lugging it from the cave to the ship – well, it didn't bear thinking about. So the captain told the ship's carpenter to take a couple of men and go find some timber and fix something up; didn't have to be fancy, he said, just so long as it worked. That pissed Amyntas off straight away; he was giving the orders round here, he said, and he hadn't said anybody could go wandering off while there was all this stuff to shift. The captain stayed calm, which just seemed to rile

Amyntas up even more; he pointed out that carrying a load like that on our backs was just plain foolishness, whereas we could spare three men out of twenty-five for a few hours, if it meant saving three or four days' hard slog. For one thing, he said, there was the little matter of food and water; what he had on board for the journey wasn't going to last more than a week, and we still had the return journey to make. So, one thing we were short on was time, whatever way you looked at it. He was all in favour of sending some men off to the nearest town to buy three or four big wagons and some horses or oxen, along with food and wine and a load of tools and stuff he reckoned we'd need. Amyntas wasn't having that. Nobody was going out of his sight, he said. Or else what, was the obvious question; after all, there were only two of them and twenty of the sailors. The captain didn't press the issue, but none of them were stupid, they all had the same idea, though nobody said it out loud. Amyntas started to look very thoughtful indeed, like he'd realised that he was probably in more trouble than he'd ever been in before in his whole life.

Anyhow, the captain got his way over building a makeshift cart, and Amyntas left him and his people alone, keeping out of their way as much as possible, though that wasn't easy in such a tiny space with so many people working. What with that, and trying to keep an eye on everybody all the time, I guess it didn't take him long to reach the end of his rope. Each time I saw him he was looking sicker and sicker; which suited me just fine, of course.

I think the captain was as keen to have a private word with me as I was with him. It wasn't easy, with Amyntas watching him like a hawk, but eventually we got our chance, when Amyntas went off to see what the carpentry detail was up to. Scamandrius and Myrrhine both took the opportunity to skive off and sit down for a breather – they weren't used to hard work, obviously, and Amyntas had been keeping them at it. The captain made sure they weren't watching, then came across and grinned at me.

'I'm not going to ask,' he said. 'You can tell me later how you two fit into all this. But I've got to say, I don't like your friend much.'

'Amyntas? He's no friend of mine,' I said.

'Really?' The captain nodded. 'I'm glad about that, because when he comes back I'm going to kill him. That all right with you?'

'Fine,' I replied. 'And the other two, while you're at it.'

'The girl, too?' He looked at me.

'Sure, why not? She'll only make trouble if you don't. I mean to say, all this gold and stuff, it's the chance of a lifetime. If I was you, I wouldn't take any risks whatsoever.'

He looked at me funny. 'There's a case for saying you and your mate are a risk,' he said, 'especially since you're neither of you exactly reliable. Do you think we ought to kill you as well?'

I thought about that for a moment. 'Oh, I wouldn't think so,' I said. 'Me and Lucius Domitius, we're no bother to anybody. I mean, we're practically members of the crew.'

He was still and quiet for a moment, then he nodded. 'That's the way I see it, too,' he said. 'Right, leave the unpleasant stuff to me and my boys. That's unless you—'

I lifted my head. 'No, that's fine,' I said, 'you crack on, it's not our line of work anyhow. Not that I'm suggesting it's yours either,' I added, so as not to sound rude, 'but I'm sure you'll figure out what needs to be done. Don't mind us, is what I'm saying.'

He nodded and turned to go; then he hesitated and looked back at me. 'One thing,' he said. 'Just to settle a bet between me and some of the lads. Your mate there,' and he nodded towards Lucius Domitius.

'What about him?' I said.

'He's Nero Caesar, isn't he?'

You could've nailed wheels to my ankles and used me for a trolley. 'That's right,' I said. 'But how did you—?'

He grinned. 'Do me a favour,' he said. 'I'm not blind, and neither are the lads. Seen his face often enough on the backs of the money, not to mention all the statues of him there used to be everywhere, in the old days.'

'Yes, but . . .' I didn't know what to say.

'Don't worry about it,' the captain said. 'Doesn't bother us, we're not fussy who we go around with. We were just curious, that's all. Once this is all over, maybe you two can tell us the story. I expect it's worth hearing, at that.'

I shrugged. 'It's nothing much,' I said. 'But yes, by all means, if you're interested.'

'Thanks.' He smiled. 'Well, fancy that, Nero Caesar. And my old dad said I'd never amount to anything.'

He looked over his shoulder, then moved away; and I saw him talking quietly to the first mate, and then moving on round the rest of his people, nice and relaxed and unobtrusive. I guess you have to be a lot of things in order to manage a ship; you need to be smart and practical, good with people, calm and sensible, good at getting things done without a lot of fuss and argument. I guess you have to be the sort of person who can take a decision like that – these three people, two men I've only just met, who may not be the nicest people in the world but they never did me any harm, these two men and a pretty girl are in our way and they've got to die. You've got to be the sort of person who makes that decision straight off, no messing, and when you've done that you've got to look round at your crew, the nineteen people you spend most of your life with, and you've got to choose which five of them are going to be the killing squad, while the other fourteen get on with the job in hand. Then, when you've made that decision, you've got to figure out the quickest and safest way to do the killing, with the least risk of them getting away or doing any harm to your people. You've got to be the sort of person who can make all those choices in the time it'd take you and me to eat a dried fig, and all your choices have got to be right, and the way you've chosen has got to be the best, most efficient way, and you've got to know how to tell the five men you've chosen what they've got to do quietly and without drawing attention to yourself, and you've got to be able to make them do what they've been told at once, no questions, no mucking about. If you aren't that sort of person, I guess you aren't fit to skipper a ship, or run a farm, or rule an empire. Our captain took it all in his stride, like he was telling the helmsman to come about on such and such a course, because the wind was getting up and he didn't like the look of those clouds. All life and death stuff, you see; the greatest good of the greatest number, the main issue always being to get your boys home safe and get the cargo from here to there unspoilt and on time. I could never do that job; neither could Lucius Domitius, goes without saying. Show me one man in ten thousand who could. Odd, isn't it, how we choose the people who steer the ship of state? (I know, it makes me want to puke too; but every time a Roman senator gets up on his hind legs and makes a speech, you'll hear all about there may be storms ahead, but with a firm hand on the tiller we can cast our eyes on the safe harbour ahead. Well, if they can say that kind of stuff, why not me?) There was our captain, and I'd have voted for him for consul designate like a rat up a drain, but he could never stand, being a foreigner and common as pigshit. And there's Lucius Domitius, pitchforked onto the curule chair by his bitch mother, allowed to stay there a while because – well, basically, because everybody else was dead and he was the only one left who hadn't been murdered or sentenced to life exile on a rock in the sea no bigger than our kitchen table. Crazy way of going about things, though I can't say as I've ever heard anybody suggest a better one.

So the captain shuffled over and said a few words to some of the lads: Tityrus the helmsman, and Ofellinus the boatswain and Speusippus the forecastle-hand, and two blokes I recognised but I can't remember their names; and they nodded once, as if to say, Yes, skip, right away, and they picked up the stuff they were supposed to be carrying, big gold mixing bowls filled up with gold cups and plates and brooches and necklaces and vambraces and the gods only know what else, and they set off towards the door; but before they get there they stop and put their stuff down and quietly walk back, not making any fuss, and Tityrus grabs Amyntas from behind, palm of his left hand up sharp under his chin, right hand takes a firm grip on the shoulder, one smart twist and there's a crack like a charioteer's whip. Scamandrius looks round, wondering what's going on, not worried, because he doesn't realise there's anything to worry about, just curious, is all – and Ofellinus and one of the other two whose names escape me are suddenly there at his sides, taking a firm hold of his arms so he can't move them, and the other bloke whose name I've forgotten reaches down, twists the knife out of his hand and draws it across his throat, like he's carving cheese. Blood squirts out, splashes the bloke right in the face. Myrrhine hasn't turned round yet; she didn't hear the crack over the clanking of the goldware she's carrying. Speusippus nips in behind her, gets his long fingers round her slim neck, holds on tight like a carpenter holding two pieces together till the glue starts to take. She drops all the gold junk with a clatter and starts shaking and jerking and dancing, trying to kick backwards with her heels, thrashing with her arms like her hands are flails, arching her back and acting crazy, like a fish on a line when it's lifted out of the water, and then, quite suddenly, she stops and just hangs there off Speusippus' hands; then he drops her and she flops on the deck, and the metalwork underneath her graunches and creaks. All very quick, very neat. Job done.

(But that's the exception, not the rule. Mostly when people are murdered, something goes wrong or somebody screws up, you can bet your life. Like, when Lucius Domitius gave orders for his mother to be killed, it wasn't all swift and sure, crack-slash-crunch and no messing. Oh no. First they had to have a council of war, with all the trusted advisers and their people and their people's aides and their people's aides' hangers-on; and they sat around for hours what-iffing and how about if we did this or maybe we could try that; and they tried poison, but she was too ornery for that and ate it up like jam; and then some genius figured out a contraption that'd bring the ceiling of her bedroom down on top of her while she was asleep, but they installed it without bothering to test it first, and it didn't work; and then they called in a consulting engineer, who went away and came back with blueprints and sections and elevations for a collapsing ship, with a sliding panel in the bottom that opened up, operated by a brilliant system of weights and pulleys and counterbalances and cantilevers and gearwheels and bits of string, and the collapsing ship worked like a charm, went straight to the bottom of the Bay of Baiae with all hands, only Lucius Domitius' old mum happened to be a really good swimmer, and she doggy-paddled ashore and stormed off to her villa down the road, squelch-squelch in her fancy heels, cursing and swearing like a platoon of cavalry on latrine duty; and then I guess they must've said the hell with it, because they sent a soldier with a Spanish-pattern sword to sort her out, and he had the job done quick as farting, and back home to the barracks in time for evening roll-call. There's a nice story about how she told the soldier to plunge his sword into the breast that had suckled such a monster, but I don't credit that for a moment. I expect she looked round, said, 'Who the hell are you?' and next thing she knew about was the Ferryman, holding out his hand for his twopence halfpenny.)

So that was that. The captain said the best thing to do would be to stick the bodies down the hole once we'd finished getting the gold out, stuff the hole full of bits of wood and stone and rubbish, and nobody'd ever know a thing about it, since nobody except us knew where they'd been headed, or even that they'd decided to stop off in Africa on the way to Sicily. Neat as a key in a lock. But, like I was telling you just now, it takes a special sort of person; not me, and not Lucius Domitius. We couldn't organise a donkey race at a country fair.

You're asking me, did I feel sorry for them, Amyntas and Scamandrius and Myrrhine? Well, yes, I suppose I did. Amyntas, mostly. His mistake was, he never ever expected to find Dido's treasure, or so much as a plated drachma, so he didn't plan ahead, figure out what he'd do and what he'd need and then suddenly there it was, enough wealth to pay off the Roman national debt, just lying there like turnips waiting to be pulled. Then things started happening so fast, before he even knew he was in trouble it was all over with him, and it could only end one way. I can sympathise with that, because my whole life's been like it; and when all's said and done, only a lunatic would think there'd be buried treasure where buried treasure's supposed to be. If you went around believing in tales like that, you'd fry your brain. I guess the gods had their fun with him, drowning him in honey, and you can't argue the toss with Heaven. Scamandrius; well, he was the younger brother and did as he was told, so you can't blame him really. He saved the Romans the cost of two bits of lumber and three penny nails. Myrrhine well, I see her face in my sleep sometimes, all purple and bursting, with her eyes popping out; or I get this weird dream where we've been married for years, and I wake up one morning, sunlight streaming in through the window, birds singing, and she's there next to me dead, strangled, the bed sopping with piss where she wet herself as she died, and my hands are stiff and sore, and the joints of my fingers ache like hell. I generally wake up at that point.

'Right,' the captain said, 'that's better. Now, what the hell are we going to do?'

Everyone stopped what they were doing and looked at him,

waiting to hear the orders for the day; apart from Ofellinus' mate, the one whose name I can't remember, who was still wiping blood out of his eyes. Then I realised the captain was looking at me; and my insides sort of went all runny, because after all, we were in the way too, in a sense.

'You two,' the captain said, 'what's going on here? Who are you, and who the hell were those idiots?'

Well, you don't even bother trying to lie to someone like that. Lucius Domitius was standing there like someone had flayed him and stretched the skin out over a statue, so I reckoned it was up to me. I tried to keep it short, figuring he didn't want all the fiddly details, just the basic facts. I said that my friend there was Nero Caesar, and him and me had been dodging around the place for the last ten years trying to make a living; but this Amyntas, who was a big gangster back in Rome, had got hold of us and was going to turn us in to the governor of Sicily, for good money; but then it turned out Myrrhine had heard about this treasure, which only we knew about, so they'd decided to stop off here just in case it really existed. As for the other time: we were desperate to get out of Sicily because the governor was after us, and his ship just happened to be passing. I said I was very sorry about conning him over Lucius Domitius being my slave, but we didn't have any money and if we didn't get off Sicily we were dead, and it was the first thing that came into my head; anyhow, I said, I hoped that all this gold and stuff would make up for that.

The captain stared at me for a very long time; then he said, 'Well, bugger me,' and I could see him shoving it all to the back of his mind, because whether or not it was true, it didn't have any bearing on the job in hand, which was getting a million tons of gold out of the temple and down to his ship. Was I ever relieved, because it meant that Lucius Domitius and me weren't going to go the same way as Amyntas, or at least not right away. Doesn't take much to make my day. Let me off being killed, and I'm as happy as a pig in shit.

All right. So how would you have gone about it?

And it's not a fair contest, either. You can sit there and think about it, take your time, maybe mull it over in your mind for a day or so, or draw little plans in the dust with a bit of stick. And you can say to yourself, sod this; so I can't figure out a way, so what? Quite; I'm never going to hear about it if you chicken out of my challenge, or give up in disgust, or can't be bothered to try.

The captain, now, he didn't have that luxury. He'd got to come up with an idea, one that'd work, using the stuff we had to hand and the people who happened to be there; he had to do it fast, and he couldn't afford to screw up. That last bit was the most important. Probably you had to be there. I can't put over to you what the atmosphere was like: nineteen blokes who were suddenly looking at more wealth than you'll ever see in your whole life, and it was theirs, free and clear; they'd be richer than Roman senators or kings of Bithynia, them and their children for a hundred generations, all their troubles would be over – if only they could get the stuff out of there and onto the ship. And figuring out how to do it wasn't up to them, they had no say in the matter. It was the captain's job, his alone. Talk about a matter of life and death – their lives, his death (no question about that) if he didn't deliver. And he wasn't trained or qualified, he wasn't an architect or one of those blokes who makes his living shifting huge blocks of stone down rivers on rafts; he couldn't just send for a consulting engineer, like Lucius Domitius murdering his mother. There were nineteen people standing there, all dead quiet, holding their breath, waiting for him to say, All right, this is what we're going to do. He had to say those words, or sooner or later they'd have ripped him into shreds and he'd have gone to the Ferryman in a scent bottle; but when he said them, he had to mean it.

Bummer, don't you think? I'd like to see what sort of a fist Alexander the Great or Hannibal or Vespasian Caesar would've made of it (and they were great leaders of men, they reckon) our captain was the skipper of a grain transport, did all his figuring on his fingers, wiped his fingers in his hair when he blew his nose. Times like that, I'm glad I'm pond-life. Nobody's ever going to lay something like that on me.

'All right,' the captain said. 'Here's what we're going to do.'

It was really very simple. Forget about carts, or carrying the stuff down the winding cliff path on our backs, or any of that shit. Forget about cranes and lifts and ropes and blocks and tackle. The temple was perched on top of a cliff, right? Down the bottom was a nice flat sandy beach. No tides in the Mediterranean. So, bring the ship in as close as they could get it, and simply chuck the stuff off the edge of the cliff. Gold's heavy, it falls in a straight line. Chuck it off the cliff, go down the path, pick it up and load it onto the ship. Easy.

Crazy as a barrelful of angry polecats; but nobody argued. Wasn't up to us, see. We may have said to ourselves, This is bloody stupid, it'll never work, something's bound to go wrong; but that was his problem, not ours. All we had to do was what we'd been told. So we did.

It may have been simple, but it wasn't easy, if you see what I mean. It was starting to get dark by then; we fired up all the lamps we'd got and made torches out of bits of old rag soaked in olive oil and wrapped round sticks, and got stuck in. Sleeping or stopping for a rest wasn't going to enter into it, we had work to do. Eight down in the cave, scooping the stuff up and pitching it up onto the temple floor. Nine blokes to carry it from the edge of the hole to the edge of the cliff. Five more to grab hold of it and throw it into the darkness, as far out as they could get it to go. Lucius Domitius got put on that job, along with Tityrus the helmsman and the three strongest men in the crew; the idea being that nobody wanted stuff getting snagged up on the side of the cliff. It had to go straight from the top to the bottom. I was put on getting stuff up out of the hole, because I'm small and suited to working in tight places. That didn't bother me. I don't think I could've done Lucius Domitius' job, standing on the edge of a cliff flinging armfuls of pure gold out into the night, not even being able to see where it went to. You'd have to be a nutcase to do that. It'd be like heaping up your whole inheritance, live and dead stock, furniture, clothes, tools and seed-corn, and setting fire to it. I wish Seneca could've seen it, because it'd have freaked him out; because he once told me, the only way to be truly wealthy is to be poor, the only way to truly own anything is to throw it away (otherwise it owns you, rather than the other way round; and the miser who's got a million but can't bring himself to spend fourpence is poorer than the man with just fourpence who buys himself fourpennyworth of bread when he's hungry. Whatever. Sounded better when he said it). I'd have liked to hear what he'd have made of that: twenty-odd blokes who could only get to keep this amazingly huge fortune by throwing it off a cliff.

We kept it up all bloody night, and by the time dawn came, we were barely half done; but now at least, Lucius Domitius' crew could peer down at the beach below and tell the rest of us, Yes, it's still there, we can see it down below, shining in the sun. That made us feel a whole lot better, and we stopped feeling so tired we could've curled up and died, and kept up the pace. Not that it wasn't killing me, all that bending down and straightening up. It was even worse than smashing clods of baked dust with the ponderous hoe. Not quite the same, though; not when we had a dream of limitless riches hovering an inch from the tips of our noses, every moment of the time. That sort of thing keeps you going, the way a cup of water and a bowl of greasy soup doesn't.

We worked at it all that day. We were still at it when it got dark the second time, and the lamp oil had only just lasted us through the previous night; there was none left now, not if we offered to pay a pound of gold for a pint of it. But buggered if we were going to stop; no, we kept going in the dark, by feel, until our gang down in the cave were down on our knees groping in the dust with our fingertips for the last straggling bits and bobs. Came the moment, round about midnight, when we couldn't seem to find any more, and there was nothing for it but to stop. We didn't bother to shift, just lay down on our backs where we were. And could we sleep? Are you kidding? Couldn't sleep, didn't have anything to say to each other; we just lay there in the dark waiting for the dawn, like a young lad waiting for his girl to show up at the orchard gate, and she doesn't show and doesn't show, and time crawls past so slow you imagine you died and rotted and your bones crumbled into dust; and you glance up at the sundial, and it's not half an hour since you last looked.

Have you ever lain there staring at a patch of dark sky, trying to see it turn from darkness into light? It changes so slowly you can't see it, but there's a point where it's still as black as ten yards down a wellshaft, and another point where it's a sort of middle blue, and then another where you can see things, just about; and you've been watching all the time, and never noticed it change. Well, soon as we were able to kid ourselves it was starting to get light, we were up on our feet – God, how my back hurt, and my arms and legs and thighs and shoulders, about the only bit of me that wasn't aching was the hair on my chest – and we were ready to go, poised like the chariots on the start line in the Grand Circus. Finally, the light seeped down into the cave, and we found – I think it was two small cups and a pair of earrings – and that was all we'd missed. The rest of it, that whole incredible treasure, was down the bottom of the cliff, where we'd slung it.

At least, we bloody well hoped it was.

Only one way to find out. I couldn't tell you how we managed to get down the cliff path without breaking our necks; it was a miracle, that's all I can say about it. We didn't run and we tried very hard not to push and shove, because we knew without anybody saying anything that we were a hair's breadth away from smashing each other's heads in with rocks at the very slightest provocation. Also, we weren't looking where we were going; we were all peering and craning our necks as we went down, trying to see the gold, if it was still there.

It was. Bloody hell, it was there, a damn great pile of it, like King Midas' shitheap. It was pretty well scattered, of course, and all those lovely cups and graceful vases and ewers and whatever you call them were bent and squashed and bowed all out of shape, where they'd bounced off rocks or had heavy stuff fall on them from a great height. Fat lot we cared, since it was all going in the melt anyhow. The main thing was, it was a cliff's worth nearer the ship than it had been, and as far as we were concerned, that'd do us.

Now maybe you've already asked yourself, if there's so much of this stuff, is it all going to fit on one ship? We hadn't; thought hadn't crossed our minds, or if it had, we'd shooed it away, like you chase crows off a sown field. Now, though, we couldn't hide from it any more. On the one hand, there was a hell of a lot of the stuff. On the other hand, the ship wasn't some poxy little cutter or a slim, pared-to-the-bone warship. It was a big, fat, broad-beamed grain freighter, with an enormous arse and round, chubby sides. We looked at the heap of gold, and we looked at the ship; and one moment we thought, we'll never manage it, and the next we thought, get out of here, it'll go in there with room left over, no problem. Then we figured the only way to find out was to give it a try.

Closest they could get the ship in was about a hundred and twenty yards; the rest we'd have to do the hard way. No more shortcuts, it was a simple matter of bending our backs and trudging, down the beach, dump a load, up the beach, over and over again. Talk about your rotten jobs. I don't think any of us was thinking about riches and luxury and troubles being over by that point; there was just the job, which had to be got done, one load at a time, one step at a time. We'd stripped off our tunics to use as sacks; the sun was hot, and I could feel it cooking my back and neck, like I was a slice of prime veal in Alexander and Pony-tail's best frying pan. By this stage, we'd forgotten what tired meant. You can get to that point, where every bit of you is screaming so loud you can't hear any one part, and so you keep going, numb from your neck to your toes, simply because you know that if you stop now, you'll never ever be able to start again. But we got there.

Well, sort of. We filled the ship. There was still gold left over, but not very much, hardly enough to buy a medium-sized island (Sicily, for example) and the ship was riding painfully low in the water. 'That'll do,' the captain said, and we dropped what we were carrying, stepped over it and stumbled like the walking dead towards the ship.

'Piece of cake,' the captain said. 'Right, let's get out of here. Anybody got any place they particularly want to go?'

Hadn't thought of that, of course. Where do you go, with a ship full of gold? Not back to Rome; show up at Ostia, and as soon as the customs saw what we'd got in the hold, we'd be in the prison, trying to think of some tale for the city aedile. We'd be luckier than we deserved if we got off with our lives, and as for the gold – forget it. Nearest land was Sicily, but Lucius Domitius and I didn't want to go there, obviously. I guess the captain realised that, and (bless him) reckoned we had some say in the matter. On the other hand, we couldn't go very far, not with that much dead weight on board. We could sail up or down the coast. West; we'd be headed for Hippo, or Rusicade or Igilgilis, and just the sound of them was enough to put us off. East; well, there was Carthage, but that'd mean rounding Fair Cape. Neapolis, or one of the Greek cities of Byzacium, we'd have to get round Fair Cape and Cape Mercury as well. Catch us doing that. Otherwise, our only other options meant crossing open sea – northeast to Sardinia, to Nora or Sulci. The food would just about hold up, if we ate like bridesmaids, but what the hell were we going to do in Sardinia with thirty tons of gold?

'All right,' the captain said, after we'd discussed the various options to the edge of hysteria. 'How about this? There's an island north-east of here, Calatha. I landed there once years ago, when my dad and me used to work crew on a freighter. We got blown off course out of Lilybaeum, a freak squall turned us over, Dad and me hung on to a barrel and a fishing boat out of Calatha picked us up the next day. They took us home with them and we hung about there for a day or so till a ship called in for water, on its way from Spain to Sicily. They gave us a lift, and they were in a hurry, so they didn't hug the coast round to Utica, they headed straight for Selinus across the open sea – and I'll say this for them, they weren't out more than a mile or so, which I think was a bloody good bit of navigation. Point is, a few hours from Calatha we passed by a little island, just a rock sticking out of the water with a few trees on top. I asked one of the men. He said nobody lived there, it didn't even have a name; no water, so nobody ever had any call to stop there. Now I reckon I could find that island again, and it seems to me that we could do worse than go there, dump the gold, backtrack to Calatha for water and food, back again to this island of mine, and do what we've got to do to turn all this shit into something useful. Strikes me we'll stand a better chance if we build a furnace and melt this lot down into ingots; that way, it'll be easier to haul and there won't be so many questions about where it came from. After that, off the top of my head I'd say Massilia. It's a regular Greek town, I never heard they were fussy about who they do business with there.'

Now it seemed to me that all we'd achieve that way would be to move the gold from one secret cave to another; but I wasn't about to call attention to myself, so I didn't say anything. The bit about melting it all down struck me as sensible, anyhow. Massilia I wasn't so sure about; never been there, but I'd heard a few things, like it was the sort of place where you can get your throat cut for spitting out the wrong side of your mouth. Then again, I've heard that about a whole lot of places, and ninety-nine times in a hundred it's turned out to be true. Fact was, wherever we went we were going to be in a great deal of trouble, human nature being what it is. The sort of people who'll buy a huge consignment of gold off you, no questions asked, are by definition the kind of people you wouldn't ever want to do business with, at least not unless you happen to have a couple of legions to back you up. We had a wolf by the ears, all right. In a way, it was a bit like being a king or an emperor. You know, without even having to look, that at any given time, everyone you come across is probably out to get you.

Long story short; we set sail and headed for this island of the captain's. We all knew it was a crappy idea, but we also knew that none of us could think of anything better, probably because there weren't any better ideas out there for us to think of. We found it all right; it was just where the captain said it would be, though why that should've been a surprise I don't know. Islands don't just get up and move away when they get to feeling lonely.

He'd said it was nothing but a lump of rock, and he was right about that. There was a little apron of sandy beach, a couple of caves, and the rest of it was a single tall, sheer mountain. Now I'm from Attica, where we know a bit about barren, rocky hillsides. After all, we spend our lives trying to grow stuff on the sides of them, which just goes to show that we aren't nearly as smart as we think we are, or we'd all have packed up and moved somewhere else when Theseus was still a little boy. Phyle, where I grew up, is tucked away under the armpit of a great big mountain ridge that keeps on going up and up until you're almost over the border into Boeotia. So we take mountains in our stride, down our way; folks from other cities say we're born with one leg shorter than the other, for spending our whole lives standing on a gradient. Be that as it may. You wouldn't have got me up the side of that mountain, not for a half-share in Dido's treasure. No wonder nobody ever bothered with that island. It was completely useless. You could count every blade of grass growing on it, and not run out of fingers.

Ideal place, in other words, for a stash. We explored a couple of the caves, and found one that could have been dug out for us specially. The entrance was narrow, you had to duck down and scramble through. Once you were inside, you sort of half-crawled down a short, narrowish passageway and then you found yourself in a big, airy gallery. It reminded me a lot of the main receiving room at the Golden House, in fact, except that it was rather more comfortable: airy and pleasantly cool, but it didn't get cold at night. Anyhow, it was plenty big enough to hide Dido's treasure in, so that's what we did. We were well used to lugging it around by now; it was like we were taking it for walks, as if it was a dog or something. We did the human-chain thing to pass the stuff through the cramped gateway and down the passageway, and that worked out pretty well: two days and a night, this time stopping for a breather every five hours or so. We couldn't be any more leisurely than that; we were short of time because we were low on food and especially water, if you see what I mean, and we had to allow a little over to get us across to Calatha. By this stage, none of us needed telling what to do. We worked together as easily as the hands work with the arms. It was a good feeling, actually, being part of that outfit. It was as though we'd all been together for years and years, like we'd all grown up in the same village. It wasn't so much that we all liked each other or got on particularly well. Rather, you didn't have to think when you were with those guys, you just knew automatically what they were going to do or say. It felt right, somehow, is what I'm trying to tell you.

We finished unloading mid-afternoon on the second day; and, in spite of everything, we decided to spend the rest of the day and the night in the cave, and push on for Calatha first thing in the morning. Basically, this meant no dinner and no more than a cupful of water each, but that wasn't such a hardship in the nice, cool cave. We parked our backs up against the nice, smooth walls, snuffed out the pine-resin torches to save fuel, and were all fast asleep in next to no time.

Now, I'm not one of your big dreamers. In fact, I don't dream very often, and when I do, it's usually one of a fairly limited and unimaginative selection of nightmares, like the repertoire of a little touring theatre in up-country Italy. There's the running-away dreams, where I'm being chased by soldiers or wild animals. There's the drowning dreams, and the trapped-in-burning-buildings dreams, the buried-alive dreams, the condemned-cell dreams, the ones where I'm a gladiator in the Grand Circus, unarmed facing a legion of huge blond Germans, and the ones where I'm nailed up on the tallest cross you can possibly imagine, so high up that I can see the whole world, from Spain to India, stuff like that, and most of it rather gloomy and depressing. That night, though, for some reason I chose to have a completely new and original dream, and it wasn't even particularly nasty or scary, by my standards at least.

I dreamed, would you credit it, that I was Lucius Domitius, back in the old days. That's right. I was Nero Caesar, emperor of the Romans, and I was standing on the balcony of the Golden House looking down on the crowded market square (there wasn't any such balcony, of course, but it's like that in dreams, as I'm sure you know) and in my hand I had Lucius Domitius' harp, the one we'd been at such pains to nick off the musicians back in Rome. Actually, for some reason I can't fathom, we still had the damned thing with us; Amyntas had fetched it along, God only knows why, and it was tucked away on board the ship inside a coil of rope at the back of the hold. Anyway, that harp was in my hand. I was playing it, in fact, pretty well too, and every now and again I'd stop, and the crowd down below me would go wild, cheering and clapping and shouting for more; so I'd play something else – weird thing was, I'm sure I was playing actual tunes, good ones, only I'm sure I was making them up as I went along and when I finished, all the people would start up cheering again. This seemed to go on for ever such a long time, and in the little bit of the back of my mind where I knew it was only a dream, I remember thinking how unfair it was that I should be getting this dream and not Lucius Domitius, except that if he'd been dreaming it instead of me, we'd never have managed to wake the bugger up. Then, in this dream of mine, Seneca was standing next to me, and this woman who was Agrippina, Lucius Domitius' mother, and next to her the Lady Poppaea, Lucius Domitius' second, or was it third, wife; anyhow, the only one he ever cared a damn for. Next to her was this doddery old git with a nervous twitch, and next to him was a little boy, who coughed all the time, they could only be Claudius Caesar and his son, Prince Britannicus. A respectful distance behind them, I could see a big mob of senators, all wearing their dress whites with the flashy purple stripe, which only the Roman nobility are allowed to wear. Behind them (only now we were all at ground level, in the street, staring up at me on the balcony) was a thick crush of Roman knights, all of them ostentatiously flashing their big gold finger-rings. Out beyond them, stretching away pretty much as far as the eye could see, there was a huge assembly of ordinary people, farmers and soldiers and townspeople and even some riff-raff like me; also, for some reason, I could see Licinius Pollio and Amyntas and Myrrhine and Alexander and Pony-tail, even though they were just tiny specks in the vast crowd; and Callistus, he was there as well holding a towel to the slashes in his neck. Then, while I stood there on the balcony, still being Lucius Domitius and playing the harp, it suddenly struck me who all these people were, and what they had in common. They were all the people Lucius Domitius had killed.

Well, when I say killed, been the death of'd be closer to the mark. Even so, there were ever such a lot of them; but they didn't seem angry or bad-tempered. Quite the reverse, in fact; they all seemed to be listening to the music, enjoying it, too. You know what people are like when a song or a good tune on the harp gets their attention; they don't fidget or cough or scratch themselves, like they would if they were listening to a boring speech or a lecture. Some of them'll have their eyes closed, the rest will be staring into space, some of them with soft grins on their faces, some of them keeping time with little twitches of their hands and feet. All these people – these dead people, who got that way because of my friend Nero Caesar – were like that, and I was the one playing for them; me, mark you, and not him, which was a bit odd in itself, except that in dream-logic (which at the best of times is as screwy as an Egyptian accountant's second set of books) I was him, and me as well. In fact, he was nowhere to be seen, if you follow me (and if you do, see a doctor and have your piss tested).

Well, I kept on playing for a very long time, like I was afraid of what'd happen to me when I stopped. You remember the story of Orpheus, who could calm down wild animals and sozzled women with his music? A bit like that, I guess, only Orpheus ended up in small pieces, so he can't have been all that good at it. But eventually I got to the end, and I held the last note five beats, took my hand off the strings and waited to see what'd happen.

To my great surprise, not to mention relief, they all began clapping and cheering and shouting, 'Encore!' to the point where I got the impression that they might cut up rough after all if I didn't give them something else. So I grabbed a handful of strings and started to play, and then realised that I was playing the intro to a song, which meant I'd have to sing.

Now Galen the Athenian doesn't sing, not if you pull out his toenails and stretch him on a rack, because pretty well any torture you can put him through is going to be a summer picnic compared with what you're likely to do to him to make him shut up. Galen the Athenian can't sing worth a tanner's snot, and the best that can be said for him is that he appreciates this, and never ever tries. But there I was, warbling away like some girl's caged bird left out in the sunlight, and I tell you what – it wasn't bad singing, at that. A trifle reedy, maybe, on the high notes, but a pleasant, lightish tenor voice, with good phrasing and all the other tricks singers use to make up for what they lack in the natural talent department. By an odd coincidence, Lucius Domitius had a pleasant, lightish tenor voice, a tad on the reedy side but excellent phrasing, so I guess it must've been him, singing through me.

I was so surprised to hear myself making a noise that didn't sound like a camel trapped in the works of a waterwheel that I'd sung two or three stanzas before it occurred to me to listen to what I was singing and find out what the song was about. Stone me if it wasn't the tragic history of Orpheus Caesar, the tormented artiste who strove to quell the uncouth violence of mankind with his divine music, and ended up dying, alone and betrayed by all, in a dingy cellar full of rats. Soon as I realised what I was singing I tried to stop, but I couldn't. Nothing I could do seemed to have any effect, the ludicrous shit just kept on coming, verse after unspeakable verse of the horrible thing, and the audience, bless their deceased hearts, were lapping it up, hanging on my every word, transfixed with the essential beauty of it all, or some such crap. I felt awful; I mean, quite apart from everything else, Callistus was down there in the audience, I could see him plain as a boil on a pig's bum – but he was stood there with this dumb grin on his chops, nodding his head gently in time to the music; in fact, if I didn't know better, I'd have sworn he was humming along, like he already knew the words.

Well, by this point I really wanted to wake up. Crazy part of it was, I really did know it was just a dream, but at the same time I knew it was actually happening, and that I was Lucius Domitius every bit as much as I was Galen – who featured in the song, by the way, in a totally unfair and inaccurate light, and it was only knowing I was dreaming that stopped me jumping out of the crowd and yelling for a lawyer. On and on it went; the sensitive, misunderstood, enormously talented youth, hated and spurned by everybody around him because he dared to sing and play the harp; the rival poets and musicians, mad with jealousy, urging on the corrupt senators to plot a coup; the gormless, shit-for-brains petty swindler Greek hanger-on—

—And then I heard a familiar voice, shrill and loud enough to be heard above my caterwauling and the sudden eruption of applause from the victims' reunion: of all the weird things, it was my mother, calling me in for dinner. Just a minute, Mum, I was yelling back, I'm in the middle of a concert. It's on the table, she shouted back. Get in here this instant or it goes on the back of the fire. I sighed, right down to my toenails. Coming, Mum, I answered sadly, and I took my hand off the strings and turned to go. The audience weren't having that. They were booing and hissing, telling me to get on with it and finish the song, but I knew what'd happen to me if I didn't come in when dinner was on the table, and it didn't bear thinking about.

So we went in, Lucius Domitius and me; we washed our faces and hands in the big stone basin and sat down at the table, me opposite Mum and Lucius Domitius opposite Grandad. There wasn't any dinner after all, because as Mum explained, times were hard; if we reckoned we wanted to eat, then why didn't we get up off our bums and do some work, especially since Grandad had bought Lucius Domitius that beautiful harp, so there really wasn't any excuse. We sat there quietly while Mum and Grandad ate their nothing (we didn't get any because we'd been late, and it'd gone on the back of the fire, along with the city of Rome, twice), and then Callistus leaned across and whispered in my ear, I thought I told you to look after your brother; and I said, Well, I did my best; and he replied, Well, that clearly wasn't good enough; look at him, for crying out loud, he's dead. He wouldn't have got in that state if you'd done as you were told. And then Mum brought in Dido's treasure in a brown pottery dish for pudding, and said that since I'd been bad I couldn't have any, served me right, and she'd given my share to the dead people. And then (about bloody time, too) I woke up.

Never thought I'd live to see the day when I'd be happy to wake up and find I was in a cave along with a load of pirates. They were all starting to wake up, and there was the captain, walking up and down with the last torch in his hand, kicking feet and telling us to get up and get a move on, we had work to do. I guess there were still bits of dream stuck in my head, because I muttered, Coming, Mum, and closed my eyes, ready to go back to sleep; only Lucius Domitius elbowed me in the ribs, the cruel bastard.

As I told you just now, the plan was that we'd all go over to Calatha to pick up food and water for our long haul out to Massilia. Someone, it could've been Tityrus the helmsman, not that it matters a damn who it was, said he reckoned we ought to leave a couple of blokes here, to guard the treasure. The captain wasn't having any of that. Two blokes couldn't defend a pot of onion soup, he said, let alone a cave full of gold; furthermore, though he was prepared to trust each and every one of us with his life, that was beside the point, since his life was worth something in the region of a hundred and seventy denarii, with his tunic and boots thrown in; he wouldn't trust his own mother on her own with Dido's treasure in case a ship happened to call at the island while we were away and some half-baked notion of screwing the rest of us out of our shares happened to float into her addled old head. No; the treasure was well hidden, there was Sisyphus' chance of anybody stumbling over it who didn't know it was there, and if we all stuck together, there wouldn't be any risk of misunderstandings and temptation, which tend to be serious problems where there's large sums of money involved. Like I said, he was smart, that captain. Maybe the prospect of ending up like Amyntas if he put a foot wrong was making him act smarter than usual, but that doesn't take anything away from him, if you ask me.

So we piled back on board the ship, all eager to be off, because the sooner we left, the sooner we could get back and make a start on the long job of melting all that fancy artwork down into boring old ingots. A stiff wind got up almost as soon as we were under way, and that pleased all of us, at first. Better still, it was shoving us along in exactly the direction we wanted to go, as though the gods were mucking in to help us out. Good feeling, that.

But the wind kept on blowing. Now I haven't got a clue when it comes to boat stuff, which can get pretty technical and complicated; it's all tacking into the leeward sou'westerly and taking in sail to bring her about when you see Sirius rising on the starboard bow. Nautical types understand all that kind of thing, but you might just as well stand there barking at me like a dog for all the sense I can make of it. So when the crew started muttering about the wind, I couldn't figure out what the hell the problem was; whether we were going the wrong way, or the wind was slowing us down, or whether the boat was about to tip over and drown the lot of us. Besides, I was too busy trying to keep down what little there was in my stomach – since we were so short on supplies, it struck me it'd be a criminal waste if I puked everything I'd eaten recently over the side. Lucius Domitius was looking pretty green as well, so we decided the best thing for us to do would be to crawl away somewhere we wouldn't get under the feet of the professionals, and hope the wind blew itself out before it turned us over or sent us to India.

I've got to say, I don't like the Mediterranean very much. Most of the time it's all right, as seas go, but when it has one of its temper tantrums, it can be a real pain in the bum. Pretty soon it was scooping the water up into big fat waves and dropping them all over us, soaking us to the skin and giving the crew something else technical to jabber about. To begin with, though I was worried (and anybody who goes out on the sea in a boat and doesn't worry is either simple in the head or asleep), I kept telling myself that this was probably the sort of thing sailors have to put up with all the time, just another day at the office as far as they were concerned, and there wasn't any danger, just a certain amount of discomfort; and anyway, I wasn't made of salt, so getting drenched wasn't going to kill me. But it did seem to be going on for rather a long time, and the crew were sliding and falling about all over the place and shouting, and quite a bit of sea was coming up through the bottom of the ship, and we didn't seem to be going sideways much, just up and down in the air, like kids on a see-saw. Then I saw a great big wave swell up and come rushing at us, like an angry pig in the yard.

It gave the ship a ferocious shove, which sent me sprawling against a rail, and when I looked up, I saw Tityrus the helmsman sliding on his face across the deck and over the side into the water. I shouted – I believe the right thing to say is, Man overboard, but at the time I couldn't remember that, so I yelled, 'Here, Tityrus just went in the sea.' Nobody answered or did anything, so I yelled it again. I knew they'd heard me, because one or two of them turned their heads and looked at me, but they just carried on with what they were doing, which was mostly hanging on to ropes and rails, or skating about the deck. Then it sunk in that we were in real trouble, and that scared the shit out of me.

Don't ask me to tell you what happened next, because I wasn't paying attention to the big picture, just my small, desperate corner. Either the ship hit something, or something hit us; anyhow, it was like when you're walking along in the dark and you march straight into a tree or something you didn't know was there. I'd hooked my elbow round a post, but I guess it must've given way, because I found myself slithering across the deck on my right thigh. My shoulder slammed into something hard, and then I felt that something snap off too, and I was in the air, and then the surface of the water hit me, and I was under it, flailing and kicking with my hands and feet. Part of me was saying, stay calm, they won't just leave you in the sea to drown, they'll turn round and come back for you, or lower the boat or something. But I knew perfectly well they weren't going to do any such thing, because when their colleague and friend Tityrus went over the side they hadn't been able to do a damn thing, just glower at me for pointing it out.

So there I was.

I wonder what they say about me, down there in the kingdom of the dead. As you might have noticed, I'm no stranger to what you might call certain-death situations – condemned cells, crosses, tumbrils, armed escorts en route to gallows, gibbets, prisons and the like, the wrong end of other people's weapons, burning buildings, all that kind of stuff. So what's the deal, I ask myself, as far as King Pluto and his people are concerned? Each time I find myself on the spot, do they rub their hands together and mutter, This time we've got the bugger, for sure? Or do they fly into a panic, terrified that if I weasel my way past the Ferryman and the three-headed dog, I'll lower the whole tone of the neighbourhood and drive them up the wall with my incessant chatter? That might be it, you know. They might be saying, Fuck, not him again, do something quick; and suddenly there's the unexpected amnesty, the cell door left carelessly ajar, the inexplicable massacre of a platoon of cavalry by someone who later turns out to be a notorious city gang boss, or the personal intercession by the emperor of the Romans. The way I look at it, I've never been exactly what you'd call the welcome guest anywhere I've been, so why should it be any different in the palace of Tartarus? Stands to reason, really. Most people freak out at the prospect of having to put up with me for a day; once I'm down there, they'll have me on their hands for ever. Doesn't bear thinking about, really.

So anyhow, there I was in the water, trying to work out how to swim. I managed to scoop-and-kick my way back up to the surface, just in time to see a massive great wave hitting the side of our poor old ship. It was like watching a man in a bar fight getting punched on the chin by someone he hasn't even seen; one moment, the ship was upright and sort of level, and the next it was sprawling and rolling in the water, tipped over just that little bit too far, to the point where it's never going to be able to bob up straight again. Then another wave crashed down on it, and I got the feeling that King Neptune, having knocked it over, was getting in close to kick the shit out of it now it was down. That was when I changed my mind and decided I was probably better off where I was.

Oh well, I thought, that's that, then. Not just for me, but the crew and Lucius Domitius. Seemed silly, really. After all, we'd just found Dido's treasure, every single one of us was now officially rich – not just comfortably set up for life, but seriously, Roman-senator rich. A cock-eyed way of carrying on, I thought. I mean, why go to all that trouble of letting us find all that gold, and then snuff us all out five minutes later? It wasn't even as if the gods were using us to send humankind an eloquent message about presumption and greed and the vanity of worldly possessions, since we were the only living creatures on earth who knew the story.

That was all very well, but there's a time and a place for everything, and I had a lot of rather urgent swimming to attend to. First things first. I spat out about a gallon and a half of sea, which I'd swallowed at some point. Then, remembering to keep my little froglike legs kicking so I wouldn't sink, I looked round just in case there was something I could grab hold of – a bit of busted mast or a plank or whatever. No chance; and I was on the point of giving up (because my arms and legs were so weary I couldn't move them any more to save my life, quite literally) when something bashed into the back of my head, and under I went again.

Odd, how you've always got a little bit of effort left in you, even when you're sure you're completely played out. I scrabbled my way back into the air, and when I came up, there bobbing along next to me was, of all the crazy things you ever saw in your life, a coffin.

SIXTEEN

I have my faults, but I'm not picky. Even though this coffin was obviously some god's idea of a really funny joke, not to mention the fact that the bloody thing had just belted me over the back of the head and damned near killed me, I made a grab for the side and hauled myself up on to it. Thinking about it, I don't know why I was surprised to find there was a dead body in it; after all, what else would you expect to find in a coffin, apart from dead people? Very dead, this one was, with skin like dried leaves and bones the colour of pottery, poking out through the remains of some old bandages, and as a rule I'm a bit squeamish when it comes to such things. This time, though, I managed to get over it pretty quick, in roughly the time it'd take you to sneeze, in fact; I clamped both hands on the side of the coffin, lined myself up as best I could and sort of jumped-flolloped in, landing with my nose in the dead guy's mouth.

Something in the way the coffin lurched and wobbled told me that there wasn't room for both of us on board; so I got my fingers under his shoulder and ribs, and boosted him overboard into the sea. He went quietly, bless him, leaving nothing but a few toes and some bandage behind, and I snuggled down in my beautiful cedarwood ark and threw up with extreme force over the side.

About that coffin. You probably don't need me to tell you that crating people up for their journey to the Other Side isn't the Roman way, or the Greek way, either. For choice, we like our dead cooked, not raw. But other people see these things differently, and it wouldn't do if we were all alike, I guess. Anyway, this coffin was rather a splendid thing, once I had a chance to give it the attention it deserved. For a start, it was painted, inside and out, and in places there were patches of gold leaf, about the size of my hand. Whoever made it was a damned good carpenter; the boards were lovingly grooved together, close enough to make the thing watertight. Furthermore, it was sort of rounded underneath, which made it a pretty efficient boat on stormy waters, rather better suited to rolling with the waves than our poor old flat-bottomed grain freighter. On one side you could see where hinges had been, so my guess is it was made with a lid, like a fine lady's jewellery box. I'm only telling you this because I'd actually seen something quite like it once before, when Lucius Domitius and I were in Halicarnassus. In one of the temples there, they've got a coffin just like my one, set up on trestles. It's a real work of art, with the lid carved like a man's body, with a head wearing a great big wig, and a face and everything. The one I saw in Halicarnassus was painted and gilded, too; and I seem to remember someone telling me it came from Egypt – it'd been fetched out to Asia by a Persian governor, hundreds of years ago, and he'd robbed it out of a king's tomb, along with a whole load of gold and treasure. He'd planned on taking it back home to Persia when his term was up, but he died and the family must've decided to leave it there. Anyhow, I think my coffin was Egyptian, just like that other one. Don't ask me how it came to be floating about in the sea, because I haven't got the faintest idea. Nor, to be honest, do I care. I'm just grateful it happened along when I needed it most; and if it really was an Egyptian king I rolled out into the sea, I'm grateful to him too, and I hope he's happy and contented in wherever Egyptian kings go to, because he did me a good turn.

Well, that solved one of my problems, in the short term. Even so, I was still comprehensively fucked, as far as I could see. True, I wasn't in the water; but I was being swept along in a storm in a small wooden box, bouncing up and down on the crests of huge waves, surrounded on all sides by water, with the nearest land I knew anything about being a very long way away, in an unspecified direction. It still added up to certain death, whatever way you looked at it, and the best you could really say was that if the bloody thing kept from turning over or springing a leak, I'd enjoy the privilege of crossing over to the next world stylishly, in a mode of transport that was uniquely appropriate and genuinely fit for a king. Probably this should have cheered me up; but guess what, it didn't.

One thing I will say for being adrift in a coffin in the middle of a terrible storm, it's relatively undemanding. You don't have to do very much, because there's nothing you can do, apart from cowering, and prayer, if you're so inclined. I'll be honest with you; I'm not really very religious. Seems to me that a god who gets his jollies from beating up on a poor, miserable little sod like me isn't the sort who'll be likely to stop just because I ask him nicely; and I've never been rich enough to be in a position to bribe the gods with offerings and sacrifices and statues and shrines and all. Now, you might say that this probably accounts for why I keep landing in mortal peril; or you could look at it another way, and argue that it's why I keep landing in mortal peril and surviving, depending on whether you think the gods like listening to a whole lot of snivelling humans all day long. Be that as it may; I lay there on my back in the coffin with my eyes shut, on the grounds that anything I did was more than likely to make things worse, and I waited to see what'd happen.

I waited a very long time, and it was no fun at all, but eventually I got the impression that I wasn't heaving and diving about nearly as much as I had been, and so I risked opening my eyes and taking a look.

What I saw was stars. That, I felt, had to be good, because if I could see the stars, chances were that the storm was over. I closed my eyes again, and believe it or not, I think I fell asleep, in spite of everything, because the next time I opened them I found myself staring up at a cloudless blue sky, and listening to the distant thunder of waves on rocks.

That was good, and bad. You don't get rocks out in the middle of the sea, only close to land. On the other hand, rocks do horrible things to boats, and most likely coffins as well. I remember thinking, it'd be a bloody shame if I'd come all this way, kept company for ten years with the emperor of the Romans, found Dido's treasure, been miraculously saved from a watery grave by some god with a coffin, all that, just to get smashed into sausagemeat on some rocks. Any fool could do that, I thought, without going through any of the preliminary stages.

You ever tried steering a floating coffin? Not easy. All you can do is trail your hands in the water, and for all the good it does, you may as well not bother. I could see the rocks quite clearly. They made up a reef (I think that's the right word) round an island, and I was being shunted along straight at them at a hell of a lick. It wasn't looking good. Beyond the rocks, which stuck out of the sea like teeth out of an old man's jaw, I could see an ugly great big cliff, with the waves pounding against it; so even if I missed the rocks, I wasn't going to be much better off. I could only think of one thing I to do, though it struck me as bloody stupid: hop out of the coffin and see if I could swim for it. So that's what I did. Of course I went straight under – only just missed being brained by the coffin as it rushed past me – but when I came up again, I was just in time to see my coffin slamming full tilt into a rock and flying apart, like chaff blown upwards from the threshing floor. Well, it's nice to be proved right once in a while.

So much for the getting out of the coffin part; the swimming for it bit proved to have been just a trifle ambitious. I froglegged and scooped as hard as I could, but it didn't seem to make any odds, I was still headed straight for that ugly old rock. I'd just about given up hope when I saw it looming up in front of me, then dodging off to the left – in other words, I'd been carried past it. That was great, absolutely wonderful, except that I was headed for another, even bigger and uglier rock behind it. Screw this, I thought; but somehow I managed to fend off that second rock with the palms of my hands, so that I glanced off it rather than going into it, splat. Then I had a bright idea, and grabbed for a chunk of stone sticking up out of the side. Caught it, too, and contrived to hang on and drag myself up onto it, both feet out of the water.

So there I was, crouching on a breaker surrounded by white foam and nasty, bad-tempered waves. It meant I was back on dry land, up to a point; but I couldn't get round the fact that my new dominion, of which I was emperor and sole tenant, was slightly smaller than the seat of my bum, so there didn't seem much point in making myself at home, building a city, dreaming up a model constitution or issuing decrees. Not that I'd have had the chance, because a moment later another wave sloshed up round me and hooked me off my rock like it was picking a bogey out of its nose.

So ended my reign as king of my own little island, which was so short I think I even managed to beat Otho's record for how quickly an absolute monarch can be slung out on his ear.

That left me back in the water again; but for some reason I can only guess at (assuming I could be bothered, which I can't) the current behind the rock wasn't nearly as ferocious as it'd been when I was in front of it. I swam like crazy, and found I was actually making headway, cutting across the current. It was still wavehandling me in the general direction of the cliff, but for every yard forward I went, I reckon I must've gone four feet sideways. So I kept going, even though my arms and legs felt like they belonged to someone else, with the result that I missed the cliff and found myself heading for a narrow apron of shingle and pebbles between two vicious-looking rock spurs. By now I'd given up on the swimming, because the current was stronger than ever, but that was fine, the waves were bundling me right at the scrap of shingle, which was the direction I'd have been heading in anyhow.

I was saying to myself, if only I could wind up on that little beach, all my troubles would be over. I was dead wrong, of course. The sea carried me to the beach all right, but then it started dragging me up it on my stomach. This was awful, because – well, have you ever watched a carpenter finishing a piece of wood by rubbing it down with a bit of sharkskin? I'm here to tell you, it hurts. I could feel my clothes ripping away, and I also had an idea that the backwash would haul me back out again, so as to give the pebbles another chance to grind me down. I didn't fancy that; so, when the backwash started pulling at me, I dug my fingers and toes into the shingle and tried to hang on. Result was, for a second or so I turned myself into a human rake, dragging a furrow of gravel and small pebbles down the beach. Then the force acting on me slackened up, and I knew, that was my one and only chance. I scrabbled up the beach on all fours, racing the tide, and contrived to get two or three yards higher up the beach than I'd been when the raking business started, before the backwash began hauling me back again. When that happened, I dug in once again, and repeated the whole business; and again, and again, with the sea's grip on me getting a little bit less each time – and then at some point, I was free and clear. I don't know what changed exactly. Either the storm finally ran out of puff, or I simply made enough ground to get free; in any event, I was lying on my face in the shingle, with an ache in the bones of my hands and legs like you can't begin to imagine, but I couldn't feel the sea dragging at me any more. If I'd wanted to, I could've stood up and walked.

Just then, though, it was simply too much bother, it'd have meant too much effort and pain. Instead, I lobster-crawled about ten yards before flaking out, and if you ask me, that was quite an achievement in itself. Maybe not up there with the Labours of Hercules, and I don't suppose it'd have inspired Lucius Domitius or any of his brother poets to write a twenty-book epic poem, but it was enough to be going on with, for a little rat-faced Greek with no particular reason for fighting so hard to stay alive. And then, you may ask, what did I do with this freedom I'd fought so hard to win; now that I'd torn myself out of Neptune's grasp and cheated the Ferryman yet again? Well, of all the things to do, lay there with my nose in the gravel, and fell asleep.

No idea how long I was out for. I just remember coming round, and it was starting to get dark, and what woke me up was the horrible pain in pretty well every part of me, except possibly my hair. I'd have given anything to go back to sleep, but that was no good; it was as if it was my ninth birthday, and all I wanted in the whole world was to go back to being eight again – couldn't be done. So I made an effort and got to my knees, then tried to stand up. No way; my legs weren't having that, my body'd suddenly got much too heavy, and I sort of toppled slowly forwards, like a rickety old building collapsing. I gave it a while before trying again – not too long, just in case the tide made up its mind to come back looking for me. Also, it occurred to me that it'd probably be a good idea, now that I'd made up my mind to stay alive a bit longer, not to be stuck on that little snippet of beach once it was too dark to see. Four goes it took me before I managed to get on my feet and stay there; then I began walking.

It wasn't a cliff, not like the ones on either side. It was just a bloody steep hill where a cliff had used to be until at some point it had collapsed and fallen into the sea, leaving an untidy mess of huge squarish boulders. The only way to tackle them was piecemeal, one rock at a time, like climbing a whole series of tiny mountains.

When the light gave out I was still at it, and I had to finish the job in the dark, by feel. Finally, though, I felt grass under my hands instead of rock, and so I made a sort of unilateral declaration of having got up the hill, and passed out again. Next thing I knew was daylight, and warm sun, and some horribly loud birds yelling their stupid heads off at me.

So there I was, cast up alone and naked on a strange, deserted shore, rather like someone or other famous, only just then I couldn't remember the bugger's name. I say naked; actually, that's a slight exaggeration. My clothes had been well and truly shredded, to the point where you couldn't really call them clothes any more, but I did still have my belt. I wouldn't bother you with this minor detail, except that – maybe I should have mentioned this before – when we were back in the cave under the temple in Africa, shifting the treasure, my trusty old leather belt, which had done me sterling service for a dozen years or more, been my faithful companion in all my adventures (condemned cells, guardhouses, hiding in empty oil jars, the lot) had finally given up the ghost and disintegrated. Well, a bloke needs something to keep his shirt from flapping about in the breeze, and it just so happened that in the treasure heap there was this rather fancy, actually pretty vulgar and tacky, solid gold belt, made up of linked plates as thick as your pinky finger with jewels and stuff set in it. Well, beggars can't be choosers, and I really did need a belt, so I wrapped some old sacking round it so it wouldn't chafe and put it on (pretty good fit, actually) and I guess it must've slipped my mind after that, because instead of leaving it in the cave on the captain's secret island along with all the rest of the loot, I just sort of kept on wearing it. Please don't get the idea that there was anything dishonest about it, like I'd intended to steal that belt from my new friends – I ask you, would I do a thing like that? No, it was an honest oversight. Really.

Anyway, after all that, the only thing I had left to me was that stupid belt, that stupid solid-gold-and-gemstones belt, which was probably only worth the price of a medium-sized farm, or at most a very small country estate. Still, a man with nothing but a splinter in his bum is better off than a man with nothing at all, as my old mother used to say. So I wrapped the few last tatters of my clothes round the belt (to stop it chafing), chose a direction at random, and started to walk.

It was only then that it occurred to me to wonder where the bloody hell I was. I'm no great shakes at geography, believe me, but even so, I felt sure that if there was a country, or even a fair-sized island, parked in the sea between Africa and Sicily, someone would probably have mentioned it at some stage, and I've had got to hear about it. But apparently not. The further I went, the more obvious it became that this wasn't just some pimple of rock, like the captain's secret island. This was a proper island, with mountains and valleys and forests, as big as Aegina, say, or Salamis, or Elba. But there didn't seem to be any people on it; no fields or vineyards or terraces or boundary stones, no houses, no smoke to be seen rising from chimneys, no light flashing off the bronze cladding of a temple roof.

Bloody marvellous, I thought. Old-timers back home used to say that a man could feed himself perfectly well in Attica off nuts and berries and wild onions and easily trapped animals, such as stoats and rats and the like, but that was as far as they went; they didn't actually explain how. Besides, I've never been any good at roughing it. I'll eat stale bread and the grease stuck to the side of the soup pot, but that's about as far as I'll go. Dump me down in the wilderness, with no baker's shops or sausagemonger's booths, and I'm fucked. I got myself thoroughly miserable thinking like this, and after a bit I couldn't really see any point in going on. Might as well sit down under this nice shady tree, I said to myself, and wait for the inevitable end.

So I did; and maybe I closed my eyes for a couple of heartbeats, because next thing I knew, there was this bloke standing over me, looking down at me with a daft grin on his face.

He was a sight, no doubt about it. Tall bugger, he was, thin and stringy like a vine that's outgrown its strength; you could see the bones and veins in his arms and legs as clear as anything. He could've been anything between fifty and a hundred years old; his hair had all fallen out, apart from a little sprinkle of white stubble on his chin, and his skin was the colour of new dark honey. His teeth had gone the way of his hair, and he had only the one eye; at least, his left eye was more or less normal, but the right one was half-closed and there was just a bit of the white showing, as though that side of his face was staring straight up at the sun. He was wearing a newish shirt, bright purple, the colour that only Roman senators are supposed to be allowed to wear, and a pair of smart pigskin sandals.

I looked at him, and he looked at me. Really weird way of looking, he had, like I was some strange object that'd just fallen out of the sky, curious and unusual but perfectly safe and unlikely to be worth anything. For some reason I was so shaken up that it took me a long time to pull myself together – which was bad, because this old scarecrow was the first indication I'd seen since I fell in the sea that I might actually get out of this whole horrible adventure alive. Eventually, though, I got a grip on myself and squeezed out a smile. 'Good morning,' I said.

He frowned, like he was thinking it over. 'Reckon so,' he said, in Greek. 'Beans want rain.'

I didn't want to talk about beans. 'Excuse me,' I said, 'but can you tell me where this is?'

'What?'

'I said,' I repeated, 'can you possibly tell me where this is?'

'You'll have to speak up,' he said. 'I'm a bit deaf.'

Exactly what I needed, I said to myself. 'Can you tell me,' I roared, 'where this is?'

He looked puzzled, like he didn't understand the question. 'This here is Long Meadow,' he said. 'Five Firs Copse is away down over . . .' He waggled his left hand in a vague circle. 'And down there in the dip is Blackwater.'

'Thank you,' I said, 'but what I actually meant was, what country is this?'

He looked at me. 'You're foreign,' he said. 'From the shipwreck.'

I nodded. 'That's right.'

'Reckoned so. Watched you last night, coming up the beach over to Needles Cove. Reckoned you were going to be drowned, for sure.'

I didn't know whether to thank him for the compliment or apologise. 'Have you seen anybody else from the shipwreck?' I said. He lifted his head.

'Reckon not,' he replied. 'Just you, and a whole parcel of driftwood and stuff, washed up on North Point. Where you from, then?'

'Athens,' I replied. Fortunately, he seemed to have heard of Athens. 'Is there a town near here, or a village, somewhere I could get some clothes and something to eat?'

'Pretty bad storm,' he went on. 'It's a wonder you wasn't drowned, or all busted up on the rocks. Terrible bad, they can be, sometimes.'

'Don't I know it,' I said. 'I was wondering, is this Africa? Only I don't really see how it could be anywhere else, there aren't any big islands between Carthage and Sicily.'

'Two or three times a year we get a wreck on the Needles,' the man went on, 'and pretty nigh every time they're all drowned, or cut up on the reef. Less you know the way through, you don't have much of a chance in these waters.'

On balance, I said to myself, I think I'd rather starve. 'Well, aren't I the lucky one, then,' I said. 'Here, is there some reason why I shouldn't know where this is? Like, is this a secret military base, or a pirate hideaway or something?' I was kidding, of course. It was only when I said the bit about the pirates that I realised I'd said a stupid thing. But the old man just kept looking at me. 'Really,' I said, losing my grip just a little, 'all I want is something to eat and somewhere I can get some clothes, I don't want to be any bother to anyone, and if you don't want to tell me where this is, then that's just fine. Only I've just spent a day in a floating coffin, all my clothes have gone, and my best friend, and unless somebody helps me, I might just as well die. You do understand what I'm saying, don't you?'

The old man looked at me for a long time, didn't say a word; and while he was doing that, I was just starting to wonder where on earth an old goat-chivvier would have come by a luxury-grade purple tunic. Then he leaned forward, put his hand on my shoulder and said, 'You'd better come on up to the big house.'

'Fine,' I said. 'Thank you.'

Well, my excuse is that I was tired out and hadn't had anything to eat for a while, stuff like that. Truth is, I don't suppose I'd have been able to keep up with the old bugger even if I'd spent a month at a training camp for the Olympic games. He charged ahead, didn't matter whether we were going uphill or down, and all I could do was trot behind him like a little dog. We went up one mountain, then down it and up another, round a third, sideways across the face of a fourth, till I'd lost my bearings altogether. My knees and calves were aching like the muscles were about to bust out of the skin, and I was breathing like I'd been diving for pearls. Sad thing is, when I was a kid back on the farm, walking all day backwards and forwards to the fields or up the mountain after the stock, I could have gone on like that and never felt it. Still, that's the penalty you pay for leaving home to go gadding about.

When we reached the top of the fifth mountain, at last I saw where we were headed. Could easily have missed it, even so: just one building, snuggled away in a deep combe between two mountain ridges, next to a sparse little trickle of water. It looked tiny from right up there, but as we went down into the valley, I realised it was quite a big place, long and narrow, no courtyard or anything, more like a huge shed than a house, with a thatched roof like a barn. I didn't see any people, or animals, or growing crops or vines, and I was wondering if the old fool lived here on his own, just him in that enormous shed. It was only when we were right up close that people started to come out of the house, a whole mob of them, two or three dozen, standing there watching us like we were a comet or something.

Talk about the old boy and his purple tunic, they were all dressed like princes or senators, in fine wool and linen, purple and military scarlet and God knows what else. There was one bloke I took to be the leader, he was stood out slightly in front, as if he was waiting to receive us with a prayer and a speech. He looked like he was in charge; you can tell, once you've got your eye in. He was a big man, thick-set, a bit on the chubby side, with hair the colour of tarnished bronze just before it starts going green. He didn't look Greek, or Italian, certainly not like an African or an Arab; in fact, none of them looked like anything I'd ever seen before, though you had to look twice to realise the difference. I can't quite place what it was, something about the nose and the cheekbones.

'I found this one,' the old boy sang out. 'Off of the shipwreck.'

The big man didn't seem surprised. 'Just the one?' he said. The old boy nodded, and quite suddenly, I felt—

There was this neighbour of ours back home, and one day he was up on the mountain carting a load of big old boulders to shore up his terraces. Something went wrong; either a busted spoke, or his axle pin dropped out. Anyhow he hopped down from the box and knelt beside the wheel, having a look to see what the trouble was. Rotten bad luck on him, the wheel or the axle gave way while he was knelt there, and you can guess what happened. The whole load of stone slid off the bed of the cart, squashed his legs like you'd crush a fly. He must've passed out from the shock, because the next thing he knew was waking up in bed back home, with a circle of anxious faces round him. His first thought is, the cart, were you able to fix it, can you arrange for the wheelwright and the smith to get it sorted out, because we're going to need it next month for the vintage. But nobody says anything, they're just looking at him with these really tragic expressions, and that was when he realised he couldn't feel his legs. So he asks what the matter is, and they explain, the only way they were able to get him out without killing him or shifting the stone so it rolled him over the edge down into the valley was to cut his legs off just above the knee; in fact, if a neighbour and his son hadn't been passing with a big crosscut saw to fell a new mast for their fishing boat, he'd probably have been dead before anything could be done. Well, the bloke just lay there, completely wiped out, like the facts were a huge dumpling he'd tried to swallow that'd got jammed in his throat.

And that's more or less how I felt, I guess; because that was when it dawned on me that Lucius Domitius was most likely dead, drowned, lying somewhere at the bottom of the sea. Everything he'd been, everything he was, all his education and upbringing and experiences, all the bloody aggravating things he used to do, the way he could be so stupid and so gullible, the way that sometimes he could be brilliant, but never quite got anything right, the way he'd at least always been there, surviving one horrible mess after another, getting so far − but not, apparently, any further. It didn't make sense to me, because why would the gods fish him out of death's mouth so many times, like those birds in Egypt who live by picking the teeth of crocodiles, just to let him drown in a sudden, unexpected storm on the way to buy groceries? I could see them snuffing *me* like that, because damn it, I've never mattered; but to save me, send a bloody floating coffin to save me, and let him drown, it'd be like setting fire to your house and taking nothing out of it but one odd slipper.

So, after I'd been shown into the house and sat down in a very posh-looking chair on the high table in this one enormous long room. 'Excuse me,' I said, 'but does that mean I'm the only one who escaped? You haven't found any more of us, from the ship-wreck?'

The boss-man looked very grave. 'I'm afraid not,' he said. 'Let's say, our reef is very thorough; it's the main reason we're here, in fact. Unless you know where the gap is, you'll never find it, and your chances of getting through the rocks – well, you're only the fifth man to be washed up alive in two hundred years, to my certain knowledge. That's why nobody knows about us, see,' he went on, though I wasn't really interested, not then; I couldn't feel what he was saying, like you can't feel a needle stuck in a numb toe. 'Ships do come this way from time to time, but once they're close enough in to see the island it's too late, they're in the current that draws down onto the reef, and that's the end of them. For what it's worth,' he continued, 'the name of this island is Scheria. Ring any bells?'

I tried to think, because the name was vaguely familiar. But it was so unimportant; like I was a carpenter, and someone had called me away from my wife's funeral to see to a stiff hinge.

'Well,' the man went on, 'if you have, it's because we're mentioned in the *Odyssey* – not us, of course, we've only been here a few generations, but the people who lived here before us, or strictly speaking, the people who were here before the people before the people before the people before us – Homer calls them the Phaeacians, and he says Ulysses got washed up here after his ship was wrecked and he was nearly killed getting through the reef. Anyhow,' he finished, because he could see I wasn't in the mood for literary history, 'that's us, and that's where you are. And,' he added, taking a deep breath, like a doctor breaking bad news, 'here's where you're going to have to stay, I'm afraid; either that, or we're going to have to knock you on the head, because we do rather value our privacy, in our line of work.'

So I'd been right after all. 'You're pirates,' I said.

The man grinned lopsidedly. 'Best in the trade,' he said. 'In fact, we're about all that's left of a fine and noble tradition, thanks to the

Romans. They don't like pirates, see. Never have. My family came here first back in the time of Pompey the Great, when he chased us out of Cyrenaica; and the Romans've been trying to wipe out the profession ever since, on and off. It's getting so bad, we have to hide ourselves away here, daren't even live up on the coast for fear of being seen, just in case a ship did manage to get through the reef in one piece. In fact, we're seriously considering giving the whole thing up and taking up farming instead; it'd be less work, easier living, and we wouldn't feel like we were hiding under a table while the soldiers run by all the time.'

I shrugged. Didn't matter, did it? Besides, who knew more about running and hiding than me? Living here, it'd be next best thing to normal. 'All right,' I said. 'Only I'd better tell you, I know fuck all about ships and sailing and stuff, so I don't suppose I'll be any use to you. Truth is, there isn't anything I can do, except maybe mend sails, if someone shows me how to do it.'

The man smiled. 'Don't worry about that,' he said, 'we'll find a way for you to make yourself useful, you'll see. Fact is, we don't get to pick and choose the people who join us here. We take them on because they're all we can get, and we've got to keep our numbers up somehow. There's two hundred and seventy-nine men on Scheria, and five women – and you wouldn't fancy any of them if their fathers were senators, if you see what I mean. No, you crack on and make yourself at home, we'll be glad to have you.'

And then they brought me stuff to eat and drink: some very nice soft wheat bread, sausage and cheese and two apples, and a jug of pretty drinkable Greek red wine sweetened with honey and nutmeg; and they looked at me for size and fetched me a virtually new wool tunic and probably the best pair of boots I've ever worn in my life, and someone knelt beside me and washed out all the cuts and scratches in my hands and knees, and put some sort of ointment on them that stopped them hurting, and dressed them up as neat as you like with clean wool bandage. I've got to say this for them, they had no need to go doing that, all they knew about me was what I'd told them, and they didn't seem in any hurry to ask anything more. At any other time I'd have sworn I must've drowned after all and got into the Blessed Islands by mistake. You could say it was typical of my stinking bloody luck. First time in my life anybody's been really nice to me, just for myself, not because they were after anything from me, and I'm too wrapped up in other stuff to enjoy it or pay proper attention.

I don't know how long I was sat there, being waited on and tended to, but by the time they were through with me, people had started coming in for dinner. Apparently they all ate together in this one huge room – it was long and narrow, with a row of tables and benches running the length of each wall, and this extraordinary fireplace that went all the way up the middle. They laid a place for me right where I was sat, on the top table, which was at right angles to everybody else, on a little raised platform. I guessed that this was a great honour, me being a new recruit and all. Excellent food and wine – plain and simple, but all good stuff and masses of it, bread and cheese and a whole lot of different dried and preserved meat. Anyhow, when we'd been eating for a while, I thought it was about time I told them something about who I was, because otherwise it was just going to be embarrassing when they found out. So I nudged the boss-man's arm and just came right out with it, the whole deal (only I didn't say anything about Lucius Domitius being who he was, or how I'd come to be with him). While I was talking, I was expecting any moment for them to grab me by the scruff and sling me outside, or bar me up in a pigshed or something, but not a bit of it. You hear people talking about someone hanging on a bloke's every word; well, that's what the head man did while I was telling him the tale (only I told it pretty well straight). He sat there with his mouth open, staring at me like I was something wonderful, except for when he interrupted me to ask for details of some point or other – how many soldiers did Strymon kill on the mountain road in Sicily, what was it Alexander and Pony-tail cooked us for breakfast, excuse him but why did I keep talking about the ponderous hoe, is that some special sort of hoe they use in that part of Italy – which only went to show how closely he was following what I was saying. Well, naturally, once I realised he was interested, I spun it out a bit, put in bits of talking, made a performance of it generally. By this time, pretty well everybody in the building was crowded round where we were sitting. They'd finished their food, and crouched on the floor or craned over each other's shoulders, with their big silver-gilt winecups in their hands; and when I got to the part about the coffin, you could have heard a gnat fart. You'd have thought I was two dozen performing monkeys and a pantomime act, but all I did was tell the truth. If I'd known people liked it so much, I guess I'd have tried it years ago.

When I'd finished, there was this eerie long silence, with nobody hardly even breathing. Then the boss-man sort of shook himself, and said, 'Well, if that doesn't beat cock-fighting. And to think, you said just now that you're just an ordinary bloke, nothing special, not particularly good at anything.'

I frowned. 'Well, that's right,' I said. 'I am, and I'm not.'

The boss-man lifted his head. 'Oh, sure,' he said. 'I don't think. Why, if only a third of that lot's true, you're the biggest hero we've had in these parts since Ulysses himself.'

He'd lost me. 'I'm sorry,' I said, 'but I don't follow. What's heroic about what I just said? I'm a thief, and a pretty crummy one at that.'

Boss-man gawped at me for a moment, like he couldn't believe I was serious, then burst out laughing. 'Dear God, man,' he said, 'you're the very essence of hero. I mean, what makes a hero, if it's not resourcefulness, enduring endless desperate trials, leaping from fire to frying pan to fire like someone crossing a river on stepping stones? And if you're seriously asking us to believe that you managed all that without at least one god guarding you night and day, snatching you out of the snares of death and pitching you into something even more terrifying and demanding – well, we're simple folk here, but not that simple. No, it's plain as snot on your beard that you're the darling of the gods, and they're taking extra-special trouble with your thread, spinning it out long and thick. Just getting through the reef proves that. Didn't we tell you, nobody gets through the reef alive, not even if Neptune's sleeping with his sister?' He shook his head, and sighed. 'Sorry,' he said, 'but whether you like it or not, clearly you're a very special and important person indeed; a hero, there's no other word for it, and it's an honour and a privilege to have you here with us.'

Well, I thought, fuck me; but I couldn't let it pass, somehow, not with Lucius Domitius lying in the mud on the seabed. 'Yes, but it wasn't me,' I said. 'What I mean is, even if there really was anything special about all that stuff, I couldn't have done it on my own, I wouldn't have lasted an hour.'

The boss-man smiled. 'You're thinking about your friend,' he said. 'Well, that's understandable. He was obviously a fairly exceptional person too, no doubt about that. But when push comes to shove there's only one way to decide these matters, and it's really very simple. Which one of you made it, and which one of you didn't? Answer me that, and I'll tell you who's the hero of the story, and who's just the sidekick.'

He made it sound so straightforward. But of course he was wrong. Any fool could see the flaw in his argument, because the best of us, the only one out of the trio who was worth a day's feed, was the one who died first, my brother Callistus. Only, I realised, I hadn't mentioned him at all, so how was the boss-man to know? Still, I knew; and that was why I couldn't go along with what he said. I mean, suppose everybody's life was an adventure, a fairy tale, an epic poem. You tell me, how would you pick out who's supposed to be the hero? The way I'd told it, Lucius Domitius, emperor of the Romans, most hated man in history, was just some bloke I went around with. But I hadn't explained to boss-man why he was important, so once again, how was he supposed to know? That's one of the reasons Life sucks. Unless someone tells you, you don't know all this important behind-the-scenes stuff, and you can end up thinking the shepherd's daughter is the princess, through no fault of your own.

Even so, I thought I'd have one more stab at explaining. 'Maybe I told it badly,' I said. 'Because really, it was him, my friend, who . . .' I was stuck; what I wanted to say was, all the adventures were because of him, who he was, or who people thought he was. I'd sort of muffed round this when I was telling the story. I'd said we were the only ones who knew where Dido's treasure was, and I'd sort of given him the impression we'd got the lowdown from that old knight, the one who told Lucius Domitius. Maybe that's where he went wrong, and as I said just now, you can't blame him for it.

'I know what you're thinking,' boss-man said. 'It's because – well, I'm going to be blunt about it, because sooner or later you've got to face up to it. Your friend is dead. Naturally enough, but wrongly, you feel guilty about it – you're thinking, you should have been the one to die, and he should have survived. And you're laying this feeling over the way you're remembering the things you did together. But the facts speak for themselves. I'll say it again. He's at the bottom of the sea. You're here. That tells me all I need to know about who's who in this story.'

I was getting fed up with this conversation. 'Well, anyway,' I said, 'that's who I am, and how I got here, so now you know, and you can make up your mind what you want to do about me. I know this sounds pretty bad, but I'm not really bothered one way or the other. I'll join your gang if you want me to, or if you like you can tie a rock to my ankle and chuck me back in the sea. I'd rather you didn't do that,' I added, 'but I won't make a fuss, if that's what you decide.'

Once again, boss-man was peering at me like he thought I was kidding him around. 'But it's obvious what we're going to do now,' he said, 'surely. After all, we've got ships, we know the way in and out of the reef, and you're the only living soul on earth who knows where to find this island where the treasure's buried. As far as I can see, the only thing left to sort out is how we divide it up once we've recovered it.'

The treasure, I thought; that old thing. 'I'm really sorry,' I told him, 'but I couldn't find that island again if my life depended on it. I don't know spit about sailing and navigation and stuff, and I spent the time while we were getting there from Africa hanging over the rail puking. And if you think I'm just saying that because I want all the treasure for myself, and I'm planning on sneaking back there on my own to get it, then it strikes me you weren't listening when I told you what happened to Amyntas and his family. The treasure's completely useless to one bloke on his own, and – no offence – the only man I'd have trusted enough to help me go and get it was Ahenobarbus' – I'd nearly said Lucius Domitius; remembered just in time that I'd been calling him by his family name – 'and he knew about it anyhow, and he's dead. I'm sorry,' I repeated, 'but that's how it is.'

Dead silence. Boss-man was looking at me like I'd just risen naked from the sea foam with a sprig of holly stuffed up my nose. 'Just a moment,' he said. 'You're saying that you know about a vast fortune in gold and jewels, nobody else in the whole world knows where it is, and you can't be bothered to go back and look for it?'

I nodded. 'Yes,' I said.

That threw him. 'Really,' he said. 'That's – well, please don't take this the wrong way, but I'm having trouble believing it. I mean, you've actually seen all this stuff—'

'*Seen* it.' I grinned. 'I've helped shift it, twice. Three times, if you count loading it off the beach.'

'Fine,' boss-man said, a bit nettled at being interrupted. 'And it's all there, for the taking; it's just a matter of finding this little island and showing up with enough ships and men to cart it away. Please,' he said, rather more urgently, 'think what you're saying.'

'Oh, I know it sounds crazy,' I told him. 'But I think – in fact, I know, it's got a jinx on it. Everybody who's had anything to do with it is dead – the Roman knight, the gangsters in the city who wanted to know where it was hidden, Amyntas and his brother, the grain-freighter crew, my friend; all of them, dead, except for me. Wouldn't you call that a jinx?'

He lifted his head. 'I'd call that inheritance,' he said. 'You know, what happens to property when everyone else with a claim to it has snuffed it. Look,' he went on before I could say anything, 'I know it's hard to expect you to trust us. We've only just met, and besides,' he added gravely, 'we're pirates. But be practical. Where are you going to get ships and men from? You said it yourself, a man on his own'll never be able to get it home. Tell you what, we'll split it with you, straight down the middle, half for you and half for us.'

I lifted my head. 'No fear,' I said. 'No disrespect, but that'd be like sealing my own death warrant. Look, here's the deal. I've told you absolutely everything I know about where that island is. If you want to go sailing around looking for it, you bloody well carry on, and good luck to you. But don't ask me to come along.' He narrowed his eyes at me, as though he was trying to figure out whether I was crazy, lying, or both. 'First,' I told him, 'I haven't got the faintest idea about navigation, and even if I had, I wasn't looking where we were going. Second, I'm too scared. I've seen what that stuff'll do to people. I'm quite happy to have got out of its way with my life,' I concluded, fingering my rag-wrapped belt under the table. 'If this experience has taught me anything, it's that all the good things in the world won't help you if you're dead. Now, if you want me to stay here, have you got a job scrubbing floors or mucking out horses? I might be able to manage that, so long as you aren't particularly fussy. But if you want to help me, put me on the next ship you send out, and dump me on the first inhabited bit of dry land you come to. I swear by the River and any twenty gods you'd like to name that I won't tell anybody about this place. And so what if I can't be trusted to keep my word, I'd never be able to find it again or tell anybody where it is, and nobody'd believe a low-life like me if I told them fire was hot. In return, I solemnly bequeath you all my share and interest' – good, stuff, that; I remembered it out of an old legal document, from my very brief career as a forger – 'in Dido's treasure, free and clear of all encumbrances, in front of the witnesses here present. Can't say fairer than that, can I?'

Long, long silence. Then the boss-man stood up. 'Deal,' he said; then he spat in his palm and grabbed my hand with a grip that'd have cracked walnuts. 'God forgive me for taking advantage of a lunatic, and God forgive you for giving away your birthright, like the man who swapped Cyrene for a bowl of bean soup. Now, you go with Niceratus here, he'll find you a blanket and a place to sleep, and in the morning we'll go over everything you remember about this island, while we're getting a ship ready.' He paused, like he'd just remembered something. 'Any place in particular you want to go?' he asked. 'You name it: Britain, India, the Clashing Rocks, Thule? Least we can do, in the circumstances.'

It hit me like a thunderbolt. Anywhere I wanted to go; my own floating sedan chair, door to door. It was the most wonderful offer, and I hadn't got a clue. After all, where the hell would someone like me want to go? Wherever I end up, any place on earth, when I get there I'd still be me, so where in the gods' names is the point?

'Athens,' I said. 'I think I'd like to go home, please.'

SEVENTEEN

So there I was—

Actually, I was fast asleep when we got there. I hadn't been able to sleep the previous night, because we'd anchored off Salamis when it got too dark to sail, and I could feel home in my bones like the itch you're supposed to be able to feel in an amputated toe. Finally I dropped off just before dawn, and was still sleeping like a kiddie when the ship made Eleusis Bay, which was where I'd asked them to drop me off – not Piraeus, because I didn't want to go to the city, I wanted to go *home*; to Phyle, and our crummy little village, with the dogs fast asleep in the thick road dust at midday. Well, the nearest spot on the coast to Phyle where you can put in a ship is Eleusis; four hours' walk and you're there.

Whether it was a practical joke or they just couldn't bear the thought of disturbing me, they carried me off the ship, still snoring blithely, and propped me up against the trunk of a small fig tree, so I wouldn't burn in the sun. Next to me they put a new pair of boots, a purse with thirty denarii in it, a skin of good wine mixed two to one, and a little wicker basket of bread, cheese and olives, and then they must've got back on their ship and sailed away, back to Scheria or off to look for the gold or whatever. I never saw or heard of them again, never mentioned them to anybody. It's like they were a dream, except most dreams don't carry you halfway across the world for free, and give you money while you're asleep.

So I opened my eyes, and instead of seeing the mast and sailors fooling about with ropes and buckets, and the sea bobbing up and down in the background, I saw the incredibly familiar shape of the north-east Attic mountains, looming up in the distance on the far side of the plain, with the Cephisus sparkling in the sun in the foreground. I was stunned. It was all still there, exactly how I remembered it. They hadn't dug up Mount Parnes while I'd been gone, or built a new city on the plain, or flooded the whole thing to make an artificial lake for rearing table swans.

Well, I said to myself as I stood up and yawned (pins and needles in both feet; nothing's ever bloody perfect), here I am, then; what in God's name possessed me to want to come back here? Offhand, I couldn't think of a reason; seemed like a good idea at the time, or something of the sort.

Then I remembered something fairly important, and felt my waist. It was still there: a bloody fortune in gold and jewels, wrapped up in bits of old rag, my salvation, my future, all my troubles over. Just to make absolutely sure, I untwisted the rag just a wee bit and peeked down. There it was, gold, glinting between the coils of cloth like a pretty girl winking. *Yes!* I thought. Just for once, I've walked away from the game and taken something with me. True, I'd managed to lose everything else, my brother, my best friend who'd been just like a brother, twenty-four years of my life, and the few bits of me that'd been decent and good; but on the other hand, I had a fucking great big gold belt with gemstones the size of camels' balls. It was a better deal than I'd ever managed to strike before. Was I complaining? Well, what do you think?

I shuffled my feet a bit till they stopped hurting, and said to myself, Well, it's no good hanging around here, time I was on my way. I felt like I had an appointment up there on the hill, and if I didn't get a move on I was going to be late, and the opportunity would slither by. So I picked up my feet, and off I went.

It's not in my nature to complain, as you know, but those Attic hills are *steep*. Trust my shit-for-brains ancestors to settle in Phyle, right up in the mountains. If my old mother was to be believed, we'd once been rich noblemen, with estates all over Attica, but time and inheritance and bad luck and lawsuits had all taken their toll, until all we had left was the one poxy little bit of dirt; and we couldn't have clung on to the land in the Mesogaia or the Paralia, or the nice fat, flat stuff in Acharnae. Oh no, it had to be bloody Phyle, the roof of the world.

But I had a new pair of boots, I was rested after my luxury boat ride, well fed, Roman money in my purse. There are worse things than walking uphill hour after hour after hour on a searingly hot day. And I was going home.

If you remember (no reason why you should) Callistus and I left home when Grandad died. My cousin Therion got the farm, my cousin Plutus got the inn, and we were slung out with our inheritance, which you could fit in a scent bottle without taking the scent out. I'd never exactly got along with Therion and Plutus, the way rats don't get on with ferrets; the chances of them running out to greet me and killing the best goat for a celebration dinner were as thin as a day-labourer's dog. But so what? The point about an inn is, they're obliged to feed and shelter you so long as you've got the money to pay, and I'd be lying if told you I wasn't looking forward to seeing the expression on Plutus' ugly face when I plonked down a silver denarius on the table and said, Sorry, I haven't got anything smaller. Petty, I know, but I'm a petty sort of guy. What I was going to do after that – hadn't though that far, to be honest. Sooner or later, I was going to have to take my courage in both hands (assuming I could find it again after so long) and go into the city, find a goldsmith who didn't ask irrelevant questions and turn my wonderful belt into clinking money. Once I'd done that, I supposed I'd take my time, look around for some land to buy, build a house, hire or buy some workers, settle down, make a start on my life (twenty-four years late, but better late than never); and then I'd really have come home, I'd finally be free and clear, and all my troubles would at last be over.

I trudged up the last mile of the road thinking, well, one thing for sure, I'm not going to buy any land that's up a fucking hill, and while my mind was elsewhere, suddenly I arrived. There it was, my home village. It'd sort of snuck up on me, and pounced.

Years ago, Lucius Domitius and me, we were stranded in some ghastly garrison town out in Asia, and because there was absolutely nothing else to do, we wandered along to the old Greek theatre to watch a bunch of local actors putting on a play. It was one of the classics – that means the writer's been dead for centuries, so he doesn't want paying – *The Bad-tempered Man*, by Menander. It was billed as a comedy, though I've seen funnier hunger riots. The point is, I'd just snuggled myself down on a hired cushion and was peeling an apple when this bloke came on in a mask and said the first line of the play, which happens to be:

Imagine this place is Phyle, in Attica—

I remember, I jumped so much I cut my thumb with the paring knife. Bloody nerve, I said to myself If I'm going to pay three copper pennies to imagine I'm some place, it sure as hell wouldn't be Phyle. It's not a lovely place. In fact, it's a dump. Now it's perfectly true to say, I grew up there, of all people I should have known it was a dump, so what was I cribbing about? But somehow, after everything I'd been through, all my horrible adventures, crowned by my amazing run of inexplicable, amazing good luck, I'd been expecting it to be different; let's face it, better. Not sure how better; burned to the ground and grown over with bindweed would've done. But it was just how it'd been when I left it, and for some reason I felt that wasn't good enough, as if I'd come home after a hard day and the dirty dishes from breakfast had still been on the table. Still, I was here, the place I'd chosen out of the whole world. I walked down the street, and there it was, inevitably, exactly the same. Our inn. One long stone building, rounded at the far end, flat roof, crumbling plaster; stables at right angles to the square end, across a scruffy-looking yard. It'd been there since Theseus was a kid, and nobody'd got around to giving it a name. There was the gate, probably the same bit of mouldy old string holding it on to the post as when I'd left; there was the mounting block, half crumbled away, with weeds growing up through the cracks. There was the well, and the staked-off rectangle of gravel we tried to grow beans in, and right next to the back door, the midden – maybe a tad taller and nastier-smelling than it'd been in my day, but you can't really call that progress. And there—

I blinked. It couldn't be. Dogs live – what, fifteen years, if they're really lucky? I never heard of a dog living to be twenty-four. But just before I left home, the old three-legged bitch had had puppies, and one of them, scrawny little thing with four black socks and one ear bigger than the other, had this disgusting habit of sprawling all over the side of the shitheap during the day, then treading muck all through the house at night. Speedy, we called him, because if you tried to catch him to give him a dip in the rain butt, he'd be off like a shot from a catapult. And there on the side of the midden was this incredibly old, blind, decrepit excuse for a dog, with four black socks and one ear bigger than the other.

'Speedy?' I said.

He lifted his head, and barked feebly. For some unfathomable reason, I was in floods of tears. I sort of stumbled across the yard, and reached out my hand to pat his head. He bit me.

Yes, I thought. I'm home.

Nothing for it but to knock at the door, so that's what I did. No reply; the dog growled uneasily, but no voices or footsteps. So I knocked again, louder; I didn't call out, just in case Plutus recognised my voice. I wanted to give him a surprise.

Well, I was standing there thinking it had all gone wrong, nobody was at home, when I heard rushing footsteps behind me, and there was this short round man with a shiny bald head. Not Plutus, not even after twenty-four years. 'All right,' he puffed, 'just a moment, hold your water, I'll be there in a tick. Just the one night, is it?'

I looked at him. 'Excuse me,' I said, 'but I'm looking for someone.'

'Oh.' The expression on his face changed, as he reclassified me under 'time-waster'. 'Who'd that be, then?'

'My cousin Plutus,' I replied. 'He owns this place.'

The fat man lifted his head. 'Not any more,' he said. 'Sorry to have to tell you, he died.'

'Oh.' That came as a bigger blow than I'd anticipated. God knows why, since I'd always hated Plutus, possibly even more than I hated Therion. I guess I thought he was cheating, skipping out on me like that and not being there to see my triumphant local-boy-makes-good homecoming.

Porkchop nodded. 'Must've been, what, ten years since. Fever, there was quite an epidemic. Of course, keeping the inn, he was one of the first to catch it. Sorry. I guess you were close.'

I didn't answer that. 'How long have you been here?' I asked.

'Me?' He looked surprised that I was interested in him. 'Oh, it must be, what, six or seven years now. His brother inherited, you see—'

'Therion.' I read the look in his eyes. 'He's dead too, isn't he?'

'Afraid so. Heart, they reckoned.'

That didn't sound right, or it was news to me that Therion had one. 'I see,' I said.

'Well,' the fat man went on, 'after he died, which was, I don't know, nine years back; after he passed over, of course, it went to his aunt.' He stopped, looking awkward. 'Would that be your mother? Sosistrata?'

'That's her,' I said. 'Her too?'

'What? Oh, no, she's still alive.' Oh, I thought. 'Anyhow, she got the farm and the inn, but she couldn't make anything of either of 'em, so she sold up, and I bought this place, with my retirement from the army—' He stopped, as it occurred to him that, if I was Mum's son, I should have inherited, not her, which meant his purchase might be invalid. Suddenly he didn't like me any more. Not one bit.

'Go on,' I said.

'That's all there is to it, really. Mate of mine had the farm, if you can call it that. I had this place.'

'You aren't from round here,' I said.

'Too right. We're from the city. Did twenty-four years in the army, took the cash instead of land when we came out – wanted to come back to Athens, see, and the land they offered us was some godforsaken swamp on the German border.'

'Twenty years,' I said. 'It's a long time.' Then an idea hit me, and I added, 'Isn't it?'

He looked at me again. 'Right,' he said. 'So you're ex-service too, are you?'

I nodded. 'Pretorians,' I added. I don't know what possessed me to say that, because they only take the biggest, strongest, meanest blokes for the imperial guard; but then, it was practically the truth, since hadn't I just spent ten years guarding the emperor of the Romans?

'Get on,' he said. 'You too?' Oh fuck, I thought. 'I was in the Guards eight years.'

'Small world,' I said. 'I was in for four. Who were you with before that?'

'Tenth.'

'Ah, right. I was with the Twenty-First. Started as quartermaster's clerk, worked my way up to QMS. You?'

'Mules,' he replied. 'Well, if that doesn't beat bull-wrestling. Was old Lasher still CSM when you were with the squad?'

I lifted my head. 'CSM in my time was a bloke called Barbillus. Spaniard, filthy temper.'

'Barbillus.' He scratched his nose. 'You know, that rings a bell. I'm sure I was billeted with a Spaniard called Barbillus. In fact, I'm positive.'

'There's a coincidence,' I said; and it was, since I'd just made Barbillus up. 'Well, who'd have thought it?'

He didn't hate me quite so much now, though he was still a bit wary of me. 'Odd how things turn out,' he said. 'So,' he went on, 'how long've you been out?'

'Few months,' I replied. 'I dossed about for a while, but I'm like you, I guess, I always figured on coming home.'

'Well, it beats getting shunted off to Germany,' he said. 'So you're back looking for a place, then? Retirement burning a hole in your purse?'

I nodded. 'Most of it, anyways,' I told him. 'I'll be honest, I've pissed some of it up against the wall, who doesn't? But I've got a tidy bit left, so that's all right.'

He hesitated; then I suppose he decided that since we were old comrades in arms, followed the dear old eagles together and all that shit, he could probably trust me with the truth. He said: 'Strictly speaking, I suppose, you might have a claim on this place. In law, I mean. Like, if you're the old – if you're Sosistrata's son, by rights this place should've come to you . . .'

I tried to make it look like the idea had only just hit me. 'Good God, no,' I said. 'Well, maybe in law,' I went on, 'but who gives a shit for all that lawyers' stuff? No, if you paid my mother good money for this place, then as far as I'm concerned it's yours; and if you want to go along to the prefect's office, I'll swear to that, no worries.'

Poor fool looked at me like they'd cut him down off a cross and said, Sorry, just kidding. 'Oh, we don't want to go bothering with any of that crap, not a couple of old boys like us. So.' He breathed out, a bit ragged. 'You're looking for a place to buy, then?'

I nodded. 'Well, first things first. Before that, I want a bed for the night and a bite to eat, not to mention a jug or two of half-and-half.'

'Oh, I think we can manage that,' he said, just a shade too cheerfully. 'On the house, naturally,' he added, and I sort of got the impression that he didn't say those words all that often; they seemed to hurt his throat coming out, like he was puking up thistles.

'That's very kind of you,' I said.

'Least I can do, for an old boy,' he replied, grinning lopsidedly.

So we went inside; and if anything had changed, I couldn't see what (except that Plutus was dead, and so was Therion; and Callistus too, of course, which left me. And mother too, I reminded myself). My old army buddy, whose name turned out to be Apollodorus, parked me at a table, then went stomping and yelling for food and wine. I'll say this for him, he turned on all the taps for me. Bacon and bean stew with leeks and fresh bread, good domestic wine half-and-half, with honey, oatmeal and grated cheese; he even turfed his old dad out of the second-back loft room so I could sleep there (strange coincidence, since that had been mine and Callistus' when we were kids, and the big ugly damp patch on the wall was exactly like it'd been as far back as I could remember). At any rate, when the sun woke me up the next morning, I was feeling extraordinarily bright and breezy and cheerful. So, first order of business for the day was to change all that. I went down into the yard and found Apollodorus on his way to the stables with a big jar of horses' barley.

'I think I'd better go and see my mother,' I said. 'Where can I find her?'

Speedy the dog, curled up on the dungheap as usual, put his ears back and snarled at me. I could see his point. Still, if the gods had meant us to be happy, they wouldn't have given us family.

'Right,' Apollodorus said. 'Turn left out of here, down the street about two hundred yards till you come to an old house with a double door—'

I nodded. 'You mean Telecleides' place?'

'Of course, I forgot, you were raised here. Yes, that's the one; only, the old boy who used to live there—'

He didn't have to say any more. Pity. I'd liked Telecleides. 'Joined the majority?' I said.

'About ten years ago, so I was told. Your mother's got it now; at least, it belongs to the Roman bailiff, but he lets her live there.'

I frowned. If she'd sold the inn and the farm, how come she was living on grace and favour? But I could ask her that; no need to discuss family stuff with an outsider. 'Thanks,' I said. 'I think I'll wander down there now. After that, I've got to walk down to the city—'

'No you don't,' Apollodorus said. 'You take my mare, she needs the exercise anyhow.'

'Thanks,' I said, a bit taken aback. 'That's very generous of you.'

He shrugged. 'Why walk when you can ride? Anyway, if you want something to eat or a drink when you get back, give me a shout, don't worry if it's late. Well, obviously. I mean, I don't suppose I could tell you anything about running an inn.'

I thanked him. He said not to mention it. If we'd been any friendlier, we'd have had to get married, if only for the sake of the children.

Well, you can't put off horrible jobs for ever, so I strolled down to road to Telecleides' old house to see my old mum.

Now if you've been paying close attention, you may have got it into your head that I didn't like my mother terribly much. You'd be right, too. Truth is, we'd never got on, not since I can remember. I'd never quite been sure why she didn't seem to like me very much. Now, that'd have been understandable if it was just me. But it wasn't. She never seemed to like Callistus much, either, and how anybody could not like him, I could never figure out. He was the original model child – good, obedient, clever, good-looking, you name it – but she was always yelling it him, same as at me, only in his case he never did anything to deserve it. Nothing either of us did was ever right, and a lot of the time she'd just look at us like we gave her a pain. Well, sixteen years of that sort of thing, and are you surprised I wasn't looking forward to seeing her again? Also, she always did like a drink or twelve, and working in an inn, there was always spare booze around, though generally not for long when she was about. One of my earliest memories is Mum in the common room, going round gathering up the winecups and swilling down the last knockings and the dregs before stacking them in the tub. I'd often wondered how she got that way, and over the years I'd explored every possible explanation, from a tragic experience when she was a girl down to liking the way the stuff tastes. Of course, I never asked her, never said anything, in fact, simply did my best to keep out of her way, drunk or sober. Well, that's as may be. They say there are Furies whose job it is to punish people who don't do right by their mothers, and if it's true, I guess that'd explain a lot about the way my life's been. But even a Fury would have to be pretty hard-hearted, or worried about losing her job, to punish me for my bad attitude. Still, I suppose that's the way Furies are, meaner than a bailiff's dog and as keen on rules as a tax collector.

So I stepped up to the door and knocked. No answer. Could be she was out, could be she was pissed out of her head and sleeping it off face down on the floor like when we were kids, or maybe she'd died last week, and nobody'd noticed. I knocked again, and secretly I was hoping the door would stay shut. If I could say I'd tried, it'd keep the Furies off my back, and I wouldn't have to see her.

So there I was, stood out in the road like a kid serenading his girl, when someone walked past me, stopped dead, turned round and stared at me; an old boy under a huge wide-brimmed leather hat that made him look like a giant field mushroom.

'Galen?' he said. 'Is that you?'

I'm good at voices. 'Hello, Mnesicrates,' I replied.

'Galen?' I'd known him all my life, on and off; not close, he wasn't family or anything.

Once when I was about thirteen he'd caught me stealing figs off his tree and chased me halfway to Thebes before he put his foot down a pothole and twisted his ankle. 'Well, bugger me,' he said. 'Didn't think we'd ever see you again.'

He came back down the road towards me. When I saw his face under that daft hat, I was shocked. He'd turned old since I last saw him, his eyes had sunk back into his head, his cheeks had caved in and his skin seemed to have grown too big for his face. 'Well, here I am,' I said stupidly. 'So, how've you been keeping?'

He stared at me. 'What? Oh, not so bad. Leastways, my wife died, about ten years ago, my son Polycharmus – you remember him, you had a real nasty fight with him once, over some girl—'

I grinned. 'If you can call it a fight,' I said. 'More like a massacre, if you ask me. Still, she'd have been wasted on me.'

He shrugged. 'Well, anyhow,' he said, 'he died about this time, year before last. My other boy, Polyclitus, he passed on beginning of this year – fell out a tree, of all the damned things, bust his neck.'

'I'm sorry to hear that,' I said.

'Yeah, well. Lost most of my flock, four years ago come pruning season; scab, they reckoned it was, though I ain't so sure. Then I had a landslip on my terraces, lost my best two-acre of vines. Well went bad on me eighteen months back; I dug a new one but it's barely a trickle, dries up altogether in the hot season. Long barn burned down, year before last, and that was all my seedcorn gone into the bargain, so I had to borrow; don't suppose I'll pay that debt back before I die. Then my eldest grandson – 'Charmus' boy – he ran off to join the legion, so it's just me and Eutychides, though he's no more than a kid still, and he lost an eye in the spring, infected, had to get a barber up from the city to cut it out. How about you?'

'Me? Oh, can't grumble,' I said. 'Tell me, who's got our place now? The farm, I mean.'

He scowled. 'Some damned soldier,' he said. 'But he doesn't work it hardly, just stays in the house and drinks himself into a state, then comes out roaring and bashing on trees with a sword. Your grandad, it'd break his heart to see it, rest his soul.'

'Ah,' I said. 'So you reckon he might sell, then?'

Mnesicrates looked blank. 'Might do,' he said, as though the idea of buying and selling land had come as a bit of a shock. 'Can't say as I've talked to him much, him being drunk all the time. Don't reckon he's took to farming. I guess you could ask him, anyway.'

'Thanks,' I said, 'I might just do that. Well, I won't keep you,' I added hopefully.

'Oh, I ain't in any hurry,' he replied. 'Just been to look at my beans, but don't reckon they're going to come to anything. Not worth the sweat fetching them in, hardly. Soil took sick a while back, can't grow a damn thing in that parcel any more. Reckon I'll just plough 'em under and have done with it. Well, don't know if you're planning on sticking around, but welcome back. Didn't I hear you and your brother went off and joined the legion or something?'

'That's right,' I said. 'Just got my demob, and now I'm home.'

He scratched his ear thoughtfully. 'Home's best, that's what they say,' he said. 'See you around, in that case.'

I wasn't sure if that was a greeting or a threat, but I made nice and said, 'See you around, take care.' He shrugged and walked away, taking his personal black cloud with him. At least I knew now what people in the neighbourhood thought had become of me. As far as Phyle was concerned, I'd gone for a soldier. That suited me just fine.

All the time I'd been talking to old Miseryguts, there hadn't been any sign of life inside the house, and I was just about to walk on when I saw someone else coming down the road towards me. This time it was a little tiny old woman, bent almost double over a thin walking stick. It didn't occur to me until she brushed past me and went into the house that it could possibly be my mother. Surely not. Last time I'd seen her, she'd been almost the same height as me, a big woman with a round boozer's face, plump stuffed-looking arms like giant sausages. Besides, she'd glanced up at me as she went by. Surely she'd have recognised her own son? After all, I hadn't changed a bit (more's the pity). Couldn't have been. The old soldier back at the inn must've got his reins tangled.

But it was no good trying to kid myself. I knew, in spite of everything, it was her all right. I sighed, gritted my teeth, and banged on the door.

Seeing her face close up, I knew, there wasn't any doubt in the matter. It was as if someone had put her out to dry, along with the figs and the raisins, and then forgotten to fetch her in again. Her cheeks had slipped down under her chin, and her nose stuck out like a rock when the sea goes out; apart from that, she was pretty much the same. 'What do you want?' she said, like she'd just bitten an apple and found me in it.

Well, I couldn't think of a single thing to say, so I said, 'Hello.'

She looked at me, and I knew she'd recognised me. 'I don't know you,' she said, 'get lost.'

That was a bit hard. 'It's me,' I said. 'Galen. Your son.'

She always had that habit of staring just to your left when you caught her out in a lie. 'What're you doing here?' she said. 'I had word you were dead.'

'No,' I said, 'still alive, more or less. Can I come in?'

She clicked her teeth; she still had practically the whole set, the only gap being an old one, from before I was born, where someone had knocked out one of the lower fronts. 'Yes, all right,' she said. And you know what? I was scared.

Well, you're saying, so what's unusual about that? Fair point. I'm a born coward, I'll happily admit that; no point in denying the screamingly obvious. I've been scared all my life – scared of being caught, mostly, scared of what they'll do to me after they've caught me, scared of going anywhere, scared of staying where I am, scared of death, illness, hunger, cold, heat, old age, spiders, snakes, big dogs, small dogs, middling-sized dogs, cows, thunder, birds of ill omen, the gods, justice, fate, boats, bridges, heights, confined spaces, open spaces, chickens, soldiers, the numbers three, four, seven and twelve, left-handed women, tall men, weapons, bats, chariots, clifftops, wells, cripples, fire, snow, the dark, change, any food that's bright red or moves, strangers, pigs, you name it, I'm scared of it. Wouldn't have it any other way, because I've always reckoned that the dumbest last words a man can ever say are, I thought it was safe. I think the gods gave us fear to protect us from all the dangerous things there are in the world, and I'm truly thankful, believe me. But who'd have thought a grown man would ever be scared of his own mother?

Still. They say that true courage is facing up to something that frightens the shit out of you, though I've always thought that was a pretty fair working definition of stupidity. Anyway, I followed her into the house.

First thing that hit me was the smell. The place stank of shit, with accents of stale pee, rotting food and vomit. It was as dark as a bag, and the floor crunched when you walked on it. When I got used to the dark, I could see it was a shambles in there. Funny, because when we were kids, she'd always been on at us about tidying up. There were pigs' bones and shrivelled apple cores all over the deck, jars stacked against the wall, cups with furry green mould growing in them, flies everywhere. She sat down on a little wooden stool. I stayed standing up, for fear of catching something.

'Well,' she said, 'you're back, then.'

I nodded. 'Yes,' I said.

She tutted. 'Where's Callistus? He with you?'

'He's dead.'

Hadn't meant to tell her like that, of course. Of all the ignorant things to say to a mother. But she shrugged her thin shoulders a little and said, 'Well, then.' What was I supposed to make of that?

'He's been dead for ten years,' I went on. 'In Italy,' I added, like that somehow made it better. Then I remembered something I'd heard once. 'He died well,' I said. It sounded really, really stupid after I'd said it.

She thought so too. 'What's that supposed to mean?' she said.

'He died saving someone's life,' I told her.

She tutted again, like somebody had told her we'd been stealing apples. 'Yours?'

I lifted my head. 'His friend,' I said.

She sighed. 'Stupid bloody fool. You weren't there, then.'

'Actually, I was,' I said. 'I tried to stop him—'

'Didn't try very hard, I don't suppose.' She shook her head, to show that the subject was closed. 'You just passing through?'

'No,' I said. 'At least, I was planning—'

'You can't stay here,' she interrupted. 'I don't want you stopping here, I haven't got the room.' Well, that was no lie. 'It's all right,' I said, 'I'm staying at the inn. You know, our old place.'

She looked up at me sharply. 'Got any money?' she said quickly.

'Yes,' I said. 'I've got plenty of that.'

She looked at me. It was the sort of look a polecat would give a rabbit. 'You done all right for yourself, then?'

I nodded. 'I had some good luck,' I said, and left it at that. No point telling her about Amyntas just happening to hire my friends on the grain freighter, or the floating coffin. I could tell she wouldn't be interested.

'You could do me a favour,' she said, assessing me like she was buying livestock. 'You always were a good boy, kind to your poor old mother.'

'Sure,' I said.

'You could go down the inn,' she said, 'and bring me up a jar of wine. Needn't be anything fancy, just the plain stuff.'

'Of course,' I said, no expression. 'And how about something to eat? Are you all right for flour?'

'Don't fuss me about that,' she said irritably. 'Just get me a jar. Go on, you can do a little thing for me, after all I done for you.'

For some reason I said, 'Such as what?' She didn't like that at all, she gave me a look you could have picked out whelks with, and sort of arched her neck, like a cat spitting. But what she said was, 'Don't be mean, darling. A little jar, that's not so much to ask for your old mum, is it? Only, I been working, up at my veggie plot' – her hands and the knees of her skirt told a different tale, unless there wasn't any soil in her garden – 'and it's given me such a thirst, on a hot day. Won't take you a moment just to run up to the inn, fetch down a little jar.'

So I left the house and walked back down the road, shaking like it was perishing cold; and most of all, I wished I never had to go back in there again, with that terrible old woman. But I found the landlord, mending the sole of his boot outside in the yard with a strip of parchment and a little pot of newly boiled glue, and I bought a two-gallon jar and hoisted it on my shoulder. He didn't ask what I wanted it for, and I didn't tell him. As I trudged back up the street, I felt like that giant in the fairy tale who carried the sky on his neck for the gods, as a punishment for something or other.

'That you, Galen darling?' she sang out as I nudged the door open with my foot, like I was a kid again, back from fetching the goats in off the hill. 'You're a good boy,' she went on, 'didn't I always say you were? You bring that here, and I'll mix us both a nice drink.'

'Not for me,' I said, thinking of all the green stuff in the cups. She didn't press the point.

After a while (she drank off the first cup neat, didn't touch the sides; the next one she mixed half and half, with water from a little coiled jug I remembered from the old days), she seemed to loosen up, like a tired man in a hot bath. 'It's good to see you again, my little darling,' she said, though she was looking at the jar. 'I been ever so worried, not knowing what'd become of you. But you never came to see me, you never sent word how you were fixed, might as well have been dead for all I knew. And things haven't been easy. I had to sell the inn, that's been in our family for gener-ations, and the farm, it'd have broken poor Grandpa's heart. But what was I supposed to do, on my own like that, not knowing if I'd ever see my darling boy ever again?'

If that was a roundabout way of saying she was sorry for pissing my inheritance up against the wall, I didn't think a whole lot of it. Still, that's mothers for you, always making it sound like it's your fault, but of course they forgive you. She went on and on like that for God knows how long, and never a mention of Callistus, or a question about him; it was as though I'd been an only child. I told her, when I could get a word in edgeways, that I'd been in the army – a cook, I told her, just in case she was listening, because even in her state she'd never believe I'd been a fighting man, and now I'd got my demob and my retirement, and I was back looking to settle down and farm. 'That's nice, dear,' she said, mixing some more half-and-half, though it was more three-quarters-quarter, as if it was a dry season and water was scarce. 'Always knew you'd do well for yourself in the world, you always were a good boy. It'll be nice to live up at the farm again. I miss the old place. I was so sad, letting it go.'

Fuck, I thought; did I say anything about having her up there to live with me? But I didn't say anything, of course. And maybe, if she came to live with me, we could get her straightened out a bit, or at least it'd be cheaper, when I had my own vines. I thought about that, and doubled the amount of ground I'd planned to put down to vineyards.

Halfway down the jar she fell asleep, and I tiptoed out and left her. Back at the inn, I found my pal the landlord again, still mending his rotten old boot, and asked him to send up another jar next time his boy went up the village. Then I set out for the city to sell my beautiful gold belt.

Nice thing about going from Phyle into town is it's downhill. I was a bit preoccupied along the way and didn't really pay any mind to looking about me; I'd done the coming-home bit to death, I reckoned, and I had the rotten bloody uphill to look forward to on the way back (one look made me change my mind about the innkeeper's mare: wonderful set of bones it had, and you could see the lot of them through its skin). Athens is a small place compared to some of the cities I've seen, but there's plenty of money about, what with all the rich Romans coming here for their bit of culture, which they gobble down like medicine, fast and with their eyes shut. That's good if you're after an upmarket goldsmith who's looking to buy. I had my pick, chose one up by the Tower of the Winds who looked a bit left-handed and shifty, rather like me. I think he nearly pissed down his leg when he saw the belt; didn't ask where I'd got it from, just how much I wanted for it. I grinned, and said it was a legacy from my old aunt, I hadn't got a clue how much it was worth, but I was sure he'd give me a fair price for it. We spent a little while play-acting – me pretending to walk out the shop, him pretending to let me go, all that tedious old game. In the end, I left him with the belt and toddled away with about as third as much again as I'd been expecting, knowing I'd been screwed rotten. Didn't care; after all, it wasn't as if it was mine to sell, not really. It did cross my mind that if one poxy little belt was worth more money than my family's seen since Alexander's time, maybe I should've taken the jolly pirates of Scheria up on their kind offer. But I'm not as stupid as that. They were nice people, some of the nicest I've ever met, genuinely so. But if I'd gone into partnership with them like they wanted me to, right now I'd be a few bits of bone three foot down in the sea-bottom sludge, and you'd never have heard of me or known I'd ever been born.

Athens is a quiet place, except at night when the drunks are about, but even so, it doesn't do to wander about the streets buckling at the knees under the weight of your coined money. I wasn't quite sure what to do at first, but then I thought, Well, why not? And I couldn't think of a good answer. So I headed for the Market Square, where the bankers have their tables. Athens is a great place for banks, because of all those Roman visitors needing money from home to buy up old statues and the like. I never thought I'd see the day when I'd be leaning up against the table of Gnaeus Laberius and partners, offices in Rome, Athens, Lyons, Alexandria. Certainly never thought I'd see the day when the senior manager, having seen the big fat bag of coins sat on his table, suddenly noticed I was having to stand up on a hot day, and sent his clerk scurrying for a stool for me to sit on. He gave me a drink too, several drinks – Falernian, all the way from Italy – and said it was a pleasure doing business with me. Another first, goes without saying. Mind you, it's easy to be a pleasure to do business with when you're rich.

Which I was, apparently; and as I walked home, I was asking myself, Well, how in God's name did that happen? I hadn't really noticed at the time – the belt was there, I stole it, it was sheer instinct, like scratching an itch. From that moment on, though, it appears I stopped being low-life, scum of the earth, and suddenly transformed into a splendid, godlike person who it was a pleasure to have dealings with, someone who gets given Falernian and has stools fetched for him, just for doing a spot of business. I hadn't felt terribly splendid or godlike when I was bobbing about in the sea, mind you, or when I was alone and naked on the beach. But then I suddenly understood, and it all made sense to me – the kind and generous Scherians, their lavish hospitality, everything going right for once, even the gods sending the floating coffin to see me safe to shore. All that good fortune had started only after I'd pinched the belt; and once I'd done that, of course, I was rich. It was clear as mountain water after I'd figured that out. Once I'd become rich, it goes without saying everything would be different. Of course the gods would take care of me and send floating coffins for me and arrange for me to be taken straight home on a private yacht. Only goes to show how thick I am that I hadn't figured that out at the time.

Well, I took on a dozen gold pieces and some silver, just for walking-around money, and left the rest of it safe in the hands of Gnaeus Laberius and partners. First thing I did after that was to stroll down to the horsefair and buy a nice little mare, complete with harness, so I wouldn't have to walk home up that bastard hill. Hardly seemed to take any time getting back to Phyle with my four-footed pal doing all the work. I parked her in the stable at the inn for the grooms to take care of, and lit out for the farm. I thought, no time like the present, while I'm in this firm, confident, heroic-Achilles frame of mind. Long story short: I found my land-lord's old army buddy asleep under the pear tree out the back with a jar next to him. I prodded him awake with my toe and came straight out with it: would he consider selling the farm? He blinked at me, like I was the leftovers of some really weird dream he'd been having, and I said it again, only more slowly – was he interested in selling the farm? I'd give him what he paid for it, I went on, and a quarter again on top for luck and goodwill, provided he could be out inside the month.

He looked at me like I had snakes growing out of my nose, and said, 'Yes.'

'Good,' I replied; and then we sorted out the details, dates and terms and what he'd be taking with him and what had to stay, live and dead stock, felled timber and standing crops, all that stuff; and then I said thank you, all gracious like a gentleman, and walked away. Simple as that, all very pleasant and no shouting or bad feeling or blood spilt in the dust, and I remember thinking, old Ulysses, instead of all that business of drawing the great bow that only he could draw and shooting down a hundred men in cold blood – all he needed to do was haul out the big fat purse of gold coins he got off the Scherians and buy the old place back, and everybody would've been happy as lambs, nobody dead, and no great deeds to make a song and dance over. All I could think of was, he'd been poor and on the hog so long he'd forgotten he was rich and didn't need to do all that heroic striving and suffering. Silly bugger.

Then I went back to the inn and ordered a big meal, with good wine; actually managed to make it sound like I meant it, instead of it being me playing at being a rich bastard, as part of some scam. Well, I thought, if Lucius Domitius could learn to be a toerag like me, I could learn to be a rich bastard, it comes with practice in the end, like playing the harp or singing.

Well, I've been poor, and I've been rich; and I'm here to tell you, rich is better. Rich is waking up in the morning and wondering what you're going to have for breakfast, rather than whether there's any chance of you getting a meal today. Rich is standing in your porch looking up at the sky when it's burning hot or freezing cold, and saying to yourself, Screw it, I'm not going to go to work today, let the hired men do it all. Rich is not having to patch the patches in your cloak, it's being able to ride rather than walk, it's having choices, being able to do what you want and not do what you don't want. Compared with rich, poor sucks.

Now I don't want you thinking I was throwing money around like two drunk sailors on shore leave. You can't just paint over the habits of forty years; and besides, it didn't take long to find out that lots of rich food gave me heartburn and set me off farting all day long, or that more than a couple of cups of wine in the middle of the day left me useless for anything. I had a woman in the village make me up three tunics and two cloaks out of decent quality wool cloth, and I bought two pairs of good boots from a shoemaker in the city. Soon as I was moved in to the farm, I hired a carpenter to build me a proper bed and a table for the house, and I took on a couple of lads to help me get the place back in order, mending the barn roof and refitting the house door so it shut. I rode into town and bought two slaves. I chose middle-aged men, Syrians, who turned out to be quiet, hard-working types, who knew what had to be done around a farm and could be left to get on with it. I gave them the small barn to live in, let them do it up in their off time so they'd be reasonably comfortable. Ptolemy and Smicro, their names were, and I never had any trouble with either of them.

Needless to say, Grandad's little farm wasn't going to be enough to keep me and two hands in the style I was hoping to become accustomed to, but that was all right. It's a wonderful thing, the Roman army. Not only do they keep us safe from all the hordes of savage Germans and Parthians (not that they've ever done me any harm, especially compared to, say, the Romans), and they do a bang-up job of patrolling the streets and chasing unscrupulous thieves and conmen down narrow alleys; best of all, the army lures gullible young men away from the farm and either kills them or gives them money to settle down in a distant land when they've done their time. The upshot of this is, the small farmers end up with nobody to leave the old place to when they go on, and more and more land comes up for sale every year. This mostly benefits the Roman senators and their kind, who buy it up and put in slaves and stewards to run it; but it also means that someone like me, if he happens to come into money unexpectedly, can gradually build up a good-sized holding without having to find a huge fortune all in one hit. In this case, it all worked out just fine. One of my neighbours, old Polycleides (who was amazed to find I was still alive, and maybe not best pleased) had lost both his sons to the legion; last heard of, they were colour-sergeants on the Eastern frontier, having far too much fun boozing and chasing skirt ever to want to come home to small-town Attica. So I offered him a good price for his six-acre patch that separated my two biggest parcels, and he nearly took my hand off at the wrist. Mygdon, who never had managed to find a husband for his daughter (though he'd set the dogs on me when I was fifteen and came round with a basket of apples; fair enough, desperate's one thing, but a father's got to draw the line some-where), sold me four acres of good olives on the southern slopes. Maybe I paid over the odds for the three acres of flat I got off Icarius' family, but I'd always liked the old boy back in the old days, and I couldn't be fussed to strike a hard bargain. In any event, I made up for that by more or less stealing eight acres of hillside from Eurymedon; I paid him the going rate for scrub and stones, but a blind man in the dark could see that all it needed was terracing and it'd be as good as any ground in Phyle. All told, I tripled the size of the farm, bought in vinestocks, seedcorn and olive saplings, treated myself to a new plough, five good oxen and two mules, and I still had over half of the belt money safe in Laberius' bank. Amazing transformation, like one of those fairy tales where the gods turn people into trees or animals: a few months and a handful of shiny round metal discs turned me from the scum of the earth into one of the biggest landed proprietors in Phyle. When all the formalities had been sorted out, the boundary stones earthed in, all that kind of thing, I sat down at my handsome new table with a wax tablet and a potful of dried beans for counters, and figured out my likely annual income; it came to a whisker over or under the magical five hundred measures of produce, wet and dry, which used to be the qualification for belonging to the ruling class back in the days of the old Republic, before anybody'd ever heard of the Romans. By the standards of your senators and knights, of course, I was just another dirt-scratching peasant. My little empire wouldn't have been enough to grow the grain it took to feed a senator's tame peacocks. As if I cared. One of the really nice things about being a country gent in Phyle, as far as I was concerned, was that there was no earthly reason why I should ever have to talk to another Roman again as long as I lived. That alone made the whole thing worth-while, in my opinion.

About the only bad thing about my new life was the company. I tried to persuade her she'd be happier living in town where she'd have all her friends about her, but she pointed out the undeniable fact that she didn't have any friends; practically nobody had said a civil word to her for forty-odd years. I reminded her that the farm-house was a poky little dump of a place, hardly more than a shack compared with her nice, well-appointed house in town, but she replied that she didn't mind that, and anyway, it'd be no bother to build on a couple more rooms. I even offered to buy her the inn; I could tell she was tempted, but she didn't go for it, worse luck. No, she said, her place was by my side. She hadn't been much of a mother to me in the old days, but now at last she'd got a chance to make it up to me, and that's what she was going to spend her last few years this side of the River doing, whether I liked it or not. So she rented out her house in the village (never a chopped obol did I see of any rent money, mind) and moved in with me; her, a big cedarwood chest of clothes, her mangy old polecat (called Galen, for some unaccountable reason) and the goddess Thirst, who'd been her constant companion for fifty years and couldn't bear to be parted from her.

Well, she was good for agriculture, because with her in the house, I found I'd much rather be outdoors, triple-ploughing the fallow or earthing up vines with the ponderous bloody hoe. It worked out that if I stayed in the fields till sundown, by the time I got home she'd have drunk herself into a coma and wouldn't bother me except in small ways, like suddenly yelling in her sleep or throwing up noisily in the fireplace (unforgettable smell, evaporating puke). My neighbours were terribly impressed by the way I was always up and on my way to the fields with my hoe on my shoulder just before dawn, and you couldn't find a weed or an unbusted clod on my property, though I say it myself as shouldn't.

Even so, there were occasions when I didn't quite time it right, and came home while she was still more or less conscious. Those were the days I really missed Lucius Domitius, because if he'd been there he could have explained to me exactly how they built that clever self-scuttling ship, the one he had made for his old mum. Not that Phyle's all that close to the sea, but I'm a resourceful bloke, I'd have thought of something.

It was on one of our jolly evenings together, me mending a broken shovel-handle with rawhide and her slumped over the table with a winecup the size of your head gripped in her claws, that she said it was a shame and a scandal, the mother of a rich bastard like me having to make shift for herself, when every carpenter's and smith's mother had a lady's maid to do the housework. I looked round at the pigheap I'd been living in since she'd come to stay and thought, if shift's what she makes, I really don't want it; but I didn't say anything, and next day, I got on my horse and rode down to the city.

Usually, Athens is a good place to buy people. With all our free-spending Roman visitors there's plenty of money about, and all the ships from the Islands stop at Piraeus before dragging on round the coast, including everything going to and from Delos, which is still the biggest human cattle market on earth. Just my luck, though. Oh, I could've had my pick of field hands, factory hands, craftsmen, teachers, houseboys, you name it. But the only female slaves on offer, apart from the usual flute girls (obviously a staple commodity in a good-time town like Athens), were some scraggy old boilers advertised as laundry and general household, who'd probably have dropped dead from exhaustion halfway up the hill to home, and a few specialist embroiderers, not what was needed and way out of my price bracket in any case.

I wasn't quite sure what to do. There'd be a new consignment along in a day or so, no doubt about it. But that meant going home empty-handed and getting moaned at, and then having to traipse back into town again, and the whole wretched job to do again. I'll be honest with you, I don't go much on slave-shopping. It only goes to show what a disreputable, dodgy life I've led, one step ahead of the watch if I was lucky; but every time I see a line of slaves up on the boards with an auctioneer prancing up and down pointing at them with a little stick, I can't help but reflect that, but for a couple of lucky throws of the dice, it'd have been me up there, and quite probably that was where I rightfully belonged. So screw it, I thought, I'll get it over and done with, and that'll be that.

So I went to the bank and got a letter for their office on Delos; sent a runner back to the farm to let them know I'd be away for a few days, stabled my horse and wandered down to Piraeus, where I had my choice of ships leaving for Delos on the afternoon tide. It was funny being back on a ship again. I had to keep telling myself, The Islands are a long way away from Africa and Sicily, and it'd take a real bitch of a freak storm to drive us off course and land us there. I spent most of the journey curled up in a sorry heap up the shard end of the boat – one of the few times I've ever been seasick; amazing I could do it so well with so little practice – so I didn't see much of Andros, Tenos or southern Euboea. Didn't bother me; I was just delighted when they yelled out 'Delos', and I was able to get off the ship and onto something that didn't buck and weave under my feet all the damn time.

If I'd known what Delos was going to be like, I'd have stayed home. Oh, it's a pleasant enough place, if you like scenery and stuff, and of course there's the world-famous Temple of Apollo, which you can just about see through all the stalls and booths selling little pottery statues and piss-thin bean and leek soup and surefire cures for blindness. I didn't bother with sightseeing; the ship I'd come in on was stopping only one night before going back to Piraeus, and I was determined to be on it, unless I could find something leaving earlier.

Even including Rome, I don't suppose there's any spot on earth that's got more people per square yard than Delos. Also even including Rome, I'm absolutely certain there's nowhere with more pain, suffering and misery per square yard, either. You couldn't call me the soft-hearted type, compassion's a luxury for people who don't have any great call to go feeling sorry for themselves. But I didn't like Delos. It made me jumpy as a cat. Any moment I expected to feel a bloody great big hand on my shoulder, or hear someone yell out, There he is, grab him before he gets away; and then I'd be up on one of those platforms, collar round my neck, holes punched in my earlobes, and that'd be that. Guilty conscience? I don't think so. Call it twenty-four years' accumulated twitch, the instinct you get when you've spent a lifetime on the hog, that tells you this is the sort of place where your sort of people come to harm. And, no doubt about it, there were plenty of my sort of people there, and none of them were buying.

Far as the eye could see, there were these wooden platforms, like little stages or boxing rings, and on each one, a little gaggle of people, all different shapes and sizes and colours and ages, the only thing they had in common being the obtrusive wrought iron jewellery. Running Delos must be a logistical nightmare, just making sure there's enough grain in the bins to feed them all, even on slaves' rations. The noise gets to you, and the smell, and the tiny gaps between people's shoulders that you've got to squeeze through to move about. There must be over a thousand auctioneers in the market any day of the year, and of course they all have loud, carrying auctioneers' voices, like professional singers singing ballads with numbers instead of words, and they're all going at it at the same time. It's like you're on an anvil, and the voices are like hammers, when half a dozen strikers are working the same piece. If it hadn't been for the fact that I'd spent several really uncomfortable days getting there, I'd have turned tail and gone straight back to the ship.

But I didn't. I wandered round from stage to stage, trying to take an intelligent interest. But I ask you, what's a good-quality, value-for-money lady's maid supposed to look like, anyhow? Do you want something middle-aged, nice and quiet and steady, or are you after young and strong, that won't wear out after six months' use; short or tall, round or square, Greek or German, or doesn't it matter a toss? And are you allowed to notice that they're people, or would that screw up the whole system – and that'd be a disaster for the whole Empire, I know that, but surely it wouldn't hurt too desperately much, if I promised not to tell anyone.

In other words, I felt like I was completely out of my depth there. Dumb, I know. It says in Aristotle or somewhere that some people are born to be slaves, and some people are born to be masters. Stands to reason. But where it seems to me the system breaks down is when a bloke like me – no prizes for guessing which category I fall in – finds himself plonked down on the wrong side of the platform. Then it stops making sense, and once it stops it's like a cart on a steep hill: a bugger of a job to get it started again.

Anyhow, there I was, walking up and down between the stands, painfully aware that I hadn't got a clue what I was supposed to be doing and thinking how nice it'd be to be home in Phyle, beating the shit out of clods of dirt with the ponderous hoe, when quite suddenly I saw a face I recognised.

Instinct, instinct; it says so much about you, doesn't it? My instinct is, when I see a face I recognise, to get away from there as fast as I can without making myself conspicuous. This time, though, I managed not to, purely and simply because I was able to put a name to the face before the instinct (in this case, indistinguishable from panic) kicked in. Instead, I stopped dead in my tracks and slowly turned round, to make sure I hadn't imagined it.

No, I'd been right. I have the knack of being able to recognise someone from a fleeting glimpse out of the corner of my eye. I'm told pigeons can do the same thing. They can tell the difference between a man with a slingshot and a bloke out walking his dog at a range of half a mile, when they're facing in the opposite direction. Well, in that case, I'm an honorary pigeon.

The question was: what was the evil bitch Blandinia, last seen in a burning mews in Rome, doing standing on a platform on Delos, while a huge bald fat man was telling the people a whole lot of lies about how sweet-natured and docile she was?

Well, I thought, it does no harm to listen, so I went over and stood at the back of the crowd, tucked in behind a tall bloke so I could see over his shoulder with precious little chance of being seen myself.

Yes, I'm a liar, been one all my life. But there's little white lies, such as, Yes, I own this mule, or, I inherited this handsome silver-gilt dinner service from my auntie; and there's great big steaming whoppers, like what the fat man was saying about Blandinia. To hear him talk, she was this sweet little moppet, slave-born, brought up nicely in a quiet, respectable house, unexpected tax liability forces sale. Let that be a lesson to you: *never trust an auctioneer*, even if he tells you your mother was a woman.

Just looking at her, you'd be forgiven for taking the fat bloke at his word. She was looking down at her toes, all bashful modesty and droopy shoulders, picking at a loose thread on her cuff with her tiny, dainty little fingertips. It made you want to wrap her in a warm blanket and feed her bread and milk, like a sick hedgehog; proof, if you're stubborn-blind enough to want it, that you can tell fuck-all about a human being just by looking.

And then I thought: Well, why not?

Part of me wasn't keen on the idea; in fact, it reckoned I wanted my head opening up and the bits of dirt and crud cleaned out of the works, because only a complete idiot would want to be on the same continent as that murderous little waif, let alone pay good money to get her back in his life after two narrow escapes. But another part of me was saying, This can't be a coincidence, the gods dragged you out here on purpose so you could buy her. There was a certain amount to be said for that line of argument: I mean, what'd possessed me to come all this way, getting my guts shook out of me on a boat, when I could've stayed home, waited a month, and got a perfectly good lady's maid in Athens? There was no reasonable explanation, it'd just been a sort of impulse thing – or some god had put the idea in my head, for this express purpose. Furthermore, I had a score the size of Euboea to settle with Blandinia, and offhand I couldn't think of a nastier thing to do to any female person than hand them over to my mother to be her personal servant. In fact, the idea was so utterly evil and nasty, I was sticking up my hand and bidding before I realised what I was doing; and by then it was too late, the other interested parties had dropped out and the auction-eer was singing out, Sold to the weasel-faced gentleman at the back.

EIGHTEEN

Fuck, I thought, but it was past helping. They do really horrible things to people who make successful auction bids on Delos and then don't want to pay. It did cross my mind to turn her loose, or knock her on the head during the journey home and shove her over the side. Nobody would suspect anything if I did. True, Roman law says you can't go killing slaves, even your own, just because you feel like it. But what kind of aedile's clerk would suspect a bloke of killing his slave when said bloke's just forked out a grossly inflated price for her? No, if I wanted to kill Blandinia, so long as I was reasonably discreet about it, my chances of getting in trouble were practically nil.

But then my inner voice said, Don't be stupid, you wouldn't do a thing like that, you aren't the killing sort. True enough. Which meant that as soon as I handed over my letter of credit from Laberius' bank and got the paper title, I'd be lumbered with her until one of us died. Talk about holding a wolf by the ears; if I let her go, she'd know I was still alive and race off to tell her gangster friends; if I sold her on to someone else, there'd still be a chance that she'd find some way of getting word to the bad guys; and if I kept her, it'd be like sharing the house with an invisible scorpion, waiting for the disgusting thing to sting you to death. Wonderful; and to think, I'd just parted with good money for the privilege.

The auctioneer's clerk came over and looked at me, like I was something he'd found floating wrong way up in his wine. The sight of Gnaeus Laberius' seal on my bit of parchment changed all that. For what little it's worth, the Laberius seal showed Mercury in flight, looking back over his shoulders at his own rather overdeveloped bum. Still, it impressed the hell out of the clerk. He scuttled away, leaving me to brood on my stupidity for the rest of the auction. Afterwards I went up to the desk and did the paperwork – they got a bit snotty when I told them I hadn't got a seal of my own, being a working farmer, not a gentleman; in the end, one of the auctioneer's people lent me his, and I used that to counterseal the draft. I don't suppose it was strictly legal, but I had other things on my mind just then, and couldn't be bothered with meaningless details.

After that, there was nothing for it but to step up and claim my property.

As I think I mentioned a while back, this wasn't the first time I'd bought a person. But when I got my two Syrians, it was all quite different; more like a proper hiring fair than something involving taking possession of another human being. When I got the Syrians, all I did was look at them, make my mind up, hand over the money and sort of beckon, and they followed me quite quietly, like welltrained dogs. It was a bit awkward starting a conversation with them on the way back home – I wasn't even sure they spoke Greek – but at some point I think I said something about the right way of forcing fennel seedlings, and one of them said, That's not how we do it where I'm from, and after that we just talked about farming and stuff. It's easy when it's men. We can always find something to talk about, activities or objects or places we've been. After all, men work (unless they're senators or rich bastards) so the chances are they've always got something in common; and I've never come across two women who haven't had something to say to each other; in fact, the trick is knowing how to make them shut the hell up. But when it's a bloke and a woman, it can be really hard at the best of times, and when you mix in other ingredients, like the fact that the man' s just bought the woman, or the woman's to blame for a whole bunch of horrible things that the man's only just managed to get out of alive, it's no wonder if the ice is hard to break.

Best thing, my old mother told me once when she was sober, when you can't think of anything to say, is not to say anything at all. Like most of my mum's pearls of wisdom, it's a lemon. The longer you go on not saying anything, the harder it gets. I didn't say anything when the clerk brought her over. I just grunted awkwardly when he handed over the rather pathetic, tatty little cloth bag that contained her one change of clothes – the fact that he handed it to me rather than her wasn't lost on either of us – and after he'd shoved off, I couldn't think what to do. So I didn't say anything; I just sort of beckoned, like I'd done with the Syrians, and started walking towards the docks.

Well, she followed, just like a well-trained dog; only she wasn't a dog (a bitch, yes, but not a dog), she was a human being, Plato's featherless biped. All sorts of dumb ideas skittered across my mind. I could pretend I hadn't recognised her (yeah, as if); or I could be stony-faced and hard and cruel, so she'd be too scared to look at me (only I'm about as scary as a plate of endive salad); or I could start talking loudly about the weather. I was turning this shit over in my mind when she said, 'Galen.'

I turned round. 'Yes?' I said.

She wasn't looking at me. 'Galen,' she repeated, 'where's your friend? Nero Caesar, I mean. Is he all right?'

Couldn't make out what was behind that; she made it sound like she had to know, but that could easily have been play-acting. Still. 'He's dead,' I replied.

'Oh.' She didn't say anything for a bit, then went on, 'What happened?'

'Drowned,' I said. 'In a shipwreck.'

'Oh.' Another pause. 'I'm sorry,' she said.

'No you aren't,' I'd replied, before I realised it. 'That is, unless you reckon drowning was too good for him. Anyhow, he's dead, so I hope you're satisfied.'

Rather cruel, yes; but I can be like that, a bit short and churlish when I'm feeling awkward. Anyhow, why the hell should her feelings worry me? Even so, I felt the need to say something else, to plaster over the crack, as it were. 'So,' I said, 'what's the story with you? Last I heard, you were a free woman, Or were you telling lies when you told me that?'

She made a sort of snorting noise, not at all what I'd expected. 'Oh yes,' she said, 'I was free, for a while. Only, there's a law in Rome, when a man's declared a public enemy and all his property's confiscated by the Treasury, that includes all his slaves he's recently set free. I was two days inside the limit, would you believe.'

'I never knew that before,' I said, just for something to say. 'Well, that sounds like just the sort of thing the Romans'd put in a law. But hang on,' I added. 'Where does all this public enemy stuff come in? Your old master – god, what was his name? I can't remember.'

'Licinius Pollio. When you started that fire, it did so much damage there was an enquiry, and somehow they got the idea it was a gang war thing and he was one of the gang bosses. So they rounded me up, and next thing I knew I was in Delos. Funny,' she went on, 'when Pollio gave me my papers, I really thought I was free and clear, and all my troubles were over. Should've known better, really, shouldn't I?'

I didn't say anything. No doubt about it, she'd had a raw deal. Quite apart from being born a slave, and whatever it was Lucius Domitius did to her when she was a kid, she'd definitely got cause to complain about so-called Roman justice. But then, she had been responsible for a lot of deaths, just out of malice and greed. A bit like Lucius Domitius himself, don't you think, except that he'd been thoughtless rather than vicious or greedy. All comes down to the same thing in the end, though; him, me and her, none of us were what you'd ever call nice people.

'Anyway,' she went on, 'it looks like things must've worked out well for you.'

'Can't complain,' I said. 'Actually, I had a slice of good luck, for a change.'

'Good for you,' she said.

We walked on in dead silence for a long time. It was only when we were in sight of the dockside that she asked, 'Excuse me, but where are we going?'

Of course, I hadn't told her that. 'Athens,' I said.

'Oh.'

'Actually,' I went on, 'it's not Athens proper. Phyle; it's a village up in the hills—'

'I know,' she interrupted. 'Where you were born.'

Should've guessed she'd know all about me, after all her careful research and intelligence-gathering. 'That's right,' I said. 'And now

I've moved back there. Is that all right by you? Or would you rather I sold up and moved somewhere else?'

That seemed to hurt her, God knows why. 'I'm sorry,' she said, 'I know it's none of my business, but I was just curious. I didn't mean anything by it.'

I shrugged. 'That's all right,' I said. 'It's only fair you should know where you're being taken.' She lifted her head. 'Actually,' she said, 'it's not. But you're new to all this, so you wouldn't know. You don't have to tell me anything; I mean, we could get on a ship here and off again the other side somewhere I didn't recognise, and I could live there the rest of my life without even knowing what country I was in, if you didn't feel like telling me.'

That made me feel bad, but I tried not to let it show. 'Anyway,' I said, 'we're going to Phyle. It's a nice place, if you don't mind the simple life.'

'Thank you,' she said.

I looked round till I saw the ship I'd come in on, and headed for it. And I was thinking of something I'd heard Seneca say, at some party or gathering or whatever. He'd said that when you buy slaves, you should always look at them naked before making your mind up. When you buy a horse, he said, you tell the bloke to take off the horse blanket so you can look at it properly; same thing, he said, with a slave. And at the time I'd been a bit surprised, maybe even just a little shocked, because Seneca had always made a point of chatting to slaves like they were people, listening to what they had to say instead of just ignoring them or telling them to shut up. But then, he was a Roman senator. If senators didn't ever talk to people who they reckoned were totally inferior, the only people they'd ever speak to would be each other. So, to him, a slave or a soldier or a farmer or even a Roman knight were all pretty much the same: all human beings, all more or less equal with each other, just not with him.

We got on the ship, and I found the captain and said, This one here's with me; and he asked how much, and I told him a figure that was about half of what I'd really paid, the way you do, and he said I'd got a bargain there; also, if I wanted a bit of privacy on the way back, he could have the men curtain off a bit of space in the hold, where he had a load of wool bales.

Straight up, it was a moment or so before I figured out what he was on about. Honestly, the thought hadn't crossed my mind. Not that she wasn't nice-looking, in a crab-apple sort of a way; but she was also a murderer, or next best thing, and it wasn't so long ago that I'd had to talk Pony-tail and Alexander out of killing me on her orders. The truth is, I was still more than a bit terrified of her; and that isn't my scene, really.

But I thanked the captain anyway, said it was a kind thought but not to bother; didn't give him any reason why not, just left it at that. He shrugged, and said we'd be ready to sail soon as they'd got the last of the cargo on board. Then I found a bit of deck that didn't have sailors all over it, dumped my bag so as to have something to lie on, settled down and tried to get comfy.

I wasn't sick at all on the journey home. She was. I don't know what they'd fed her on in the slave compound, but there must've been a fair amount of it, judging by what she sent over the side. At least it solved the problem of what to talk about, since when she wasn't leaning over the rail making revolting noises, she was curled up on a pile of ropes groaning and clutching at her guts. It was probably as well I hadn't planned on taking the captain up on his thoughtful offer; it'd have been a right Hercules' breakfast, the state she was in. But sitting there on the deck, fairly comfortable in the warm sun, watching her chuck her guts up into the wine-dark sea, it was hard to believe I'd seriously considered killing her, not all that long ago. You can't really take someone seriously as a threat when they're bright green in the face, with bits of sick dribbling down their chin.

By the time we made landfall on Tenos she was over the worst of it, though she wouldn't eat, just sipped a little water straight from the ladle. We were talking by that stage, too. It'd started cautiously enough – 'Are you feeling any better?' 'No.' – but we'd gradually got beyond that, though none of our chats lasted very long, mostly because she had to keep breaking off in order to sprint to the rail. Little by little, though, we both loosened up a bit; the awkwardness had gone, though we still didn't have a lot we could talk about safely. For my part, I couldn't see any harm in just talking; I'll talk to anybody, pretty much, assuming they can bring themselves to talk to me. True, she was a murderous bitch who'd tried to sell

Lucius Domitius and me to the gangsters like we were beef cattle. On the other hand, I'd just bought her, which sort of evened the score, if only because it dragged me down to her level. Besides, there was a case for saying that since it was my best buddy Lucius Domitius who'd been responsible for her ending up all savage and twisted – and he was a monster of depravity and a matricide, and that had never seemed to bother me much – I couldn't very well come over all snotty where she was concerned. Most of all, though, it was just nice to have someone to talk to. That may sound rather strange; after all, I was back living in Attica, where everybody talks all the damn time. But there's talking and talking. I'd had to face the fact that I'd been away for a long time, and since I'd come back I'd found it strangely hard to get back in tune with my neighbours, even the ones I'd known since I was a little kid. Not so strange, maybe. I'd been places they hadn't even heard of, done things they couldn't have understood (and probably just as well, though of course I never said anything about that sort of stuff; I'd come home from the army, remember, after twenty-four years blameless service, never been drunk on parade or absent without leave). So all right, I didn't really want to talk to anyone about those places or those things. But I missed having someone who'd understand what I was going on about if ever I did feel the need; put it another way, someone who spoke my language, because it wasn't pure unsullied Attic Greek any more. Often I'd caught myself using a word my neighbours didn't know, or having to stop and think, How do they say this in Attica, rather than Cappadocia or Cilicia or Italy? It wasn't just the dialect, mind you, I could've put up with that until I'd picked up decent Attic again. It was all the stuff that lay behind the strange words, ideas and experiences, a way of life – one I was bloody glad to have left behind me, but even so. That's who I really was, not Sosistrata's boy from Phyle who'd never been further from home than Athens City. You can do a lot to change who you are; you can even pretend to die, and then make believe you're someone completely different. But you'll never convince yourself.

So anyway, once we'd got on speaking terms, I found I enjoyed talking to her. Sure, there's nothing much else you can do on a ship except talk, and a cleft-palated German would've been better than nobody at all. It was more than that, though. Hard to explain, really. Twenty-four years on the road; I'd always had someone I could talk to free and easy, without having to think before I opened my mouth – first Callistus, then Lucius Domitius – but since I got home (the one place on earth you'd have thought I could loosen up and be myself) I'd been going around feeling like it was all a scam, a con, a part I was playing in order to deceive and defraud the honest folks of Phyle. It'd started to get to me, to the point where I was spending all day lurking out in the fields, hiding not just from my loathsome mother but from my loathsome self.

What all that'd got to do with Blandinia, I couldn't tell you. But coming across her again, it was like being in a foreign place, where they don't even talk Greek, and suddenly running into someone from your home town, when you least expected it. Or whatever. In any event, I don't have to justify myself to you. So I'm the sort of bloke who'll chum up with nasty horrible people. So what? I never said I was perfect, or even halfway decent.

By the time we got to Piraeus, then, we'd sort of made our peace, if only on the basis of a mutual exchange of insult and injury; we were quits, and there didn't seem any point in fighting any more. Not that I trusted her at all. No way, she was still a wolf by the ears, and I knew that if she got half a chance to get her freedom or any advantage at all by turning me in to the Romans or selling my severed ears to the sausagemaker, she'd do it easy as sneezing. But we both accepted that, it was out in the open, lying on the table between us, as it were; so, somehow, it wasn't a problem.

All right, I'll own up, because you've guessed anyway, and what have I got to gain from lying to you? Hands in the air, I admit it; I was falling in love. Falling isn't the right word. Think of what it feels like when you're out walking in the wet, and you go to jump over a steep ditch and you almost make it but not quite; you balance for just a moment, and then you feel yourself slipping backwards, out of control, and you slowly slide down the bank and end up in the mud up to your knees. I was gradually slithering down into love; probably because, well, living my kind of life you don't get to meet many nice girls, or many girls of any description, and then only long enough for them to tell you to drop dead, or yell for the watch. And, like I said, she was sort of nice-looking in a sparse kind of a way, and twenty years younger than me; and, most of all, she was there. When, over the course of twenty-four years, you only find one girl who'll hold still long enough for you to say more than a couple of dozen words to her . . . and yes, I'm not forgetting Amyntas' sister Myrrhine, but I think that proves my point. I fell for her in the time it takes to peel an onion; not because we had loads in common, or we were the two halves of one soul severed before birth, like in Plato, but simply because in my life, when it comes to quality time with the opposite sex, as long as it takes to peel an onion is practically for ever.

Right, we've got that sorted, now maybe we can get on with the story.

We got off the ship at Piraeus, and I went round to the livery and collected my horse. This presented me with a problem straight away. The way I'd seen it when I left for Delos, on the way home, I'd ride the horse, leading my new slave behind me on the end of a piece of rope. Now that I was in love, of course, that didn't seem appropriate. If things had been otherwise, needless to say, I'd have let the object of my affection ride the horse, while I walked. But I wasn't so far gone in daffyness to risk letting Blandinia get on the horse, because of the very real danger that she'd kick me in the face and ride off in the general direction of Thebes and points north as soon as her bum hit the horse blanket. So I compromised. We both walked, and I led the horse.

She can't have grasped the subtleties of the position, because she asked me after a bit 'Why aren't you riding?'

'Oh,' I said. 'I just feel like some exercise after being cooped up on a ship, that's all.'

'I see,' she said. 'So let me ride the horse. I've only got these thin sandals on, and my feet are killing me.'

I lifted my head. 'You wouldn't like my horse,' I said. 'Very bony back, he's got. I'm used to him, but you wouldn't like him at all.'

She shrugged. 'Suit yourself,' she said. 'Only, I'm not used to walking – well, not in the country at any rate. Inside buildings, up and down stairs, in streets, yes; you spend all day on your feet when you're a slave. But all these stones and ruts and things hurt my ankles.'

I didn't say anything to that, and she let the subject drop, which was just as well. Instead, she asked, 'When we get to your place, what've I got to do?'

I felt like an idiot; I hadn't told her. 'Lady's maid,' I said. 'For my mother.'

'Oh.' She seemed pleased, the poor fool. 'I've never been a lady's maid before. But,' she went on, 'I've seen enough of them, God knows, back at the Golden House. Always struck me as a good life, for service. Mending clothes, helping the mistress do her hair, reading to her in the evening sometimes – is that what you mean?'

I thought about my dear mother, drinking unmixed straight from the jar and spilling soup all over the floor. 'That sort of thing,' I said. 'And a bit of general housework, now and again.'

'Sounds all right,' she said. 'Better than a lot of things, anyhow. You know—' She stopped, and I stopped too, though the horse carried on walking till I pulled him back. 'I suppose I ought to say thank you,' she said. 'I mean, after some of the stuff I did, back in Rome. Some of it was pretty mean.'

You could say that, I thought. 'Well,' I said, 'that was then and this is now. I think it'd be better if we didn't dwell on all that.'

'No,' she said, 'maybe not. But some people would've wanted to get their own back. And really, I'm not a horrible person – oh, I know it's easy for me to say that, and there's no reason for you to believe it, but I don't think I'm a horrible person, anyway. I've always just done what I could to get away from all the bad stuff – at the Golden House, you know what I mean. I've had this idea that unless I could be free and clear, completely on my own, not answering to anybody, there'd always be the chance I'd end up back there, or somewhere just as bad. It's just because I'm scared, I guess. But – well, I know now that you aren't like that, and if you're prepared to give me another chance and believe me, I promise you, I'm through with all that stuff. I want to be somewhere I can do my work, whatever it is, and know that if I carry out my side of the deal, nothing bad's going to happen. That's all, really. Sorry,' she added, 'that sounds totally dumb and pathetic. But for what it's worth, I do mean it.'

There was a long silence, broken only by the sound of the horse having a piss. 'Like I said,' I told her eventually, 'far as I'm concerned, all that stuff's behind us, so why don't we just carry on as though it'd never happened? Better for all concerned, if you ask me.'

I still didn't let her ride the horse, though.

It was nearly dark by the time we reached Phyle. For the last mile or so she'd been asking, 'Are we nearly there yet?', and I'd been saying, 'We'll be there soon,' and she'd been saying, 'Is it soon yet?' – at any rate, she'd been telling the truth about not being used to walking on Attic roads, because the closer we'd got to home, the slower she'd gone, dragging herself along like she was dying of exhaustion in the trackless Libyan desert. So, when the farm was no more than a hundred or so yards off, and she asked again, 'Are we nearly there?' I nodded and said, 'Sure; only about ten miles to go, we'll be home well before dawn.' She was still making whimpering noises when I pushed open the gate and headed down into the yard.

'Is this it?' she asked.

'Yes,' I said.

'Oh,' she said.

Smicro, one of my two Syrians, happened to be coming out of the stables just then. He said, Hello, have a good trip? and I replied, Not so bad, and gave him the horse to see to. He looked at Blandinia but didn't say anything. Don't think she noticed him.

There was light showing under the house door, which meant either Mother was still up, or she'd zonked out with the lamps still burning. Fortunately it turned out to be the latter, because I wasn't in the mood to do the necessary introductions after a long walk up the mountain. Mother was lying on the floor in a pool of red stuff when we walked in. Blandinia tried to jump out of her skin and made a loud squealing noise. Luckily, it took more than that to wake Mum up when she had a load on.

'My God,' Blandinia was gibbering, 'oh my God, she's been murdered.'

I shook my head wearily. 'That's not blood, it's just booze,' I said. 'She'll be all right. Either she'll wake up around midnight and drag herself over to the bed, or else she'll just stay there till morning. You'd think at the very least she'd crick her neck, but it never seems to do her any harm.'

It was fun seeing the look of surprise and, yes, disgust on Blandinia's face. 'You mean she does this a *lot*?' she whispered.

I nodded. 'Every day, practically,' I said. 'That's not to say she always fetches up on the floor. Some nights she passes out in her chair, or on the couch. Some nights she manages to put herself to bed. One time I went out at dawn to feed the pig and there she was, face down in the pigshit, snoring like a boarhound.' I yawned. 'Since you've only just got here,' I said, 'we'll say you don't start work till the morning, so don't bother cleaning her up or putting her to bed tonight. There's a spare mattress in the corner, look, you can sleep on that. Goodnight.'

To be honest with you, when I woke up the next morning, I wasn't sure she'd still be there. Judging by the look on her face the night before, I wouldn't have been at all surprised to find that she'd snuck out while I was asleep and legged it, and the hell with the horrible tortures prescribed by law for runaway slaves. But when I opened the door of the inner room and looked out into the main house, I was amazed to see it was looking – well, near as dammit clean, and neat, and tidy. Mother was still fast asleep on the floor where we'd found her, and the space around her hadn't been touched, it was a little island of squalor in a sea of hygienic order. Blandinia was down on her hands and knees with a bucket of water, scrubbing a stubborn mark off a flagstone. Amazing, I thought; it was like walking in and finding a wolf darning your socks.

You've got yourself a little treasure here, I told myself. 'Morning,' I said. 'Sleep well?'

She turned her head and snarled at me like a snared fox. 'Lady's maid, you said,' she growled. 'Nice light work looking after a dear old soul who'd be no bother at all for a year or so, then die and set me free in her will. I've been at it since before dawn, scouring five-year-old vomit off the furniture.'

I smiled. 'You're doing a grand job,' I said encouragingly. 'Only,' I added, pointing, 'you missed a bit.'

She didn't throw the scraper at me, but probably only because she preferred to close in hand to hand, like the Roman army. 'I should have guessed,' she said. 'Vindictive bastard like you. And all that stuff about let's forget about the past, make a fresh start.' Words seemed to fail her, which was probably just as well. I edged past her and got my hat off the hook.

'When you've finished that,' I said, 'how about fixing us all some breakfast?'

I left before she'd finished replying. Some of the words she used I hadn't even heard before, but I think I got the gist of it.

I spent the morning terracing with the Syrians. They were curious about the new addition to the household, but too polite to ask outright. I said I'd got a maid for my mother while I'd been away on business, and left it at that. At midday, I said I thought I might wander back down to the house for something to eat, since I'd missed breakfast. The Syrians looked at each other, but didn't say anything.

Well, naturally I'd been dying of curiosity all morning, wondering how Mum and Blandinia had got on with each other. As I pushed open the door, I expected to see smashed furniture, bits of potsherd all over the place, maybe even a pool of blood. Not a bit of it. The two of them were sat round the table – Mum on her chair, Blandinia on a little three-legged stool I didn't even know we had – and there were two winecups beside the jug. That aside, the place looked neat and tidy, Mum's hair was combed and she was wearing a clean dress. She was pissed as a rat, of course, but no worse than usual; and she was smiling. I didn't think she knew how.

'And then,' Blandinia was saying, 'I rolled him over and stuck a sprig of parsley in his ear, and then the watch arrived.' Mum burst out laughing, did the nose trick with her wine. Neither of them seemed to have noticed I was there.

'Hello,' I said.

Mum looked up, realised it was me, and scowled. 'What do you want?' she said.

'Nothing,' I answered, 'just wondered if there's any food.'

Mum glowered at me as though I'd just asked for a quart of her blood. 'There's bread and cheese,' she said, 'and if you want olives, you'll have to fetch in a new jar.'

I lifted my head. 'I'm not bothered, thanks,' I said. 'So, you two've been getting to know each other, then?'

Neither of them seemed to think that was even worth replying to. Instead, Mum poured out two full cups of unmixed, and said, 'So then what happened? Did you give him his clothes back in the end?'

I got a bit of cheese and the stale end of the loaf, and went and had my dinner in the barn.

Over the next month or so, we got a hell of a lot of work done on the farm. It was just as well I'd chosen a couple of good workers in Smicro and Ptolemy. They stuck at it and didn't complain, even when we started and finished in the dark, and had to walk home from the fields by moonlight. All right, you can call me chickenshit if you like, but after Blandinia had been there two months, I took to sleeping in the bunkhouse, and kept clear of the main house altogether. Well, I was getting home so late and starting work so early, there didn't seem any point, there was plenty of room in the bunkhouse for one more, and Smicro and Ptolemy always fixed up a good breakfast of fried oatmeal and sausage, which they were perfectly happy to share with me. Oddly enough, I felt much more comfortable that way, like it hadn't been right for me to kip down in the main house, like a gentleman or something. Believe it or not, I was quite enjoying the farm work, even the ditching and earthing up and the clodbashing. It's different when it's your own dirt, after all, and doing something constructive and honest for the first time in my life was so much less hassle than conning or thieving, and when you count in the time I used to spend hiding in haylofts and under market trestles or running down alleys, the hours were better, too. Add in a dry place to sleep and all the food I could eat, and I was as happy as a jarful of crickets. I only wished Lucius Domitius could've been there to share the pleasure; only he'd have moaned like hell about the long days in the searing heat, and how his hands were getting calloused all to buggery.

(And once or twice I thought, This is a better ending than the one in all the books. Far better this way than the big fight scene, stringing the great bow and shooting down the noble lords of Ithaca like stray dogs. So much more sensible, if you will insist on coming home, to settle down in a quiet way, do an honest job of work, raise a good crop of corn and grapes and beans, and not worry about who rules over who, or what the right and wrongs of it all are. It's as if Lucius Domitius had come home after his ten years' wandering among the savages and the seat monsters, and got himself a job teaching the harp, maybe singing at tables in the evenings. But the trouble with Ithaca is, when you finally get there, you find out it's moved on, and the place where it used to be is called something else now, and strangers live there who don't hold with your sort. Different in my case; I'd been lucky, amazingly so. It'd taken a whole skyful of gods, not to mention a vast hoard of buried treasure, a secret island and a perfectly timed floating coffin to win me my corner of the bunkhouse and my two square meals of bean porridge a day. Most people don't have that kind of luck. I guess there simply isn't enough of it to go round.)

So there I was, from worthless parasite to blameless peasant in one roll of the dice. Better still, Mum seemed to have taken on a new lease of life, thanks to my thoughtfulness in supplying her with a congenial companion, which got the Furies off my back and meant I'd probably turned into a Good Son. Oh, she was still on the booze, more or less permanently zonked, but at least she seemed to enjoy it more than she'd used to. Often when I passed the house I could hear her roaring her head off laughing, presumably at one or other of Blandinia's dirty stories about her time in the cathouse. Quite why the two of them were getting along so well I didn't know, or care. Obviously they had something in common other than a really piss-poor opinion of me, but whatever it was they didn't say and I couldn't be bothered to ask.

I once heard someone in a barber's shop say that the lives of mortal men are nothing but a story the gods tell each other across the dinner table up on Mount Olympus; they call us up out of the empty darkness to serve some purpose in the story, and when we aren't needed any more, they send us back where we came from, and start the story off in some new direction. Well it sounds clever enough, like so much of what you overhear when you're having your hair cut, but I don't believe it. For one thing, if our lives were meant to be entertaining enough to keep a bunch of gods from falling asleep over their wine, there'd be more comedy and sex in them, and not quite so much farming or weaving baskets. More to the point, the theory was true, there'd be some kind of shape or pattern to the way things happen, not to mention a damn sight more happy endings. Take my life, for instance. There's me: I'd been away, done all sorts of adventures and stuff in the big world, gone around for ten years with one of the most famous, hated people in history, found this amazing stash of Carthaginian gold, come home again rich. Now, wouldn't that be the right place to end, with the Blandinia bit tacked on at the end as a sort of comic tailpiece, showing how what goes around comes around, or whatever? Damn straight it would, if it was you or me making it up. No need to go on any further. Or suppose that the story was really about Lucius Domitius, and I was just a supporting role, a sidekick or a funny servant or whatever; fine, that'd fit well enough, with all the roles being reversed, neat as a daisychain, even down to me rescuing Blandinia from Delos, just like Lucius Domitius rescued Callistus and me off the cross, the first time we met him. Only difference would be, Blandinia would've fallen in love with me, like Callistus did with Lucius Domitius; that didn't seem to be happening, but then again, I'm not one of your literary types, so maybe I'm missing a point somewhere. I couldn't care less, actually. What I'm trying to say is, this ought to have been where the story got neatly tied up and put to bed, or at least petered out, and the gods who'd been listening to it should've yawned loudly, drunk up and staggered off to bed. Everything had fallen more or less into place, like the wards of a key in a lock: Lucius Domitius had escaped the death he deserved through Callistus, just as Callistus had escaped the death he deserved through Lucius Domitius; because of Lucius Domitius, I'd had the ten years of misery and aggravation I deserved, and at the end of it I'd been paid back, also all because of him, with my gold belt and my nice little farm. All the other bad guys had been dealt with in the way they deserved – Amyntas, Strymon, even Blandinia, reduced to being the drinking companion of my unspeakable mother – and our Ulysses (that's me) was back home again, everything bolted down tight, job done. That's all for now, folks.

But that's not how it happened, which just about wraps it up for that particular theory. What's more, the sneaky bitch of a story did its best to make me believe it was over, to get me off my guard, by slipping into happy-ever-after (or at least, not miserable) mode for best part of six months, during which time I did my work in the fields and shared breakfast with Smicro and Ptolemy. When it all started up again, I wasn't expecting it at all. Downright dishonest, if you ask me.

I was pressing olives when I first heard, which is probably why it took a while for it to sink in. You know what it's like, working one of those contraptions. You've loaded all your bagged-up olives into the drum, and your men have filled the sack that hangs off the end of the beam with stones to act as the counterweight, then it's your job to grab hold of the beam, scramble up onto it with your arms and legs wrapped round it, and cling on like a monkey on a rope, edging your way down it so as to get the leverage. It's not a dignified position for a man of property. In fact, you feel like a clown, hanging in mid air off a long bit of wood while the press goes squelch, like an elephant farting. But you can't leave it to the help, it's too important, and besides, if you told one of the men to do it, they'd reckon you were chicken and lose respect. The one thing you've got to do is concentrate, or else you're going to end up on the deck with bruised bones, and most likely a busted beam. It's really not a good time for chatting, and only an idiot would stroll up and start a conversation with you while you're at it.

Unfortunately, my neighbour Eurycleides was just that kind of idiot, particularly when it came to timing. No matter what you were doing – raising a roof tree, tempering a ploughshare, boiling tallow, having sex with someone else's wife under a thornbush, all the tricky things where you really don't want to be disturbed till you're done – if he saw you he'd stroll up and launch into some topic of conversation, usually starting in the middle so you didn't have a clue what he was going on about for quite some time; and taking no notice didn't work, because he'd just keep saying 'Well?' and 'So, what do you think?' until you answered him.

'Hello there, Galen,' he called out. He had this knack of seeming to appear out of nowhere, like doves round a granary. 'I'm surprised at you, really. I'd have thought there was enough needing doing round here for the both of you.'

I was two-thirds of the way down the beam, hanging on by my toes and fingers. 'What?' I said.

'And it's not as if there's not enough in the place to support two men,' he went on. 'Nice little spread you've built up here, since you've been back, I'll say that for you.'

'Thanks,' I muttered, managing not to scream at the pain in my finger joints.

'But it's a poor show,' he went on, 'and I don't care who hears me say it, when a man goes buying in foreigners to do the work, and leaves his own flesh and blood to go day-labouring. Sorry if you don't like it, but it's got to be said.'

That went clean over my head, like a flock of starlings. 'Well,' I said, 'there you go.' The press was making that really gross squidging noise that means you're nearly done; all I had to do was hang on a little bit longer . . .

'All right,' Eurycleides went on, 'it's not quite the same as grape-picking or coal-mining, but that's not the point. A man shouldn't have to go standing out in the market place looking for some stranger to give him work, when his own brother's got enough land for two men. I'll be straight with you, I thought more of you than that. Well, cheers for now.'

And the clown started to walk away, just about the moment when that phrase 'his own brother' bit me like a sledgehammer. 'Hang on,' I shouted, and tried to turn my neck. Bad move. I lost my grip with my left hand, and a heartbeat later I was lying in the dust groaning and rubbing my shoulder, where the busted end of the beam had smacked down on me. I was bloody lucky it didn't break a bone, at that.

Well, what with the pain and the buggeration of having broken the press, and the Syrians fussing round asking if I could feel my arm (of course I could feel my arm, otherwise I wouldn't have been sobbing in agony), it clean slipped my mind, that stuff about my own brother. It was only next day, after we'd finally managed to lash up the beam with soaked rawhide and rope (it was a real botch job, and it bent like a twig, but it just about held together; and after all, they don't hand out prizes for Neatest Olive Press, so who gives a damn?), that I remembered; and, of course, nothing would do but I had to set off right away for Eurycleides' place to ask him what the hell he'd meant by it.

He wasn't home. Oh no, he wasn't even in Phyle; he'd set off at dawn for the poxy little two-acre he had in the Mesogaia − not quite the other side of Attica, but near enough. So I went home and got out the horse − this was right in the middle of oil-making, of course, when I really couldn't spare the time to go prancing off on bloody stupid errands − and traipsed off down the city road, north-west around Hymettus, and on to the plain. Luckily I knew more or less where Eurycleides' place was – we'd been out there helping him with trellising one year, back when I was a kid – and since I was riding and he was on foot, I managed to get there shortly after he'd arrived.

'Hello there, Galen,' he said. 'Nice day, though if this heat keeps up we'll be eating the seedcorn come vintage. What brings you out this way?'

I didn't bother getting down off the horse. 'What you said, the other day,' I started. 'When you were up my place, and I fell off the beam.'

He nodded. 'Doesn't look like you did any serious damage, though,' he said. 'I had an uncle, fell right out of a tree on his head—'

'You said something about my brother.'

He sighed. 'There,' he said, 'I knew I'd upset you, probably that's why you fell off the press. But it's always been my way, I speak my mind and that's all there is to it. No offence intended, but if the hat fits—'

I waved my hands about. 'Listen,' I said. 'I'm not pissed off at you or anything, I just need to know what you meant. What's this about my brother doing day-labouring? Hadn't you heard, he's dead?'

Eurycleides thought about that for a moment. 'No,' he said, 'you're wrong there, because I saw him myself. Never forget a face, me. I'm shocking with names, mind, but champion with faces. It was him all right. Your brother . . .' And he scowled, clicked his fingers. Like he'd said, he always was lousy at names.

'Callistus,' I said. 'Is that who you mean?'

'That's it.' He looked thoroughly relieved, like a constipated man wiping his bum. 'On the tip of my tongue, it was. Your brother Callistus. Good lad, I always liked him.'

'He's dead,' I repeated. 'Been dead these ten years. I should know,' I added, and only just stopped myself in time from saying exactly why.

But Eurycleides lifted his head. 'Oh, it was him all right. And like I said to you, it's not like digging or picking, granted, there's some as calls it a profession rather than a trade, but I still reckon it's degrading, a grown man having to go around asking for work, even if it is indoors, and meals thrown in.'

'Eurycleides,' I yelled, 'what the fuck are you talking about?'

Eventually, I got it out of him. About a month earlier he'd been in the city about some family lawsuit or other, and as he crossed the market square he'd happened to look across to the bunch of stalls where the jobbing cooks and caterers and musicians hang out, waiting for someone to hire them. He thought he saw a face he knew, so he stopped for a closer look; and he was positive that there, among the harp-players and flautists and people who pretend to swallow fire while doing double-back somersaults off a sawhorse, he saw my brother Callistus. He was late for his lawsuit so he didn't stop, but he was certain sure that's who he'd seen, because he never forgot a face (which was true, in actual fact; I could vouch for that), and so Callistus couldn't be dead, could he, not if he was stood in the market along with all the other long-hairs—

He was still talking when I rode off. Trouble is, you can't really get up any speed on the Mesogaia–city road, not if you don't want a horse with a busted leg, so I didn't reach town till well after dark. I went straight to the market square, but of course it was no use. Went without saying, all the jobbing musicians would've got their gigs for the day while it was still light; if you're holding a dinner party you don't wait till the guests arrive and then send out in the hope of running into an all-night harpist. So I had to stay the night, and, since I'd come out without any money, that meant knocking up somebody I knew in the city and asking for a bed for the night. Problem was, I knew only four people in Athens proper. Three of them were out on the piss (typical thoughtless behaviour) and the fourth was a dreary old git called Dexitheus, who was deaf as a post and didn't hear me knocking till I'd woken the whole block.

I tried to get some sleep in Dexitheus' hayloft, but I might as well not have bothered; I just lay there, trying to make sense of it. Well before dawn, when only the charcoal-burners and the people who're on jury duty are up and about, I was in the market square, pacing up and down. I was still there when the farm carts came in, and then the fish, and the first wave of shoppers, and the bakers and the sausagemongers; all the trades of Athens reported for duty around me on every side, except the bone idle, good-for-nothing, the-hell-with-work-let's-have-a-lie-in hired musicians. They didn't deign to put in an appearance till practically mid-morning, and then only in dribs and drabs, like the stragglers from a defeated army.

I thought about grabbing a harpist at random and asking him if he'd seen anybody answering the description; but I didn't. Maybe I was afraid of hearing him say, No, never set eyes on anybody like that; or maybe I'm just shy. So I mooched around a bit, so the market police wouldn't take me for a thief; I looked at some imported Egyptian honey, and some ivory-backed mirrors, and some cute bronze bath-scrapers with pornographic handles. I eavesdropped on the cooks (but they reminded me of Alexander and Pony-tail) and pretended I was interested in the price of two hundred jars of slightly spoiled wheat flour, f.o.b. a grain freighter due in the day after next from Syracuse, owners just gone bankrupt, a real opportunity for a man with the necessary nerve and vision. Come noon I was ready to go home (by way of Eurycleides' place, where there might just be bloodshed); there were enough journeymen musicians hanging round to man a full-strength legion, but nobody whose face seemed familiar.

Then someone tapped me on the shoulder, and a voice I knew (I'm good at voices, like Eurycleides with faces) said, 'Galen?'

There's this fairy tale, I'm sure you know it. Orpheus, the greatest musician who ever lived, goes down to Hell to fetch back his dead wife. King Pluto tells him to fuck off, the dead don't come back, it's the rules; but Orpheus stands there playing his harp, and the music's so utterly wonderful that finally Pluto says, All right, you can have her back, but on one condition. You set off walking back into the light, and I'll send her on, she'll be right behind you. But whatever you do, whatever you hear, don't look round at her till you're back topside, because if you do, that's it, she stays here for ever. So off he goes, and behind him he hears his wife's voice calling his name, Orpheus, Orpheus; but he knows the king of the dead doesn't muck about, he means what he says, so he doesn't look round, just keeps on going, one foot in front of the other. And still there's this voice behind him, calling out to him, Orpheus, is that you, look at me; and he knows it's her, the voice he's heard in his mind every day since she died and he left her, since she died and he went on living, since he swam to shore and the gods sent a floating coffin for him to save him from the reef – hang on, I'm getting my legends muddled here, that was someone else, Ulysses or one of those people. Anyhow, he's almost there. He can see the bank of the River and the Ferryman's boat, bobbing up and down on the water like a floating coffin, and beyond that he can see the light, and then the voice calls out to him, Orpheus; and without thinking he looks round and sees her face, and in that moment when he realises what he's done—

I looked round. It was Lucius Domitius.

NINETEEN

'Galen?' he repeated. 'What the bloody hell are you doing here?'

He said it in Greek, but didn't he ever sound Roman, like he'd come down to breakfast in the cloister of his villa and found some scruffy old tramp dossing down under the table. I thought, bloody cheek, he makes it sound like he owns the place (and then I thought; well, fair enough. Arguably, by rights, he does).

Anyhow, I stared at him. 'I thought you were dead,' I told him.

'What, me? No.' He was wearing a fairly new tunic, good stuff, quality Attic wool, and a pair of quite decent sandals – better than what I had on, at any rate; and there was a cute little lyre tucked under his arm, carved frame, with the grain still clean and open. He looked different, mind; not back to how he'd been in the old days, but noticeably plumper, without the bags under his eyes or the stringy muscle tone that comes from regular exercise and not quite enough to eat. His tan was starting to fade; it hadn't quite turned into the dead-fish pallor of your urban gentleman, but he'd never have passed for a grape-picker. And he was scowling at me like I was a bad oyster in his seafood salad. 'You seem to be all right,' he added, managing to make it sound like I'd done something wrong, probably out of spite.

'I'm fine,' I said. 'Look, can we go somewhere and talk, instead of standing out here in the street?'

'What? Oh, right, I suppose so. But I haven't got all day. There's supposed to be some people hiring for a big dinner party.'

But before we could go anywhere, one of the other musicians came up and looked at me. 'Morning, Narcissus,' he said. 'Who's the farmer?'

Narcissus, I guessed, must be the name he was going under these days. The farmer was, presumably, me.

'Oh, just family,' Lucius Domitius replied awkwardly. 'Look, I'm just nipping across the road for a moment, I won't be long. If the bloke turns up while I'm gone . . .'

The other man nodded. He was tall, spare without being thin, long black beard, just this side of fifty, maybe. 'Don't worry, I'll put in a good word. But hurry it up if you can, this promises to be a good job.'

'Who was that?' I whispered, as we hurried across the square towards a wine shop.

'Oh, a friend of mine.' He sounded defensive. 'We work together. He plays the flute.'

Well, fine, I thought, that explains everything. I ordered a half-jar, two to one, and two cups. They took their own sweet time bringing them, but that's Athens for you.

'You didn't answer my question,' he started up, before I could say a word. 'What're you doing in Athens?'

I wasn't expecting anything like that. 'I live here,' I said.

He frowned. 'What, here in the city?'

'No, in Phyle, my grandad's old place. I own it.'

His expression seemed to be telling me the other one had bells on it. 'But I thought your grandfather was dead,' he said.

'That's right, he is.'

'And he left the farm to your cousins. You didn't get anything.'

'Absolutely. But my cousins are dead, too. I bought the place.'

He looked stunned. 'Bought?' he said. 'Where the hell did you get money from?'

Not, how did you escape from the shipwreck, or anything like that. No, just, What's a dirtball like you doing with money? Charming.

But I wasn't in the mood for starting a fight. 'From Queen Dido,' I told him.

'What? You mean, you went back and got the treasure?'

I grinned. 'No fear,' I said. 'I managed to sneak something while we were loading it. You won't believe some of the things that've happened to me since—'

'But you're farming now, right? You're through with the thieving, for good?'

I couldn't think of the right words for what I wanted to say, so I nodded.

'And you were discreet about fencing this thing you stole? You didn't go splashing your money around, drawing attention to yourself?'

'Of course not,' I said angrily. 'I'm not stupid.'

His face said he wasn't so sure about that. 'Well, anyway,' he said. 'Can't be helped now, I suppose. But what prompted you to come back here, of all places? Why couldn't you have just gone off somewhere else, where nobody'd know you?'

I could've said, What, you mean a place you and I haven't been chased out of by the law? Name three. But I didn't. 'Bloody hell, Lucius Domitius—' I started.

'And don't call me that, for crying out loud. My name's Narcissus, got that?' He glanced over his shoulder as he said it. "Narcissus, son of Porphyrius, from Mitylene. You won't forget that, will you?'

'Whatever,' I said despairingly.

That made him angry. 'For pity's sake, Galen,' he said. 'It's important.'

'Oh,' I replied, 'I'm still allowed to be Galen, then?'

He sighed. 'Not if it was up to me,' he said. 'Last thing I need is you parading around under your own name, in a place where someone's bound to recognise you. But it looks like it's too late to do anything about that now.'

I decided to change the subject. 'Honestly,' I said, 'I was convinced you'd got yourself drowned, when the ship went down—'

He clicked his tongue, like he'd just resigned himself to wasting time on chatting with some boring old fart when there were things he should be doing. 'It was pretty damn close,' he said. 'I came up, and there was a bit of timber floating, so I grabbed hold of that and hung on. Don't know how long I was in the water, but just when I was sure I'd had it, a ship came along. Real slice of luck, that was.'

Right, I thought. All I got was a floating coffin, good condition, one careful owner. Might've known he'd get a proper ship. 'How about the others?' I said. 'The skipper and the rest of the crew?'

He shrugged. 'Never saw anybody else,' he said, 'so I guess they bought it. Terribly sad, but these things happen. I remember thinking at the time, this is a judgement on me for what I did to my mother, that damned ridiculous collapsing yacht. But no, a ship happened to be passing, and it picked me up and rescued me. And that,' he added, 'is where I met Philocrates.'

'Who?'

'My friend. The man who talked to me just now.'

Your *other* friend, I thought; and then, your *new* friend. I decided I didn't like Philocrates.

'And that was a stroke of luck, too,' he went on. 'Turned out the ship was headed for Corinth, and Philocrates had booked a passage all the way. Soon as he found out I was a musician too, he suggested we should team up and try our luck in Athens. He paid my fare, out of his own money, and here we are. We're doing well – he's a damned fine flute-player – and that's all there is to it, really.' He drank some wine, then remembered something he'd forgotten and added, 'How about you?'

Somehow, I didn't feel like telling him about the reef and the coffin and Scheria. 'More or less the same,' I said. 'I got picked up too, and I couldn't think of anywhere else to go, so here I am. And it hasn't worked out too bad, as you can see.'

'No.' He frowned a little. 'No, it hasn't,' he said doubtfully. 'So long as you're safe, that's the main thing.'

He said that like he meant it, a bit. Then he looked over my shoulder. 'Look,' he said, 'I really do want to hear all about what you've been up to, and there's a few things we've got to get straight about the future, but right now I've got to run. If we can get this dinner-party job, it could be the making of us. Be sure to look me up,' he added, getting to his feet, 'next time you're in town. All right?'

I tried to grab his tunic, but he'd gone. Wonderful, I thought; if he'd been that quick and agile when he was going around with me, maybe we wouldn't have wound up in so many condemned cells. Anyway, I didn't follow him. I just sat there, feeling like I'd just come home from the war after ten years' wandering, and immediately been slung in the coop for loitering.

There wasn't anything I wanted to do in town, so I went back to the inn, paid my tab, got my horse and went home. A drink would've been nice, but Blandinia and my dear mother had recently moved all the jars of wine out of the barn and into the inner room, where I used to sleep, presumably so they wouldn't have to leave the house when it was dark or raining. I pushed open the bunkhouse door and drooped in, to find Ptolemy and Smicro on the mattress, making love. 'Sorry,' I muttered, and pushed off to the barn, where the cow gave me a nasty look and the dog tried to bite me.

Oh well, I thought.

It's boring, sitting on your own in a barn, so I got a hoe and a shovel, and walked out to the two-acre to trench up the vines I'd planted there. At least they seemed pleased to see me, though maybe they were just being polite. My back started hurting but I kept at it in a desultory sort of a way for an hour or so. Then someone called out my name, and I looked round. It turned out to be another neighbour of mine, a nice enough bloke in his way, name of Demetrius.

'Someone was round my place looking for you,' he said. 'Foreigner.'

That made me stop and think. Of course, in Phyle, foreigner doesn't just mean non-Greek, or even non-Athenian; it could just as easily mean a city type, or someone from Pallene or Acharnae. 'Really?' I said. 'Did he tell you his name?'

Demetrius lifted his head. 'Just asked me if I knew where a rat-faced bloke called Galen might be. Truth is, I didn't like the look of him much, so I said I'd never heard of you. Sorry, were you expecting anybody.?'

'No,' I said. 'What did he look like, this bloke?'

'Foreign,' Demetrius said. 'Big, rough-looking, sandy hair going a bit thin on top. Smart dresser, though. I reckoned he must be either a loan-shark's runner or the government. Anyway, I hope that was all right.'

I shrugged. 'I don't think I know anybody looking like that,' I said, 'and I'm getting too old to make new friends. Thanks.'

'That's all right. If he comes round again, I'll let you know. It was only when he'd gone I thought he might be an old pal of yours from the army or something.'

I lifted my head. 'Turns out I never had any friends in the army,' I told him. He wasn't sure what to make of that, but he didn't say anything. We chatted about the vines for a little while, and then he went home.

I'd managed to play it cool while he was stood there, but I'm telling you, I was scared. There was nobody out of the past I ever wanted to see again – not now – and I didn't suppose he was a lawyer come to tell me my long-lost uncle in Corinth had died and left me a fortune. The only question was, what to do next. My instincts told me, clear out. Don't even bother going back to the house for a change of clothes, he might be there waiting. After all, I had shoes on my feet; it wouldn't have been the first time I'd set out on a long journey with my entire fortune invested in footwear. But I was feeling weary; tired from my journey, tired of pretty much everything.

I knew a bloke once, a great big fat guy, and he was in a field one time, and didn't realise till it was too late that the bull had got in there somehow. It charged him, and he started to run, but there was a hefty stone wall all round that field, too high for him to hop over, so he had to keep on running, with the bull after him, and he ran and he ran, until finally he was completely out of puff and his legs felt like octopus feet, all floppy and bendy. 'And so,' he told me, 'I said to myself, Bugger this, he'll just have to gore me.' So he stopped running, and the bull stopped too, and after they'd stood there looking at each other for a while, the bull wandered off and started feeding, and he strolled over to the gate and let himself out.

And why not? I said to myself. It can't be Amyntas, because I saw him dead with my own eyes. Don't suppose it's Strymon, because he's supposed to be dead too. Could be any one of about a million other people I'd pissed off rotten over the years, but then again, it might be something quite other; some layabout, maybe, looking for work and he'd got my name somewhere as an easy touch. Truth is, if I'd heard the news any other day apart from that one, maybe I'd have done something different. But that day, what with one thing and another, I couldn't be bothered.

I looked up at the sky. It was starting to get dark, and I figured that Ptolemy and Smicro must be finished by now, so it was probably safe to go back to the bunkhouse and get some sleep. So I walked home, taking my time. There was nobody about when I got there, so I kicked off my boots, lay down on my mattress and fell asleep.

I woke up because some bastard was prodding me in the ribs. I opened my eyes and saw it was my mother, of all people. And not far off sober, at that. 'All right,' I groaned, 'where's the bloody fire?'

'There's a man to see you,' she grunted. 'And don't use language like that, talking to your mother.'

I pulled on my boots and tramped over to the house. There, sitting behind my table, looking like he was the one who lived there and I was some tramp, was Tityrus, the helmsman from the grain freighter.

Well, yes, I thought, now you come to mention it, he's a big, mean-looking bloke with sandy hair. But I'd been sure he was dead. Still, I'd been known to be wrong about that sort of thing.

'Hello, Galen,' he said. 'You look like shit.'

I saw he had a bloody great big army dagger stuck through his belt; you notice weapons when you've been around like I have. But I'd never done him any harm that I could remember. 'Tityrus, for God's sake,' I said. 'I thought you'd drowned.'

He grinned. 'Came pretty close,' he said. 'I was swimming round for hours, round and round in circles. Saw a ship, but the buggers didn't see me. Thought I'd had it for sure, but bugger me if another ship didn't suddenly pop up out of nowhere, just as I was about to give it away. Took me to Acragas, and there I signed on with a crew headed for Alexandria, the long way round up the side of Italy, down the Thracian coast, in and out of every poxy little inlet. We're laying over three days in Piraeus, shore leave, and I was hanging round the market square wishing I hadn't spent all my pay when, fuck me, I saw you. In a right hurry, you were, on a horse; I ran, but I couldn't catch up with you, and then I remembered, Phyle, where you said you come from. So I took a chance and came up here, hitched a ride on a carrier's cart.' He shook his head. 'Don't know what you've done to piss off your neighbours, but nobody round here reckons they've ever heard of you, except this lady—' He nodded towards my mother, who was looking mustard down her nose at him.

'She's my mum,' I explained.

'Ah, right,' he said. 'Anyhow, it's good to see you. For a moment there I thought I'd seen a ghost, probably comes of drinking too much salt water.' He frowned. 'You've done all right for yourself, by the looks of it.'

When dealing with people from my past who show up out of the blue, I've always been guided by two rules. When in doubt, lie. When not in doubt, lie anyway. 'Nothing to do with me,' I said. 'When I got here, I found out my cousins had died. So now this place is mine, for what it's worth.'

I was half expecting my mother to jump in and tell him I was lying through my teeth, but at least she had the wit to keep her face shut; after all, it was her home too, and she was prepared to take it on trust that if I was telling fibs to my old mate here, I had my reasons. 'Well,' said Tityrus, 'that was a stroke of luck, I guess. But how did you get out of the wreck alive, for crying out loud? I was sure I was the only one.'

So I told him; most of it, anyway. I left out the floating coffin, made it sound like it was the first ship he saw that picked me up, and I didn't say anything about Scheria, either – I guessed he might not've been too thrilled to hear I'd given away all subsisting rights in Dido's treasure when his claim to it was every bit as good as mine. Which reminded me; I hadn't given it a thought since I'd been home. But I didn't really think Tityrus had flogged all the way out here just to chat about old times on the Acragas to Ostia run. I didn't mention Lucius Domitius, either. Apart from that, and my gold belt, I told it pretty well straight.

'Amazing,' he said when I'd done. 'And talk about your freak chances, me catching sight of you like that in the market. Like it's destiny, or something.' He looked at me. 'Fancy a stroll?' he said. 'You can show me round this spread of yours.'

I looked up at Mum, standing behind him, ears flapping like an elephant in a thunderstorm. 'Why not?' I said. 'And you're staying to dinner, aren't you?'

Mum made a sort of snorty-grunty noise, but I ignored her, and Tityrus and I went out together. Soon as we were clear of the house, where the women wouldn't hear us, he grabbed my arm and said, 'All right, Galen, what's the story? You didn't inherit this place, you bought it. Bloke at the inn told me you'd come home with money. Where'd you get it from?'

I sighed. 'Where'd you think?' I said. 'I nicked a little something from the treasure, while we were loading. I suppose you want your cut.'

He looked genuinely hurt. 'That's not a very nice thing to say. It's your good fortune, you enjoy it, mate. Besides.' He grinned, and reached inside his tunic, pulling out a big, chunky gold bracelet on a bit of string. 'You weren't the only one. Soon as I can fence this, I'll be just fine. Charter a ship, get a crew together, blokes I know in Sicily, they're all right; we'll go back, find that island, we'll all be rich as Caesar. No, reason why I came chasing out here after you is so you can join us. After all, it's your treasure as much as it's mine.'

No kidding, I was stunned, like you'd just bashed me on the head with a fencing mallet. He was telling the truth, no doubt about that; I can recognise lies, the way a fish recognises water. Here he was, this evil-looking thug with a dagger in his belt, and he'd searched me out just so he could give me a second chance at being unspeakably rich. I could've burst into tears on the spot.

'Well,' he said impatiently, 'what about it? Got to be worth giving it a go. It'd be mortal sin to leave all that stuff just lying there, where any old toerag could come along and find it. I was steering the ship, remember. I'm positive I can find the place again. What d'you say?'

I could hardly say a word. 'Tityrus,' I told him, 'for God's sake, don't go out there looking for that stuff, it'll kill you. Sell your bracelet and buy a farm, settle down, get a life for yourself. You saw what happened to Amyntas. Anybody you take with you, they'll cut your throat in a heartbeat. Take the hint, can't you? You and me, we got out alive. All the rest of them are dead.'

He looked hurt and bewildered. 'Don't be a prat, Galen,' he said. 'I'm not some shithead Roman, I know who I can trust and who I can't. And this time we know it's there, we know what's involved, we can make plans, get everything we need ready in advance. It'll just be a case of getting there, getting the stuff and we'll be free and clear. All our troubles will be over.'

I really wished he hadn't said that. 'Tityrus,' I said, 'it's a wonderful thing, you giving me this chance and all, you're all right, no doubt about it. But I'm not going. See, I'm free and clear already. All my troubles are over; and I really don't want to start them up again, just when they look like they've wandered off and decided to leave me alone. You find the treasure, and bloody good luck to you. You have my share. You deserve it, I don't.'

He looked at me for a long time, then shook his head. 'I don't get you,' he said. 'You ungrateful little shit. When I saw you today, I thought, this can't just be a fluke, this has got to be a sign, from the gods. And now you just stand there and spit in my face. What did I ever do to you to deserve that, Galen?'

Ungrateful little shit, I thought. Must be catching, or something. 'I told you,' I said, 'I don't want it. Don't want to be as rich as Caesar, it's a mug's game. You know what? All I ever wanted, as far back as I can remember, was to be a nice quiet little farmer, here in Phyle.' (Who's the farmer, Lucius Domitius' friend had asked him. Me, that's who. And that, looking back, was the moment when Ulysses must've come home.) 'Really and truly, I want you to find the treasure, get it away safely, have everything you ever wanted. Just like I've got,' I added. 'Right here.'

'Don't talk daft,' Tityrus said. 'Just look at this place, it's a dump. Just a rotten little farm like they give you when you've done twenty years in the army. And you've got a pisshead for a mother, and a wife who's not much better—'

'She's not my wife, actually,' I said. 'Just the maid.'

'Well, there you go. Man of your age, hasn't even got a wife. Before you know it, you'll be a shrivelled-up old man leaning on a hoe, like a million other dirt-scratchers. You can't want this. It's a dump. It's shit.'

'It's what I deserve,' I said. 'Actually, it's a whole lot more. I never deserved anything, except a cross and two busted knees. Can't you see, Tityrus? I'm home. I don't want to come out and play any more.'

He stared at me, or where he guessed I was in the darkness. 'Well, fuck you, then,' he said, and walked away. I called after him – don't be daft, come in and have some dinner, stay the night but he didn't answer. I could've run after him (like he ran after me) but I was afraid I'd trip over something and hurt myself.

I went inside.

'Where's your friend?' Mum asked.

'He had to go,' I said. 'Remembered something important in town.'

She looked at me like I was the place where the dog had just squatted. 'Oh for God's sake,' she said. 'I've just fried some fish, and there's chickpeas to go with it.'

I sighed. 'Enjoy,' I said. 'Don't worry, I'm not stopping.'

'That's all right, then,' she said. 'Blandinia, fetch out a fresh jar, it's just you and me for dinner.'

I went back to the bunkhouse. It was dark, the Syrians were asleep. I kept quiet, so as not to disturb them. I lay down and tried to go to sleep, but instead I just lay there, thinking about ungrateful little shits I'd known: both of us.

Next evening, on my way back from the fields, I ran into Demetrius again. He waved at me to stop, and hurried over.

'Guess what,' he said. 'That bloke, the one who was asking about you.'

'Oh yes,' I said. 'What about him?'

He grinned. 'He's only dead, that's what. Last night, Iphicrates and his boy fished him out of the creek down on their three-acre. What they're saying is, he must've been going back to town in the dark where the road's narrow, on the hillside there; slipped and fell, bashed his head on a stone on the way down, pitched in the creek, drowned.' He shook his head. 'Well, I told them, it's entirely possible it could've happened that way. Course, I didn't let on I'd ever seen the bloke, or that he'd been asking for you.' Then something seemed to strike him; he looked up at me sharply, then looked away. 'Anyhow,' he said, 'I thought I'd mention it. Just in case you hadn't heard.'

I said thank you, nicely as I could, and went home. Looking back, I realise now, Demetrius must've thought I'd killed the man, because he'd come looking for me and seemed like trouble. That's the thing about people, they're never happy with the obvious explanation; because of course it's possible, perfectly possible, more than likely. A man can drown in a little creek in Phyle just as easily as in the deep, dark African sea, when his ship founders in a storm and every soul aboard her is lost. A man can drown pretty well anywhere, it's just a matter of how he chooses to go about it, and what for.

Now I never studied philosophy. Best I can ever hope to be is an enthusiastic amateur. But there are times when I seem to visualise the great, all-spanning arch of Being as a big brown cow; and this cow wanders along through Time, munching bits out of the Past, digesting them in her double-chambered gut (which we call the Present) and finally shooting them out her rear end in the form of enormous, squidgy cowpats, which is to say the Future; and we blind mortals, straying haphazardly along life's path and seldom looking where we're going, will sooner or later put our boot right in the middle of one of these cowpats – namely our Past, transfigured into the shit we find ourselves in in the Future.

I guess Plato would've come at it from a different angle. But Plato, and the rest of that crowd, probably never had to put up with the kind of rubbish that I've always seemed to end up with, by way of a life. When you've lived like I had, with a fair proportion of your meals coming at you through a hatch in a cell door, it's not surprising if you find yourself trying to make sense of the workings of the cosmos in terms of huge steaming cowpats made up of all the really dumb things you did twelve months or five years earlier.

That's by the by. After my run-in with helmsman Tityrus, I made a real effort to watch my step along life's highway. As far as I was concerned, I never wanted anything to do with my past life ever again, or any part of it. The way I saw it, everything that had happened to me up to the moment when I scrambled into the floating coffin was all horrible garbage, and no good could possibly come from having anything to do with it. Here I was, Farmer Galen of Phyle, with everything a man could reasonably want, so long as I put the time in behind the plough and the shovel. I had a roof over my head, food to eat, clothes, somewhere dry to sleep. Anybody who wants more than that is like someone who tries to fish a honeycake out of the mouth of a crocodile; what you stand to gain is never worth the risk.

Which is a roundabout way of saying that when Lucius Domitius failed to get in touch with me, I didn't go looking for him. Screw him, I thought; he's got a new friend now, he seemed happy enough, and I sure as hell didn't need him. I mean to say, what good would he be, in my new life? The Syrians and me could handle all the work about the place, with a little help from hired men in the season, which I could well afford to pay for. He'd just be a complication, a nuisance, in the way and not needed on the voyage, as they say in the navy. He always did have this knack of attracting hassle, the way a magnet draws filings. Proof of that:

since we'd parted, when the ship went down, pretty well everything had gone right for me, or at least nothing had gone badly wrong. While we were together: ten long years of hardship, danger and filthy rotten luck, and bugger all to show for it. As time went by, I found myself starting to believe the tale I'd been telling ever since I got back, that I'd spent the last twenty-four years in the army. Might as well have done. After all, I did all the things people do in the army – sleeping rough, eating crappy food, wearing damp, raggedy clothes, constantly having people trying to kill you or capture you. The only part of the army experience I'd missed out on was killing other people; and if I'd done my time as a cook or a muleteer, I'd never have done any of that stuff anyway. And, of course, for ten of those twenty-four years I'd been principal bodyguard to my emperor, so my little white lie wasn't so far off the mark, at that. Anyhow, I thought, there's nobody who's going to contradict me, and it's nobody's business but my own.

So, best part of a year went by, and the seed I'd sown grew into barley, and the shoots I'd planted turned into vines, and my beans survived the dry season, and my olives didn't get the blight or the canker or the rot; and if my dear mother was still alive, well, you learn patience when you're a farmer. The flipside of that, of course, is that you start putting down roots of your own. You wake up each morning with a pretty fair idea of where you're going to sleep that night, and what you're going to eat. In other words, you lose your edge. Then, when a celestial cowpat pops up in your path, you aren't ready for it. Bummer.

I don't know why I was having dinner in the house that night, instead of over in the bunkhouse where I belonged. I seem to remember Blandinia was sick in bed with the guts ache, and Mum yelled at me across the yard to fetch her in some charcoal, and when I brought it she said she was all alone, and surely it wouldn't kill me to spend an evening with my old mother once in a while. So there I was, perched awkwardly on a stool while she sprawled on the couch, playing cottabus. (Don't know if you're familiar with the game. It's where you try and flick the dregs out of the bottom of your winecup so as to hit a specified target, like the vinegar jar or the fire dogs or the flute-girl's left nipple. My mum loved playing cottabus, goes without saying.) Time went on, and Mum got more and more plastered; to start with, it improved her aim, and then her shots began to get a bit wild, and then the handle came off her cup and it fell on the floor and smashed, and I had to go to the chest and get her out a new one. It was that sort of evening. Crazy fun.

'You know,' she was muttering – I was trying not to listen, but it was like when you're lying awake in the wee small hours, and however hard you try, you can't help but listen to the sound of the rain dripping in through the hole in the roof. 'You know, it's really nice having a quiet evening alone with my little boy. Really nice. God knows why it's got to be only once a bloody year. You'd think you hated me or something, and you don't, you're a good boy really, just fucking selfish, that's all. Rather sleep out in the bunkhouse with a couple of dirty wogs, instead of here with your own flesh and blood. Disgusting, I call that; but still, on the whole you're a good boy, and I forgive you.'

Gee, thanks, I thought. 'It's not as bad as all that,' I was dumb enough to say. 'I mean, you've got Blandinia for company.'

'That stinking little whore?' Mum spat, and knocked over the oil jar. She could spit straighter than a Persian shoots an arrow when she had a mind to. 'God only knows why I let her in the house, filthy bitch. Oh, I've seen her, smirking at me out of the corner of her eye, when she thought I wasn't looking, like she's saying, I know all about you, you old tart, you were no better than me in your day. I mean,' she snuffled, 'what kind of a son do you call yourself, letting a filthy whore look like that at your own mother?'

I shrugged. It was late, and I'd far rather have been mucking out the pigs. 'What does she know, anyhow?' I said.

'Oh, she knows,' Mum sighed. 'Because I told her. God only knows why. Subject came up, so I told her all about it. And now she's taken to coming on all superior, when she thinks my back's turned. Well, she's got no call, and that's the golden fucking truth. I mean, there's no comparison, none at all. She was just a halfpenny tart in a funhouse.' She straightened her back a little. 'Nothing like me. *I* was a Roman general's special mistress. There's a difference, you know. A difference. But can she see it? Can she hell as like.'

I really didn't want to hear this. 'Go on,' I said.

'Oh, that's all there is to it,' she said. 'Nothing to tell. Here, this jug's empty. Are you just going to sit there, or are you going to make yourself useful for a change?'

I got a fresh jar from the corner and broke off the gum. 'You're right, of course,' I said, casually as I could manage. 'Her trying to make out she's anything like what you were. Damned cheek, if you ask me.'

'That's *right*.' She banged the table with her fist. 'When I took up with Gnaeus Domitius, I was just fifteen, never been with a man, never been away from home before, and everybody said, I was as pretty as a picture. And wasn't he ever a splendid man, in his armour, sat on his big black horse. And so kind, such a gentleman, not like these fart-arse types that call themselves gentlemen these days. Oh, he had a temper—'

'Mum,' I tried to interrupt, but she wasn't listening.

'He had a temper,' she went on, 'he could be a vicious bastard when he'd a mind; but that's gentlemen for you, real gentlemen, they don't have to bow down and lick shit like ordinary folk. Never paid his debts if he could help; and there was one time, we were in Rome, this fat old knight came up to him in the market square whining for money, like some pissant little Greek. So he grabbed him by the scruff, stuck his thumb in the fat man's face and popped out his eye, just like podding a pea. Oh, he was a fine man, just like a great lion. I loved him, Galen, God's honest truth. I loved that man like I've never loved anybody before or since.'

'What did you say his name was?' I asked. 'Gnaeus something?'

She ignored me. 'Proudest day of my life,' she went on, 'when our son was born. It was just after his wife had their boy, little Lucius. He picked up our son and took him across the courtyard. I said to him, Where are you going? He said, I'm going to introduce our boy to his brother. Just like that. My little Callistus, and his own honest son; he didn't care, they were both the same, far as he was concerned, his boys. He loved me, you see, just like I loved him. And it was all my fault.'

I frowned. 'What was your fault?' I said.

'Oh.' She spat again, though there wasn't anything left to aim at. 'Your bloody father, that's what. God only knows how I could've been so stupid, when I had everything I could ever want: a man like that, and living in a fine house, like a princess. I was free and clear, no more troubles; and I had to go and fall for your stinking bastard father, who was just a servant; not even that, a dirty slave. When he found out, I was so ashamed; I really wish he'd killed me too, it was only what I deserved. But no, he said, he wasn't going to do that; for baby Callistus' sake, he said. You see?' She was crying, fat salt tears plopping into her drink. 'He saved my life, my darling little boy; and you fucked it all up, you and your dirty bastard father. Threw me out, that same day, me and Callistus – and you, of course, you weren't born yet but you were there inside me, like a bad splinter. If only he'd killed me too, my baby would've been all right; he'd have looked after him, brought him up decent, he'd have been a fine gentleman, like he deserved. But now he's dead – he's dead and *you're* alive, you little shit – and I'm here with you and that whore. What the hell kind of a life do you call that, then? What's the point of being alive, like that? Oh yes, sure, I brought it on myself, I deserved to come back here, with a fatherless kid, another on the way, and my dad yelling at me, calling me filthy names and making me scrape cowshit in the yard. But there was a time.' She emptied the winecup, and dropped it deliberately on the ground, where it broke. 'He loved me, and I loved him, and I threw it all away.'

'What was that name again?' I asked. 'Gnaeus . . .'

'Gnaeus Domitius.' She was staring straight ahead, like I wasn't there. 'Gnaeus Domitius Ahenobarbus, grandson of Mark Antony, father of Nero Caesar; Nero Caesar, my little boy's brother. He introduced them to each other, you know, the day Callistus was born. I wish I could've seen that. It must've been something to see.'

'Right,' I said. 'And my father,' I went on, 'the one Gnaeus Domitius killed. What was he called?'

'Him? Oh,' she sneered, 'he was just a Greek, or a Thracian, something like that. A slave, anyhow, answered to anything anybody cared to call him. Didn't deserve a name of his own. Gnaeus Domitius hit him so hard with his sword, he damn near cut him in half. Served him right, too. He was strong, my Gnaeus, like a bear.'

'Excuse me just a moment,' I said, getting up. 'I just want to nip out for a while and throw up.'

So I did that, and it made me feel a bit better, but not much. And all the while, at the back of my mind, a little voice was saying,

Well, that accounts for it, how come Callistus and Lucius Domitius looked so much alike, always knew there had to be a perfectly simple explanation. Probably my dad had a sharp, pointy nose, like a rat or a weasel. Marvellous thing, heredity.

When I went back inside she was fast asleep on the floor, where she'd slid off the couch. I looked down at her, and at the sharp shards of the winecup, and it crossed my mind that it might not be a bad idea to do what Gnaeus Domitius Ahenobarbus had neglected to do all those years ago, with a quick flick of the wrist, like podding a pea. (Gnaeus Domitius Ahenobarbus, Lucius Domitius' old man – what would he be to me, I wondered. Stepfather? Was there a term for it in heraldry? Bound to be, it's such a fussy science.) But I decided not to bother. Not the sort of thing I do, and besides, she wasn't worth getting lumbered with the Furies for. So I left her lying there in her muck, trudged back across the yard and went to bed.

Now you wouldn't have thought I'd be able to sleep, not after all that lot. But it'd been a long day, out in the hot sun, and I'd glugged down a certain amount of wine that evening, just to be sociable. So I fell asleep; and I dreamed that I was back in the Golden House, in the small courtyard with the five small pear trees, and I was sat on an ivory stool while Seneca explained to me, with the help of some complicated diagrams scratched in the dirt with his stick, how it all balanced out in the end: Mum and Gnaeus Domitius loved each other, but so did Lucius Domitius and Callistus. Gnaeus Domitius had killed my father, but I'd killed Callistus, to save Lucius Domitius. I'd loved Lucius Domitius but he'd left me for a flute-player, so it was quite right and mathematically necessary that I kill Lucius Domitius; which left my mother over, like the bit you carry when you divide and the first number doesn't go exactly. He tried to prove it for me with calculus, and he'd got as far as explaining why Lucius Domitius raping Blandinia when she was a little girl was the product of me and Gnaeus Domitius, minus Callistus, squared, when suddenly a giant cowpat dropped out of the sky and buried him completely, with only the tip of his ratlike nose showing. And then my mother called us all in for dinner, and I woke up.

TWENTY

Everybody, my old mother used to say, is good at something; and by and large, I'm inclined to believe she's right. For example, I once knew a bloke who was as thick as the plaster on an Italian cheese. Ask him what two plus two came to, and he'd stare at you helplessly; it was a miracle he ever learned how to talk, he was that dumb. But give him a chisel and a hammer and a saw, there wasn't hardly anything he couldn't do. Or take Lucius Domitius; generally a waste of space and provender, and a trial to everybody who ever knew him, but he could play the harp pretty well.

Or take me. The list of things I'm useless at goes on for ever, but though I say it myself as shouldn't, I'm quite a dab hand at ploughing. Shouldn't be, of course, I'm short and skinny and light, so I have to keep one foot on the shaft to keep the share in the dirt, which means I hop along on the other foot like a dainty little thrush pecking worms, but I can hold a straight line, and lay down the next furrow level with it, as well as any and better than most. I've had old-timers in Phyle come up to me and say my ploughing's pretty near as good as they could've done it when they were my age, and that's praise.

So, the morning after my visit with Mum, I yoked up the mules (did I mention I hate mules?) and set off to do the half-acre down the end of our lane. Funny little field, that. Far as I can gather, we've always owned it, right back to old Eupolis' time. It's surrounded on all sides by other people's land, so you've got to traipse round their headlands to get to it, and it's a long, long way from any of our other bits and pieces. But it gives back five to one even in a bad year, and once when we were kids my grandfather got eight to one out of it, God only knows how. It's a long, narrow terrace, with a steep old drop, so you've either got to waste a good quarter of it at the end, or else go at it fairly steady if you don't want to find yourself lying on your face under the plough, trespassing on the next terrace down.

But that was fine by me, because it meant I was going to have to concentrate like mad, a good thing when I didn't want there to be any danger of my mind wandering off and worrying away at what I'd learned the previous night, like a bad dog chasing hares.

So I ploughed all morning, taking each furrow right up to the edge, making sure they were all arrow-straight, doing the best job that I possibly could. Then, when I'd done, I took the plough and team home, fetched a hoe out from the barn, and went back to bust up the clods and generally get it ready for sowing. The Pleiades had set several days before, and I was behindhand as it was, what with stopping to get the olives in and press them before they started weeping.

As I may have told you before, clodbusting isn't my favourite occupation; and it didn't help that I'd taken on Smicro's hoe by mistake. Smicro's hands were much bigger and wider than mine, and I could hardly get my fingers to meet round the handle. As you'd expect, this made the job a whole lot more awkward, and pretty soon my wrists and forearms were starting to ache like buggery. A sensible bloke would have stopped, gone home and fetched his own hoe, but not me. I just stuck at it, as though for some reason I reckoned the pain served me right. Come nightfall, when I'd managed to get about a third of it done after some fashion or other, I decided I'd had enough for one day, and started off back to the house.

Halfway along the headland of my neighbour Aeschines' top two-acre, there used to be a funny little fig tree. I was tramping along past it when it suddenly called out my name in a sort of shouted whisper.

I'm not used to having trees talk to me in that tone of voice, so I stopped and looked back. 'Galen,' the tree repeated. 'Over here.' And who should walk out from behind it but Lucius Domitius.

Put yourself in my position, will you? Truth is, all the thoughts going through my head right then were just too complicated for me to handle. I hadn't got a clue where to begin, it was like trying to unravel a horribly tangled piece of rope. And what the hell was I supposed to say to him? On top of all that, I was still mightily pissed off with him for dumping me and going off with his new flute-playing chum, dropping me like I was something he'd been tracking round on the sole of his boot till at last he'd had a chance to stop and scrape me off. What with that, and the stuff Mum had told me, I think I did pretty well choosing my words. I said, 'Hello.'

'Shut up and listen,' he replied, looking over his shoulder. 'I don't know if I've been followed here; it's only a matter of time. Look, I need a place to hide, and you've got to find a ship that'll take me to Hibernia, soon as possible.'

I couldn't make head or tail of this. 'Hibernia?' I said. 'What the hell do you want to go there for?'

He scowled at me. 'Because it's the furthest country in the world,' he said, like it should've been painfully obvious, even to a dumbo like me. 'You going to help me, or what?'

'Slow down a moment, will you?' I said. 'Who's after you? What's going on?'

He scowled mustard at me. 'Have we got to have this conversation in the middle of a field?' he said. 'Why is it you can't do the simplest thing without arguing the toss first?'

'All right,' I said, 'fine. Follow me.'

He was a right pantomime, the way he ducked and crept along; I guess he was trying to keep out of sight or something, but all he achieved was to make himself as conspicuous as possible. If we'd happened to bump into one of my neighbours on the way back to my place, they'd have taken one look at him and gone straight home and told the family 'I saw our Galen walking along with this strange man who kept bobbing up and down,' and the story would've been all over Phyle by sunup.

'So,' I said, trying to ignore his idiotic behaviour, 'now can you tell me what's going on?'

'Trouble,' he said. 'Philocrates has been arrested.'

How terribly sad, I thought; oh well, never mind. 'You don't say. What's he been up to, then? Thieving tableware at one of your gigs?'

'Don't be ridiculous,' Lucius Domitius snapped at me. 'He

wouldn't do anything like that, he's an *artist*. No, I was supposed to meet him in the market square, but I was late; and when I got there, he wasn't there. So I asked a bloke I knew if he'd seen him, and he said yes, he'd been standing by the well minding his own business when two soldiers and a big, ugly man who looked like a gladiator had come up and grabbed him. Didn't say anything, just twisted his arms behind his back and hustled him away.'

I wasn't sure I liked the sound of that; not because I gave a damn about Philocrates, obviously. 'Any idea why?' I asked.

'Shut up and I'll tell you. Anyway, I went over to the prefecture; thought I'd try one of our old routines you know, the ones I used to get you out of stir when you got yourself arrested. God knows, I've had enough practice over the years. Thought I'd try the one where I'm the master and you were my good-for-nothing slave, always getting into trouble. So I went up to the lodge, asked if they had anyone answering his description, told him the tale; but they reckoned they hadn't seen or heard of anybody like that. Well, that meant it wasn't the regular law that'd taken him in, so it had to be something other than ordinary stealing or disorderly conduct. But of course, I hadn't got a clue where to start looking. So I wandered around the town for a while, trying to think of a plan of action; and then by pure fluke, I caught sight of someone.'

'All right,' I said. 'Who?'

He sighed. 'You remember when we were in Sicily,' he said, 'and we ran into the governor's entourage, and you made a damn fool of yourself when he started asking us questions?'

I wasn't sure I remembered it quite like that, but I didn't say anything. 'Yes,' I said.

'Well, do you remember his front outrider, the one who killed our mules? Him.'

Took a moment for that to sink in. 'Here?' I said, stupidly. 'In Athens?'

Lucius Domitius nodded vigorously. 'No doubt about it,' he said. 'I saw him straight on, no more than five paces away. Thank God he was talking to somebody and didn't see me. Or at any rate, I don't think he did. Anyhow, I made myself scarce as quick as I possibly could. Got out of town and came up here, asked a couple of old boys I met on the road where your place was; when I got there you weren't home, obviously, but there was a farmhand in the yard who told me where you were likely to be. Point is,' he went on, 'if I could track you down so easily, so can he. For all I know, his men are up at your place this very minute, waiting for us. I mean, it's no secret you and your brother came from here. Why else would the governor be looking for me here?'

I felt like someone had just punched me in the guts. 'So what do you reckon we should do?' I asked him.

He shrugged. 'Impossible to know what to do for the best,' he said. 'But here's my idea. You leave me in that little olive grove near the top of your lane, and go on down to the house, see if the coast's clear. If you don't come back straight away, I'll know there's trouble, and clear out. If not, you can hide me while you're finding a ship for me. Once I'm on my way, you sit tight and wait for them to come to you. They'll search the place, obviously, and question you, so you'll have to tell them something misleading, like, yes, I'd been there a day or so earlier, and I'd said something about going on to Corinth via Megara; anything to send them off on a false trail.' He thought for a moment. 'Best thing'd be to let them knock you about a bit first, so they think they've forced it out of you. That way, they'll be more likely to believe what you tell them.'

I nodded. 'I could provoke them into burning my barns and cutting down my vines,' I said. 'Maybe even break both my legs, or chop my right hand off.'

'Whatever,' he said. 'I'll leave the details to you. But everybody knows you're a born coward, so probably you wouldn't have to go that far. Just as long as it's believable. I reckon I'll need at least four days' clear start, so when they do find out which ship I'm on, they won't be able to cut across overland and catch me up. Oh, and I'll need money, of course, and a change of clothes, stuff like that.'

I looked at him. 'You could have the shirt off my back,' I said, 'only it wouldn't fit you.'

He just nodded. 'That farmhand of yours I saw,' he said, 'he looked to be about my size. Some of his stuff'll do me, I'm not fussy.'

'You bastard,' I said. 'You selfish, thoughtless arsehole.'

He hadn't been expecting that. 'Now what've I done?' he complained.

'Oh, for crying out loud,' I said. 'You turn up in town, practically back from the dead; and do you even want to know me? Do you hell as like. Oh no, it was, well, I might be able to spare a moment or so to look in on you somewhen, but right now I'm too fearfully busy with my new chum Philocrates, so go away. Did you hear what he said?' I added angrily. 'He called me a farmer. Who's the farmer, he said, and I was standing right there.'

Lucius Domitius looked surprised. 'But you are a farmer,' he said.

'That's not—' I had to make an effort to keep from yelling at him. 'That's not the point,' I said. 'The point is, you come here and you treat me like I'm a bad smell, and now you expect me to let myself get tortured by the Romans, just so you can escape. Well, fuck you, because I'm not going to do it. No way,' I added, in case there was any doubt.

He frowned. 'That's a stupid attitude,' he said. 'I mean, let's be realistic about it. They're going to find you and they're going to come here looking for me, whether you decide to help me or not. Probably they're going to beat you up a little, no matter what you say. After all, you're known right across the world as a habitual liar. They won't expect to get the truth out of you without a bit of persuasion.' He lifted his head. 'So, since it's going to happen anyway, you might just as well do me a good turn while you're at it. No, the only question in my mind is whether you're up to the job. But I've got to rely on you, because there isn't anybody else. I just hope you'll be able to pull it off, that's all.'

Well, what was I supposed to say to that? I sulked the rest of the way home. We stopped at the little olive grove, like he'd said, and I went on down the lane to my beautiful farm, feeling like I was walking out into the circus at Rome, with the lions roaring at me from behind the bars of their cages.

But it all seemed to be all right. No soldiers came rushing out to grab me. There weren't any horses tied up in the yard. Nobody about, in fact; which was how it should be. So I went over to the bunkhouse, where there was a light under the door.

Smicro and Ptolemy were there all right, fixing up dinner. Ever since I'd barged in on them at that rather bad moment I'd been a bit wary about going in the bunkhouse when I knew they were there, so I made a point of knocking three times and waiting a bit before pushing open the door. I asked them, had there been any strangers round, but they said no.

That sounded all right, but I reckoned I'd better be a bit more thorough than that; so I took a deep breath and went across to the main house. I'd far rather not have done; after all, last time I'd seen Mum, she'd told me a tale that had me puking my guts up out in the yard. But either she hadn't remembered anything about last night when she came to in the morning, or else she'd made up her mind to act like nothing had happened. Either way suited me. She wasn't precisely sober, of course, but she wasn't lying slumped on the floor singing the Harmodius either. Anyhow, she said there hadn't been any strangers at the farm that day. Also, she added (like I cared), Blandinia was feeling a bit better, but she still wasn't right.

Well, thank God for that, I said to myself as I shut the door behind me; what a tremendous weight off my mind, knowing Blandinia was on the mend. I trudged back up the lane and told Lucius Domitius it was safe to come out. He'd told me to whistle twice like an owl as the signal that the coast was clear, but really, I wasn't in the mood.

That just left me with what to do with him. Not the main house, obviously. Not the bunkhouse either, because the fewer people who saw him, the better. That left the barn, the stable or the pighouse. I decided on the pighouse; out of spite, mostly. Then I went back to the bunkhouse and had some soup and bread with the lads. Pretty good it was, too; and it crossed my mind that really I ought to take some out to Lucius Domitius. But that would have meant thinking of an explanation for Smicro and Ptolemy, and I was all thought out for one day.

Next morning, though, I woke up early (hadn't got much sleep, in fact, what with one thing and another), which meant I was able to nip out with the crust end of the loaf and a jug of water from the trough in the yard before those two were awake. Lucius Domitius was fast asleep, snuggled up in some dried-up bean helm like a baby kitten. I woke him up with my boot and said, 'Breakfast.'

He was obviously hungry, because he hardly bitched at all about the bread being stale or the water being a funny colour. He actually thanked me, which sounded pretty strange.

'Don't mention it,' I said awkwardly. 'Look, about finding you a ship. It's not going to be easy, if you insist on going to Hibernia. It's not what you'd call one of your regular destinations.'

He nodded. 'I was thinking that, too,' he said. 'Even if there are any, it could be months. So what I thought was, if you could find me one that's going to Massilia – that shouldn't be hard – I can either look around for another ship there, or I can go across Gaul overland and get over to Britain from there. Actually,' he went on, 'it doesn't really matter where I go, so long as it's far away. See what's in dock at Piraeus and use your own judgement.'

Coming from Lucius Domitius, that was next best thing to an apology. I was almost touched. 'Sure,' I said. 'I'll ride into town today and see to it.'

'Thanks.' There was an awkward silence; but it seemed like it was more awkward for him than for me, so I let it carry on. Finally, he swallowed a deep breath and said, 'Just getting away, that's all. Not too much to ask, is it?'

I thought about that. 'No,' I said, 'not really.'

He shook his head. 'I really thought,' he said, 'after I'd survived the shipwreck, being the only one left alive – well, I didn't know about you then, of course – I really managed to kid myself into thinking that maybe the gods had saved me for some purpose, like they were stopping the game and letting me go. I honestly thought I was free and clear.'

'All your troubles would be over?'

'Something like that. And now here I am, about to set off for the ends of the earth. Funny, isn't it?'

'Hilarious,' I replied. 'Want me to come with you?'

Don't know which of us was the more shocked at that, him or me. I'm betting it was me. I hadn't meant to say it, but once it was past the gate of my teeth, I knew I meant it. And that really shook me.

'What, you mean leave here and come with me to Hibernia?'

'Yes. Or wherever it is you end up going?'

He looked at me. 'Why?' he said.

I could've hit him. 'Well,' I said, 'I thought maybe you'd like some company. I don't know, do I?'

'But you seem like you're happy here. Settled. Doing what you always wanted to do, and so on.'

I nodded. 'That's right,' I said, 'I am.'

'Then why in God's name would you want to throw all that away to go traipsing off to some godawful place you've never even heard of?'

'Because—' Oh hell, I thought, I'm buggered if I'm going to say it. 'So you don't want me along, then?'

'It's not that,' he said, a shade too quickly. 'But what'd be the point?'

No point at all, I thought, so I decided to lie. God forgive me, I can be really pathetic when I set my mind to it. 'Listen,' I said. 'This is where I was born, I grew up here. Fine. I can't think of any place on earth I'd rather be. When the – when the captain of the ship that picked me up asked me where I wanted to go, anywhere in the whole wide world, I told him here. And now, here I am. I sleep in the bunkhouse with two Syrian farmhands because I daren't go in the main house because I can't stand being in the same building as my pisshead mother for longer than it'd take to pit an olive. I start work at sunup, flog my guts out, fall asleep at sundown. I guess I wasn't cut out for this life after all.'

He looked at me. 'I see,' he said. 'You see, that's where you and I are so different. All my life, the one thing I wanted was to play music; didn't matter where or who to, didn't even matter if there was anybody listening. And all my life, that was the one thing I couldn't do – not back in the Golden House, because it wasn't allowed, not when we were on the road, for fear of being recognised – until, as I thought, suddenly the gods changed their minds and they staged my death for me, so that everybody in the world would be sure I'd died. After that, I was so positive about it, I *knew* it was all clear from now on: I was in Athens, the best place in the world for a poet and musician, and I was earning a living – an honest living, damn it – just playing music, with a friend who loved music as much as I did, someone I could talk to, about poetry and art and all the things that matter to me. It felt so right, if you see what I mean. And the thought of going back – you and me on the road again, lying and cheating and staying one jump ahead of the law if we're really lucky – damn it, Galen, I'd rather be dead than go back to that. It wasn't life, it was a really spiteful punishment for all the things I did in the old days. King Pluto himself couldn't have dreamed up anything nastier. No, I'm going alone; and as for you, for God's sake try and make the most of this chance you've been given, to be what you were always meant to be. So it's not perfect. Life's not like that. For crying out loud, Galen, you don't know how lucky you are. You know what? I'm jealous of you. Really, I am, if you can believe that. You've come home. It's as if you'd gone to sleep when you were sixteen and woken up twenty-four years later, got up and gone to work same as usual. You're so fucking lucky it isn't true.'

I stood up. 'Fine,' I said. 'I'll go into town and get you on a ship. And then I'll never see you again, and you'll never see me again.' I looked away. 'I expect you're right,' I went on. 'It'll be best for both of us.'

'I think so,' he said. 'After all, ten years on the road, and can you remember one single good time? I can't. Look at it this way. Callistus died so we could both have a life. If we don't take our chances now, recognise exactly what it is we're meant to be doing and stick to that and never let go, then we're wasting his death, he'll have died for nothing.' He sighed. 'You know something?' he said. 'When I thought you'd drowned, to begin with I was really upset . . .'

Upset, I thought. Well, there you go. Almost as bad as missing a boat, or losing your pet rabbit.

'But then,' he went on, 'I thought about it for a bit, and I had to face up to it. You and me, we were never any good for each other. Both of us, we were holding each other back, like two men in the water, each trying to save the other, so we both drowned. When I realised I was on my own at last – I know, this sounds really terrible, but you know I don't mean it like that – suddenly I felt like a slave who's just been given his freedom in his master's will. I was sad, of course, and grateful too, in a sense; but mostly it felt like this terrible weight had gone from round my ankle, and I could swim up to the surface and breathe at last. I expect you felt the same way, didn't you?'

I turned back and looked at him. 'I'll tell you the truth,' I said. 'I was more worried about saving my own skin. I didn't think about you till much later.'

'Well,' he said, 'there you go, then. I mean, we're friends – I guess we're that, after everything we've been through; sort of like army buddies, if you like. We never had anything in common, apart from the dangers we faced and the horrible shittiness of our life, and the people we'd shared and lost. But that's all; comrades, allies in a common cause, it served each of our interests to stay together for as long as it took for us both to get free and clear. That's all. We don't belong together, you and me; it's not like we're lovers, or brothers. Now the common purpose has been fulfilled, it's to our mutual advantage to go our separate ways. You do see that, don't you?'

'Yes,' I said.

'I thought so. I mean, it stands to reason, really. And I want you to know, it was sort of nice of you to say you'd come with me, even though I know you don't really want to, because you thought I needed you or something. I guess you were thinking it was what Callistus would've wanted. But it isn't, I promise you. He'd have wanted the two people he most cared about to find their proper place and stay there. Don't you agree?'

'Sure,' I said.

'That's all right, then.' He grinned. 'You know what? I was worried you didn't see it that way. Only goes to show, you think you know someone really well, but when it comes to the point, you find out you don't know them at all. I'd got it in my head that somehow I'd got this duty to look after you – because of Callistus, I mean; that somehow I'd have to take his place, be a brother to you because I'd cost you your real brother. But that's silly, isn't it?'

'Very silly,' I said. 'It's like you just said. Army buddies, puts it exactly. I mean, it's always the way, isn't it? They demob and go their separate ways, swearing blind they'll always stay in touch. And then, two or five years down the line, either they've forgotten the other bloke completely, or they meet up and find they've got nothing to say to each other, because they never had anything in common. And that's dumb, really.'

He nodded. 'Let's just pretend we've been ten years in the army together, and leave it like that.' He peered up through the corner of the doorframe. 'I don't want to rush you, but if you're figuring on getting into town, finding me a ship and getting back before dark, you ought to be on your way.'

'You're right,' I said.

So I got the horse saddled up and set off for town; and along the way, what I was mostly thinking was, well, at least I'm not having to walk. Things can always be worse than they are, even if it's only by a little bit. I couldn't remember who used to say that when I was a kid. My old mother, probably. It sounded like one of hers.

Finding a ship proved to be much easier than I'd thought. Fourth ship I tried, in fact; turned out they were headed for the Black Sea – Tanais, in the territory of the Roxolani, wherever-in-hell that might be. The bloke on the ship said it was a fairly desperate place – scorching hot in summer, bollock-numbing cold in winter, no scenery to speak of apart from endless rolling fields of wheat, and the savages – well, savage, and that was if you caught them on a good day. I replied that it sounded like just the sort of place my friend was looking for, and paid him fifty drachmas.

Since I'd finished earlier than I'd planned, I had time to nip round the market stalls and pick up a few things. Two pairs of boots, for instance; three tunics, two heavy winter cloaks, a belt, a goatskin satchel, a wide-brimmed leather hat; I even bought a sword off a second-hand stall (well, it was cheap, and you never know). Then I went to my bank and drew out two hundred sesterces. I'm soft-hearted, but not as soft-hearted as all that.

Then home again, back up the hill, with the purse of money clinking on my belt, the sword stuck between my knee and the horse blanket, and the do-it-all explorer's survival kit slung over my shoulder in the satchel. All told, I'd blown close on three hundred sesterces, none of which I'd ever see again. Still, I could afford it, and there was an argument for saying it'd have been cheap at twice the price.

It was as dark as twenty foot down a well by the time I reached Phyle; just as well I grew up there and knew the way. I rode into the yard, led the horse into the stable and tied him up; dumped all the stuff I'd bought for Lucius Domitius there, too, since there was no point taking it with me into the bunkhouse, I'd only have Smicro and Ptolemy asking what I wanted with all that gear. First things first, I thought; something to eat and a good stiff drink, and then I'd go back out, see to the horse, take Lucius Domitius his stuff and tell him about the ship. For that I'd need a lamp, if only because I wanted to see his face when I told him about Tanais and the savage Roxolani. Not that I'm a nasty person or anything, but I reckoned I'd earned that small pleasure.

I opened the bunkhouse door and walked in. Someone else closed it behind me.

There were five of them. Two I recognised. One was the Sicilian governor's outrider, the man who'd killed our mules. The other was the governor himself. The remaining three I hadn't ever seen before; though if I'd ever been into watching gladiator shows, I might've seen them in the arena at some stage. No mistaking their type. It's the shiny white scars and the enormous shoulders that give them away, every time.

Also present were my two Syrians – they were hanging by their thumbs from a rope slung up over the rafters; Mum, looking sober and as white as fresh cheese, tied up and sat on a low stool; and Blandinia, leaning against the wall with a smug expression on her face. No sign of Lucius Domitius; apart from him, everybody present and correct.

Absolutely no chance of me getting to the door; one of the gladiators had moved across and stood with his back to it, arms folded across his chest, looking professionally mean. No point in me saying anything; so I stood and waited to see what'd happen next.

The governor got up; he'd been perched on the rim of the big oil jar, like a huge mutant butterfly. 'Galen, isn't it?' he said. 'I was sure I knew you from somewhere.'

I nodded.

'Very well,' he said. 'So that's one of you, now we just need the other one.'

I acted dumb. I've had the practice, after all. 'Who do you mean?' I said.

He laughed. 'Well,' he said, 'it's Nero Caesar I'm really after, but I'll settle for your brother Callistus, if you prefer. Either will do. After all, what's in a name?'

At this point, Mum burst into tears and started screeching – least she could do in the circumstances, all things considered – until one of the gladiators whacked her across the face. It shut her up so quickly, I wish I'd thought of it myself. The pet cavalryman grabbed my right arm and cramped it up behind my back. In case you don't know, that hurts. 'Please,' I squealed, 'I don't know what you're talking about.'

I've said some dumb things in my time, but not many dumber than that. For a moment I thought the cavalry bloke was going to break my elbow joint — that was scary, because those things never heal right, and I'm a farmer, I need my arms in good working order. But he stopped just short, gauging it nicely from long practice. That was me told.

'All right,' I said, 'I'm sorry.'

Blandinia laughed; fine hero you turned out to be, she seemed to be saying. But there's no heroism in having your arm broken, because any bloody fool can do that, even a coward like me. The heroic stuff lies in finding a way of not getting your arm busted. So I ignored her, and said, 'He's in the stables.'

The governor nodded. 'Fine,' he said. 'You two,' he added, nodding to a couple of his men, 'go and fetch him. We'll kill them both here, I want to watch.'

Well, he would do. Great watchers, your Roman senators; that's why they built all those huge theatres and stadiums and arenas and racetracks, as a monument to the rich bastard's taste for sitting on his bum under a sunscreen while a load of other poor buggers feel the pain. Of course he'd want to watch, to experience the moment and savour it, roll it round his tongue like a good vintage (fetched to him at his table in his villa from some faraway place). For my part, I was thinking, this is no good. I'll be slaughtered like a chicken in my own house while the senator watches; and then he'll go home, maybe stop at an inn on the way back to Athens, grouse about the food and the bedlinen, get on his specially chartered ship and sail home, carry on with his life; and I'll won't be there any more. Everything about me will be over, all gone, just because I got into the wrong place at the wrong time, and strong men held me down so there was nothing I could do to stop it. Bugger that, I thought. After all, only a complete loser goes quietly.

'Hold on,' I said.

They were fools to listen to me, but they did. 'Well?' said the governor, and everybody held still.

I was frantically trying to remember the layout of the stables, inch by inch. 'He's a slippery customer,' I said, 'those two clowns'll never catch him on their own. He'll get out the back way or through the hayloft in the dark. If he hears someone coming, I mean.'

The governor looked at me. 'Well?' he repeated.

'Whereas,' I went on, 'if I go into the stables and call out to him, he'll come out, won't suspect a thing; and then you can grab him. Provided you let me go, of course.'

The governor thought for a moment; balancing potential gains and losses, a hard-headed business decision. 'No,' he said, 'I can't do that. But I'll tell you what I will do. If you make sure I get Nero Caesar, I won't kill your mother. How's that for a deal?'

He thought he was being clever. Very good. 'But you can't do that,' I said. 'I mean, she's got nothing to do with this, there's no call to kill her.'

He nodded. 'I'm inclined to agree,' he said. 'So on balance I'd rather not, which is why I hope you'll take me up on my offer. Otherwise—' He shrugged. 'I'm not really bothered either way,' he said. 'It's up to you, really.'

'All right,' I said quickly. 'We'll do it like I said, and you'll let her go. But I'll need you to place your men where I tell you to; otherwise, there's always a risk he'll get away after all.'

He thought again, then nodded. 'But Calpurnianus here,' (the pet cavalryman, presumably), 'he'll be standing behind you with his knife across your mother's throat. Agreed?'

'Sure,' I said.

'Fine. Then let's all go. You can't imagine how much I've looked forward to seeing this.'

Where he'd made his mistake, of course, was in bringing so few men. Arrogance, you see. I was finding it bloody hard work just breathing, in no fit state to do anything straightforward, let alone complicated and delicate. But what the hell; treat it like just another condemned cell, I told myself. It'll be all right.

I arranged the gladiators round the stables, making sure they were quiet, so there wouldn't be any noise to startle Lucius Domitius. Blandinia had come too, which was handy. It pays to be tidy when you're doing precise work. I took a lamp and slowly pushed open the stable door.

'Lucius Domitius,' I called out. 'It's all right, it's only me.'

Now if you're as smart as I'm giving you credit for, you'll remember that Lucius Domitius wasn't in the stables at all, he was in the pighouse. I hadn't forgotten that, if that's what you're thinking. On the contrary, I knew exactly what was in the stables and (I sincerely hoped) exactly where; otherwise, there simply wouldn't be time, I'd come up three or four heartbeats short and the whole thing would be a washout. If only I'd known earlier, I'd have paid more attention, got everything ready. That way, the nice new double-tined hoe I'd sharpened the day before would've been placed just handy, next to the big pile of fresh straw and bean helm.

'Lucius Domitius?' I called out, taking a couple of steps further into the stable. 'It's all right, I'm on my own. I got a passage for you, on a ship.'

There was a gladiator right behind me; also the cavalry bloke, with my mum. As I'd hoped, they hung back in the doorway so they wouldn't be seen. That gave me five paces, which is two heartbeats' worth of time before they could figure out what I was up to and get up close enough to stop me. If the hoe and the straw were six paces from the door, I was fucked. It all depended on my memory: my life, Lucius Domitius', the whole cockfight. Wonderful odds.

I took another slow step, then my five planned quick ones. As my right hand reached out for the hoe (gods be praised, it was actually there), my left hand threw the lamp onto the stack of bean-helm. As all that dry stuff was taking fire – you want to watch that stuff, by the way, it'll burn like lamp oil if you're not careful – I was twisting round on the spot, swinging the hoe round my head and bringing it down on the place where (if I'd figured it all out right) the head of the gladiator ought to be. No time to look, you see, it all had to be done by blind reckoning.

I screwed up. Fortunately, though, not by much. Instead of smashing the gladiator's head like an egg, I caught him smack on the right forearm, sinking both tines in until the bridge got stopped on the bone. I hadn't realised I could hit so hard; but maybe I'd forgotten, I was a farmer now, not just some skinny little Greek thief, and I'd put enough hours in with the ponderous hoe, God knows.

Anyhow; the gladiator opened his mouth, but no sound came out. As I twisted the hoe to free the tines, he screamed; out of the corner of my eye I caught sight of the cavalryman slicing through Mum's neck, but I'd allowed for that in my calculations, so that was all right. After all, I knew from the start that I wasn't going to get out of this free and clear, and rather her than me. I was already at least three heartbeats behind schedule; soon as I felt the hoe was free in my hands, I swung again, and mercifully the gladiator was so shocked with pain he held still to be hit. I got him just above the left eye with the right hoe-tine, and he went down like a stack of apples you've barged into because you weren't looking where you were going.

Fine, I thought, now I've committed murder; still, there you go. The cavalryman had dropped Mum and his knife, he was fumbling for his sword, but he'd got the pommel stuck under the crossbelt. The last thing he'd been expecting was to have to fight me – after all, I'm just a rat-faced little Greek – and he wasn't ready. He made the wrong choice, kept on trying to free his sword instead of using his feet to get out of the way. Sloppy. I killed him and let him drop, didn't have time to watch him fall. For one thing, I had a lot of work to get through in a short space of time. For another, the stable was on fire, and I didn't want to stay in there any longer than I could help.

I heard the horse screaming (another anticipated loss; omelettes and eggs, as they say in Rome) as I pushed through the doorway into the open air. I reckoned I had maybe four heartbeats to kill the governor before the gladiators I'd so carefully placed all round the building arrived to stop me – and that was allowing for them being thrown off kilter by the fire; I'd deliberately torched my own stable just to buy myself another heartbeat.

But he wasn't there – the governor, I mean. Either he'd heard the gladiator yelling or smelt the smoke, or I'd made a mistake in my mental geometry, or he was just being awkward. Anyhow, no governor where I'd been expecting him to be, just Blandinia, her eyes wide as fruit plates. I considered killing her, but decided there wasn't time (balancing potential gains and losses, a hard-headed business decision) and left her stood there while I hared off, looking for the governor.

I nearly missed him, at that. He was smart enough to try hiding in the deep shadows around the corner of the barn wall. But he screwed up, too; the blade of his sword made a tiny scritching noise as it dragged over the chape of its scabbard, and that's something I've heard quite a few times in circumstances that mean it's a sound I recognise immediately. I swung round and brought the hoe down hard and hit something solid enough to jar my elbows painfully, but not as solid as a wall; also, the tines were stuck in something, and I had to waggle the hoe about frantically to get them free. The governor answered the question of whether he was alive or dead by falling across me and knocking me off my feet. By the time I'd scrambled out from under him, I knew he was well out of it.

And that was as far as I'd planned; never expected to get there, if the truth be told. I'd expected I'd be dead quite some time ago, the last thought crossing my mind as I died being, Well, it seemed like a good idea at the time. But there I still was, alive and in the game, and my mind had just gone a complete blank. Bugger, I thought; now what?

Well, three dead, three from five makes two (and I managed to figure it out without counting on my fingers). I'd just finished when I saw the two remaining gladiators, nicely backlit by the blazing stable. They didn't see me, of course, in the shadows. I had a brainwave.

'Over here,' I called out, in Latin.

They turned their heads like trained dogs hearing a whistle, and headed towards me, arms by their sides. 'What the bloody hell's going on?' I shouted, also in Latin, while I did my best to gauge distance in the dark. 'Don't tell me, you let him get away.'

'We thought we heard—' the first one said; and I found out my estimate was close enough for government work, as they say in the dockyards. His mate was going to be the problem, since I'd just given away all my advantages – surprise, darkness, shadow, position – and I had to face the grim fact that it was likely to be a fair fight. Well, I'd managed to go one better than I'd dared hope, so it wasn't bad going for a country boy. I swished at him with the hoe, and he hopped back, neat as a cat. Then, quite unexpectedly, he floundered wildly, lost his footing and sat down hard on his bum, just nicely so I could spike him through the top of his skull with both tines. Turned out he'd slipped in a cowpat, of all things.

A little voice in the back of my head said, It's over, but I didn't believe it. Couldn't be over; I couldn't have made it, couldn't have *won*. I stood there panting like a dog, trying to pull all the threads together in my mind, only all I could think about was that bloody stupid old story, Ulysses single-handedly slaughtering his enemies all together in his house, the day he came home. What that had to do with anything I had no idea; but you know how it is when you're all overwrought, your mind gets full of the damnedest things.

And then there was someone behind me, and I said to myself, there, I knew it wasn't over. So I wheeled round – getting to be second nature by then, of course – and had the presence of mind to move my feet to give myself room before striking down with the hoe. I made it a good one, too, every last ounce of bodyweight behind it. Felt like when you sink your hoe into a thick seam of fat, sticky clay.

Whoever it was slid off the tines and went thump. I took a step back to catch my breath, while I checked my mental arithmetic. Five enemies; two in the barn, plus the governor, plus two in the yard here just now, makes five. Mum was dead, I'd seen her blood spurting out of her neck, so who the hell did that leave over?

Blandinia, I thought; and then, oh well, never mind. She'd been marginal in my calculations, and I'd only spared her the first time because I'd been on a schedule. I swung the hoe up on my shoulder and walked slowly over to the barn steps, and sat down. The hoe felt heavier and more ponderous than ever before, but I wasn't letting go of it, not for Dido's treasure. And let that be a lesson to you, by the way, never to piss off a farmer.

So there I was; and I was thinking, All I need to do now is collect up all these bodies, load them in the cart, take them a long way up onto the mountain and dump them, over the side of a canyon or off a cliff; sure, some nosy bastard will find them sooner or later, and it won't be long before someone else starts wondering whatever became of the governor of Sicily. But who the hell would ever associate me (blameless ex-soldier, hard-working respectable farmer) with the death of a noble senator? Also, who in their right mind would ever believe I could've killed a cavalry officer and three gladiators, all on my ownsome? I'd have to make out that Mum and Blandinia had died of some nasty disease, and we'd had to burn them fast to stop it spreading, hence no public funeral; but Smicro and Ptolemy would back me up on that, what are friends for? Oh sure, I wasn't free and clear quite yet, but all it'd take would be a little care and discretion, and all my troubles would be over.

And then someone moved in front of me. I looked up, and it was Blandinia.

'Did you get— oh.' She stopped dead still. Stupid bitch had taken me for one of the gladiators.

I grinned at her mistake; and then I realised, something wasn't right, suddenly the books didn't balance any more. But first things first; I jumped up and went after her, and I caught up with her after six paces. First, though, I pushed her to the ground and put my boot on her neck.

'You told him, didn't you?' I said.

'The governor? Yes,' she answered. 'I wrote him a letter, sent it by the carrier's cart to Athens. He promised me a reward, money and freedom. But I didn't do it for that.'

'I'll bet,' I said, and I held her head steady with my boot as I swung the hoe. And that really was murder, and I couldn't give a damn.

As I straightened my back, I was figuring again. Maybe there'd been a sixth man; quite likely. Someone they'd left outside as a guard, or just to hold the horses. At any rate, I probably ought to find out. So I went back to the barn and looked for the body. Couldn't find it, of course, in the dark; so I went over to the corner, found the senator and the two gladiators, then retraced my steps from there. Found it that way, eventually, and dragged it over into the light of the burning stable, where I could see.

It was Lucius Domitius.

TWENTY-ONE

So there I was, stood in the middle of my yard. Dead people all over the place. My stable burnt to the ground, with my horse in it. Just lucky I'd turned the donkey and the mules out onto the bolted vetch to graze a day or so earlier, or they'd have been roasted too. Well, you've got to look on the bright side.

Could have been worse. The barn and pighouse could've caught fire too, and quite possibly the house, with all those sparks and hot embers flying about. The governor and his men could've trampled my vines and slaughtered my poultry, out of spite. I could've been killed. In fact, it was nothing short of a miracle that I'd survived, considering what I'd done – odds of four to one, not counting the governor, and them all trained fighting men. If I hadn't done what I did, we'd all have been dead anyhow. Looked at that way, it was like saving one piece of furniture out of a burning house, or one jewelled gold belt from a lost hoard of buried treasure; everything you get away with is pure profit.

Well. You can see why I never managed to make my fortune telling the tale. My old mother used to say, how can you fool other people if you can't fool yourself?

I went back inside the house. Smicro and Ptolemy were still where I'd left them, hanging by their thumbs from a rafter. Poor buggers. Weren't they ever surprised to see me? They were sure I'd been killed, along with everybody else. I cut them down and they flopped on the deck looking miserable and scared, hugging their wrecked hands under their armpits like cold children.

'It's all right,' I told them, 'they're dead, the Roman and the gladiators.'

Smicro stared at me like I was crazy. 'What happened?' he said.

'I killed them,' I answered. Couldn't be bothered with long explanations just then. 'Mum's dead, though, and Blandinia, and my friend. How are you feeling?'

'All right,' Ptolemy replied. 'My hands hurt.'

I nodded. 'Look,' I said, 'we've got work to do, and we can't afford to waste time. I know you're hurting, but I need you two to help. We've got to get rid of the bodies, or we'll all be in the shit. It won't take long,' I lied, 'and then I'll set you two free. Is that a deal?'

They looked at each other. 'All right,' Smicro said. 'What needs doing?'

So I told them what to do. While they hunted round for the bodies in the dark, I went out and caught up the mules (contrary bloody animals; did I tell you I've never had much luck with them?) and backed them into the shafts of the farm cart. Then we loaded up. A real performance, that was. I was completely knackered by that stage, only keeping going because I knew I had to. Smicro and Ptolemy couldn't use their hands at all, and their arms and shoulders weren't a hell of a lot of use, so lifting the bodies up on to the cart was a right old pantomime. We managed it, though, in the end, even if it took us the rest of the night; the light was just starting to seep through when I goaded up the mules and we set off for the mountains; me up on the box with all the dead people in back, Smicro and Ptolemy walking along beside the wheels.

A man in a cart and his two slaves on the road in the early morning; most natural thing in the world. Walk down any road in Attica and you'll see something similar, a farmer off to market with a load of olives or corn or wine or pigs, live and dead stock. So nobody took any notice. You hear in stories about the heroes with their helmets and cloaks of invisibility, magical gifts from the gods, but who needs stuff like that? There's nothing on earth as invisible as an ordinary bloke going about his business; nobody sees you, nobody cares. Makes you wonder why the heroes bother with all that enchanted hardware, when all they really need to do is stick a bashed-up old leather hat on their head and slouch down on the box of a ratty old two-wheeler behind two thin mules. I guess the kit doesn't really matter, so long as the job gets done – like, for instance, who needs a gold-hilted blue-steel magic sword forged by Vulcan himself when you can smash someone's head in with a plain old hoe?

The going gets rough north-west of Phyle, as you head towards Boeotia. It's useless country, only fit for sheep and skinny goats to wander about on. The roads, if you can call them that, wind round the sides of mountains that fall away sheer into canyons and goyles, and it doesn't take much for a cart to go tumbling over the side and get scrunched into splinters on the rocks before it reaches the bottom.

Or so you'd have thought. Don't you believe it. We picked a likely spot, where a fat lump of road had crumbled away, with a sickening drop below. I stopped the cart and jumped down, and we tried to get it to go over. Could we manage it? Could we hell as like, mostly because of those miserable, ignorant bloody mules. Never had any luck with them. Soon as they figured out we were trying to edge them off the road, they started backing and stalling, making a hell of a racket and refusing to budge an inch. Smicro and Ptolemy weren't a lot of good, not being able to use their hands. All they could do was kick and swear, while I got on the inside and tried to nudge the wretched animals sideways. Eventually, after what seemed like for ever, we contrived to get one wheel of the cart over the edge. Then I fetched a long bit of branch, and with all three of us heaving on one end, we managed to lever the cart sideways bit by bit, till suddenly it started to go. The mules got stroppy and tried to pull it back onto the road, but the weight was more than they could handle; it pulled them backwards off the crumbling path, very slowly and gradually, until at last they were dragged off their feet and sent tumbling down the mountainside in a flurry of broken limbs. We watched them all the way to the bottom, as the cart broke up, scattering bits of timber and wheel, dead people and dying animals, all eventually coming to rest among the rocks and scrubby rubbish of the canyon floor.

'Well,' I said, 'that's that done. Let's go home.'

On the way back, I explained, best as I could. I told them about how I'd figured my best chance was surprise, in the dark; how I got the other two gladiators out of the way by posting them round the back of the stable; how setting fire to it bought me the precious extra moments I needed; how I had the wit to call out in Latin, so the last two gladiators thought I was the senator. I told them the cavalryman had killed Mum, and I'd killed Blandinia for selling me out (though I didn't give any reason why the senator should want to harm me, a respectable ex-soldier with twenty-four years' blameless service). I didn't say anything about Lucius Domitius. It'd have complicated the story, and I've always found it's best to keep it simple when you're telling the tale.

I was dead on my feet by the time we got home, but there wasn't any time to rest. We had the yard to clear up. There was stuff all over the place that shouldn't have been there; swords and hats and boots to be gathered up and buried deep in the shitheap, the governor's sedan chair to be smashed up into firewood (fuck, I thought; we could just as easily have pitched that bloody thing off the cliff, and in fact it'd have been more convincing, a senator and his escort travelling in a chair rather than a peasant's cart; and then I wouldn't have had to waste a perfectly good wagon and two expensive mules), a funeral pyre to be built and lit for Mum and Blandinia – at least we were able to use the busted-up chair for that, instead of good lumber, which is never cheap. When at last we'd done everything, and been round three times checking just in case there was something we'd overlooked, I yawned till I nearly broke my jaw, and staggered towards the house to get my head down.

'Just a moment,' Smicro said, sounding a bit embarrassed.

'What?' I muttered.

'Our freedom,' he said. 'Remember?'

I'd forgotten; genuinely forgotten, not trying to cheat them or anything. 'Oh, yes, right,' I said. 'Look, can't it wait till tomorrow? I'm shagged out.'

They looked at each other. 'We'd rather do it now, if it's all the same to you,' they said.

I couldn't blame them, of course. After all, I could have died in my sleep, and then they'd have been really screwed. So I did the business, mumbling the words with my eyelids feeling like lead weights, and then I went into the house, and they went off to the bunkhouse. Normal sort of thing; except that now, of course, they were free and clear, and all their troubles were finally over.

And I – I'd just killed seven people, watched my mother being murdered, cold-bloodedly staved in the head of a girl I thought I was in love with, accidentally slaughtered my best, my only friend – I dropped down on the bed like a sack of charcoal and was fast asleep before my back hit the cords.

Oddly enough, I dreamed about the captain of the grain freighter. I dreamed that I was him, and that I was in charge, like a captain always is. What I was in charge of, I'm not sure; at times it was the ship, taking Lucius Domitius and me away from Sicily, with millions of sesterces' worth of gold plate and bullion crammed in the hold; at other times, we were back on that clifftop in Africa, that temple where we'd found Dido's treasure, and we were trying to load up a huge consignment of dead bodies we'd discovered down in the crypt – hundreds and thousands of them, there were, all people we'd killed at some time or other, and how we were meant to pack, ship and embark all those thousands and millions of dead, stiff bodies without any carts or cranes or derricks or winches, I just couldn't begin to imagine (all we had to work with, I remember, was one coil of rope, a ponderous hoe and a sedan chair), and then it struck me, it was obvious what I had to do: I reached inside my satchel, where I'd got all the provisions I'd bought for Lucius Domitius' journey, and fished out a copy of the collected works of Virgilius Maro, because it was all in there – complete instructions, everything you needed to know about ploughing and harrowing and planting, shifting heavy loads, lading ships and transporting dead bodies. It seemed to take ages to find the right place – I kept scrolling down through the roll and missing the bit I wanted and having to go back to the start – and when at last I finally found the bit I was after, it was all in some weird language and I couldn't read it. Then Amyntas and Tityrus and Smicro and the governor of Sicily and all the rest of the crew started muttering, and I knew I had to come up with something fast or I'd be in real trouble, they'd kill me and share out all the bodies among themselves; so I turned to Seneca and asked him what I should do, but he just shook his head and said I was the emperor, it was up to me and nobody else could help me. All this time, of course, the fire was getting closer and closer; I could hear the crackle of the flames, and the screaming horses. So I made up my mind, we'd have to go with the collapsing ship idea, even though I knew it probably wouldn't work; but it did – at least, it sank like a stone, but everybody managed to get out and swim to shore, and there we all were, standing naked and alone on the beach on Scheria; and we were all free and clear, and all our problems—

And then I woke up.

First thing I did was wander across the yard to the bunkhouse. I wasn't even sure those two would still be there, now they were free men and could go where the hell they liked (and I was free too, once, and I went all over the world, but never found anywhere I liked). But there they were, sitting at the table looking quiet and subdued, with their hands all wrapped up in cloth.

I couldn't help grinning. 'It's all right,' I said, 'you're still free, it wasn't a dream or anything.'

We had a chat. Upshot was, they were quite happy to stay on indefinitely, having nowhere else to go, and carry on working for me same as before. In return they'd get board and lodging, plus basic wages – which worked out at a few drachmas a year more than I'd been giving them anyway, since I'd been fairly generous with their *peculium* (there isn't a Greek word for it, Greeks don't usually pay their slaves, it's a Roman custom, mostly. I guess all those years going round with a Roman must've turned me soft, or something). To be honest, I couldn't really see it made any difference to them being free, but they seemed to think quite highly of it.

There wasn't any question of them being fit for work for a while, after what the governor's men had done to them, so I told them they might as well take it easy, and left them to get on with it. That left me in a fix, with just me to do all the work. In a way, I was lucky. Between the setting of the Pleiades and the rising of Arcturus, there's not a great deal that needs doing around the place. You've got your late ploughing, of course, and there's always the pruning to be done, though you can usually fit that in to suit. Otherwise, there were just the usual daily chores: milking the goats and the ewes, mending and ditching, a new cart to be built to replace the one I'd shoved off the cliff, all boring stuff that's got to be done whether you like it or not. I'd probably be able to cope, so long as I didn't mind starting early and finishing late. Comical, in a way; for the next month or so, I'd be working my guts out to support my two ex-slaves in comfortable leisure, like they were

Romans or something. But that's farming for you. The idea that you just stick stuff in the ground and come back when it's finished growing is all very well, but it never seems to work out like that, somehow.

Anyway, once I'd made sure I still had a household of sorts, I went out to the barn and put my hoe away; then it was off to town, to buy a couple of mules, and the nails and tyres I needed for the new cart. No horse any more, I had to walk. Oddly enough, the mountain hadn't got any less steep while I'd been riding around like a gentleman.

I've never done any good with bloody mules. At first, I thought I wasn't going to be able to find any at all, not even for silly money; the army buyers had been round, scooping up everything on four legs that brayed. But someone I knew slightly in town told me about some bloke out the other side of Phalerum who'd come in to the city a day too late and missed the buyers; he might still have a pair of mules for sale, if I was lucky. So I trudged out to Phalerum and found the bloke; he reckoned he'd never even considered selling his mules, but he did have an uncle at Halinus who might still have a pair, if I felt like taking a chance that he hadn't flogged them to the army after all. Well, I'd come that far, and Halinus was only just down the long, rocky, dusty road, so off I went again. When I got there and asked, they told me the bloke's uncle had died a month or so back; however, his son-in-law, who'd had the mules, already had a pair of his own, so it might be worth my while paying him a visit and seeing if he was minded to sell them. By this stage I'd made my mind up that I wasn't going home without a pair of mules, even if I had to walk to Sparta to get them; also, the son-in-law lived a short distance outside Eleusis, which was practically on my way home (assuming I'd lost my way, or was wandering round in circles like a drunk after a festival). So I dragged myself down the road to Eleusis, found the place where the bloke lived, and bashed on his door. Obviously I wasn't expecting to find him at home during the day, but his wife ought to be able to tell me where I could find him.

No answer; either he wasn't married, or his wife was in the inner room with next door's houseboy, and didn't want to be disturbed. Screw it, I thought; and then it occurred to me that it was getting late, and there was no chance at all of getting back to Phyle before dark, or even as far as the city. Also, even if I could find space at an inn (Eleusis was jam-packed with visitors for the Haloa Festival; just my bloody luck), I didn't have any money on me, aside from what I'd need to buy the mules. Choices were to hang around on the doorstep until the bloke came home, buy his mules (assuming he had mules to sell, of course) and then beg a bed for the night by way of luck-money, or bugger off and try and find a barn or a ditch fit for sleeping in while there was still enough light to see by.

Miserable choice, whichever way you care to look at it. I opted for the barn or the ditch, since by now I'd come to the conclusion that mules were entirely mythical beasts, like centaurs or hippogriffs, and the bloke would probably regard a stranger turning up out of the blue asking to buy them as a dangerous nutcase, and set his dogs on me. I walked away, head bowed, feet dragging, and headed in the general direction of Eleusis.

Barns and ditches are a bit like the market police: ten a penny when you don't want one, impossible to find when you do. For two pins I'd have stretched out on the side of the road and gone to sleep, I was that tired, but the month of Posideon isn't a good time for sleeping rough if you value your health, so I kept going until I found myself in the town.

I said the place was heaving because of the festival; I wasn't kidding. It'd been bad enough during the day. Darkness seemed to have drawn them out like bats; there were people everywhere, torchlight processions gumming up the streets, good-time drunks smashing things up wherever there was enough room to get a good swing with a walking stick, vomit underfoot and the sound of music everywhere. As far as kipping down in a doorway or a portico went, it was hard enough standing still, without getting swept along in a crowd. Eventually I found myself in the market square, where I got wedged into a crevice behind a statue, with no prospect of getting out again. So there I stayed; and I was weighing up the chances of getting some sleep standing up, like a horse, when I happened to look up and see a face I knew.

In Attica, of course, that's always a possibility; there's neighbours and friends of neighbours and relatives and neighbours of relatives and friends of neighbours of relatives, so the odds on bumping into someone you know are generally pretty good. But I couldn't place this bloke straight away; I knew him, but I wasn't sure who he was, if you follow me. Still, there was a chance that if he was local he might have a hayloft or a pighouse I could doss down in, so I pushed and heaved my way through the mob towards him. Might as well have tried to swim through the current off the reef round Scheria; all that happened was that I lost my comfy little nest behind the statue, and found myself out in midstream, so to speak, at the mercy of other people's feet and elbows. The bloke I knew, who-ever he may have been, was long gone by this point. I stopped trying to control my destiny and let the crowd shove me around. My natural condition, after all. I just wished I'd trained as a pick-pocket rather than a con man when I was young. I could've nicked myself a fortune in that crowd.

After a long, uncomfortable time, I found myself flat up against a wall. It was marble, nicely finished, and I guessed it was a temple or something like that; too posh for a private house. The crowd seemed to have ground to a halt, like they'd reached the place they'd been heading for and were standing around waiting for something. Well, I had nothing better to do, so I waited too.

Not for long. Turned out the big deal was a music recital, of all the bloody things. In front of me, about fifteen ranks of bodies away, were the temple steps. At the top of these appeared a bunch of blokes in fancy frocks, the sort of thing priests wear, only they had harps and flutes and cymbals and stuff; and as soon as they looked like they were going to start playing, everybody shut up and stood still, like they'd just seen the gorgon's head and been turned to stone.

I'm not a great music fan at the best of times, and this wasn't one of them, either. I was dog tired, there was a fat bloke to my left standing on my foot, and I was bursting for a piss. All in all, I wasn't in the mood for the finer things in life; in fact, I'd gladly have traded the Nine Muses and the collected works of Virgilius Maro, sung by the author with Apollo on harp and Orpheus on castanets and the doggy whistle, for a bed of damp straw and half a mildewed sausage. But I didn't have the choice; so I held still, and listened.

They weren't bad, I suppose, if you like that sort of thing, which in this case was an incredibly long hymn to Mother Demeter, quite possibly the least interesting of all the gods and goddesses on Olympus. But they tootled and twanged and yodelled competently enough; at any rate, the people all round me were lapping it up like dogs round a leaky wineskin, which meant they were staying put, and therefore so was I.

I guess we've all got our own ways of staving off terminal boredom. Some people count sheep or recite poetry in their heads or think up their all-time great chariot-racing teams. For some reason I've never been able to figure out, though I think I might have told you about it before, I imagine sea battles. Crazy, because I've never ever seen a sea battle, for which I'm profoundly grateful, and – well, you know what I think about boats generally. But that's what I do. I picture the two opposing fleets standing off against each other like forests of cherry trees in blossom. Then they close in, and I try and follow one or two particular ships as they jockey for advantage, trying to get a ramming line or snuggle in close to grapple and board; and here and there I'll see a ship on fire, where the other side have managed to land a direct hit with fire arrows or a catapult shot of burning straw; and there's a ship with its oars shorn off all down one side, helpless as a bird with a busted wing; and over there the marines are at it hammer and tongs on the top deck of a trireme, jumping about on the gangplanks and the oarsmens' shoulders. Exciting stuff, you'll agree; a damn sight more entertaining than some mouldy old hymn.

Well, by the time the musicians finished the third part of the hymn I was well into my imaginary battle; I'd already sunk two triremes and a couple of little galleys, and things were starting to look pretty grim for the Cilicians, or the Parthians, or whoever the enemy were. And then, just as my best trireme squeezed through a gap and ploughed into the side of a helpless four-decker (splintering timbers, sailors and marines jumping over the rail the sea gushing in through the gaping hole in the four-decker's side) my mind suddenly cleared, like a writing tablet when you shave off the old wax. It was as though someone had tapped me on the shoulder and said my name; and I had the weirdest feeling I knew who it was.

'Galen,' he said.

I didn't turn round or anything; I couldn't have done if I'd wanted to. Lucius Domitius, I said inside my head, is that you?

'Oh for pity's sake. Honestly, don't you know me by now?'

Sorry, I replied. But you startled me. And anyhow, you're dead.

'Well, you ought to know about that. I just thought I'd say goodbye, that's all.'

Goodbye, I thought, stupidly. Why, are you going somewhere?

'Of course I am, idiot. Don't you remember? We discussed it, that night in your barn.'

Oh yes, I thought, right. Only it's too late; the ship I booked you on is long gone, must be halfway to where it's going by now.

'Don't worry about that,' he said. 'I've made my own arrangements. The Scherians have said they'll take me anywhere I want to go. You don't turn down an offer like that.'

That's true, I thought, only, how come you know about them? They're a secret.

'Bullshit,' he replied, 'everybody knows that story. They live on the island at the end of the world, which isn't really there, except at the moment of death. And when you die and the water closes over your head, you stand up on the beach on Scheria and they come and take you to wherever you're meant to be. Well, it's my turn now, but I just thought I'd drop by first and say so long.'

Hang on, I thought. That's not right. I've been there.

'Been where?'

Scheria, for crying out loud. It's a real place, somewhere off Africa, not far from where our ship went down. I got washed up there, in a floating coffin, and they rescued me—

'And took you where you really wanted to go. Oh come on, Galen, even you ought to be able to figure that one out for yourself.'

No, straight up, I told him, it's a real place. A real island. I've been there.

'Oh, sure. Maybe you'd care to point to it on a map. This is the Mediterranean Sea we're talking about, there's not a square yard of it that hasn't been charted. Something the size of an island would be pretty difficult to miss, don't you think?'

There's this reef, I told him; it protects them, because every ship that ever gets near there is smashed to bits, and all the people die—

'Yes,' he said patiently. 'And then the Scherians take them where they need to go. Think about it.'

Oh, I thought. And then I thought; but that's still not right, because I'm still alive. I must be alive, or how did I kill all those people? How did I kill?

'Me, you were about to say.'

All right, yes, you. Tell me that, if you're so damn smart.

'Ah yes,' he said, 'but I was dead already, remember? I died over ten years ago, in Phaon's villa. You killed me. I asked you to do it, and you were kind enough to oblige. You stabbed me; I dropped to my knees, muttered, "What an artist dies with me!" and snuffed it. That's what happened. Ask anybody, they'll tell you.'

Yes, I thought, but that wasn't how it really was, that was just telling the tale. But he didn't need to tell me that the tale is all there is, because of course I knew that already; like I knew I hadn't killed the senator and his gladiators, because they died when their cart went over a cliff; and I didn't kill Blandinia, because she died of the same disease that did for Mum; and I didn't kill Nero Caesar, because he'd died years ago; and I didn't kill Callistus, because he and I died on the cross, that day I first met Lucius Domitius. Ask anybody, and they'll tell you.

'Anyhow,' he was saying, 'I'm off now. I suppose I ought to say thanks, for keeping me company and all; but I've got to be honest, all you ever did was keep me from being where I needed to be, what I always should have been. You meant well, but it was really just an unfortunate mistake. You know, seemed like a good idea at the time.'

I see, I thought. And now?

'They're waiting for me,' he said, 'down at the dockside, and I don't want to keep them hanging about, they're very busy people. And I also wanted to say, don't worry about what happened. It was a bloody stupid accident, is all; but it's all turned out for the best. After all, but for you I'd still be in the wrong place, instead of finally free and clear.'

And all your troubles are over, I thought. Heard that one before. But he'd offended me, so I just thought, well, so long, then, and didn't even try to look round (like Orpheus, in the story, remember?). And then he wasn't there any more.

The musicians had finally ground to a halt, and everybody was cheering and yowling like they'd just had a most amazing treat. The fat bloke next to me who'd been standing on my foot elbowed me in the ribs and said, 'Wasn't that grand?' and I nodded, just to be polite.

'Wonderful,' I said.

'Yes, wasn't it? And so brave of them to perform it, too. I don't suppose it's been heard in public since he died.'

I had a bad feeling about this. 'Sorry,' I said. 'Since who died?'

The fat man looked at me. 'Nero Caesar, of course,' he said, like I'd just asked him what the big white round shiny thing up in the sky was. 'That was his Hymn to Demeter, his masterpiece. Brilliant,' he sighed, 'absolutely bloody brilliant. He may have sucked as an emperor, but what an artist.'

'Absolutely,' I muttered.

Of course, there weren't any mules, next day, when I went back round the bloke's house, after a few hours' sleep on somebody's shitheap. So I went home; and here I've been ever since.

You know, I think Lucius Domitius was wrong about the Scherians. True, nobody's ever heard of their island, and yes, you'd have thought somebody'd have noticed it, by now. But I'm pretty sure I'm still alive, at least when my back aches after a long day with the ponderous hoe, so I guess he must've been telling me the tale – which is what artists do, after all, and I have it on good authority that he was one. And I think someone must've been to Scheria and lived to tell the tale, because it's there in the *Odyssey*, after all. And nobody's ever been to the land of the dead and then come back to tell about it, except maybe Ulysses, if there ever was such a person (and he went to Scheria too, so maybe there was). Talking of which, a year or so back I was in town with time on my hands, and I found myself outside a bookseller's stall; so I found a copy of the *Odyssey* and looked up the relevant bits, about Scheria, and visiting the land of the dead, and all. And there was this bit that's stuck in my mind, where Ulysses is down in the underworld and he bumps into the ghost of his friend Achilles, the great hero; and Achilles tells him that it's all very well being a great hero, but then you die and that's that. 'Don't you go telling me the tale about death, Ulysses,' he says. 'I'd rather be alive, and be some poor man's slave, with no land of my own, making a piss-poor living, than be king and emperor of all the glorious dead.' Which made me think, though generally I don't go a bundle on philosophising; all in all, I came out of it all right – better than I deserve, that's for sure – because I got home in the end, and now I'm free and clear, and all my troubles would appear to be over.

Anyhow, so here I am; and if I'm in a condemned cell awaiting execution, then isn't that always the way?